In Winter's Moment

❦

C. Dád Murphy

In Winter's Moment

A Novel based on a true story

First Edition - Oct '05

Christopher David Murphy

C. David Murphy
 # 271/300

I was left with myself and the brisk wind which blew about, still wondering, always wondering. Sandra had abandoned me once more to my impressions, and perhaps my illusions of what may have caught us in a world of similarities. Our lives were somehow tied together by a single strand of silk, born from two different spiders; this very cross I was clinging to.

iUniverse, Inc.
New York Lincoln Shanghai

page 197

In Winter's Moment
A Novel based on a true story

Copyright © 2005 by Christopher David Murphy

All rights reserved. No part of this book may be used or reproduced by any means, graphic, electronic, or mechanical, including photocopying, recording, taping or by any information storage retrieval system without the written permission of the publisher except in the case of brief quotations embodied in critical articles and reviews.

iUniverse books may be ordered through booksellers or by contacting:

iUniverse
2021 Pine Lake Road, Suite 100
Lincoln, NE 68512
www.iuniverse.com
1-800-Authors (1-800-288-4677)

ISBN-13: 978-0-595-36754-2 (pbk)
ISBN-13: 978-0-595-81174-8 (ebk)
ISBN-10: 0-595-36754-2 (pbk)
ISBN-10: 0-595-81174-4 (ebk)

Printed in the United States of America

Dedication and Remembrance

To a mother now hidden in the vast blooms of Heaven. You gave me life and then taught me how to live it. That dreams should never die and you should live within them. To all that you were to me. To all that, by your loving hand, you gave me a chance to become. When I fell, you picked me up. When I shed tears, you gave me a shoulder to dry them on. Your graceful thoughts and kind love were always the loving grace to humanity. I am convinced through your example and teachings there is no greater power than almighty Love.

This book is for you mother. I watched you fade in life while I began writing this script. But you never gave up, nor ever gave in. You gave to me then the strength to continue on without pause. Your dream never died; nor will mine.

So I live on; knowing those treasures so passed down from you to me; what words passed between us; what affections we shared. Nothing was left undone. The lifetime of endless memories will cast a comforting shade through the long remainders of my life. There is no greater gift a mother can pass to her son than what you gave to me. Thank you mother, for all that you were, for all which you still are to me, and how even today you forever touch the lives of so many.

Contents

Chapter 1	Memories and Reflection.	1
Chapter 2	Our Family Portrait.	12
Chapter 3	A Family is Born.	25
Chapter 4	Our Time in the Gardens.	38
Chapter 5	When Times were Younger.	56
Chapter 6	The Treasures of my Early Life.	67
Chapter 7	I Say Goodbye to a Friend.	84
Chapter 8	The Irish Grandmother.	97
Chapter 9	The Firehouse Gang.	110
Chapter 10	The Day I Fell from my Childhood.	119
Chapter 11	The Procession of Honor.	138
Chapter 12	I Begin to Grow Up.	161
Chapter 13	I'm Too Young to be a Chaperone.	177
Chapter 14	The Years Go Quickly.	190
Chapter 15	The Mystery is Revealed.	206
Chapter 16	Fate can be Friend and Foe.	219
Chapter 17	Courtship and Union.	242
Chapter 18	Into the Dawn of Lights and Shadows.	251

Chapter 19	The Colors of Reality Show Like a Rainbow.	264
Chapter 20	The Portal Eye into Night.	276
Chapter 21	Into the Season of the Unknown.	287
Chapter 22	I Have a Dream.	300
Chapter 23	Out of the Eternal Springs of Hope.	310
Chapter 24	My Friend Calls for Me.	322
Chapter 25	The Serpent Strikes Again.	337
Chapter 26	We Call Upon the Children.	351
Chapter 27	The Lost Birthday.	365
Chapter 28	Father, Please Come Home.	375
Chapter 29	The Long Journey of a Dream.	385
Chapter 30	A Season With My Brother.	397
Chapter 31	The Shadow in the Mirror.	412
Chapter 32	I am Home Again.	421
Chapter 33	The Light Grows Dimmer Still.	433
Chapter 34	I am Visited by the Past.	450
Chapter 35	Friendships and a Story.	465
Chapter 36	One Final Dream.	479
Chapter 37	Into the World of Another Land.	486
Chapter 38	A Promise Kept.	507

Chapter 1

Memories and Reflection.

Life. With a bit of reflection, and with some time spent on this road, you can actually sense the memories like a shadow growing with each passing day. You often revisit much of what you experience and pull about the most cherished events to reminisce on. It was my attempt to do such a thing. Reach back into my mind, find some happiness there, and to relive the world from which I had come from. Those clippings of time are but the moments we know most intimately; of a lost yesterday, that when they suddenly and most unexpectantly re-appear, not as shadows, but as spots in your thoughts, you realize just how much of a friend they really are to you. I would recall the happier times, along with the emotions and the feelings that were like fine silk threads interwoven into those occasions; pieces of history; my history; moments in time; my time.

Anything can trigger a reflection. Voices that can echo without warning from days gone by, and which huddle close to your every waking thought. At any moment they might spring about and ask you to recall the long and seemingly still ghosts from your wind-blown past. There, when something you hear is something you had heard from long ago. It moves you to remember. Do you hear it? Those whispers and sounds buried in that endless treasure vault of experiences. It awakes from what seems to be a dream buried within time itself.

In the most troubled times you find time to reflect; to ponder the world as it was. Perhaps the smell of an ancient fragrance will guide you there; or the whiff of some childhood candy you hadn't enjoyed in years. But you remember, and only forget until that same memory comes again to visit you; to say hello and remind you of what used to be.

I thought I was too young for this; to reminisce, to think, to ponder; to relive seemingly glory years that didn't seem so glorious while living in them. But here they are with me; fragments, pieces of treasures that are but a puzzle until you put them all together. I have always been told trauma bears trial; and in trials, a person discovers what they are truly made of. It is like a rainbow of emotions; where both sorrow and joy were born and brought out to look like a distant, beautiful rainbow. In this case, distance would need to remove me from the present and eventually make it a part of my past. Then, perhaps then, I could reflect on this moment I am living under, and see some scrap of joy that was produced.

It is true what they say of the heaviest showers. There is always a most beautiful rainbow after such a rain. Here, now, it was as if I were looking within a brief scope into my past and to where that shower had just passed by, still having no clear explanation on it; no rainbow still to be seen. I could not tell you precisely what it was, yet I observed all theses senses for clues to place with me adequate reasoning on it all.

But to see the puzzle pieces to my life flashing before and through me, gave me pause to escape on those aimless winds. They appeared to have no direction or navigation in them. I lost myself from the present, seeing now those traveled worlds like a good tale to review once more. Memories and Reflection—the particles of that which makes up the very essence of who I am, and who I have become.

Now, I suppose this story has some virtue in its tale. How do I know this? Well, there is virtual truth in the belly of it. And where there is truth, then virtue is soon to follow like a good ending to a story. It was as if I had devoured life and all there had to be experienced, and when you come to some form of conclusion and resolution to what lays in that belly after all this, you know you have been well fed. It is true I have been most fortunate. A wondrous life, some would say. But inevitably; unexpectant trials trip you up and over, and you suddenly are in need of defining what the words hope and faith truly mean.

But here I sit. I am the silent inhabitant of an only island; mine.

I could see the block, white screen stare empty back at me. The sounds of a 38 mm film reel rotating and clipping against the aging projector at a constant beat, softly snapping close to my left ear. The weak, humming purr sound of that projector was playing a tune and rhythm of its own in that backdrop. I heard its echo swear at me with every top-turn to its reel. I was alone and only companioned with my daydreaming thoughts.

The room was vacated out now. I was sitting to myself, along with those vagrant memories still keeping me with good company. The screen never changed or altered. It stared back pure white as the flow of light expanded from the small cylinder lens of this projector and widened until it nearly took up most of the back wall to this room. But I swear, all the while, it was playing my entire life back to me.

Styrofoam cups were sparsed about. Some cleaned empty while others still held some of their drink at the bottom. My daughter Tyler had left her favorite doll propped upright in the small chair. I am sure it was staring back at me; smiling, holding its short stumpy arms wide open to me as if it wanted to embrace. I, too, needed a hug. My son Cory had also left some of his mementos about. Several of his army men were displayed on the far table with no reason for their positions. He still had yet to learn the true art to that playful warfare. I suppose he placed them about where he saw fit at that time.

I could smell the sweet aroma of pipe smoke drifting about this room and chalking the air with dust, wandering as freely as my thoughts were. My father Allen had only been puffing on his usual brand just a few hours before. It always seemed to put him at ease when he did so.

The lights about the room had long before grown dim. Yet I could sense the pondering shadow of someone lurking from my rear, appearing to stretch in quiet observation of me. I knew who it was however; it was Sandra. Her ways were always of soft measure. She had the charm to smooth out all the rough edges of the world, and somehow make the rainbow appear on every occasion. This time would seem to be an impossible act of nature if she could perform the feat.

I did not turn so suddenly, but feeling her head drop slightly around the doorframe; her frozen eyes, watching and staring over me. I could sense her presence as if it were as vivid as the dreams and memories I was currently visiting on. It was a loving shadow that bent over me there, like a good guardian angel she was. Sandra possessed the finest skill in timing. She was waiting, collecting herself, and then announcing when the time was appropriate to do so.

"And what would my husband find so fascinating about a blank screen?" I heard her voice softly whisper from behind.

"I don't know," she knew the answer before I could say it, "I really don't know."

I heard her steps draw near on me, and I felt the gentle passing of her arm around my shoulder as she bent to stare on my profile. My sight remained constant to that empty screen.

"A college-educated man; the top of his class. A brilliant representative; a consummate husband, father, son staring silently, absent-minded in the privacy of his own home; spending his evening hours watching a blank wall...what would the public think of this little skeleton in his closet?"

I could feel the breath of her smile as her expression turned upward, though I remained on my fixation for just a spell.

"Every man has his moments," I weakly proposed.

"And what is yours?" she employed, turning her face in front of mine.

"Which one?" I tried to smile, but it fell short.

"Your being very deliberate here maestro," she grinned.

"A man is not a man without mystery."

She frowned on this, held to her thoughts, then spoke, "A man with too much mystery seems to abandon those close to him," she paused, "You know Conner; Cory and Tyler are like tremors to your every earthquake. Don't put barriers up to them for them to see. They're too young to get over these obstacles. They watch your every move and they see how you are neglecting your relationship with them," her face became slightly more drawn now.

"It just takes time," I spoke, "is all. But I hope they would never think that of me…trying to keep them at a distance and all…"

She paused for that moment, and in her usual wisdom, she replied, "I won't debate the things you already know, but just think about what they are going through. Sometimes we just have to mask our emotions a little, to protect the children. They feel it most when you withdraw from them, and they are confused by it. Kids are never blind because, in their small and bright world, we are the center to their universes…but you know this."

"I can't change any emotion that's honest."

"I'm not asking you to," she smiled, "just camoflauge them a little and you will see a big change in your children. It's ok with me. Let me be your sole sounding board if you want. I'm a big girl. But don't take it out on the kids." She paused, "Even if you don't mean to…"

My eyes captured hers in our looks, and I thought openly about what she was saying. I bent over to console myself in that instance; finding a silent tear dropping from my cheek as I brushed my hair back from my eyes.

"It just happened so fast; so suddenly. I had no way to prepare for it. I had no idea it would be this way," I could sense her arms linger around my shoulders and pull me close to her, "Nor had I ever imagined how it would be."

"I can't tell you how to feel," she hugged me closer still, "but feel as you are, and how you are supposed to be."

"This has changed me," I quietly replied.

"I know," she responded, "I suppose we are all finding out more about ourselves…in the end, we will know."

"Cody and Tyler aren't the only one's confused."

"Don't lose yourself Conner," she returned, "The way home isn't so long. You just have to trust in your beginnings, and know what is right—don't lose sight of this."

"We were both blessed with good parents," I remarked.

"The best," I could feel her smile start up against my cheek, "They say great parents in the morning make the sunset glow brighter for us. And in the end, you will own more wisdom than you will ever know. But you have something else to attend to." Her expression came across more constant to me.

I curiously looked on her. I wondered what that might be.

"Your children, they are so young. Go to them. They have been asking for you."

I looked to her and I caught that blank screen out of my corner stare. She was moving about the room as if this were her final speech, and that I knew exactly what to do from there. Sandra was right; I did know what to do. She went about, collected the cups and plates round, and so gave them more attention than me. I stood, took her hand into mine, and made her pause for that time.

"Not just the children…I have a wife to attend to as well." I replied, and so caught the edge of her grin meeting with mine. Silence broke on us, though we knew what I must do. It was time for me to see my children before they fell asleep and into their dreams.

I was hesitant and reluctant to do so, not knowing what to say; to give them ease and normal perceptions to live by. I had been stretched away from them for a bit. As if the circumstances had pulled our relationships apart like a strained rubber band. Their room was so close, but it felt like such a journey to get there. Those self-taught emotions seemed to be playing havoc with my strong will. I knew what lay ahead and I was hard-pressed to find the right words for them to live by. I paused; Sandra smiled, then she gently pushed me free of her; all the while she mouthed the word 'Go' in a repeated fashion.

I traveled from room to room. The air felt quiet and as much asleep as the night had seemingly become. Each room was empty and scarce, but for the sound of my dress shoes clapping on the hardwoods floors. The stairs creaked and echoed out their wheeze as I went cautiously up those flights of stairs. The banister likewise gave a little as I leaned on it from step to step. There, to the end of the hallway, sat my children's room. The door became slightly ajar but unmoved. I could hear the rustle in their sheets as I came still closer.

I pushed the door free, saw the long shadows grow longer still. I watched them as they apparently slept quietly without a diversion, though I knew they were play-faking sleep this early in the night. I moved to Cory's bed first and I sat on the edge of his bed.

"Hey," I wiggled him awake, and so he turned to see me, "How's your tooth?" I whispered as he grinned on me. I took to wiggle that top, front tooth, "Still there." He nodded in agreement. "Are you ready to pull?" He disapproved on this statement and I reacted with a smile. I brushed back his hair; felt the silence pass between us as we stared on one another for a moment. Such the likeness of me he was; that temperamental way; the soft freckles of youth I once owned myself; the reaching-back dimples whenever I smiled, poised themselves as well over his cheeks. I could see the memories of myself when I looked on him, noting how reflection plays such a stare with me while we were frozen in moments like this. Cory was my shadow and I knew this. His disposition; his mannerisms; his boyish performances were as I was so many years before. As if he were walking down the same pathway that I had first traveled on. Memories and Reflections—now came rushing on me like a past wind I once remembered, but had so recently forgotten.

"You know, we are only delaying the tooth fairy." I suggested with a silly grin.

"She can wait…" he fearfully proposed.

"She might forget," I further suggested by a sly grin.

"She won't," he smiled, nearly popping out that tooth when he did so, "She never forgets."

"If you say so…" I whispered. I brushing back his hair once more, taking a move to wiggle that tooth back and forth myself, "It seems mighty ready…"

"Not yet…"he pulled his covers up to his chin as I leaned in on him. I placed a kiss to his forehead and I sent back a serious expression like a shadow hovering over his bedposts.

"You remember what happened to the last tooth?"

"Yes," he shyly proposed.

"Then I think we should pull it…" I came again.

"He'll never let you pull his tooth dad…" I heard Tyler turn, rustle about in her bed, and roll to face the both of us, "Not me. Let dad pull three of them, and I got three dollars to prove it," she said this with such an air of pride.

"Will too!" Cory lashed out.

"Will not!" Tyler volleyed back.

"Will too!"

"You haven't before," she grinned on this.

"Cory," I shot a firm glance to him, "Tyler," I did as much the same to her, "I am sure when the time comes I will be able to collect your tooth for the tooth fairy. No need for arguments here for the sake of arguing…you both still have a full head of teeth to lose, and will become more than 'well to do' by it at the expense of the tooth fairy herself," I eyed them both as they had grown more silent. They both shot me the expression that somehow I was angered by their little quarrel.

I paused. I made a sigh in hopes to defuse the situation and allow myself to collect my thoughts to speak on further.

"What chapter were we on?" I said.

"Chapter 7," Cory cautiously remarked.

"Which book?" I had forgotten.

"Dad?" Tyler pleaded with me to remember.

"Oh yes," there was a pause, and it seemed to be sent my way, "Robinson Crusoe."

"No dad," Cory softly replied.

"Black Beauty…" and by the look on their collective faces, I was in error again, "Heidi…Oliver Twist…The Call of the Wild?" I could only venture then, and still be fiercely abandoned by my more usually keen memory.

"You used to never forget…" Cory employed. I felt his words softly pinch me with its most accurate accusation. I had failed them again, and so I felt the most inept of our trio. To sense that these moments we shared; these very moments which held the utmost meaning to them, had failed to hold any relevance with me. That pause brought me into shame and embarrassment in front of the very two little people who held me so in high regard and invincibility. I wondered where the right words would come from. I was holding still, gazing but into the reflective stares of their eyes while they were sitting, wanting me, hoping even still, that perhaps, if all were to go as it should, that I may remember the book we had stopped on before. I thought for a moment as I tried to discover the magical title which would appease them so. I could not find it.

"What can I say?" I only mastered this phrase.

"Huckleberry Finn…" Tyler spoke out, disappointed as she was with me. I was so finding more failure within myself.

"Yes…Yes," I threw my finger into the air as if it had come to me only a fraction of a moment after she had said so, and would have darted back into my memory if she had not blurted it out to me so premature. My look found theirs to be so full in acrimony that perhaps I had lost them for a second "Where were we in the story?" I defused.

"Huck was being chased by Pap with a knife…" Cory said.

"And why was he doing this?" I shot them a confused expression, as though I had never thought of reading that section before.

"Pap thought Huck was the Angel of Death, or something…" I saw the despondent stare resonate from my daughter's soft and engrossing eyes, which all but tore over me. I could sense that lump drive upwards in my throat; my inner tears remained within. They couldn't see my own sorrow.

The gaping hole of silence in our conversation seemed to frustrate them further; my lack of comfort; my inability to set things right and make the world as it was before; to somehow turn time backwards and give back those dear things which were so recently lost to all of us.

Surely I would have been an awkward clockmaker. I believe I would have brought to heir the revolution of having the hours spin counterclockwise. But I suppose I would have been just as well the smart clockmaker as a good father to these children now. It was true. Somehow I had lost my step along the pathway; turned a corner I was not meant to travel on. And in looking back, and so seeing the ways I should have gone, I was in struggle to redirect myself.

Sometimes life throws shadows in your way without the light to guide you by. Your hope is to discover the way as you see fit, but sometimes, even in the most winter of times, there isn't enough light to be sure on. Then, when the hour is most dim and the air the coldest still, you just have to discover the way.

I saw their worried eyes; their most early precepts of childhood where everything was to be of fancy and play. Nothing bad was to touch them in their lives, where security was as great as life itself. This infant bubble had somehow burst by the pin of fate itself. And now they felt the world seemed as cold and dim as I did.

Tyler moved from her bed to sit most near to me, to see more closely the weakness in my own eyes. Cory leaned up, intently eyeing in me the same thing as Tyler did. I felt the weight of their stares expose the very expressions I did not want them to see, which so caused me to wilt under that pressure. The mask seemed not as strong as it did before, but I held to a sigh; looked away briefly until my daughter's soft voice caught me back again.

"How long will you be sad daddy?" Her five-year old voice nearly struck the beat strings to my heart. I could not deny the sword in her words, yet I still refrained from my weep and I kept it silent.

"Only until the spring dear," I whispered back. She placed with me a hug, and too, did Cory lean further until they both were within my grasp. I squeezed both into a tight fit within my embrace. We held each other still there; time eclipsed and spun now on that same moment as we locked into that comfort and embrace. We did not want to let go, but let everything pass until we were all sure that everything would at least heal a little in that time we could share together.

"We should attend to our reading tomorrow…can we?"

"Huckleberry Finn?" Cory hopefully said.

"Oh yes...and while you are at school I will be sure to review the first six chapters again," I smiled, "In fact, I will become the best expert on it."

"And the voices?" Tyler chimed in.

"Of course," I replied, "What is a story without voices?"

"Not a good one..." Cory leaned back with arms placed over his head. He stared back on the ceiling tiles like they were bright stars in the night sky.

"Then I will have to make good practice on different ones," I placed Tyler back into her bed.

"I like it when you do an old man..." she giggled aloud.

"Like this??!" I grew my face old, rolled my eyes in retreat, gummed my lips over my teeth, and dried out my voice until it sounded like the one who needed a long and deep glass of whiskey, "A varmint! A heathen!"

"You sound like the way Pap would sound," she giggled once more and she smiled broadly as she looked to me.

"Pap..." I softly whispered that word through my lips and I so stared out into some unforeseen distance. As if my mind was venturing away again; eyeing the prodigal notions of a son lost in his own history; poking that long scope in retreat into the way I had come. I could see my own childhood as I peeped backwards like a good Tom, "Pap...I used to call your grandpa that."

My words trailed off at the end of that sentence.

"Grandpa?" Cory shot in.

"He was Pap to me..." I looked back onto Tyler's shining face, "You're a giggly goo one, aren't you?"

And she laughed once more as I tickled her to clear it out of her system.

"What did he call you dad?"

"Just Conner," I paused and winked a smile, "But when he was really angry with me, he used to call me Connnnniiieee!"

There was a general roll-call of laughter which hit the room. I looked back at the shimmering light and open door. I could see Sandra's shadow standing off in the distance; silent and motionless, staring into our audience to overhear what was going on between us three.

"Time for bed," I returned my attention their way, "Butterflies and bats need their rest too," I imposed a metaphor to each of them.

They drew snug in their beds. The soft, cupping blankets rolled back just underneath their chins. Their eyes were in a droop, and yawns consuming the full expressions in their faces. I could see that they had had a full day. The tiny-tot children closed their eyes, fell to a slumber, and so tumbled into some dream and sleep I could only imagine. I left them as they were, but better still than before. It seemed perhaps they would have good dreams rather than nightmares now, as long as Pap did not show up in them.

I had often heard Tyler crying in her sleep. When I went to comfort her in those moments, the tears kept flowing even as she awoke. They were so very long to dissipate. Tonight perhaps would be different.

I drew the door closed and I stepped down the hallway where Sandra was leaning up against another doorway.

"Good job Maestro," she smiled, and grinned in the same expressive way.

"I'm just a natural," I said modestly.

"Six chapters…" she had to remind me, "And all those voices. You know Huckleberry has as many characters in it as words," she reminded me still further.

"I can handle it," I said, "I will just have to spawn some riverboat magic, if you can do the female roles."

"Oh no," she shook her head on it, "You're better at voice alterations than I am. This is your job."

Then she stopped, and her grin was replaced by a serious look.

"They have missed that…more than you know."

"As I have…" and I left her side.

I knew Sandra would be gathering herself for bed soon, as well. I moved outside our old Boston home and I caught the early winter air in my face. The ancient light shimmers in the wintertime there, and so the cross-town streets were gleaming back on me when I would look out their way. The soft spray of headlights moved about the nearest streets like lightening bugs in search for new companionship. I could hear the rain quietly pelt round the trees with a soft peddle thump, and sidewalks with the hoof beats of a tiny horse in a long and constant trot. The air was cool; not biting, though I could see my smoking breath rise up whenever I was exhaling into the night itself. I could see the mist swirl about like a cotangent stew; muddle about, drift in sways, brighten every porch light up and down the street, and so drip from the dark sky. As if Heaven was softly weeping in her sleep. I looked upward through the grand-perching trees in our long front yard. Clouds were constantly drifting to cover the glowing stars in that particular constellation; and so as such, clouds moved in their stealth and unseen ways. I saw the moon peek through for a glance, then drop out of sight once again.

Times like these a person has to reflect on. The urgency of those times makes you see the world from a different angle altogether, though not self-imposed. I saw those memories loom like a big spinning yarn in my mind again; of birth; of youth; of burgeoning age; of life in all its wonder. The scene I suppose called for such a thought as I had there.

I drifted further into the lawn and closer to the street edge. There, in the very midst was an old, entangled, grossly enlarged oak tree; as old as earth itself. One burly limb hung out longer than all the rest; and there, as its big arm cast out along those grassy shores, it held a heavy swing out from its base. I was sitting there, swinging to and fro, watching the world about me seemingly move by my locomotion, and my eyes falling to dream. There, as was always in the fancy of my imagination, I could alter the way of fate and bring back to life the days gone by.

Those sterling dreams; those memories of old; those employed reflections never grew old or appeared to fail me. There, the world was perfect again and I knew it to be so.

I would see tomorrow for what it was; a new adventure strung from the collective pages of the past. Like a book only half-chartered. A connection and a bridge to what had become was so now affecting what 'will be'. Through turmoil; through joy; through grief, life will still commence by its own stage. Fear can drive one to resist what is just there before us. Not me. I had seen that storm, and so knew its brash wind and its violent spray. I had survived, though not unchanged. Life will do that to you. Transform you; make you into the person of your own destiny. Like an eagle still growing its wings; a deer still learning to prance about and run; as a kitten captivated by its own play; and as a person still evolving and discovering what life yet has to offer us.

I was once told there was a beautiful rainbow after every heaving rain. Perhaps this is true. But perhaps, even still, the beautiful rainbow comes only after a long journey. It makes the walk seem nicer still when you get there. I had cried my ocean of tears then; saw the bounty of my emotions roll and heave like that storm. Now it was time for the rainbow to appear.

I stopped the swing there. Silence became more still than the dead empty space it resided in. I sat alone, eyes closed, and so I bent my head into my chest while wondering when the rainbow would come.

There was one last cry for me to go through; kind of like a brisk shower that was never forecasted. But it came and I went through it, so giving sustenance to the flowerbed to my emotions. Someday the world would seem brighter than that moment did.

I felt a soft hand touching to the sides of my face, and then a hovering cloud enveloped me. This stirred me to let the tears fall uninhibited and I felt the touch turn into a full embrace. Sandra had shadowed me. In this time of memories and of reflection, she too shared her tears with mine. There was more rain that night than in the skies above, for Heaven was not alone in her sorrow. And as the clouds above softly pelted us with her dew, I felt Sandra's warm heart take to comfort me.

Chapter 2

Our Family Portrait.

I was raised in the heart and soul of Boston, within the middle of a section called Charlestown. Our clapboard house stood on Elm Street; a long and narrow way just a few blocks down from the Monument Square. Our particular setting was a simple, gray, wood structure home with white-framed windows. The lamplights rose from the sidewalks and lit about the evening at six every night. The house beside ours was of a darker gray tint. What always stuck out in my mind was the rather unusually large bay window that protruded so indecently from the main structure and the gated flower garden which surrounded it.

We lived on an incline that bent higher and further up for blocks on end, past Tremont and Bunker Hill Street. The foliage of trees sparsed about; the magnolias and lilacs in bloom always brought great rebirth during the month of March. The dogwoods also were cutting out their white tusky blooms about the same time.

The residents here always parked their cars on the street in front of their homes, being that so very little space was available to park ones' car. Everyone scheduled their days in the winter months about forty-five minutes earlier due to the harsh weather; and the car windows would need constant cleaning off from the ice and snow. I could often hear my father scrapping the windshield of our car, chatting about with a neighbor of ours doing the same thing. Kind of like the early morning water cooler discussions, except with ice and a scrapper instead.

Life was considered as normal for me as anyone I suppose. I was the oldest of four children, though we were born tightly together in time. I had been no more than eleven months older than the next in line, my sister Lorie. Soon thereafter, no more than a year later, Amanda came to be. Then four years after which the youngest, Adam, was born. My parents always jokingly said they wanted their family and quickly; all in attempt to get the 'birthing process' over with as soon as they could.

I was the leader and the more curious of the brew. Everything found its way into my mouth. I had such a sensation to see, touch and feel, then eat everything in my path. So much so, I nearly choked to death on a nickel when I was barely one. But for the sake and expertise of my mother in reviving me, I would have been lost. I had an intrinsic fascination with pictures and books. My parents would often find me silently in a sit in one corner. An assortment of books surrounded me, fully open and on display, and so I would go from book to book searching out those things that would stimulate me the most.

My mother always told me how quiet a child I was; rarely fussy, even when I was teething and had colic as bad as I did; though my training to the full functional potty was a difficult chore for both my parents. It nearly took me into the age of three to finally master that individual feat. They said, fondly, that when I used the portable potty and I took an attempt to do 'the number two' as they put it, I gathered myself from my seat. I looked down horrified at the mess I made and I would not return again for some time. It seemed I preferred to sit 'in my mess' rather than look at it.

I was broad, blue-eyed, and tussled with silvery white hair. I rumbled about the room with a glib and a smile on my face and I never appeared to be unhappy. I thought each thing was unique in its own right and I held such a will to investigate and inspect all that was around me, sometimes to the point of being a nuisance. I did not like to be carried or held, but wanted so much to go about my own way at my own pleasure, as soon as I took to walking.

Lorie was an adversely shy child in her own right, but she always was curious from a distance. Caution kept her step in that distance and it seemed to always accompany her. She was prone to accidents from the outset, so I suppose this being the reason for her continual hesitant nature. She hardly ever reached for anything but waited for it to be brought to her, unless she knew it would bring no harm to her. If it didn't move in her direction, she never cared for it nor bothered to inspect it. Lorie doted over being held by her mother, and was quite affectioned by this. She enjoyed running, yet was never really very good at it in the beginning. We seemed to find her face first into everything for a time. It was not uncommon to discover Lorie bandaged, cut, or bruised about her face before the age of four.

When she smiled, her humorous gab filled up her face with that expression. She always held her tongue fully out when she giggled; a laughter which repeated so rapidly in succession, you thought she had been filled up with laughing gas. Her eyes sparkled brown and hid behind her smile as her lips rolled upward and spread from ear to ear. Her black locks of hair hung straight down to her neck, and she possessed such an insatiable habit to sucking and pulling her hair into her mouth, that my mother had to put vinegar on the ends of her locks and braids to prevent it.

As Lorie grew older, she was a primper with her clothes and mother's makeup. Whenever the opportunity arose she would sneak into our parent's bedroom, parade about, find eyelash, rouge, liner, lipstick, blush, and whatever other materials were at her disposal; sit about the mirror and paint herself so silly with lipstick running over half her face, one would think she had more than her fair share of drink before she set out to making herself appear as the artsy, modern, flashy, deco-type of woman she wanted to become.

On one occasion, while mother was involved with her garden work, Lorie made her way into mother's wardrobe, sat in front of the vanity for a good thirty minutes before being discovered, went about to paint her face all shades of blue, yellow, green, ruby red, and brown; fixate seven beads of necklace around her neck and shoulders; take grandmother's ancient and tired hat from the lower regions of the closet, and wear it tilted on her head, with a brim which was so rounded and worn, it drooped in front of her face; loop four separate pairs of earrings and place them on either ear, and even a ring or two in her nose. And when all was said and done she took mother's highest heels, plopped them on her feet and she came from that back bedroom, down the long corridor as if she were the most graceful model ever to step on a runway.

It took mother an hour or two to clean Lorie clear off, yet little Lorie was not a small girl for mischief, just gregarious play.

Amanda was the most studious of the brew. Her golden hair always strung simple and straight right into her face. Her eyes were pearl gray and her dimpled smile brought light even into the darkest rooms. She was a regular to pull up her dress in the front whenever she got so excited. Even at the labored attempts my parents used to keep her from doing so. Still it was such a spontaneous act on her part. She simply could not help herself. My mother had to lock the bathroom door from the inside when she gave Amanda a bath, for fear she would dart out skin-naked into the other rooms, and out the front door. There were times when mother turned her attention just for a moment, and out went Amanda full head of steam, through the front foyer and door onto the cold pavement. We caught her one time circling the front sidewalk with her hands fully stretched into the air, while she soaked in the evening sun rays on her giggling face.

"Allen!" my mother would direct feverishly, "Pull her in before the neighbors see and call the social services on us!"

And without pause, my father would slide down the front chill-covered stairs and make a play to grab Amanda. How she would dart about as if it were a game of tag.

"You can't catch me!" she would laugh, "You can't catch me!"

All the while flopping down the sidewalk a few doors down, looking back, and seeing her father half-dressed himself; he also was slipping and stumbling from the curb to the street.

"You better hope I don't, young lady!" my father sternly proposed. He bumped about the sidewalk and neighbors bushes.

"Sorry Mrs. Goldstein!" He pulled himself out of our neighbor's prized bush once when he landed square to the base of it and tore its limps to shreds. Mrs. Goldstein looked out her lower window, caught all the commotion in her snoopy, prying ways, frowned out on my father with such clear disdain, huffed a measure or two, then drummed her fingers continuously on the open window ceil while raising her eyebrows; left, right, then left again.

Amanda was never one to seem to take after either of our parents, though my aunt on my mother's side had hair as golden as Amanda's was. She always held a fascination with birds, the outdoors; deer in general, and of all things, roosters. Each month, at various times, she would ask mother and father for a rooster; either on Christmas or her next birthday. Our father eventually gave into her desire for one. He purchased it without my mother's consent, and in the same stroke he acquired her fury for doing so.

"What?" mother shouted; dad asked her in the kitchen, "She's been asking for one since she could speak 'rooster! rooster!'"

"But a rooster Allen?" my mother held a knife out in a menacing fashion. You could feel the heat rising in the kitchen from more on their conversation than the stove itself.

"That thing will cackle all hours of the morning; our neighbors Allen!"

"Just wait," he proposed, "You'll see; all is well."

Particularly myself, I was deathly frightened of the thing. It nearly attacked my friends and me as we came and went from the house. That contagion rooster always stood guard as if our home was a chicken coup, and we were the foxes who planned to carve out a meal from a chicken or two. He roused his feathers, stood erect in a soldier stance at the base of the front door; one leg pinned up underneath its belly feathers, and so ready to strike at the least movement he saw.

The neighborhood dogs took to badgering it incessantly, barking with such fierce anguish that the rooster would cackle, bob its head, prance around the dog in semi-circle, and duck-walk back up to its spot on the porch when it was done.

Of course the only remedy my father saw in the situation was to allow the rooster residence in our house. This brought out more ire from my mother, even still.

"I'll NOT have a rooster in our house!" she harped. She was carrying two kitchen knives this time; one for my father, and one for the rooster itself, "This is NOT an animal farm!"

"Lauren," my father pleaded, "Think of your daughter."

"No Allen," she firmly held her voice down, though she gritted her teeth through those words, "That rooster is very aggressive. It might one day attack our children."

"Then we will leave it in the basement."

"Oh good," she swore, "and hear the call every hour of the morning. No Allen! The rooster must go!"

And with that sweeping edict, the decree was final and set by the script of my mother's own words. Certainly Amanda was disheartened by the news when my father told her in her room later that night. She had often carried the rooster with her throughout the local neighborhood. She always looked behind to see if the rooster had finally laid an egg. It baffled her as to why the rooster did not do so.

"Come on Chicky," she would call it, "Lay your egg now." Amanda would pause, swirl about her as she held the rooster in hand, round and round, and searched for the egg that must have dropped but had somehow escaped her detection of it.

Father had a friend who owned a farm several hours north of the city and he had so inclined that his friend needed a watchful rooster to guard his hen house from the neighboring foxes. They popped in and about when they had a mind they were hungry. Amanda gave the rooster her dramatic 'goodbye's', short-tear farewells, and off the rooster went in the station wagon. That night, Amanda went to her room alone, crept into bed, and cried softly till she fell asleep.

The youngest was my only brother, Adam. He was nearly six years younger, and so my mother had some difficulty carrying him through her pregnancy. There was much mystery and privacy about that time; especially as she drew closer and closer to having Adam born. I do remember my father, on one instance, running to me frantically and saying we must call emergency.

"We've got to call the doctor son! Mind your sisters....your mother is bleeding!"

I drew into a freeze at that moment. I had no clear thinking on what I must do. My eldest sister was stammering about while Amanda was sitting on the floor, staring aimlessly with a pacifier in her mouth. My father quickly placed us all in a room together, shut the door, asked me to make sure none of us left, but remain until he came to retrieve us. My fear traumatized me there, as I inched to the door. Quiet as I was, I placed my ear to the door and I heard the muffle sounds of my parents as they struggled through that crisis. My eyes grew to a bulge as I turned about, checked on my sisters who were in play, sat in a lonely chair by one corner, and so stared out into nothing. I waited anxiously for the roof to fall in on us. Time had no meaning there, but it seemed to play out into eternity.

I waited; my sisters grew tired and Amanda cried when the pacifier popped from her mouth, though no one came. I made my best attempts to console her through her own trauma, not knowing fully what to do.

"There, Amanda," I held her as best as I could.

Eventually the door pried open and my aunt came forward. She told us that we would all be staying with her for a few days. She gathered our things, what she could quickly shuffle about with, and so we went to ride home with her. I remember that seclusion so vividly; the foreign manner of the cot I slept on; those misty windows from the cold; her german shepherds which never seemed to take any liking to us; the cold sandwiches she fed us for dinner and supper. It seemed such a long time before father came to retrieve us.

I could often see myself peeking through the one bedroom keyhole. I looked about directly into the den. His expression was worn and tired, as if it had sat on his face for days, and near to a week that we had been apart. His eyes drooped and were despondent, near to tears; grief lingered constantly in his face. My aunt swiftly came to his aid and placed about him a hug.

"I'm so sorry Allen," she wept in my father's shoulder, though my father's glassy stare remained in his look. The moment stood still for a while as neither moved from the spot. And I so feared, even at such an early age, something terrible had happened to mother and my soon-to-be-born sibling.

As it were, father gathered us all into the station wagon for a most silent ride home. He said very little as I watched him, as he paid no mind to my sisters while they sat in the back seat. He took to glaring out onto that dark road ahead, never flinching nor seeming to blink, as though it were a passageway onto nowhere. His soul apparently either escaped him or appeared to sleep inside. His usual, youthful, gay self was somehow in a pause. I looked about my window there, watched the stars above flicker in their light; it was an odd thing to see them twist and turn casually as our car went from south to east. The moon seemed to pop out from its hiding place with a quarter stare, as so the clouds drifted by. I was eager to see my mother.

I found her softly tucked in her bed. I captured a smile from her as soon as she saw me. Mother held her arms about for me to come forward. I ran to her, felt her grip entrap me with the warmth and love a mother gives to her child. The smell of her raven hair engulfed my face as it lay across her shoulders. I felt all was well at that moment.

My sisters soon followed and we all crawled into bed with mother. I felt her stroke out our hair, one by one, as we lay beside her. Amanda quickly took to sleep with that same pacifier dripping from her mouth. Lorie pretended to be reading her book until she, much the same, fell asleep. I leaned up on my mother as I watched her contently show care to my sisters, then to me. The hours drew deep into night; my father away again for an overnight shift at the firehouse.

"Mother." I asked, "Are you alright?"

She leaned down on me, gave to me a comforting kiss, "I am son. The Lord takes care of you."

"The baby?" I questioned.

"It will be here soon," she smiled down on me, "The Lord will take care of that too."

Adam was born a month later; a strapping, hardy, bouncing boy which took to delight both my parents on his arrival. Balloons, party hats, cake, confetti all were strung about our home when my mother rose from the back seat of our family's station wagon the afternoon of her return. The air was brisk and sprightly cold; the flowers yet to bloom; the timber trees still yet to cast out its green foliage for the spring. But I do believe, by the happy occasion which ensued, spring had already come. There was a full entourage to greet her and the baby. We all were standing just outside on the porch, and freezing in that bitter air while we were still heavily clad in thick coats. Though, as odd as it may have seemed then, I could not recall such a celebration when either of my sisters first came home. I would eventually learn the thundering and consequential reasons for this.

It was my promise and my joy to finally have a brother in which I could play with. No dolls, but sports; no tea parties, but army men; no make-up dresses and slumber parties, but wrestling and bicycle races. Adam was to be the brother I endeared myself to have. And I was to be the older brother he would always admire on and say, 'he's the best older brother a guy could ever have!'

I knew from nearly the beginning however, Adam was not to be such a brother. He was a most quiet child, as I was but in a different way. Absent of any social bearing, he rather enjoyed keeping to himself but for the attention mother mainly provided his way. There seemed to be a wall there; a distance of travel between Adam and I. Others observed his behavior, and though he appeared a darling boy with a cute smile, a twinkle stare, and a loveable giggle, his skills for engaging others were never realized.

Even in sleep, Adam would often hide behind the couch to be alone; or if placed in his bed at night, you could find him settled nicely underneath his bed. There indeed was something quite different about Adam. My mother encouraged him to garner friends and to attend gatherings from church and school. But he took a better liking to wandering out in his mind to a place he would neither speak of, nor tell. It seemed to be such a mystery; in particular when we had supper together. Often solemn and somewhat aloof, he could not bring himself to show interest in the 'goings on' of the other family members. And when asked of his day, he said the least that he could, to skirt out of being the center of any attention.

Now mind you, Adam was extraordinarily gifted in many respects. From the very early stages of his life, he would initially sketch out images roughly so, then quickly progress to depth, colors, measures of dimension, then at last adding 'spirit' to the watercolors, sketches, and eventually full portrait and drawings he would characterize. Colored pencils and empty blank pages were more to his liking than picture books and children's stories. He was found stirring often in his room; alone, by the dim light of a desk lamp, and even a candle or two; quietly, almost religiously poking along on his configurations. His gift for concentration and careful study to sights were a marvel to me. I wished I had such the gift as he possessed. It was as if God had taken the pricking of his own finger, and touched Adam with it.

But most rare than this, Adam had the great ability to write. He studied the finest masters of word and literature. He began around the age of twelve or so. Dickens, Shakespeare, Twain, Faust, Homer, Poe, Whitman, Lord Byron, and Austen were some of his favorites. I knew where to find him during the school hours when he had available time; down in the dungeon, sitting alone in the corner of the library, as he read contently away at a pound-thick novel or gazing through a Di Vinci or Rembrandt collection of paintings.

It seemed vastly odd at how intelligent Adam seemed to be in these two arts; nearly mastering the unmasterful methods of its imagination. He did quite horribly in school; almost to the point of failing on every level. I made my best efforts to be a good brother to him throughout our growing years and I am sure he appreciated this in his own aloof and distant ways.

"Stop," I remember him saying once to me, "Sit still."

He looked at me as we sat out on a bench during a spring day. There, he proceeded to pull out his sketch book, eye me in a deep-thinking grimace, continue to eye me further, step his mind into his sketch and lose me in the process.

"No, no Adam," I refuted, "You're not sketching me."

"Yes I am," he was assured.

"I said no, Adam," I was not one to enjoy my picture taken, let alone to have myself under the pen of an artist; even if he were my own brother.

"I've already started…" he went quickly to work, eyeing me through his right eye, and charting the sketch with his left.

"But why Adam," I wondered.

"Because," his jaws locked, "there is a thought in your look; something reflective in your expression. Your look has a story to tell right now…now hold please."

I said nothing further; Adam was more determined than anyone I knew, and he had the talent to back it up.

"Done," he proclaimed twenty minutes later. He spun the pad around. My eyes locked on it as my heart stopped. I had never known the perception of his ability till then. Not only to capture my appearance in such a real life form as he did, but to also snag the very core of what I was thinking when he drew me. As if my soul sat in the shadow of his drawing and he conveniently painted it for me.

My father was a long-term and highly-decorated fireman; nearly a legend amongst his peers within Boston's inner city. Station 112 was where he began his tenure as a fireman, and that is where he would stay his entire career. It was something his blood was built from; a passion; an undying submission to; apart of his culture and entire character. There were times when I would feel the faint tingle of a kiss on my cheek around four in the morning, when either he was going on duty or coming off. He carried his dedication like armor; his duty around like a badge of honor. He believed credit was earned and not freely given. That to walk into a firehouse, become assembled into a group of individuals whose design and purpose was to help others, and to become a life-saving team, was much of what he lived for. There was indeed love he held for his family, but his heart was there in that firehouse. From the soup kitchens and late evening meals or early morning breakfasts that could easily be resoundly interrupted, he lived for the rush of being on that edge.

I was never forbidden to enter the fire station. In fact, it was often encouraged by my father for me to attend and be 'a man' amongst the group there. By the time I was born and of the age when I could make my visitations on him, he had become a sergeant and was quickly moving up the ladder, so to speak. He was always noted as unrepressed with his bravery. His skill was second to none and his instincts were far greater than any other which came out of his class of 60'. He knew danger and could smell it before he was at risk, or any others within Fire Station 112.

My visits were gradual and became more numerous as time went along. Before too much time I had met most of the crew in my dad's normal shift. There was Fred 'buckles' Willis, with those bright and shining gold and silver buckles he always liked to wear. I could never catch him without a smile on his face; regardless of the large gaps between his teeth. He loved coffee, a bagel, and afterwards I never failed to find him sucking on his teeth to get the particles out.

There was Gerry 'grumble' Show; a big brown-eyed black man who was as large as my father, but with a barreled chest and thick forearms the size of Popeye's. He giggled incessantly when he laughed, which stood out to be often. His voice was as deep as the deepest ocean, and how he could sing when he heard the old Nat King Cole songs hit the radio. He threw me in a roar when he made his grand attempts to swing dance and sing all in the same motion; and how he tried so hard to get me to be his partner when a 'catchy tune' was 'strumming' out over the airwaves.

"Come on little boy blue!" he would smile on me.

"No, no," I confessed my desire not to, as the others laughed on me, "I can't today Mr. Show."

"What's to it??" he smirked, twinkled those enlarging brown eyes; and grinned a hefty grin, "Oh comes now! You got the rhythm; I knows you do! The beat! The rhythm! We will make the firelights above us swirl and dance!"

Reluctantly I would give in and be his partner through his 'one-of-many' favorite songs. Needless to say his voice talents far exceeded his dancing ability.

Next was Hank 'two-time' Hinkle. Why 'two-time' you may ask? He always repeated himself. But he could make the best waffles in Charlestown, being a marketable chef in his former life, and so deciding he would try being a fireman in his second. His salt and pepper hair, slicked straight back, stood out with me; along with his constant, habitual nature of primping in the mirror when he could get half the chance.

Then there was Captain 'Buck' Wilson; the eldest of the group, and the one who held onto an old man's wisdom, worldly travel, and the acute ability to tell a great tale. He always found the best in everything and he drew on his vast ability to spin a thought-provoking yarn. A yarn that was pulled from the reserve of experiences he had during his life. I felt him to be more of a grandfather figure to me than anything.

Joey 'lippers' Habershack was another; 'lippers' because of all the girlfriends he had calling the firehouse. A dead on look-a-like of Elvis; even sang as well. Lamar 'caps' Singleton forever had a hat on his head due to the flaming red hair he was born with; which he preferred to hide as much as possible until he went to dyeing it a silver tint. His body-tattooed freckles were a different story, for there was not a place on his body he did not have a freckle bulging from. Kelly 'baby' Foster worked the small and cramped office just inside the main corridor leading to the restrooms. She drew the most attention with her golden blonde hair, dimple smile, city-girl approach, and her classic dress style. Kelly always exuded confidence and knew how to keep all the guys at the fire station in place; including me.

There were nearly thirty men and two women working at fire station 112, with two full-sized fire trucks in active duty around the clock. And of course, not to be the least, was Skip, the black-spotted Dalmatian the entire fire station adopted.

I have been told Dalmatians are not very akin to children. But whenever I walked into that firehouse he would gravitate to me, and I to him. It was an instant and long-lasting friendship. I would be sitting in the eatery and I could hear the shuffle sound of his food bowl. A few moments later, after turning around, out crept that bowl around the corner and he just behind it; all the while he was pushing it by his nose. Once I saw him I smiled. He would bring himself to a full stance, drop his lower chin, flip out his tongue, and wag his tail so violently that he would nearly flop his 'Behind' to the cement floor. There was never a doubt when Skip was hungry.

This was my father's home away from home. I could see why he felt such the attraction to it. There were times he would cast my tiny body into the back of the fire truck, like a father placing his son in a swing set. I felt the overgrown fireman's hardhat droop down below my eyes. And no matter how hard I pushed it upwards, it would drop down again until I settled my hand to hold it back. This always brought a rustic laugh from my father.

That heavy, overbearing, twice-as-large-as-me fireman's jacket was soon flung over my shoulders. I felt the axe in my hand that I nearly dropped the head of it to the hard floor below. They made a 'clank-tee-clank' sound when I walked in those buckled boots of his. Before long I could hear the flash bulbs going off and my father at the other end of the camera, as he took a large array of pictures to show to family and friends later on.

We would often find ourselves watching the sunset dip between the two arched and tall buildings behind the fire station there; lawn seats all stretched out as some of the men took to washing and cleaning up the fire trucks. Skip would play in the soapy water, make a dash between the fire hoses, lick up the excess flood running down the wide driveway, and then come to a sit by my lawn chair and take a quick nap.

I believe father wanted me to someday walk in his shoes. To become a fireman like him; to find triumph in tragedy; to build friendships that were lifelong and beyond any measure, and live in the world he had become accustomed to. He wanted for me to have the same joys he held so to himself. This was his dream and I was glad to experience this time with him.

As for my mother, she was a rather articulate woman. She held a teaching degree from Agnes Scott College in Georgia. Her father was a prominent businessman in the local town she grew up in, and at one time, stood against the president of the United States in disfavor on his policies about labor issues. It was not a popular stance but he stood for it, and so remained with his convictions throughout. This very trait, the trait for duty and diligence, was the very backbone to my mother's own personality. She never wavered; not once in her ardent belief system.

She was affectionately referred to as 'Annie' throughout her life, even though her name was Lauren. I never knew the purpose for this but it always seemed to fit her so well when that name sounded out. There was love behind it when she was addressed this way; and such deserving love at this.

Mother had deep raven, thick, bushy locks of hair; clustered gray-pearled eyes that hid behind her prescription glasses when she took the mind to wear them. A soft-tempered voice; not easy to rile, but simmered the Scottish heart she held to a heavy boil when provoked. Non-effacing and quiet in nature, she had the sense about her of calm confidence, yet remained within the confines of her own demeanor, as to dissuade anyone she was either cocky or arrogant.

There seemed an unknown brilliance to her manners; that genuine virtue and esteemed assurance radiated around her, and it could be most easily detected without a word spoken on her behalf. It didn't take a fluently-perceptive person to see this. Nor did it take much conscious effort for anyone to realize the real and true sanctity of my mother's presence. It simply just glowed from her.

But the deepest element my mother held in her possession; the rare jewel so many acclaim to have but so very few actually do carry, was a golden heart. It was so rare to the human race that mighty kings would fawn over to posses it. There was an unforgivable drive to never give in; to always persevere; to live the dream most see as impossible yet to be always seen as possible; to harbor hope at every angle; to cherish the longing of family and tradition; to never settle for less than what is deserving of you, and above all; to carry humility throughout the days of your life.

"Conner!" I heard her voice call back to me as I was leaving to walk myself towards school, "Young man!"

I would stop, pause, and think for a moment, then return to the back door, "Yes mother?"

"Conner, my boy," she placed both fists on her side and frowned, "You forgot something."

I thought for another moment, crossed my eyes back and forth, "Oh yeah."

I leaned up and kissed her on the cheek.

"That too," she slightly grinned, "but something else."

I thought again; my mind drew a blank.

"Don't remember?" her eyebrows shot up, "Take this and read it on the way to school," she displayed the paper she held in her hand. The words folded inward and out of view for me to see directly, "turn around," I felt her stuff the piece of paper in my back pocket, give me a pat on the behind, "now scoot son," and I was off. I heard the back door slam behind me. I had not traveled too far along when I reached back in my pocket, as she asked me to do so.

"Son? Do two things today…Ready? Good…Give joy to others, and always show yourself to be humble…"

I knew what she meant by it.

Chapter 3

A Family is Born.

My parents met in Georgia. Mother was in her last year of studying to be a teacher; father had traveled to Georgia for training as a fireman. A friend offered my father a ride to 'Jimmy's Soda Shop' where my mother was sitting in a booth with three of her friends. The attraction was instant; the engagement was brief. Very soon they found themselves snuggled down in a small but adequate apartment off of Sycamore Street near the waterfront; third floor in 'B' section, closest to the sounds of the ships coming in and out of harbor. The waves would gently push at the docks, and the long shore men who quite often found a ruckus in song and merriment while they worked.

They were married in 61' and I came along four years later in 65'. And so the family began. In quick succession our family grew until all were settled within the home they purchased in Charlestown around 71'. A perfect life; a good life; built and harnessed by the American dream.

We were brought up in a religious setting; protestant no less, within the boundaries of a very large Catholic population. Both of my parents taught Sunday school on a regular basis. Mother was one to coach and teach the youngest class just outside of the pre-school age. Father, on the other hand, preferred more the high school groupings. It was not too far along in time that he would be recognized as a gifted, vibrant speaker. One who held people's attention like a kite to a string; so much so that my father was often asked to give sermons whenever the minister was away from the pulpit.

I could remember how packed the church became on those Sunday's. The sanctuary would fill to the rafters; the air stifling with the hand fans waving about frantically to keep everyone there cool; the choir so tugging on the necks of their robes to keep from over heating; the bad-tuned organ and off-key piano trying to play in unison, but rather sounding like a dying quail after it had been shot.

I would say over four hundred climbed into those pews when it was established my father was to be speaking on a particular Sunday. I marveled at their dedication, and how people felt my father was as gifted as a true witness for God. Mother had the measure to shy away from attention, and would always have us ready early so we could be settled us in the back of the sanctuary on the Sunday's he would be preaching.

After a few hymnal songs and a scripture reading my father would gather himself up into the pulpit, pause majestically, hold both hands straight out on the podium, send out a stern but yielding expression, clear his throat to gather everyone's attention, and then begin about his saving of souls. The minister constantly remarked that my father had a second calling to speak for the Lord. My father always considered it just a matter of saving the other half of the person, since he was in charge of saving those whenever their lives were at stake. This just seemed the more natural to him.

There was one Sunday which always stuck out in my memory more than any other. It was a hot July, just after the Fourth of July celebration. Some were in travel, but most stayed close enough to hear my father preach that following Sunday. All were dressed in garb; ties and suits, flower dresses and bright apparel that had been sitting in their closet since Easter. I could see the church fill in quickly which brought my mother to some worry.

Lorie had been dragging the whole morning, and nearly keeping us from getting to the church on time. But there we were; in our polite dress attire, hovering about the back of the church. Mother held my hand to her right side; the fussy Lorie to her left, with Amanda still wrapped in her arms. Adam was still so young. We had a babysitter watching over him.

I looked about and saw all the tallness of the people standing by, so smiling in the usual affectionate way. Some were giving out nickel and dime hugs on me, which I detested then. But I did concede to give out a return squeeze to keep my mother happy, and not embarrass her. The heat nearly made me sweat my hair into a drench; my greasy collar felt much more tight than normal by the thickness of the tie that hung around it. I fidgeted most of the time till we took to a pew three rows back from the rear.

Lorie made a jab on me while I sat all huddling next to mother; staring about the ceiling, eyeballing the bright images shining through the stain-glass windows all along each wall. I turned and gave her back the offense. My mother was not amused, and so grabbed my hand and Lorie's in a stern grip.

"Children," she whispered strong and flipped her head back and forth, "I'll not have this! Remember your manners!"

I could see Lorie bend past mother's waist, make sure I saw her, and jerk out her tongue on me and go, "Naaaaahhh!"

"Naaaaahhh!" I copied her tongue for tongue. My mother looked straight up and almost seemed to converse with God there. I shrunk back as far as I could in the pew.

"God forbid," she growled, "Conner; you're the oldest and here your sister is showing you the manners of a chimp! Look at you Lorie...be a lady for a change. If you two can't behave? I'll have you after church, standing in the middle of the kitchen, tongues out, with an ice cube stuck between you!"

I shivered at the thought, though I thought an ice cube around my collar, at that moment, would be good.

"Oh mother," I weakly objected.

"Don't Conner," she put her finger to me, "Don't! I have already had it out with your sister this morning...one more word in either direction? The ice cube is coming!"

We all drew somber and quiet on this last command. My mother, through her love, discipline, and beauty, was always good on her word.

I clapped my hands between my legs, being they were too short to set back on the carpet floor; there, they just dangled about as if I were on a dock somewhere fishing (not for souls of course), whistling a tune, and passing the earliest part of the morning away. My eyes wandered about. I caught the accidental glimpses of all the people I had seen from Sunday to Sunday. They were still very much strangers to me. Many would smile and tilt their heads to acknowledge me as a polite gesture. I, in turn, would halfway grin and roll my look away.

It was here that I felt such a strange occurrence; the need for food. I had just eaten no more than an hour before. But still I had those hunger pangs people always talk about; so much of an urge that I tugged on my mother's yellow-flooded dress to get her attention. She bent her ear back behind my hand as I whispered so no one else could hear.

"Can we go to McDonald's after church?" I asked.

"You just ate son." she advised.

"I know," I kept to my whisper in my pause, "But, but, I am really hungry," my plea was so taken note of.

"We will see..." she patted me on my leg as the service settled into an introduction. Now my mother knew this was my most favorite place to eat. Even though to save money they would get one order; half the hamburger and fries for my sister and me. Still half a hamburger was better than none in my eyes. I made the valiant attempt to take my mind off the hunger urge that was surging in me. There, it happened.

As the silence went into a pause, a solemn prayer arose.

"Growl!" my stomach went off like an alarm clock in the middle of a library crammed full of studying students.

"Growl!" It went off again.

This time as if I were a rooster in the middle of a sleeping hen house.

Some looked around with an expression saying, "What was that?" My sister just giggled aloud until my mother brought her back in bay.

We stood on the next hymnal. My head mostly covered by the back of the pew in front of us, yet I held to my song book and tried to mask the words on page 67 like everyone else did there.

"Growl!"

I looked up to my mother, though she kept to her reciting on that hymn and she sang while not stirred to look down on me.

My father soon entered the pulpit, dressed in a purple robe that shinned and nearly clipped the sun with its brightness. He had an open bible in hand and a forceful look in his eye. Then, without credence, the 'fire and brimstone' sermon began. I tugged on my mother's yellow dress during an undetermined time in the sermon.

"Mother," I whispered, "Can we go to McDonald's after church?"

My plea was more to begging than anything there.

"Son," she appeared more pestered than ever, "we will have to wait and just see…"

I sitting, wandering about with my mind; hoping, even praying my stomach would keep quiet. As my father took a sip of water, and after a long dialect of turning everyone else's stomach, there was a spot of silence that came over the sanctuary once more.

"Growl!" my stomach echoed throughout.

This caused my father to stop drinking his water.

"Growl"

Snickers rumbled in and out of the pews while the entire congregation looked seemingly at each other.

"Somebody is hungry for the Gospel!"

I just thought a McDonald's hamburger would do me some good right about then. My father went to roaring through his sermon like a lion casting eyeshots over his domain. At times he held that bible on high, flipped it to and fro to get everyone's attention on his word.

When my father expended all his energy, he at last asked for conversion; those to step forward during the final hymn; to accept Christ as Lord and

Saviour; to enter the bounty of Heaven that very day and have your name written on the book of Life. The invitation was opened and he instructed the entire congregation to rise. That old wheeze of a piano started to play the hymn, and for all to sing aloud and rejoice.

We all rose in unison as my stomach rang out one final time, and so perturbed my mother that she tugged on me lightly to stand straight. I felt the push of that hymnal in my hands as I came to a pause, sung a verse, and then pull on mother's dress with one, final attempt.

"Mother," I said as she bent to me, "Please, can we go to McDonald's?"

It was urgent this time.

"Just wait, Conner," she urged, "We will see."

"Can we go to McDonald's after church...Please?"

I could see by her look on me with those gray stone eyes, she at last thought and persuaded herself perhaps she should give it a second thought after all.

"You'll just have to ask your dad."

The second verse began to play as I settled back into my hymnal. I was not singing, but pondering the meaning of what she had just said. So far no one had come forward; the isles empty; my father standing alone at the front while I was peering around the mound of people in front of me. He had his head down as though he were trapped in his thoughts; standing there, and resting his chin onto the back of his right hand.

I wonder; hmmm, ask dad.

I flipped the hymnal closed without another thought. I placed it on the pew rack in front of me, stood out into the isle before my mother could even detect what I was doing, and so I marched forward. I would settle this final; once and for all.

I could see the sun glaring at its highest pinnacle point there. The strong cache colors were flowing through those windows like a dry rainbow without any water in them. I came from the outward seat of that pew.

I was amazed by those nearby who turned in curiosity and paused from their singing, nudged one another, and whispered about as I ascended forward.

"Look, the Fireman Pastor's son, Look!"

"He's accepting Jesus," another woman gasped.

"Minister's son," I heard others say, as I looked left and right at all the heads that turned in my direction.

My father was the last to notice. I took a quick glimpse back as I did and I saw my mother squarely with her stare cutting back at me with a, 'When I get you home son?? You'll need Jesus to save you!' look on her face. She thrust such a heavy expression my way.

I turned back and saw my father taking full notice of me now. His arms were spread as wide as the smile he held on his face. I went to his waiting embrace; he leaning down and turning a receptive ear to my lips.

"Father?" I whispered right next to his ear, "Can we go to McDonald's after church? I really am very hungry!"

My father turned his face to meet mine, with so the strangest and oddest look, "What?"

"Mother told me to go and ask you…"

It wasn't bad enough that I had done the unthinkable there. But to throw my mother into such a bad light, and so suggest it was her idea would have only doubled my trouble.

"Son!" my father grizzled, "Go sit in the front pew."

I nearly froze at the thought of what would come next, stiff-legged as I was on that pew. My father closed with a prayer and a benediction, and there seemed a sense of urgency in his words. I hoped as I did he would perhaps say a prayer of grace for me in the process. None came.

The crowd mulled about as my mother came forward. My father had already descended to the rear to greet those as they left. I looked for an alternate way out and I so found a side door when I felt the pull of my mother's hand grab onto mine.

"Not so quickly young man," I knew her voice so well, "That was a mighty embarrassing stunt you just pulled."

"I didn't mean anything by it," I cowered. I turned around to face my sheepish look onto her gritty stare.

"I think a nice hot bowl of cooked broccoli would suit you when we get home."

She knew broccoli was the food I detested more than any other. Castor oil to me had more of a taste than broccoli ever could.

"Oh," I tried, "but I don't like eating little bushes."

"It will suit you just fine," she pulled me closer, "It's good for you…"

"But what about McDonald's?"

It was my one last gasp to speak on before I was required to say nothing more.

"You should bring that up now."

"But…" she quickly halted my sentence with her eyes.

"One more word," she remarked, "and it will be two bowls of broccoli. Now get to the car and smile all the way out. Don't want to disappoint the Sunday folk."

I felt her hand leading me through the masses, smiling and conversing with those who were wishing her husband, my father, to be permanent resident minister at the church; his gift for the oratory; his calling most profound; etc, etc. And at each stall step, my mother was still continuing to hold my hand high by her firm grip; with me standing in front, waiting patiently (or impatiently) for her next movement forward. I felt like a cattle head with a noose around my neck. And so all could see the grand embarrassment I was encased with.

Those before who thought I was accepting Jesus just then. And how so I was the sparkle darling in their eyes; how so things do change quickly. I could sense the eyes of a thousand looks pressing on me; with all thinking I was the evil soul and miniature demon which had been so irreverent by making my march forward during the invitation.

"Spare the rod, spoil the child," I overheard one elderly lady whisper out to my mother as we passed by.

To my most grief-stricken self, I soon found my father standing tall before me; right near the vestibule. His robe made him even more of an authority in my eyes and I nearly crumbled under the weight of his downward gaze.

"You've got a spirited one there," an old man poked his arthritic finger over my shoulder, laughed a chuckle or two, and went out the front door.

I looked about, right on the outskirts of the tall wooden heavy doors. There to my amazement was Lorie cackling and carrying on like a liquored-up child; waltzing and prancing about in a stupor; pulling up her dress in the front while she was marching with the other girls, and seeming as if she were a go-go girl dancer on stage. All the while some of the most elderly ladies stood close by with such a shocked and incredulous stare that they were nearly fainting and huffing off in a fermenting stew. Their eyes nearly bulged out and fell onto the sidewalk at such a sight; my sister had been the sure leader of that parade pack.

"Oh My!" mother hurried out to Lorie, "Lorie James!"

I made a try to follow mother.

"Not so quickly Conner," father grabbed me by the shoulder and pulled me to his side, "your mother can handle the situation rightly enough. You can stay here."

I did as he imposed while I watched the array of stares plopped down on me during the congregation's 'filing out' one by one. They made consistent comments on how wonderful his sermon was and how they could not wait for him to get back into the pulpit soon.

Needless to say I did not have my trip to McDonalds on that bright Sunday day. Yet I spent two hours at the kitchen table trying with all my powers to devour a FULL bowl of heated Broccoli. As so it goes on the appropriate punishment with the crime I had committed during that particular Sunday day.

* * *

Early in my youth, father would often take elongated trips out west. Especially during the late summer heat months when there was such a lack of rain and the risk of uncontrollable forest fires was great in the nation's western parks; most notably in Yosemite and Yellowstone. He would often seem to wrestle with himself in his sleep whenever he heard of the national parks being endangered by forest fire.

I believe the forest fire was his haunting ghost at night. He would toss and turn for hours before falling asleep, grunting and swaying through the long hours. Sometimes the sleep would never come and I would find him awake; watching the late hour news on our old nineteen-inch black and white television. It sat propped on a cart in the den. The shallow reflections mirrored back on his blank stare from the set itself. He was like a man who had been pulled into another land; wherever the news cameras would take him.

It wasn't long after this that he was off to the western states to assist in fighting the fires. He felt so compelled to 'do his share' as he put it, leaving us for weeks on end, perhaps even months at a time. No sight of him; little word, if any. Our family was fractured during these endless days and listless nights. Part of ourselves gone with him; our history stalled, the family broken from itself with everything on hold till his eventual return.

My mother felt the most anxiety from it all, though she never appeared to falter from it. She took it upon herself to play the dubious role of both mother and father. And so she might put on one hat then the other when it was necessary.

Through the birthdays, the holidays, the bumps and bruises from school, the temper tantrums, and the major tests we all feared at this time in our lives—to this, she seemed to correct everything and place it all in the appropriate order.

But there seemed a longing which was lost there; like a bird that had just awakened from a bad dream, only to discover it had only one wing to fly with and could not remember how the earth looked from the sky's point of view. And I to see how helpless this tiny bird was in its struggle to fly out into the skies once more; crying, silently for some measure of hope or goodwill to intercede. Where the laws of nature would somehow have grace on its shoulder and alter the seeming course of things; while at last giving this bird a new wing to fly with.

Each summer felt longer than the last. It seemed to be as some right of passage for him. My father would head west in his dire need to assist the lands we had never seen, or only knew of from pictures or lectures in school. Our normal ritual for bed felt all the more hastened, as if mother had a need to have time for herself; to escape even for a time when we would settle into bed, and until she found resolve to drop off to sleep. I somehow knew mother was trying to drown her thoughts in the four corners of her bedroom.

One middle summer eve, after being tucked into bed nicely for our evening sleeps, my sister Lorie was in her own room. The light darkened and the door went ever so slightly ajar. She had fears of being totally isolated at any one time, and she always insisted the door to her room be lightly cracked during all segments of the night. Amanda and Adam were still quite small, and so in the room nearest the master bedroom.

I, watching the breeze drift through my curtains, and having no conscious reason to sleep, while I was tossing onto my back and gazing up at a dark and empty ceiling.

A dim light crept through underneath my door and it kept my room from what would otherwise be complete darkness. It remained in a flicker deep within that night. I spotted my watch every twenty minutes or so, read the lit-up dial through these intervals. Midnight came and went; then a quarter till one. I heard the grandfather clock chime on through into one, then ring out a quarter after when I could no further lay in my bed than sit up and read, or do something more useful with myself.

I crawled from my bed and I sounded off the creaky wooden floors below as I stepped on them. The gentle hush of a whisper wind tossed in from the outside like a tiny rock that hit the floor about me. I felt a slight chill even in that heat, as the damp air forced its way into my room. I huddled to myself, scooted quietly through the door leading into the long and narrow hallway. I looked for the origin of this weak light which kept homage with some fading tint, yet somehow I knew instinctively where it was coming from. There, simmering through between the door and the floorboards just below, this single light was coming from beside my mother's bed. I cautiously moved down that hallway.

I came within earshot of her room and I could hear the faint echoes of a sniffle, a ripple tear, a sweet but complacent cry, and then silence before it began all over again.

Her door was cracked, and this bedside light showed me her faint silhouette as I approached; a kind and giving mother sitting up in bed. She appeared to be matching wits with her solitary despair and individual dilemma. She was wilting beneath the struggle. Her expression appeared locked into a face I had never seen before from her; a face of some level of realized delusion; a thought which extended a thousand yards long and so kept her mind in turmoil; a stare so distant that even the horizon could never hold it. Her emotions were on a rampage, as though it were a curse with no reason to exist, but was haunting her much the same. As I think on it now, it seemed to me to be the shadow of some misguided truth that had captured her thoughts within her eyes and her expression. One so powerful it would not let go.

I stepped back for a moment and I watched this unseen being wrestle her. It was like some lost and forbidden spectre that had just hit her hard, and so settled in for that battle during the long night.

I knew she had been up the entire time; the wrinkled eyes; the heavy gaze that wished and desired to fall into a peaceful sleep. I could see she felt no recourse; trapped in a world which frightened her so. She shivered. I paused but yearned to comfort her. Still, I remained like a hush with no breath in it. The silence numbed me as I watched her further.

She buried her face in a tissue already drenched by her former tears; but so worn and tattered from its constant use, it had now fallen apart all over her nightclothes. These sorrows were for father. His absence was as if it were an unexpected push in her back while she stood looking out from the highest point of a cliff; overlooking some boundless, emptied-out, roaring sea. Now she felt the falling of herself, and then drowning into the ocean of her own tears. This convergence; this manner of her trauma exposed to me a mother I had never known or seen till that time. I so made war with myself as I watched her; fear battled my desire to give her what she needed most—comforting.

I stalled for just a moment when I pushed the door free. She watched me enter without a second to re-collect herself.

"Mother?" I wondered aloud as I stood silent in her doorway. I held an obvious, dumbfounded expression on my face.

"No, no," she rushed about as though the light exposed her for all the world to see, "You can't son…give me a moment."

"Mother?" I softly pressed forward; my eyes sat affixed on her. She shivered more so now.

"Mother…"

"I hate sad endings…" I could see the television was on but mute beside me, "they can be tiresome, but also have a poignant meaning to them."

"Are you alright?"

There was concern in my voice.

"There's nothing wrong."

She collected another tissue.

"What's wrong?" I took another step to the foot of the bed, "There's no sound to the T.V."

"I didn't want to disturb your sisters and brother," she tried, but failed to hold onto her tears. They were all but dripping down each cheek like a constant stream of water running down a window, "they're hard to get back to sleep if they should wake up."

I saw her pat the foot of the bed. This was an offering to me to climb aboard. It was not often that she would do this. I moved to her side, felt her arm kindly reach over me when I bent lower to meet with her embrace. I placed my hands just underneath her chin and I felt her hug grow tighter still. I could sense the side of her cheek bending down on the top of my head.

"You will be very good about this Conner," she proposed, "and never tell your father."

"Why are you crying?" I knew the answer already.

"Because," she responded, "we can't go through our entire life without crying some. It's been awhile for me. Without the tears, the joys will never follow."

"It's about father..." I said.

She pulled me tight.

"Some days will go quickly; some days will grow longer...this day has just been one of those long ones," I could feel her cheek turn up into a tiny smile, "Like when you have to go to school, knowing you have a hard test ahead of you."

"I don't know about that..."

I had never been to school. I was still too young for it.

"Oh," she grinned more widely there. She cleared her throat as she went, "well, imagine having to sit through a very long sermon in church. Not one of the times your father went into the pulpit. But just imagine, going into church on a hard pew without any cushions. And the minister preaches what seems like a bible full of lessons."

"Yeah," I giggled, "I know about that one."

"Well then," she said, "You know what it is like."

"When will father be home?" I asked.

"I don't know son," she answered honestly, "When all the fires are put out, then I guess he will come home."

"He sure has been gone for a long time."

"Long enough, I know," mother said. I looked up to her gray-stroked eyes, "but no longer than it has been before."

I pulled up the McNally map my mother had sitting on the bed with her; the leaf bent over was on the state of California.

"Is this where father is?" I questioned.

"California?" she inquired, watching me point to that map.

"Yes Conner, he is there."

"How far away is it?"

"Very far," she replied, "a long ways away."

"Can we go see him?" I seemed to have a continual question on my mind, "Maybe tomorrow?"

"No son," her chin wrinkled a bit on that thought and I felt the tears would begin again.

"Not tomorrow. We will have to wait for him to come home."

"I miss dad," I wondered, which nearly crushed her.

"I know Conner," she wept a tear on the top of my head as I played with her map book, "So do I."

I could feel her kiss the top of my bushy head.

Suddenly, little Lorie appeared in front of us. Her tiny gown was pulled up as she wiped the sleep from her eyes.

"What are you doing up?" mother asked.

"Couldn't sleep," she wined back, "I had a bad dream."

"Then come to bed," she offered Lorie. With a pat from mother's hand on the bed, she vaulted forward and landed on the same side I was on. Lorie gave me a slight push.

"Move over," she demanded, "I like being on this side of the bed." I decided to only do what she asked, considering I wanted to cause no trouble for mother in her state. I climbed to mother's other side; she being wedged between Lorie and I.

"Do you suppose we can all sleep in this bed?" mother asked on both of us. She shifted her return gaze on one, then the other, "Don't you suppose?"

"I suppose," I said.

"I suppose," Lorie echoed.

"Then turn off the television; I'll get the light."

And within an instant everything was off. We climbed beneath the covers and we said our 'night's' and 'sweet dreams'. I found the darkness to be so settled into a stillness that it allowed all of us to fall into a deep sleep quickly.

I was the last to slide off into my own dreams, as my mother and Lorie were nearly asleep within the first few minutes. I took a peek at my watch. The hour read upside down on my wrist as I had hastily put the watch on backwards. I thought it read something like a quarter after seven, though it was actually a quarter till two in the morning.

My mother was always an ardent proponent of teaching. This being her trade, she preferred her children to learn as quickly as possible. From early on she gave us all the loving care. She would always read to us and allow us to participate with her reading. I learned rather soon; talking by one, reading sentences by two-and-a-half, telling time a year later. Lorie however was more resistant to teachings than I, and consequently was on a slower pace.

There, in the vast well of that dark night, I felt very close to my mother. Her raven hair flopped about the pillow when she softly turned from one side to the other. Her motherly love always appeared to override all other concerns. The gentle sway of her manners and genuine love to all her children carved out such a secure blanket for us, that nothing seemed to interfere with that increasing bond we held together.

It was in that moment I felt content enough to fall into my own sleep. My mother now found more comfort in a cramped bed of three instead of a semi-empty bed of one.

Chapter 4

Our Time in the Gardens.

Father would attend to many weeks of firefighting out west; some stretches being for a month or more at a time. This gave us great time to expend as a family in waiting for his eventual return. Even during his homeward stays there were gaps of days where father would be continually at the firehouse, brewing up some hysteria of his own with 'the guys'. I often wondered during these early years when time would dictate his return. I had always the curiosity as to why he was gone as much as he was. Many of my friends had their fathers close by and attended to them during the normal course of everyday life, but mine often remained as he was, with pure dedication to his craft and work.

During the fading seasons of spring and the early days of a new summer, mother would make ready plans to take us on assorted field trips about Boston. She had as much curiosity about history as I had about life, in general, at that time of our lives together.

There was Trinity Church which I found delightful to attend. The vibrant stained glass windows showed the sun's light in so a heavenly setting when it hit in the afternoon days. I would stand in awe at the immaculate show of rainbow colors. The bell tower's sound tickled on the ears at every hour; the sanctuary burned a dim candlelight appearance as you walked from front to back; the baptistery and the chancel; the grand pulpit and its carved scenes of Christ's life. Mother would come quite often go to the front pew of the church, with us tagging along, and have us sit directly behind her while she stayed in prayer for a time.

Beacon Hill and Charles Street were also of frequent visits. My mother desired to spoil herself while she looked at all the old shops and antique stores.

We were finding ourselves as 'tag-alongs', going from window front to window front, occasionally ascending within to view all the assorted antiques one could imagine, and then some. It never failed for us to take a trip around Louisburg Square, and though the bow-fronted townhouses were nearly impossible to see, we would stretch our eyes past the high iron fences and try to imagine what they would be like in full view, inside and out.

Park Street Church and its 'sky-reaching' steeple also caught all of our fancies; the Massachusetts State House and in particular, the Hall of Flags; the site to the Boston Massacre; the Old North Church; the Waterfront, and especially Paul Revere's House where he began his midnight ride; all made us constant visitors throughout the spring and summer seasons.

My personal favorite was very apparent. It was the one I vied for on many occasions, whenever mother threw up for vote 'where should we go?'. I was the first to respond; 'Old Ironsides! Old Ironsides!'. I enjoyed the seamless majesty of her sight; the tall distinguished masts; her contained canvas sails; those mighty side cannon portholes; her streaming decks. I got such a thrill whenever we went to the Charlestown Navy Yard.

However, all in all, our most common visitation was the Boston Common, Public Gardens, and the Central Burying Grounds. It was here where we roamed to play; where mother found her comfort and grace; where we 'would be of little bother to anyone, and we had the grasslands to 'play in', so mother would say.

We were early to rise on those days we went there. Packing a lunch, basket, drinks, blankets, Frisbees, and balls; enough food and water to last us until sunset. Mother always felt it to be such a harbor of nature in the middle of Boston. We began our trek at the Parkman Bandstand, where Lorie took a liking to those columns, running circles around the circumference of it, darting up and down the stairs in a giggle, light a fuse in her belly, and head out in a direct line to the cemetery.

"Mother, are you coming?" I would look back at her, as she carried all the utensils of the day, and a continual smile while she strode along in our rear. She told us the purpose of this was to keep a constant watch on our activities, as well as watch over Adam, who at this time was barely a toddle and still struggling to walk on his own.

"As always son," she was a few yards behind us, "Now mind your sister; she has her tendencies to stray."

I would bolt out and relocate Lorie. If I could not find her in body initially, I could always discover her in spirit, due to the echoes of her laughter as she scampered about. The wooded area just before the cemetery would have her prance and dance around every tree she could find; then, off to the old church as it appeared to govern the cemetery about.

"You want to help me read headstones?" Lorie turned and asked of me. She found such fascination in dates, names, and the quotes that were sometimes left as an inscription.

"I'll need to help mother first," I would look back.

"You two know the rule." mother said, setting a blanket about, taking the picket basket, and throwing out the food.

"If you don't see a 'stone', you go no further," Lorie and I said this in unison. We had heard that quote enough times to know it by heart.

The rickety stance of those headstones; how some arched backwards, others cracked, while others were barely readable, especially to two young urchins now beginning their attempts on the English language. We found some stones as far back as 1756.

The grass was thin and bare in spots, though there carried a lush phase of green wherever grass lay. Trees of overhang and heavy foliage would create long shadows throughout the entire cemetery. The hovering branches always kept us in cool shade, like overcoats to keep off the hot sun and heat from us. The flowers of bloom, especially in early spring, held the talents of every color. The bristles on that early spring wind blew in amongst the cascade of trees, and sounded off those leaves at it rumbled through. Butterflies danced along the tops of the tombstones as Lorie found adventure in trying to catch one, then another, and another. I kept my eye to mother whenever I could. I found her sprawled long-legged across the blanket as she kept both Amanda and Adam in tow.

"Conner," Lorie proposed, "Look at this one."

I could see the back of one stone. A crack directly down its middle; though by the looks of it, it may crumble at even the touch on the top. I saw weeds assemble at the base. No one had attended to it for many years.

"How old?" I questioned her.

"1804," she looked back at me.

"I say 1793," I responded.

"What do I get if I am closer?"

"Nothing," I replied as I followed her.

Lorie landed on the back of the headstone. She leaned up against the base of it where she found a daffodil close by and picked it clean.

I saw the marveled look on her face, "What's this?"

"A flower," I suggested, not knowing what it was.

"Yeah" she squinting her eyes out and up to me, "But what kind?"

She twirled it about her fingers.

"A flower," I repeated.

"You don't know," she laughed, twisted her dark hair, and began to place it in her mouth.

"It's a flower," I said, "Ok?"

I sat beside her at the base of that tombstone.

Suddenly we felt the presence of a moving cloud rise up above us in a strange shadowy form.

"Daffodil," we heard a voice above us say.

There set a man leaning about the top of the headstone; his eyes in a glare. He wore a deep green cap over his hairless brow, as if his scalp pinned the brim of it on a prop there. The wrinkles were set deep into his expression and they gave the appearance his look was chiseled in stone.

I leaned back as far as I could, up against that high slab and template, and I caught the very wears of his eyes upon me. My sister, in counter reaction, seemed to be all too traumatized by his presence; her mouth was as wide as her eyes had become.

"Daffodil," he remarked, "as plain as the nose to your face Laddy," then he perked to look onto my sister, "Lassie."

"Mother!" my sister backed away and screamed, "Mother! There's a ghost in the cemetery!"

"Why lassie," he defended, "you've caught the cold in your eye. I'll be far from a ghost yet...I may be white, but no ghost," He smiled a grin with teeth sprawled apart that further agitated my sister as she cried out more.

"Mother!" she curdled a high throat scream, "The ghost is talking to me!" she retreated farther away.

"Ladd," he looked down on my stunned face, "Is she always like this?" he gruffed out a laugh like a choke and a cough, "As skittish as a bird out of flight."

"Are you real?" I could barely bring the words out.

"Of course," he grimaced, "I'll do haunting to the weeds and long grass of sorts, but no people, least of all children...I have six grandies myself."

I stood and kept my distance in a shy manner.

"What's the name?" he still leaned out over the headstone, with pruning shears lodged between his hands.

I said nothing, yet stared cautiously on him.

"Cat took out your tongue Ladd?" he smiled.

Still, I said nothing.

"Elijah Haberstaff's the name."

I kept to my silence even still.

"You think me to be a ghost then?" he questioned, "More of an angel than a ghost Laddy," he gruffly laughed once more, though to his dismay I could say nothing.

"Well Laddy," he shorted on our conversation, "Best be back to my work," he tapped his hat rim, "Good day."

He moved off slightly to the next burial spot, stooped low, and showed particular consideration on his work as he gleaned over that square landscape.

"Johansson Rails," he read the name aloud, "A great man lives on after death when the heart of another remembers him."

He was stooping further and he took great care in cleaning off around the headstone itself, then taking a flower from a basket he was carrying with him, and laying it about the very foot of that saying he recited to me.

"You still there?" he turned on me to grin, "An old man like me doesn't usually get so much attention from a tot like you…Where's your mother?"

I turned to see my mother standing off in the distance; her hand just over her eyebrows and she trying to spot on me with her stern look.

"Conner James!" she yelled into my vicinity. I saw Lorie had finally reached her, and was so instructing mother on what we discovered.

"Ahh," he leaned back on his legs to look at me, "Good name…almost as good as Elijah," he winked and laughed a gregarious laughter. It came out in such a way that it felt he had just discovered a humorous joke, told it to himself, and it seemed to him as though there could be found an incredible joy sitting somewhere in the punch line.

"I would have been a great poet," he sparked, "if I had written down all the epitaphs to these stones and placed them in a book."

"Conner James!"

I heard the stress in my mother's voice more prevailing.

"You better go son," he leaned back onto his work, "Never acquire a woman's scorn, I say," he smirked a glimpse on me, "least of all a mother with a ready-made-belt to use."

"Conner James," I softly said as my introduction.

"Kind of figured that one," he winked.

"Nice to meet you," I gave him a half-wave where I stood.

"Likewise," he waved back.

"Are you from here?" I asked.

"Conner James!"

Mother's voice was getting closer, and so was she. I turned and saw her stammering down the embankment directly towards me.

"You better go save yourself, and plead insanity."

"Why?" I was uncertain to what he meant by that.

"She's got a hickory switch in her back pocket."

"Conner James!" she was now in the cemetery, full steam, just behind me, "If I ask again…"

"Don't let her finish that sentence," Elijah whispered over, "if she does, it means trouble."

It was too late. Mother had found me standing just beyond the stone I had fallen behind.

"Oh…" my mother stopped when in sight of this elderly man, "I've come to retrieve my son."

"Quite alright madam," he began on his work again.

"See?? Mother," my sister said. She stood behind the right flowing side of mother's dress, "It's a ghost."

"Dear," my mother laughed, "I don't think a ghost he is."

"Quite alright madam," he repeated.

"I am sorry," she apologized, "My daughter has quite the imagination."

"Oh," he said, "They were tantalizing over a Daffodil. I've seen them all. I run a greenhouse in my spare time; cardinal flower, aster, buttercups, columbines. The nasty things here; mainly thistle, dandelions, clovers, and oh yes! The creeping bell flower and green briers are terrible pains."

"Your name?" my mother asked.

"Elijah Haberstaff," he dipped his hat again.

"Annie James," she responded, "My children, Lorie," who hid a bit further behind my mother, almost disappearing underneath her long-flowing dress, "My two youngest, Amanda and Adam. And of course, you met my oldest…Conner."

I waved on him a second time, which made him grin at me.

"They take a liking to you Mrs. James," he eyeballed us each, "No…I think they do."

"As much to their father's good grace as mine."

"Perhaps," he said, "But I see your imprint."

"You must work here," mother suggested.

"On Wednesday's and Friday's…" he smiled, "But if the good Lord doesn't part the skies for good weather on those days; well, then, I suppose Saturday's and Monday's are just as fitting to be out here."

"It's strange that we haven't seen you out here before. We do come often," mother implied.

"Well," he looked about, "I am usually restricted to the cemetery. I just care take of the grounds; the resting people's beds. Good job; they don't complain much. They usually keep to themselves as do I," he grinned about as wide as his mouth would go, "Good benefits. I get a reduced price on a plot."

"No family?" mother inquired.

"As I was telling your son, Conner here, got six grandies; one on the way. Three kids—one in Oakland-technical engineer, one in Florida-scuba instructor, and the other one is in Wyoming working on a cattle farm…"

"And your wife?" my mother was full on questions.

"She died six years back," he saddened his eyes when he spoke on her, like the loving memory a husband would have of his wife, "emphysema; heart disease…She smoked."

He stalled to think on that moment; perhaps to flashback on his times with her, then he went on to change the subject.

"Worked in the Boston harbor and yards for thirty years as a dock worker and long shore man…"

There was a strange silence that was hitting the air, like a soft wind bringing in a peculiar odor; but one, with a bit of reflection, reminding you of something. You just didn't know what it was at the time.

"We are a bit upstream from here," my mother smiled and looked back at the distant blanket up on the high slope, "but if you wish to take a little time with us Mr. Haberstaff, we do have an extra sandwich or two if you care."

My mother was being polite in all this.

"Oh no, no," he shied away, "I could never impose."

"No, really," she pleaded with the elderly man, "I am sure the children would be delighted to hear your tales of old."

"Well I do appreciate it madam," he said, "I am on duty however. My direct boss isn't here," then he stared above, "but the overseer is watching."

"If you take a different mind on it later."

"Of course," he replied.

My mother began to back away with us all four clinging to her like monkeys in a tree limb. She stalled and turned, "Mr. Haberstaff," she wondered aloud.

"Yes Mrs. James," he turned and leaned up to her.

"Children can be quite venturesome. If you would please, that is if my children do come your way again, would you look over them?" hers was of a cautionary concern.

"Why certainly," he smiled, "I would be delighted."

"The offer still stands," were my mother's final words, "lunch in thirty minutes."

"I'll keep that in mind."

We were off there as I spun about on occasion to look back for the old, feeble man. I saw him darting from headstone to headstone as if he were an elf on Christmas Eve, getting Santa's checklist filled in the toy store just before the big event. I saw him stand; look about; check out his list; recheck it once more; pull about his hat and scratch that bare, bald head of his; place his hat from where it came, then spot the marker he needed to attend to next.

Mother reminded us to remain close; to play about the small grassland close by, and not to go beyond into the brush and woods again unless she approved. The wind was modest on that brisk, yet sunny day. The air brimmed with the early shadows of spring; the newborn leaves made new whistles as the breeze cast by. I could see a rabbit and her little ones hopping through the brush, inspect the surroundings, and then proceed to remain well concealed until all was clear.

I retrieved my kite that I had so longed for to fly, though I had not had a chance until now. It was a Christmas gift from that previous December. Though I was so delighted on receiving one, father had instructed me to wait until spring to give it a go for good practice; the winter air being too heavy and stiff for any chance to fly it.

It was like an angled mast with its bluish and purple design glaring back at me from the topside. I made my tumble runs across the ridge.

"Go! Go! Go!" my sister Lorie would parade me on, clap her hands together and giggle up a storm of laughter, "Go! Go! Go!"

As such was true, my tumble runs were just this; tumble runs. My eyes would catch the whipping of the tail, the bristle sound of that canvas flopping on the crossbars. And me being as astute as I was, I would spot it from behind, look back, then stumble out over a grass pothole I had never seen before, and so roll down the embankment as if I were a ball let loose in the streets somewhere.

"There isn't enough wind!" was my excuse.

"Your not running fast enough," was my mother's way of telling me to try harder, "You can do it...Know which way the wind is blowing."

I made several more attempts. I was daring in my attempts yet I was still failing on every attempt to capture the kite on the wind.

"Conner," mother called out, "time to eat son!"

Before I had a chance to assemble myself with the others, I saw Lorie full in gorge of herself, Amanda sprightly picking at her food with displeasure and more in play, while the youngest, Adam, had crawled round the blanket and had gotten his hands and knees in everyone else's food.

From the bush and without any warning, Mr. Haberstaff appeared coming to our direction.

"Food still warm?" he asked my mother with a tease.

"Why yes," mother handed him a sandwich, "hot sandwiches at modest room temperature. What changed your mind?"

"Ohh." he dug in, "Not often a pleasant day comes around to spend time with a pleasant family."

There we were like a spring thanksgiving feast, tossing about the various foods and calling out good conversation for near an hour. It was indeed a pleasant time as Mr. Haberstaff suggested. The company was warm and polite; the perfect weather a gift to us with its beauty and ease. There was a baseball field just off to our left where kids were playing a pickup game. I heard their jeers; their calls out to one another; the swing of a bat, the silence that follows; the ball lifting into the air, then the sudden cracking of the bat sound passing by us.

"You want to fly that thing?" Mr. Haberstaff asked.

"I've tried already Mr. Haberstaff..."

"And what makes a boy not try again?" he pointed a finger into my shirt, "Its Elijah."

We stood in the open, with me at the kite's helm and direction. He was looking up into the sky as though he were actually watching the wind play about just above us.

"You need a gust and good tailwind my boy," he said, "Ready yourself and when I say go; be a bird and fly as fast as you can...you hear?"

I nodded and I held the back of the kite close to my ear.

"Ready?" he softly spoke. I nodded. "Go!"

I shot out as quickly as my legs would carry me; my sister shouting 'hoorah' all the way. That kite flapped in my shadow as if I had a wing to fly with.

"Let Go!"

I instantly did so. I felt the kite glide from my hand, lift into the air, take a swirl and dive, stall for a moment, then take off higher still.

"Hold the string!" Elijah yelled.

I could feel the tug of the wind on it when my hand wrapped, hard-pressed, around it. My expression reached to spot the darting kite. It danced about the rich blue skies. The kite looked like a buck that was kicking and flapping its mane at the first sign of a rope, pulling me as it did along that embankment. I felt the exhilaration and fear all at once punch into me as I struggled to hold it at bay. Elijah came to my aid, and though he never took it from me, I could tell he was pleased at the sight of seeing such a grand smile over my face. His kind hands guided me through the process; his soft voice held me with its instruction.

"How did I do??" I looked at my mother. Her eyes were so charmed with pride in seeing me succeed there.

"I didn't have a doubt Conner," she clapped a couple of times, and pulled Adam back to her knee. I thought I had just landed on top of the world there;

the highest peek at my footstep, and the bridge of eternity now sitting in my every view—I just wished father could have seen this.

Before the day had drawn into the afternoon, we all sat round this large blanket. Mr. Haberstaff took center stage with his grand stories of old. He captivated us with his knowledge; his humor; his experiences in life; the joys he appeared to hold in reminiscing. Even my mother fell silent to his jolly and carefree ways.

It wasn't long until we found ourselves along the rim of the large lagoon within these gardens. The boats were trimming the watersides; lovers reciting poetry to one another; others out on a day trip and traveling the parameter of that clear, blue lake. We went to the dock and watched people cast out by boat. I wanted to go myself but I was too young. I felt Mr. Haberstaff's hand lean around my shoulder and so pull me to his whisper.

"You'll be out there someday soon enough young man."

Mother had taken the children down by an embankment while Mr. Haberstaff and I walked onto the Lagoon Bridge. We peered down over the sides to look into the foaming waters. The ducks paddled by and underneath the bridge. Some would look up at us, quack a bit, then wait for us to throw down the leftover bread from our earlier meal.

The sprinkle ray of sunshine moved with the heart of that lake. The reflection spawned such brilliance that it nearly blinded me when the sun bent lower in the sky. A few clouds moved through the plain of that old day; it bringing shadows which were dancing across the bridge, embankments, and lake itself. Spring was almost near and it held a certain rebirth to that season; a bridge to something that was better than the past; the guidance to new hope, a dream long-last realized. I had just begun my life and I had not seen that much in the seasons changing. But this I do remember; on that day, in that hour, I had met a friend for a time in moment.

"Look below young Laddy," he pointed to the waters beneath where we stood, "You see?"

"See what?" I looked up at him with a confused stare.

"Look deeper," he said and he lowered his voice.

I crumbled through the deck, came to a squint, reached deeper and more concentrated into that realm; past those ducks and geese, and so sighted my own reflection as it rolled in the waters, "Me?"

"It's a sign boy."

"Sign?" I asked, peering up to his ancient face.

"It captures you," he smiled, "in a time, when you give the waters your attention, it will look back at you. You will see what it gives back to you."

"I don't understand Mr. Haberstaff," I was being my normal self; a confused, little boy.

"It reads your face and tells of the boy you are," he said, "Now. A part of you will always be in these waters…To say, Little Conner James once past this way, like all the little boys before you once did. It will ripple and cast off wherever the waters go."

"It will?"

"Without a doubt…"

"I suppose," I got to my feet.

"Some even say," he began, "the rivers, lakes, streams, oceans, and seas are an entrance way into another world."

"Well, I wouldn't know about that," I splattered in a mater-of-fact way, "Don't suppose they lead to anywhere."

"Oh you think?" he gruffly smiled at me, bent down to spot my eyes with his, "And how do you suppose a boy of such small stature knows these things? Eh?"

"I don't," I was sure, "I just hear them…is all."

"You're not an easy Laddy to convince, are you now?" He let out a cantankerous laugh that seemed to echo throughout the areas surrounding that bridge.

"Just a boy is all I am."

"Well I have heard," he started, "that some waters are the waters of the past….they show you what has already been; fond memories that your remember from long ago…"

"I don't remember much," I shrugged my shoulders.

"Oh but you will," he giggled and wrapped his old hand around me, "when there is more time that you have seen, and the more time you can remember with, then you will my boy."

"I suppose," I was still rather confused.

"But there are," his stare was reaching out along the bay, finding solace on the tiny boats that were crisscrossing the horizon in front of us, "some rivers which are about the future…they show you what will become. You look into their waters; very deeply mind you, then they will show you a glimpse; just a glimpse of what is to come."

"I'm just a little boy Mr. Haberstaff. I don't know about those things."

I climbed up on the railing.

"But," I wondered aloud as I climbed back to lie across the bridge. I looked over the edge and I peered out on my reflection once more, "which one is this, do you think Mr. Haberstaff?"

"It is the sea of the future Laddy."

"Really?" I bent back to look at him while he stared down from the top railing onto me.

"For me, it is only the seas of the past. For you it is quite a different story."

I looked back in these floating waters, concentrated mighty heavily then, "I don't see anything Mr. Haberstaff."

"I do..." he softly spoke.

"What do you see?" I asked.

"Come up my boy," he asked. I stood as he leaned down in a kneel and brushed the dirt clean from my pants. He grabbed my waist with both of his eyes and he squared his expression at even-eye level with mine.

"Do me something Conner," he had a most worried look on his face.

"Will you?"

"All right," I was becoming confused again. It was here that I looked away to spot my family by the shoreline. I heard only the last fragmented words of what Mr. Haberstaff said to me there.

"When the time comes," he paused, "be there for your mother. There will come a time when she will need you most."

He never blinked on this, nor did he flinch from his serious, engaged look. His brow became more cross and dark even; never breaking for a smile or flinching from the importance on what he was trying to say to me.

"I don't understand."

"You will need to do for her as she has done for you. You will be ready. I assure you...but be brave and ready."

I was speechless, not knowing what to say. I looked past Mr. Haberstaff. My mother was sitting by a small inlet where she was staring out our way. I leaned about one of the many stone columns and I caught a glimpse of my mother standing to that shore side. Our eyes did connect in way which would have launched a thousand thoughts between us. She carried such hope in her gaze; the fixed, gray eyes posed something only a mother and a child will ever know; that connection; that inner language of dialect that only two people born of this relationship could ever communicate with. It was like a single harbor for my ship. She was standing there along those shores. My siblings were strapped to every side of her. I had no meaning and understanding on what Mr. Haberstaff was trying to tell me then. But by her gaze, there stood a thousand definitions of how our love was between us; this, in so my simple stage of life, I could understand most completely.

"Someday you will return," he said, "and remember what I have spoken," there he smiled as we heard the ducks give a uniform quack our way, in want of more food, "Time is an adventure Laddy...Enjoy your stay in Life!"

We threw out more food. All manner of fowl jockeyed for position on the next morsel we tossed that way. Mr. Haberstaff took me down below and so said his farewells to us all.

I thought of all he had said during our drive home. It constantly wore in my ear like an echo that spouted off when it had the desire to do so. Weeks passed and I wandered about Mr. Haberstaff and how his well-being was. I asked mother for us to make a return trip to the gardens and cemetery, but she slighted me off for another day. I still persisted. After nearly a month had passed, mother took us all back to the gardens for the next visit.

A day that was much similar to the day when we had last seen him. The sun was rising and casting the grounds more green. The early morning breeze chased us through the meadows; spring was more to arrive and giving hints of flowers abloom. Different sights and sounds of sing-song birds paraded through the trees and seemed to give life to every limb about. My mind was set; I wanted to see Mr. Haberstaff again.

When we got there I asked mother for permission to go to the cemetery and find Mr. Haberstaff. She obliged in her usual manner and said 'No.' I was never one to find that word to have any appealing prospect whatsoever, so I pursued it further.

"No," my mother was more quick and firm about it. I would wait a bit for my opportunity again.

"I said no Conner." When she spoke my name, I was pushing it for sure, "Help me with lunch."

I decided to get on her 'good graces' and do as she had asked of me, then spring that request on her a third time.

"In a minute Conner," she was beginning to concede.

I waited. My mind was persistent now to the point I would no longer enjoy the day, the sun, the gardens, if I did not get my way.

"May we please mother?"

"Alright Conner," she proposed, "You lead the way."

I shot out through the long gardens, down into the thatch of woods which led to the cemetery, and I did not give care that they were following me.

No one could match my pace. I found myself out and about on my own in a matter of minutes. My breath was nearly lost as I reached the cemetery's outskirts. The lawns appeared strangely long and unkept. The weeds had begun to linger; the wildflowers more afoot. The strong array and assortment of beautiful flowers were gone, and the cemetery looked more distilled and dark without them.

I felt the strange bellowing of a gust of wind cross over my path. I lingered from one side to the other; its tiny gail blows followed me in my path; my gaze pressed my eyes to nearly come from their sockets while I went through these unguarded stones and posts.

"Mr. Haberstaff!" I called out, "Mr. Haberstaff!"

Nothing, but for the shimmering wails of the tree limbs overhead that seemingly were in a shudder at my presence.

"Mr. Haberstaff!" I came full circle. I found myself surrounded by the very mist of this cemetery. I saw the dotting of sunrays peeping through the heavy overgrowth trees. The shadows would pop through, and then suddenly disappear when the clouds were playing about overhead. I was sure he would be here; he to be amongst the images and shadows of the treetops which skirted along the lawns throughout this entire cemetery plot. I felt the silence consume me, but for the high-perched bird that lofted above me. I am sure it was in watch of every move I was making. I went from plot to plot, looking past every stone.

"Mr. Haberstaff!" I would call out periodically, but to no avail.

My mother came into a distant view but she stayed there watching over me. My siblings climbed aboard her like she were the mother monkey of many chimps.

I felt a wind push through; the leaves rattle some call when it came to surpass me. A melody of nature, in sorts, hovered most nearby. These plots and gravestones had been here for many-a-years, and they would so remain long after I was gone. But somehow they seemed alive here; carrying the eyes of those they represented, and so seeing the charm of a little boy running about these grounds in search of something he did not know, yet they knew more of.

Mr. Haberstaff was their friend. He took care of them; gave them the soft smell of freshly cut flowers; kept their grasses cut clean; the weeds and unsightly wild vegetation out. And without the love and care of such a man, it would appear less a harbor of love and more the harbor of neglect. There, in that moment, it felt as something was missing and I was in search of it.

I kept to my ongoing pace. I leaned over a headstone large enough to shelter that kind old man. I heard the clipping noise and I saw a bent figure huddled over near one stone.

"Mr. Haberstaff!" I ran to him. I spotted the figure as it turned round on me.

"Mr. Haberstaff?"

"What is it boy?" a grizzly, bushy-haired man with tiny-framed glasses stood to face me, "You lost your family?"

"You're not Mr. Haberstaff?"

"Who?" he kept to scratching his head.

"I thought you were Mr. Haberstaff."

"No son," he appeared frustrated with me, "Gilbert."

"I am looking for the groundskeeper," I spoke hesitantly, as not to offend him further, "He comes here regular."

"That would be me," he puffed out his chest.

"No," I responded, "The groundskeeper; Mr. Haberstaff."

"I said boy," he snuffed, "That would be me."

"I don't understand," I said.

"Neither do I son," he smiled with barely a tooth behind his lips, "Don't know this Haberstuff. Been here working nearly twenty years and I never saw anyone by that name come around here."

Just then my mother came to my rear.

"I'm sorry my son disturbed you."

"Quite all right lady," he made his way back to attend to the plot which, just a moment ago had his fullest attention.

"He was just looking for someone," she politely defended me as she pulled me back by the shoulder.

"Haberstuff," he gruffed again.

"No, Mr. Haberstaff," I correct him.

"Elijah Haberstaff," my mother proposed, "The groundskeeper, you have seen him…"

"Listen," he stood, "I am the only groundskeeper of this place; been so for years. If there was a Haberstuff here, he was here long before me; and hasn't been here since," and he snapped his head down as if to prove his point.

"We saw him here recently," I conjectured.

"You say Haberstuff?" he thought with a queer expression on his face, "Can't hear good boy. Speak up."

"Haberstaff!" I pronounced more affirmed.

"Haber…"he stalled on the word.

"Staff," my mother calmly swayed on him, "Mr. Haberstaff…do you know him?"

"Haberstaff," he bent down and stared at the ground just in front of his feet, "Haberstaff, Haberstaff…Hmm…Let me think," he would say over and over again, as though he were in a conversation with himself, "Seems like that name does ring a reminder with me," he opened up his blackened mouth wide this time and he barely showed us a tooth in the process, "Ah! I have it," his eyes lit out like two fireflies dancing in the darken air, "follow me…"

He led us through the maze. We crisscrossed over several rows of tombstones until he came to one smaller and nearly split-out stone; the etched out wordings were barely readable after all the harsh weathering it had been through over the long years.

"There you go," he lowered his head in presentation, "Mr. Haberstaff," he smiled once more; filling the air with a goofy grin and silent laughter which never made it to sound.

"This isn't right…" my mother questioned.

"Well miss," he sounded perturbed, "that's the only Haberstaff I have seen in these parts."

I had lost this man in my mother's conversation with him. The stone so lost in the ages, felt hard to the touch. I bent to remove the debris before it. The cryptic signs were barely recognizable; the words harsh and chiseled poorly out by a heavy hand. There was a crack embedded through the stone, and so cut through the name, "Elijah Haberstaff."

I could not blink, nor think to do so. I touched each letter in shock; the wording seemingly dripped down onto my palms as I lifted myself free.

"It must have been an ancestor who comes to visit his family often then," my mother suggested.

"No miss," the man replied, "Even the redcoats have visitors from time to time. But this one? No, never seen anyone come by this plot in all my years. This must have been a rather lonely soul through his years," he laughed.

"Well then," my mother angrily sparked, "there must have been an exception."

I knew by my mother's words she was in as much disbelieve as I was. Her tone told all that she too was thinking much as to my thoughts; Mr. Haberstaff was a figment of a ghost who had crept back into our world to shower a day with us.

For whatever reason, the lonely man from the past had found us and made his presence felt; in hopes of giving back something that was lost to him. His life was unknown but for the name he told to us, and it seemed now to be but a shelter to his real purpose.

I could feel his eyes looking upon me there, staring back from that distant history he had so long ago lived in. The talents from crossing time, like an echo which found its way to us. He had given me a message that had yet to be fully realized; and one I had passed away as nothing more than another sentence in our conversation. It had slipped by me then, and I was so lost in that confusion.

I replayed what was said before; even the manners to his ways; nothing. I looked out across the fields of headstones and I swore I could hear them call to me.

"Don't you remember Conner?" they spoke out in unison, though in a sudden blast which rippled through the trees, I was brought back again. I found my mother's hand still settled over my shoulder.

"Remember Conner?" she said, "we have to get to the store," I felt a nudge come from her hand when I looked up.

I had forgotten everything at this point.

"Thank you sir," my mother said in parting.

"Not a problem lady," the old man shot back. He leaned down to continue on with his duty. We drifted away from him and mother pulled us along whether we wanted to go or not. We were to escape now, more so from our own fears than anything else.

"You are not to talk to your father about this," she tugged, pulled, bantered, dragged us along, "And furthermore, we are not to speak of Mr. Haberstaff again; probably a local miser playing a trick on an unsuspecting family—nothing more than this."

"I don't," I tried, but the words were lost.

"Young man. Mr. Conner. You abide by me. You hear? There was no Mr. Haberstaff; just a man playing foolery and trying to make us look like a fool. You are not to go into this graveyard again," she turned to Lorie and so smartly pronounced, "Nor you young lady."

"I told you he was a ghost," she whispered over to me.

"Stop it!" mother warned, "Mind your sister. This discussion is over with."

Nothing more was said again. I took hold of Amanda and helped her carefully walk through as we went along. All the while, Lorie just skipped in my mother's shadow. Mother clung most tight to Adam until we made it to the open grounds.

Later that evening, while sitting alone in my bed, I could hear the raptured sounds of that day in the park playing in the back of my memory.

The sky was so blue a painter's dye could not have made it more perfect. We were lingering along frog pond, while watching other children wading in; and how I would soon take part by Mr. Haberstaff's constant encouragement; the swan boats and lagoon rides; playing about the bandstand; skipping rocks across the ponds, and settling out on Lagoon Bridge while feeding the geese and ducks as they passed underneath our stage. It was a most glorious day to be reminded of.

I would sit there in my first reminisce, even at such a young age; toiling about in my mind the times we shared, if ever so brief. It seemed a day made from Heaven's own hand to me.

The moon was white bright that evening and it cast a hollow gray hue through my window shade. The strange and iridescent misty shade filtered an odd radiance into my room. Everything appeared to light up, as if a spotlight were being flung from the tree limb just outside. I was at comfort then, remembering Mr. Haberstaff's smile whenever I closed my eyes. And as much to all this, I tried to think of what he said to me that was so important. I spun the day's events back and forth in my mind, rewinding to every crucial segment for any clues; nothing came. It was lost when I was least paying attention to him. And no matter how hard I tried it would never come to me. Just the soft temper of his nature found its way back. The laughs; the grins; the drenching stories of old; the soft confidence he displayed to me was what prevailed.

    I thought he would be lost forever; to somehow fade by my young inability to remember the particulars of him well enough; just another character to enter my life and then leave. But little did I know that he and I would meet again, and the words he relayed to me in my youth would play such a profound role in my life. There was more to Mr. Haberstaff than meets the eye you could say. Ghost? Angel? Or just a vanquished soul drifting in and out of life, I could never speak of with any certainty. Someday however I would discover just how important that one day was; those hours we spent together, and the words he sent my way. How all of this would resolve itself to me in the end.

Chapter 5

When Times were Younger.

My beginnings were humble and astute. As I have spoken, I was raised on the north end of Boston called Charlestown; a quiet, sleepy, and homely plot where families had lived and died for generations gone by. The streets were narrow and angled, barely allowing for two cars to travel side by side on. But it made for a tight and most intimate setting from house to house. This is the world I have grown up in and I have always known. Some will say I am an ordinary man, raised from ordinary beginnings. I would have to believe this to be most true above anything else.

My life as a child was as normal as any I suppose. I grew up in the shadows of the Red Sox struggling, and eventually falling to the Reds in a seven game series. I remember staying with a friend of mine who lived close to Fenway; and his father and friends taking us to that climatic sixth game when Fisk hit the most gigantic blast over the green monster. Surely the Red Sox would win after that dramatic victory. The sounds in that ballpark were deafening then, with the initial hush as all the fans were perilously watching before the final pitch was thrown. Then as the subsequent roar of the crowd lifted when that single ball was belted out, cleared the fence, and meant victory for the Red Sox nation. It was like watching a warring hero return from battle as Fisk came rounding those bases for the final run. All was well in Red Sox land that night.

Jason 'Gum' Winchester was his name; a friend from the start, and one who followed me through into my adult life. We called him 'Gum' because you never saw Jason without a stick of gum fumbling in his mouth; as if it were rambling through and trying to steal some of his teeth. Others would quite often call him 'Stick' because of his general stature and physique in those days, and that he only used sticks of gum to chew on. He didn't enjoy this adjective too much so I just stuck to 'Gum'. There were times he must have been chomping 5 or more pieces in his mouth at one chewing session. And in this case, his speech impediment became so great we could barely make out the words he was speaking on.

Jason and I became very close during our early years. His father was a firefighter, as was mine. Both were stationed at Charlestown for several years until Jason's dad was eventually transferred further south, close to Fenway Park. On many days Jason and I would go after school, pack an evening supper; one that was quite easily transportable, get to the local vacant field, pitch ball initially in catch, hit grounders to one another, then fast pitch in turns until darkness set in.

"You want to pitch first?" he would always ask.

"No," I came in simple response, "You have to get me out—remember?"

"You always go first…" he shot back.

"You fussing again Gum?" I was smarting at him, picking up two bats, and swinging them about me.

"Well, I gotta learn how to hit in order to play."

"You'll get your turn," I assured him. And so this went time and time again; me hitting all his best pitches.

"See! That would have been a hit," I would say, as I shot a fastball of his over the third base line.

"No it wouldn't."

"Yes it would Gum!" I refuted once more.

"Nope," he replied, "I had my third baseman holding the line…it's late in the game."

"You're taking an out away from me then," I suggested.

"Yep," he sent the next pitch hard at me while I stood in the batters box, and he nearly took the shirt off my chest.

"Ball," I cried.

"Strike!" he smiled.

"Ball!" I insisted.

"Strike," he responded, "The ump has a large strike zone."

And he laughed and cackled on this. Next pitch came barreling down into the box and I sent a whizzing shot right back up the middle, nearly taking Gum from the mound. He dove to save himself rather than stick his glove up to field with. I eyed his expression while he cleaned the dust off of his jersey.

"Hit!" I laughed, "A lousy fielding pitcher couldn't handle my cobra strike!"

"Two outs," he calculated, but his math was as poor as his fielding skills.

"One!" I was more irritated this time.

"No," he quietly implored, "Two. My shortstop had to cover second on a count of the runner at first was stealing second."

"What runner? There was no one on."

"Yes there was," he explained, "Don't you remember? I walked the first batter of the inning."

"No you didn't," I held the bat down to my waist.

"Yeah, I did," he got into pitching position once again.

"No," I moved closer, "you didn't."

"Yeah," he took to his wind up, "I did."

And so he hurled a pitch directly at me. I took a rather unkind offence to this, charged the mound, and tackled him in his midsection. We landed in a puff and cloud of dust. We rolled our bright clothes into a dusty, mangy, and 'mother-to-be-feared' punishment for sure.

"Boys!" I heard a voice call out.

It was Mr. Simpson reading the evening paper. He was casting out white rings from his pipe while sitting on his second story perch, just above and down the first base line.

"Boys! You do this every time! How many times have I told you; if you're going to play here, play fair!"

We came to a stop, looked upward and about, and saw that middle-aged, ball-headed man stare directly down on us.

"Right Mr. Simpson," I gathered myself up, dusted myself off as best as I could, then gave a hand to Gum.

"Your turn," I whispered in a mild-mannered, most polite way.

During those times when we had nothing more than the evening, waning sun; that old dusty field; and ourselves, we would talk about our future lore with the Red Sox's, among other things. Going off to college; Jason the resident staff ace; me being the consummate, booming third baseman. We would make our legends there first; then, when the draft came, we would both be selected by the Red Sox. Next we would travel the lonely roads of the minor leagues together, bust up a few hotels along the way, then finally make it to Fenway and become heroes to all the fans there in Boston. That was our dream, and all along the way we would be together, exploring life as two unkindred, kindred best friends that we were.

One of those late summer evenings when the sun seemed to set at its latest time for the year, Gum and I had a most intimate conversation. It was after practicing much that late afternoon and sitting out in centerfield. We took to a talk; one that I can still recall even today.

"How did you do on the butcher's test?" he asked. He was lacing up the leather fingers on his worn glove.

"Same," I responded. He knew what that meant.

"Failed," he smirked, fell back, and tossed the ball straight up in the air.

"Terribly," I spit in my glove, rubbed the palm through, and smelled the leather seep from the glove's joints. "There is no hope for me now."

"So what will your father do when he finds out?"

"Not worried about him, it's my mother."

"She'll give you trouble, I know…"

"Trouble? I'll get horse whipped. Then she will tell my dad. Then I'll get horse whipped again."

"You can call in sick to school the next day," he kept tossing the ball straight up into the sky.

"Then let the butcher McEwing have her way with me—good!" I smarted back.

"How did you get her anyway?" he missed the ball on one turn and he shot out to retrieve it.

"You tush!" I remarked, "Don't you figure? I'm in the J's-J, Ja, Jamesss; you're in the W's….you got Wilhelm; the push over. He would give A's to toilet paper if it walked into his classroom, sat in a desk, smiled, and asked smart questions. You have it easy Gum."

He drew into a serious expression there; his smile wiped clean from his look; his eyes grew a cherry red color, "No, I don't."

I stopped and said nothing right away. I could feel the wind blow between us with a hot summer gust that nearly choked us as it went by.

"How come you say this?" I asked.

He paused and seemed to be in a long, careful collection for his words to come. He thought, spirited the silence in a sort of anticipation of something I had no clue of; for which appeared to burden him beyond my own imagination of knowing it. There was a matter deep within him he had been holding for sometime; waiting, wanting to spurn it to my attention. A sort of silent calamity that is more punishing to keep in secret and in hiding than to have the experience of altogether. I could tell Gum would be cautious on his words; to tell, but not to tell so much for the mere release of it might give him as much peril as he felt at that moment. This would be the bonding of our long-enduring relationship together.

"You have good parents," he softly spoke.

"So do you," I replied, though he said nothing; kept to himself and his silence, "You do have good parents Gum."

"Some would say so," the implications were far reaching on those words.

"And you wouldn't?" I asked. I felt the silence from him again, "Gum?" I watched him pitch the ball up several more times, though he would not take to look at me there.

"You ever wanted to be someone else?"

"What do you mean?" I pressed.

"Like in another body; not start over. Just see the world in another way. Somewhere else; be someone else."

"Don't suppose I have," I pondered for a moment.

"I have," I heard the ball snap and pop in his glove as it landed very hard in the palm, "A lot of times."

"But—why?" I dared to ask.

I was not thinking of what response might come next. But thinking rather how hard it would be for my friend to tell me anything at all in that moment.

"Swear," he spoke out one word.

"Swear?" I echoed him back.

"Yes, swear," he bore down on me eye to eye, "Swear; never to tell; never."

"Swear to what?" I was more lost in this.

"Swear!" he grabbed me by the shoulders, pushed me down like a big cat in play. He sat on top of me and would not let me up until I made good on the promise, "Swear, Josiah Conner James!...or I won't tell."

"I swear," I felt him loosen from me a bit and let me free to sit up once more, "Ok?....ok."

I felt the silence once again surround us and create a sort of eerie presence in our conversation; one that would have the crowd at Fenway Park in a hush, if we were sitting in the outfield there.

"Your dad, did he ever touch you?"

I was merely in my early teens at this juncture of my life, so there was no measure of understanding on this statement, other than the simple gestures a loving father would display to his son. My look towards Gum gave all away. As if the oddity of what he said sought to confound me more and more, while my thoughts grew deeper on it.

"Touch you?"

I must have held a rather large question mark within my expression there. One so large that it must have bent down on the arch and plunked ole Gum on the top of his head for having been so dinky in his ways.

"Yes," he was looking away, fumbling the ball about in circles inside his glove, as if the world was rotating in his hand, "Touch you."

"What do you mean Gum?"

"Touch you," his look shifted out of range behind me, then deeper into left field, "Isn't that normal?"

"My dad doesn't tuck me into bed anymore," I was laughing, thinking I had a revelation on what Gum was speaking of.

"No tush!" he shook me a bit and I could see the serious nature of his look spread all over me, "Not like he touches mom, nor my sisters, but touches me. Sometimes, I don't think it is right—but I don't know. Maybe seems most natural in other families, but it don't seem right to me. Sometimes I go home and I am afraid when I go to bed; hoping that bedroom door stays closed and never opens."

"What happens when it does Gum?" I became more serious then, thinking I was being spooked by a ghost, but not seeing it like you would think it might scare one; there, late at night in the shivering darkness of a room and carrying with it an evening chill. But I felt it then; as real to me as if the spirited hands shook my bed covers and brushed against my shoulders in the empty black.

"He comes."

The air about us became deaf. I felt it keep me from speaking directly until I could say only, "What does he do?"

"Touches me," he whispered, as a tear dropped down from his far cheek, and dripped to his glove.

"How does he act?" I inquired.

"Real silent like," he quickly, though softly replied, "as if he didn't want anyone to know; as if he might get caught."

"What do you do?"

I nudged a little closer.

I saw him look about the world like he had been just born in it; he staring out and feeling like it wasn't the place for him. That somehow God and fate had made a mistake to bring him about like this. It was the first moment I saw the horrible vulnerability in my good friend Gum. Nothing would change our friendship. I knew this and so did he. Why else would he risk telling me? He was like a brother to me, and I a brother to him. We had shared so much up to this point in our lives, and I knew Gum even better than my whispers knew what to say to me when I was alone; bored, and decided to talk to myself in an attempt to keep me company. He was close to tears, but he fought it back as hard as he could. He was quite still while sitting next to me.

"I keep quiet," he paused, "Still," another pause, "and pretend a little."

"Pretend?" I was supposing, not knowing what he would say next to me, "pretend…"

"Like I am not there," he rubbed the ball hard into his open glove, "Like I am somewhere else."

"Like you wish to be; like you want to be."

"Only then though," he stopped, "Not any other time."

"What does he say?" I was reluctant to ask.

I felt another hard gush of hot wind encircle between us and move on. I could see by his corner stare this conversation was beginning to wear on him.

"Don't that feel good son?" his voice became soft as a baby's cuddle sounds, "And I don't answer....I never answer."

"How long does this all last?"

I tried to figure out the reasoning in all this. I had known Gum's father as long as I had known my own. It was an impossibility for me to have forethought all this, nor believe in an instant on the validity of this story. That is, until my good friend Gum told me on that fateful summer afternoon in the abandoned ballpark.

"Few minutes," he stalled to think, "Maybe more. I lose track when I pretend."

"Mother know?" I asked.

"No," he was most hasty to answer.

"Sisters?" I imposed once more.

"No," he came again, "Your it Conner."

I felt the weight of the world pass from his shoulders to mine all in that second.

"We should tell someone, don't you think?" I offered up to him.

"No!" he snarled, and then he came back to some calm, "It isn't bad...besides; I can pretend a little longer."

I sat beside my friend Gum for sometime there and I said nothing further on the subject. But just speculating inside my own thoughts how a man can do this to his son. I wondered how Gum would do, not telling, but believing 'to pretend' was the answer to all the questions he may have in the matter. All I knew was I would be his friend; then and from there on-no matter what.

We sat close to one another for a little, yet we were more like two sand pebbles at the opposite ends of a twisting and winding desert. The late sun torched us for a bit more as we watched it curl back over some of the city's nearby, elder buildings. That light dropped and sprayed everything into a seeming haze of gray, white, and black.

I saw a coach pull on by near to us, with a bride and groom on board. They were toasting the beginning season to their marriage. They laughed and carried on like two drunken fools in a stupor and a merry brawl of joy. I heard the clomping steed spur into a grunting sound, hesitate for a spell, and then continue on at the insistence of the on-board driver. I saw the groom look our way, smile, and toast us as the carriage was to pass us on by.

"Good joy, young boys," he giggled like a silly schoolboy who had just had his first kiss in life. She, in turn, smiled, raised her glass in the same sort of ceremonious salute to us boys of summer.

"Think you'll ever get married?" I asked.

"I don't even like girls," Gum remarked and chomped on the ancient, three-hour piece of gum, which by now must have been hard as a rock between his teeth. I pushed him along with my glove, smirked a half-wrinkled smile as he turned on me; pushed me back, and off we went scattered dance along the sidewalks. We tried to catch one another.

I nearly caught one boy on a bike when we turned the corner to the soda shop. Old man McKenzie always had an empty stool or two for us to hop up on. I think they must have stood more than five feet tall, greased down with slippery oil, and nearly spun off their platforms. I always went first, being the better athlete, and then I would help Gum on board his own stewpot seat.

"How is it chops?" McKenzie would always ask. He was rubbing down a dingy, ten year-old glass with a rag I even wouldn't wash my dog with, "Hey, check out the rug."

"Nice dooooo there Mr. McKenzie," I replied while I watching him flip up his hairpiece just a bit. He smiled and winked out a happy expression our way.

"Dooooooo," Gum followed to say behind me.

"Best threads this side of Manhattan," he quirked, "Shaved my dog last night from tip to tail."

"Glad you did it in the summertime." I said, "It'll take a good six months for Chip to get his coat back."

"You economizing on the restoration project Rock?" an old man beside us said, pushed out his empty soda glass as if to ask for another. Mr. McKenzie snickered and groped a laugh, though his expression told us he didn't like the old tart too much.

"Cheaper than water," he poured out another dark soda for the guy, "but better than wine." He looked our way, "What'll it be chops?"

"Cream soda," I said first.

"Butter Scotch Waltz," Gum mumbled his reply that sounded more like, "Butha Scocth Woo."

"They teaching him English in school," Mr. McKenzie frowned on that suggestion, "or Gaelic?"

"English," I responded.

"Then spare me on the translation," he bent his ear closer to me with a light-hearted gesture.

"Butter Scotch Waltz," I was much clearer than my counterpart; as we both looked on Gum. Gum was grinning ear to ear like a wet dog caught with the chocolate sticking through his gapping smile.

"Well listen boy," Mr. McKenzie looked Gum square in the eye, near to the point I thought Gum might very well digest that huge wad of gum laced in his mouth; clean through to his stomach, "You got acne in the mouth?"

"Noaa," was Gum's simple reply.

"Can you spit?"

"Noaa."

"Can you swallow?"

Gum gulped a try, but failed, "Noaa."

"Seems like your going to lose your teeth before they come in completely. Don't you know gum is terrible for your teeth?"

"Noaa," Gum shrugged his shoulders, and looked about.

"Well," Mr. McKenzie shrugged his shoulders in a mocking manner, "Now you know. Can't say you're ignorant on that fact now, can you?"

"Noaa," the gum seemed to protrude from his mouth, and gape from the hole in the middle of his face. Mr. McKenzie took an old, seemingly tired glass and stuck it under Gum's chin. There was a pause.

"Come now boy," Mr. McKenzie urged, "Spit." shaking that glass in fine fashion. I heard that huge tumor of gum topple from Gum's mouth and into the bottom of that glass.

"Now," Mr. McKenzie winked, "Don't you feel better?"

Gum shifted his eyes back and forth, "No."

"Keep on the chew, and you can take that nickname of yours most literal then. Try gumming a tomato sandwich?"

Gum said nothing, but remained quiet.

Without warning, Mr. McKenzie pulled his false teeth out and plopped them full-face on the counter in front of us.

"I have!"

He smiled without a single tooth to show for it. To Gum's horror I saw his brow grow to a sweat there; his eyes roll white and nearly hide in his head; his hands shiver; his tongue leap back into his throat, and he nearly choke in front of me. I surely thought Gum had seen the ghost of the Almighty there as we sat.

"Hee hee! It isn't a pretty sight!"

I stuck my nose in that cream soda of mine as I burst out a laugh. It was echoing through the glass as my eyes were tearing so hard from the uncontrollable humor of it all. So much so that Gum took exception to even a whisper I might have spoken then, though I kept my giggles encased in the glass and I never looked to eye on him; not once.

"What's so funny?" he pushed me nearly off my seat.

"Looks like you saw a gremlin there Chops," Mr. McKenzie grinned out an empty, black grin; winked on Gum with a flirty wave, then picked up his teeth, clapped them a couple of times near Gum, and said, "Chops! Chops!"

"You have a glass eye too?" Gum snorted.

"Your friend doesn't take pardon to much ribbing does he?"

Mr. McKenzie nudged me and began to talk about Gum as if he were not present there. I had been to this soda shop on numerous occasions and over time I had discovered the off-brand humor and notorious manners of the owner himself. He was always full of life; a bit of a gabber, but he held such a way with happiness, that it seemed to follow him wherever he went. Gum had only managed to be present with me once before in that shop, but Old man McKenzie had a recital to attend to that afternoon for his granddaughter.

It took a bit of adjustment and warming up to for Gum, though as the day drew out further and the city lights caught a glimmer and light, Old man McKenzie had Gum in laughter before too long. The soda shop was a merry place and I always found enjoyment there whenever I went in.

It was time for us to leave, as my mother would take to worry on Gum and I; that is if we were too much later than we already were. I gave McKenzie my 'see you soon' and my promises to return very soon. We darted out the glass door and onto the sidewalks. We passed on several blocks and we found refuge in the streets close to my home. I gathered up a stick the size of a baton, kicked it around the open streets a bit, and then tossed it back and forth for the rest of our journey home. Gum and I passed it out around while we hit the roadsides and made it slightly rattle with a kind of warping, saw sound. Then we plucked a few picket fences along the way, which nearly made my teeth chatter when we did as much.

We were in bed before too long. Gum took to a sleeping bag on the floor and I lying in my single bed, with the loft window just above me opened halfway. The curtains were twisted and rung by the wind as I watched them as they danced just above me and to my right. I could hear the hollow sounds of cars with bad brakes rattle down my street, come to the stop sign, and wheeze from the nearly worn down pads to the rotors. Every once in a while sirens would go off as the paramedics and police made off on their duties; and others, I could hear mumble sounds of people conversing on the walkways, across the street, and the outlaying cars with the windows rolled down.

"You think you will ever get married?" I heard Gum whisper up to me.

"I don't know," I said. I was still watching the twirls of those curtains; my hands propping my head up, "I suppose some day I might. Never thought about it too much myself."

"Girls," I could tell he was still in defiance of that gender, and then he grunted, "Girls."

"Gracie Fran thinks you're a peach."

"Yuck!" he spat out that vile medicine.

"She does," I smiled, "Really."

"Girls," he swore on it once more. Then a pause and silence came; I knew we were thinking the same thing.

"Conner?" he spoke back in his whisper again. I could feel him get on his knees and lean on the side of my bed, and look out the window on the unknown world with me, "Thanks…for today."

I said nothing, though I looked square on him down at the edge post of my bed.

"Whatever I can do Gum," I finally spoke.

He reflected on this in that moment, though I knew he was most reluctant at replaying what passed between us a second time. Harsh memories, even so fresh, are hard to digest. There was no need to dwell further on their meaning. Our silent pact remained. We were to remain friends through it all, no matter what.

Gum retired back to his sleeping bag. Soon I could hear the gurgling sounds of his snoring resonate through the lower portions of my room. The hallway light cut past the little sliver of door-opening my room allowed through, and I could see someone peering in on us for just a moment.

I myself thought of this time, with the deep melodies of this night dropping down beyond the draws of my window. Like a cushion pillow to my mind, I spent away into my sleep by accident; into a dream only meant to keep me company until the new day dawned on the other side of that night.

Chapter 6

The Treasures of my Early Life.

I remember, often during those summer Saturdays how we would go to the park and catch a Red Sox game. It didn't matter who they played; only that we were able to get in and see our Red Sox team vie for that long elusive World Series title. We met an old man one early spring, after we watched one of the team's pre-game warm-ups. His name was Wes 'Spike' Shanks. A bit ancient and rather the more eccentric, yet we grew very fond of Spike. He had worked for the organization for decades as the consummate, manual score keeper in the outfield. He always kept tabs on the other ballgames, posted scores as those changes warranted them, and placed up on the scoreboard those 'egg zeros' as he would call them, whenever our team or the visiting team did not score. He always giggled in glee when the other team 'put up the goose and made it cackle!' as he would say. Every time an opposing player struck out, he would bark out, 'SCRATCH!' and throw out such a torrent laugh, it sounded like a rusty harpoon whistling through its cage as it was being shot out.

Jason and I would sit out behind the scoreboard, watch him work and cackle like a crow. And so we would keep that old and decent man company. A few games turned into more, and then the season vaulted from one season to the next. It became a ritual on many Saturdays for Spike to make a special request that we were invited into his area and we often got in for free. He even got us jerseys signed by all the Red Sox players.

"Hmm!" he grunted, watching through the peepholes, "Yankees…pin-stripes meant more for jail than baseball!"

"Why do you say that?"

"Cause," he shot back, "They're a curse," then he would walk over to me, poke his pudgy finger into my shoulder and snarl, "And—I—don't—like—that—Bucky—Dent!. You better not like him," he seemed to swear on us.

"No..no..I don't" I tried to assure Spike. He swung his finger into Gum's direction and started towards him.

"Neither do I!" Gum shied back, "Trust me."

"Good!" I saw him frown up his chin, bob his head up and down as if it came up for air in the water, "Irish and the Red Sox—the best two kin there is. Your Irish aren't you Peewee?"

He was looking at me with a left eyewink, sitting by his chair, widdling away at his apple, "Don't like the skins…pesticides and all…kind of like those pesky A's."

"I'm Irish," I spoke, "I think."

"You a Red Sox fan?"

"Why of course," I was more certain on this one.

"Livin?" he pointed the sweaty knife right at me.

"Why yes," I spoke more profoundly this time.

"Breathin?" his knife shook more; his eye more in a squint. I felt the knife nearly puncture the air between us.

"Dien for then?" the last hurdle.

"Yes," I gave my final allegiance.

"Good!" he rocked back in that cranky chair of his between innings, that I thought it may very well crumble just by his slight weight. He still was cutting the apple skin free, "You can sit with me then. Quite a privilege you know Peewee; sitting behind the great Fenway monster. The crack of the bat, the roar of the crowd, the whistling ball as it steams overhead, some thirty; no forty feet above until it whips into that upper screen. You can hear their cheer as the Sox'y boy rounds those bases!" He nearly cried and laughed with pride in saying all this.

Now old Spike was indeed the character. He had been the scorekeeper for twenty-five years, or the 'gatekeeper' as he was fondly referred to. A man of large stature, he once played second base for the Red Sox lower level minor league club for two seasons, but could never advance any further.

'He just could not hit-it was like watching a toothless man try to suck a grapefruit through a straw; defense nearly stellar; best reserved for later inning 'fill in's' when his position had batted through the game.'

This was the etching on his scouting tombstone, which concluded his baseball career. He spoke admirable on the game however. The thurst and yearning passion for it stirred him, and love of it always remained.

He wore wire rim glasses that mostly hid on his nose, and they seemed to drown in the wrinkles of his face. Hair so white, I thought the weather had snowed on him even in the clearest days. His arms were short; his legs more like stumps than legs, and he wore the cheapest cologne he could find, or something a soup kitchen must have thrown out a day earlier. I could imagine old Spike rummaging through the city's alley dump heaps in hopes of finding 'that new deodorant'. He always seemed to wear something in the plaid family; with lapels that were so wide they appeared to be splitting his shirt in half. He enjoyed the color pink for whatever reason. I could never take to it, but old Spike constantly wore it as if it were a badge to his honor.

Then there was his whimsical personality; a fancy brew of 'age-old stories' and heartfelt memories. He rarely talked of his family; his wife having died some years ago. His son off in San Diego in the military-half the time he never took to see Donnie.

"The boy has a life of his own," Spike would smartly say, grin; look down with a tinge of sorrow. I knew it caused him some measure of pain when he reflected on it, "I gave it to him. Now it's his time to live it…It's his time."

"Did I ever tell you about Brew Johnson," he would go off on his wild tangent of old baseball lore.

"No," Jason and I would uniformly speak out, "You didn't," and so the story would begin.

"Well," he always started his introduction this way, "He had a cannon-for-an-arm. He would cock that arm from deep center field, launch his bullet towards home plate, and it would land one skip home. He could break the back of any catcher with his dead fastball. One time I caught one of his furious relay throws, and I had a thumb blister for a week on my glove hand. You follow me Peewee?"

I was alert, as he would always tell us the tidbits between innings, "Yes' am."

"We were in first that year, with three games to play; 72-44 that year. It was the best team I ever played on; two games up with three to go. We had our last three games at home against the team just behind us in the standings."

Then he would pause for a moment, stare skyward, and smile.

"I'll never forget what Brew Johnson did in that series."

"What did he do?" Jason asked.

"At that time, Brew was playing in the field for four games, pitching on the fifth game. It so happened, if need be, he would pitch the final game of the regular season. First game? We lost 9-8. Brew took out the last three pitches he saw for homers. One to left field, one to right; the last a towering shot that left the stadium so fast, we never saw it leave his bat. Still, it wasn't enough."

He stalled on this point as I began to whittle on my own apple.

"What happened in game two?"

"Came back, we were down 8-1 by the fourth inning; the home crowd now getting antsy. To lose a lead like that, it began to ring down the 'boos'. Brew came up in the fifth; two out, bases loaded-no where to put him. They walked him the first two at-bats. This time, he would shove the ball down their...He waited; first pitch? Nasty 12 to 6 curve that nearly hit Brew. He snarled at the pitcher; the crowd nearly cursed that young left-hander into his grave. Second pitch was a fastball as close to his chin; knocked that hefty Brew on his backside. He stood nearly six foot five; barrel arms; legs like a python grip. I saw Brew dive straight back so fast his helmet shot off his head and nearly rolled all the way down the third baseline. Brew got to his feet, shook the bat barrel right on aim at the pitcher and told him the next was his."

"Really?" I admired and laughed on this, "I wouldn't mind being like Brew then."

"Now Brew could have taken a shot in the back there, go to first and get a run home; but Brew was greedy then. He wanted his swings; he had to have his swings! Like an itch that had to be scratched; Brew was going to get his swings."

"He hit a homerun on the next pitch...yes?"

"Oh it came," Spike was in full reflection now. He replayed that moment like it was the soft song he remembered from ages ago. Like a whisper in the trees on a June day. The sweet embers of a rose long past its prime. He recollected all the joys in that memory with us.

"That pitcher ducked the lip of his cap; 'Ok'd' the catcher's sign, bent down, leaned back, heaved a mighty throw towards the inside lower half of the plate. I could hear the ball sizzle in the air.

"How so?" I asked.

"Son! I was standing on first base as I was. Old Brew swung so rapid a swing; he clocked that ball right on the bat's trademark. Shot it like a bullet from a gun, right between left and center."

"No homerun?" I inquired.

"It thumped against the outfield wall so hard, the ball spun all along the warning track; past the centerfielder and leftfielder, rolled clean across the foul line to the corner. I could see Brew bearing down on me as we rounded those bases. Click scored first, Desmond second, then me. I turned back and I saw Brew kicking dust around third base as he headed for home. The crowd stood; I could see the throw from that corner send the ball barreling just past Brew's right ear."

"He was out wasn't he?" Jason asked.

"Now that's the strangest thing," Spike simmered on it for a spell, and then finished his tale, "Catcher caught the relay just in time. But I was sure seeing the catcher as he stood; he had a Popeye view of Brew's grunt expression as they came to a collision. I swear that catcher gulped down his tobacco chew when he braced for that tackle Brew laid on him. The ball exploded out of his mitt. And down he went, flat out of conscious, like a baby who had his last bottle and was now doing his sheep counting. Brew stood, stomped on home plate, looked down sneering at that retired catcher."

"What did he do?" we were both drawn into the story now, as was always the case on Spike's stories he told.

"He fired out at him, saying 'You called the pitch bud!'"

And how Spike laughed on this as he nearly tumbled backwards out of his creaky old chair.

"Well? Did you lose the game?"

"8-7. Funny; the catcher was out cold. He left the field and they brought in the utility infielder to catch out the rest of the game, but we still lost."

"So last game," I said, "Brew to pitch."

"Pitcher's duel it was." Spike began, "No score until the eighth inning. Brew had struck out twenty by that time."

"Twenty?" I marveled.

"Twenty," he again recalled.

"How did you score?" Jason inquired and bent forward on his own chair, "Did you win?"

"Did we win?" Spike laughed aloud, "Now would I spout out a tale and we not resolve it to some victory? Of course we won!"

He took a huge bite out of his apple and he drew up the hard core in his mouth as he chewed on.

"How many did he strike out that day?"

"Twenty four went down."

"Is that a record?" I wondered aloud.

"Till 1963," Spike had a memory more sharp than any whip, "Someone did 25 in an eleven inning duel."

"Whatever happened to Brew Johnson?" I asked, "I mean. He never made it to the big leagues. I never heard of him."

"Let me tell you a spill there Peewee," Spike became all serious with me, drawing closer, and eyeing my expression as if a father to a son, "Most greatness is never realized. There are many-a-stories of 'what could have been'. The past is littered with lost hope and ancient dreams. Fate gives virtue to so few, and plight to the many. We all weigh our fortunes on a scale; and rather count what we could have had, rather than what we do have. There are no promises; not for you, nor I, nor Brew Johnson. Now, I will tell you in all, Brew Johnson, if he had come to his fame rightly, he would have been a Hall-of-Famer for sure. I've seen many come and go. Most with less than half the baseball talent than what ole Brew Johnson carried," Spike was so enthralled by all this; we had mostly forgotten the game in hand.

The crowd was in a stir as Spike went to peer out anxiously through the outfield walls; take to a look and try to measure what was going on, "What's the score? Who's on first! SCRATCH!"

We looked out our own peepholes.

"Yaz is up!" I yelled.

"No, Freddy Lynn," I think!" Jason spewed out his suggestion and winked through his own eyehole.

"Isn't Fisk on third?" I cried out.

"No tush!" Jason swore, "You bat blind goon! Fisk hits after Lynn!" Gum and I were nearing another one of our wrestling brawls again.

"Ohh!" Spike became all too frustrated, "I'll call the dugout."

He got on the heavy black phone close by; there was a hurried pause, "Sam-score please. We still a goose this inning? Hits? Two? How many outs?"

He paused. There sounded a crack of the bat. A thundering fly was sent out of the infield and how that crowd rose and bellowed out a roar so deafening that Spike tried in vain to hear what the dugout was telling him, "Who hit it? Drago? You said Drago right?"

I could hear the profound stress in Spikes voice while he shoved himself forward, still barely attached to the phone. He was looking out his own peephole to see what was happening on the field of play.

"Laid three eggs this inning!" and he let out a resounding hi-grunt laugh which nearly cracked the phone in two.

"Put those Pin-stripers back in their cage! That-a-boy!"

We cheered as if we all three were amongst the players in the dugout. It was like we were waving home the runners as they were passing on by; hitting home and returning back to their spots alongside of us. We were caught in the collective heat of that moment, and the story of Brew Johnson somehow escaped us. The joys of our beloved Red Sox taking a lead on the Yankees stirred us to forget those faint whispers from so many years ago. In those yards, when the past was not so, but the fresh daisy to life itself; they were king. But now the Red Sox and their hopes to somehow make it to the World Series was our current plight; our riches to scour through and find, and so find the wealth of what may come to be the most important venture for us all.

We did not speak of Brew Johnson any further that day, nor do we ever again. Spike never told me what happened to that minor league legend. Yet so it remained, as it was, the reclined mystery that had disappeared from years gone by. That is…until.

Gum and I had spent those many-a-spring and summer Saturdays at the ballpark. We were taught how to be a meticulous guide for the box scores through on every game that was being played on that particular day. On occasion we would peek out to see the long outfield grasses stretch into the infield. We watched intently the comings and goings of every batter who came to the plate. Most would fail, as life is, while a few met the glory with the tradition, and so became heroes in the hearts of the fans who saw them. Some were heroes only for a day; others for a career. Still more met with folklore and legend, and thus became part and parcel to the tradition of this glorious game; stories that were to be told years down the road. All with the purpose to create legends and folklore all in the same story, and give to the newer generations the reasons why the game of baseball was married with its tradition.

There was one Saturday which Gum and I were most unusually left to ourselves. Both of our fathers had to pull a three day shift and as such, a relative of mine took guardianship for the day; an uncle who took us to Fenway Park, gave us directions to which seat he would be in, and placed with us specific instructions to meet him there by the end of the seventh inning; and no later. We were as good with our adventure as we had always been. We went through the turnstiles with abandon, and so ran to the same lady attendant in aid, who knew us quite well.

Her name was Katie Blanch with bright hair, a gleam smile, freckled from head to toe. She had glorious waves of fire red in her hair that when the sun sat directly upon it, there seemed to be a rich sunset right in front of us. She would always guide us through the maze of security till we reached the outer skirts of the outfield walls. Here is where Spike would be sitting, waiting patiently for us. I could still see him peeling that apple just before game time; his whisky smile sprawling in our direction upon our approach. He gave a grand 'Hullabalue!' with a tilt of his head and a stiff, gruff rub on his chin.

Today, above all others, would not be the same. I spotted Katie first, though she kept her eyes in attendance to the fans most immediate to her. The moment my eyes met on her expression I knew there was something wrong written in it; a distant stare; a place where her mind went yet her body remained; the place where we go to escape when a person is not able to venture out physically; the place of security, of eternal sunsets and eternal sunrises; a place for peace.

"Katie!" I ran to her. She turned.

"Conner," she forced a hapless grin; her eyes told of that distant shore of some far away place.

"What is it?"

"Gum," she deferred, with yet another displaced smile, "Boys, you best follow me."

She said nothing more. But as she went in such a formal manner, she could say little more. I dared not quiz her any further, but only to say, "Where are you taking us?"

There was a painful look in her expression. It seemed I had stung her for even thinking more than keeping quiet there.

She walked away from the activity on the field, down three winding corridors and into a vacant, enclosed room with sparse seating about, and a door that read 'Administrative.' Katie led us into the room; said nothing more; gave all her needed conversation in the last stare. I saw her glance at us on final second while the door slowly came to a close.

"Katie?" I spoke out as I watched her eyes fall to the floor; the door closed behind her, "Katie?"

There was a pause; Jason and I passed a distressed look to one another, and neither could mince words for a bit.

"What was that all about?" Jason came whispering to me, staring out with a disoriented stare. His jersey was off-center and hanging limp from his left shoulder; his cap turned in a tilt.

"I don't know," I speculated, though we waited for a few minutes in that silence, until we heard the lone walking steps of dress shoes faintly snapping down the far end of that front corridor. I could hear the haunt echoes of each step as they passed by our door and went further down, as if in search of us.

We waited with a frighten stare; a pause in an empty room, not able to swallow when we could see the doorknob turn. In came a man who wore a pinstripe suit; elder, with an empty hairline, thin rim glasses, heavy wrinkles that surrounded his cheeks and lips, ruffled and heavy brows, and a stern, concentrated look on his face.

"Gentleman," he spoke out in a strong voice, "You may wonder why you are here…"

We could say nothing, but could only stare up at him like a grandfather who was readying himself to give us the most resounding punishment from a switch.

"I didn't think so," he brooded, "I am the General Manager of the Red Sox," he guided us with his hand in a stature for us to take a seat. We found ourselves, all three, sitting in a triangle. Jason and I watched and waited for him to explain.

"I won't make this into a grand speech. I have had many hard choices to make in this position during my tenure with the Red Sox; many announcements I have had the terrible displeasure of relaying to others. It's inevitable that from time to time, I have to perform duties which I do not care for."

He took a deep breath, grew painful in his gaze on us there.

"But this….this perhaps is the hardest of all."

He stopped short once more, almost as if he desired to wait for us to say something, anything.

"You are Conner," he tried to smile and asked on me; I nodded.

"And you are affectionately called…Gum?"

Jason nodded as he nearly swallowed on his gum.

"I have heard good things about you," he said, "Many good things. In fact, much of the team is aware on the both of you."

"How?" I asked. I was noting I had never met any member of the team, "We just come to see Spike."

His face drew worn once again.

"The reason for you being here…Spike has been affectionately a part of this team; a part of this organization for decades. He has been here longer than me, and will always be so…even in spirit."

I could feel the sense of terror overcome me, as the shockwave rode through my face like a lightening rod of electricity just ignited. I felt quite taken away from that moment then; a snapshot of my life stilled into a prevailing surreal time, like a dime dropped into a heavy, deep, and dark well with me waiting for it to make its haunting sound when it hit the bottom. As if the world had stopped breathing but I continued on without it. I caught the air of some lingering chill when he spoke those words.

"I am sorry boys, but Spike passed away in his sleep last night….apparently from a stroke. The family has been notified." His look grew even most grim while he awaited us.

"But that can't be?" Jason's jaw dropped open, "We just saw him last week. He was fine."

"I'm sorry son," he looked on Gum, "It's been a terrible loss and shock to us all. Spike held a deep love for the Red Sox, as the Red Sox held for him."

"I don't believe this…" I stared off to a place that could not be seen to the naked eye. But that which so locked my mind into some internal dream; that my eyes could only follow suit on.

"Spike was greatly fond on both of you. So much so, that I think he would want me to suggest what I am about to say,"

I saw this elderly man make the best attempt to comfort us both, though my heart wasn't in it. I had never had been a personal witness before to someone dying who was so close to me. I felt I had been sheltered from the world so conveniently, then as unsuspecting as things in this nature come, I had been thrust into a most unsecured reality of all. My heart sank about my ankle as I watched on Jason. I saw him too, holding his head low, looking as it seems for his heart around his feet.

"We would like for you two young gentleman to spend the entire game in our dugout, with the players, wearing your own uniforms. We even have your names stitched on the back. We will have a prayer in honor of Spike during the middle of the seventh inning…I think Spike would have wanted it that way. I know he would."

"I don't know…" I could only say.

"It is for you to decide. I just want to honor what Spike would have wanted. I owe him more than this, but unfortunately, this is all I can give."

"Is that what you think Conner?" Gum spoke to me.

"Yeah," I looked back to him, " I think he would."

It was settled at that point. The General Manager led us directly into the locker room where all the players and staff surrounded us. They were giving us a hero's welcome, adorning our jerseys and caps, and then escorting us to the dugout. The open air did us welcome, though I stared out into centerfield and I immediately saw the flag lowered to half staff, in honor and in loving tribute to Spike. The players were as hearty and heartfelt as I imagined them to be. Yaz was the more gracious, as he specifically asked Gum and I to sit on each side of him.

"You know," he softly spoke from the large man he was, "Spike spoke of you two everyday I saw him. I always thought of him like a surrogate father myself…and I am sure you did too. He was pepper to my salt. He always kept me grounded."

I was very intimidated by this larger-than-life hero of mine. He was sitting there, chatting with me as if I were his equal. He made me feel this way; a boy so young as I, though to be treated like a man in his eyes. Yaz smiled often with his hair turned off from the side. I saw his spirit in him and I saw Spike's spirit in him too. Like a ballplayer who had been so affected by the charm and genuine nature of this long-lasting man. And with so a bit of reflection we could see the shadows of Spike walking in our own souls.

He paused for a moment there, wrestled his arm around my neck, and gave me a bear hug that was more gentle than strong, saying, "Life is flavor my friend; Life is flavor."

Gum and I sat in the dugout for the main duration of that game. All that day Jason could say very little, but he silently chomped on his barrage of gum; spit out one, then took another one in. Before long this too came to be flying out of his mouth and another would take its place. I, on the other hand, was reflecting with my thoughts, except to dream myself into the game that day; finding myself on the playing field of my dreams.

During the middle of the seventh inning the announcer came to the loud speaker and talked of Spike and his presence with the Red Sox. I looked about. Many had a solemn expression on their face. Others already had their heads bowed and I was certain their thoughts were exclusive to Spike. My eyes went deep into the outfield. I stared out over the scoreboard where they had posted all zeros in honor of Spike.

"Scratch! Scratch!" I could hear the whisper echoes of Spike yell out in a howl, then a raucous laugh he always spread about in his happy ways. I nearly wept, not knowing how or why that emotion overtook me, though it nearly did. I took a deep breath, collected myself, paused, lowered my expression to the dugout floors, lifted my hat about my face, and wondered one last time how this could be.

The game was tied 2-2 with the heart of the Red Sox order coming to bat. Yaz came by to sit by me one last time before he would come to the plate.

I wondered. Had he heard?

"Spike ever talk to you about Brew Johnson?"

"Brew Johnson..." Yaz gazed down on me like a father to his son, gleamed a smile that nearly made an expression on his face.

"Why certainly. Everyone knew about Ole Brew."

"Is it true?" I asked.

"The stories you mean..."

"Yes," I pinpointed myself more precisely.

"They are very true..." Yaz winked and smiled.

"What ever happened to Brew Johnson?"

"Well..." Yaz stammered a moment, thought, then spoke, "After the war, being a rather decorated pilot, he returned home...found his way back into baseball—the game he loved since he was a boy. He did so until his last day."

"What did he do?" I wondered; I looking up to Yaz as a boy to his father might.

"He became a scorekeeper for the Red Sox..."

I nearly dropped to the dugout floor while I saw Jason take the biggest gulp and swallowed his gum, and nearly choked on it. It was him; all that time, it was him.

"But...He played third...He was a big man in his day?"

"Wasn't big enough you say?" Yaz laughed and grinned on it, "Son...He was a legend in minor league play. They say he would have been one of the best players of all time if he had come to the big leagues."

"Why Didn't he?" Gum inquired.

"Man had his principles; love of country was greater than his love of baseball. He had to serve, and he felt the duty was worthy enough to risk it all. He went into service in 41', and didn't come out until 'V-Day' in 45'." He paused, and I could see a slight tremor exude from Yaz's voice, "Spike is a good man. He touched so many people, and gave more than anyone knew. A man I respect more than any other…"

"He could have played when he returned…" I suggested.

"Too many injuries in war son…He had a few medals for bravery, included three purple hearts. The injuries were too severe for him to ever play baseball again. So he did the next best thing," Yaz smiled broadly there, reflecting on the man he loved and endeared himself to.

"If he couldn't smoke the cigar, he sure as heck was going to smell it as long as he could…"

Yaz gathered himself up, went to the plate soon after, drove in two runs with a smash double to the deepest part of the ballpark. I leaned over the railing as he took his swing. The crack of that long wooden bat of his took out the silence which preceded it, and it brought thunder from the crowd afterwards. The dugout erupted like a volcano spewing its lava. I was proud Red Sox fan watching the players climbing from their seats and embracing the runners as they crossed home plate; so descending back into the dugout, tossing out their helmets and crying, "That was for Spike! That was for Spike!"

Goosebumps ran all over my body as the chant descended from the dugout and made its rounds into the front bleachers. Eventually it brought everyone in Fenway ballpark to a chorus of chants. I went out to get Yaz's bat from the umpire from where it had settled on home plate.

"Spike! Spike! Spike! Spike! Spike!" the crowd roared out as if they were the lion standing atop of its domain and showering the lands with the long shadows of its presence. I swirled around and I saw the many faces of the crowd in near chaos there. All the while I was standing briefly on home plate.

The moment was filled by magic; like a sweet smelling wind that just crossed my way. The kind reflection; the sun peering high in the blue sky as though Spike were smiling back at me; the galactic chants above us. It was a drama that could never be scripted, though it happened by the very decent nature of that moment. We all could feel it, including the White Sox players who stood out in the field. They glanced about and marveled in that same wind. They paused it seemed, to reflect on this very special man who appeared to have touched so many.

I saw Yaz give me one final grin, pause and reflect, blow out air, raise his helmet slightly, and settle it back down on his head in satisfaction. He sent a wink my way.

"Spike would have been proud," I thought I heard him say in that look he sent back to me, "We got one for Spike."

I returned back to the dugout. I sat in my same seat where Dwight Evans gave me a smile and a silly rub on my cap. He passed by and seemed to act purely out of impulse. It was there I truly felt like a Red Sox player.

The Red Sox won that day 4-2. A late-inning, come-from-behind victory as Spike had so often performed in his prime; playing just on the edge of the big leagues and so creating himself as a legend in minor league play.

An announcement came over the intercom, once the game concluded, for Jason and me to please proceed to the main ticket counter. We came as requested. We were bypassing all offers to go back into the clubhouse, and so finding ourselves in front of my very angry uncle. He quickly reminded us both that we should have met him at his individual seat in the middle of the seventh inning, yet he conceded that as long as we said nothing against my father's wishes, he wouldn't tell or reprimand us.

I remember the ride home as we waited for an hour just to leave the parking lot. I heard the muffled laughter of those fans through the car windows. They were making their way past us. As was his custom, my uncle said nothing at all. I suppose he felt more of an obligation to take us to the game than for it to be an enjoyable outing. It was always his nature to be more quiet than silence itself.

I felt a greater loss still; the game would never be the same again. My mind wandered about as I leaned my head up against the enclosed window, though Gum poked me a couple of times with his glove as he hoped to pull me from my trance. Still, I persisted. I paid him no attention and kept to my daydreams there. The reflections of the past; the memorable days I spent coasting about with that old man; set in his ways. I could now see the joys of his particular personality each and every Saturday home game the Red Sox had over the past two years.

So many occasions to reflect on as I played through those thoughts; one by one like a series of old records I would play in sequence. Take about a spot on my old porch, close my eyes, and listen to the tunes as they came and went, and so reminisce on what they all meant to me. But Spike was like the best record of them all; the one you listen to the most. The one you savor the longest and leave the last to play.

I thought of Spike like a surrogate grandfather to his grandson. I had never known either of my grandfathers, but I imagined then how Spike would have been a most pleasing substitute on their behalf.

It was early evening when I found myself home. Feeling tired, I told my mother that I would rather be alone for a while in my room. The house drew strangely silent behind my enclosed room. No one rarely moved about, nor made hint of passage by my room. The house was old and scant, and had boards that would wail and creek a huge snore of sounds when the other members to my family walked past. I knew they were most concerned about my unusual behavior that evening. Father would be home soon from his three-day stint at the fire station, and surely mother would have him come and have a talk with me as soon as he got home.

It wasn't long before I heard his heavy walk cause those old planks to cuss at him on his every step. He seemed to pause at the door for a moment, and then proceed to dangle on my door handle and push himself through.

"How was the game?" he asked, though I kept to my thoughts and my full silence.

"Son?" he spoke in half-whisper and half-talk, "What seems to be the problem?"

I was lying on my bed; stomach down, with the pillow propping my head up so I could have partial view out my window. I saw nothing to entertain me.

"Why do people have to die?" I wondered more aloud than to have asked him a specific question. My father's presence was always a strong one. His eyes were deeply-set, though they were as blue as the clearest blue sky above, which somehow penetrated from their deep set ways and glowed even in the dimmest light. He wore a frame tall and forceful, wrapped by muscles that would crush a bull if he got a hold of one. His skin was patchy dark and hairy in most places, though he kept himself quite clean-shaven.

That Musky hair of his had such a wave in it that it seemed to wave at you whenever you were to pass by. Nor did he appear to care how it looked. He would often wear a hat which had the name of his precinct unit and fire station on the front. 'Station# 112' always inscribed on the base rim, yet he wore a wide variety of colors from green to gray, yellow to orange, and back to blue and purple once again.

I could sense him standing off in the deepest shadows of the room; close to where he had shut the door. His eyes were in warm glow then. He moved from shadow back into the rays of light as he softly stepped and bent to the side of my bed; close enough to whisper and hear out our conversation, though far back enough to keep me from seeing unless I should bend fully back and catch his eyes with mine. I remained however as I was.

"I don't know son," his voice was more soothing than trite, "It's one of the great mysteries."

"How often do you see someone die?"

"Once, is one time too many," he responded before a pause, "In my job, we do our best to prevent it. But sometimes we can't avoid the outcome."

"What do you do?" I was full on asking. A new world had been opened up to me. One of terror, fear, yet it held on me a sense of curiosity I had never felt before; as though it were an undiscovered country I had just found, and I so wondered what exactly I had stumbled across.

"Deal with it the best you can," father imposed to say, "And go on. It's what we do. It's what we are."

I felt his large frame bend on the frame of my bed, and he seemed to be leaning me closer to him by his own weight.

"Why the questions son?"

"Spike," I called out his name.

"Spike," my father repeated, and so hesitated, "Spike…yes, Spike; the man at Fenway; the scorekeeper."

"He died last night," my voice tailed off just at that last word, "In his sleep."

I could feel my father lean upwards and capture his stare over the open window. It was time for another lesson in life.

"Do you remember how often we go to play catch Conner?" he questioned me.

"Two, maybe three times a week."

"When I can," he started, "I come home, grab my glove, ball; you do the same. We look forward to the fun we will have and we can't wait to get out on the playing field. Because we remember how it was the last time we did it."

"Yeah," my pillow felt as if it were sinking, "I know."

"But it had to start somewhere," he said, as he placed his hand on my back, "The first time you never knew. But I remembered when my father took me to play catch. And so, from that time on, I wanted to pass it along to you. A time for us; a time for father and son to enjoy moments together, as it was for me and my father…"

He stopped for a little when a faint gust of wind blew my curtains inward, and so caused such a ceremonious wave that I thought of Spike and his wondrous ways. I could sense an unintended tear tilt down my cheek, and softly touch on the dry pillowcase below.

"Life is kind of like this," he began again, "There is a beginning to a time, a place for it to live, then at some point in time, it ends. Very natural; it just was meant to be…"

"When was the last time you played catch with your dad?" I announced his way. I hoped he would answer.

"It doesn't really matter. It ended at the time and place that it should have. I think we both knew that life had changed us into something different."

My dad leaned in, and my tear grew into another. He could feel my pain like it was his own.

"You'll learn son…Life can be hard, and it can be good. But in all, it still gives to us something of value to remember on. Spike gave you something to take with you; something you'll always think of."

"What is that?" I buried my head in my pillow to wipe the tear off as quickly as it came.

"A touch of a soul on yours," he whispered, "Something you will always hold dear, even at my age."

He shook me about in an attempt to rustle me out of my stupor. I turned round to finally face my father there as he looked down on me with pride and prejudice; but most of all, with love.

The man had such a gift with his heart, which was merely masked by the largeness of the man he was. I watched as he stared on me for that moment; the glow of something so enduring; a connection of thoughts and blood that could foreshadow a thousand lifetimes of meaningless conversations. For in this time, my father and I were as one, and knew one another more than we knew ourselves.

"You have been invited to the funeral," he said.

I shook my head in approval.

"How do you feel about that?"

"I don't know," I looked him straight in the eye, and so he saw that I had yet to develop the great understanding for what all this meant, and will mean to me throughout my life.

"Do you want to go?" He asked.

"I suppose," I shot back; lying in my bed.

"How about Gum?"

"Don't know," I replied, "Maybe he wants too."

"How about you asking him tomorrow at school," father gave me a reassuring wink, "I'll take you both."

I instantly leaned up and I gave my father the largest hug a boy my size could give. I felt his heavy grasp squeeze me all the more tighter. He retreated, sent the overhead light into the dark, while he spoke his 'good nights' and 'I'll see you in the mornings'. The door clicked quietly behind him as I watched him go.

The shadows formed once more in that endless darkness; lights flickered to fade; the curtains took to whip one last time for the evening, as a smart wind made its howl past my room. My eyes grew heavy while I held that single moment in review of when I was standing at home plate, watching Yaz send me a wink and a stare, and the crowd cheering on in unison Spike's name. As if the ghost of him were still watching behind that scoreboard. Fenway must have been his Heaven. At least for that game today it was. His wings surely were spread out like the puffy clouds which danced about the stadium the whole day long. His fingertips seemed to brush around the baselines whenever a gust would blow and cause a miniature dust storm; the balls; the strikes, all his calling behind home plate. The hands of time wiped clean as eternity rose up and came to claim the game today as a special occasion.

   Whenever the sun slightly dimmed and hid behind Spike's lofted wings, a Red Sox player would look skyward and catch a pop fly. He waited for his moment like the tradition he always held. The point of his choosing; when, by some galactic and miracle storybook ending, the Red Sox would come from behind and win the game. The fireworks would dash out from behind the green canvas backdrop afterwards, and explode as they touched the sky. I felt then on every sunburst, as we watched the show in silence, I thought I heard ole Spike yell.

   "Scratch! Scratch!" and then a resounding echo of his vivacious laugh send my heart into a warm glow. He touched my soul alright, as he did so many others. You'll be missed Spike.

Chapter 7

I Say Goodbye to a Friend.

It was the first time I had experienced the misfortunes of death, let alone someone so close to me. I remember how uncommonly cold it was; damp, misty, as if nature had sneezed out an odd day in the waning days of summer. The dampness to my outer window stuck to the pane like unrelenting glue. The soft pits and patters of water droplets cascading from the trees about and the window ceil were appearing to serenade me with its own version of a song.

I had been properly dressed for some time that morning. My suit was black with very faint designs in its fabric; the tie red with fire and plainly clad. I felt cramped in such attire, where someone had cloaked me in an overbearing jacket which made me itch all over. My eyes concentrated on the small floods and puddles that formed on the brick around my window, and how those formed trails of water moved in a consistent stream down into those basins just below.

"Ready?" my father peeked in to disturb me; he too, dressed in all black dress suit and a fiery red tie.

"Yeah," I slouched.

"Call Jason?" he pushed the door wide.

"He's ready too," I walked by him and headed downstairs. I could see my mother standing in the doorway with her raven thick hair sheltering her face. Her hands clasped in front of her as if in a rest; her grayish eyes pestering mine with her constant stare. She bent to one knee before me, once I came into the small foyer.

"Now you mind your manners Conner," she said and she fiddled feverishly with my suit; checking my pockets, and pulling out a pack of gum, "No gum! You hear? No gum!"

"No gum!" I heard my ancient grandmother walk by in her ancient clothes, snub on me with her expression, and pass by without a care for me.

"Not fitting for boy in a funeral to be chewing or popping gum," she swore on me, "especially during the favored speeches of his eulogy; or when the minister is in prayer."

"I won't be popping gum," I fussed a sort, which she soundly tempered with a sharp stare of her own.

"You mind your manners!" more sternly she spoke, as she shook that pleasantly smelling gum in my face, "And make sure Jason minds his!"

I said nothing, but looked down and away.

"Conner," she appeared to warn by the tone in her voice.

"I wouldn't do anything," I pleaded, but to no avail; I had been caught red-handed with the gum.

"No Gum!"

I heard my nosey grandmother sound off in the far room a distance away. My mother rolled her eyes and retook her standing position in front of me.

"You mind your father," she softly whispered. She brought my face close to hers. I felt the kiss of her lips on my forehead; her hand went to grab onto mine and shake it with affirmation. There was always a genuine and tender emotion about her; a grace indescribable; a haven of comfort; a prerequisite joy whenever you were close to her. She was the backbone of a large, robust family, with as many diverse personalities as one can imagine.

I felt the tug of my father.

"You look great young man," he smiled on me like the sunshine from a bright day, as if his pride was in that glow there.

We were out the door in a short step or two, and we found the day full of a constant drizzle. The mist condensing into a blanket, with the pattering pellets of rain drenching everything about. Our yellow station wagon sat out front of our house, though the windows were all foggy with the car in steam.

I peered back for a second to take note of my mother, who was standing in that unrelenting spray. Her eyes warmed to the heart with her smile, as it ignited the gleam in her expression about. She waved and I returned the sentiments as such. Her dress, so coarse and gray, seemed to illuminate in that mist. Like the hallowed ghost of some angel looking through an open window from Heaven; and so gazing back at me.

I would have never imagined my life without such a woman in it. My reflections there were caught in an instant emotion; where time no longer ticked a trail of seconds. But paused, ever so slightly, in its' own way to memorialize that moment there.

I stood by the open car door while my father made the attempt to pull me in. I felt my mother's thoughts converse intimately with mine, and so tell me how proud she was.

"Come on son," my father roared, "Jason is waiting!"

I climbed in and I felt the car move forward. The cars were parked all along the way, yet the sidewalks and streets remained empty and void of anyone. I heard the squeaky sounds of the windshield wipers make way for my father to see and drive by. The lamplights flickered to a fade; the streams of water cut across my sight as I watched everything move by us while we went from street to street.

I could see the clouds were heavy and laying low with that weight of so much precipitation. It seemed as if they to were in tears over the death of Spike, though mine had yet to come. The skies muffled a sinking gray, and so crowded the roads about with its fog. The solitary pedestrians, cloaked in black and deep blue rain jackets, huddled to themselves so to gather and retain warmth. They appeared as mourners, all the while as they slowly walked in their own single parade; marching if you will, so they could see Spike one last time.

I thought everyone knew; the baker; the doctor; the seamstress; the mailman; dentist and accountant; the turnstiles worker at 'The Constitution'; the harbor man who watched the ships come in and out of port; the kind teacher who let her children home early for the event; all coming for Spike's funeral.

I did not rightly know what to think then, but I kept to my thoughts and my silence. My father quizzed on me.

"Son," he glanced over, "Are you ready for this?"

I said nothing, though I kept my concentration to the window. I was hoping someone would stop, look about us, and wave when we were to pass by. No one came with a smile.

"Are you ready for this?" he spoke again and nudged me in my ribs, "You don't have to do this..."

"How long will it be?" I connected his look with mine.

"As long as it takes son."

"How long is that?"

I could no longer stare on him, but to return back to my former, transparent gaze.

"Thirty minutes," he estimated, "maybe an hour. Then there will be the gravesite service."

"In the rain?" I asked.

"Even still," he responded, "I have an umbrella. We can stand close to the back if you want."

"No," I replied, "I want to see."

We crossed down Briar Street and onto Willow Grove, where Jason's home was the third house on the left; small, square, graying by the weatherworn shudders with steps somewhat out of place. The railings raddled so when you touched them; a porch, damp, cranky on your every step, with the screen door which wheezed every time you opened it.

I saw Gum peeking out just behind the screen, with a blank look to his face. The door facing appeared like old drift wood set out to sea for years. He waved a slight finger roll, a shy and sheepish glance; kind of like a boy first caught with his pants down and his underwear showing. He appeared dapper in his suit; the one I had seen on many-a-Sunday's. Jason I believe was beginning to outgrow it. The pant knees were now slightly worn and a little shiny from the wear; the lapel slightly frayed but still suitable for show. The white shirt he wore was not pressed but held wrinkles in the cuff and collar.

My father parked the car, jumped from his side with the umbrella in tow, held it out for Gum as he descended with my father, and so jumped in the back seat of that station wagon. I leaned back with my arm over the seat and I cared to give him a side glare, which caught his attention.

"Pat! Pat!" I snapped on my fingers in attempt to have him give it up; I rolled my nimble fingers to me.

"What?" he looked nearly shocked.

"You know," I spoke and rolled my fingers further, "Give it up. Give it up."

His mouth appeared in a gaping, wide manner, and so showing the massive mound of gum sitting limp on his tongue.

"What?" he nearly lost it then.

"Come on Tush!" I snarled, "You can give up the chew for at least a little while."

Out it plopped into my hand, and I quickly made disposal of it while my father jumped back into the car. We were off.

The rain drew into very heavy downpour as we came near to the red-brick church where the funeral was being held. There was a large crowd muddling about close to the front door; mostly men dressed in black. The long church doors were fully open, with glimmering vestibule lights peering past the tops of their heads. Candles aglow deep within the belly of the sanctuary, all but froze the scene in time. The three of us walked up those wet and frigid steps. There were many eyes that caught us in their view; the solemn stares like ghosts not yet dead tremored my soul into a shiver. Those frank eyes weighed strong with thought, and so passed through us as we divided them into some parting sea of suits and musky cologne.

"Do you wish to see?" my father bent to my level, gazed into me, eye to eye, with a most serious of stares, "Do you wish to see?"

I was confused and he knew it.

I looked round with a curious and strange expression on my face. I was struggling as my eyes shot from the left pews to the right, searching for what my father meant.

"Son," he tugged on my tie and pulled me back to him, "Do you wish to see Spike one last time."

The cast of fear riddled my expression back to him. I had not anticipated this, nor had it ever entered my mind. I quickly thought, not being one for much impulse, and I could say nothing more immediate than what was the need.

"Don't worry son," he sighed, "You don't have to."

"I will," I quivered in my voice.

"You want me to go with you?" he asked.

"No," I spoke without thinking.

I felt his tender push away from me. The main isle looked free, narrow, and lit about by candles at the pews' edge. The glow was most odd, disturbing, yet feeling a sense of comfort for me as I went. I saw the looks of those already in their seats. They were gazing back on me as I slowly made my way to the front. A hush ascended on the church there. I was THE boy, most touched by this man. And a man most touched by this boy; now coming forward in host and tribute to his fallen friend. My eyes rose into the heart and center of the pulpit. There, casket lay open and exposed, free for the viewing. I kept my hands close to my sides; the lights glimmered and beamed to a sparkle, deep red hue passageway.

In the midst of all this I could see Spike lying there with his profile staring to the Heavens; silent, peaceful, hands crossed over his belly. It seemed his spirit lingered nearby his vacant body there. Perhaps he was waiting for me to come to say goodbye. My fear danced about me like a legend once thought to be a hoax, but it seemed more real in that moment. It stifled me; haunted me; chilled my soul to the bone.

I was thrust into a foreign world; a strange land. As if my father had just put me on a lonely boat from my homeland shores, and so sent me into the seas of the unknown. I was afraid; most deathly afraid then. The hands of an invisible monster had taken me and were now forcing me to see what I thought was truly unreal. I stalled just before coming to his coffin. I discovered the surrounding candles that brought wafts of shimmers and trailing shadows in the fellowship of his soft, unmoving expression.

I drew closer still. I could hear the whispers of our times before gather in my thoughts; push out my memories into a collective rush, and so seem to make those words he spoke to me resonate along those church walls. I briefly smiled when I thought I heard him cackle one last time; his finger appeared to rise in the air, and he making sure that I would always love his Red Sox, no matter what.

There were no flowing tears from me; there, as the world watched and waited for my motion to continue, though my heart bled with tears to see Spike so. It felt like a dream which had awakened me and decided to continue to play for me while I wrestled to wake myself free of it; but it remained. I felt for Spike's finger; no warmth inside; cold; a harboring land of stillness and stone. I could not say anything, but only stare and try to imagine what Spike might say to me in that moment. One last vestige of truth; one more meaningful word he could pass to me; that I may, in turn, be able to carry with me as a treasure for the rest of my days.

I sensed a hand roll around my shoulder. I shuddered but looked to my right. It was my father's strong arm pulling me gently away. His guiding force brought me back to where Gum still was standing.

"You did well son," my father whispered in silence to me, "I think the family was very touched by that."

Soon the service began; in dignity and respect. The rolling sounds of heaving rain and distant thunder played out in the background. Even the candles shivered weakly as the storm persisted and played out through the service. I could see the shadows of those faces along the walls; the quiet movements of their heads as they tilted their looks back and forth while the minister spoke; the words of scripture most dear to Spike; the solo hymnal song from Spike's favorite tune; the eulogy from a son living so distant on the west coast who had now returned to remember the man who raised him, and so gave him the imprints on the man he had become.

I watched the tears drip in ceremony through his expression when he spoke so tenderly of the man he always loved and respected. His words reached from his heart and they touched all those who heard them; like gentle, individual fingers caressing their souls. He was a powerful speaker; an affluent man of emotions; his loss greater than all others.

I could see all the Red Sox players, coaches, and head brass were in attendance. They would be going out on a flight that night for a west coast trip to play the Athletics. For now, their thoughts and prayers were with Spike.

"Conner," Jason made an attempt to get my attention.

"What??" I whispered strongly back at him.

"What was it like?" his curiosity must have played on him for some time before he had to ask me.

"Nothing," I responded.

"What do you mean nothing?" he pushed further.

"Nothing," I said, "I can't say…"

"Boys," father took to correct us with one solid word and a steel-like expression, "Be mindful…"

"Where do we go from here Mr. James?"

"Soon," father bent on us both, "to the gravesite."

It wasn't long after this that eight men marched to the front, took their hands on the casket, and left the church where a hertz was waiting. The church disassembled and disbandoned out to their individual cars; most would ride in train to the gravesite some four-miles south of the church.

The rain had quickly subsided as the deep gray and misty air resumed. The haunting shadows of the mid-day storm still prevailed as the candles within the sanctuary were blown out one by one, and so the heart of that sanctuary had grown dimmer and dimmer until the darkness took over; as if its spirit had been blown out when Spike left.

We were the thirty-fourth car in line along the way (I counted, but Gum swore we were the thirty-fifth car in line). The police escort slowly drove through the winding trail as we followed in single file. Cars pulled along the side in every direction as the drivers and passengers viewed us when we passed by. I knew their thoughts; it was most evident in their looks to us.

"That person must have been important!" they told themselves in awe. "So many cars; so very many cars."

I watched from our window again, and I saw the city streets move more to meadows and grassy lands as we went closer to the gravesite. Soon the main car pulled into a very large and rolling cemetery. The grasses nicely cut; the lawns sweetly manicured and kindly cared for. I could see from a distance where Spike was to finally be put to rest at. The green overhanging tarp and medley of flowers dotted all in a surrounding array there.

One by one, then in clusters, we marched to the spot where Spike's casket had been set. The Arms on Guard, with rifles in bay, stood firm and distinctive, without fanfare and prepared to sound off the twenty-one-gun salute. An American flag was now draping his coffin; the pawl bearers standing close and to the ready. The family drifted into the scene in single file, and they were seated most near to the casket. The minister held to his gown and cloak; stared softly on the family as he held each of his hands to the small bible close to him.

There was a bittersweet silence that prevailed for a bit, but for the tiny drips of rain, which sounded off as they struck the canopy and the umbrellas that had sprung up about. I kept my eyes square on the casket; thought of Spike in that loneliest of places now; wondering if he were as cold as I was then. My father held to me close, so bending the umbrella down on me so I would stay dry from the rains.

The service was short, brief, with a single song; a gun salute and the playing of taps intermixed in that affair. I was stoned to my feelings as such; not knowing quite how to react. This was a new discovery to me; a land of unknown knowledge; a place where I had yet to roam. I stood mesmerized with a blank and uncertain look to my face. The black-laden crowd slowly dispersed about. While some gave into hugs and gentle pats of reassurance, others moved quietly away to return home.

Spike's son came up to me with a distracted smile fixated on his look. He approached with care and caution, with two men by his side.

"You are Conner James?" He inquired.

"Yes," I held close to my father, "I am."

I saw him look down over me with a broad and more sharing smile.

"My father always spoke of you," he said, "quite favorable. We talked by phone at least twice a week, and he never failed to mention your name."

"Conner has always had a good way with people," my father interjected.

"And you must be Conner's father…"

"Yes I am," my father shook his hand. I could feel this man now bending to meet his glaring eye with mine.

"And as you know," he spoke, "my father also had a good way with people. He was much loved."

I could say nothing, but meekly stare at him and watch his smile transform the occasion into a slightly more pleasant one.

"What better way for him to hand down the most precious thing he owned, to someone who is like him."

I waited and wondered what he meant by that.

"Recently, my father had thought of what he might want you, Conner, to have. Something he valued more than anything else."

I saw a second man beside him hand over a box. There was a pause once more.

I could feel Spike's gentle manner had succeeded him, past down from his own father.

"I am sure my father spoke of Brew Johnson. Well, in fact, that was his name. He actually came to the big leagues for spring training in 1935 with the Boston Braves. They brought him up to see what this strapping, young player could do. Tried him at catcher briefly; didn't work. Outfield? Too much quickness, but less speed. So they placed him at third, and how he could guard the corner. He seemed to glue himself to the bag when he played defense. His arm was a cannon rifle; so much so they tried him at a stint on the pitching mound."

I saw him converse with his thoughts for a moment; smile about my father, Jason, and myself, then return.

"It was an unusually warm early spring day; more uncommon than most. The aging Babe Ruth had been partying all the night before. His bravado was legendary as was his ego. Well, my father took to a challenge; one that the Babe would never back down from. Dad made a bet with him. '*I strike you out—you buy me the best stack box of cigars in town*'. Ruth laughed and stood at home plate, and he swore out to my green-horn father, '*You strike me out; I'll buy you two boxes of cigars. But! If you don't? A round of drinks for me for a month!*' Ruth laughed so hard on it that his belly nearly shook bottom buttons free from his shirt."

"He challenged Babe Ruth?"

"Didn't even flinch on it," the man quickly and most proudly shot back.

"Now that would have been more than my father's month wages, so he had no choice—he had to strike Babe Ruth out. Babe Ruth came to the plate, sliced the air with his left-handed swing. The catcher got to his crouch, flashed a sign, then a second one. My father threw a fastball high and away which nearly pulled the catcher from his stance."

"What did he say?" I asked.

Spike's son smiled ever so slightly and seemed to go into the voice of Babe Ruth himself.

"'*Ha! I'll need a poll ten feet wide to hit that one! You got fear boy! Or your liver dropped to your knees and crawled back in its hole! Trust me boy! You're heading back to the minor leagues after I'm done with you!*'"

He paused there for a moment.

"Now my father straight at Babe Ruth and said, '*At least my liver isn't a rock George!*' No one called him George or Herman; least of all a sniffling rookie. He saw Ruth's eyes burn red then and his cheeks grow stiff; chin up and jaws locked."

I looked up to my father. I saw him intently listening as much as Gum and I were. The rain had nearly subsided as our umbrella went down and I felt the cool air brush across my face.

"You see," he continued, "Ruth was quite angry with my father, '*Quit fumbling you caddy rook and pitch the ball!*'"

"A strike?" I questioned.

"Curve ball dipped right under Babe Ruth's armpit, snuggled right up to the black of the plate. He swung and tipped it into the catcher's mitt. My father called for the ball back, tipped his hat, turned around and looked beyond the centerfield walls, then stared out into the blue skies," he paused and reverted back to the voice of Ruth.

"'Ain't you coming?? Or you going to squat there and lay a goose egg??' My father turned around, and told the Babe, 'I am going to strike you out old man!'"

We all hushed when we heard this.

"Ohhhhhh!" my father leaned back and rubbed on his chin, "I suppose he didn't take kindly to that."

"No," Spike's son grinned, "Babe Ruth tried to charge the mound, but the catcher held him back; my father never flinched. He just stood there, straight-faced, eyes just under the brim of his cap, and looked dead on at Ruth."

"What did Ruth say on that one??" I wondered with more interest than before.

"'You'll fetch my water boy, all season long you keep this up!' Spike just stood there high on the mound and never moved, 'You hear me boy?? I like my water with a pinch of lemon, sugar, and two ice drops!'"

"I'll bet Spike had something to say then," I grinned.

"'I can taste those cigars now' my father joked as the Babe headed back to home plate. Next pitch? Curve ball that scuffed in the dirt about two feet in front of the plate. Babe Ruth laughed on that one, spat in his hands, and shook a fist out to the pitcher's mound. Next pitch? Fastball caught the outside of the plate. The count now two and two…. 'I thought as much,' the Babe laughed on my father, 'nothing but prissy balls to hit from you. Why don't you pitch like a real man??'"

I watched as Spike's son gathered to his feet, stared about the scenery, and he noticed a few people still mingling around.

"That's when my father told Babe Ruth what was coming, where he would throw it, and what to expect."

"What did he throw?" Gum questioned.

"Fastball; down the heart of the plate," he replied, "Foul ball straight back. Then another fastball on the inside; another foul ball. Next came a fastball high and away; another foul…Seven straight fastballs and not one of them, the ole' Babe could straighten out into a hit, and each one he knew what was coming. Still, no hit."

"Two balls, two strikes?" I asked.

Spike son just winked and nodded as he freed the box top open and showed us what was inside that mystic box. Like a newborn puppy, I was glowing an awe-filled expression when the two objects came to light; one being an old glove with thick, overgrown fingers on it; heavy laces as thick as the width of a pen. It had a musty smell to it; brown and somewhat tattered; worn distinctly around the edges where the fingertips were ragged and rough. There, in the belly of that glove was the signature of Babe Ruth himself. The second object he pulled free, and I could see beyond the scuffing of its sphere was a baseball also signed by Babe Ruth as well; the strokes to the pen broad and agitated as if the Babe were angry about something when he signed it. I gazed at that baseball like it was the crown jewel to the game itself. Gum's lower jaw nearly dropped onto his chest; his eyes nearly rolled white and bulged from their sockets when he too took fixation on the object.

"Last pitch?" Spike son began, "He didn't tell the Babe what to expect. Spike took to his windup, looked straight up, shot his arms to the sky; this very ball."

There he laid the ball squarely into my palms. Babe Ruth's signature was staring back at me.

"This was the very ball he pitched with. He lofted it like he was tossing it over a rainbow. The Babe waited and waited; nearly swung three times as it fluttered back down and gently began to cross home plate. The Babe roared back, and with all his might he took a cut that could have split a tree in half."

"What happened?" I intently said.

"You see the ball," he smiled, "his signature is on it. What do you think?"

"I don't know…really," I stared on him with a baffled and unsure look. I looked back on my father, whose own expression caught my eyes when he looked down to me.

"The Babe missed."

"He struck out Babe Ruth??" Gum smiled.

"Not once, but three times that day," he answered, "That was my father's proudest achievement in baseball. He only told that story to his closest friends and family. Besides, he didn't think anyone would ever believe him. He always kept that story for himself. But around thanksgiving time, sitting about our family dinner, he would always tell the same story," he paused, "And we never got tired of hearing it, nor did he."

"That's a wonderful story," I made an attempt to hand the ball back to him.

"It's for you Conner," he returned both to me, "My father wanted you to have them. He knew you had dreams to play for the Red Sox. He thought it would give you the greatest joy, and perhaps be a good luck charm in fulfilling your dream."

He stood straight and moved back a step.

"I don't know what to say…"

"No need son," he spoke these last words, "He wanted you to know how he cared, and what you meant to him; to thank you for giving something to him his last few years."

"What was that?" I inquired and I looked up at him.

"Friendship," he rubbed my bushy head, smiled to us all, and began to descend away. We all silently paused as this gifted gentleman went by car down the lone, rustic and gravel road, out onto the main streets, and disappeared behind the tall bushings that surrounded the cemetery.

My father clapped his arm around me. I could not take my eyes off of either the glove or ball. The signature broad-stroked and swaged from the proud man Babe Ruth must have been.

I'm sure Spike enjoyed an array of cigars while he smoked them; each roll carried him back to that memory on the time he struck out the mighty Ruth. Each puff blown to the wind would have sparked yet another flash in his mind. I could see him there now, leaning back in his old rocking chair, watching the sun drift down into a sunset. The back porch lit at the edges; darting fireflies in the grasses below; the heat fading into a humid odor. The blink of light as he lit one, suckled the end, and took about a grand string of puffs while the aroma settled into his mouth and lungs.

That tempered smile he carried; that quaint, pleasant reflection which settled in his face; rocking as he were on that podium of his. He must have sat there for hours; rocking and reflecting, enjoying every last fragrance of each cigar. I could see he never smoked one but on special occasion. Holidays or birthdays; when a grand child was born; when the Red Sox one a pennant-all to rouse him to take his kingly seat, smoke, sit back, and reflect with fondness on that moment long ago. He must have smoked two or three when they finally reached the World Series in seventy-five.

Spike was as much as this was; always reminded of the past, like a treasure trove of memories locked within his vault. The more precious ones he could pull out at will. I suppose in a small, measurable way he was a lonely man. He never spoke of his wife; only that she had died some years previous to me meeting him. This was not a pleasant reflection and he would not strike up a special cigar for it.

I felt I was sitting on that porch of his with him; a second rocker guarding his. I thought of the evening chats we must have had if it were so. The stories he would tell; the constant reminders on times of old. He may lean back in his casual way, giggle out of sequence, then tell a funny tale he thought of just then; something which happened years before; something he had long forgotten but that which had suddenly and most unexpectedly flashed on him when he took a whiff on his cigar. Each roll had a memory locked in its smoke, I would have thought.

I was in an eclipse there. Pulled away into a time which never was; a setting and a place lost from me, but one I imagined could have been if fate had not taken Spike so soon. Things spoken from his lips to my ears; things I would have carried beyond even his own time; things I could have given to my children.

The rain began to ascend once more. Father pushed the umbrella above me and Jason. I clung to those treasures Spike found to be gems, as we three moved slowly back to our car. The smell of leather; the wisp of that stitched ball from ancient pasts, rose to me and so seemed to carry their memories with them. I had to it more than imagination; more than dreams could tell. I suddenly realized the bonds he and I shared were most important of all, and I began then to miss him so. I peered from within that station wagon; through the fog and mist of that rain; the droplets of dew sheltering my view when I saw the attendants lowering Spike's casket beneath the canopy floor, and down beyond the place I could see.

"Goodbye," I waved out to him. I hoped he could see me. My hand froze there in its wave, in silence; no whispers; nor thoughts imposed upon. I was alone in that second, as he, my friend, was alone too in his own world. I gave to him more than I ever knew, and so the repayment for me was this glove and ball which I now clung to as my own possession there.

I never knew what death meant until then; the glimpse and momentary dream it sent my way. The power of its curse; the wisdom for knowledge it showed; all, rushing into my understanding. It was a final separation; an ending to something that should never end. It was there I met with my sorrow; it having hidden itself so conveniently up until this moment. I crumbled my head onto the window, sensed the tears in my own river drip from my eyes-to-cheek. I felt my father's hand grip my shoulder as the car slowly worked its way from the cemetery, and back home again.

"Goodbye Spike," I could whisper only once more.

Chapter 8

The Irish Grandmother.

As time passed on by, father made fewer trips each year out to the western front to aid in the summer forest fires. I believe mother had a hand in all this. They would often have discussions behind closed doors. And through the muffled door sounds I could tell she was not pleased with him; not in the least. Their preference was always, if the occasion arose, to have these 'discussions' behind closed doors, and out of earshot for the children's sake (me being one of them). I was the oldest, and being so ordained I would scurry the others off when I knew the tempest storm was about to set in.

Through eventual trials mother made her case stick firm. She made sure father knew quite explicitly that leaving a family of five alone for months-on-end was not an appropriate venture, no matter the noble cause with which he felt compelled by. In mother's eyes, family came first. No matter high water or earth, family always came first. As tireless as father was in his convictions to his cause, so too was mother more convicted by this simple rule.

Grandmother Ashton lived just north of Boston in Wakefield, and so during some of the spring months we would make a family trip to see her. I always took delight in this because of the enormous strawberry patches that surrounded her home. It was like an island house amongst the sea fields of strawberries. Her house sat plain as view when we drove up onto that long and dusty track of road leading to her front steps. She was a kindly woman, though a little senile and showing good measure to her age; a bit couth and eccentric, she would always have pies and cakes baked whenever we came. There was strawberry pie with strawberry filling on top; strawberry cake with a swirl of vanilla and strawberry icing; donuts with strawberry filling; strawberry milkshakes;

jams, cookies, even strawberry friendship twirls. Certainly Grandmother 'Ashley' would have been the perfect poster person for the strawberry farmers throughout the world.

I often marveled at the ultra tight curls she placed her hair in, with a fish net never failing to be sitting atop her crowns. I suppose she felt it to be quite a fashion statement on her behalf. But however many times we went out in the public she garnered more snickers than praise. She held a very distinct Irish accent and it nearly muddled her English into very discernable words when she spoke. She was one of the few who could speak Gaelic, and she used it on regular occasion when she came into a fit or was angry with someone. Her dress was always black with black shoes; apron or lace in the front, and a collar strapped around her neck so tight I thought she might well be hung by her own dress.

Her cane was cut from ancient Irish wood as she would say, and one that had corrected more than four generations of 'James'. Sometimes she would make claims that her 'staff' had been used to herd the animals on the ark by Noah himself; it being a very 'correctible tool' in her eyes.

Now father took to an amusing stare whenever Grandmother Ashley told her tall tales; how she ventured by sea in nothing more than a raft to cross the Atlantic and settle on the shores of Plymouth when she was a young woman. How she saw the Titanic being built in Ireland just before she also went to America.

"Stand down Conner!" she would yelp and snap her cane on the hardwood floors to get my attention, "You picked your bushel yet for the morning?" she would ask as she watched the fear as it crossed into my eyes, and so found me standing at attention in her direction.

"No Grandmother," I weakly proposed.

"Well then," she spouted, "The days' nearly done and you haven't pulled your share of the plow today…don't suppose supper will be waiting for you unless you do so."

"Father said I could come in…" I stated.

"Who owns this house?" She shot back.

"It's yours grandmother," I replied and held my breath.

"Exactly!" she clapped her rod down on the hardwood floors like thunder, "An hour wasted out of the patch means that many more strawberries don't make it to market. Do yourself some usefulness and fetch me another bushel or two!"

Now don't get me wrong, Grandmother Ashley was hardly ever persistent in her demands; that is except when it came to her strawberries. It was like the cream to her cream; it was as necessary in life as breathing in air.

The long evenings we shared while we sat amongst her long room, where the fireplace lit out a bright hue which caught glimpses of each of us within its lighting, were some of the most special times. She had her particular story-telling chair near the fire, with 'Cotton', her longhaired pure white Persian cat, sitting across her lap; flapping its long tail as she spun her yarn of tales.

There was one story however that caught my fancy, and it laid great interest to my siblings as soon as they heard it. Most of her stories were built on the timber blocks of truth and fiction; this was indeed a story of truth.

Many years before, on the coast of Ireland in the western region, there was a small port city Galway. This is where she lived, where she grew up, and to where she fell in love. Grandmother Ashley would lean back in her soft but aging chair, stare about the ceiling as if there were stars from heaven about, and so begin her tale. The tale of romance, of love born, then love lost in the River Corrib. His name was Charles Lynch and he was a fisherman on a Galway hooker.

"Tell us one more time Grandmother," mother would ask while making clothes for one of my sisters.

"Oh," she laughed, "you've heard it so many times."

"For the new ones," mother replied, "they don't remember."

"Yes please Grandmother," Amanda would lean in closer as she sat on the rug floor, all stretched out; hands propped up her chin, and her legs in a constant criss-crossing.

"We like to hear about old Charles," father said.

Grandmother paused, closed her eyes in a seeming manner to look deeply into her long memory, and so pull out the fabrics of this story again. As age goes on, the details are less familiar and appear more like a stranger than friend to her. Yet she told what she could remember on. Though Charles was as fresh to her as the day she met him, and you could see it in her smile.

"Promise me five bushel tomorrow, and I'll tell it."

"We do," Amanda shouted.

"Each," she pulled out her cane to spot us all, "agreed?"

We did as much to promise her, for the sake of her telling such a charming story; yet another time than for our own satisfaction.

"There was a time when your grandmother was so young. Blond hair; soft feather-like skin; dressed in a long, flowing skirt and shawl. I used to sit out close to Galway bay and watch Pucans and Hookers sail by. Sometimes the young men would ferry out so much beer, the Hookers nearly tipped over. They didn't care. They were young, bright-eyed, and life didn't have a care; like me," she smiled and paused to reflect further, "I can still hear their calls to the girls on the shore lines; the fisherman too. We were all heavenly creatures in their eyes."

"Men are the same throughout every generation," mother said, "Never change, never change."

"And the women don't?" Father imposed.

"You ever hear a woman changing her mind?" Mother leaned back, "Change is in a woman's design."

"Continue," father looked out to grandmother.

"I would read along the Old Quay; Chaucer, Lord Byron; Dickens, Jane Austen…They were all like lovers from a book with their stories and poetry. I am so fascinated by what the mind can display with just a flint of imagination. I would read a passage, watch the sun dip around the dock, and think that they had been here before. But Charles Lynch," she smiled so brightly, "Was truly a man of the sea. He loved the water; the sails flapping from the wind above; the slight waves flipping up against the black hulls. All the women fancied Charles. I thought the darling man could ferry a whole herd of cattle in his Hooker…"

"Grandmother," mother interjected, "I think you need to explain to them what a 'Hooker' is."

"Yeah…" what is a Hooker?" Amanda looked around.

"A sail boat Mandy," grandmother bent down and smiled on Amanda's curious face, "I always fancied him. Whenever he walked by, I'd stop; that tall, angular figure; massive hands; eyes like blue pearls; black-night hair and a smile which could bring out the sun during a rainstorm. At first he didn't notice me. That is, until one day I was sitting outside a local shop. It was painted so bright yellow like a canary, and red like an apple; a little eatery place with a small patio next to it. I had been reading Pride and Prejudice by Jane Austen, and I was so fully enwrapped into story when he pushed the book from my face and replaced it with an ever-growing smile."

"What did he say?" Amanda was fully into it now.

"*'Hello Ashley Browne,*' " Grandmother spoke of it as though she were hearing his voice at that very moment, feeling the sudden pull away of her book to see him so squarely attending to her. I felt her heart flutter then, even after so many years, " *'Do you ever do anything other than read?'*"

"He asked you that?" Mother smartly shot back.

"Charles had good intentions," grandmother stroked her cat a bit harder, "he was leading up to having me sail on his Hooker."

"That day…" Amanda said.

"No better day than then," she responded, "than to go for a boat ride. I reluctantly agreed; being as bashful as I was. He walked me out to the dock. I brought my books and we set sail into the harbor. He sailed us through while I read to him, though I might say he paid little attention to my readings as we went. He just seemed to stare out into the waters and sea, and think of those things a man thinks of," it was there she stalled, as mother and my grandmother both stared with some level of judgment and conviction for our gender on my father. He just stood in the rear, drinking out the last vestige of his tea.

"What did I do?" He looked on them.

"You were born a man," mother spotted him with her look, and grinned out a sarcastic gaze.

"No harm in this," father drank up his brew, "Mother, continue please...will you?"

All eyes went back to her, there on her 'story-telling' platform. We could see the shadows pop in and out of her limelight; the crackle flames held reflections which danced most proudly about her face, as she seemed to reminisce there quietly. She looked into the fire without a word, crossing time as she did in preparation of telling her story. The glimpse was like a harbor of what she once knew; the melodious ghosts to her past streaming across her thoughts as she dared play in them once more. I thought of what I would be like when I was her age; to see for myself the matters of what I had gone through; the life that I had led years before. What would it be? It seemed rather odd to think of what would be as if it had already occurred. But I imagined in that moment what she must have felt. I thought this was the charm of living; to have that album of memories to always reflect back on like a good storybook you have to go back to again and again. Some good; some bad, but it was yours.

"Where was I?" She softly broke the silence.

"You had just met the dashing Charles," Amanda giggled.

"Charming?" Grandmother looked at her cross-eyed, "Not my words young lady; gifted, true; but not so charming. He was a radical flirt, like a buck that had sprayed his scent on too many trees I tell you..."

We all laughed.

"Mother...please," my mother spoke up.

"No, now," she was assured, "He was all that. Charles never could keep his eyes all in one place. Now mind you, there was much to admire on the man; his care-free, venturing ways; his unwavering manner without fear; his grand love for life; optimistic without pride, which is a rather thin tight rope to manage."

"He had eyes for you..." father smiled.

"Yes he did son," she laughed, "I was a beau to be had back then I suppose...and he had his fancy for me. We often went out on his Hooker, especially during the prime weather. I read of lands unknown, and he sailed us to them."

"You were in love then…" I asked.

"Yes, but I was a challenge," she responded, "But I knew he loved me. After six months it became evident to both of us we were destined to be married. But his love of the sea was a strong pull. He wanted to travel all along the coast of Ireland; from west to east, and was making plans to do so."

She bent down to gather a look on her complacent cat, still in a lounge on her lap.

"Did he?" Amanda wondered aloud.

"He enjoyed traveling across Ireland, and quite often asked me to go with him, but he had interest, especially in Belfast," she paused and held her breath, "This was the time when they were building the Titanic. Oh he marveled at the sight of it; the size; the majesty of it. Through his constant and persistent inquiries, he made connections and eventual arrangements to become a ship hand aboard her, once she set sail out of harbor."

"Charles was heading to America," mother replied.

"That was his wish," she stopped, "for the two of us. He was to work in one of the boiler rooms, and I was to be a nurse maid."

"You said no…"

"It's in my nature son," Ashley somberly spoke, "You know this. I am always hesitant. And, I told Charles so. No matter. He begged and pleaded for me to go with him. As the ship was nearing completion, he spoke constantly of going to America and beginning a new life with me. Leaving my home Ireland did not appeal to me then. I asked him about his Hooker; his sailing; his love of the sea. He always responded that being on the grandest ship was like going from the desert to the meadow. I disagreed."

"So, what happened grandmother?" Lorie spoke up there.

"It was on the eve of the last stop before sea. Titanic was to make its final stop in Southampton, but her last stop in Ireland was in Cobh. It's the last I would see Charles. He gave me something very special there; something I have always held close and most dear to me."

"You still have it," father asked, "even now?"

"Oh yes," she smiled, "Something simple, but something heartfelt. It's a gift only love can produce son."

She went to her mantle and clapped her cane on the floor as she stepped. She pulled free a purple velvet box. Grandmother Ashley returned to her chair, made her self situated again, and she peeled back the top cover to reveal a necklace. A half-heart locket, pierced in diamonds and sapphires that jumped radiantly by the firelight when she pulled it free.

"My," mother spoke in awe, "What a jewel! It must have cost Charles a month's wage for it."

"Nearly," grandmother glanced over, "But the price of love is very high indeed. To Charles, money was never an issue. It was his way of proposing to me. There, in front of the Titanic, he got to his knees and asked me to marry him," she pulled back the top cover to reveal within the oversized locket, a picture embedded deep within its frame; a picture and still photo of Charles.

"He said that whenever I looked at his picture, no matter how long I lived and where life might take me; at every moment, when I opened the locket to look at him, he'd have me with him, and he would be there with me; kind of a porthole."

"Did you say yes?" Mother stopped to ask. Grandmother smiled, "well?"

"Some things a woman keeps even to her own secrets dear," she remarked, "He knew my answer, and that is what is important."

"So where is the other half?" I questioned her.

"The other half?"

"Yes, the other half to this heart."

"Why Charles had it. And if or when we were to reunite, then so would the two halves of this heart."

"He never made it, did he?" I was more despondent.

"Oh now Conner," she slapped my knee and laughed, "Much time has long since gone. I can reflect now without any emotions. But to speak of it, as I don't do very often at all," she stopped to think of the tragedy at hand; her eyes growing cold from this chilling memory, "April 14th. Yes I believe it was. April 14th. Charles went to his grave in the ship or was buried in Iceland. I have heard varying stories that he might have survived, and came to the shores of America. But, I am rather sure of what happened. It was a miracle, he was actually near the deck when they hit the iceberg; otherwise, he would have been entombed in the boiler room he was working in. Became a hero, as I knew he would become. He helped aid the filling up of three lifeboats, with women and children, and not once asking for a seat for himself."

There was an odd sort of silence that filled the room there. Sort of an incidental reverence on behalf of Charles, or an unintended moment of silence that made us all pause before speaking further; a chance perhaps for her to reflect and go back into that moment when she last caught a glimpse of Charles.

We could almost see that reflection in her eyes; casting away as she was back into that small city of Cobh, standing alone on the dock as he must have given her one final kiss. Not a kiss for farewell, but 'until'; a continuation; something that would give 'longing' its meaning; a stir to the heart; a motion which brought emotion into a foaming.

Love was in her expression; of the lost, lonely kind; where the heart was broken, but never to fully mend. It would heal and go on, but not ever to completely recover. A shadow of something untouchable, but faintly seen; where memory was sitting on a curb, and had trouble seeing around the bend.

This was the hard part to life I feared; the part I shivered to eventually have to experience for myself. I knew rainbows and rain come day to day. This was the rain I so wished to escape from for myself.

We watched in that infinite moment as a single tear dripped from her eye, and so glimmered the light from the fireplace when it moved from eyelid to cheek. She still loved Charles; more than she could remember or recall.

The locket dangled in front of us while it lay in it's wrapping around her middle finger. I could see the brilliant fire in its stone as it must have charmed her so many years before. But the wisp of seeing him glow in that evening light; his kneeling before her out of duty and respect; the pause; the question; the anticipation of hearing her answer, must have all seemed to roll life up in a ball there for him, as well as for her. His heart must have roared from his chest when he requested her hand in marriage on that dock.

I imagined what she must have said; the proceeding regrets afterwards, and the long years to remember all of this with. Truly a whisper from some time ago, unleashed from its cage of long forgetfulness. Like a shadow of transparency, yet once viewed in the mirror, it only cast a startling reflection.

"Charles was an admiration and an idol," she whispered as if it were a hush from yesterday, "An adorned rose; all that was good."

"That's the reason why you came here, wasn't it?" Father asked of her, "To find Charles."

"Partly," she responded, "and partly to see why America charmed him so. Out of respect for him, I came."

"Any regrets?"

Grandmother Ashley paused, silently, quietly, with an endearing grin, "I had you didn't I?"

She looked at all of us round.

"And none of you would be here if it had not been so. I can say these things now, long after your father did pass. It's not to say I didn't love your father, or that I loved your father less; I did. But the love I held for Charles, and still hold. It is vitally different and something very special and appealing in one's life."

"It must have been grandmother," mother grinned and bowed her head slightly, "the most special kind of love."

"A love which makes the memory of it worth having to look back on," she patted my mother's knee like she did mine so often before.

"It's that kind of love." She winked on us all.

The fire brandished a dimmer glow. The kids were worn from the long day, and the soon-to-be early rise to start all over again. Mother gathered us all up and sent us to our individual beds, with a kiss 'goodnight', a story of her own, and a gentle brushing of the hair back from our faces as we looked up to her.

"What do you dream of Conner?" she whispered while in a sit by my bedside that evening.

"Baseball," I grinned.

"Oh Conner," she shook me, "there's more to life than baseball; you know this."

"Travel?" I knew we were getting into a serious conversation.

"Travel can be good," she wrinkled her chin. "But what about someone to spend your life with..."

I looked at her quite confused.

"One to marry, one to grow old with..."

I looked on her even more confused now.

"I know son," she laughed, "It will come to you in time. But hopefully, and I pray for this; that you, your brother, and your sisters find those most especially meant for you. So that you all will find the love which your father and I are so richly blest with," she paused and stared out at me with a corner stare, "Not everyone is so fortunate to have that...but we are."

I felt her kiss on my forehead and then she slowly descended. She gently closed the door and the room went dark.

The next day, as with many days on our visitations to Grandmother Ashley, we were out and about in the strawberry patch picking bushels and bushels, bright and early before the heat came on. Lorie and Amanda were more apt to play; Adam too little to do much more than sit in the wettest part of the field, pull one strawberry one by one, inspect each, toss them about in play, then pick the dirtiest one he could find and devour it half. The other half would spill out all over his shirt as he grimaced at the combination taste of dirt and strawberry. Once he discovered he could squeeze them into a squirt and make more of a merry mess, he found much more game in this, and mother so found her self repeatedly cleaning Adam up.

Lorie skipped along between the rows until father called her back. Grandmother stood out on the porch and watched the work as it proceeded. Father was the more diligent and had bushel after bushel picked before anyone was aware. I, on the other hand, made a furious attempt to 'copy cat' my father and his efforts, but with little affect other than making a more grand mess than Adam seemed to be making.

This was our tradition through the growing seasons with Grandmother Ashley. During the other times of the year, especially during the holiday seasons, she had her house all in decoration for us to visit in.

The Christmas tree all nicely attired; sweet roasted walnuts and peanuts and their intoxicating aroma drifted throughout all the rooms of the house; pecan pie; apple struddle; eggnog nice and primed for the drink; the stockings draped precisely and equally apart from one another along the mantle; Christmas cards hung along each door frame from top to lower tips; the old 45's playing ancient but melody Christmas tunes in repeated, though warped fashion; the fire always in heat and crisp to burn; the logs glowing as they melted away into embers; the presents, large and small, all neatly wrapped and carefully placed over the tree skirt; garland strung over every railing, indoors and out, and wrapped in cautious symmetry; the candles burning from every tabletop and stand; all giving a seasonal cascade to the Christmas at hand.

Much as we were enveloped by such an occasion, grandmother nearly bettered herself during the Easter, Thanksgiving, and Halloween season. And without fail, we would be present for each and every one of them.

There came a time in the midst of my early teenage years where great tragedy struck in our lives and hers. One fall evening, when the weather turned most unusually cold, grandmother decided to take her dog out walking for a spell. Just a short trip of no more than a mile or two, and it was still early enough to do so. Little had she been aware that an old cord to a heater she quite often used had become worn and exposed. She accidentally left the heater running, and so left it unattended while walking out on that lonely roadside. It took little time for her entire house; all the remnants to her past; the memories'; the souvenirs; the pictures and paintings; the fondly-written letters; memoirs and sentimental objects; the children's boots; clothing her children wore; the uniforms; the recital outfits; dancing shoes and old provenance china and glass wear; the trinkets and knickknacks from Ireland; the treasure trove of hand-me-downs from generations ago; all lost in the escapable time of a single hour.

She returned to discover her home engulfed from foundation to rooftop, in an unrelenting fire and smoke. It was told to me she simply dropped to her knees, huddled to the cold and harsh ground, and wept while hearing the faint sounds of fire sirens going off in the distance. Alas, it was too late; all was to be lost.

During the proceeding morning, firemen sifted through the rubble and pulled free that diamond locket Charles had given her just before leaving on the Titanic. The picture was charred, but miraculously it somehow survived the full-fledge fire.

Grandmother Ashley was despondent over the loss of her home for many months. We quickly had her stay with us in Charlestown where she remained for the rest of her life. She was never the same; always drifting in and out. At times she was attentive; at others, nothing more than a blank stare, or in incoherent comment coming out of nowhere.

Mother always had taken a wonderful liking to grandmother, but she felt the most sadness in seeing grandmother within the state she was in. I, on the other hand, tried my ways to comfort her. In the end I felt an odd distance had come between us. I no longer knew what to say or how to react to her. She became another woman to me.

Grandmother Ashley had drifted into her own lands then, or had found a boat much like the Titanic, and so sailed out into her own solitary seas; perhaps to reunite with Charles once more. She continually wore the locket she so lovingly coveted before and revered, to the point of always keeping it locked away in a safe place. Now she would never be parted from it. She would spend long hours sitting by the window in the most front part of our house; so watching the world about in a dazed trance, and so casting out ambiguous expressions through the window. How she held firm to the locket as it lay about her chest, strumming it gently along the braided chain and latch, and so keeping the locket itself buried in her palm.

I wondered where she had gone to; the world she seemed to have left us for. I was always in the hope she was happy there, and had found her peace. The constant and fixating stare; the chiseled manner by which it never seemed to change; the statue gaze and prolonged glassy view staring out into nowhere, or a world we could not see from where we sat.

Mother was most loving and caring for Grandma Ashley. Making sure she was blanketed when cold, cool when warm, fed when hungry, and so giving to her every convenience possible.

Discussions came quite often on whether she should be placed into a nursing home or care facility. Mother would have none of that; strongly objected to any and all forms of solution which would result in Ashley being removed from the home.

"Family is family," she swore when the siblings were gathered in meetings about their mother's welfare, "I can only speak for what my gut tells me, but the only peace she will ever have in these later days of her life will only come in being around her own children and grandchildren…This is family, and not something that can be replaced."

I was most proud of mother when she had her dandruff in a tizzy, nearly snarling at them as they sat in a circle. I knew by her words and her strength of character, if this were to ever happen to me, mother was never the one who would give up; ever.

"Hope," she spoke through her tears, "There is always hope. No matter the cause or calamity…we have this. If you think you have it bad; look around you. You'll never have to look very far to find someone who has it worse. Then you have cause and reason to always count your blessings."

This was forever her motto; her stone of truth she lived by. She would never waiver in all her days from this. This is her adorning legacy and the law of her individual nature she lives by.

It would be some years after the fire and loss of her home, before Grandmother Ashley would succumb to such a reduction in her life. The times were special; the joys many, and the happy moments clipped into the treasured photo book of our mind.

Thanksgiving, Christmas, Easter, the fourth of July were made that much more special because Grandmother Ashley was living in our home. We took particular interest in decorating all about without care during these times; and as such, due to our dedication, this brought to her more joy than the holidays we celebrated in her house from the prior years before. Father even brought in carolers to sing, within our long family room on Christmas Eve; just for grandmother.

How her eyes popped in a glow; her hands huddled about her cheeks in anticipation of the tears that would soon flow freely, nearly bringing tears to my own eyes. I took pictures of her expressions as the carolers set into a semicircle about her; now saturating her with carols, one after the next.

It was a time when life was special and flowing with the milk and honey of our dreams. There was a particular emotional economy which burst around us during these moments. We were at harmony, and we learned most especially what the joys and havens of a family meant. The drawing near of Christmas; the days as we were to count them down; preparation of all decorations, and so dressing up the entire home as if it were a big fat turkey at Thanksgiving; the sudden appearance of wrapped presents below the glistening Christmas tree and how, in private, we would shake, rattle, and roll the ones addressed to us; the eve service and the caroling afterwards, and so the eventual rise to Christmas morn and all the unwrappings which followed. The hugs, the kisses, the sweet timbers of emotions and display of affection were there to reinforce the closeness of our family. And at last the grandest occasion of all would have us in community; Christmas dinner in so the most wondrous of scales.

Family members from near a hundred miles away all gathered for the big feast. Every manner of food came out to be admired; the coffers full; the tables running over with the most glorious of aromas and smells; the congregation of love and uniting brought us all once more to celebrate. And as the seasons passed by with the fruits of such what these seasons bring, Grandmother Ashley, at least in these God-giving moments, so found her home again.

Though amongst the rubble scars of that tragic night when all was lost to her, the greedy fire which came as a thief and stole from her all that she knew, and how this horrible memory consumed her for much of the year, she could finally peel back the scars and rediscover the joys of family she always knew was there.

I often saw her when a single moment let her be alone with herself. Quietly, timidly, and so softly, she would pull free that half heart which hung from the back of her neck. She supported it in the very deep pocket of her palm; smile, reflect, caress it a few times, and then flip open to the bed of it. There, in the very center of it all was Charles smiling back at her, and how she would return to him a smile, as if it were a wave of 'hello' and 'goodbye' all in the same motion.

A thousand memories must have flooded her then, like an endless snapshot of times' past; and though the oceans of misfortune and fate had separated them from one another for many years, this was the one moment where she could be with us and have Charles right there with her. No journey to see him, or finding a neutral spot where they both could unite in. It was here that I could see part of Charles glowing through her, as if she were the portal eye to all that he could see.

"So this is your family??" he must of asked her there, as they both watched the merriment surrounding them through her eyes, "You should be very proud Ashley; very proud."

"I am," I could hear her whisper in a soft and polite tone. A smile would creep across her expression and remain, just like the joy and peace which captured her heart in that moment. She would lean back in her chair; look about and soak in the celebrations all round, then gently fall asleep into her dreams. There was Charles standing on the dock, dressed in overcoat and heavy shoe sand smiling in the locks of that Irish night; waiting for her. The lump stuck in his throat yet the smile remained, and how, all over again, he would get to his knees and ask Grandmother Ashley for her hand in marriage.

"Yes," she must have said countless times in her dreams, "If I had hundred lifetimes to spend, they would be spent with you."

We are the harbor to our memories; keeper to those locked-away days of our past. We could blink our eyes one moment forward and catalog those times we do remember. Grandmother Ashley held much to the memory, and in this there is some glory to be had. She had seen, felt, and known what true love is, and how it so bonded her with her happiness, even unto the last days of her life.

Chapter 9

The Firehouse Gang.

In my growing years father had become more accustomed to spending time at home. The travels out west became less and less, and as a result, father became much more involved in the immediate community within Charlestown itself. Trips to the firehouse became more frequent. And as I grew older he would have me attend many hours with him there. It was said that the men were better in behavior when I was around, but there were times when my presence didn't really matter. The group was confident, close knit, protective, and fiercely loyal to the fireman's clan. There was a righteous brotherhood amongst them which I saw in no other; nearly as if they had taken on a second family crest name and so sworn to each other that 'this blood' was as sacred as their own individual family blood.

At times they were as giddy as drunken fools without the liquor. The laughter rumbled through the firehouse like some cannon in the storm. But when it came time to head out on a fire the seriousness quickly took over. As always, there were implicit standing orders to forever 'do' for one another. Protector, Brother, Saint; and to NEVER, EVER, leave one of 'yours' behind; this was the heart to their unified soul.

Father talked of the fire having a spirit and life of its own. And so going into a blazing home was akin to walking into the belly of hell itself and finding the devil waiting at the doorstep for you. Such stories kept me up all night, on the night of their telling. I had become afraid of the slightest ember; never to go near fire unless father was present and assisting. He was the finest protector, and so in my youth whenever father was around, I knew we were all safe.

I remember the trips through town on the local fire truck, I sitting in the cabin and hearing the sirens roar down the streets as we went. I was feeling like a very hip guy in the coolest sports car, checking out the women as they stared when we were passing by; and they all looking to see who was onboard. Buck drove with skip in the middle and my self on the end. The biggest joys were the Christmas and summer parades I attended; then, I knew I had the coolest sports car around. Everyone waved and asked us to honk one more time.

"HONK!" it shot off like a gun, "HONK!" The sirens in high pitch; the lights all in a swirl, and I sitting most casual in the cabin, waving at all the cute girls on the sidewalks; they smiling and waving back the same. Buck would constantly glance over at me and chuckle out loud, then reach behind Skip and slap at my hair.

"Don't get greedy son," he said, "They see the truck, not you."

I think Skip was feeling sorry for me, giving me several licks to the side of my cheek. It was my responsibility to keep the local firehouse dog entertained and in shape. I would constantly be taking sponge balls and rolling them about the station's floor to give Skip his exercise, and taking him out on leisure walks around the block and up to the local post office where Miss White and Miss Black were always at work. They took a liking to me whenever Skip and I entered the post office to check on the station's mail.

"Well now, Spic and Span," they would call us.

"Any mail for the firehouse today Miss Black?"

"Santa Claus' bag is quite full today," she would say, and thus pulling a handful for me to carry back. On a few occasions the mail was so numerous I had to have a small bag to take it back with.

They used to tease each other over their names.

"Maybe we should switch names?" Miss White would say, "That way no one will get us confused."

"I like my name well enough," Miss Black returned, "It's what I came into the world with, and rightly so, it's the name I will go out with," she grinned large and wide on that.

"Quite chilly out there isn't it Spic and Span, but it ain't no food," Miss White carried on in her happy self; and always made that statement in the fall and winter seasons.

Miss White had a continual spell of happiness about her. You knew she enjoyed being apart of people's lives on an everyday basis. Her gregarious ways were the more infectious the longer you were around her. At times I would stay at the mailroom with her for an hour or more. She always had a chair ready for me when I came, as well as a smaller stool for Skip when he joined me.

Her eyes were a deep brown texture and nearly shut when a smile crossed from ear to ear on her. She had trouble at times with her step, being that she had had a few back surgeries in her day, though she never complained when the stiffness got the best of her. Originally from Georgia, Miss White had made her way to Boston nearly twenty years ago, with the need to take care of her sick mother until she passed ten years back. However, she took a fond liking to the area and decided to remain, being with the post office for as many years. I always enjoyed my conversations with her; her bubbling-over personality; the freest spirit I ever knew. As if she was a stallion along the plains, and so enjoyed every moment of her life. Her high black curls were now peppered with gray at the very tips, and those puffy cheeks now swelled so to hide those dimples which were so prominent in her earlier days.

"Your father mind?" she slotted the mail when we spoke.

"He knows I am here," I returned, all trumped in my high chair, "he doesn't mind…really."

"You best abide by him," she warned, "I always believe there is honor, in honoring your parents."

I could see my mother in her; family is family and that is that.

Now Miss Black was from Connecticut; her family had a large horse farm which she often traveled back to. Her skin was light and on the pale side; her hair a tint of red, though more brown in the light. I found humor in her in the way she spoke. Her voice, though soft and easy tempered, would race along the words as if she were constantly out of breath; not ever knowing when to stop. She had bundles to say and she carried a constant smile with her wherever she went, though she never let out a chuckle; just a silent grin.

"I saw your mother at the grocery store and let me tell you, your mother is so beautiful. I don't know how she does it with you and your three siblings but I can see how you are and if you brother and sisters are like you, well then you must make it easy for her. Why I wouldn't know what to say with four children and all; keeping up with my two boys can be a terror at times but they have their moments of some good as well. I tell you, I can only imagine having girls in the household, since I had three sisters myself and we always have been close knit. Girls seem to be more tame in the growing up years than boys are, but boys like to play outside so that is good and you can have your quiet times…" Miss White, Skip, and my self would quietly sit and watch Miss Black carry on without interruption or pause.

"What?" she now had a curious look on her face as we must have had on ours.

"Good Child!" Miss White said, "You can put wind in a hurricane storm with those pipes of yours!"

"Oh please," she turned red and bashful, "It's a gift. Let me tell you…" and so she would go on and on.

"I don't know which is worse," Miss White whispered my way, "My constant back ache, or her long roadway for speaking."

Many of the firemen took to playing basketball, tossed around a baseball, or tidied up the two trucks in their spare time. Captain Buck enjoyed his time in the mid-day sun, sitting out on the driveway in a lawn chair with a warm coke in his right hand, and a heavily versed epic novel in his left. His most favorite of novels was Thomas Mann's 'The Magic Mountain'. Gerry had a sweet spot for keeping the floors clean, to the level of near obsession. It was nearly every time I came to visit, to always find a sign up, 'Caution, wet floor' in any part of the firehouse.

Hank's duties were relegated to keeping the uniforms and equipment in top shape and in good order, in the event a call came in and they had to leave on the hurry. Joey 'Lippers' spent much of his time making attempts to date Kelly, though she passed it off saying she had a boyfriend already, then coming over to me and planting a gigantic kiss on my cheek. This generally brought out the laughter of those close by, and the steaming ire of Joey himself.

"Maybe you should take lessons from the kid," Lamar would cackle, as if he were singing a happy song and those were the lyrics.

"Do da!," Hank furthered the jesting, "Do da!"

"They should patent your humor," Joey responded, "Ain't no man an island in this rig. A man pays dearly in this profession if he makes enemies amongst his brethren," there seemed to be a sort of competition between those two in every aspect. And through Lamar and Joey's adversarial role, a deep seeded brew of dislike continued to boil as long as I could remember.

"I'll have none of that," Buck leaned back from his propped book; with a stern and constant stare.

"Buck, he's got the nerve, not me." Joey said.

"You both do," Buck came from his chair, "True, no one lives on an island here, and I aim to keep it that way. Kelly can pick her own beau's. If she has a liking to someone? I am sure with her smarts she'll let the fellow know well enough…"

"No harm in trying Cap…"

Buck looked back on Joey with a most hard and cross look, "You do well by your nickname…'Lippers'…While you are here, I have a mind on anyone's business. Outside of here doesn't concern me. But in this house, I own the command and have a station to run. Anything contrary to this gets in our way."

"That's the rule…" Joey shied off a bit.

"That's the rule son. You're the shortest stint here. Make sure you remember that."

Buck kept his eyes solid on Joey.

"You'll stand by your brother, and be prepared to make sacrifices for him if need be," Buck was more strong-willed than even my father.

"Can do, Captain," Joey smirked, "Can do…"

"That's the fireman's way," Buck responded.

"You stick with me Conner," Gerry leaned his big massive body down towards me, and whispered with a smile, "These guys are just spirited at times; goes with the boot…"

"Goes with the boot?" I turned smartly to ask him.

"Yeah," he was grinning a goofy grin, "Just a saying. A fireman's term here. If you put it in your boot while you're out on a fire, then that means it's valuable to you. Don't you see?"

He appeared to plead his case, though I could only give him my normal confused look, and an interested ear to hear by.

"Listen," he leaned down to get to my level, "Fireman's gots things to protect, so in turn, it will protect him. Like a bible in his pocket, there the Lord sticks on his hip and stays with him; ain't no fire goin to stop the Almighty…A wedding ring around his neck, there his Misses is right by him, talking him through the mess he is in. A fireman needs something he really values; kind of like a good luck charm. He'll fret if he goes in alone, and that fire is no friend to the lonely. No sir!"

"What do you carry Grumble?" I asked.

He smiled real wide, and his dark eyes glimmered out a hard, coal-like glow, "I carries a signature!"

He proceeded to pull out a piece of paper encased in hard plastic, hanging limp around his neck.

"Gots this some twelve years ago in the summer of 63', down in a jazz hall in Louisiana on a hot summer evening…"

He seemed so proud by it; so much so, his broad smile nearly fell off his face there.

"Nat King Cole," he giggled, "Yes sir…the reverend of music himself. Got his autograph while he smoked a cigar after the show one night. I asked him politely and he obliged. I swore I'd never use the pen he wrote it with again. Got it sitting up in my cabinet at home, in a juice jar, on the tallest shelf…sitting way in the back so as the Misses can't find it and use it by mistake."

"What if she used it?"

"I died," he gasped, and nearly lost his breath.

"What if you lose his autograph?"

"I'd die again," his eyes grew bold with the whites of his pupils nearly popping from their sockets, "Man can't lose his kryptonite only once in his lifetime, and hopes to expect to live."

I took it to inspect it gently, almost treating it as if it were the holy relic Gerry viewed it as. I curled the small-encased note in the palm of my hand. I eyed it intently as Gerry watched every move I made. I knew quite frankly he was most concerned about it being out of his immediate possession. But by the script which settled in front of me, I could tell Nat King Cole had a strong hand, and by his writing there was much joy in his manner.

"Kind of like the fireman's spirit."

"Burns more bright than the fires we fight...A fireman's spirit is his lifeblood, and he needs it to survive if the blaze catches him."

"You know what I would carry Gerry, if I were a fireman?" I sparked a curious look up at him; a look so gout with wide-eyes that it grabbed his attention my way.

"What's that little Pa?" He returned with his hand clutching around my shoulder.

"I'd carry a baseball card," I grinned.

"Baseball card?" he strangely stared at me, "You don't say."

"But it wouldn't be any of the Red Sox players now," I stalled to think further, "Maybe for Yaz, but other than that..."

"Who would it be then?"

I allowed the silence to further my thoughts more; so wondering as they did until it hit me; the only person it could be.

"Spike," I said, "Brew 'Spike' Johnson," I gazed out over the open bay door. The sun gleamed back and struck out lines all along the inner driveway floors.

"It would be him for sure."

"Whoever he is," Gerry chuckled, "Must've had some pull on you, to make you carry him in the fire with you like that....Man's special...Man's special."

"What's it like?" I curiously asked another question on Gerry. His big brown, round eyes rolled white for a second, then pierced backward in a resentful, most hesitant stare.

"You don't ever want to know..." he fearfully imposed.

"Tell me," I gestured.

His pause drew out the moment longer still, like a long sliding blade from its shaft; until, "It's a beast little Papa...It's a beast. I remember a first year fire I saw. The call came in the middle of the night. It was five stories high; in a warehouse with no room to breathe; sittin' right in the belly of that building. It was dark, like the blackness could see and took out all the light. You could hear the building wheeze and ache like it were going to cough out loud. You were just waitn' little Papa…"

"For what?" I pressed on him.

He bent down near to my closest ear, eyed to and fro to check to see if anyone could overhear, then he shoved a whisper into that ear.

"For somethin; somethin to happen. Five stories up, you can be blocked off from any exit at any time. So's you got to keep good smart wits about you; let your ears do the see'n for you, when the darkness snuffs out your sight."

"Were you scared?"

"Oh little Papa," he grinned to the point that his eyes nearly shut completely, "Fireman's brother is fear. He's just got to learn how to control it, is all…. But you can hear it first."

"Hear the fire?" I asked.

"Yes'am. The fire goes to searchin. We always call it the oxygen hog; like a cancer fit to seek out its next prey. Always prowlin; first, the room gets mighty sounding like your surrounded; then, the smell approaches. Smoke leaks in if it can find a way through. The paint begins to curl; sometimes bubble on the walls. And if the fire can find a way to blow in, then it begins its crawl."

My heart nearly poised to stop while he spoke. The world caved in with my full concentration on every whisper he made, where time had clipped a moment and continued to sit on it while he told that story. The surroundings were now seemingly gone, with both Gerry and I sitting out in nowhere, talking as we were.

I kept to my calm, being so young and so the impressionable one, Gerry had my undivided attention, and he was aiming to keep me set to his story as well as every movement to his body.

"You felt it coming…" I suggested.

"I could feel it. Like a hand almost touching the edge of your shoulder in the pitch black. You knows it there, but it hasn't touched you yet; waiting, thinking for the right moment to play on you. You grip your axe double tight; wipe the sweat, smoke, and film from your sights. You sees the smoke billowing, then what seems to be a shadow of that dancing creature…Each one has a different birth…"

He stopped to let it sink in with me.

"Birth?" this time I was unsure.

"You knows," he continued, "Some from gas, others from kerosene, others electrical or matches; wood or paper. But they all have their own ways."

"How was this one?"

"Vicious," he swallowed hard, as though that fireman's fear was caught in his throat and it would not come down, "Most vicious…'Hub' was to my right;

'Goat' to my left, and your daddy just behind me. Before we knew it, the door in front of us blew open and free...and the monster came through in a burst and a mighty, most hideous wail. Knocked me clear back on your father; blew Goat straight up against a side window. We saw it."

"How was it?" I dared to ask, but feared to know more; knowing hoe keen my imagination can become when I was this excited; and how, by such precise measures, I could place myself virtually there as he spoke deeper and deeper into the story. The sweat on the palms of my hands grew out into leaks of water and perspiration.

My thoughts drew into a blank, yet they kept to the whim of Gerry's description. My senses drew me unwillingly further into his story. I felt the fireman's hat from my head blow clean off; the axe I held situated in my hand, flying to the corner of that room; my buckled coat fly about my eyes and push my mask clear from my view, then so see that unholy fire thrust into the room as though a giant mouth had blown a gust of fire, heat, and ash our way.

"It did its crawl, high on the ceiling; like fiery fingers running individual-like over us, passing down the smoke on top of us to confuse us, and so hitting 'Hub' right into his face. The fire caught him; took him down in a cry and a scream."

"What happened?" I kept my breath quiet and still there.

"Now don't scare the boy," I heard my father's voice from behind interrupt Gerry. My dad wanted the story to come to a halt, "Alright?"

"Yes Mr. James," Gerry responded, catching himself.

"Tell me," I pleaded.

"Its best son," father came over and pulled me by the shoulder with the clasp of his powerful hand, "to leave things buried where they belong. The past can be a cure; but if brought up again, can be a sin as well. It's best son; sometimes to only remember. Nothing more."

He eyed me looking back at Gerry.

"Sorry Mr. James," Gerry apologized, "Best some things not told on a boy," he laughed a chuckle, "My boys are better to know the light than the shadows."

"What happened to Hub?" I pressed weakly.

"Come over here son," father requested.

I felt his pull more firm now. He guided me into the long stairs and upper chambers of firehouse 112. A place I had not visited very often, and had never quite taken much notice to. There, in the place where their individual cots lay in rows. Straddling the back wall, I could see six pictures staring back at me. Faces unknown to me, nor ones that I had ever laid eyes on before; people who must have held some venture in the firehouse in times ago, though people who were as foreign to me as if I had just met them that day. I looked into their faces and their eyes; they were all firemen whose expressions told me so.

My father lifted me to his waist's side, gave me a tug and tight curl with his powerful grip, and then so softly lifted his one free hand to point out one of the pictures in front of me.

"There is Hub," he sighed, "He's still here. Good liking sort of a guy who always had a smile on his face, and a cigar sitting in his fingers. He's here son; as good justice goes. You never stop being a fireman once you become one. He's home, and where he should be. You remember that…ok?"

I nodded and approved, and I said nothing more about the subject again. There were many things my father felt free to speak on; others, which were as locked in some far away gate. As if they were never known to me, nor would ever be. This, being one of the more prevailing things he was not only leery about talking of, but that which held such reverence and solidarity with him, he could never find the bridge to gap himself with me on it. It was to be left as a deep measure within him, and so a lifelong mystery with me.

I respected this solemn torch he carried; the firemen who were lost into the past; ones he could never discuss on. The brotherhood of the clan; that sacred accord, bond, and covenant as if it were a religion on its own behalf; things which could only be embroidered in the fabric of that firehouse gang were so left within this exclusive membership.

Though, as father teaches his son to become, he inadvertently passes on those same traits. Traits held more deeply than any truths buried into secret; things only entrusted to one person—yourself.

If only I had known the tragedy which would await us most soon afterward; something which would make me a participant and eyewitness to the glory, and the heartache to such a creed.

Chapter 10

The Day I Fell from my Childhood.

I had marked this day on my calendar for sometime now. My father informed me of a drill fire they were to perform on an old, condemned, and abandoned home. He had asked me to attend, feeling that it would be a good learning experience for me; and perhaps one I could give a research paper on in the coming school year. I was to be ready, like a good fireman's son; with pencil, paper; plenty of this, and to make double sure I took extra-fine notes. It had always been my grand anticipation that I would join my father someday on a fire run.

As the days grew closer to that Saturday, I marked each day off as they came and went. It seemed time was as eager as I was. The days would come and go; my calendars so looking like 'x' blocked pages than anything else when I was done with them.

We were to start early that day, just before sunrise. I requested to my father that I stay over in the firehouse the night before, and treat it like it were a real fire we were going to.

"Certainly son," he smiled and laughed softly, "in fact..." he led me to a corner locker, "I took the liberties."

I felt the whole firehouse began to converge on me with the weight of thirty eyes or more; the circle grew tighter as I moved slowly to that locker. Firemen filtered in and clamored forward, as some peered over each other's shoulders, while others took to turning themselves into jumping jacks in the rear.

High atop and above my own height, there stood my name, clear as day, brimming across the locker door itself. My lower jaw faltered and dropped as my stare looked wide. I felt the world was engrossed with what I was seeing. I clipped the metal door handle free and watched as the door swung open. There was a pint-sized fireman's hat before me; cap, overcoat and t-shirt with 'station 112' penciled across the chest of each; boots, socks, belts, pants and vest; all according to my size. The silence dropped the air then into a very solemn quiet.

"You're now officially a fellow fireman, 3rd precinct, station 112," my father gleefully announced. His look spoke to me with such measure of pride and joy, and his smile cut a path across his face to the point it nearly fell off onto the floor.

"Now you're decorated for sure little Pa," Gerry moved close and wildly grinned. I could see the stark 'whites' of his teeth next to his dark and overly tan skin, "Likes us…a true fireman."

"Shined your buckles nice and proper little boy blue," Fred chimed in as he pulled a bright, shiny gold buckle from atop, lowered himself, and showed off the pride of his artwork to me, "See? 'Conner LBB James'; looks spiffy…Don't it?"

"Here…this will suit you," I felt two hands shove a hat down across the back of my head; just brimming over my eyebrows.

"Fire station 112's newest member," Lamar spoke.

"What's ya say? What's ya say cappers?" Hank doubled up his words on me, "Thing fits, thing fits better than a, a glove."

"What do you say son?" father asked.

I paused for that moment and I looked around at all the groping eyes sitting in front of my stage. It seemed no one had ever done such a thing as this for me. These men had grown to know, to understand, and to eventually become fond with affection for me, as I, in return had grown most fond on them. This was a special time in my life; a time as ingenious to the occasion as when I was standing at home plate, looking about Fenway Park and seeing all those fans chanting for Spike after he was gone.

You find yourself unwittingly so, when fate and circumstance propels you onto that unplanned stage; a partner with that individual, almost sacred moment. A pause like this in life appears almost as if it were a reverent prayer to the specialties of that special occasion; spontaneous, unrehearsed, not planned and most natural to when it occurs. It's an eclipse in time; a moment once in passing like a breath gone by, yet still remains with you. It travels so through life by your side, and evolves ever so slightly through the whims of time itself, as a collected memory you had unknowingly picked up along the way.

It's as if a kind flower had burst out in front of me and was showing me just how good life can be; the smell, the touch, the sensation of its birth came dashing my way. I fell into that moment as though it were my first kiss, which I had yet to experience. Time always shudders in such a moment; just a spell, to kindle within you the beauty and glory of it.

And so with every wonderful sunrise, there is an abiding sunset. The lantern once lit, begins to fade; the precious moment gone but not lost.

I was feeling its' passing as though it were the sorrow which follows the joy, as my mother often spoke of; but how it now was gifting me with the meaning and purpose to forever reflect on.

This, above all things, was the lesson my mother attempted to persuade me on. As life would teach to me, then so would I understand the very Truths she bestowed along my way through life.

"Little Pa?" Gerry brought me back.

"Thank you," I softly spoke, "You make me feel welcome."

"Well you are Conner," Buck spoke for the group, "As good as Skip here," and with this, the whole room burst into a roar.

That little Dalmatian cocked his ears back and forth, stood firm and curious in his expression, and puckered his nose out as if he were trying to sniff out the humor in it all.

"You got a good boy there," Kelly smiled out on my father, then to me, "And if you were a little older, you might be a lot more dangerous," she knelt down beside me, bent low inside the rim of my cap, and kissed me square on the cheek. I nearly turned a pure flush mixture of red and burgundy.

"Hmmm…" Lippers backed off; seemingly disgusted he was not the recipient of the kiss she gave me.

"There you go again with the belly ache in your mouth," Fred spoke out as he crossed on Joey's path; they standing face to face.

"What's it to you?" Joey angrily shot out, "He's just a kid."

"Exactly," Fred replied, "So if you have a bitter pill, do us all a favor…and swallow it."

"How long have you been here soldier boy?" Joey 'nubbed' his knuckles on Fred's shoulder, "Huh? Number of fires?"

"Long enough Frat boy!"

"You haven't seen the belly of fires I've seen…just enough to roast your Cub Scout marsh mellows by," he pushed up nose to nose on Fred. I could sense the tension stir the air into a fire of its own. I stood, watching Fred's Adam's apple dart up and down in his throat.

"You feel like you always have something to prove, don't you?" Fred pushed back, which caught the ire of his fellow fireman.

"Easy guys," Buck broke in, "Keep your differences out of this station. You have problems now? Just wait; you get out on the line when it really matters, and you still have problems with each other, then someone's going to get hurt…maybe even killed. Can you live with that?"

Buck looked at both of them square in their eyes.

"Well? Can you? Someone give me an answer. I am at a loss here."

"No problems here," Joey snorted, "None the least."

"Tell you what fly boy," Buck turned his full attention now on Joey, "How did you get out of the academy? Cancers don't usually make it through…"

"Like I said Cap," Joey defended himself, "I got no problems."

"Yeah you do," Buck sharply replied.

"What?" Joey folded out his arms.

"You're a rogue," Buck pushed further, "Rogues are dangerous; they get themselves in an ash pile of trouble. You want to be independent? Carry the hose yourself. I'll not have you riding in the station any further if you can't get with the program."

"I didn't start this Captain."

"So? But you're always ready to finish it."

Buck crossed his arms out over that wide chest of his.

"One thing Lippers I figured out in my days. Wherever you go in life, you got two things you have to get used to smelling. No matter what, you gotta learn both or life gets real hard to handle for yourself."

"What's that?" he inquired.

"Roses," Buck paused, "and dung. Roses are easy; you just have to figure out how to stand the dung smell…so, figure it out."

"I get you Captain," he grumbled, "More dung for me, than roses,"

He sounded off in a bitter tone.

"That's your choice water soldier," my father broke in, "As far as I am concerned, you'll be most polite when my son is around; and you'll do your job when called upon. Anything else?"

"Nothing," he grumbled as he shot out from our midst.

"I'll not have any member of this crew ostracizing Lippers…you here?" Buck warned all.

"Any problems? You address them with me…We have a big day tomorrow," he paused, smiled, and looked towards my tiny frame, "We have a new member to initiate tomorrow."

"Don't worry little Pa," Gerry came round and swung his massive arm around both my shoulders, "Stay with me. I'll take care of you tomorrow. Just like your dad did before, for me…"

I did not understand the last part of what he spoke to me, but I would wonder on this all throughout the night. That phrase darted across my mind while I made every attempt to get some sleep, but could not. The silence was nearly as impractical to sleep by as was being in the middle of a rocking sea storm, so casting my bed ship all about. What did he mean by it?

I heard the concert snores all around me. Each fireman had his own method of spouting out a growl or two. No one was ever in sequence; Tubby first, then Caps gave it a try; Buckles was soon to follow; Hank and Saggy seemed to sing out their own duet. Then, when all was quiet, my father decided he was going to perform his own solo act, which lasted nearly a half hour or more.

This was my plight and my unenviable curse. Tomorrow was to be my first experience as a fireman; a real fireman. To see the eyes of the beast; to feel the curdle echoes of that creature; sense the dangerous crawls of its ways, though caged as it may be. Still, I would have the chance to look into that mirror and see its reflection. My father was never one to ever speak on his encounters with it, so I had no premonition or warning to lean on; this, whether by wealth or by famine, I would see for myself; and in those things he respected and feared the most.

I could see the shadowy cars pass through the streets just below us; the silhouette and figures would ricochet across the broad brick wall in front of me. There was a slow, continual faucet leak in one of the long sinks in the open bathroom. I waited for each drop to splash, and I would count the seconds between each drip. My watch would drag on the minutes much the same way; and I would count the drips between each second, then count the seconds between each drip.

I was confounded by my uneasy way towards sleep that night; the manner by how eternal a single night could become, and the excitement and hesitation I was beginning to feel towards the house fire I was to attend the following day.

"Ok kittens."

I heard the captain say, as I awoke from what felt to be only a moment's sleep.

"Time to rise and shine and get your milk…" Before long they were quickly in their gear, yet I straggled behind even with the constant help from my father.

Still the time had come and we were all soon aboard the two largest fire trucks within the station. I sat in the inboard cabin seat facing the rear of the truck; my father by my side with his hand in full clasping to my outer shoulder. Gerry sat across the way with his large head seemingly to burst out from underneath his hard hat. He smiled a few times at me as he cross-buckled his jacket from waist to collar; though the nature of those grins he sent my way were quite different than ever before.

"You have Nat King Cole with you?" I asked.

"Always," he spoke and giggled, "Baseball card?"

"I didn't bring it with me," I yelled back through the roar of those sirens, "I forgot."

He pulled a baseball card out from underneath his waist jacket.

"I didn't little Pa," he handed it to me.

I inspected it closely and found it to be one from my favorite Red Sox players; Yaz himself.

"Thanks Gerry."

"You see?" he grinned out with a gaping smile, "I told you I would look out for ya…didn't I?"

He winked on me.

"You were always good with the details Grumble," my father said with a return smile

Gerry looked out over the passing streets, appeared to think about something most personal, then he turned back and patted down Skip, who was sitting most next to him.

We went from Elgin Street, down onto Barker, and into what seemed to be quite a lonely, rundown neighborhood of sorts. Many of the structures in this region were some of the oldest in the city of Boston; not of good keeping, nor kept in repair. The street led us to a home set off to itself; two stories in wood frame and structure. A home neglected for what seemed a decade or more; perhaps of an invalid or miser of some manner. A loner so isolated, he rarely was seen in public. The bushes were tall and lanky, bending and sprouting out over the lower level windows. The paint had worn badly from the many years of weathering, chipping at every nook and cranny. Shudders hung limp to each side of the windows; some had fallen off altogether. The grass was uncut for what appeared the long summers of years past; now brittle and dry, it nearly seemed to be a miniature dust bowl and thatch.

Some of the firemen had taken the smaller vehicle and were present hanging about the front of the structure, looking back on us as we sirened forward, just in front of the rubble sidewalk. There were fifteen firemen, Skip, and myself in all; so coming from the trucks and standing in file while we were observing the house before us.

"Did you check the house?" Buck caught Joey's attention.

"There's nothing," Joey replied.

"Double check?" he pursued further.

"Of course," Joey responded, "Nothing flammable; all power turned off and cut from the house; sub floors seem stable; no problems with the stairs; structure appears adequate enough…good to go Cap."

"All right boys!" the Captain turned to speak to all of us; I and Skip at the end of that long line. Just then I could see the shadows of smoke beginning to rise and billow within the deep etches of two windows; one downstairs; one upstairs.

"Listen up and stay clean! Two alarm fire; family of four; husband, wife, and two kids. There are four manikins in place throughout the house, in undetermined locations. It's our job to go in, contain the fire, find the residents, and pull them clear of the house. No funny heroism. Anything goes wrong? Clear the building. No need to have more than manikins stuck in the house. I want a hose readied on the west and east end."

He stalled and inspected us with his glare and stern look. He propped one hand high above his head.

"I want five search and rescue; ten in containment positions…Luther, Hank, Buckles, Saggy, and Crew Cut; your up! At my mark head to the structure and proceed in. You others split into crews of four each…two in the saddle and two in the rear," I could hear the fire in a fizzle then; flames in a shot-put formation, dancing on both floors now.

Its' heathen breath caused the house to ache and moan at its own impending death. Suddenly, windows and glass began to break within the house. I could feel the sudden impact of that heat move to surround the home, like an unseen inferno parading around and baiting us to enter. The creature Gerry had spoken of before was starting to rear its mighty, violent head, and I could smell its storm. I sensed my own uneasiness begin to rise as I looked out over to my father; his expression was in a stony glare and an unflinching way.

He had been through this on-many-occasions; his experience gave him the stout bravado and security to perform his duties without waiver. I had never seen my father with such a look built into his face as this; stony, cold, determined, and wild yet bridled until the moment for action. Like a racehorse at the starting gate; grunting, swaying from side to side, and giving out a back kick; eager to hear that bell go off and the front gate to suddenly fly open.

I peered back on that home as the force of sound and fury increased with intensity. Smoke poured from the ash-burnt look of those windows; the waves of its passage turning upward and creeping up the sides. The house groaned further; wheezed and sizzled a cry that nearly struck me into a scare. I could hear cabinets from the kitchen begin to collapse and tumble to the floors below. The walls yawned and bent from the excessive heat. Old parched paint flew from the outward boards, dropping like white snow onto the dusty grounds below.

"On my mark!" The captain called out.

I knew he could see the monster also. He waited; silent, observing, holding firm in his look and so dripping the sweat of heat and fear; all rolling down the sides of his cheeks. Flames ripped from the windows and poured out in search of more oxygen, so seeming to be like odd and gross fingers from a large hand; rolling backwards and holding a beacon for us to enter by.

I remember Gerry's words as I too observed that destructive beast growing in its own lair. *'A fireman's fear never leaves you; just have to figure out how to keep it contained'*.

I looked down the row of men waiting for the Captain's word. Each held that same fear, and seemed nearly haunted by it; the identical lump to the throat; waiting, eyes wide and engrossed; halting, weary in the moment, yet still and patient due to their training. The five in front held firm on their axe; their masks hovering just over their hats and ready to descend.

"Go! Go! Go! Go!" Buck cried out.

It began. Everyone ran in precise sequence; those five men pushed forward, while thrusting their masks over their heavy faces.

"Hose! Hose!" father yelled.

I saw two men leap forward; two men to the rear on each truck pushed to release the hoses while one other hooked to the fire hydrants at a frantic, almost Herculean pace. I could hear the rumble of that water pass through once these firemen unleashed it, as if it were uncorked from a long-sealed bottle.

I bent backwards, not knowing what to expect as I felt the sudden sway of the moment. I lost my breath somewhere along the way, and though I bent forward in an attempt to recapture it, somehow it seemed to still escape me.

"We have a little too much grease on the second floor gentleman. Get some water on the third window as soon as you can,"

Buck acted like an overseer to the event while he scowled about; harsh, unforgiving, barking akin to a dog angry over his lack of food. His hands were flailing in every direction like the mad man he seemed to become.

"Do you gentleman have arthritis? You'd move faster in a wheel chair! Move! Move!"

Their pace increased; their adrenaline coursed from vein to vein in such a hurried scatter. I could see Grumble nearly rip the cap from one of the fire hydrants with his bare hands. His face tore into a grimace; the sweet dropping from his cheeks as if they were puddles of water. Two firemen disappeared within the confines of the burning house; then a third, a fourth; a fifth soon to follow.

"Fireman aboard!" my father yelled out, "Fireman aboard!"

"Fireman aboard!" I had another cry out.

"Fireman aboard!" yet another echo shot into the air.

The fire whaled and bellowed out its own version of laughter. Every window, door, and opening was now engulfed in flame and smoke. Wind gusts poured in and about the home to create its own rapid cantation. The fire gushed forward, then retracted back within the confines of the house; in and out, in and out; so breathing the seeming stuffy fumes of its own exhale. I felt the house was tumbling to its own slow engrossing death, gasping for what little air it could retrieve. The paint pealed back from its surface; the timber below it turned into charred and scorched planks; the windows crackled and shattered from the increased pressure; the eaves and overhangs curling back as they burned into rubble.

Men moved closer as they leaned back from the force of those powerful hoses; pushing their hoses forward in a rush, though the flames roared outward in a seeming attempt to push them into a retreat. A push of fire would roll out like a snowball off a mountain, then so disappear from the weight of that water.

"The fire is moving rather quickly Captain," Lamar observed.

"A little too much," Buck grunted back.

"Gentleman! This one has backbone; show it you have more kick!"

A third hose was pushed to the front, almost immediate to those crumbling front steps and platform. One man rushed forward carrying one of the manikins free.

"Wife's out!" he sounded off as he descended onto the front lawn, "How should I read her?"

"Don't look at me!...What are her symptoms?" Buck moved to coach the young fireman further.

"Appears to be a contusion to the back of the head; severe laceration on one leg."

"Vital signs," Buck yelped, "Vital signs! That will regulate your urgency. Remember, its' about saving lives...and not losing yours in the process. Condition code son! Determine that first..."

Without warning, I gazed out over this structure in all its apparent chaos. Every man was in tight condition; holding to his post and not flinching. It looked as though, in that instant, the house took sort of a hiccup when the fire penetrated to the roof; slowly bend outward as if it were taking in a big blow...then.

"OH MY!!!!...." I heard a voice strike these words onto the scene, "Gaaaaaaaaahhh!"

In a swift and sudden kick from nowhere, I felt myself being propelled backwards and onto the street sidewalk. My head snapped behind me; the helmet dart from my bushy head and roll into the street; my hands were cusped in a ball as the earth felt to a shake and grumble. I heard Skip let out a single and frightful yelp, and then disappear from my view. The house blew out a hefty contagion rush of heat, fireballs, and hot-ash air from its very mist. The cannon shot had blown one fireman clear from a second story window, landing as he did in a row of bushes just below. The two head firemen with hose in hand, standing there at the foot of that platform, were so eclipsed by that shot from hades itself, and were cast into those flames until that inferno rolled back into the house.

Their cries of agony hit me first; then as horror unfolds, I could see them running in retreat, full in ablaze. My heart nearly stopped and died in that moment. Four others rushed to their aid, landing on top of them, trying in sheer desperation to put them out. They all collapsed in a tumbling and rolling mass of bodies. My father quickly ran to the other lame fireman settled in the bushes, and pulled him onto the parched and dirty lawn.

"Stat!" Buck furiously raged, "Stat! Call for backup! I've got four men trapped inside!" He pointed angrily at Joey.

By this time the entire home was consumed from within; plumbs of heavy fireballs rolled into the crisp blue sky, and as each one did, the ground beneath us rumbled as if to shake the earth by its own fear.

From inside one second story wall I could see an axe penetrate into the open. It hacked out of desperation; it hacked out of fear; it hacked out of preservation and a need to survive.

"Wham!" it struck with such force and blow that the wood began to split clean, then another blow, and another; a hand reaching through; eyes leaning forward to force themselves into our view; the face looked into the heart of agony and so collapsed from that weight. Two firemen ran to the very foot of where one of their own was trying to cut his way through.

The frothing smoke and gushing gases from each side of him were pushing now through that same opening while he continued to struggle. To my horror, which nearly put my sight into a disease of its own, those hands wrangled, flailed away, shuddered and shook violently before slowly coming to a drop into a death of their own; lifeless; still, and unmoving while they were wedged there.

"Get that truck over here!" Buck cried out, "Ladder up! Ladder up! Get him out of there!"

Another explosion, this time from the second floor, blew us all back to the ground once more. The shock wave crawled along the bed of earth itself until it rolled on past me.

I turned back; saw two firemen down directly in front of the house while four more were attending to them. Another fireman lay in one corner getting aid from another. The force of that second blast had collapsed the truck ladder onto itself, and now making it useless.

"ETA!" Captain Buck yelled on Joey again, "ETA!"

"They didn't say Cap," he lowered his hand from the radio.

"Then make yourself useful water boy!"

Buck grabbed him by the shoulder of his jacket and began dragging him to the foot of that house.

"What are you doing?" Joey implied.

"Making you a hero boy!" he screamed back, "We're going in!"

"Flank on the hoses!" father cried to four firemen holding the water lines on the east and west ends. He stood, gathered me in his sights, and spoke with the command of Thor, "Gerry, get Conner in the truck!"

And just over his shoulder, running in his most direct background, I saw Buck and Joey descending into the very belly of that awful creature.

"Crew Cut's got a concussion," Gerry was still attending to him, leaning over him like a makeshift nurse, "We gots to get Buckles and Hank! Luther, Saggy, they's still inside boss!"

"Come with me!" father grabbed Gerry as they moved passed two firemen, "You stay where you are!" father yelled into my direction.

They ran past the west corner, round about, and into the rear portions of the house. I could see Skip dart from a side street and connect up with Gerry and father.

"Skip!" I yelled, moving forward, and disobeying my father's demands all in the same motion.

"Skip!"

I could sense my heart pushing into beats beyond its normal limits; so much so, it felt as though it would rip from my chest or stop altogether from the stress. My breath was famine and nearly extinguished; my eyes were absorbing the rapid-fire events as they unfolded before me. With axe in hand, my hardhat sitting uneasily over my headlocks; jacket, gloves, and boots all inset, I moved to shadow my father's path.

I felt the roarish heat from that fire as I came closer; those flames would lick out just in front of me; crackle and pop as though it were in full laughter on my attempt to stop it.

"*Now I have you!*" I thought I heard it whisper to me.

My face caught a singe from its heaving breath; I tumbled, rolled down a slight embankment, sensed the tip of a fireball run just over me, and then dissipate into a ghastly cloud of smoke. There was a profound whoosh at the end of it; the searing echoes of its laughter sneered at me.

One section of the roof had collapsed and tumbled into the attic just below it. The side windows blew what remained of the glass towards my direction. I gathered to my feet, lept over the embankment, and routed myself onto the backyard. It was there I saw Skip enter as the last of that trio had done.

"Father!" I nearly wept there.

Still I rushed ahead as I felt blood beginning to drip from my cheek. My eyes nearly bulged free in a moments' take. There stood a long and narrow deck connected to the back of this home. I ran to its steps, looked upwards, and saw the mesh of fire and ploom cascade down those floors, then roll back inside. I stumbled upwards, slipped several times over the steps I had just crossed, and kept steady my sights in front of me all the while. The smoke and haze pushed on me to obstruct my view; still I continued.

"Father!"

Another rumble took me from my feet, and nearly crushed me where I stood. I fell to the decks' floor. Another fireball from the second story blew out from the large window above me; the ash hitting me as it curled out. Another hideous laugh bellowed from the creature.

I thought for a second I had come across one of those stand-alone moments; but not to smell the rose this time, yet to sense the sorrow on its lost bloom. This was the offset to sunshine; the very rain we all dread. To fear for a loved one's life, and see it shot away just before your eyes. It was a moment where I thought all was lost; my father captured and placed into a world for which I could never visit. To no longer know the power and influence of his ways; to see a life shortened, and me attempting to discover another direction in my own life. There were shadows of fate all about, yielding its own unmistakable powers. And perhaps, if the moment was one of grace, my father would remain and this would be nothing more than a passing episode in our lives together. I met with prayer at that moment; asked for its comfort; pleaded for its hopeful outcome; then waited for its answer.

I gazed into the pitch-blackness of that open area in the rear of that house; the only place where this creature had not fully overtaken all. From the shadows of that refuge there came my masked father first, hands-to-shoulders, and having Hank wrapped over the back of his neck. I could hear the sizzle coming from his mask and tank. I looked onto Hanks' face, and so saw the expression of a man just born again, and sighting out onto the new world as if he were awe struck by what he saw.

My father's muddled gaze bore down on me with such a stern look; his pace seemingly slow and the world had slowed with him. Another explosion rocked from above and with it came the clash and clamor of more debris all around us. Father pressed forward like the giant he appeared to me there; steady; without pause; risking all; strong to the helm, and unmoving like nothing would ever harm him.

"I thought I told you to stay put son!"

He pointed at me; the muttered sounds of his voice protruded out from the steamed mask situated over his face. Suddenly Gerry shot out from this blackened hole as well; his hands about his shoulders, and so bulking up his frame to show an impressive mass. There Saggy sat slumped over Gerry's shoulders like a lost lamb just now recovered. His eyes searched out into the open air while his expression bore a look of thanks and glee that he was pulled from the grips of this monster.

Both men were in an uncontrollable cough. Gerry and father pushed past me, down from the deck, and onto the cleared grounds below.

"Where is Buckles? Luther?"

"Don't know…" Hank coughed through, "We were paired off. Buckles and Luther headed for the second floor…Lost sight just before the explosion."

"They are upstairs?" Father stressed on them, "They are upstairs??"

Father grabbed onto Saggy with such intensity, I thought he might have well punched him.

"Not sure! Not sure! I was next to the mud room!"

Father leered back with his look as he stared down the house if though it were the enemy itself.

"I'm going back in!" he cried, "Stairs or no stairs…I'm going in!" Gerry pulled on his jacket.

"Captain and Joey already are in there looking for them!"

"I'm going in," father repeated, "Who was hanging by the opening…Second floor?" he looked back on the others, "Who??"

"Didn't get that far boss," Luther responded.

"I'm going in," father returned his attention back to the house and shot a look back up where those stairs would have been; with axe in fist and a stare which would curse a saint. No one dared to stop on him.

Father bore on me one last haunting glare, then proceeded to rush back through this opening. Smoke pummeled the deck and nearly filled our sights with a dark and misty haze. I nearly lost myself to a continual cough; the air stymied and choked with fumes. The house breathed one last great breath, paused, and then blew a mighty exhale that filled the surroundings with a converging fire and heat.

"Get back little Pa!" I heard Gerry in my rear.

So very quickly I felt his massive hand yank me full length from the outer edge of this deck and land us both full bellied to the ground below.

I stood; viewed the devastation at hand; dropped my hat to the ground as my hair wrestled free from it. The deck collapsed onto itself; the blackened opening was now filled by rage and long streaks of fire going from floor to roof. I thought I had seen the belly of hades consume this structure, lap its way through every nook and begin the final phase of having the entire home cascade into a heap of rubble. The west-end tipped to one side, moaned in its horrid ache and cries like a giant metal ship nearly ready to sink to the ocean floor; dip slightly, and crumble there to the first level below it.

Terror shocked my body into thinking this was nothing more than a dream. Those prayers long lost and not answered; I waited for mother to turn on the early morning light.

"*Wake up son!*" She would say to wake me.

Then it would be over; father still in his bed, sleeping from the previous night's shift. Nothing more than a fabric of that night; a nightmare conjured up from a bad evening meal.

"Nooooooooo!!!!!!!" I cried out as I lept forward towards the nearest window, yet only to find my path stopped by Gerry's better determination to stop me. He wrestled me to the ground.

"Daaaddd!" I reached out with a single word, "Nooooo!!!"

The east-end floors still hung in a precarious balance; the sub floors and interior walls bending, tossing to and fro as if it were casting about in its own wind. I could see a hand push out from the farthest window, disappear, then shot-put Skip in flight against his will.

I heard him yelp twice as he twisted violently in the air. I followed his freefall and I could see the stark fear in his eyes; his body in uncontrollable shakes; his paws were near to a crumble as he landed on all four. There came a final yelp cry. I ran to him, noticing without pause his left front leg had been injured. He sat most quiet and still, casting out a terrified look from his left eye, then so bending his nose upward to see me with both.

Suddenly we could see a silhouette figure center out over the crest of this window, bending down nearly to disappear from view, just inside and below the window's facing; lift up something into a prop, push it forward and send it partially out the window.

"Luther!" Gerry ran directly beneath the window. Luther's hardhat tumbled to the grounds below; his arms limp and dangling from the second story window ledge; his face buckled down and out of view. No life apparent but for the second pair of hands pushing him further and further out of that window.

"It's going to go!" I heard my father's voice cut through those increasing sounds of calamity, "It's going to go now!"

"Get to it!" Saggy got to his feet, apparently talking to himself as he began to drag one leg behind his body, "Get to it…Come on!"

Gerry took a mighty thrust with his axe. He summoned as much might as he could possibly muster into the lower wall. The axe stuck and he took to lifting himself higher by it, "Throw me your axe!" He leaned back and caught Saggy in a lame sprint towards him, "Now!"

Saggy swung the ax upward, handle first, with it landing squarely into Gerry's free palm. In one fluid motion, Gerry swung higher with the force of Thor himself. The wall gave and stuck onto the second axe at such the angle that Gerry pulled himself up another level. I could see father's ramped eyes peer full gasping out over the landscape, onto me without a blink, and there, just below him, getting full view onto Gerry who just happened to be looking upward, "Back up! Back up! Catch him!"

Luther dropped without warning from the second story, onto Gerry and Saggy; all three tumbling into a collapse.

"Grab his hand!" Gerry commanded, "Drag! Drag!"

Hank finally gathered himself to a stand, rushed to their aid, collected Luther's feet, and so they carried him out from the house.

I felt the ground muddle underneath my feet once more; the hideous prelude to one last explosion soon to erupt on us. Father began his climb from the window's opening. A pause; a rush; one last prayer for fate, then the roar of this creature's engine grasping for one final victim, and out shot a loaded fireball from that very window. My father collapsed to its base as he looked outward and down, so catching the heat on his back as it rolled out. There he let loose to hang, dangling from his post there. The east-end second floor jolted and shuttered just before it came crumbling downward.

"Jump!" Gerry hailed out with as much fear in his expression as I had ever seen on him, "Cut it! Jump!"

In an instant, father released himself and fell freefall at the foot of the house. All of the second floor faltered and so began its descent to crush the floor below.

Father rolled out as if he were an elongated ball; hands huddled close and rolled upward; his legs straight and steering him into that rapid roll. His mask was long gone and showing a face parched and burned from the fire. His hands grew into a shake and twisted out to grab a hold of something; anything that would halt his progress. I could see that he lay there in pain when he looked to the Heavens, saw the waves of clouds passing by in a drift and for an instant, I thought I saw the little boy in him. His gaze sky-struck, looking hopeful, kissing the sky with his lips, and seeming to think that life would be wonderful, 'just around the corner'.

"Boss!" Hank came to father's aid, "Boss? Where is it?"

"Side…" father weakly spoke, leaning to expose where a tiny board had punctured through just below his ribs. I panicked; came into full tears; ran to kneel at his side and collapsed onto his left arm.

"Son..." he coughed, "Take care of Skip...ok?"

I leaned back and was most silent in my stare on father; a tear dripped down one cheek and I shook my head in approval; backing away until I came over to where Skip lay.

I looked skyward myself. The cream-colored clouds perched high above and showed no signs of the peril that had just taken place; the canopy sky with its pearl blue cantation seemed to stare back on us with solemn wonder; the green grasses below and the long meadows which followed held no signs of the disaster I had just experienced. Nature had contained the horror in such a small place, yet preserved the immediate area about as if nothing happened.

I could hear the numerous sirens roar like a fortress army coming to our rescue. They piled onto one another in a chorus of psalm and rally; strumming down the main access road until a dozen or more emergency vehicles had cut across the lawns; parked to the front, side, and rear of the house; nearly surrounding the entire structure. I saw the flash of cameras, the whizzing role of newsmen running about to be the first to carry this story.

"Over here," one man rushed his panicky cameraman down close to the scene, "Set up over here! Be on in three minutes."

"No you don't!" an officer herded them away as persistently as he could, "Not on my watch!"

"But the story," the man fumbled with his microphone.

"These men have families!" the officer swore more angrily on them, "Good gosh man! Give them space!"

"The story," he pleaded, "we are in roll in three minutes."

"Not on my watch!" he pushed them further back, "It's only fair to the families. They don't need to find out this way...not this way," he pressed forward on them.

"Any shot then," the reporter negotiated one more plea.

"A hundred yards back," he forced his hands out once more, "Make no mention of which fire station...you hear??"

I gently picked Skip up within my own embrace. He conceded but for a slight whimper, so keeping his look on me while he rested his nose to my shoulder. I could see the mayhem only intensify. The full fledge catastrophe only now becoming more real as I slowly walked from the rear to the side of this house, then back around towards the front. The flames burned yards above the actual home, nipping the surrounding tree limps into a scorch and ember.

This home appeared nothing more than a pile of massive charred wood, mortar, and brick. Three firemen lay motionless on the front lawn, though being aided by three or more paramedics each. I retreated back with my view and I saw father slowly gathering himself into a stand, holding his side, and grimacing a rather painful sight while he walked with the aid of Gerry and Hank.

"We got Cap!"

Two men screamed and carried out a stretcher in arms. There sat Buck; unmoving, lifeless to the core; his hands nearly charred to black; his face chaffed from eyebrow to eyebrow.

"We're in stat! We're in stat!"

"Vital signs someone!" another fireman I had not seen before bellowed out.

"There are none," a paramedic replied.

"Then give us some!" The firemen returned; his hand clinched in a ball as four to five men surrounded Buck.

"Are you hurt son?" another paramedic interceded on me.

I looked to him, cast-eyed and set in shock; my arms nearly numb; my thoughts lost into that apparent nightmare for which I could never awake from. I saw the sudden impact of life and death and it so scared me into a near caustic mood.

"My dog," I quietly said. I turned my look down on Skip.

"We'll get him," he gently lifted Skip from me.

"Come on Buck!" I heard one-man charge. His hand landed slap down on Buck's chest; his shirt now pulled free.

"Give me something! Please!"

I stared out on them in a daze. Through the mass of hands, legs, and arms, I could view the embattled man still laying on the ground without an ounce of movement in him. I feared for Buck then, as I feared for all the men, including my father. My memory rushed back on me in that eternal moment; my thoughts of Buck and all those times we shared. How he made the world glow even in the darkest of hours; his pension for storytelling; that graphic smile; his high-spirited manners and engrossing ways. The heart of a lion, though the soft caress of a fatherly man. He was all this and more, and now, in such the torn fabric of time we were under, he seemed so far away and lost from us. I begged in my prayer for his return, but nothing came.

"No pulse!" another paramedic shot back, "Nothing!"

"Stabilize the bleeding," another sounded off, "We have a chance…He's lost half; we'll need four more units!"

The men collaborated and so cursed inevitable fate in the process; always hoping; forever trying. All grew silent for me there as I stepped closer to where my shadow crossed over Buck's frame. I dare not blink, nor move to escape from what was in front of me. Time shuddered to a stop; nothing heard, the sounds cutting through like some distant echo; something that you hear between your sleep and your dreams but you believe is nothing more than a whisper.

No one took notice of me; as if I were a ghost in the bright sunshine; unseen; undetected, and able to move most freely, to freely observe the final moments of the man I called Buck.

I thought of Spike in his last moments. What he must have felt; what he must have imagined and thought of then. And there, in this last, escapable exchange I was certain I saw Spike's expression in that fray. His eyes were pointed towards mine with one final blink; a shadow passed through and released into the vaults of Heaven. There was meaning in his stare, as if there was a message written in it, lofted out expressly for me to capture and remember him always by; a solemn goodbye from a friend.

"He's gone!" One paramedic shattered my concentration there, "There's nothing left…It's time!"

And with this announcement all stood still. They looked over Buck and so passed a sheet from one hand to the next until it was lying full length over Buck's lifeless body. I nearly froze in my stance when they performed this horrible feat; a shudder as if his spirit had just walked by me, skimmed across my shoulder with one final glimpse, and faded away into a world and place I knew nothing of.

"Come Little Pa," I felt Gerry's strong hand cross over the back of my shoulder and pull me away.

"It's best to go now…Your father asked me to get ya…"

I did not object, but turned and went silently with Gerry.

There sat an open ambulance, squarely in front, and in the direction to where we were walking. Father lay saddled up in a stretcher within those confines there.

"Wait for my son," he demanded, "He goes with me."

My heart nearly faltered a beat when my eyes met up with his. Between the pain and heartache, he held to such a dramatic and helpless gaze.

He had a tormented expression written in his eyes; his wrinkles showing a man ten years older than he actually was. I knew the look by instinct alone; a look of a man who felt he was a failure in allowing his son a profound loss of innocence. A place where you can never possibly go back from or re-invent into the childhood you once knew. It was the day I fell from my grace in his eyes. It was the day I fell from my childhood.

He pulled me most tenderly towards him. A silence set in during our embrace and it felt as though we sent a single community prayer skyward together. We had survived and this was the bounty we were thankful for. His silence spoke more than his words ever could; sometimes it's the better choice of conversation.

"Now you know the ways of a fireman," he whispered without a note of apology, "Albeit, the bitter end to it."

"I'll miss Buck," I whispered back a return.

"But he's no stranger son," father replied, "Like Spike, he left his mark; a good mark; one that we will carry always."

I felt my father's arm wrap around me; the back door to the ambulance shut; the motor start up, and we were off for the hospital. I could see the portal view of that house still in blaze, yet coming to its own death. It took enough life this day. There was nothing less that it deserved than the same end for itself.

Chapter 11

The Procession of Honor.

Three men. Three soldiers to the fire were lost that day. To whatever avenue brought them to that point in their lives, they had reached the precipice and lept forward. Without waiver; engraved in danger; holding to the passions of a fearless individual, they stood steadfast like the traditions of their forefather firemen before them, and how so they became saints in their own right.

To me? They were friends in every manner. For several years or more I had forged an enduring bond with Buck. His senior ways and gravitating approach towards Life caused me to revel and admire in the man he was. There was a powerful gift in knowing him; like Spike, a man who could touch the very tip of your soul in such a magnetic and affectionate way that you were pleasantly poisoned by his good humor. He had such a craft and art for the fine, meaningful story, and the constant persuasion his way was the best way of all.

"The most gratifying thing about being a fireman?" he would always say to me, "Is bravery, and knowing you made a difference."

As for Joey, he possessed attributes we could all reflect on and remember with some fond memories. His ways were not prone to teamwork; rather more to his individual goals. But in all, there lies a constant wage of war between good and evil. He was still in that initial stage of overcoming his obvious flaws.

"Time and maturity," Buck would remark on Joey, "Is the finest teacher to the person we should become. Give him both and he will do just fine. If the man he is to be can just look back for a moment and pull the Joey we know, forward, then he would be that man." Unfortunately there are little if any guarantees. Time was not one of the benefactors for Joey.

The final lost fireman was Fred 'Buckles' Willis. For a time I would sit near my locker and be quite distant in my mannerisms; pulling free the silver and gold buckles he had made especial for me. My fingers would comb over the letterings ever so gently, almost as if they were the reverent etchings from God's ten commandments just passed down to me. I would grin as though I just heard the echoes on one of the jokes he told long before; like a whisper that had just passed by me. My eyes shut deep into thought. There he was happily standing, mouth gaping wide with his sparsed teeth gleaming through; coffee in one hand and a bagel in the other; a toothpick to the ready for the time afterwards, and the consummate sucking of his teeth which followed.

The spirit of three men; diverse, original, and unique, were now sitting in my mind like a prevailing thought left by their own memory. I would lean far back against my locker, stare high above in the rafters, let out a purposeless tear or two, weep only for a moment in spell, and still not know the reasons why I did so.

Later that afternoon they found Joey's body lying in the stair's rubble. Investigators speculated he tried to make a desperate attempt to flee the building, though was caught on the long winding stairs when they faltered. The fall had killed him instantly.

Buck had been pulled free of the fire while still alive, however the inhalation of smoke had choked the life from him; the severity of his burns too great on his limbs, and one of the explosions had propelled an object almost near through him. They say he still tried to climb those stairs to save Buckles. He had to. If God were to take him there, then so be it. He was still going to try and save his friend. As much as I will ever know; this was Buck's legacy to me.

Finally, Buckles. It was he who made the attempt to axe through the upper floor walls and suddenly found himself pinched by them when he reached through. They discovered him later that evening, sifting as they did through the smoldering rubble; Buckles still stuck in that charred wood. His hands had never released. But as odd as reality goes sometimes, they found a transfixed expression on his face; an expression which had many words written in it—like he had seen the beauty of an angel just before he died; quiet, peaceful, as if the surroundings around him at the point of his passing were no longer relevant. It was a blink-of-an-eye expression; one quite often which comes and goes through the mortal man who lives beyond it. He, as odd as oddities goes, left this world at that very moment and it kind of stuck on his face.

They discovered the rapid nature of the fire bleed more quickly than they supposed, due to stored fumeless chemicals beneath in the crawlspace. Joey had neglected to check there in his hastiness. The explosions themselves were from firearms, small explosives, and weaponry stored in the sub floor by the former owner of this residence. It seems the old man was that rare eccentric who trusted no one. And he was fully prepared for the certain apocalyptic times he figured would happen any day.

Neighbors were quoted as saying they feared the man; he constantly watching from every window in the house. Curtains were always drawn and shuttered closed. He would peek out from time to time, looking for any manner of invasion that would soon present itself on his front steps. He had one trusted friend deliver groceries and essentials once a week. But this was all his contact he had with the outside world; nothing more.

The house was an unknown hotbed for fire and torch. I know it seems lacking to the men that died, but it was not to favor an excuse for what occurred; only to deliver a reasonable cause.

Three days had come and passed on fire station 112. Mother had desired for me to stay as far away from the station as possible. Father on the other hand insisted to the contrary. Fear was not to drive me away, but my single choice to leave. I decided to go back and stay. Through the long faces and misguided stares, the quiet and empty evening nights filled only by the darkness and silence, the nearly abandoned dinners and empty plates, I could sense every fireman sitting in his own individual trauma. Each was to handle the fresh ghost which now preoccupied their thoughts, but also what was haunting them through awake and sleep times.

There was no escape. Time had to push them all far away from it in order for it to make a difference. And time takes no hurry for anyone. So goes the storm before the rainbow.

I huddled quite close to Skip, as I was overseeing his injuries, recovery, and general care. I put out food even when he did not push his bowl around like a soccer ball, as was his custom before. Filled high and double high, he would go to the bowl without heart, bend down over the food and stare at it, take a sniff or two, then look up at me and seem to speak, "I'm not ready yet."

His tail hadn't wagged since the fire I watched him when he limped over to his resting place, get into a soft curl and tried to get some sleep. His head was flat to his paw; eyes darting to and fro, though his head lay steady and still, and he so remark with his look that he was a dog as sad as any.

The tremor of three days ago still rumbled through this fire station and it would remain a constant fixture for some time to come.

Lamar took to constantly playing cards with himself by one corner of the station. A fragile table no more than two feet high sat in front of the armless chair he always settled into. He had picked up smoking again and he never seemed to be without a cigarette on either his lips or in his hand. That dingy hat nestled close over his flaming red hair; those freckles glimmering in the light as he flipped one card after another; continuously without pause; always in quiet succession.

Hank took to his cot and made sure he was far from everyone else. He poured over magazine after magazine, in seeming constant turmoil as to which one to glance over next. His premature graying hair looked oily and coarse from the lack of washing; his grooming practices halted. Hank loved to be in the kitchen making up another batch of his 'special brew' for all the guys before. Now he would remain as far away from the kitchen as he could.

Kelly would walk about the station and make a general inspection from time to time, but no one noticed; just keeping to their solemn, individual studies and the quiet horrors they were battling.

"How are you doing Conner?" she asked me.

"There is no doing," I replied.

"I'm so sorry you had to see this," she whispered.

"I was hoping for better," I said.

"I know dear," she took to comfort me, "There is no reason for it; not ever."

"Well there must be," I spoke in a whisper.

"What do you mean?"

"Mother always said," I paused, "Time has a present each day for you; some good; some bad. But no matter; its' all in the rainbow to life. You just live to learn from it."

"Mom's a blessing," she tried a weak grin.

"Do you think they are in Heaven?" I wondered aloud.

"I'm sure they are," she took to give me a small, though most tender hug, "Maybe if we pray real hard, we will see them there in our dreams tonight."

"I looked already," I quickly returned, "You don't suppose I missed them?"

"They're there dear," she placed a kiss to my forehead, "This you can be sure of."

"How?"

"Because of the men they were," she remarked. "They made the sacrifice so few will ever make."

I nearly wept when she said this. There was a closeness we shared there, like a young mother to her son. I knew Kelly possessed the bounty of love; a heart who dared and ventured to care; the softness of her tender ways gave to me the peace and contentment only a mother can give to her son. It was there I felt Kelly had the gift of motherhood in her.

"Little Pa," I heard a voice softly call for me; it was Gerry, "Wants to show you something."

"Ok," I lowered my look away, rose from my seat next to Kelly, and I went away with my friend, "I'll go."

We stepped out into the early night air. Much of the town had quieted down but for the occasional cars which drove on by. The night air felt fresh with a calming chill, with the wind kicking about every so often. I knew the silence would draw us deeper into our walk. It was a time to share between us; a time to hold presence with one another. The depths of our feelings drew us closer still and we took our stroll out as if it were so.

The humid air stuck my clothes to my body; the whistle blows; a distant train plunders down the tracks it was on. I felt the shallow wisp of night's breeze trickle down me to give out a brief relax from the humidity. Then it stopped and I could hear the silence grow back again. The lowly street lamps hung lower still, as if to beacon our walk into their beams. The handrails and wooden posts along each road begged for my hand to rub against them, or count them one by one as I did. We heard a distant fire engine blow out its call in that night air; a signal they were in route to another call; the creature still lurking somewhere in that night.

"Some things you keep Little Pa," Gerry started off, "Some things you let go of; get them off of you."

"Dad says the same thing," I replied, "Mother does as well."

"You think you can?" he asked.

"I think I did with Spike…" I paused, "But I remember silently. Sometimes, when I am alone, nothing more to do than think, I think of Spike."

"He might appreciate that," Gerry looked down and grinned on me, "Besides, I think Buck, Buckles, and Joey would too…That is, if from time to time you would think on them as well."

"Are you going to die Gerry?" I pondered. I saw him glaringly look down on me.

"Hopes not!" He said while his smile began to rim around his face. "Nots to expect something like that. Your Pa; he's a good man. More good than you know of…why he's a hero in many eyes, including my own. He does good; he does mighty good."

"Then that means he will die too."

I was solemn in this phrase. Gerry stopped me, bent down, and looked me square in the face.

"Little Pa," he softly spoke unlike his massive frame, "You goes into life not knowing what to expect. Everyday, things will touch you. You don't figure they were even there that morning. That's the gift; that's the theft. If I goes or your father goes, we can't figure that beforehand. We will do our fine best to wait awhile, when we gets old and age, or illness makes us leave."

He stopped to reflect most deep within himself.

"I don't knows much. This is true," he waited, choked a little, and proceeded, "But I have seen more than most. I've seen Life, and I've seen death…Life is the easy part; death you just figure comes on its own, and you make do."

"You still got your Nat King?" I changed the subject on him, which brought forward the most radiant smile I had seen all day.

"Sure do!" he pulled it free, "The Lord and Natty…What a combination! Ain't no fire going to stop Grumble's; not know how!"

He laughed with a joy so forgotten for three days. Or it was kept tight to build on itself for that long that it exploded all out in this moment. I heard the echoes charm the streets near to us, and it so filter down the alleyways as it vibrated out like a ripple in the pond.

You know the ripple; a touch of a finger to the pond's mirror will do. Then you watch it go out and influence everything else; seems so simple that a single touch would carry out in such a way, and make the whole pond shiver.

"You think Buck was a ripple?" I wondered aloud.

"A ripple?" Gerry looked confused, "What you suppose?"

"A ripple," I explained, "A finger touch, like the soul to another. It touches and causes a ripple of influence…So my mother says."

I was certain I was right, but not totally convinced at my age.

"No ripple Little Pa," Gerry returned, "Just the ocean itself. That was Buck, through and through. He didn't make the water go…He was the water." Gerry looked skyward and saw the stars perched high in the night's rim. The host of speckles dotted the horizons with a solid backdrop of deep emptiness, as if they were stuck up there with glue.

"Like Spike," I sighed.

"Born of the same soul," he kept his gaze upwards, "Still have Yaz?" I could see another grin curl about his broad cheeks.

"Never left my shirt," I pulled it from my pocket and shoved it close to his face.

"Does you good," he giggled, "Don't it?"

"Like a charm," I tugged on Gerry's strong arm, "Thanks Gerry."

"For what Little Pa?"

"For being there," I weakly replied, "For watching out for me."

"Little to do, than what was done," he said.

"What do you mean?"

I felt him pull me towards a bench to sit for a bit. There was something working in his thoughts which he had to speak on; maybe this was what he wanted to show me.

"Your pa," he began, "Got me that gift. He saved me from the creature...this is before Nat King Cole, of course...Buts he saved me. That fire? I began to tell you about? Your father pulled me clear out of that fire then. I'd never thought another man could carry me; but he did...Like a man possessed or something. I owes him, like someday...you will owe someone."

"Maybe you?" I interceded.

"Maybe," he came back, "Hopes not. But if it comes to that, I'll be much obliged to do the same Little Pa."

"You brought me here to show me something," I spoke up, "What is it you wanted to show me?"

I sensed the reservation in his expression and he revealed to me he was cautious in the ways and manners he would pursue this with. I looked out over the darkened parks before us. I saw the shadows and the light play tag with one another as a wind rolled through; pushing trees all along the light posts, and making the silhouettes dance over the grassy plains. I could see the harbor lights off in the distance glisten by the moon, and if we were close to the waters we could view the reflecting sparkles glow the warm water.

"Buck had a wish Little Pa," he started out, "He had his 'Boots' too. Something he always carried like a shield."

"What was it?" I asked.

There was a vast and deep pause on Gerry, as if the cycle of his words fell inward; his thoughts crossed over his face to show what was there, but that which he was unable to speak on. His eyes shut closed. I felt the moment rush my heart into a stall. He waited, slumped ever so slightly, and then he pulled out a necklace from around his neck; a gold one, bright and shiny as though someone had taken tender care with it. The type of model most generous with the love, and whoever held this must have been greatly loved by the one who had given it to them.

The chain was interlocked and it glistened with the dim light about; kind of like a sun's sparkle on the waters in a clear day. When Gerry twisted it back and forth, the gold radiated from the very heart of it; the glow attracting, not strange. A glow that would draw one's attention to it, and so keep it locked.

Yet by the very bottom of this chain there sat a cross; silver, worn, aged by time and wear, though still in loving preservation. They were not of the same place and time; the chain and cross, but there held a charm when so united together; as though one were to be born so that it could be carried by the other.

A long lost gift; a measure of devotion and a warm heart; the gallant souvenir to love and honor; the whisper from time itself, when youth was young and the heart glowed in its brightest day. This was no ordinary necklace. It had meaning and purpose all written on it.

I dared not to blink, though keep my stare constantly on it. It mesmerized and moved me to hold my full concentration there.

"Where did you get this Gerry?"

"I am just here to hold it for the new keeper."

"I don't understand," I looked up at him confusingly.

"Something Buck once told me Little Pa," he replied, "Something solid with truth; as gold as someone's word should be; something worth repeating; something that always stays with you. Buck, a few weeks ago tolds me…this is his 'Boot's'. He tolds me he wanted you to have it, if something were to happen to him. Buck made it when he was your age. He said you reminded him of how he was when he mades this cross…in Sunday school fifty years ago. It was his most special thing in life; something as close to him as his heart was."

"Buck made this?" I was stunned.

"Yes'am," he returned, "With his own hands. He wore it ever since; had the chain made about twenty years ago just for it."

"But why me?" I said, "His family…"

"Because," he reiterated, "Buck saw you in his shadow. Said it would have a good home with you, and you would keep it in kind."

"What did he say?" I wanted to know further.

"'*Grumble?*' he says when we were alone, '*I think my time has come. Don't know where or how, but it's here. Like the storm you hear and see ahead, but not yet over you, and you know it's coming your way. Or when the wind approaches; you hear the whistle just before it hits you,*'" I saw Gerry break into tears, which nearly brought out the oceans in mine before I caught them, "He said he wants to make sure you get this; his 'Boots', because he knows if you have it, it will always keep you good and safe, like it did for him. He said you would care for it."

"I will," I took it close, careful not to drop it, "Don't suppose Buck would have wanted it any other way then."

I sniffled back a tear, closed my eyes, and felt the wetness of that emotion bring Buck back to life in my imagination; seeing him smile as he drove me in the fire truck through those many parades; telling me all the stories of his life as though he held the adventures of Marco Polo in his past. My memories of Buck had me most fond of him than at any time during his life.

I so wished there that I could speak with him once more; one more time, and tell him what he truly meant to me. I sensed a measure of regret, that when urgency rose out of nowhere and played out life and death in not only Buck's last day, but also Spike's, I was not there to fully realize the true meaning in our friendships together. They knew, and so I could resolve myself in this fact. But to hold no less than an explicit announcement to them both that they left me half-empty rather than half-full in my cup of life.

"I'll do good by him," I cried, "Don't need a baseball card as 'Boot's' if I have a 'Boot' like this to protect me."

"Two 'Boots' is better than one," Gerry giggled, "Its' a gift Little Pa; a mighty gift."

"I know," I spoke; putting the chain around my neck, "It now means as much to me as it ever did to Buck."

Gerry and I sat together for a spell in that long night. We both knew that the next morning was to be the funeral for all three men. Our silence together stretched for as good as an hour or more; sitting by our side, helping us to reflect one by one on these three friends of ours. I could see Gerry every now and then give a slight smile and a grin out over the lamplights and plains. His reflection bore out a kind memory that he was now playing back from some time before. It seemed it was like a prayer to him; a moment to pause and pull history into the forefront; pick a time of significance relating to Buck, and play it over and over again in his mind until it drenched his heart with sorrow for something that had long escaped from him.

I saw his head bend low. A soft reminder had drifted into his mind there. I said nothing, held my pause, punched him to the shoulder to garner a punch back; and so it would come, nearly knocking me from that bench onto the sidewalk pavement below.

We heard a boat whistle every now and then; the docks filling out the harbor in an array of misty blue colors and red gleams. All the tree animals were asleep now; the birds grown deaf and silent until the morning to come.

Without a word Gerry suddenly came to his feet, and so began his walk back to the fire station. I followed and kept slow pace with him along the way.

The lights of the station had long ago melted into two or three. Father had returned to the station with the attire we were to wear for the funeral. As Gerry and I entered, I could spot father still walking gingerly about, as he was still trying his best to recover from the wounds he sustained during the fire. His face appeared partially melted from the creature's long touching reach; or in the least, a severe burn from the sun.

"You'll need this son," he pulled out a fireman's dress-code suit and uniform. I was dazzled by the spectacle look it rendered.

"For me?" My mouth opened wide on seeing it.

"It's meant for special occasions; for honor, and dignity," he looked stern on me. I backed away and lowered my stare, "You'll do very good to shadow me tomorrow…in every step. Agreed?"

"Agreed," I echoed his strong sentiments.

"I'll put it away for you," he remarked, "until tomorrow."

I saw him leave around the corner, then yell back to me, "Off to bed son...we have much on our agenda; bright and early."

"Yes sir," I started my ascent to the upper floor. The lights were low or dimly lit; the soft fragrance in those shadows grew out long and muddled, as I could see all hands were in their cots and beds; turned about despairingly, but sound in their sleeps. I crept to my individual cot; undressed, made a prayer on my knees, crawled underneath the covers, and slipped into my imagination one more time before sleep would take me to my own dreams.

* * *

I heard the call for arms to ready for that day, as soon as the sun came into view on the horizon. All held to their hard faces and subsequent silence. To shower we all went; groom, then for dress; each having his own routine by it. I followed my father to the 'T', as I was so instructed to do. We were in our proper dressings; the decorative hats; white gloves; shining medals and dark blues; glossy black shoes and dress socks. Even Skip had a bow tie loosely fitted around his neck. My father popped the top of my hat, showered down a gentle smile through the mirror my way, and left me with a sense of pride he must have held for me at that moment, when I so looked back up to him.

"Keep your pace," he said, "and follow my lead."

We all moved to the open fire trucks prepared for our travels. As red as I had ever seen before, with 'Station 112' gleamed in bright white letters and numerals from each side.

"Let's do them proud!" one fireman yelled out to the others. There seemed not a mark on them, and just newly painted. I felt goose bumps ride up my spine when the general call went out for all to come to attention. The men now came huddled around my father.

"I know this will be difficult for you all," he began, "none the less for me. They were my friends; they were my brothers. You know Buck, Lippers, and Buckles as if you were born with them. You slept with them, broke bread with them; made a home away from home with them. We laughed through the tears together; we fought the enemy together, and we saved lives together."

My father paused to collect himself; the silence ran through as if a gush of wind had cut him off, as he so held back his tears when he continued.

"We have always been there for each other; no matter what, we were there. Through the first day we stepped into this place and became real firemen; through the training and learning we shared; through the kids being born and eventually cutting school; through the fights with the misses' and the makeup's which followed; through the family tragedies and victories; the happy times; the hard times. Through it all, we had one another and did by one another."

He stopped to cry, yet caught himself halfway in his tears.

"I won't forget Buck; I'll always remember Joey; keep Buckles closer to me than a simple picture on the wall."

A roar of approval came from the firemen; another goose bump ran through me there.

"When they went; something of me went with them. But, as a simple man like myself goes, a part of them remained behind with me. That's what honor and character is boys, at least in my faith book. I'll do them dignity; hold my head-high; smile when the sunshine hits me; fight every fire from here on out in their memory; give back as many lives as I can so that they never died in vain."

Another arousal went up from their crowd.

"All you men wear that uniform for a reason. And when others see you, they see you with eyes of respect. Earn that! That respect is only given to those entrusted to saving homes, and to saving lives. Do Buck, Joey, and Buckles proud today. Walk with me men, and make Fire Station 112 the finest station in Boston."

I felt the men give one another unannounced embraces, pats to the shoulder, until all had either given the other a hug or embrace.

The fire trucks rumbled their engines up; single file out from the station. The sky beamed a cream-colored blue with puffs of clouds which drifted out in the far distance and long horizons. The sun radiated a bright shimmer all about the city, and we could see the streets in full bustle and activity. Many saluted us as we passed by; others stared and were glowing a warm smile. The station had been seen citywide from newscast to newscast.

Father and Gerry both had been especially noted for their bravery and reckless desire to save their fellow fireman that day. Word quickly spread; the loss of men's souls observed and revered beyond the normal tragedies a city this size may see from one day to the next. Somehow, in an odd and most glorious way, this event had touched so many people.

The heartwarming nature and outpouring affection of seemingly all had simply overwhelmed the station. Countless of cards streamed in from every part of the city; flowers showered down on the station like they were raindrops from a heavy, brooding storm. Some came by with donations; others desired to start an education fund on behalf of these three fallen fire soldiers.

I was in awe on what had transpired in those past three days. There wasn't an hour I did not see their posters posted out on boards, on street signs, laundry mats, churches and ball fields, shops and outside vendor areas, music halls and events, windows, bus stops, stations, hotels and restaurants.

The massive outpouring of emotion had exhumed such sentiment from the masses that streets were full of onlookers and cheers as we passed on by, nearly giving out the notion we were the only participants in a parade. I looked out from the open spaces of this cabin and I saw women who were throwing out kisses our way, as well as man holding out signs of support.

During the processes of these past three days, founders, loyalists, traditionalists, Catholics and Protestants; all factors of people had come together to participate in the outreaches of this event. It had been mutually decided the funeral ceremony would be held just outside of Charlestown, at the spectacular Trinity church.

Our road path took us through the long winding streets of Charlestown, into the main corridors, down onto Rutherford Avenue, into the North End and down Washington Street. There we slowly trekked onto New Sudbury, crossing Cambridge, then flooding into Somerset, and finally Beacon Street, which led us to Back Bay.

All along the manors a trail of cars and enthusiasm grew from a small converse of people into a swath and swarm of dozens of cars in pursuit. All the while my father had this strange and unusual expression sifting through his face, as if it were trying to find the correct emotion to attend the funeral with. Kind of lost between pride, happiness, and sadness, yet he bore me a half-arched smile when we looked square eye to eye.

The red, white, and off color lights above us on the fire truck circled about continuously and sprayed the whole area with a sort of fireworks display. It certainly caught everyone's attention. Some slowly marched along our route; others waved; others saluted.

We could see countless of fire engines strewn all along Commonwealth from every possible division within the Boston limits.

'Paying last respects' I was told.

"We wears our duty like a badge of honor; we wears our uniforms like a code of pride," Gerry said proudly, "You'll see Little Pa. They all come with their 'Boots'. They knows the tradition of a fireman; that's why they come. They come to give respect, and in return, they get respect."

"Is that why you come Gerry?" I asked.

"Buck, Joey, and Buckles all looking down from Heaven," he smiled, "They see us…It's the giv'in Little Pa that matters."

"Son," father interjected, "It's the fireman's way. We never leave our own behind; we never forget our own."

I felt a sudden jolt as the truck came to a stop. The engine died to a halt, and all of us climbed onto the ground. There to our front was none other than Gum's father and Gum himself. He too, dressed in strict uniform.

"We decided to wait for you Matthew Allen James," he came to shake my father's hand and give him a half embrace.

"I wish we could have seen one another on better circumstances Andy," father replied. "But if the turn out is any indication, then these three men had great honor."

"Captain Buck was my idol Allen," he returned, "To lose one man in a fire is difficult; but to lose three, including the finest fireman the city of Boston ever knew," he paused, "If you ever need me Allen, just call."

He clapped his hand around father's shoulder.

"Good enough," father led me forward, "Son," he bent back, "I think Skip will need a hand."

"But dad," I gave off a slight heir of resistance, "I don't think I can carry Skip all the way to the church."

"Listen son," father sternly reported, "If I can carry good ole' Gerry out of a half-crazed burning building, as big as he is, then I think you'll do fine by Skip."

I did as he asked. I picked up Skip from underneath his belly and I carried him over my outstretched arms. Skip perked a bit, turned his face to mine, set off a tongue lick or two over my nose, and began incessantly wagging his tail.

"Looks like you got yourself a partner there Little Pa," Gerry smiled; all the while pulling up to my rear.

To my astonishment I could see before me thousands of people somberly and most temperedly leading their ways to Trinity Church. Hundreds of firemen were accompanied by wives, husbands, and children; all were cascading to this singular location. The boys were in their nice, primed Sunday suits; the girls in their primrose, flowered dresses. The air felt quiet and in peace, except for the shuffle and clamoring of shoes from every direction.

As we proceeded forward, the crowd stared about in retreat and looked back on us. They hushed into a silence, parted their movements, and allowed us to lead up to the church. Fire Station 112 was the first to enter, and so we led all who would attend to those abounding, nearly fortress steps. I marveled at the sight of this structure and I nearly broke my back backwards trying to capture it in full view. The Heavens seemed to be filled up by it, or at least the skies themselves.

I held my father's hand for a moment and he squeezed mine in return. I knew we would be the only ones to attend; mother remaining at the house with my three younger siblings and grandmother.

"Gentleman," a robed clergyman stepped onto our path, "You'll do me the honor."

Within minutes we were led to the side of the chancel; holding ground there and waiting for our 'queue' to enter within the sanctuary. The pause was immanent and appeared to last beyond time itself; we taking our turns looking about, but not at one another throughout.

"Come, please," he returned for us when all were seated within. And as we stood at the rear, I saw the caskets of Buck, Joey, and Buckles before me; closed, fist-ironed, and each draped over with an ornate American flag.

"Remember son," father whispered; bending to me, "Keep your pace and follow me."

I nearly wept at the lapel of my suit. All the thoughts preceding this moment were to prepare me for this time, but at that striking point of engaging it, when nothing else mattered but for that very sector of my life I was living in, what was spent before to prepare me for it felt ill-used and inadequate on the emotional rush I was currently feeling.

I could sense the looks of a thousand long faces turn to us; silently, reverently, dripping with emotion and tears, so casting out a full harbor of 'well-wishing'. I centered my hand within the arch of my father's palm, but still I managed to hold Skip up with the other. I felt the squeeze of his hand for security and then a slight tug ahead. We followed the procession of caskets forward as they wheeled cautiously to the front of the chancel.

The breath of that time stopped in its own breathing; the moment stirred time to pause and reflect; shadows loomed long and with an overhang; the chancel burnt brown with a tinge of orange and yellow glow. The Scottish bagpipes wailed in lament about the front; sounding off our procession of honor as we were entering. The dome and arch above grew wide and impressive as I passed under it. The stain-glass windows gleaned rainbow colors which crisscrossed this enormous room.

All along the way were well-dressed firemen standing at attention whenever we came close. We proceeded through and passed quietly by, and spotted these men and women from each district and firehouse. They stood to the end of every pew and looked on us with guided and prideful stares; then saluting us each as we were coming to the forefront.

Not a seat was empty or a pew available. Hordes of others stood to the rear and on the outer rim of each pew. I could hear the background sounds of sniffles and of soft cries resonate through this very hall. Buck's wife, two middle-aged daughters and their families, sat in the second pew from the front; Grace's arms were draped around both of her daughters. I quickly looked away. I did not want to bear the sight of such a lovely woman in distress, nor the anguish which registered on the faces of their children and grandchildren. I paused, held my ground, and looked about for the attention of my father. He turned, showered a look of concern over me, then one of assurance, and I continued with the soft rub of his thumb over the back of my hand.

Soon all were in attendance and settled in their seats; the minister standing firm and tall in the pulpit, with the drawn-up caskets in row at the large opening before us all.

He began when everyone fell silent. His voice echoed throughout with the authority of a magistrate in his jury box. It seemed he skimmed over each face in that large and overflowing crowd. There came a pause; a gentle press of a cloth to his forehead; a look to the ceilings above. My eyes held to the groomed and lavishly arranged front where the caskets were set. I didn't care to blink but stare my gaze into a blur. I wiped my tears off to the side when I felt a gentle tug from Skip, who sat patiently on my legs and always seemed to be looking over me; wondering perhaps why my emotions dripped from my face as they did.

"Reflection," the man began, "As we succumb to the powers of our own mortality; each, will know this in our own end; our own time. Blessed is the one who gives his or her life for another; most blessed is the one who gives his or her life for an unknown soul."

He paused and glared again over the awaiting flock of people.

"Captain Joshua 'Buck' Wilson."

Another pause.

"Lieutenant Fredrick 'Buckles' Willis."

Yet another silence.

"And Joey 'Lippers' Habbershack…" he said. I was lost from this point of the ceremony forward. I didn't take note or care on what was said beyond the moment. I stayed where he had begun, within my own reflection of what these three men meant to me, the times we shared, the heart of who they were; all playing reflection into my mind as they all sat in that vault.

Words from my mother came rushing over me; the SoundBits to life; those unrehearsed thoughts filled by such meaning, wrestled with the point and purpose of all three lives unexpectantly being taken from us. I preferred nothing more than to be lying on my firehouse cot, turning about, and seeing Buck strapping on his fire suit for another run. A giver's lot I suppose. But this would not be the case, nor ever. They were gone, by fate and misfortune's collective desire for it to be so. A road that some had traveled before them and where most left as heroes, now being graced with the admiration of those which remained behind. Still the agony; the hollow escape and tragic void that was left behind by these men's long and unfortunate break from that destiny we all thought they would hold to. Somehow they were lost along the way.

"Son?" I heard my mother's voice echo through my thoughts. We were sitting on that long porch of my grandmother's home on a hot summer day in my mind.

"Sadness and Joy are two sisters born from two different worlds. But they are cast out along the roads of your life like rivers and bridges."

"Rivers and bridges?" I would ask.

"Sadness gives you the rivers; Joy throws down the bridge to get you over those rivers."

"What was grandmother like?" I remember asking her.

She would smile abroad and cast her lot of various looks over the long rolling hills. She watched the ground below as it seemed to sweat and perspire into its own early morning dew.

"A wonder Conner," she grinned, "A wonder."

"When she died?" I pursued further.

"It was like God had cut away that part of Heaven from me that was most special. But with her, being so much in my life, God gave me a river of Love, strength, and appreciation. It's true though Conner," she bent down at me to smile, and squeeze the near life out of me, "I know this may sound odd, but God had her death take place in a most beautiful way. I suppose only our human grief lends a sad note to that song," she would stop and reflect; a tear passing from eyelid to cheek that nearly put a spell on my own emotions.

"However, this one thing I must say. The Love which passed from her heart to my heart and from her fingertips to my fingertips is all that I mean to pass along to you...This love; a mother's love is, and has always been so very beautiful."

I found myself in the pew again.

My father gave me a slight pat to my wrist, and then he rose from his seat as I watched him suddenly ascend to the pulpit above. The entire congregation came to a sullen hush, but for a few cries about the sanctuary there. You could sense the tense emotion rise on that sultry, summer morning. There was a simple gesture of solidarity when father stood and proceeded around; the haven of that crowd; those eyes attended to one single thought which unified every heart about. We all seemed to step inward to remember something good about each man as we waited for father to begin. For those who knew them? An eclipse of time was the meaningful pose with which we reflected on. I know many who were present must have dripped rich with such a memory or two.

Father came to that pulpit; the lights above sprayed about him as though he had a heavenly aura surrounding his presence.

"I was asked yesterday evening if I might wish to give a eulogy," he started and fumbled with the scrap papers he pulled from his vest, in an almost childlike manner. I could never recall seeing him so disturbed before, "I agreed…But in the same notion I wondered what I should say. How could I possibly show adequate reverence to these three men; to reflect their honor like an image in the mirror; to show to the world who they were in life, and how much respect they have garnered by their deaths…I debated and tired over this nearly all night. It was really no burden though; more of a privilege than anything. To give something long-winded and prepared seems to lessen their heroics. So I decided I would speak from where it matters most…the heart."

He was peering from one corner to the next, and then back again; all the while biting on his lower lip.

"Ladies and Gentleman, I am a fireman…and so were they. That gives us a brotherhood and a creed of fellowship we could never show with any one else. And this being said I feel I can give you a small glimpse into the great men they were, and still are with me. Some of you undoubtedly knew them; some perhaps better than me…especially the immediate family. I couldn't possibly abbreviate the magnitude of who they were in a mere ten to twenty minutes. That wouldn't be fair; most of all to them. So if you would please, just for a little bit, walk with me with your thoughts, just for a moment, and simply see the wonderful men Fred, Joey, and Buck turned out to be."

My father looked about, most proud and esteemed in his eyes with such a charmed expression. He spread his hand about the pulpit edge, collected himself within, thought in silence for what seemed an eternity, and then came with his own human 'reflection'.

"I remember when Joey first came to the fire station. He immediately showed us all he had a wealth of charisma. A spirit never tamed, but seemed to shine mostly when he felt free. I can recall those times, sitting around the fire trucks, how he and Gerry would try to outdo one another with their songs. It was always a very tight race, and each would get the better of the other occasionally, but Joey had such a kind, melodic voice. It echoed throughout the fire station; a psalm and a symphony which had you always thinking; always reflecting. It made you want to stop and listen; whatever you were doing at that moment; you simply stopped…and listened until he was done.

Joey drew out that kind of attention to himself. We knew this from the very beginning. During his first full month on the force, we noticed he always used special toothpaste. I tell you," my father paused to smile and rub out his chin, "It was kind of a dark, deep emerald blue color. One day we got this similar-colored dye, one that lasts Ohh, a good two weeks in a stain; emptied out his brand new tube carefully, mixed it all together with this dye, reloaded it back again, and just waited," the crowd snickered as my father continued, "he came in just before his dinner date; one he had been anxious about for a good week or more. Showered, washed his Elvis-slick hair back real clean-like, dapper'd himself in a nice shiny suit, then out came that toothpaste."

The snickers grew now into full-blown laughter, and one which caught me so much so by surprise, that I began to laugh out-loud myself. I saw my father stand in a still pose, lock his face into a goofy, precocious grin, and wait for all to simmer back down again.

"He brushed and brushed '*Dang toothbrush! Dang toothbrush!*" a thunderous roar came once more as my father displayed how Joey scrubbed to the fullest.

"The more he tried, the darker his teeth turned...to the point they seemed to fall into his mouth. He had the emptiest-looking mouth that night; like an old man who had forgotten his dentures. You couldn't see his teeth anymore! We were so amused how persistent he was; still scrubbing and scrubbing, then buffing out his teeth to no end....but this was Joey; persistent; spirited; never giving in; the wild, untamed horse that he was. This was something that forever garnered my respect of him. Joey, you will be missed."

I could sense the general congregation's emotion go from near joyous bedlam to reserved calm, then back to utter somber once more, so weighing their emotions by the look my father held in this pulpit there.

Father was the master of honorable character, standing high on this stage when he held us all in a perpetual realm of joy and sorrow there. That calypso persona that gilded him like a vast-armored suit; his cunning manners and streaming orator presence; his captivating strings which held the emotions of those who were listening on a virtual puppeteer's cross boards, the likes I had never known.

He had such a commanding voice. On its highest peek he could pillar the very walls which held it within, seek out those who were indifferent, and gather them into his flock of ears as well. At its softest pitch and lowest whisper, people would bend ever closer to hear the very words he spoke. He could empty out a crowd as quickly as he could fill them back up again. The waters within their cups were always in motion; the levels changing in a continual flood, like the river which could never stop flowing into the very basin of their own heart. His honestly shone brilliant even in the darkest of lights, and so everyone took notice of this, and listened intently.

"My friend Fred," he came back from his pause and thundered through with these words, "Now there was sunshine...better yet, there was the sun's glow itself," my father thought to smile, "He was a gift of friendship, and so brought meaning to the word. People such as Fred quite often get overlooked, displaced, and sometimes even ignored. It takes a sensitive person to recognize the talents Fred had. He smiled so much; I thought he was born with it, and it never went away. Throughout his life it simply remained; always; constant, as if it embraced him, and embraced those nearest to him. I suppose that was the testament to his character. He made those around him see the very sunshine, and forget about all the rainy days before.

I felt he launched a thousand hopes with this pleasant, continuous smile of his. Those who knew him were surely blessed to have him in their lives. I know; I am one of those people. I've always had this image that whenever I saw Fred 'Buckles' Willis, I saw a quiet rainbow sitting in the distance, dressing up the sky with Heaven's colors...You will be missed Fred."

The lights round, so bent in a burnt and brown tint, appeared to gleam a little less bright now; the silence tanning them into a deeper rose to view with.

"Lastly...I think of Joshua," my father fell silent.

He nearly passed into tears before he caught himself.

"Buck...Buck...This is so hard," he looked up with a glaring tear running onto his chin. It quickly was apparent to all that what he was to speak, was a most personal message for Buck.

"A man I have known nearly longer than life itself. He was there at every stage; my academy graduation; my wedding; every birth of my children. In every aspect, he has truly been the guiding angel, and with his light gone from my view, it will make the road for me ahead a darker one to travel on.

It wasn't supposed to happen this way. We talked of the days when we would retire; join the olds folks' home, sit around and pretend we were drinking beer, play chess or checkers until the sun dropped into night, gab about the fires we fought for all those years until our teeth fell out; go deep sea-fishing when the fish were ripe; climb the mountains in the autumn and count the colors on the trees in the valleys below. It wasn't your time Buck; your light was simply to bright to go out until then."

My father bent his head deep into his lapel; quiet, somber, seemingly broken. I heard the shuffle of heads turning to the rear, and there, standing upon the edge of that vestibule was my mother; she was holding her eyes directly in the location of my father' stance. I saw her move forward, glide through the crowd, and pause just in front of the trio coffins before her.

With her grace and outpouring reach of emotion she stood, calmly, collected, and she waited for my father's eyes to lift and catch hers. Instinctively, as only a husband and wife could ever do, the inner notions of presence moved him to feel her there, and he came to find her look constantly in hold and attentive to his.

I saw their secret conversation captivate the crowd in a wonderful sort of silence. It was as though a glowing, radiant bridge of love began illuminating between them, garnering their souls into a consummate spell of honor and dedication. There were words unspoken then; words of profound ingredient and language. Where the mutual look speaks a thousand volumes of soft, unheard whispers; where the voice leaps back into the heart it owns and connects with that soul linked by a life-long covenant. The conversation abounds; most privately, holding persuasion with the language they alone speak.

You feel the silence; the pause in time where their words communicate with a brilliance you can only see; a language of unknown depth and harmony causing all to stop for this moment and marvel without an heir of understanding to what was precisely said.

They never blinked, but were frozen in a place they called their own. She nodded, ever soft; he followed. She smiled a tempered grin; he reacting in an identical manner.

"There is grace in every corner; you just have to go find it. Sometimes wisdom and reason take many years to show us the purpose on such a tragedy as this. I am at a loss on that discovery for now. But I pray someday I will find the meaning to it all; until then? I suppose faith in the Almighty will have to do.

I'll miss you too Buck…You will always be the shadow I think I see at night. When I look at your picture, even in the long years to come, I will think and I will remember you with the million memories we shared together…Never say goodbye…just until…"

I could feel a pin drop if it were to fall to the wooden floors below. The sound became so deafening; the wind fans above blew out like a heavy Gail in the middle of a sea storm. The hallow grounds of Trinity Church have been most unlikely mesmerizing this day; my father now moving down to touch each of the caskets. He bent to one knee and pressed a kiss to the head of each. He stood, took about my mother's hand, and moved to where I still sat. My jaw seemed fractured and in awe on what had just transpired.

The ceremony concluded shortly afterwards. The chorus of Scottish bagpipes came before the congregation, performed two somber Scottish tunes, and began the procession of honor in its leave from Trinity Church. The three caskets were reverently pulled from their settings and led outside, one by one, with the twenty-seven other firemen from station 112, close to follow.

As we exited to the outdoors, the sun had come into its full sky then with not a single cloud to block it with. A crowd of Boston firemen, amassed in the hundreds, stood to encircle the exit from Trinity Church. Bagpipes continued to play. The coffins lowered step to step where horse-drawn single carts were waiting for their arrival. My father lowered his hand around my shoulder as I gazed up to my mother. Skip sat so patiently in my arms, and did as much to look over my parents.

"I am so very proud of you son," she remarked.

Father stepped to the front of the middle cart. He held patrol on the reins to that white, pristine horse near ready for pulling.

"I'll take this one," father whispered to the man, who then stepped aside, "I'll take my friend to his final journey home."

"Sir," a well-dressed officer from another station came to my father and leaned into him, "May we shadow you. These are our brothers as well."

"Thank you for the honor," father replied and bowed.

Gerry moved to the cart which would carry Buckles. I saw the man back away with the intimidating sight of such an enormous individual as Gerry coming towards him. Lamar soon followed suit and pulled up to the third carriage cart.

"It's only proper," Lamar whispered, "Firemen take their own."

The Scottish bagpipes forged to the sides; standing firm and in tune on that outer rim. The fireman's medals shown brightly in that sun; to think the day held so much light as if to twinkle out those medals for all to see. They were dressed in their deep blue uniforms; fire soldiers crafted with honor. Suddenly, and with slow repetition, they moved forward and in complete step.

I felt the heavy horse hoofs stamp out the road and clomp to a silent beat as they went. Those massive frames overshadowed the three men that pulled them by side-rein. The Scottish tunes and the hybrid pipes which echoed and loomed over those streets as we passed on by brought nearly everyone who watched into tears. The number of firemen to our rear grew into a mass of uniformed men and women, and held constant step with us.

Like a train that only grew bigger as we went, the number in our force rose to a thousand or more. We traveled up Dartmouth Street, through Beacon Street, back down Charles Street and onto Boylston Road. The city of Boston had been so moved by these events over the last few days, and how the general public had pulled together in support of fire station 112, that these firemen were signified as heroes and true sons of Boston. They deserved of a rightful place in history; to be buried at the Central Burying Ground within the Public Gardens themselves. I felt the irony there sweeping over me; to see my friends being laid to rest at the very place I had so often played in, enjoyed the summers with my family, and had encountered the mysterious Elijah Haberstaff. In the back of my mind I wondered if he might be there waiting for us.

I could feel the breeze from Charles River cross over us as we stepped onto Beacon Street. The numerous people were so strung along the way to such a force that they kept the grassy plains of Commonwealth Avenue out of our view. The route had been planned beforehand. Officers were laid out like human cones. Endless rounds of rope pulled out from one block to the next in a long continuous string. Children waved with a carefree notion this was a parade; mothers held onto their silence as many watched while wearing sunglasses; more so to hide their tears than to hold the sun at bay. Fathers and sons gazed on us with a steel sense of pride; their expressions seeming to say these were the true sons of Boston.

Mother walked with me the entire length. Skip bobbed his head about as I held him firm. His ears were popping out to catch any sound that came our way. I could hear the lone bugle echo out a lament when the bagpipes took to pause. Fire trucks on the byroads stopped and turned their lights on to honor us. One fireman I took note of; standing high above the reaches of the crowd, sitting, leaning out over the slightly elevated truck ladder; he so in uniform with an American flag draped over his shoulders. He was still, nearly lifeless; watching us progress forward. His hand came and cut over his brow in a salute which remained long after we drew out of his sight.

"Son," mother smiled, "This is only one color to the rainbow."

"I know," I sadly agreed.

"There are more, but together they make it the beauty it is."

"I know," I kept my concentration on Skip.

"Remember the rainbow son," she whispered, "is the life that you live."

The long procession of Honor; the vast streams to a river flowed by the very will that directs it, and turned like the streets we marched on. I sensed the long hand of time stretch to the top of one significant hour there in my life; the bell tolls and rings out the chimes of three honored notes to make a simple tune; softly, reverently, precious and most appreciative to the moment. We were that river this day, flowing and yielding to no gravity but to the gravity which lowered the feelings of our collective heart.

I closed my eyes and I saw clips of all three men; there, standing before me, playing, laughing as if they were in an old home movie reel displayed on my wall over and over again. Like a vault of time itself unearthed, I could see their smiles glow, replay, and glow again from one moment into the next; unaltered and unchanged from the freshly stamped memory it came from. I chose to remember the happy times; I chose to think of the wonderful occasions we shared.

"They'll never fade son," mother said, "As long as you give light on your memories of them…They'll always be there."

As the hour faded into the next and the day drew deeper into the afternoon, the settled crowds around the cemetery watched in respect to those three men who were forever lost. The ceremony continued without pause, though we wished on every passing second that we could stop the tradition and create a new one; a tradition where they would return and be reborn to us.

My father once told me there are always conclusions in life which will grip and shake us; where the dreams are lost and replaced with reality. Yet hope remains as the art form to our imagination, and so transforms our lives into a continual renewal and growing season. Life will teach us only a fabric of what it is to us; the rest is left for us to discover on our own.

To this, I will say, I will miss my friends until I see them again in my dreams.

Chapter 12

I Begin to Grow Up.

The seasons that followed turned over like the pages of a good book. The previous chapters freshly printed in the recent thoughts of my mind, so helped to shape and mold the young boy I was and the early man I should become. I was caught somewhere in between there. Not knowing what vintage character I had become yet. A mixture of both, or perhaps a mixture of none; the limbo stage in life called the cast iron dungeon of puberty.

My hair grew lighter, nose protruding more like a good 'James' heritage, more tall and lanky than solid such as my father; voice coming through those off-stages where it constantly was cracking and cackling like on offbeat rooster cock. Father did say however that in time, I would 'fill-out' so to speak. I was a bit awkward at times; so reading the Legend of Sleepy Hollow and seeing the specific descriptions of Ichabod Crane did me no good in the least. Especially when I found myself in front of the bathroom window, reading the script delicately, word by word, noting the characteristics of Ichabod, and so seeing these similar features staring in a glare back at me when I took to the most hideous poses. You would have thought I was more spellbound by it than anything.

The inevitable takes place; growth, raging hormones, then more growth. There were slighter things now which caught onto my nerves, shook about them a bit, and wouldn't let go; siblings especially. The late 80's were present and the 90's were just around the corner. I, being a fresh sophomore in school, was trying to make my way and my name in a much larger venue; high school. Back in the middle school I had become somewhat of a modern legend, but in this grander setting I was nothing more than 'a nobody'.

I used to watch the athletes bask in the glory of their own egos; raiding the girls' lockers and P.E. wash areas, walking around school in their uniforms as if they were captains in the military, and so taking advantage of every boy they could possibly tag as a, how should I say it; 'nerd'? I did ponder the notion, and came often to wonder in that first year if I had conducted myself in such a primal way just the year before.

Leading roosters have a tendency to strut their stuff, no matter how large the hen house they reside in has become. It seemed my former henhouse was no more than a two-chicken coup than one of any natural size, as I found myself in during my first yearling experience at high school. And with so a bit of reflection, I could see the very foolish nature of my ways. I did not know whether 'maturity' was setting in or that the mirror was showing the stupidity of my former self. Being a cautious observer can do that to you.

Baseball was my forte' however. Schooling had become more of an anomaly than anything at this stage in my life. Now mind you, I had much resistance to peer pressure, and I held to my ground when the need arose. I often looked forward to the early spring day when tryouts were to commence. And along with Gum (more affectionately called Jason now), we began our full-fledge dreams of working ourselves onto the high school team, impressing colleges for scholarship in the general Boston area, being drafted by the Red Sox, and eventually finding a roster spot with them. Jason of course was to be the star pitcher, and myself to be playing the hot corner at third base. So goes the plan of mice and men.

Shortly after the tragedy from several years before, it had been announced father would be the new captain at fire station 112. He first withdrew his name for consideration, citing the awareness he never would want to profit in any manner from the loss of such dear and close friends; especially Buck, his mentor. All the men at the fire house rallied around dad. And with brute persuasion, they convinced him to accept the honor, but not without much internal deliberation. My visits to the firehouse grew longer between each time. I had grown more interested to be around people my own age. I felt more akin by the trials we shared than to spend time at the firehouse, as was my normal case before. I thought this bothered my father for some time, yet he knew the day would come when I would 'spread my wings' more. He began to accept it as nothing more than nature and the inevitable. Still, I would make my timely runs and visits there.

"Little Pa ain't so little anymore," I saw Gerry run up to me when he first saw me enter the station, "Hey Hey! Toddler to a strapping young man...Good golly, what a sight!"

"Still got Nat King Cole?"

"If you gots your Yaz?!!" he laughed a notorious laugh.

"As always," I grinned and pulled out my bent and creased Yaz baseball card, "Who taught me to always be prepared, huh?"

"Now, now," he would step around the hard floors, "Can't lay any claims to the duty of your own father. He makes you the man you are…not good ole' grumble…got my own pigeons in the roost to make fly; don't need a fourth to toss out of the nest."

Father had turned a tad to the gray side now, yet his smile would always shine him to look younger than he ever was. He wasn't on the verge of salt and pepper just yet; just more streaky gray on the sides like I saw Charlton Heston in the 'Ten Commandments' years ago. Every time I set foot into that station, I felt it growing smaller still. Those Fire engines still gleaming the brightest red; the floors to a spickle shine; Skip still laying about near to his bowl, occasionally scooting it around to the closest fireman in hopes they would fill it up with food; top hat level with all those bed carts still nicely laid in order; and to the wall facing the rest area were now nine infamous men to the wall; Buckles, Joey, and Buck included.

"I told you, you would be a bit dangerous when you got older," I heard a female's voice call from behind me; it was Kelly, "How's the new school Conner?"

"Hello Miss Kelly," I responded.

"Drop the Miss please," she smiled, "make me sound like a middle-aged librarian. Don't read enough to be called that."

"School's fine," I said, "little adjustment from last year, but I'll manage well enough."

"Your father was smart enough to teach school himself; mother too," she grinned, "you are trying out for baseball this year?"

"Oh! You bet!" I about leaped out of my skin at the thought.

"Tell me when you're playing?" She slyly spoke, "I'll come and watch. Make sure all the fire hats off-duty are there…Deal?"

"Deal."

I still made my rounds to the old drug store these days, and occasionally Jason would partner up with me there. The structure had a bit more paint wear than before, but it always felt like the warm place to go. Suppose old man McKenzie brought the fire in it.

"Well look what my old dog Chip brought in!" he said, "Chops; the dead ringer for Ichabod!"

There was a muddled laugh that rose when he spoke this. All heads were turning my way, and finding the similarities there that I so constantly rediscovered in the mirror every time I looked.

"Your hair hasn't gotten a day older, but you have," I shot back, as Jason followed me through the door.

"Oh! Smart tongue for a smart whit!" he giggled, "Age does different things to different people. Rug's still the same," he flipped the front up just a tad, "So are the teeth," he dropped his top denture down just a spell to show off, "Oh, but the heart is as warm as ever. I've been smitten Chops!"

"By whom?" I said, gathering to a swivel stool.

"You would think, by the physical features I possess, she might be blind for sure," he poured out some coffee in a customer's cup.

"If I was a lady, I would pucker up for ya Rock!" an old gentleman gaped wide, stamped his hand down hard on his knee, and laughed continuously at his tired, bad jokery.

"Then pucker shut," McKenzie sent him a fowl glance, "Well she's a fine lass," turning back to me as he did, "her name is Gypsy June."

His eyes grew white-eyed on this.

"Juuuuuuunnnnnnneeeeee," we heard a unison groan from the masses around, a flicking roll of the eyes, and everyone taking a taste of their drink at the same time.

"No, her name is May," he sarcastically spouted.

"Maaaaaaaaaaaayyyyy," they all were more vocal this time, taking another sip in their silence.

"Ok...Let's go down the list," McKenzie turned around again, "April," he paused for another announcement.

"Aaaaaaaaaaaaaprilllllllll," the swan song sounded again; another spike to the drink they went.

"Alright! Alright! You want the whole calendar. Bunch of Vivaldi's...I'll give ya The Four Seasons. I had to pick one shop in Boston to run, and I had to be sooo lucky to find the funniest sidewalk to come to work to everyday."

"Come on Rock," one man pleaded, "I am sure she is a speckle."

"Speckle," McKenzie echoed, "Speckle? Listen Potty, when was the last time you and the misses..."

"Don't have a Misses," he grinned, "Just got my Caaaa."

"Good," he said, "Drink up and drown."

"Sounds like your looking for a healthy tip," another laughed.

"Thump the forehead," McKenzie leaned over, pushed the old man's hat upward to expose his forehead, and flicked his middle finger on it.

"Good gosh Dorothy!" the man was leaning back, with his eyes nearly bulging out like a light that not only flashed in his head, but blew his brain into a million sparklers, "I think I have a Brain!"

"You don't say," another chimed, "Ruff Ruff! I' I' ammm the Lion wizard, and I think, I think I need cur, cur, courage!"

"You don't say," yet another sang his tune, "I am the tin man...and I need a heart!" he began to whimper as a poodle.

All the while, Mr. McKenzie leaned over and to one side, now with a goofy grin plastered to his face, "You see what I put up with Chops? Everyday. I got the 1924 Red Sox rejects."

"Hey!" one said, "I resemble that remark!"

"Most astutely, I would say."

"Most astutely."

"What about Gypsy June," I brought Mr. McKenzie to a whisper shot.

"Oh yes! Gypsy June. Hair as hot red as the fires your daddy takes to fighting, and she's got the spirit to go with it. A bit on the tart at times, due to her English background, but she has more whim than any woman I know. Yes sir."

"I am happy for you Mr. McKenzie," I smiled, closed my eyes, and shook my head in quiet approval, "Truly I am."

"Do me the delight young man!" he sparkled about as good as he did before, "What will it be?—Ahh! Cream Soda!"

"The same as always."

He spotted Jason sitting next to me. He pointed his finger out at Jason, as if to appear to give a lecture, then pause, remain silent, and hold his finger and mouth in that framed pose.

"How's your dentures?" he peered on Jason with a Popeye, one-eyed look.

"How's that?"

Jason leaned in as though he did not hear him clear enough.

"Come again?"

"Dentures," McKenzie replied, "You know...Falsies."

He chomped down a few times.

"Looks like who ever your orthodontist is, he did a whale of a job!"

"I don't follow you..."

"Hmm..." McKenzie took to eye Jason more closely, "You're that Gum boy. Yes. I remember you, and that frightful wad of gum you consumed in that cheek of yours. I figured by now you would have lost all your teeth."

"No. No." Jason laughed, "All present and accounted for."

"Don't remember the name," McKenzie said while cleaning a glass, "Just that fibish language you spoke."

"Jason," he said, then cleared his throat, "Sir."

"And that hybrid, intolerable, odious, steam-rolling, mushing, witch cantation-of-a-drink you ordered on a most regular basis," McKenzie reported, "I believe it was a Butter Scotch Waltz, if memory serves me in good faith."

"Yes, it was."

"Still drink it?"

McKenzie stared at Jason as though he were a new-found ghost sitting on his stool.

"Sometimes," Jason replied, "On Occasion."

"Hey Potty," McKenzie laughed, "You should get some of that needed Courage from this young lad," he turned his attention back on Jason, "More of a noxious, heavy-duty window cleaner than a drink for the soul son."

"You mind?"

Potty leaned over and flicked Jason on the forehead. He so then leaned back, wide-eyed and gooney-faced, "Ah! Ah! Be Praised! I got Courage now Dorothy! Someone catch me!"

"Shall we?" another one roared up with his drink.

"Ohh!"

He waited for the others to come into tune.

"Ohh! We're off to see the McKenzie! The wonderful McKenzie of Oz! Because! Because! Because!..." and they held their ear-crushing note for the longest of time. They nearly broke the heart of every glass in McKenzie's place.

"Alright! Alright! A little too much morning cider for you guys!" McKenzie blurted out, "I'll have to cut you off!"

"I'll bet that's what Gypsy June tells him all the time!" they all laughed, "Juuuuuunnnnnneeee!" again they came, "No! Aaaaaaaaprilllll," and, "Maaaaaaaaaaayyyyyyy!"

"Just a soda for Jason as well," I whispered over to the exasperated McKenzie.

Jason and I drank on our soda for as long as the juice would last. Slowly we felt the belly of our glass to empty out as we chatted and talked amongst ourselves, and with Mr. McKenzie the same. We talked of old times; we talked of the newer days, as if we were soldiers of history just back from a gallant fight.

We had tryouts again that day for the high school baseball team. It was the final cut, going from 30 guys to 25; I having impressed the coach well enough to get a good hard look at third. Jason was more on the fringe of making the team since his fastball was a little faster than most, his command being more his trademark, though you would not have thought so during our earlier playing days.

I remember riding our bikes up to the high school, then clomping along the sidewalks in our cleats; bats hung high and upside down over our shoulders, and so carrying our ball gloves on the handles. We appeared as though two lanky soldiers in some march to the war of baseball. We moved from the front entrance to the rear of the school, past the soccer field, tennis courts, football stadium where the cheerleaders were practicing on that nice spring Saturday morning. There she was; the gift from Heaven itself.

Her name was Sandra Miller, the daughter of an executive with John Hancock Agencies based in the John Hancock Tower. I had viewed her from afar for some years now. I never attempted to make contact with her. There had been a few times during the last grade or so where we nearly walked into one another, made conversation, and eventually became acquainted. She was quite the intimidating presence; tall, long-blushing, golden-blonde hair which sprung in her bounce. They say she carried a time-stopper in her blouse wherever she went. For when she took to walking down the halls, along the school sidewalks, during the pep rally's, lunches, proms; anywhere one might encounter her, the boys all stopped and gawked in awe, nearly heart-struck at the sight of her.

There was much envy and rivalry amongst the other girls in our sophomore class. Sandra was perilously brilliant in every way; from class work to her studies, coordinating events, charity work, extracurricular activities, council, and church. You name it, she was involved. It seemed there was a pedestal underneath her wherever she went, though she apparently took pride in none of it. She captivated the attention of all when she came around. I suppose this was the reason why we never had any contact to this date; I, being in the homeroom with the J-K-L's three doors down from her; she being in the A-B-C's three doors up from me.

A 'high-bred' young lady who was fit for a social kingdom once she arrived at a certain age. Her father was a Harvard graduate of business; her mother a master's graduate from Duke in 'technical studies'. The first of three daughters they had, Sandra was to be the charmed princess of them all.

Now, as Jason and I had made our way about, we were just skimming the outside area of the football stadium. Cheerleaders were in practice and of course, Sandra was the consummate lead. We stopped and sighed in that moment, and so paused to view her bright shining face while she was guiding the cheers. She appeared to be a dance pro of her own. I swear I could see the stark blue eyes glistening as bright as the sun, shining those sweet pearl drops out to us there.

"She looked at you!" Jason nudged me in the ribs.

"It was a blink Tush!" I nudged him back.

We took out a few more steps along the pathway; making what sounded as a rutting noise by accident. The girls simply stopped in their steps while the music continued on.

"Now she's looking," Jason giggled, pushed me to the side, and darted off ahead of me.

"She's was looking at the prissy way you were carrying your bat…"

I caught up with him and he swung around to meet me on that infamous word, 'Prissy'.

"You got a lot of nerve bumpkin," he replied, "Get in the batter's box and I'll make you dance like a priss…"

"Dare, dare," I smarted back.

"All right," he said and shoved me to the shoulder, "Dare."

"You got it tush," I remarked, "You bring the heat; I'll bring the smoke…"

And I walked by him.

"Spoken like a true Fireman's boy."

"And what are you?" I poked at his eye, though he pushed me off and swung his head to the side, "Cat's got the eye! Whoa!"

And in a fierce and mighty bolt, I ran at full speed down the embankment to the baseball diamond where all the other teammates had assembled, "Whimp can't catch! Whimp can't catch!"

I felt his breath on my shoulder as he made every attempt to get a hold of me. I felt the wind push out my wave-locks and hair behind my ear. Jason touched my shoulder in a brush. Then as I kicked out in full stride, I could feel my legs tumble from underneath me; Jason nicely tucked beneath me there.

"Got ya Whimp!" we rolled sideways down the rest of that embankment in what seemed like an eternal tackle and roll.

"Ok Gentleman," the coach barked out, "Save the warfare for inside the diamond!"

We got to our feet and went directly to his side.

"I'll have you two up first…Seems spirited rivalry between two good friends never hurt anyone. I'll have you remember though, these are still tryouts, and someone is going to get cut."

"Us?" Jason grinned, and pointed to himself.

"I'll cut God himself," he replied, "If he doesn't want to play team ball. Now get into position. That goes for team A. Run! Hustle! Run!"

The boys moved into position in an instant. Jason was on team A, and I designated to team B. The coach enjoyed pitting close ties between one another. He figured it would bring the best out of our instinctive, competitive nature.

But nothing faired more to bring out the competition between two close friends than when a woman came into the mix. Kind of makes the water and oil mixture to be such a poor combination; and it being nothing more heightened when none other than Sandra Miller and two of her co-cheerleaders showed up on the third base side bleachers.

"Did you see that?" Jason looked over and whispered down at the batter's box, as I began my warm up swings.

I could see the sweat begin to pour off of him even before the first pitch. He anxiously looked about from one side to the next; like a doe standing stone cold on the road, and with car headlights staring right back at him.

"What should I do?"

I saw the lump on his throat stick prominently out. It changed his voice out from a deep resonation into a high-pitched, squalling, fingernail-scratching, puberty-cutting speech.

"Pitch the ball," I mouthed those words most plainly for him to see.

I watched him wipe his brow, tug the brim of his hat, and slap the ball in his glove. He kicked back the dust from the mound like a bull, and grunted in an attempt to impress Sandra.

"What is he doing?" the catcher muffled through his mask.

"Being a Tush," I replied, "Like he always is."

I took a round of two more swings.

"You ready Horn Head??" I exposed a handkerchief from a back pocket of mine, thrust it about in front of the plate, and so let the wind flap it around as a mocking gesture.

Jason peeked over at Sandra one final time; the lump in his throat now growing into a bowling ball of fear and anxiety. He wiped on his brow again. I am sure he thought it was the manly thing to do. He spit out over the front of the mound; and must have thought this was quite the 'cool' thing to do. He then tossed back a few more clouds of dusty smoke with several more back leg kicks; the haze nearly choked his shortstop and second baseman into a coughing crouch of sorts.

"Are you going to pitch or grunt?" I said, while lowering my bat.

In a swirl of activity, Jason flung around in full circle, cocked his arm back with the most grievous stare over me, pulled the trigger right down the inner corner of the plate, and nearly took the shirt off my back. I went crashing and kissing the dust on home plate with my face.

"Pitch." He calmly said afterwards.

I pushed myself back up with the bat, kicked the dirt off my cleats, and I took in two more heavyweight swings just outside the batter's box.

"Pitch my…" and before I could finish that statement, another pitch dove right in on me, just underneath my chin; causing my reaction to have me flattened backwards on the ground. At this point my jersey was entirely covered in brown dirt.

"You enjoy the dance yet Priss Pot?" Jason dug into the mound, "Have two more coming…You know."

"I'll take my chances…" I swore out at him.

"Dare," he grinned, "Remember?"

"If you get on next inning," I replied, "just make sure you don't make it to third base...you here?"

"Come on Flyboys!" the coach yelled out to us.

"Keep it in the game! Keep it in the game!"

There was a pause. A high and tight pitch suddenly dipped into a curve. It cut the black part of the plate. I heard the umpire yell out "'Striiiiiiike!"

Jason smiled wide on this one.

Jason took to stammering around the mound for a moment, and making a glance over towards Sandra to make sure she was looking his way. She wasn't in the least, which agitated him further.

"This time friend," I shouted, "You're going to have to really get me out. No magic here."

"What's that suppose to mean?"

"Is what it means," I chuckled, "No imaginary friends."

Jason gripped his jaw hard into a lock, pushed the ball into his glove with a slap, came into motion, bore back, kicked high and lethal, drove to home plate, and let his hardest ball fly.

The pitch was carrying no movement, but holding straight like a sail in a strong wind, so cutting through the heart of the plate. I jerked the bat around, drove hard into the ball without taking my eyes away from it; the thunder rose; the crack from my bat; the echoes which followed and sounded off into the fields. I could see the ball immediately jump from my swing and become a mere dot in the sky as I looked skyward. The hush that followed and the jaws that dropped wide as it propelled deep; the sudden turn to the head on all the fielders. Even the coach and his assistant rose from their seats just to see how far that ball would fly.

The outfielders didn't a step back, but just turned to view it as it lept out of the yard. It looked as though it were a streaking comet in space. I held the bat firm and I stood close to home plate. I had never hit a ball quite that far before.

Jason turned and spotted me while I took glory in my homerun. He turned, kicked up a huge cloud of dust behind the mound, and eyed me with a sneer-eyed look all along my prance around the bases. It seemed to be a 'still-shot' moment and an eternal stroll for Jason. I looked at him after crossing second; his gaze brushing past the rim of his hat, and so taking a scowl on me.

"Everyone has a lucky shot," he growled.

I knew it was eating him alive now.

"Catch a star next time Conner."

I said nothing, taking my long gallop around third base, and seeing the catcher backing away as I began my final approach. Suddenly I felt a jolt to my left and before I had my full senses about me, I was landing around the third base coach's box on my right side. The whole world appeared to turn sideways when I found Jason glaring down on me. His hat must have fled off that thick bush of hair of his. Because, when I first caught sight on him, he appeared nothing more than a full face of brown locks.

"Take it easy!" I said. The others came to aid by rumbling in, and pulling Jason into a mini headlock.

"Break it off!" the coach pushed on us both, "Break it off!"

I could see the perspiration pumping from his forehead.

"You got Spirit, both of you! But you need to channel it the correct way!"

He stuck Jason's ball cap halfway over his face.

"You two are friends?" he looked on us both, "The two of you?"

His look nearly strained his eyes from their sockets.

"The best," I wiped my lip off.

"We go way back," Jason shot in.

"You could have fooled me!" The coach shot out, "Get a shower!" He yelled, "Both of you!"

"But the tryouts?" Jason pleaded, almost in despair.

"Your through with the tryouts!" he barked, "Now get your shower...The two of you!"

"Nice move," I whispered over to Jason as we were trotting off, "You just cost us the season."

"Gentleman!" the coach yelled back on us; we turned, "Check the Athletic Center Building tomorrow...Noon sharp!"

"We made the cut?" Jason looked back, nearly in awe.

"You made the cut," he groaned, "But pull another stunt like that and I'll have you working the charity dunking booth the rest of the year. You'll be so wet, you'll have to grow fins...then you will wish you had never made the cut."

"Here that Tush?" Jason gave out a yell, "We made the cut!"

He jumped about my arms as if I had just proposed to him.

"Shower boys!" and with this, we took full flight as fast as our legs could carry us, straight to the athletic building.

Jason and I snapped towels at one another for what seemed an hour, giggling and carrying on like the two schoolboys we were. The back of my calves had become fiery red from the shots I had taken from his towel. He would wind up a tight wad, flip it clear, and snap it back so fast it nearly took me to my knees. At one moment we found ourselves in the hallway, nearly bucknaked, with only a long draping towel around our midsections. I fell to one knee in that hallway, and looked back on Jason whose own sudden transformation from a happy and gay soul turned into a morbidly shy look. I quickly spun around and saw my own fears rapidly materialize in front of me; Sandra

Miller had been watching us at the long end of the hallway, no more than thirty feet away.

"Ohhhhhh," we were stuck, dashing about, running, then slipping, running, then slipping further; all in a tangle while holding our towels as tight as we could, "Ohhhhhh!"

"Do you think she saw us?" Jason whispered aloud, well enough to here.

"Of course," I spat.

We could hear the lonely footsteps protrude, moving ever slowly forward, towards our direction. This above all else was not the way I wanted my first encounter with Sandra Miller to turn out.

"Hello," I heard her heavenly voice bend around the corner and into our stall where we were hiding.

A silence, pause, and then Jason returned like the quick thinker he was, "No one here!"

"You don't suppose," she giggled.

I peeked up over the top wall; my ripe, dark hair flopping wet over my eyes. She stood and stared square on me.

"Hello," I crackled a response.

"Am I interrupting anything?"

"No. No," I refuted; I flinging my hair across my brow, "I would have you sit down," I laughed, "but there is no place to sit."

She moved forward. My legs were shaking from her presence.

"One of you boys dropped this," she said; pulling free the cross Buck had left me years before; the one that was his most special 'Boot'. I nearly jumped from that stall to retrieve it but I quickly retreated back to my wet cell.

"Yes," I replied, holding the towel tighter still, "You can leave it on the rack if you like."

"I had a question," she ignored my request.

"Be quick about it," Jason blurted, "We're dripping here."

"If you would like for me to go..."

"No!" I shot back, "No..." I was more calm there, "It's just we're slightly indisposed here."

There was a pause to the silence, I clearing my throat.

"What's the question?"

"I have a cross just like this," she said, "Where in the world did you get it?"

"It was given to me," I started, "If you'll excuse us...We'll be right out," I ducked back beneath the top of the wall. I looked over at Jason as intensely as I could.

"Quick! Get your clothes on!"

"But I'm dripping wet!" he bellowed.

"I don't care," I insisted, "get to it!"

"Oh good," he grumbled, "Now my underwear is going to feel like I just came out of a swim…All gushing!"

"Show off!" I remarked, "Wouldn't be here if you hadn't tried to impress the Miss there!"

"Why didn't you strike out?" He asked.

"What?" I curiously insinuated with that single word, "No gifts! You earn it buddy! The strike out! The spot! The team!"

"And I did!" he propped his hands on his nude hips.

"You look like a grand Tush!" I laughed till the echo rang throughout the entire hallways, "Standing like that."

He said nothing further, though unwillingly forced his clothes about him until we were both fully-clothed. We sprang out from the showers where Sandra had been waiting patiently.

Our eyes met on this turn. Her smile brought out the sunshine and pushed all the shadows away. Her meadow, golden hair glistened when she turned with those soft flaxen strands; all the while they were changing into different arrays of colors on her rotation. Those soft eyebrows were waves across her forehead like graceful ripples to water. She leaned about the brick of that wall, hands folded and adjourned around her front, with my cross dangling from one of her fingers.

"The clasp broke," she said, "Otherwise I would have thought for sure it was mine. I figured it might have dropped off when you passed by us coming to the ball field."

"Thanks," I cautiously moved forward, wary to look at her directly in order to avoid possibly contracting a sudden speech impediment, "That was very kind of you."

"Your Conner James," she looked confused then, "The famous fireman's son…Right?"

"My father's the decorated one," I grinned, "He's been medaled a few times."

"Now to my question…" she pursued.

"Conner," Jason popped me on the back of my shoulder, and moved by us both, "I'll be up at the front, when you're ready." She turned back her attention on me. And as I was peering over her shoulder, I could see Jason give me the 'two thumbs up', the semi-twirl, the roll of the hands and bending of the back dance; ending it as such with the flailing of the arms upward as if he were in a dancing parade. I looked on him mortified, which so caught Sandra's attention, and caused her to look back on Jason while he was making a fool of himself.

"Strange one," she said, "Isn't he?"

"At first," I replied, "He can be a little intolerable. But he rubs off on you after a little while," I paused to clear out my throat, "You know you didn't have to bring that down here. You could have caught up with me in school."

"I know," she smiled, "I'm always into meeting new people though. You and I have been going to school together for sometime now, but I suppose we just never met."

"Different crowds," I lifted my arms to my sides and rattled my eyebrows up higher, "Haven't been as involved with school activities as you have all these years. Our paths just never crossed."

"So what have you been doing with all that spare time, all these years Conner?"

She laughed with a shy, smirkish grin that pulled over her expression, and so batted her eyes out at me.

"Home mostly," I resigned to that fact, "Spent time at the firehouse growing up, ball field with Jason practicing our dream; soda shop…mainly."

"How was that?" She was more curious now, "the firehouse."

"Guys are a unit," I said, "You feel the bond almost immediately. They have to be close. Their lives depend on it."

"So what is you dream Conner James?"

I paused for that single moment, as we stopped our step just before reaching the outdoors' edge, "Play baseball I suppose—for the Red Sox someday."

"You really believe that," she gasped a little.

"Yeah," I replied, "I do. I really do."

I looked on her, as our eyes greeted one another with an heir of earnest friendship; thinking of what the other may be thinking, and holding still without a blink.

"What about you? What's your dream?"

She turned away. Her eyes grew into a sparkle of hope; her shoulders came to a shrug, "Go to a prestigious school, graduate with honors; travel the world; Paris, Rome, Morocco, Greece. Just be as the wind goes…and find adventure wherever it will take me."

"Your stars are as big as mine," I shook a finger out at her.

"Why do you say this?" offensively, she spoke.

"Because," I replied, "I could never dream of something like this for myself. I am the son of a middle-class, working fireman. Our hopes are always pinned on either sports, or doing what our father has done, and his father before him."

"It doesn't have to be that way…"

"Nor does it not…It is the way it is," I suggested.

"You know Conner," she said, "You can have more than your father ever had. Even if you only get halfway there; it's still more."

"Maybe I don't want more," I refuted in a pleasant manner, "Maybe what my father has is as much as I need…"

"Maybe your father works as hard as he does," she returned, "so you can have the chance for more."

"Then that is his dream," I replied.

"And not yours?" she came back, "Somebody gave you this cross for a reason Conner; someone very special. Someone who had dreams and cared enough about you to place this in your trust; I know."

I paused with a most confused look on my face.

"Wait a minute," I wondered, "How do you know?"

"It's not important," she fussed.

"Yes it is," I pressed. By this point I had lost all my inhibitions around Sandra, and I felt I had known her longer than I had first imagined.

"What is it Sandra?"

"It doesn't matter," she implored.

"Yes it does," I softly whispered, as if it were a plea from some affectionate ghost standing right next to her, "Please…There is something you need to tell me. So, tell me."

I could see her step away with her eyes. Her face was sullen and wrought with the showers of some coming tears. There looked to be hidden pain there. Like the pain buried by a soul for years; unreleased, hidden in the doors and closets of a person's thoughts. It had stung her again like it had many times before; in private, holding her to her secret and never wanting it to be released. A secret not shared for as long and as deep as it had been buried within her.

"No really," she refrained, "I have to go…"

She softly pulled away. I could sense the wound in her heart trying to mend itself over as she wiped back her tears from her face. I felt Buck's cross slip from her hand to mine, and my prevailing silence only captured her further into her own sadness. I didn't know what to say.

"Wait, Sandra," I gazed on her as she left and descended out along the ridge; not once looking back in retreat. What words to measure with; what magical saying to impose on Sandra to return. Nothing; simply nothing could come to mind. I felt the blank words from my mind fall into a blank look on my expression.

I wandered back up to where Jason was waiting.

"Boy!" he observed, "You look like you just saw the dumbest ghost, and he left a stupid look on your face."

"It's nothing," I said, "Really."

"What did she do to you?" he looked most odd at me, "She got some kind of strange power there Conner."

"Let's leave it alone," I insisted, "Alright?"

Jason leaned over my shoulder with his arm, patted me to one side with his hand, and frowned a rather heartless frown, "It will be fine. Loser's club isn't so bad after all. We all get there one day."

"You should know," I said in a cross manner, while catching my bike out in a hurry, "You're the founder…"

"Hey!" he yelled to me, "Stanton ball field. Seven o'clock tomorrow. Practice…Ok?"

I heard little of this but I kept the pedals rotating on my bike. From street to street I went, though I felt an out-of-body existence all the while; contemplating, thinking, observing, and replaying what had just transpired between Sandra Miller and me. There was much more to tell than what she was willing to tell me. Perhaps the continual separation between us was pre-designed for some reason. Or perhaps we had been accidentally destined not to meet until today. Or perhaps it was an accident all together that we met.

I looked down on that cross; studied it, observed it from every angle when I came up to a street corner and I waited for the long light to turn. There was more to the mystery; a stroke of embers to burn that I had not seen in its initial spark many years since; something far hidden from my knowledge, and kept from me as the very same secret which seemed to scar Sandra to her very core.

We were not finished, Sandra and I. For the very source of this empty equation now would play on me like the lingering sore born in Sandra so long ago. I forgave her for her intrusion there, and I wished she would intrude further. It was my hope that beyond this moment we shared, the future would somehow allow us to share more.

Chapter 13

I'm Too Young to be a Chaperone.

"Wake up you dumpster!" I felt a pillow come crashing down on me while I slept. My snores and dreams were both interrupted all in that swift and unprovoked act.

"What?" I said; half-awake when I felt another pillow pile-drive me back onto my covers, after I had just managed to come to a sit, "Quit streaker!"

I made an attempt to fight back.

"You're a late bloomer again Conner," I knew it was Amanda this time. Mother must have sent her to retrieve me, "Mother said to grab Adam on the way down."

"Alright," I stumbled from my sleep, felt the cold rush of the floor on the soles to my feet; my hair wobbling over my forehead as I went walking about.

"Why don't you get him," I argued, "He listens to you more than me."

I began to fumble through my dresser drawers.

"Because," she was emphatic; nor was she one to take direction too well at this stage in her life, "It was mother's specific instructions," she huffed on this one.

"You know how she gets on her 'specific' instructions."

"I know, I know," I waved Amanda off, "*Follow to the 'T' what I expect or the choirs will double.*"

Mother was always involved with making out a 'to do' list for us all. The weekly schedule would sit on the refrigerator, stuck about with magnets. Our requirements would rotate from week to week, but it seemed I always had to take the trash out to the curb every night.

I drunkenly walked down the hall to Adam's room, knocked two pecks; had no answer, and then I stepped through.

"Come on Picasso." I remarked.

I saw him sitting quite lonesome in one corner of the room as he took a very concentrated dive into his sketching of all those stuffed animals. They were sitting well situated all nicely at the top of his bed, and he capturing their poses, expressions, and arrangements there.

"Hey, Picasso…Breakfast is up; you can eat your sketches later."

"Hold on Conner," he stayed steady to his work.

"Now Adam," I explained, "You know how mother will get if I come downstairs without you. That's her pet peeve…well, one of them." I said, "Drop the pencil cowboy."

Adam gazed back hard on me. His staunch look only dug a deeper foxhole in his mind. Those rimmed glasses shaded his eyes well, with such a tiny peephole to see through by. Every now and then you could see that twinkle stare sparkle about and play within his expression, like an odd ghost which would come to poke its head out on occasion.

He held such a sorted disposition; totally consumed by his artwork and writing; like a fire raging without the lack of fuel to burn with. Adam had sprung a bit in the last year and he nearly held some comparable size to me. He enjoyed sweaters even when it was a tad bit too warm for them; reveled in the dapper, courtier look, which in the adult stage of life would be most appropriate. But not at the cumbersome age of ten or so. I was quite sure the other kids poked and picked on him; I now being at a newer school. I could no longer provide him with adequate protection against such onslaughts and attacks. No matter. He did as much with that as with any other thing; just ignore it.

"Too much delay, and mother will make a fuss over it," I spoke, which garnered yet another stern gaze back.

"So much distress over a little food."

"No Dickens," I warned him, in a shallow voice and cold whisper, "It's the fussing that we feel the fuss over."

I marched him down, though he kept to his usual posture of hiding behind his glasses in a shy and sheep-glare pose. Adam took to his seat and waited, patiently, absent a word and rather feeling more comfortable in doing so than to raise a notion otherwise.

Mother was galloping in a frazzle about the ring of that kitchen. Her smile was as warm as always; her age creeping a bit more in the sight of her look. That thick raven hair drew a few streaks of off-color gray now; the wrinkles bore more to frown-lines, or happy lines in her case. Grandmother was still settled in her bed; mother not wanting to get her up just yet. Commotion such as a full family meal brought her undue stress. Mother would wait until we were all done, and then attend to grandmother.

Grandmother had lost more of her presence now. Time had shadowed the real world from her, and made a strange, newer one for her to revel in. It was not uncommon to find grandmother grabbing the air for flies that were not there; mumble into the open room as though she were in a formidable conversation; stare at her empty glass down into the very bottom of it; pause, contemplate it, and so drink the air as if it were liquid. Certainly, most of the children had lost their ability to communicate with her in any extensive manner. The shell of a woman; the graceful butterfly lost from her wings; the life lived and longed for, now seemingly misplaced in the drifting vaults of her mind. Somewhere out there, still, a portion of who she was, still yet remained.

We settled about our chairs; the food nicely displayed before us like the wonderful sight and smelling temptation that it was. I grabbed for a piece of bacon, yet mother was quick to slap my hand back into place.

"Grace first," she looked at us all, "Adam, grace please."

We all bowed our heads in a moment of fasting truce; fingers locked and ready for pray. The pause came, waiting, still waiting for Adam. I peeked out of a corner stare and I saw Adam wandering with his own look. I persistently kicked about his shin.

"Grace!" he blurted out in one graphic word. He turned his attention to ending his ten-second fast, and feasting as if he had lost valuable time in the process.

"Hush Pooh!" mother scorned on him, "How is that to say grace?" She stuck her finger on him as if it were God's finger.

"But mother," Adam complained, "I'm not good at grace."

"All the better," she replied, "You need the practice."

"But I'm not able…" he returned.

"No Adam, grace please…"

"But," he tried once more.

"Butts are for disciplining," she warned, "if a child of mine which owns it doesn't do as I request."

Mother paused.

"Now. Grace please Adam."

We all took our positions once more; some were munching down their last morsel of food before mother had intervened on us. Adam began, slowly, irregular in his speech and step with the word, as if he were most afraid to talk to God there. He came across muffled, hesitant, and lacked the correct words to say. I peered over to mother all the while; she keeping tabs on Adam with her own stare; yet in a loving, most prideful pose. I could see in her thoughtful expression she hoped this was the start of something; something special for Adam.

Halfway through our breakfast, mother festered and began.

"Conner," she stalled for a moment, "You know your sister Lorie is fifteen. She has a friend who would like to take her out."

I looked on mother, then Lorie, with no response.

"A date." She continued.

I said nothing, but just kept to my chew.

"Tonight," mother kept her stare on me.

I took another bite. I did not quite realize what was to come.

"I won't be able to take her. Your father has his shift work at the fire station until the day after tomorrow."

My eyes grew wide and bold as it hit me; my chewing took to a sudden pause, "Mother; no, I can't."

"Conner, I have a very important PTA meeting tonight. One I am unable to get out of. You will have to take your sister."

"Mother," I pleaded.

"You can drive Conner. You are quite responsible and its time for you to learn more responsibility. Your father even said you could drive his Mustang convertible."

"But what about my plans?"

"They can wait," she replied, "This is a giving time for you."

"But mother," I tried one last time.

"Why do you fester so!" she exhorted on me, "This is your sister's first date; one that she has been wanting with this young boy for some time. The other day he asked her to go out. Your father and I spoke of it, and approved."

"So let his parents take them out then," I suggested.

"Your father and I don't know them," mother stated, "We'll pay for the gas, food, movies. I'll need to be at the school by seven, and I will be home no later than ten-thirty. Another thing; you will have to take Adam and Amanda along with you."

This raised the ire of all the children in one spontaneous, combustionable moment.

"That wasn't part of the plan mother," Lorie shot in.

"Mother," Amanda harped in, "I had planned to talk with Carol on the phone this evening."

"What about?" mother asked.

"Boys. What else do girls talk about; what else?" I smarted.

"That's enough Conner James!" mother pressed her finger out over the table at me; further still.

"I have to finish my sketch," Adam calmly said.

"Who's going to look after grandmother?" Amanda said.

"Grandmother will be fine. Your aunt Penny is coming this morning to take Grandmother to stay with her for a few weeks. You know its' her time to take care of your grandmother; that's the arrangement we have," mother replied, "Children, look at it this way. Think of it as a night out with one another. I want you to spend more time together."

"But mother," Lorie exclaimed, "not on my date though. This is so embarrassing."

Lorie dropped her fork on her nearly empty plate; causing it to ring out.

"I know Lorie," mother sympathized, "But as it stands, in order for you to go out tonight with Brian, it has to be this way. I didn't know of the PTA meeting when your father and I initially spoke of it. You'll need to make do."

The remaining three of us siblings all stared down over at Lorie. I knew she felt the strong weight of our looks and sneers as they pressed hard on her. We all had that unified hope that Lorie may very well back out of this situation and rearrange her date for another time. There was a pause while she scoped out all our looks.

"Ok. I promised Brian we would for sure tonight," she said.

Adam dropped his head nearly back on his plate. I rolled my eyes as if I knew now I was in store for an evening prearranged as enjoyable as going to see my dentist; for three hours no less. And Amanda, in her own quirky way, seemed to relish in the venue; perky smiling with her dimples cascading between her cheeks; her hands propped about her chin in support, and that fork she held so dangled from one side to the other. Regardless, we all had a rather odd night in store.

For the remainder of that day I had a certain dread-look stuck on my face. If someone were to take acute notice of it, it would bulge into a full frown like a balloon being blown up with helium.

Mother passed down kisses before she left for her PTA meeting, and a roll of sixty dollars was given to me.

"Take good care Conner," she smiled, "I am relying on you. Spend only what you need; nothing more. You're the oldest and it is time for you to show your siblings how to conduct themselves; to behave and keep the 'James' name in good standing."

"Mother," I softly spoke, "You sound like you just came from the 1800's or something."

"Well good Etiquette never dies. It's very resilient and it has lasting charm," she paused while her gooky smile turned into a curious look, "That sounded old too didn't it son?"

"Older," I replied, "More like ancient Greece."

"I wouldn't suppose that far back," she turned about, and readied herself to step out into the evening air.

Lorie came from her room and displayed herself. Her black hair was strung out straight as though she had combed it a thousand strokes; and so having a nice sheen to it that was glistening when the light struck it. Her jeans were of the baggy sort; cream-pink shirt with a soft yellow sweater tied over her shoulders, and with brown sandals to boot. Amanda and Adam dressed according to their personalities, as I did the same.

"You look very graceful Lorie," mother replied on the sight of her; pulling Lorie close, and casting out on her a final hug and kiss, "Give my regards to Jimmy."

"Brian," Lorie corrected her.

"Brian?" mother wondered aloud, "Yes, it is Brian, isn't it."

She was quickly off to her PTA meeting and I wrangled up all my siblings into my father's new mustang convertible.

"You are going to put the top down?" Amanda's mischievous in her ways, and asking so quaintly.

"Oh no!" Lorie replied, "It took me a half-an-hour to brush out the curls. And my mascara is sure to run. The top stays up."

"It's your date," I said, "Do as you like."

"But I want the top down," Amanda moaned.

"It's not your date sis," I said, "When it's your date, you can ride out on your bicycle if you want."

"We should make Brian sit in front…" Amanda smirked in a grin and a wink to us each, "with you Conner."

"No No," Lorie riled, "You get the front saddle on this one sister." She waved Amanda off with a shake of her finger, and a stern look, "You're not going to be this way all night are you?"

"What way?" Amanda came back.

"A pest," I moved in the driver's seat, "Don't be a nuisance. Adam? You're upfront with me."

Adam said nothing but followed my instructions. I needed him this evening, even if he didn't say a word otherwise. It would seem more 'natural' for him to tag along. At least it would not appear I was carting my sisters around like an older brother who had nothing better to do.

"Where does he live?" I asked of Lorie.

"Booker Street. I have the directions. We are about five miles out. I think."

That last phrase gave me pause.

We all settled in our areas, roared the high-strung Mustang up, and took off about our way. According to Lorie, we had to take a series of turns down four back roads to find his house. I did as she suggested. But on our final left turn, we came across 'Robin's Street' not 'Booker's', then onto McHulty, Walford, Eden, Pearl, and lastly Salem. Bookers' was nowhere to be found.

"Lorie," I said in frustration, "Where is it?"

She pulled out her map, flipped it about; left, right, full circle, semi-circle; there came a chuckle.

"What?"

"I had the map wrong," she chomped on her gum thirty times or more, "Would you believe?"

"Yes I would," I looked out in my rearview mirror, "And you're driving next year…"

"I know," she broadly smiled, "Isn't it great?"

"You better learn to navigate," I said, "Or you'll be spinning doughnuts in the bathroom."

As we made our way back, reverted our direction, found the chain of streets to maneuver through, we at last found our place in front of Brian's house; though fifteen minutes behind schedule.

"Lorie," I said, "Why don't you go get Brian."

"I want to go," Amanda announced.

"No you're not," I insisted, "Stay put. You can watch from the back window…"

"Some view," she shrugged, "It's like looking through a dot out there. I can't see anything."

"Amanda," I said, "If mother finds out about tonight, she'll be furious. You're not starting out so good on this one."

"You'll tell," she grouched.

"Of course," I was most explicit there, "Do you ever want to go out on a date you're entire life?"

"Maybe," she snobbingly proposed.

"Mother will fix it where you won't…not ever."

It was silent there as Lorie ascended from the car, waltzed up the walkway and to the front door. I could hear the distant sounds of a doorbell ring, a cordial 'hello', and 'you must be Lorie' from a woman inside who must have been Brian's mother.

There was a lag in time there while we all waited. I counted the streetlights just ahead of me; so hearing the steps of two people returning our way.

"Hey!" I heard a boy's voice call out, "It's the partridge family!"

I turned to my right, saw Brian (though I wished at that moment it was an imposter and the 'real' Brian would come out), slap his hands down over the open window. His smile reached from universe to universe; his teeth gleamed out over me as though they were slicers from a horror film. He wore a notorious tie which didn't match the other garments he wore. His hair was so pasted with goo, I thought he might be a mobster of some sort. The jewelry he flashed around sparkled in such a gaudy manner, I was sure he was a spokesperson for a costume jewelry store.

"Hey! Pops don't look so old!"

"Hello," I forced a smile through my gulp, "My name is Conner; Lorie's older brother."

"Nice to meet you Donner," he shook my hand wildly.

"And this is Adam, and Amanda," I did the further introductions; pointing so to each.

"Hey!" he shook on Adam, whom I knew he most thoroughly detested already, "Nice to meet you Allen! Mandy!"

They quickly got into the car.

"Times-a-wasting there chuffy!"

Brian laughed at his own ill-performed humor, "Coach away!"

"Isn't he a dream!" my sister leaned up, placed her hand gently on my shoulder. I could see a giddish smile cross over her expression as she settled back into the back of the car. I knew then this night would become longer still. I was sure then my sister Lorie had lost her ability to make appropriate judgments, and that she would need private counsel after all this was said and done.

I gripped the steering wheel hard, bit my lip into a quiet simmer, and I drove to the fish restaurant we were to eat at.

The place was called 'Captain's Purse'. I had never taken to eat here before, so noting the 'cheesy' nature of the layout, the poor harbor view, and the odd, half-baked, corny large fish head seemingly to burst out of the roof with a wispy look on its face. I would have preferred another, though Lorie wanted to try this place out. I decided to abide by this since it was her first date.

We were seated promptly; the crowd and air ruled by a misty and nauseous cantation that appeared to sift and simmer in the air. It was like a smoke which had no meaning, but only to make the room look more like a mist drifting off the sea ocean into the bay. I couldn't bear to look at Brian too long; with that silly, corndog, mutated, gasping grin stuck on his look. It seemed to be pasted with Elmer's glue on one side and laying limp on the other.

Lorie huddled close to him; gushing her eyebrows into a rapid succession of blinks and starry gazes.

"Oh don't do that," I looked on her almost with disgust.

"Please don't do that…"

She looked at me with the word 'what?' on her mind, yet she said nothing more, other than with her expression there.

"The children," I defended, "Please…"

Adam gazed around with a sort of indifferent, inoculating stare; a look never to be planted about for very long at all. Amanda, on the other hand, huffed slightly; but kept her tongue behind her drawbridge. The waiter came over politely.

He stalled in front of us, looked about rather like a shore man, placed his hand over his forehead as though to be looking out at sea for a wayward boat; then pulled from his pocket a whistle and blew on it to call us to supper. He wore a modestly fake mustache; all dressed in navy blue but for the white scarf dangling around his neck; and that long, over-bearing hat which stretched from here to china, looping about like a broken umbrella that had been bent disproportionately by a recent, heavy rain.

"You must be the captain," I relayed to him.

"Waiter Dave at your service," he pronounced, "What will it be?"

He was standing at attention all the while.

"Menus on board sir," he pointed directly to the middle of our table. We then scrounged around to gather one menu each. I could tell by the silence we were all flopping through our choices.

"You are going to wait for our orders?" I asked.

"A good waiter always attends to his guests."

I nearly dove headfirst into my menu when he said this. We went around the table and ordered like we were in single file at a buffet counter.

"I'll have the flounder mix with perch; light on the sauce; melted butter with the greens and softly baked potato."

"Crab legs," Brian blurted about. I looked at the price and was nearly floored by it, though he wasn't finished, "lobster tails, touch of the vinegar; fruit cup; candy yams; extra slaw; how about an extra round of hush puppies," we waited to see if he was through; I now counting the money and calculating to see if I would have enough for the entire evening, "how about salmon patties to finish her off! Lightly-breaded."

He smiled through all this.

"I'll just have fried shrimp," Amanda reacted. She closed her menu shut. She cast over an obvious look on Brian.

"Me too," Adam quickly shot out, without a care.

"And what will my Frunchkin have?" Brian doted over Lorie. I nearly choked on that word as he spoke it, and he so pinching her cheek.

I wanted to ask Brian what he wanted to do with his life when he grew up. But measuring the state of his situation, I dare not ask what the adult form of him would turn out to be.

As the waiter began to leave, Brian raised his hand one final time, "And yes waiter; a Michelob please…"

"Excuse me?" the waiter turned.

"Waiter," I intervened, "a round of sweet teas for us all."

"Very good sir," he bowed like a diplomat.

"So Donner," Brian leaned back, cock-eyed and all, "You're a year older than Lorie here. You enjoy high school now?"

He talked as if he were a middle-aged man, and had already surpassed all of this before. I would be more tight-lipped than usual through dinner. I did not wishing to excel on expounding about myself in front of this terminal fellow.

"It has its moments," I replied. The teas were swiftly placed in front of us and I took my breath in my own drink.

The dinner parlayed out like a rather bad occasion. Amanda bore her soul in her expression with the most painful of sights at all of us. There was much she wished to say. But I had virtually sowed her lips together by my verbal lashing earlier. Lorie batted her eyes, grinned a love-swoon grin, and looked on Brian almost with near submission. Brian wished however to tackle with me on every turn in an arrogant tone. I just sipped on my tea and tolerated the bloat. I suppose he desired to show he was a better teenage boy than me, or to continually congratulate himself on his, as-of-yet, uneventful life. I guess I loved my sister well enough to let it all go.

Adam however gazed over at Brian as though his voice was the direct result from fingernails on a long, never-ending chalkboard. On one instance, Adam retrieved his trusty pad and buried himself immediately into a sketch.

"What do you have there little tike?" Brian barfed.

"Oh nothing," Adam glanced over and continued.

"Let me see," Brian snatched the pad from Adam, "Well, a good likeness," he grinned that horrible grin of his, and then proceeded to flip onto the next page to perform his own drawing. He yielded out nothing more than a stick figure.

"The same likeness!"

He laughed to the point his tongue might drop out of his mouth.

"Adam," I defended, "Considers it a very serious ambition of his."

I sent Brian a cold, reserved stare that shadowed out a glare from the low-lying lights about us.

"And he has the talents to pursue it someday, I believe."

Our food came out in short order and it diverted our attention from the tension, which was beginning to rise around the table. We ate mainly in silence, though I asked Lorie and Brian not to feed one another when this tradition began.

"Oh please," I sounded off, "Lorie…We are ALL eating."

They discontinued this practice quite immediately.

"Your brother is quite a stiff," Brian leaned over to Lorie's ear and whispered. It was rather obvious he wished for me to overhear, though I paid him little, if no attention on the matter.

After dinner, we barely had enough money to continue our evening out together. I went to the bathroom stall, nervously counted out the coin and currency remaining while I sat, and calculated I would be a buck twenty-five under, as long as the bottomless pit Brian did not want anything more than a coke at the movie theater. We all jumped back into the Mustang; I watching the 'going-on's' in the back seat.

"That's my leg," Amanda huffed out and stared Brian down. He grinned, kicked his chin up, and threw his arm around Lorie. I drove us as quickly to the theater as I could get us there.

We stood about the front, gazed at all the posters lit up on the outside, made a decision to see the movie of Lorie's choosing.

"Dirty Dancing," she spatted.

"Dirty Dancing?" this was not my first choice, "Alright."

We went inside, paid for our tickets and of course, Brian wanted not only a Coke, but also a hefty bag of M & M's. I decided to forego my own drink for his delight, paid for the others, and held three quarters in my hand; the bitter remnants of the sixty dollars my mother had entrusted to me. I foraged about all four of my pockets; nothing further. That was it; three whole quarters.

We went to our seats directly in the middle. All that remained was a ninety-minute movie to grind through and I would have that detestable Brian home as quickly as the last credits rolled through. My seat was next to Lorie's; my preference, with Brian to her other side. Adam sat next to me, with Amanda on the tail end of our group. Brian chomped and crunched, slurped and battered, licked his lips and burped, all through this movie. I kept more eyes on Lorie than the big screen itself.

"Whoa!" Adam seemed dazzled by it all, "Whoa!"

As the dancing escalated throughout the movie, Lorie and Brian became most giggly. I leaned in on Lorie to gather her attention.

"Not on my watch." I whispered.

I glanced over at Amanda and noticed she had a strange propensity to continually sip on her drink, even after she had emptied it out.

We left as soon as the last scene faded. It was nearing just past nine-thirty and it was quite the time to get Brian home. I hustled everyone out to the car, made my cordial get-away, and sped out toward Brian's home. Brian had seemed to be rather subdued by his full belly; his generic lack of consideration now tempered toward a sleepy, glassy stare out of the car. As we came to Brian's home, Adam pulled out from his seat, let Lorie attend to Brian on their walk back to the front door. A minute or two passed when Lorie reappeared.

"Wasn't he great?" she said in a gleeful tone.

"No," Amanda replied, "He wasn't."

"Amanda," I leaned my eyes back to spot her gaze out the window, "Enough said. We all have our own opinions."

"He could have at least said 'thank you,'" she returned.

"Some people are brought up differently," I said.

"That's simple, common courtesy Conner." Amanda shot back.

"I agree," Adam softly spoke, "He was a jerk."

"I think you are all jealous…" Lorie defended.

"Of what?" Adam looked onto Lorie, "Mafia king pin here?"

"I have a boyfriend, and you don't…"

"I don't want a boyfriend," Adam replied.

"You know what I mean," Lorie crossed her arms and settled back into her seat with a frown which dribbled from her expression there.

We were able to pull in the driveway just a few minutes before ten. Mother had yet to return but was sure to return within the next half hour. The four of us bolted into the house, made our way into our rooms, and we began to settle down for the evening. I, sitting in my silence, reading a book I had just purchased the day before, and having my back to my door.

My door squealed open from the lack of greasing. I kept it this way so I would know beforehand if someone were trying to enter my room predisposed. It was a soft push to a crack. The pause let me know who the intruder was; Lorie. I felt her enter, silently and with caution. Her arms came to drape around me with a hug and she sat to the edge of my bed.

"What was that for?" I asked, in turning.

"You didn't say anything."

"What do you mean?" I pursued.

"That's just it Conner, you didn't say anything," she smiled with a tear pushing through her eyelid, "Brian was horrible. I never imagined he would treat my family that way. I'm smart enough to know what he did, and what he didn't do. But you Conner…you tried to make it the best first date possible for me, even when he was at his worst. You didn't make a scene."

"I knew what it meant to you," I looked back on my book, "No since in trying to make a bad situation worse."

"I won't be seeing Brian again," she took off the cheap necklace he had given her, "I'm going to give this back and tell him to give it to the next girl he decides to take out…but it won't be me," she stared out on me with her admiration beaming through, "You're a great brother Conner…you care."

"Thanks," I smiled; not knowing what further to say.

"Maybe I can do a better job picking a second date next time."

"You're on your own there," I laughed, "You're lucky though."

"How's that?" She inquired.

"Some boys are not as upfront about themselves as Brian was; a little more calculating. At least you got to see the real 'Brian' early." I forced my lips together and passed to her a slow right punch on her arm.

"Boy; did I ever!" she laughed through her sniffle, "Promise you won't tell mom or dad."

"Tell them what?" I smiled.

"Thanks Conner," she burst out and gave me another quick hug; went to the outskirts of my room, held the doorknob in one hand, looked reassuringly on me, and slowly moved the door to a shut.

I turned about to my reading once more. I felt the words run across my mind in a blank imaginary stare, and I thought of my family in the most endearing way.

I could have read the volumes of books that night; read through the travels of Dickens, Steinbeck, Austen, and Twain; taken myself to the highest peaks or the lowest valleys of emotions and dreams. I thought more on the reality around me however. The family I adored and cherished beyond my own life. Now this was something far more significant than where my imagination could take me to. The home of the heart; the house which resided by that estate, and which gave me a sense of who I was, and who I would eventually become.

There are tragedies in life; there are joys in life, the same. The spectrum broad and expanse; so much so, there will be events in life one can only experience and yet, can never be prepared for. The future was as unwitting to those events as I was, but as masterful as the greatest artist to carve out their existence within my path.

I would so learn these truths when the coming years came into being within my life. The dawning of those moments were to be like the horizon sunshine and the dimming sunset all in the same blink of an eye. "*The rainbows of life*," my mother would say.

Chapter 14

The Years Go Quickly.

High school was a capsule of short and rapid change. I had become, in my first year of school, a district all-star; hitting .350 with twelve homeruns and helping our team get to the state quarterfinals. We lost however to the eventual champions that year. Jason had been lesser used, though eventually he posted three wins late in the season; three more in the playoffs. It appeared we both had assured ourselves a spot on the team for our junior year. Our dream of one day staring in the majors; taking field on the hallowed grounds of Fenway Park could come to reality. It seemed to be an improbable journey, but one journey Jason and I were dedicated to.

"Son?" my mother spoke on our porch one evening, "I want you to take the impossible, and make it possible. Take the possible and make it probable, than take the probable and make it happen."

"And where will that lead me to?" I asked.

She smiled, waved me off with a little twist of her hand, drank from her cup of lemonade as she watched out over the horizon, then settled her head back to take a rest and gently rock in her chair two or three times. I could see the measure of her aging grace shining through there, like a flickering light now glowing it's brightest from its own breath and strength. The warm luminescence shown through her eyes as if she were a star beaming back its glow to earth for me to marvel at. Perhaps she was looking out at the stars from Heaven, and so spotting the very star she would become when she passed on.

I nearly froze on her look there; the force and weight of its mass struck me cold in that single moment. The thoughts overwhelmed me to think of her now reaching the very pinnacle of her life; she looking over the shores that were touching the seas, or gazing out from the top-most peak of a mountain and becoming so the dayspring of a sunrise and sunset all in that second. I nearly wept when that rush unexpectantly hit me.

"Do you remember when I spoke to you about my mother's passing?" she softly said.

"I remember," I replied.

"Conner, it was the only time in my life I felt my intellect had to sooth and calm the emotions to my soul. I perhaps would have faltered otherwise, and lost myself totally in that loss. It was a time when I felt the greatest need to be closer to God, but in the same breath, felt the most distance in. It was truly a moral dilemma unlike I had ever experienced before," she grinned to look at me, "And I suppose it would only be second to the loss of one of my children."

I could say nothing, but listen intently.

"I hope I have been a good mother to you children…"

"Oh you have mother," I quickly responded.

"And you have been the most precious children to me. I am so proud of you all, truly I am. The way you have grown, the people you are becoming, always brings a smile to my heart."

She patted me on the top of my wrist when I looked onto her.

"And looking back, and stretching myself to remember what all occurred, has given me some self-taught lessons. None have been too invaluable to stop thinking on or stop remembering the purpose of those times."

"What was the purpose of them mother?" I weakly said.

She paused and held to her thoughts. I knew she wasn't quite ready to release all to me. The silence overcame us in that moment; while we watched the neighbors play in their backyard.

"Your grandfather was a glorious violin player. You didn't know that did you?" she chuckled once or twice.

"No I didn't."

"He was indeed. Every year, while mother made the Christmas turkey, yams, stuffing, and all the fixings to fatten a pig with; father would drag out his old violin, spend a few hours dusting it off and cleaning it up, then play about countless old hymns on Christmas Eve. Some we would sing to and ask him to play again and again," she closed her eyes, her head pulled back to the chair support, and she seemed swept away to that breath-taking past of hers.

"I can still hear the old strings rubbing that good bow into a melody. It was so sweet Conner; and so powerful I can still hear those tunes call me back even today…I wish you had known him Conner.

At night, in some summer evenings, when he had smoked his pipe an hour or two, every once in awhile he would pull out his violin, play out over their balcony like he had the stars above as an audience…He would just play and play Conner…Oh goodness! I would be sleeping on my side towards the window. But when I heard that sweet echo coming through my window, I would open my eyes, listen quietly, and watch the moon glow and smile back at me."

"It's a nice memory mother," I whispered.

"Memory yes, but not lost," she replied, "I always wanted you children to have memories of us, like I had of my family; to be carried by you into your day; your time. I wanted for you to have these simple joys to be like a present you can continually unwrap every day of your life."

"Do you think you haven't done this?"

"I don't know," she honestly appealed to me, "I hope; I always hope," her emotions were becoming softer by the moment.

I stood from my seat and looked out over the dimming horizon. I knew then I must speak without the covers over my heart holding over me like a warm blanket. The hidden treasures not to stay so hidden; the words were meant to be shared in this moment.

"I wouldn't have any other mother," I said as I looked away into the distance, "And I thank God that I am constantly reminded of this everyday of my life…when I look at you mother."

I took to step away down those back stairs, jump over the fence that separated our home from our neighbors, and then find myself in full play with the younger kids. I would gaze out over and see my mother still in her rocker. She was looking out over me like a mother who was proud of her son. I paused; our eyes and thoughts connected as before when I first went to Spike's funeral in that downpour and rain.

I was older now, and it seemed I had better understanding on the words and meaning to those emotions which were now passing between us.

She smiled with an air of conclusion in it, and slowly pulled herself to a stand to re-enter the house. The words of Elijah Haberstaff came rushing through my thoughts like the engorged river it seemed to be at that time.

"*Be there for your mother. There will come a time when she will need you most,*" was the echo which vaulted back at me.

Like a long-lost whisper, perhaps the tireless instrument of experiencing life itself, or an old sound from my memory that played as on old record going round about the turntable in an endless cycle of tunes. I stopped my play with the children, and I stared out into nowhere.

"*You will need to do for her as she has done for you. You will be ready; I assure you…but be brave and ready…*"

I gazed back at her abandoned rocker and saw it still tipping by the weight of her rising. It seemed the wind had blown it about for a spell, swirling in motion, and keeping it on the move. Would I someday return, and find my mother had just left that same rocker to never return to it once again?

Could it be the shadow of tomorrow now brushing into the melodies of that day? Could it be the string memory from my past that somehow had influence on the days to come? I contemplated more than what it was due; and so proceeded to place with it reverence most undeserving. But still, I wondered, and I played in that thought for what seemed longer than a moment.

"Conner!" a voice brought me back, "Conner!" it was my sister Lorie. She came rushing from the front; glowing by the conquest of her day.

"I sailed my first boat out of the harbor! My very first boat! Even went into Boston Harbor; it was so, so exciting!"

"How did you manage that?"

"Well you know Uncle John loves to ride his boat out on clear Saturdays. They asked me to go and he allowed me to sail on my own for at least an hour. I was so thrilled!"

"I am happy for you Lorie," I weakly smiled as we conversed between that fence separating us and our neighbors.

"Ate at the Pier, then sailed out from the dock," she paused with a strange and twisted look on her face. It dwindled down into a blank, nearly incoherent stare.

"I was quite surprised that we ran into someone you know. They sat right next to us, and overheard our name 'James', and she inquired on you."

"Of me?" I asked curiously.

"Yes," Lorie replied, "You know her, Sandra Miller? Who hasn't heard of her? She was with her boyfriend Dirk Ballard."

My heart nearly drowned in my chest when she said this.

"What did she say?" I meekly proposed.

"Just wanted to know how you were doing. Since school has been out, she hasn't seen you…In fact, she made mention she hasn't spoken to you since the last few months before school let out."

My sister looked out on me to see my reaction.

"Oh?" I simply blurted out, "How did she seem?"

"Conner!" my sister rolled her eyes and huffed, "I have heard she is always cordial. I don't think she meant anything by it."

"Oh," I forced my hands into my pockets, shrugged my shoulders, and made mince of any possible insinuation my sister felt I had made by that remark, "Just to be curious; didn't mean anything by it. We've only talked once, by accident; of course."

"You like her don't you?" she shyly grinned.

"Oh no!" I refuted, "No! Not in the least…Just friends…distant friends."

I continued to stutter while my sister Lorie watched me hang myself.

"Off distant friends…one you say 'hello' to once or twice a year in the hallway…Nothing more,…really."

She kept to her silence, but continued to look me over.

"What?" I exclaimed, "What? What did I do?"

"Yeah," Lorie laughed, "You like her…"

"It shows," I winced, "That bad? Huh?"

"Real bad," she giggled, "As bad as it gets brother."

Ever since my engagement with Sandra Miller, the mystery behind what we had spoken to one another on never left my mind. It rather played an inconceivable game with me; darting in and out, and showing up when I least expected it. I would be totally involved with one matter, then, without warning or frank candor, I found myself thinking on her and the vast mystery still unsolved. It was made worse by the long evenings of that summer; I was always sifting through my bed and counting how many 'rollover's' I had performed before falling asleep. The night air was most stale and stifling hot in late July and August. Sometimes I would pull myself into a sit, drop my hand out to turn on the lamplight, pull out Buck's cross from underneath my t-shirt, and watch it dangle in a twist. I could feel that boyish grin fall over my expression and I could sense Sandra waiting for me in my imaginary dreams.

I knew Sandra Miller had captivated me from the moment I first saw her; the years of which had made it only worse. Puppy love as I have been told, you grow out of; this, however seemed to stir about in a melting pot stew for as long as I could remember. It was only enhanced by my sister's mentioning of it. The new school year was quickly approaching. And so I had both hope and reservation on what was to come the moment we again laid eyes on one another. Would I see the curious force of that mystery sitting in her expression; like a longing that I too had possessed since we spoke last?

Little did I know, on the very first day of our return, my junior year in high school, we would finally see one another.

I had made a noteworthy name for myself in the preceding baseball season. My picture was quite often plastered in the sports section of our local newspaper within our district. It seemed rather extraordinary how one year can be altered from the next. I at least heard my name 'Conner' being pronounced correctly, rather than the diverse and offbeat names from the previous year; 'Comet', 'Cornhead', 'Corky', 'Cody Co', to name a few. I had also grown three inches over the summer; 'filled out' as my father put it, a few more pounds, yet my hair crisscrossed in the wind in the same manner as before, and as if it were as carefree as I had become. No more of the 'Ichabod Crane' similarities I had detested the year before, which so gave me the greatest of relief. One 'new sophomore' even asked me for my autograph, and my friends who were about me at the time were astounded by such a request.

"Wow!" one spouted, "Whoa! That is so cool!"

My sister Lorie was now a sophomore, and I sat with her out on one of the connecting walls during lunch break.

"You see Brian of late?" I asked.

"I thought I told you?" she said, "He moved to Wisconsin over the summer…Green Bay, I think."

My sister looked over my left shoulder, smiled a devil's grin that had the most evil thoughts behind it.

"Here's your chance."

I was more than baffled by her witless announcement.

"Better make the best of it sick puppy," she hopped from the wall and gave me a quick peck to the cheek, as she passed by me.

I turned to catch her exit, and caught another arrival heading directly towards me; it was Sandra Miller.

She stopped; I turning to meet with her in her smile; the look from that gaze; the power of a divided moment when expressions tell a thousand thoughts without even a whisper.

"Hello Conner," she held her newly-acquired books in front of her, "When I left you before, I never thought it would take so long to see you again," she remained at her distance.

"Nor did I," I chuckled.

"I knew you would do well during the season," she said, "You can tell. Baseball is like a second nature to you."

"We all have passions Sandra," I softly replied.

"The passion of a firefighter's son?"

I looked away briefly and caught myself smiling, "I suppose."

"How was your summer?" she asked.

"Spent some of it playing ball, a trip to Vermont for a week; worked in the harbor most of the days. Need that 'working man's money.'"

I sat back down over the top of this brick wall while she stood in front of me.

Her classic blue embryos eyes now were showing a misty gray in the direct sunlight. Her long blonde hair being fluffed out by the occasional wind blowing, and played havoc with her expression as she made every attempt to hold her locks back from her look on me.

"You?" I asked in return.

"I went to Italy for three weeks, California for two more."

"Someday," I looked around, "maybe you can tell me about it. About those places I like to dream of; those ones you have gone to."

"I would like that Conner," she smiled, "What classes are you taking this year?"

I looked down at my list. I knew I couldn't remember them all in her presence, "Calculus, Advanced English, German, basic that is, Coach has me in Physical Education…"

"I know," she smiled, "P.E. doesn't sound as sophisticated as Physical Education," she looked onto her books, "Micro Biology…"

"Mr. Hanahan," I nearly folded from my seat, "I heard he is a winner. When he gets very angry, he drools. So you will have to sit close to the rear on that one…"

She had this radiance about her that the clear day we were now sitting under could have turned into a torrential downpour, and I would never have known the difference.

"Shame we don't have a class together." She suggested aloud.

"I know," I looked about and kicked a rock some clear five feet, "I could always stow-away in one of your classes. You can feed me doggy biscuits while the teacher is at the chalkboard. Let me tell you this."

"What?" she saw the exasperation in my face, and how her expression lit up so.

"My mother told me of a friend of hers that went to Georgia Tech. He and five college fraternity buddies had a mascot German shepherd name 'Busky Walls'. They signed up this dog for the four-year curriculum. Paid the tuition; each one taking turns in their specialty. They would pass that individual course under this assumed name, 'Busky'. So when it came time after the four years to graduate, and 'Busky Walls' was to get his degree and walk across the isle. His name was finally called. They all stood, escorted good ole 'Busky Walls' to the front, and had the chancellor put the diploma in the dog's mouth. Dog graduated with a 3.50 GPA."

"How in the world did they get away with that?"

"One of the boys was the College President's son." I squinted in her direction, "that's how."

She paused, began to collect herself, and gather up her things for the next class.

"It's good to see you again Conner. Wish I had more time to talk."

"Yeah," I stammered a bit like that lost schoolboy I felt myself to be then, "So do I."

"Well, I have a class in ten minutes," she took steps in retreat.

I watched her with an air of simple innocence and helplessness as she turned and walked from me.

"Listen, Sandra," I said; she spinning back to address me for the last time there. Our eyes met like they had only moments ago.

"Didn't we leave something undone before?"

"We did," she took a deep breath on this. I could see that mystery shadow her expression, like the night had fallen and cloaked the sky with its' endless darkness.

"Perhaps sometime we can continue…"

"I think we should," she weakly smiled in a thoughtful glance, "When time gives us this opportunity…We should."

"And when this time comes, you will let me know," I pursued it further. I could view, from her reflection staring back at me, the severe hesitance which had so disturbed me before and followed me throughout everyday since we last spoke.

"We will both know Conner…"

"Why the mystery Sandra?" I asked.

"Its' not that simple," she pondered, and then eased on her aggression, "When the time comes, I promise."

And with this said, she spun and walked from me. I never felt more 'emptied-out' than at that moment; this cussing equation of not knowing; that temperamental, yet fond engagement left me abandoned once more.

I was left with myself and the brisk wind which blew about; still wondering; always wondering. Sandra had abandoned me once more to my impressions, and perhaps my illusions of what may have caught us in a world of similarities. Our lives were somehow tied together by a single strand of silk, born from two different spiders; this very cross I was still clinging to.

I pulled the cross from underneath my shirt; simple, not gaudy or premium in its metal or makeup; plain, straight-line, and without the makings of a pure craftsman or qualified maker. But what it lacked in design, it made up for in tradition and soul. This simple component; this emblem and charm had the weight of the world behind its spirit.

*   *   *

The year went along without too much more fanfare in my life. Father had spent as much time at the station as before; if not more. Mother meanwhile kept good attendance on the welfare of her children; seemingly to live her life through ours.

"Fill your life with the making of pleasant memories Conner," she once said to me, while we again sat on that back porch of ours. The dimming day of a late autumn evening burst into cascades of deep red, orange, and long streaks of yellow across the slumbering skies. It was here when we could the see the airplane fume trails cut the sky like a comet in white tails.

"You owe it to yourself…Because, in the end, that is what we are left with."

"Would you come to see one of my games this year mother?"

"Oh son," she paused in her sweet smile, "Perhaps I may. Adam takes a hardship approach sometimes. The walls he builds are very hard to overcome. A little love may improve this. I will try."

"You know," I spoke freely, "Father never came to a game of mine last year."

"I know son," she gave me a pat, "It worked against his schedule so much last year. A most unfortunate thing, but I am sure he was with you in spirit; as I know he always is."

"Mother, you shouldn't make excuses for him."

"I think you know your father well," she replied, "to talk with him on your own terms. It's a simple thing being a son or daughter. But to be a parent; this makes the world a much more delicate matter. In his own way Conner, your father loves you."

"Sometimes I believe he loves the child I was," I stood from the porch and I looked out over the dipping horizon, "Not the man I am becoming. It's like we are two people in his eyes."

"Well." She looked over me softly, "You used to visit him on many occasions at the fire house. You hardly go there anymore. It's been years since you sat foot in the station. Still, he doesn't blame you for this; he never has, nor has he said so."

"I have changed," I spoke out, "I'm seeing there is more in the world to interact with…and finding myself in it."

"And this is only natural," she grinned, "It's a part of growing up son. So how can you blame him for change when you, yourself admit you have done the same? No Conner, your relationship is changing, as it always will through time."

"I suppose I don't understand."

"Imagine that," she chuckled, "Someday you will see these visions in your own children. From the point of your first step, you are beginning your own journey through a life, meant only for you. I blink? You change. I blink again? You change more. It shocks and stuns a parent sometimes. You see shadows of yourself in your own children; the little things that go so far to help you reach back in your own life and see the world as your child is now experiencing for themselves. It's a thrill and a fear Conner; to see the very same things in you son."

She came from her seat, turned me to her, and cupped my face in her hands.

"The gift of your past is the memories that you have Conner. Don't lose this, and don't be afraid. Embrace it, like it were your own child. You're no villain for growing up, nor is your father a villain for being afraid of you becoming a man. The bridge of life extends a very long way, with turns in that road which can't be seen sometimes until you are right upon them."

I thought my mother to be the wisest person I knew. Her eyes spoke to me a thousand virtues to be entrusted with there. The overwhelming warmth of her grace struck me like a rainbow I was now seeing in my mind. Her words had the wings of angels to fly by.

It was true, as my mother had spoken; Adam was going through even more depths of changes in his life, at the tender age of eleven. He had withdrawn more in his days. He was lurking back in his bedroom soon after arriving from school each evening. He would never talk very much, but stir in the well-depth stewpot of his mind, and make conversation with his soul it seemed. I worried about Adam immensely; as a brother should for his younger sibling. There were times when the family 'get-togethers' were not so complete. He would surely be present with us. However his mind wandered about as if he were in a park and saw the carefree notions of looking at everything around him.

The world had become a venture for him; a ponderous and wielding trap of confusion he desparately was sifting through, and he attempting to try to make sense of it all.

I forever made my advances to include Adam in nearly everything; to reach him and make some level of connection. He quietly and respectfully declined. There was nothing more he wanted than to descend to his room and read, write, or sketch another 'vision' he was currently having. As Adam grew older, his work became on the near side of brilliant. Teachers at school who often shivered at his inept manners during class, so longingly adored the very art he was producing. He was not a mere mathematician with the paint strokes; he was rather a master connoisseur of the soul when he brought his ideas into a painting or drawing. They told a tale of their own, and he was soon to be vastly recognized for them.

Lorie had met a young junior by the name of Matthew McDonald. He had moved to Boston just the year before. Matthew came across as a smart, witty, quite engaging boy from North Carolina, just on the outskirts of Charlotte, where his father had been transferred from, as an engineer with a sifting particles corporation. I enjoyed him much more so than Brian just a few years before; a diverse change from that overly-cultured and abusive attitude.

There was a bit of charm about Matthew; a southern, slightly-dribbling drawl which festered a bit early on, shortly after his move from the south. He held an abstract quality of sincerity, and had not an ounce of insecurity or flamboyance about him. I came to the custom of calling him 'Matty Mac' and he appeared to enjoy the gesture. Yet it was in the way he treated my younger sister that influenced my positive stance on him the most. He truly adored Lorie, and I loved him for it.

Amanda was still trapped somewhere in purity's time vault. Her spirit only grew with her ability to make longer strides in life. She was quickly turning into quite the beautiful young lady, though by her traits and personality, you might have thought she had been the quintessential offspring of the spunkiest woman alive. Not only had she provoked the attention of every boy in her grade school, but also her very active nature had landed her in virtually every conceivable after-school club. Needless to say I saw very little of Amanda during this stage in her life.

Grandmother was slowly, though inevitably spiraling down into her own enclosed world. The times of her conversing and communicating with those around her had become less and less over time. Sure, there were moments where she appeared to convey herself as she had so often before; during our holidays at her home, but they came out more remote and not quite as often as times gone by. It was a difficult sight to encounter; watching her sitting alone through much of the day as she took to viewing her favorite episodes of wrestling. That high-bred lounge chair was never to fail in giving her comfort while she rocked back and forth in it, and staring out to the screen, there occasionally petting on her tiny poodle. I made my attempts to engage her, though more often than not she said nothing. There was always a kiss left on her forehead at the end of our 'one-sided' conversations.

My father had become strangely distant with me over time. The times at the station, milked with so much warmth and humanity between us, now seemed to pass off in the distance and sit in some age of history so long ago. I did not fret over it, nor did I confront him with the matters that were sitting between us. My attention grew elsewhere as I immersed my entire energies into school, my friendship with Jason, baseball, and my thoughts of Sandra Miller.

I eagerly waited for the new season with a grand roar of anticipation. When it had finally arrived, I delved into it with all my passion and drive for success. We had won our division for a second year in a row. My batting average had escalated to well over .400, and so had my power numbers increased with my size. Jason had been one of our vital starting pitchers the full season, and having amassed a 9-2 record throughout his junior campaign.

Scouts were beginning to come and take a look at me, including scouts for the Boston Red Sox. The dream, as I had so often longed for spent many waking hours dreaming about, now seemed, in the dawn of that new and wonderful horizon, to be coming true. I think Spike would have been most proud of me. On occasion I had even seen Sandra coming to the ballgames; however Dirk was to her side at every one of them. My mother made the travels when able; Lorie was there with consummate support always; even Amanda and Adam would show up when the moon seemed to turn blue; still, my father never took any interest to attend.

We had reached the semi-finals again that next year. Up one game in a two-out-of-three series, we had taken a decisive lead late in the second game. Six outs to go for the state championship round and the coach made a decision to keep his regulars in the game. I was in my usual position of third base. The New Hanford Cardinals had the middle of their lineup due up. First man struck a ball deep between left and centerfield; a hard blazer on the base paths.

He ran about first and second as though he had fire cannons coming from his shoe soles. The shortstop took the deep throw from the leftfielder, wielded around and threw a liner which sailed nine feet high, and nearly over my head. I jumped; stretching as far as able, and then catching the runner with my left cleat as he barreled into a dive for the base bag. I spun in mid-air and twirled about in a haze and violent collision. The lights rotated so fast I had lost all scope into an incredible blur, as if the world had suddenly taken to a crazy spin.

The crowd rose, stood in silence, and came as quiet as a pin dropping on a carpet floor. I slammed hard to the ground, and slapped the earth with me shoulder in a twisted, horrible motion. I felt the pain rush through my right side like a hot poker thrusting straight through my shoulder. My body forced itself to pull away, come to a sit, and then crumble from the pain all over again.

In one fleeting moment, time had collapsed my once-promising baseball career into a fading dream. My rotatory cup on my throwing arm had been crushed beyond repair. The doctors confirmed the diagnosis a few days later, and so informed me I would never be able to have the strength in that arm to throw with the necessary force and accuracy to play baseball again.

I spent the entire summer that year fretting over this mis-guided fate. Somehow this was all a horribly confused dream and I was to soon awake from it. All it would take was a firm pinch or two from my conscious and all would be right with nature once more. It was not to be, and I had to learn to deal with personal misfortune.

There were days I sat on that porch of ours. I sifted through my thoughts as I watched the days dim on by; thinking in the same fashion as Spike must have when he was in his last days. I imagined smoking that favorite cigar he kept locked away all those years. And finally, after years of anticipation, I would pull it out, smell it from end to end for hours going on forever, and then at last take to light it. This would be the porch to my kingdom while I sat viewing those neighborhood children around in their continual play.

The puffs of smoke would rise from my exhales; the aroma smooth and sweet from the years of aging, and I would stare out with a glimpse of what could have been in my life; I now shedding a tear or two on my behalf. It was not the conclusion I had dreamed of.

"I am sorry Spike," I whispered out, "So very sorry. I let you down," was where all my thoughts seemed to end up.

"Hey Tush!" Jason came by one, unusually cool evening. He leaned his elbows over the fence, "You're going to fret your life away?"

"What's it to you frat boy?" I returned.

"A friendship," he said, "So it goes with me. Want to catch a movie?"

He seemed to smile in the face of my disappointment.

"No, I don't think so Jason. Not this evening."

"How about ice cream," he saw the shake of my head, "Doesn't appeal to you...I see."

He thought for a moment.

"I heard the Dodgers are playing the Giants tonight..."

"The last thing I want to see is baseball," I tried my own smile on for size; it didn't seem to measure up to his.

"Well—how about I pal around with you; here, at your home?"

"Maybe another time," I came from my seat and started for the door to our home.

"You know Conner," he yelled back, "You can't fret forever."

"Easy for you to say," I pulled the door open, "You still have a choice." I entered on this last phrase and I quickly went to my room.

My final year of high school was marred with the anatomy of nothing new or special to observe. I attended classes, though only half-heartedly; yet I made my grades adequate enough to enroll into Boston University. What my major would be? I had no clue at this juncture in my life.

I had seen very little of Sandra through my full senior year. Whenever I did see a glimpse of her, Dirk was always to her side. There was never a moment when we would speak during the course of this year; our lives so much more in difference than in similarities. I kept my distance and allowed nature to carry her where it may. Though still, in the soft temperament of my dreams, I hoped that someday we could share more than that mystery between us.

Jason and I decided we would attend our final Prom in stag. It was not an uncommon venture to do so, though I suppose I hadn't found anyone to match my admiration for Sandra, and it would be rather useless to make an attempt to fool even myself.

I carried the torch of a forest fire for her, yet she never knew the large extent of that flame. If she were to ask, then I would be most willing to tell her of my general and particular affections for her, but not until then. I remember coming to the front entrance and so finding my family all waiting for me to leave for the prom.

Even Jason decided, for once, he would drive for the both of us and not the other way around. My sister Lorie was all bubbling with excitement; her date Matthew by her side. Grandmother sat aloft in her chair, though she took to stare past her glasses on occasion. Adam came over and gave me a simple handshake, an earnest attempt with his smile, then a brief hug for congratulations. Mother came most tender to me; brazened with her uncontrollable smiles, and a kiss lofted on my cheek for happiness.

"I know things haven't turned out for you son as you have often dreamed, and imagined them to be," she spoke in the softest tone, "But God has a window out there for you…go find it."

"Thank you mother," I hugged her.

Father approached and gazed on me with a stiff, yet moving expression.

"Son," he said, "This is your gateway. Listen, whenever you get a chance, I would like for you to come by the station."

"How is Gerry?" I asked.

My father smiled, nearly to falter into tears, but he caught himself.

"Good," he said, "He asks for you often. He's still looking for a good singing and dancing partner."

"Still has his Nat King Cole?" I pursued further.

"Always," father laughed.

I saw the shadow of the man I once knew, and had so idolized all my life. There were memories so vast that sat in our past, like rivers and oceans of the endless seas. I could have painted then my own Picasso's with that rich texture of our connected pasts.

I gazed deep into my Father; not so much with the idol stare I once possessed, but with the enhanced view of a boy who saw his father simply as human, now growing with age in life. His temple was wrinkling and fraught with the lines of an elder statesman; those massive arms and shoulders more brought into size as I grew taller; his ears and nose now supporting reading glasses when he became tired in the evening light, and it so gave him the vintage look of a proper and decorated librarian.

I still longed for those tender talks we shared late in the evening, just before I went to bed. He would climb into my room, send a slight embrace my way, and send me off to my sleep with a gentle kiss. Those were the 'pleasant memories' my mother spoke of that were instilled in me. The days of spring when we went to the fields to play catch, pitch, and bat for hours on end. Then, as to my amazement, it struck me to the very core of my soul. My father once told me, as this echo ventured to ring in my ear; as it was with his father many years before, things change and those days of playing in the fields were left behind. Their relationship had been altered forever. This had come full circle with my father and myself; no one to blame, nor to convict of a crime never committed.

We both had simply imposed on ourselves the laws of nature and time itself. That fate had incriminated us with the inevitable spells long ago prescribed even before our times. Shadows always live in the vaults of mirrors; the reflection stares back, and one can see how time can fly as fast as an eagle in full flight. The promise and hope remain, but time pushes us forward into its own natural span and occasion.

I had grown nearly to adulthood now; father had been pushed as many years in advance as I had. The tempered spirits of us both still there; unaltered, though yielding to a new time and place we now found ourselves in.

"Father," my emotions ruptured as I came to give him an embrace. I felt his strong arms pull me back to his love.

"Son," he whispered into my ear, "Now you go and make your father a very proud old man…You hear?"

I shook my head on his release of me. Our eyes dropped and I could see my mother near to her own tears. The silent sins of a family can go years undisturbed, like someone buried in a tomb for as long. And as emotions arise, the sins are unearthed to be set free. I felt at this moment in our lives together the vault had at least been opened a portion of the way, and we found ourselves free to discover one another again.

My mother was the glue; always the glue, and held the charm to always keep the family together. Her strength was like a shield to our security. And no matter the material differences between us, we survived in that wondrous unit together.

"You'll forgive me," I backed up a bit and I sheltered my eyes from view, "This isn't the time for this."

"It's alright son," father patted me on the shoulder.

"It just shows a son that is human," mother gave me a kindly hug, "Now you do as your father asked."

I bowed my head, caught Jason in my eyesight, and we backed out the door. I could feel the calm air, sweet as the freshly cut grass smell, so burn into a cool night aroma.

"Touching," Jason said as we went from porch to sidewalk.

"What do you mean?" I stopped to look straight on him.

"Your folks," he kept in step, "Touching."

The thunder of what had happened to Jason when we were still boys dreaming of the big leagues, there as we sat on the ball field that day, so came rushing towards me like the ghost he had deposited in his own grave many years before. I felt a sense of sympathy settle in me.

"Oh no Jason," I sounded off.

"No, no," he waived me off, "It's ok…really."

"I know we would never discuss this again," I said, "I promised you that. I'm one for my word."

"Don't." He stopped me short, "Just remember, next time you want to fret over losing your baseball career. Think of what you have; the good things," he paused, "I may have a nickel on you for a baseball career now, but you have a whole dollar over me when it comes to family; maybe more. You don't forget; not for a second."

To this day, I would never forget.

Chapter 15

The Mystery is Revealed.

As the tradition goes, the yearly prom is held directly on the bay at one of the towering hotels adjoining the inlet. Whether stag or with a date, it was always enjoyable attending this affair the three years I had gone. This year however, Jason and I had decided to go as good-ship rogues, and to be the fancy of the party; dancing with whomever we liked; courting whomever we wished to court.

I thought it might be prevalent to put a good front; inwardly noting how I fondly felt for Sandra Miller all these years. It was easier on me to 'show' myself in one manner, than to make it apparent I was a love-lost puppy, and I would be cast out by the ire of all my friends.

The hotel was a mass of beautiful, modern ingenuity and its sister gardens unmatched by any within the city of Boston. I could see the lighted structure as if it were sitting on the shoreline like a lighted castle drawing me within its drawbridge.

We entered somewhere about six or so, and found the largest dance floor packed from outer wall to outer wall. I was quickly greeted by a mass of classmates; girls and boys, meeting with smiles and hugs from all over.

Jill English was the first to arrive (as was always the case). Tall, fluffed hair to the tower length over her crown, speckled green eyes, dazzled teeth that were cut through by her smile and a constant bevy of shorter girlfriends to her sides. She was quite the angel to look upon, but the problem arose when she spoke. It sounded as if her throat was draining through her nasal passages, and somehow her tongue was caught in between both. This made for a most abnormal resonate which did nothing more but to sit painfully on my nerves when I was close to her.

Beth Rochester was the next to greet me; the class president and brilliant mathematician who had the prestigious honor of holding a scholarship to Harvard for the coming year. I always held great admiration for Beth. Through the years of her painful teenage upbringing and hard-nosed transformations she went though; above and beyond her times, there was no one who suffered more repetitive jokery, picking on, and general torment than her. I always thought she would be the perfect plaintiff in a lawsuit against those who made fun of her all those years. This alone would have made her independently wealthy for the rest of her life. It was non-stop and hard core, yet somehow she managed to prevail. And in fact, excel far greater than most in our class.

She was the most perceptive person I had known in high school, and was only second to my mother in this regard. We had many conversations; Beth and I, and I had always known we would have a fruitful friendship long after high school. But she was a dismal sufferer in the 'looks' department. Call me 'shallow' if you may, but our relationship stopped at being good, quality friends.

Frail, engrossingly bony and shapeless; you would have thought of her more of a stick than to carry a figure. Her throat protruded from her profile, as did her long, down-turned nose, with glasses sitting atop of it that never really seemed to fit her. Her hair was coarse and plastered all about her head, though she carried a lovely smile when she took to grin or even laugh.

"She is here Conner," Beth smiled and composed herself, "And she has asked for you."

"Who?" I looked around, knowing full well who that may be.

"Oh Conner," Beth smiled and pushed me by the shoulder, "I think after three years, word has gotten around."

"You're speaking of Sandra," I inclined.

"Who else would it be?" she said, "She's a lucky girl."

"And how is that?" I gazed down at Beth with a curious stare.

She said nothing; though smiled one final time, took a sip of her punch, as the glass she lifted seemed to drown her face in its juice.

"Why the mystery Beth?"

"There's no mystery," she said; dropping the glass down, "Mystery to those who don't know it."

"Beth," I was trite, "Stop with the riddles."

"Dirk left early," Beth replied, "She seemed most hopeful to see you Conner."

I saw a smirk rise out of the corner of her lips.

"You presume too much," I pulled her chin into my hand.

"I just hope she responds the same way I would," she looked deep into my eyes, "If you looked at her in that similar fashion…She's in the garden; waiting, wondering if you will come."

"And what if I don't want to go?"

"You do," she quickly responded, "You always have."

I looked atop and saw the enormous chandelier above the master floor glisten with bright sparkles as I past away from Beth. The nut cake, fingers and sandwiches all strung out along the tables; the punch bowls lined up with cups turned downward on others; the banners reigning high 'Welcome Seniors! Last Dance!'; the rolls of different colored paper hanging about in angles; the band enroute to another rocking tune, slow melody, and then another current hit; the echoes, the cheers.

I looked about at the faces of my classmates. I wondered how they would change over time; what would be our reunion picture in another twenty years; where some would stay, where some would go. We to be sprung out of our safety nets like tadpoles in a very big pond.

My hands grew into a sweat; my thoughts nervous with some unknown anxiety; the heart into a flutter and sensing some trauma and resolution coming all in the same stroke. I could have wished on this moment for a thousand years and never believe it to come, yet find the strength to let it be or proceed with promise. I felt the wage of war within me, like the battle of two unidentified forces wrestling for a distinct cause.

I pressed to the outer reaches of that wide dance hall. There, in the glittery realm of that enchanting garden, I could see the black light posts beam soft shadows and embers all throughout those grounds. The elegant benches were trimmed in black, unattended and sprawled about in every seeming avenue. There sat every imaginable flower color in pockets of individual segments, as if a rainbow had landed from the sky and planted all of its beautiful colors there. My hand pushed the door free and I could feel the cooler air grow colder still.

My eyes trimmed around the immediate surroundings; no Sandra. I walked a lonely step; my tipped shoes clipping the sidewalks as I went; my hands now resting in the bed of my pant pockets. I appeared to be the body of a restless soul there; stepping as I did in some unforeseen pace, and holding the trance look of a dazed man in my expression. I was losing my breath and I could feel it. I stalled, leaned out over a fountain; the dance of a woman; her eyes sitting out in Heaven; her hands raised and aloft, and her tears flowing through the fountain and dropping on the makeshift rose petals below. I wondered what she must have been thinking then.

"Hello Conner," I heard Sandra's voice behind me.

I turned, engaged her from eye to eye. That most powerful locking, as though we were meant to stare at each other for an eternity. Those soft-glowing pupils were staring directly over me; unwaivered, intent, and sheltering no reservation this time, nor harboring the thoughts of another. I knew this was our time now.

The earth stood still; the dotting nightlights above were brimming out their own special, engaging glow. I could sense Heaven's softer ear now pressed on the window of our conversation.

"I am at a loss Sandra," I couldn't bear to look at her.

I thought she had the dream of a princess in her there.

"Why should you be at a loss?"

She took a few steps towards me. I still kept my look at an angle; feeling the weight of hers on me and staring down my very essence.

"So stunning," I blew out some air, "I never thought…"

"We would speak again?" She finished my sentence.

"Maybe," I glanced over at her.

Sandra was dressed in a flowing, tapered white dress that seemed like the bright glow of sunshine in the middle of that night. Pure white gloves trimmed all the way up her elbows; her hair was to flow the golden spinster weave of the most glorious meadows, and so radiated when she turned her head about. Her smile nearly fell off her lovely expression, and then some distant thought evolved it into a frown.

"I guess we can both be at a loss."

I paused; more cautious to my words, then, "We haven't talked in nearly two years; again. A guy might become quite self-conscious, waiting, perhaps, for a chance to speak with a girl like you again."

I waited for her approval.

"You think?"

"It wasn't by design Conner," she moved slightly forward.

"How was it then?" I wondered, "Accidentally," I grinned, "Consciously," thought again, "Sub-consciously?"

"None of the above."

"Suppose I am at a loss again Sandra," I nearly fell back into my turtle shell, "Have I ever done anything to offend you?"

"Not ever," she moved a little closer, "You shouldn't think such a thing. Perhaps I was waiting for the right time."

"You seem pretty picky," I giggled.

"Particular," she closed her eyes and shook her head.

"Must be important," I kept hiding in my empty shadow there.

"Important enough to wait for that perfect timing."

"Well," I finally took a step towards her. There was a measure of silence as I looked out over the fountain, and I could feel the trickle of those waters in my mind.

"It's a shame things meant to be said, were never said."

"Never said," she placed her hands behind her back; twisting even closer, "but not lost. Sometimes you dream of something, and no matter how hard you try, the dream just seems too wonderful to awake from. You're afraid, that if you cause that dream to try to come true, then maybe what does come true, doesn't seem like it should have been at all. So you keep that dream, safe, secure; hoping someday that a perfect time does arrive."

"Are we talking about the same thing?" I asked.

"I think so," we were now only a few feet apart from one another; our eyes no longer hidden in the distance, nor cast in the shadows of any other than our own gaze. I nearly could feel her thoughts penetrate mine; her eyes motioning with words and a language of their own; wanting, needing some validation from mine.

"I have always wondered Sandra," I whispered.

"What is it?" she whispered back.

"How it would be," I said, "like you."

"How do you think it would be?"

"I can nearly taste it Sandra…"

"Then why don't you?" Her expression nearly engulfed mine.

Our lips met only for a brief interlude; that warm touching from two lives meaning to connect; the heart stopping in the very drowning notion of that moment; time spilling its seconds into what seemed an infinite spell. The magic; ever breathtaking and once so illusive, now stirring emotions and affections never imagined before that time.

"How was it?" she whispered through a smile.

"Umm," my voice cracked, "more than I ever dreamed."

"Like; kissing a dream?"

"Kissing hope; and finding it better than kissing a dream."

"Mr. James?" She pulled me into a hug.

"Yes Sandra," I held her close.

"I've never known anyone in my life that I felt more comfort with, and yet spent so little time knowing."

I pulled her away as we sat at the foot of that fountain. I found myself staring entirely on the necklace hanging about her neck; the very necklace which I had sitting beneath my coat and shirt.

"There's more of a connection than a necklace here."

"There's more to this than you know."

"Then tell me Sandra."

I brought my look into the deepest well of her eyes; searching, hoping to find the very substance of it all; to compel the mystery to be no more; to have the certainty of knowing rather than to ponder the variable reasons for everything, and not knowing, not ever knowing.

"Someone gave you this," she cupped my necklace with her soft, engaging hand, "someone most dear to you, more so than you ever realized. This someone gave me the very same gift."

"I felt that might be the case Sandra," I replied, "But I never knew for sure, if in fact Buck may have or not. How do you know him?"

I felt her hand grasp into mine.

"Do you know how much he cared for you Conner?"

"No," I swallowed deep. I caught her look as it began to smile. She was reflecting; her head tilting to one side.

"There were days he would speak of you. It was like looking in a window and seeing a young boy though the eyes of my grandfather, and seeing someone who was more special than special."

I nearly choked on her last sentence when she said this.

"Buck was your grandfather?" I asked.

"He was more than that Conner," her head bowed on this.

"I never saw you Sandra," I said, "In all that time; in the fire station; going to his home; being around his wife. I didn't see any pictures, no talk of you; just his daughters."

"I was there Conner," she whispered, "You just never noticed me before. I was simply invisible to you."

My heart nearly froze when she uttered these words out to me.

"How can I be so blind?" I shuttered, "It was me…all these years, it was me; not you."

I looked out from us. I was nearly stunned by what I felt and how it was all revealed to me. The mystery now wearing away, and I finding that the very heart of it all lay not behind some corner, nor in the belly of some unknown secret, but right before me; so close to me as to have blinded me from its very presence there. I looked back on my past for some evidence that I had overlooked her so long ago.

"I believe the apology is all mine Sandra…"

She grinned and nearly wept in that same expression; so grabbing my hand into a tight squeeze. It was there I first saw her cry; a tear dripping into the pool of her face.

"No need to regret anything Conner. You were as warm as if I had known you long ago. My grandfather had given me more than a glimpse of you. I saw, through him, the very boy you were; and now, the very man you are becoming; now with my own eyes."

She wept freely, "I wouldn't change a thing…"

"My mother always told me that whatever you do in life; never do anything you can never forgive yourself for…"

"What is it about my grandfather you regret?"

"That I miss my friend," I cried in the shadow of her tears.

"I miss my grandfather," she said; pressing her lips to mine, "He had the rare gift of giving; giving not of things, but of himself."

"Well he brought us together," I softly spoke.

"It was what he wanted," she agreed, "How was he on that day? Can you remember?"

I took in a deep sigh, closed my eyes into my thoughts, and looked backed on a time I would have rather forgotten. But a time I would revisit just for Sandra.

"He died trying to help others." I began. "They pulled him from the burning building. My father and Gerry went to the rear of the house, as I did. We were looking for an entrance to pull him and the other firemen free. When I returned to the front, there he was laying on the front lawn. They tried to save him."

I shook my head.

"But he was gone…Sandra."

I looked back on her expression with a thought-provoking look of my own.

"I felt him leave; at that very moment. I could sense him pass by me, touch my shoulder, give me a final look, and then slip away. Gerry later gave me the necklace; told me Buck had wanted him to make sure I received it if anything happened to him. He said I would know how to take care of it; to honor it like it was my own."

"And now it is your own," she smiled halfway.

"Only half to its purpose Sandra…"

"So what is the other half?" She asked.

"I don't know. When one mystery is solved; another is born."

"Devotion?" she supplied a possible answer. I watched her stand and walk about me. Through my glancing at her, I could envision the moonlight coming to brush her hair with its white fertile glow.

"Perhaps duty? Maybe Love?" She paused to stare me down.

"Don't know Sandra," I could barely keep my eyes on hers.

"Think about it Conner," she sat next to me, "My grandfather picked you like a flower out of a whole garden."

"I'm just a simple fireman's son; nothing special; someone who is willing to work hard and make a living for himself."

"And make do?" she questioned.

"Yeah..." I replied.

"Conner," she fretted, "Whatever happened to your dreams of becoming a baseball player?"

"They died," I said, "when my shoulder gave out."

"You don't understand," she pressed her hands in mine, "Those dreams came from somewhere. Invent another one, or two, or even three. Conner; blink for me one time. Close your eyes, and invent a new life and hope for yourself."

I thought in that moment while I had her attention fully engaged with me. I pressed my eyes into a shut, thought of something; anything I could to appease her with, and then slowly re-open my look to find her still staring directly over me with a goofy smile on her face.

"Well?" she asked.

"Well," I echoed reluctantly.

"Well?" she forced the issue.

"Well," I repeated her word like a stupid bird.

"Well..." her stare tossed over into a stern look, "The world doesn't end on the baseball diamond you know."

"I know," I tried to calm her, "But it's not so easy; takes time to think of something."

"Well, you don't have much of that left. You're graduating in a few weeks." She insisted.

I stood and spun about the circle of that glittering fountain we sat around. The stars were all in full beam now, as the night drew deeper into its course. The caress of a lonely wind curled about me and gave me a shiver. Sandra stepped to my side, and so aided me with her arm underneath mine.

"We come from different places."

"I know," I replied, still eye-cast on those stars above, "Is that why we have hardly spoken all these years Sandra?"

"Partly," she bowed her head from me, "Fear has as much in the equation as anything."

"What are you afraid of?"

I grabbed her hand into mine.

She leaned up to me, with a shadow of worry mixed with sorry in her expression. There were more answers in her look then than I cared to see for my own self; the connection, so gifting that so few people have, now playing robbery with my hope. I too had fear. For this very reason, I felt Sandra would reject me.

"Of you," she was more cautious, "Of what 'us' will bring. That our worlds would never mix. That I could love you more than I would have ever known love to be like, and then discover what I had so wanted could never be for me. Like standing on the sidewalk of a shop just before Christmas; seeing the most favorite doll I could ever want; asking for it, but I could never go in to get that doll. Somehow, something I wished for was never meant to be."

"So you turn away from your dream," I remarked, "we are not as different as you might think. There are more alike than different Sandra."

I felt her pull away, cross to the other side of the walkway, and bend over to smell the flowers near to her feet. She picked out the tallest purple tulip, bent it close to its stem, turned about to face me, and hand me the flower as if it were the very core of her heart she was giving to me.

"I love you Conner. I have always loved you. Even before we ever met, I loved the dream of you. The little boy my grandfather saw growing up in that fire station, to the young man you are becoming; to the man you will become. I see shadows and I see the shades of you. And I know deep in my heart that if there was ever a man I should love all my life, that it would be you Conner."

My eyes grew double the size they normally were. I felt the pronouncement of her words strike me with the unexpectant force of their enormous meaning. I placed my hands about as if I had been kindly stung by an air of a sudden gust wind. It was futile for me to attempt to gather my balance, though I bent back on the rock wall and pulled her with me, into a sit. This was more than a shock to me; to hear these words coming from Sandra, from the very breath she swore on me at that moment.

"Conner?" she made tries to get my look back on hers. I stalled, gathered my emotions in check, and then took to kneel there before her.

"I never imagined Sandra," I nearly cried and laughed all in the same sentence, "That the one I had fallen for when I first laid eyes on her so many years before; the one who kept my thoughts and dreams trapped in her every care from that moment on; that she would ever say those words to me that I just heard. I simply never imagined it to be Sandra."

"What are you telling me?"

"In my heart, I knew you long before we ever met on that baseball field. The feelings and emotions for you had long-started; the meeting we shared was only a preclusion to it all."

She bent close to me; face to face, with her hands now cupping my cheeks in a wealth of affection. This nearly made me crumble from its strength.

"Then it wasn't my imagination," she smiled in high fancy, "Tell me Conner; a woman never wants to be deprived from hearing…"

She interrupted herself in hopes I would continue.

"That I love you Sandra," I spawned, "That I have always loved you. Like the virtue of a first-born memory that is never forgotten, that such a love like this exists for you; from me."

I felt her lips press to mine and lovingly impose the rapture of a dream I once envisioned. It was now turning into a time, a place, a setting, a reality.

"I will always value this," she nearly wept.

"What do you mean?" I pulled back in confusion.

"My life is already set," I saw the gushing river of her tears drip as though they were droplets from a window, "I'm to leave for Stanford soon after graduation. My father has me in a pre-law program."

"But Sandra," I was angry, "Why would you say these things; knowing full well you were leaving to go across country?"

"I have my own mysteries as well," she said.

I stood to face her; my breath pulsating, my heart racing like a lions' roar.

"To be satisfied?" I fussed, "Then when all is well made like a good bed, you just get up and leave?"

"It not that easy Conner."

"You're right!" I shouted, "It's not that easy."

I pulled her close by her shoulders, and I forced her look into mine,

"It's never that easy. This is about Dirk, isn't it?"

"He's going as well," she shied away from me, "It was a mutual agreement we made several years ago."

"Love," I snapped, "There are two kinds of love aren't there Sandra…"

I moved over to the fountain with my face away from hers.

"No," she stepped, thought better of it, and remained, "Only one. There is always only one."

"Then you love us both." I suggested.

"I didn't say that," she countered.

"Then what are you saying?"

I spun to meet with her again.

"Enlighten me. What is this all about? The purpose; the reason; me being here with you…here; now; like this; as we are."

"If I had met you a few years ago; really met you, and knew how you felt, then none of this would have ever occurred."

"I suppose fate slept too long then."

"The princess did," she caught her tears and weakly grinned, "and the prince as well…"

"You can't reduce this into a fairy tale."

I pushed past her, yet she took hard grip on my hand and pulled me near. The trimming blues of her eyes made me gasp. The reflections bore a soul which mirrored mine. The deep waters of her gaze floated from their surface and showed to me more than a glimpse of the woman she was, but a whole lifelong endeavor of that search she was currently under to find herself.

"I hope someday you discover the very things you are looking for."

"I already have," she whispered, "But this isn't a farewell."

"Then what is it?" I asked.

"Until…"

"Until?" I pushed her further on it.

"I don't like 'goodbye's,'" she brought her face closer to mine. I felt the kind shelter of her stare glow like a mid-summer's day, bright sunrise.

"Don't ask me to wait," I shut my eyes from her, "I couldn't possibly bear the want of someone I can never be with."

"Who was asking you to?"

"Maybe you; maybe me; maybe the both of us."

"Perhaps," her hand wiped away the stray tear which was falling from my one eye, "I can always believe in miracles."

"I am at a loss Sandra…"

"Tell you what," she smiled in a reckless sort of way, "How about you and I take a walk. Think of time as nothing more than a passing car on the road. Just you and I making up for time lost, and enjoying the evening we can now share together. It's our last prom, and I want the memories of you and me sitting, here, always," she took to cup her heart with her soft hands.

I said nothing more, though I captured her hand in mine for that promised stroll she held so dear to her. We strayed through the gardens as if we were the proud owners of them. The rising moonlight glittered all along the waters there; reflections bore a thousand stars flickering on that bay front. Lamplights gleamed in single file and streamed out along the other side. I could feel the soft pats of our shoes echo in sweet temperament as we walked in slow procession; her hand in mine. I saw her smile gaze up to me a multitude of times, that I most quickly lost count of. I could tell she had never quite been so happy before our time that evening.

My heart bled with joy and bittersweet thoughts there. The counter emotions of having all that I dreamed of more near than I could imagine, and the restless notion it would all disappear in a few short hours, so made the hourglass tip on its side and quit counting the sand droplets rushing through its cylinders. Our conversations were warm and inviting; filling up with laughter and the sweetest reflections.

Our lives had finally crisscrossed in a rather unique way. The joys of that moment so readily outweighed the reality which awaited us for the 'tomorrows' to come. It was our single refuge. Like a box of a 'temporary time' where we could see the worlds of each other, now together and happily engaged. I felt myself to be a star who had lived all its live for this moment; to grow in intensity and shine for all to see, as if there wasn't another brighter soul out there except for Sandra's. It was inevitable we would fade from one another, for as we moved outside the gardens and along the walkways, and having a sudden brush of wind blow us into one another, we made our final kiss escape from time itself.

I could feel her heart beat the same breath and rhythm of my own there. Our eyes closed into that escaping world; a world where we found Heaven had stopped by to give us a glimpse of what true happiness meant. Her hands gripped onto mine as though she were falling from her cliff; mine holding on tighter as though to prevent her from going. The world had suddenly disappeared and we were at last alone. Silence prevailed in what seemed to be an infinite measure of stringed-together moments.

The waves dipped to clip the dock, cup the walkway, and then secede out into that harbor night. Moments later, it would begin again, like a water dance in spring. I felt Sandra touch me with her soul.

We parted; our eyes rose into one another; the words elapsed into further silence; nothing said; the moment striking us into a mute persuasion. She nearly stalled on her heavy breathing; I touching her with the back of my hand to her cheek.

"Mr. Conner James," she delicately whispered, "If a woman's heart could ever be permanently captured, then you have done so tonight. I have been truly swept away by you."

"And what will tomorrow bring?"

I whispered in return.

"The knowledge of knowing I have lost something more dear to me than anything," she nearly wept and bowed.

"It doesn't have to be that way," I was careful not to try to influence her anymore than necessary, "But, in the same fashion, you are free to do as you wish. Sandra, if I were to have to persuade you to remain, then you weren't meant to be with me anyway. And I couldn't live with this."

"A life already set," she pondered, "The wrong life."

"Only you know which life is for you..."

"Conner James," she smiled and placed her arms around my neck, "For a fireman's son, you are a pretty smart fella..."

"And Sandra Miller," I included, "For a fireman's granddaughter, you're not so bad yourself."

We walked a short distance further before we found an entire clan of fellow prom-goers holding display out over these gardens.

"Is it midnight yet?" I sorrowfully spoke out.

"Conner," she whispered, "I'll love you for a lifetime of midnights."

With one further squeeze of my hand, she was quickly led away by that mob. Our eyes touched the sight of one another for one, last parting glimpse; and so I mouthed the word 'until' to her; waving a partial wave, and seeing her fall from my view. I spun to the walkway railing, moved to the edge of that water, and contributed my own tears to that bay then.

"Conner!" I felt Jason come up to my rear and slap my back, "Where have you been??"

I hid my expression away from Jason in order to recollect myself once more.

"Jason, you have rotten timing."

"Sorry friend," he backed off a bit, "You with Sandra?"

"In a manner of speaking," I remarked, "yes."

"You game for somewhere else?"

"Just for home," I gathered myself, "I think I'm ready."

Before long I found myself driving home with a complex, sullen daze riding in my face. I felt my heart had been discovered, and then become prodigal all in that same evening. I could hear a hundred violins dribble weakly through a never-ending love song, and so cut my heart from its own, normal sensibility.

I believe I wrestled with my soul the full evening through. I stared out that same window from early childhood. I wandered about aimlessly in my thoughts; dreaming a world of another place, seeking asylum to where my hopes had laid a passageway to. Every ending, ended with Sandra; every scenario played out with her in it; every future memory basked in the sunshine of her lighting. Yet, even still, as I crossed into every moment afterwards, I had become accustomed to that disappointment of not having her with me. It was here that sleep caught me from behind and took me into my rest. The night was no more; I would awake into tomorrow.

Chapter 16

Fate can be Friend and Foe.

Four years had passed and I was soon to graduate from Boston University. Not a grand scholar mind you, but adequate to the purpose. I had pondered my major for as long as able; and still suit the requirements of the college to garner a four-year degree in that similar amount of time; in political science with a minor in theater no less. This was a far cry from the young boy who wished to be a professional baseball player for the Boston Red Sox. To feel the pine; smell the freshly cut grass of Fenway Park; hear the constant roars from that eager crowd, and so make myself a legend within the city; as much as my father had become in a different sense.

As pertaining to Jason himself, he went on to gain a scholarship with Boston College, pitch for two years, and then would be drafted in the fourth round by the Boston Red Sox. It was rather surprising that he was assigned initially to their double-A team in Portland, but I suppose the scouts were very high on him. Jason became a tall, thoroughbred style pitcher with long, lean strides, powerful legs and a limber combination shoulder and left arm. Left-handed pitchers were a high commodity, especially one who had a 12-to—6 table dropping curve, and a fastball with late movement, which reached 95-96 mph late in games.

During Jason's first year in the minors, I managed a trip out west to see him pitch a pivotal game late in the year. He ended up 12-2 with an impeccable earned run average. The next year, he spent his entire season at Pawtucket, and so going 11-4 and becoming the Red Sox's top pitching prospect. He came into spring training the year of my college graduation as a probable fourth or fifth starter in the Red Sox's rotation. A duo achievement, since we both were on the verge of accomplishing something most prolific in our lives, and we were treating it as a double victory on both our parts. In a great sense I felt Spike would have been most proud for the both of us.

I was indeed balancing late season exams with coming out to see Jason during practice and warm-ups. My pride for him swelled beyond my wildest dream when I first saw him step to the mound with that Red Sox jersey number 44 saddled over his shoulders. Was I disappointed I had not joined him on that rise to our mutual dream? In a small way, yes. But I also felt him living our dream for the both of us, and so by that honor to our friendship, the victories were always for 'us'.

Lorie had achieved significant success in her own right; landing a prestigious award during high school. This ultimately won her a partial scholarship to Harvard. She had created a fancy for chemical engineering, with a particular interest in biochemical studies. Lab work appealed to her in every sense, and the hope was she would work for a pharmaceutical company upon her graduation.

Amanda evolved into quite the show woman; so diving into the disciplines and voyages of the theater itself. She had become quite accomplished in her attributes there, been the headliner to many school and local community plays, held rave reviews from many district newspapers, and soon found her self being accepted into Boston University as well.

Adam still remained as he was. Now a late-blooming junior in high school, he hardly ever ventured much beyond his room or the crypts of a library. He was constantly summoned to his drawings and sketches like the mad man he seemed to be becoming. I knew he was hard driven; that inert passion which wreathes a man's souls sometimes, and equates his life to that single virtue he wishes to acclaim. I feared my brother Adam was quickly closing in on this. He had virtually shut off all those close to him, and so swindled himself out of all the social worlds he could have involved himself with. School was a by-product; something required so you scrape by, barely making it through. He excelled in art and English but brutally failed in the far reaches of his other studies; such as biology, mathematics, and economics.

The world had become estranged to him, and he, an equal partner in this relationship. His work was nearing the stage of brilliant, maddening, and all-consuming. Mother fretted mostly over Adam. He was her baby charm, and it did nothing to appease her to see him fail away into what seemed a matter of his intent and destiny. I shadowed her, watched her, felt the pains of her wound, and sensed the inner struggles she bore herself in keeping 'hope' alive for Adam. There were times I made attempt to break through his icy ways, yet to no avail. He turned me away as though I were a light switch on the wall.

My relationship with my father began to improve over time. I was no longer the studious and eagerly attending son I used to be; the pint-size boy who always wore his father's fire suit whenever he asked me to. I began to visit the fire station 112 once more. Gerry had aged a bit; the others likewise, though from time to time I would stay and rekindle the times we all shared many years before.

Mother had graced her beauty with age now. The raven hair and locks were more distinct in their premature graying. There was a settled look in her expression, as if she were aging with ease, and allowing it to happen without any complaints. Our relationship had blossomed into a realm I could never have anticipated before this time. The memories were growing into a long-stretching movie through life. And I felt her engaging words commence with mine with just a look, or even a slight off-centered glance towards me.

Our conversations held more of her teachings and the times we shared. The reminiscing was long, slow, and had been engulfing the better part of our evenings together. During the winter months she would ask of me to make out a fire, stoke it high and warm so as not to disturb it for another hour; then our conversations would begin. During the summer evenings spent together, we would settle on the back porch as we always did, and see the sunset dive into a surreal, evening glow. She talked of Easter; her joy in making the girls matching dresses for the grand Sunday service; of the times when she would allow us to have friends over to stay overnight, having the sleeping bags all sprawled out, or making up the tents in the backyard. There was even a Christmas where she played Santa Claus for all the children; of course having a pre-recorded 'dub-over' of a man's voice playing in the background.

On one occasion, she read me her thoughts of when her own father passed away.

"'*I feel a sense of departure from myself. I pray these words and writings carry my thoughts through time and are sufficiently inscribed for those beyond me to read; to reflect, and to understand the joys and sorrows I experienced through my own life. It's the true witness and testament to the woman I was, I am, I will become. These are the cherished lessons I transfer over to you.*'"

"Why didn't you write mother?" I asked.

"Then I would never have been the mother I am," she smiled in her sweet, happily-induced manner, "In the hopes you become the man I think you should be. Conner? My greater service has always been to you, Lorie, Amanda, and Adam. What other greater quest could I endure and love better? No…I'll let the word masters tell a good tale…You have always been my greatest concern."

"What about father?" I asked.

"Oh!" she waved me off and giggled, "He can take care of himself."

Grandmother had remained with us through many of those years. Her general demeanor had spiraled more prominently into the worlds and outlays of her hallucinations. It had come to the point that she neither indulged conversation with us, nor made any conscious choice to be a part of our lives. She would sit in her rocker in one corner of the family room, look disconcerted and most involved with her delusions, grabble with her inner spirits, and only occasionally come out to eat or nap.

However on that year's Mother's day, the oddest occurrence took place; one where Fate could either take a turn as friend or foe. Our celebration lasted much of that early afternoon; I sitting across the way of my grandmother and drinking about my tea. Mother and Amanda were gathering up all the dishes and cleaning about the kitchen. Lorie had left for the day while father had duty at the firehouse till Tuesday evening. Adam, as always, expired quite early to his room, nearly mute and oblivious throughout the Sunday lunch.

I watched grandmother seem to wave a fly from her face that didn't exist. Her stare was most constant and without blinks; her mouth went into a fanatical though silent muttle, and her legs nervously bounced up and down on her stool.

"Grandmother," I leaned in on her with an inspectful eye, "Do you hear me? Grandmother," I jiggled the glass near her face; still, no response, "Well, I would hope you at least try."

Still nothing.

I leaned into my chair, gazed skyward to the ceiling, and watched the fan lazily move counter-clockwise. I still was hoping I could count the number of revolutions it made in one minute.

"Grandmother Ashley," I turned my attention back to her, "Are you ever going to come back to us?"

Still, only silence.

There was a bit of grace which fell over her expression; eyes now dimmed from the long years of experience. They seemed to be swimming in those long years from a place and time ages ago. We sat about; my look shadowing hers, though she was somehow displaced; deaf and mute to her surroundings all the while. I watched as she pulled that half-heart locket from below her blouse, and began slowly stroking it with her three fingers. The knots in her joints were overgrown and brittle; the fingers coarse and ancient that now presently hurt when in use; her glassy stare still remained.

I pulled myself from my seat, spun about to face the exit when I heard the softest voice reach for me.

"Conner," grandmother muddled out a whisper; I returned to see her still thumbing her locket, "Is that you Conner?"

I came closer and I felt the weight of her call, calling me. I pulled my body into a single knee before her. She took her hands, lowered her once hollowed-out eyes directly into mine, cupped her fingers squarely about my face in support, and frowned in confusion.

"Is this you?" she asked, "You have certainly changed."

"A bit older grandmother," I responded, "but it's me." I smiled.

"My," she swore, "You have changed."

"Just grew up a little," I was sad-eyed, "is all."

"I have missed you boy," she faintly grinned; those parched and hungry eyes for her grandson now glowing.

"You have been good to your parents since we last spoke…"

"I tried," I responded.

"I knew you were a good boy," she kept her smile locked, "I'm glad you have come to see me. Not often a woman my age has visitors. House is a mess, but you will have to excuse me. I haven't had a chance to clean it lately."

I looked about and kindly gave her a pat on her hands as she lowered them to her lap.

"How have you been?" I asked.

"Lonely," she grimaced, "But still in good spirits."

"So where have you been grandmother?"

"Why Conner," she nearly laughed, "been right here, at my house. Was wondering when you would come to see me."

"Well," I smiled, "I am here."

"Oh!" she looked strong on me, as if to dispatch her own investigation, "You loved once."

"What do you mean?" I whispered.

"You loved once," she winked on me, "I can see that spark in you. It only comes when you have loved once."

"How perceptive," I replied, "Yes I did."

"Find her," she stressed; pulling her locket out further, and strumming it with her fingers more quickly.

"Find her…" I repeated.

"Yes…Find her," she drug out the cross from underneath my shirt, and started to strum it in the same fashion.

"You see? She carries the other half, as Charles did for me."

"I don't know where she is."

"Find her," she continued.

"It's not that simple grandmother Ashley."

"Easier than living your entire life without her," she pressed on me, with a point of her finger, "Now you go find her. Don't dally."

"And what if I don't?"

"You will," she gazed more deeply into my eyes, "The winter of life will be easiest for you if you do. It will become the most important thing you ever do Conner. Don't live your life always looking back; forever looking back, and 'regret' staring back at you."

"You're something grandmother," I smirked.

"She must be a most beautiful woman," she stopped me.

"The most," I looked off to the side, then back to her, "Like a sunrise and a sunset. She made a choice to go."

"Then find her…" she leaned back into her rocker, "I must go now Conner. Little tired…Must get my rest…"

I could see by that dimming flicker in her eyes she was returning back into the isolated world she had resided in for so many years. That lost hope she spoke of, when the history of your life is unchanged, yet grips and holds you in the remainder of your days, is something you never take lightly. It was the first moment I had placed my prom evening with Sandra in such importance. I had not seen Sandra since that evening; nor had I mentioned her to anyone in the past four years. She had been buried with that hope for as long as I could remember. No one else was allowed to enter. And I found myself doing the very same withdrawals that my brother had encircled himself with, though with a different motive. Still, the end results were the same.

I knew I was still in love with Sandra and there would never be another who could ever come as close to knowing my heart as she. Grandmother was right; I noting the long affects to that incurable disease she was still possessed with. There was no cure; not even a prayer for one. Just sustain the symptoms and go on with your life as best as you can. Grandmother had found her remedy; the memories of old to replay again and again.

"You rest now," I sweetly whispered to her as I rose from that kneel. I placed a tender kiss to her forehead.

She leaned back and disappeared from me without a trace. That glassy-eyed stare returned and softened by the light.

"No one has to know grandmother," were my last words to her.

"Son?" I heard my mother's voice call me from my rear, "Its' Jason. He is on the phone and wishes to speak with you."

There was a pause in that silence when I kept my look to my grandmother. I had hoped she might glance up at me once more; nothing came, but for the constant shadows of her placid expression.

"Is anything wrong?" Mother asked. I turning to her, walking to her side, and placing a hug around her neck.

"Happy Mother's day mother," I announced as her hug came more firm now. We released and I spotted her happy smile grab a hold for my affections.

"Thank you son," her chin wrinkled through her grin.

"Conner," Amanda smarted, "telephone."

I went into the back bedroom; saw the old glimmer of my mother's lamplight shower light over the black phone next to her large cast-iron bed. It was sitting atop the nightstand next to it.

"Hello Jason," I picked up the phone.

"You busy?" his voice returned back over the line.

"Well," I reminded him, "It is Mother's day."

"Ahh," he sarcastically proposed, "Good observation bright one. Now. I have something for you."

There was a pause as we both went deaf over the phone.

"Well," I insisted.

"You know where the Vinesia Hotel is?"

"On the waterfront," I continued.

"The one with the gold and bronze dome. You got it?"

"I remember where it is..."

"Ever been in it?" he asked with a sense of urgency.

"Not that I can recall," I answered, "No"

"It's magnificent Conner," he replied, "You should see it. The main hall is second to none. There's a main dance hall there thirty feet or more in height, with a big dome as big as the capital dome in Washington; chandeliers all along the ridges with an enormous chandelier in the main section; as big as a space ship. Beveled glass everywhere; checkerboard floors in all shades and colors; winding stairs with ivory staircase posts; mahogany doors and furniture strung all throughout. The main dance floor has the acoustics..."

"I see—what you are saying Jason?" I cut him short, "You called me to talk about a hotel...What does this have to do with me?"

"You're going tonight friend."

"Going where?" I was becoming a little agitated.

"The biggest dance of the year. Singles dance; this year's theme is the big band, Glen Miller era. Even have a band leader who looks like him,"

I could hear him chuckle with that wisping snare in his voice.

"Tonight at seven until...well, whenever."

"I have class tomorrow Jason."

"So?" he pursued, "Skip it."

"I am almost at my finals," I argued, "I don't have the available time. Who needs a single's dance?"

"You do," he ensued.

"And why is that Tush?" I persisted.

"Listen. Only a dumbbell would not notice how you have moped around for Sandra for as long as your life is. You need to go out and enjoy life a little. You've been clustered up, way too long."

"I don't have a thing for Sandra…"

"Yeah, yeah," he ignored me, "That torch you carry never went out. Why? Because you refuse to see anyone else."

"What if I don't?" I insisted emphatically.

"Then find another woman who is named Sandra," he suggested, "Better yet? Find another Miller. Surely there is another Miller in high town Boston somewhere."

"Really Jason," I affirmed, "I'm just not interested."

"This is by ticket-only friend!" he growled, "Only one thousand invited. Through my influence, I was able to get two tickets for us to go."

There was an air of pride in his voice when he said this.

"Because you are playing for the Boston Red Sox…"

"Why not?" he said, "It has its' privileges. What do you say?"

"No Jason…" I nearly hung up then.

"No?" he sounded offended on that one.

"I said no," I was ready to go.

"Practically a hermit," he grumbled, "Aren't you?"

"Just have other interests right now."

"You need to diversify," he implied.

"You sound like a financial broker," I laughed.

"Ham hog or Sushi…" he shot back.

"What?" I thought there was an odd measure in that question.

"Answer the question Tush," he asked, "Ham hog or Sushi?"

"Ham hog of course," I replied, "I hate Sushi."

"Sushi is your school work. Let's just say Ham hog is finding a little female companionship. Throw the book out your window for the evening and enjoy a little time with your old friend."

"I'll make a deal with you," I tried another angle.

"What's that?" he answered with another inquiry.

"Flip a coin," I remarked, "You call it. I flip; however it lands is the way we go. You get it right. I'll go."

"No, No," he wasn't keen on it, "How do I know?"

"Creed of honor," I said, "We go as it goes—game?"

"If it will get you out there, then yes," he spoke as I fumbled for a coin through my nearly emptied-out pockets.

"Find one?"

"Got Mister Washington sitting right in my palm."

"Then flip it and I'll call," he waited, "Ready?"

"Ready…" I responded back with a word and a flip.

"Heads," he chose, "Let's ride Mr. Washington!"

I tossed it about the air. It rotated and flipped in mid-flight at least a dozen times or more; ricocheting off the nightstand, and rolling about the floor directly underneath that massive bed of my parents. It rolled entirely out of view from me.

"Well?" he inquired.

"I don't know…" I bent down to make my attempts to spot it.

"What do you mean…" he cackled, "You don't know…"

"It went underneath the bed," I did the play by play.

"Don't touch it!" he warned.

"Why?" I responded back by impulse.

"Read out the verdict as the coin lays," he swore, "Bad luck to touch it. Get a flashlight and look."

I did as he asked. I leaned deep beneath the framework of that bed. I could sight out where the coin lay, though I could never determine precisely how it fell.

"Well that is just super," I groaned, "Can't tell a thing."

"Move the bed then."

"It's a heavy bed Jason," I whined.

"Need help moving it Popeye?" he giggled, "Forgot your spinach didn't you?" he laughed further.

"Hold on."

I laid the phone over the nightstand, and with a mighty thrust upward I shot the mattress and springs on their side, and vaulted all the pillows across the room.

"Heads!" I yelled out to the phone.

There was nothing more than a muddled response in return. My mother made her way down the hallway at nearly the identical time; she catching me in the strangest positions.

"What on earth are you doing Conner?" she said in a very shocking tone, "Put down my bed."

"Not looking for anything mother," I laughed, "Not what you might be thinking. Just flipped a coin and it rolled underneath your bed…Heads! Heads!" I repeated again for Jason's benefit.

"What was that?" I heard him say.

"Conner," mother insisted, "Please."

I dropped the bed and grabbed up the phone, "Heads."

"I think you have lost yours," she shook her head in an abrasive manner, "Now…do me the honor and put my bed back together. Will you please?"

I mouthed out to my mother in approval and asked her for a few more minutes in private; she let me be as I requested.

"You win," I came back to Jason, "It was heads."

"Good; I'll be there in forty-five minutes."

"Wait," I stressed, "You said big band era. Yes?"

"Of course," he replied.

"What about costumes?" I expressed, "I don't have anything even remotely associated with the forty's to wear."

"Already taken care of…"

"Wait a minute," I was more to the cautious now, "What are you up to Jason? I know you very well Tush."

"And you do," he agreed, "Like I said. It's all handled. Just make sure you are ready to leave then."

"No dirty tricks," I warned.

"None," he voiced, "Just be ready."

By the strike of that forty-five minute time span, Jason's car pulled up to the curb in front of my parent's house. I darted out like a boy just let out of school or prison, and we were off as quickly as he had drove up, "Very little time," he muttered.

"Where are you taking us?"

"The theater district, near china town," was his one-worded answer.

"The theater district??" I shockingly imposed on him, "Why the theater district?"

"Yes, the theater district," he stared on me as though I had become a nuisance, "Don't sweat the particulars here Tush!"

"I'm not," I defended myself, "Just want to know is all."

"We'll have to snap on this faster than a hare," he advised, "if we have any hopes in getting there on time."

Jason drove as fast as legally possible and then some; exceeding the speed limit where he could, and taking all the risks in other areas, though it was in a small measure for time when we arrived at the theater district. Before I could take another breath we found ourselves diving into the Colonial Theatre. A solemn, single flashlight met us at the door.

"You know I can get into hot trouble for this Jason."

I heard a voice behind that sparkling flashlight fume out.

"Keep in step," Jason stressed, "we have little time."

We were escorted hastily through the main, formal entrance; past the highly decorated auditorium, and into the back stage area.

"Look at this Jason!" I grabbed the flashlight from our unknown guide as we passed through the main auditorium. I toured the high vaulted ceiling and gold, gilded trim work; frescoes, friezes and statues about. I darted that single light as if it were being led about by a drunken man. I felt I had been thrown into a movie theater with all the lights now dimmed out. I gawked freely at all the artwork.

"Give me that!" I felt a hand pull the flashlight frantically from me. By the force of his blow, and his weak, though tight grip, I could sense he was a small man of seeming stature.

We could hear his shoes clipping along the hard floors, with the flashlight in low flicker about the seatbacks; his step brash and clapping at an extreme pace. Shadows dipped and rose like mice forming into genies along the far-gazing walls; statues with silhouettes forming into imperial gods of the Greeks, holding stance and figuration where the light and shadows met.

The frescoes about would show faint yet distinct flurries of colors, as the light would dance across its paintings.

"You're not very cultured are you?" The voice asked me.

"Not prim-nosed and snooty, if that's what you mean."

"Ever been in a theater?" He sharply shot back.

"Plenty," I grumbled.

"Then you're not to touch," he said, "and I mean everything."

"Don't patronize Applegate," Jason replied.

"The hired hand puts himself at jeopardy," he stalled, "and you think I am patronizing. I have ten years in this place. I'm not ready to toss it out on the sewer line just yet maestro!"

"You're not hired help," Jason chuckled, "You're the prop, slash, costume director."

"Correctly put," he said as we entered into the back-staging area, "And it's no small feat to get Anna Karenina on stage. Lot of material; lots and lots of material I say."

"Quite an accomplishment then," I smarted.

"Thank you," he took me quite serious to the bone.

"So Jason," I inquired, "Why are we here? You left that part out."

The light suddenly flickered on. I could view more costumes than I could have ever fathomed if my mind had to begin from scratch and make an adequate imagination out of it.

"So this is why we are here?" I looked around.

"My!" the little guy was in full view, "You are as big as he is. This will be difficult; very difficult."

"Something military perhaps," Jason suggested, "Usually the actors playing military roles were larger men."

"Not necessarily," I could see Applegate thumbing his mouth with several fingers; downtrodden and glass-eyed. He seemed to fit the persona of someone in the theater workings. His vest settled in with an assorted three-piece, old-hand suit. It appeared quite outdated; his tie lacking the modern version of its form, and seeming to step him back into the twenties, "How about subtle, gangster style."

"No," Jason stopped him, "too forward and flashy. If at all possible, two matching flyboy suits would work best. If not both, at least one can go but not gangster; better secret detective than gangster; Humphrey Bogart style and with charisma."

Jason was running his hands through the racks of costumes as if they were posts out on a picket fence.

"Now I don't want to get in trouble impersonating military," I cracked out, though my expression backed off when Jason took to look me over with a glaring stare or two.

"How about a nurse's uniform soft-hand Luke," he flung a white skirtish nurse outfit over me, "Little tall for the hem line?"

"Funny bunny you are," I sneered, "Ha Ha."

I threw back the skirt towards Jason, and smacked him out over his face, "Military will do fine."

"More like it," Jason agreed.

"We'll need to measure," Applegate stood us both on a stand and in front of a three-mirror semi-ring. He hastily went from arm length to arm length; shoulder blade to shoulder blade; round waist; pant length, and then ring around the chest.

He hustled off deep into the room, and rustled past rack after rack. We were watching his progress from over the top as though he were dug deep into the grounds of those costumes; like a mole pillaging through the dirt. Ten minutes past and he prevailed out with two uniforms in hand; world war two army pilot lieutenants in dusty brown, light brown shirt with matching ties, fly-boy wings, and lapels decorated with medals; side patches and double scarfs to boot.

"They'll need to be altered, but its close."

"Altered?" Jason questioned.

"Yours will be two inches shady in the waist. They'll drop at the first sight of wind," he raised his beady eyes beyond the light rims of his glasses to spot over Jason's costume, "Pants are a little off, but not enough to notice."

He stalled, gimpy-eyed over mine.

"Now yours will be a tad more delicate. Have three inches to suck in on your pant waist; let out a little on the shoulders; have to cuff yours, excess inch at the bottom. Looks like your head is a little off on the hat; here."

He gave me the hat.

"I figured," he watching me in a grimace, "Little tight."

"Manageable," I remarked.

"No, not manageable in the least," Applegate smarted off, "Military man prides himself in precision. Precision in duty, precision in work ethic, precision in dedication, precision in following and taking commands, and of no less," he paused; pulling the hat from my head, "Precision in uniform. He takes pride in that. Having an off-centered uniform on for a military officer, is like being naked at Times Square just before the apple hits the top to start out the new year," he grinned, "Rather them cheer the apple than you. I'll get a hat that fits more suitable…"

Within the hour, Applegate had worked miracles with the Army uniforms, and we were fit to perfection.

"Scarf is suave," Jason dropped a scarf in a loop just underneath his lapel, "Here, you should try it. Makes you look more distinguished."

I pulled a second one over me.

"Quite nice," I checked myself out in the mirror; army hat in a tilt with a firm clasp, tight-lipped expression sitting just beneath that brim, "Very savvy."

"How much do I owe you Applegate?"

"Season tickets," he demanded.

"Season tickets?" Jason nearly choked on that one.

"You heard me," he peddled at my feet, "Season tickets."

"I'll arrange it," Jason brushed himself off and lowered himself back to the floor; all the while admiring the debonair way he posed in that multiple mirror setup.

"Have them back by nine in the morning," he pointed at us, "or I'll be the one hanging from the top of that apple in Times Square, this New Year's Eve. They take inventory once a week."

"Thanks Applegate," Jason snickered, "Never saw an apple on top of another at Times Square. Might ring in the New Year more phonetically, don't you think Tush?"

"Don't even think about it," he slapped, "You best be here nine sharp, and to the dot tomorrow morning!"

We ran down past that elongated hallway, through the auditorium, and into the main entrance with a roar and a cheer. Our echoes tumbled through the crevices, high-beam walls, and arches; as if we held the chorus sounds of a thousand voices. Our shadows danced along the sidewalls like two Peter Pan's entering Wendy's room for play. The distorted formations were twenty feet tall and quite menacing even to us.

"The master of charm," Jason's ego was beginning to burst, "Is my weapon of choice."

"The king of charisma is mine," I fluttered about him.

"We shall see," he cocked his head, "which the ladies find more appealing; which shall they choose. Like magic with no remedy for cure; they'll be begging for our number."

It was nearing the drop of the hour past six and our travels were only a few streets closer to the bay. The lines filtering in were long, but pacing quickly towards the entranceways.

"Now!" a lady with a greasy face, cat-like glasses, and misty lens came up to us, "Take a card."

"What is this?" I ask when she shoved the deck nearly up my nose, "Didn't come here to play cards lady."

"Ohh," she whimpered, "You're not being fun. It's a game sweetie!"

She nearly chomped her gum out of her mouth. The spots she wore on her black and white dress nearly jumped off her skirt and danced to the prevailing music we could hear thumping in the dance hall before us.

"Go on!"

I reluctantly took a card from her. It was the six of diamonds.

"Your turn," she gaily displayed the cards for Jason to grab from in the same manner as she did me, "Only one now."

"Do I have to?" Jason leeringly spied on her.

"What are you two? Brothers or something?" she spawned out another high-pitched, curdling cry. I though she might break down and fall into tears right before us.

"Alright, whatever you say," he took a single card; it being the six of clubs.

"Oh great!" she hoped and giggled, "Two sixes. What a duo! The ladies will be most especially beautiful for you!"

"Don't suppose you know any of them," Jason sarcastically spewed out with a fake laugh. She returned in kind.

"Oh no sweetie!" she cackled, "The rule is this. All the ladies have two cards each; skip over two in between. In your case, you have to find the lucky ladies who have the five and eight cards. Then you bring them back here for a prize!"

"With your enthusiasm little lady," Jason hoped once for her, "Who needs this game."

I nearly snickered myself into a sneeze.

"Oh stop! You're too kind. I just work here," she smiled out large and deep; well enough her gums showed as though they were the ear to a corn, and her teeth all lined up like the kernels in a row.

"Now! Scoot! Scoot! Scoot!" she gave us a forceful push directly to the front entrance; her hands almost reaching below our back pockets.

We herded out hastily to avoid her otherwise indecent indiscretion there.

"Good luck!" she waved us off with one final lift of her hand, tipsy-toe stance, and an even larger grin.

I turned about, pushed the tip of my hat upwards to gather in a better view, and stare out into that vast-estate-of-a-room with the look of utter awe on me.

"Will you look at this?"

"Didn't let you down, did I Tush?"

"I'll say otherwise friend," I couldn't blink for fear of losing sight of that magnificent hall; not for one second.

The high arches ascended as though they were as high as Heaven. Frescoes adorned from corner ceiling to corner ceiling, with figures so in grace that they would stare back at you with equal wonder. The band platform rose from the center back of that immense hall, and it was nearly showered by glistening blue marble and lime green looping drapes; dipping almost thirty feet from top to base. Each side held miniature arches decorated in high wood, crown moldings, mahogany wood-paneled doors, and gold-plated, see-through ball handles.

There must have been five hundred small round tables disbursed evenly throughout the vantage points; some candlelit while others held tiny covered lamplights in their centers. The chairs were solid cherry wood with Victorian knee curves, and nearly rocked when you sat in them. All along every angled wall were these column windows which illuminated the streetlights that were all surrounding this structure. This created such an array of iridescent sparks that it seemed we were being surrounded by fairy fireflies swirling in the night air.

I could barely keep my eyes from the dome sets above me; the moldings, by far, danced in every formation conceivable with swags, loops, and trails which made you follow their path all through the designs.

"Did you come here to check out the surroundings," Jason popped me about the waist, "Or did you come here to check out the surroundings?" he sneer-eyed about with the cache of wolf eyes at all the women, "Did you ever see a better litter to pick from?"

"Gum," I groaned as I went close to a table near us.

"No, No," he wagged his finger on me, "Not this Sandra thing. Not now! You are not pulling this '*I am lost in love for Sandra pouty routine*' now. You hear?"

"You keep bringing her up," I balked, "not me!"

"Look," he half-smiled, "Let's enjoy the evening. Better yet, at least let me enjoy the evening, and let you swoon over the four-year-old ghost of Sandra Miller."

I immediately grabbed hold of his hand and dragged him through the quandary of people standing about; my head set into a 'b-line' stare and head strong gaze until I came to the first well-dressed forties woman I could find; though her back was most conveniently turned away from me. But her hair looked nice and I decided to take the better part of assertion here.

"Ma' dam," I said with hard authority, "Will you please dance with my friend here. He's going off to war tomorrow with death staring him down, and he needs a little female companionship."

She turned around to face us with the harshest features on her expression. I knew Jason would take to murdering me afterwards.

"Why certainly," she looked Jason over; sipping out the lip of her straw and drink, "Flyboy."

She firmly gobbled up Jason's hand in hers, and while he felt the full tug and yank of her thrust, he managed to grab hold of me for a whisper.

"And you're grounded flyboy! Just you wait!"

And to make matters worse, it was a slow dance.

The band was dressed in cream white suits, black bow ties, and sunny-side shoes that one could use as a mirror if had be. The bandleader however was appareled in black, white shirt, and fancy alligator shoes.

On the next song, the music vibrated the floor into a fever pitch; the trombones scowled the airwaves; clarinets back-dropped into the musical arena; the saxophones hypnotized the sounds, and the collaboration of instruments produced such the hopping mood that I felt myself tapping my own rhythm in consort with it.

A few women, clad in velvet red dresses with frills from head to toe, asked politely on me to make a dance with them. I, in my initial shy state, respectfully declined for the moment; so stating I had just entered and wished to see the surroundings before I attempt on any dance. I, in turn, requested them to check back with me later. They frowned as customary, and left.

Jason returned back after a few trips around the dance floor; his brow in a dogged beat, and his breath heavy from all the activity. I handed out a drink to him, which he gladly took and engulfed.

"So how was it?" I asked.

"It's my turn to pick a doe for you!"

He began to grab my hand and tug me like the tugboat he was.

"Wait! Wait! Wait!"

I locked, and then set a shocked look about for everyone to see as he made a scene on us.

"No! No! No!"

He had me clean to the gild then.

"Be a good friend!"

"I am," he growled back, "Now let's see!"

"No, really now Jason," I nervously laughed, "You don't have to do this, really," I laughed more nervously.

"My pleasure," he kept on the lookout, "Quit balking; I'll carry you if I have to. And you know I will."

"Easy," I bit on my tongue, "Easy now! Anything Jas' I'll do anything! Please."

I could feel the eyes of all now penetrating our jokery; the snickers humming into a louder spectacle while he was dragging me about like a dog with a sled attached to its neck.

"I'll look out for you buddy," he swore, "I got just the thing for you…now, close your eyes!"

"I know you," I whispered, "And I can't bare to look."

"There," he spoke when we stopped.

"Where?" I looked all round me; nothing but the mass of people clouding my view with their forms.

"Where Jason?"

He softly took the sides of his hands, twisted my head in the correct formation, and allowed me to see.

"There," he dropped slightly behind me, "Now isn't she the most beautiful woman you ever saw?"

My eyes slowly fixated over a mass of people huddled close to the dance floor; people of all shapes, sizes, frames, looks, distinctions as well most bland sorts.

"Listen," I fussed, "I don't see anyone."

"Take a closer look," he forced my head away from him; making me strain as far as my eyes could clearly see with.

Again, there was a fog of people muddling around. The lights, though bright to some clarity, still held enough dimming in their wattage that I could faintly make out who was there.

"Closer Conner," Jason whispered, "Closer."

I turned to look at him growing in distance to me.

"Closer," he waived me further, "Closer."

I reverted one final time. The dance floor light grew to a slow flicker; the music dying into a soft melody and slow-parading dance. I could here the soft temper of the piano dabbling its keynotes to light a sort of perfume sound all nearby where I stood. The saxophone blew in a chord or two, and then dissipated once more for the piano to take full stage.

There, in the bloom of my surprise, was Sandra Miller standing with the backdrop of painted stars on the walls behind her; seemingly to dance around her as if she were the glowing moon itself. I nearly fainted with shock; a gift from Heaven and its stars all-a-bright. In one instance, my life had been transformed from bland into sunshine and rain. The dips and valleys of what was to come all appeared to shake the 'ordinary existence' all away from me.

She was there; indeed, she was. A haven and a harbor; a beacon and a torch, which felt to brush by my heart and make it glow again.

She was all I could love; she was all I could ever love. The sunrise I dreamed of when I first awoke; the sunset I reflected over just before I went to bed each night. There she now stood; peach coated, v-necked, frilled-covered, sleeveless, white-glass slippers, hand-sown long gloves, soft pink rose pinned to her breast, charm-gold necklace with glitter-to-glow when she swayed—and above all the graceful elegance of an elite princess standing aloft.

For a moment I stood in my silence. I watched her gleam like the sunrays of a meadow. I could see the lilies in her eyes, the ham-sung rose in her cheeks' dimple whenever she smiled. Her blue-tone pupils would squint near a close when her mouth parted out to let her bright white teeth exposed. The golden turns of her hair flowed from her soft temples, just above her thin eyelids; rolling as if they were caressing waves to the shoreline of her expressions. Eventually they reached about her shoulders and sat in a glisten while surrounding her face.

I felt the existence of no one then. Not the audience, the people around; the band, nor Jason. I had been right; I had been always right. My love for Sandra never went away. It just slept for a little awhile and might have slept for a lifetime but for this fateful time. And now it had come to wake up on this very moment.

"You see?" Jason came to my side, "Your friend looks out for you. I think you should go to her Conner."

I was in a sweet, ethereal dream until, as I turned to her right, a man who stood close to her had her undivided attention. He was proper, elegant in his own right, and he was dashingly-handsome. He appeared my superior in every respect. Someone I knew who could capture her interest nearly to that moment. I thought my heart a few moments ago had wings to fly with, but quickly discovered they were merely tears dropping from its base.

My jaw simply gaped into a wide opening as I stared on in disbelief. Their banter and appearing joyous nature showed me beyond resolve, there was chemistry brewing between them.

"Well?" Jason nudged me, "Aren't you going to her?"

"She's in the middle of something."

"Just like that," Jason fumed, "You give up. You're here. She's here. There is purpose in that. Conner. Sometimes fate does shine a little in cloudy weather."

He nudged my rear again.

"Go on!"

"I am not going to intrude…"

"It's been four years," he argued.

"So?"

"Ah la la," Jason performed a three-sixty pirouette, "You can't Conner. You can't throw this opportunity away."

As I refocused on Sandra, she had left her spot and disappeared. My look became most desparate as I pushed my eyeshot in every direction; now seeing she and this gentleman had gone to the dance floor to dance a few rounds.

"You're going to wait," Jason pinned his expression over mine, "And wait you shall…until that young lady comes off the dance floor."

One song, second song, then a third; finally a fourth and they were back in that same spot as before. Laughing, joking, carrying on even more pronounced than before the frolic on that dance floor.

I took to slightly excuse myself to speak with Jason.

"Do you think she will remember?"

"Oh Conner," Jason rolled his eyes in every manner, "Tush! She told you she was in love with you! Unless she is so frivolous with her feelings; of course she will remember. I promise you. There hasn't been a moment that has gone by that she hasn't been a love-sick, google-eyed, grease-pit, heart-dripping puppy for you. Good Gosh!" he stammered.

"Do I have to do everything for you two?"

And on this very queue, I felt a tap to my outer shoulder. It was that dashing fellow all was, just a moment ago, all enwrapped with Sandra.

"Excuse me," he pronounced, "Are you a six or seven?"

"Excuse me?" I thought it a very odd proposal on his part.

"Are you a six or seven?" he repeated.

"Excuse me?" I followed his lead.

"Are you a six or seven?" he drilled me further. I knew then what he was referring to. I gently pulled the card from my sleeve and displayed it out for him. I had the six of diamonds.

"Well, yes I do…come to think of it."

"Then go to that girl," he suggested.

"What did you say?"

"Go talk to her," he pointed in Sandra's direction, "Just do it."

I looked out on Sandra; all mesmerized as I was once more, stuck in my stance with that card limply teetering in my palm. She was standing alone, eyes dipping to watch those twisting about that floor. Still, she had not taken to see me. I looked back to find the dashing fellow had completely disappeared from view.

"What do you need?"

Jason peered over my shoulder like the angel in conversion.

"Does Jesus have to come and give you a pep talk? Or do you need a royal carpet rolled out in her direction."

"You go," I ignorantly employed that idea.

"Ah!" his hand went up, "Mr. Darling came to you. Not me."

"Give me your card," I was hasty.

"Why? He wondered aloud.

"Test fate," I scrambled, "Oblige me. I just have to know."

He stuffed the card in my hand. My eyes were entirely pressed on Sandra's every movement. My walk began; slowly; drunk appearing; stumbling; intoxicated by every step; balance-wrecked, yet somehow I made my way right before her.

The glass lowered from her expression; those golden blues' were temptuous and stunning as they were lightly peering to gather me in their viewpoint. She stopped; motionless, nearly without breath. I felt the soft pedals of her loving countenance all seem to be in a blur with emotions there. I stalled just within earshot of her.

There was a cupping smile, a slow-lid blink, and then she stopping to catch herself once more.

"Some man just walked up to me."

I nervously smiled.

"And asked if I were a six or seven, but I thought I was a ten."

Her laughter nearly fell off the side of her drinking glass; her expression lit up with all the fireworks of joy there; she remembered and never forgot. I must have looked timid in my approach.

"Well handsome man," she grinned, "You are."

She paused, and her face fell straight and sincere; the walls now fully withdrawn, and her heart and soul stood there face to face with me.

"Hello Conner."

"How have you been Sandra?" I moved closer.

"Waiting," she paused.

"Waiting?" I pursued.

"Waiting," she grinned a sly grin.

"Hmmm," I returned with a smirk and a grin; casting my hand to meet with hers, and pulling her close with a gentle tug.

"Waiting. Interesting. So what ventures has the world taken Miss. Miller to?"

I watched eagerly for her reply.

"Well," she rolled her gaze to the ceiling, then back to me, "After three long years at Stanford, and discovering that the wishes of my father were not my dreams, I decided to leave there and come home. It wasn't for me Conner."

"I'll bet Dirk was most disturbed by that."

"Dreadfully," she laughed, "Stanford, and he, went along with the same package. I figured, if it is my life? I have to figure out how to live it myself."

"And what has the soul-searching time brought you? What mild wisdom have you acquired since the drastic announcement?"

"I missed home," she took another shy drink, sipped a bit, and tendered to move closer, "Father was quite dispelled by it all."

"I'm sure," was all I could filter through my apparent happy look on her. I could feel the music continue in rapid shift until, finally, at last, a slow-moving sympathy of song and loving dance made a mood swing over the entire hall.

"Shall we?"

She took my hand, bent her elbow straight, and pulled me forward; leading me through onto the floor's very middle section. I tugged her into posture, hand-to-hand about our shoulder with the other hand sliding around her waist; her hand now dropped over my shoulder. I could see even the dimples in her eyes cause me to quietly sigh. Our checks at times fell side to side, pull free, and allow our looks to start up once more.

"Waiting for what Sandra?"

"Someone was missing out of my life."

"So why didn't you call?" I asked.

"You know how fate works?" she asked, "Do you?"

"I believe I have met with it a time or two tonight."

I slowly pulled both sixes in front of her, as we danced.

"You have a five and an eight, no?"

"I do," she sweetly remarked.

"Then pick one of these sixes," I said, "one is from me; the other one is from Jason."

"Oh no," she was hesitant.

"Ah," I soothed her in a word, "You believe in fate don't you?"

We paused for a spell in silence.

"Now pick. Fate will guide."

I saw her eyes dart back and forth with debate; fixating on one card then the other, and then gazing up over the lip of those cards directly at me. I was playing poker with my expression, never giving her an ounce of indication which way to go. She fiddled with her lips nervously; criss-crossing them, and taking to a bite or two out of their sides. I giggled on her constant fidget, then.

"Decide?" I winked her way.

"Yes," she stalled on one last stare, pulled out the one she wanted, "This one…they say diamonds are eternal."

I said nothing, still in poker uniform.

"Well flyboy," she huffed, "Which one is it?"

"This one," I showed off the six of clubs, "is Jason's"

I looked over her shoulder and I spotted Jason grinning at the edge of that dance floor. She spun about with a fanatical gaping, jaw-spreading, distorted air, and so planting a gregarious hug over my body.

"Fate it is!" she kissed me as my eyes bugged into their whites, "Fate it is!"

"Did you propose?" a couple next to us looked on in a gasping wonder, "You proposed."

"They proposed?" another muddled through, then another.

"No," I professed; looking around, "we…we…we,"

I grabbed Sandra's hand and I ran off with her onto the outer perimeter, past two double-door sets, and suddenly we found ourselves in the mist of another garden; it overlooking the bay shores of Boston.

"I know this is real," I was huffing out of breath.

"Uh huh?" she was near into full-blown joy; stuttering with that single phrase.

"Sandra," I became more serious, "There hasn't been a moment these past four years which I went about without you being there with me. Not a moment. You see? It's crazy, a silly sort of preoccupation, but, I know, that there, well…What I am trying to say Sandra is…"

I stalled.

"Yes Conner?" she paused with me. My eyes were darting from side to side as though I were the frozen tin man, "Conner?"

"Darn!" I splattered; now holding the sides of her arms, pulling her near to me, and so kissing Sandra with the passion only love owns. The bursting stars counted out into explosions and blooms right above our stage. The night sky was clear and clean, and became filled by the warmth of the spring air. I could sense the extinguishing fires of those fireworks lofting high, and were now dripping into starlights and dusting simmers until they had touched earth.

We paused, gasped for air; our gaze in a trance by the others' power to absorb. The wisp of a glancing wind; the cool bay-like breeze; the single blows of small ships coming into harbor as they passed by; all filtering the occasion with its special tone and carriage. Heaven was surely smiling over us now.

"You say it so eloquently," she made attempts to gather in her breath, "If I only had your diction Conner."

That pond in the bay was showing the reflections of those quick fire flickers and bursts out along the bed of those waters. The blues, yellows, greens, and oranges smoked into the sky; re-shimmering their reflections on this glassy-eyed pond. I came from my hug on Sandra to wonder.

"Sandra?" I pondered, "Are those, those, those real?"

She turned to look out over the bay; the fireworks dripping through her eyes as she looked on me, "Of course silly. You didn't know?" She broadly smiled.

"No," I grinned, "What?"

"They are testing the firework mechanisms tonight for the upcoming fourth," she slid back into our hug, "You see? We get a brief picture show for our troubles."

And so we re-affirmed our true love for one another on that intimate stage. Fate, as I believe the verse goes, can be indeed friend or foe. Well, at least tonight it turned out to be my best friend. This time there would be no letting go of Sandra. We were to see this out to some outcome, to what end might resolve itself in our lives. I remember what my mother always said to me. Sometimes the sorrows have to come before the Joys can follow. I could only see the joy in all this. If there was some sorrow built in it, then it must have escaped out the back door.

The harbor was like a grand meadow to us there. The ocean's edge had crept up through the bay, tickled the shorelines with its gentle waves in and out, and had given us the beauty of Boston to fall in love with all over again.

Chapter 17

Courtship and Union.

It was not long after the beginning of our sure courtship until I made plans to ask Sandra to be my wife. I thought the occasion required a special touch of ingenuity; something which would forever be reflecting back on us all throughout our lives. A moment, if you will, which we would always be in fond remembrance of.

With Jason's assistance and help in conducting such a task, and so noting how certain I knew he could keep and retain the 'hard-guarded' secret, we made our way to a local mall on that Tuesday before; attended to eleven separate stores, and asked each to contribute their efforts to the occasion. A single rose was to be placed at every store; a note commencing from the early vestige of when we first met until that moment of proposal. And at last a map to lead her into the next store.

I had asked one of her good friends to call on Sandra to go shopping for a day. And of course, it just so happened to be at the same time as my surprise proposal to Sandra; on that early Saturday morning no less. Stephanie most hardily agreed to take part in this wonderful surprise. Eleven roses you say? What about the twelfth and final rose you ask? Well, as fortune and fate shines down brilliantly in these matters, I held the final rose, along with the engagement ring, right at the main mall fountains.

It was a gracious and eye-popping setting. As I had it set out, Sandra would end up at one end of the mall in the eleventh store, and then proceed down a long, very large, straight, highly-lit and pedestrian-active corridor leading all the way up to the two-story looping fountains. There, I would be nervously standing and waiting for her arrival. Somehow I would muster the good faith and ability to get on one knee and ask for her hand in marriage.

What better time than to perform such a ceremony just before the throngs of Christmas. The mall would surely be packed; alive with the hustle and bustle of shop-goers everywhere. And so on queue, with the particulars rested and ready for action, the plan was put into place for a Saturday in the middle of December.

I arrived early; first attending to the flower shop and acquiring the finest twelve roses that were available. The notes and roses were then disbursed to the shop attendants I had spoken to several evenings before. I would return back to the flower shop and eye-watch her travels going here and there; half-witted about and totally in a frazzle. I knew the sequence by heart and I could remember precisely how long it would take her to reappear from one shop to the next. I had figured nearly ninety minutes until I would be on my knees, looking up to her soft eyes, and seeing the woman I was to marry in all her grace.

As it so became evident, rumors swirled and festered through all the shops of the mall that day. It seemed everyone was in on what was to occur. That is, except for Sandra. I first saw her cut through the mall; gabbing freely and in light step with Stephanie. Unaware and quite off-guard to what was soon to take place, Sandra moved briskly past my hiding place enroute to her first store stop. As she dipped out of sight, I reappeared under the loud and thunderous applause of those who had already assembled near the fountains.

"Shhhhh!" I waived everyone to hold the accolades until the moment arrived. I could see the dreamy look in some women's eyes as I darted frantically around to rein in all the vocals.

"You know its' quite rare what you are doing," the lady at the flower shop grinned on me when I returned. I spotted the odd and vastly, strange arrangement she was putting together.

"What is that?" I questioned.

"Oh, this?" she stepped back to show it for display, "An arrangement for a boyfriend."

"What girlfriend would order this for her boyfriend?"

"None," she replied, "Man to man." Her freckles grew when she smiled, "Not to worry, it's actually a very common arrangement. See? We have it displayed in our brochure."

"I would have never thunk it!" I looked strong at her brochure.

"Don't worry," she shoed me away with her sheers, "I'll let you know when the lassie passes by, and you are safe. Just peek through those two vases when I call you from your seat. You'll be able to see her when she goes by."

It wasn't long before Sandra came forward with two roses now straddling her folded arms. The look in her eyes; the transient glow I had not seen so far; as if there had been sweet tears that just before had passed by underneath her expression, and the rainbow in her smile had taken over only moments ago.

Her smile never left her as she moved to the other edge of the mall. There stood an entire row of people watching her when she marched by; the crowds huddled, meshed into a converging group; watching; staring the whole way through.

A third rose, then a fourth soon followed; she again reappeared to a store near the edge of that fountain. She entered the body of that store, took a moment's pause, walked to the counter, and soon left with six roses in hand. Six???

"She is only supposed to have five!" I whispered; looking back at the shopkeeper.

"Don't you remember? You left the fifth rose and the final rose; the one you were supposed to hand her at the very end, right there in the store." She was calm about it all.

"What am I supposed to do?" I stressed, "They were only supposed to give her the one rose!"

"Darling," she said in a soothing fashion, "It's not like I am out of roses. A red one will do…"

"What do I owe you?" I asked.

"Nothing…" she followed.

"Nothing?" I was more clearly nervous now.

"You're too kind," I responded.

"Oh the hard-sick nature of young love," she laughed, "It keeps me in business. But this is your special day. What's another rose to me? Let's just say prince, I am most honored to give you the rose, the twelfth one and the most special rose of all; the one you will propose to her with."

Seven, eight, nine; all were dripping over her as she passed down the final corridor. Her smile more beaming more than ever and it certainly registered that she was in full consort on what was about ready to occur between us.

The crowd had amassed in full force. The shops nearest to the fountains were now filtering out. Even the shopkeepers were amongst the attending sightseers. I nearly gassed when I saw four Japanese tourists marveling at why all these people were assembling; and so they began to take pictures in every direction.

It was time for me to take my place in front of the fountains. There was an accord and rounding applause, which brought me to a more nervous and riled state. I weakly raised my hand to acknowledge them. A woman came rushing towards me in her high-clapping shoes, and so landing an enormous hug over me.

"Oh!" she fawned, "Aren't you the true gentleman."

The crowds were now filing up in rows to both sides, and becoming a human corridor wall to guide Sandra back to the fountains.

My brow beat with sweat; my hands perspired and nearly allowed the glow-white diamond to slip free. I stared ahead; still nothing; dropped my look back to the diamond, and twirled it round as it sparkled radiantly back at me. The red rose I was holding was now dipping slightly to one side. I cleared my throat; stood in a firm stance with my hands crossed over one another in front of my body.

Still; most still; the applause rose from the rear as she made her way up that corridor. She was alone now; Stephanie following back to allow Sandra that single walk up on her own. From the distance I could see her expression in tears and smiles; the flood of emotions cascading down from her meadowy eyes like a constant streaming waterfall. I was most ecstatic, though nearly lost myself in tears to see her so much in happiness there.

I regrouped, held firm, gazed from side-to-side to see the full mass of people guarding her way as she commenced still closer. The hush of the crowd now began to rumble of whispers, and spill over further into silence. It seemed the entire world was now watching us. The flowers decorated her dress to make her out into a garden.

Our eyes connected and locked into our own world. She reached for me; I taking her hands into mine. The quiet silence consumed the surroundings completely for that most special occasion. We leaned forward to a gentle kiss, a touch to the foreheads, and then I led her to sit before the glowing fountains.

"Are you ready for this?" I whispered to her.

"I think so," she perked out; nervous to the bone.

"I believe we are being pulled together by something even greater than we really know fully about. Certainly a mutual person, influential in our lives, felt we were meant for one another. And we both know who this person is," I paused to clear my throat before continuing.

"Sandra Miller. I will always carry this cross close to my heart; in symbol of my continuing love for you. It was given to me with love, and love will carry me all the way through my life. No matter the consequence; no matter the crime. If it's a sin to love you Sandra, then let me be buried with it."

"Is this a proposal Conner James, or a speech?" She remarked.

This brought a spontaneous roar from the crowd; all in simple laughter.

"Sorry," I shyly grinned, embarrassed by my rambles, "I believe love such as ours holds on through eternity. I see it in your eyes, and I have always seen this in you, from the very first moment we first looked into one another; really looked into one another. I came into my life not knowing what it would bring; hope, happiness, and above all, true love are my ambitions to meet with."

"You're doing it again," she whispered.

"Good sir," a voice cried out, "Get on with it."

Another mutiny of laughter rose along with her wishes.

"You're going to sour the moment," another laugh rattled about.

I knelt to one knee as the crowd settled. I rolled my hand forward and pinched the ring with two fingers.

"Oh, my gosh!" she began to shake; now realizing the strong and heavy weight of that moment, "Is this a dream?"

"No," I shuttered my eyes and shook out my head, "Our time has come. Sandra, I love you for as long as I can see a day and night come together. I want our lives to be a continual affair of the heart. An adventure; two lives always interlocked into one. Our spirits born like our hearts were, and so meant to spend time and life with each other. Sandra, please, will you marry me?"

I placed the ring onto her finger.

She gazed upward to the skylights above us; a measured tear dropped from her eye, and so glittered a warm glow within that reflection; her hands shivering like they were cold. The hush poured through all about like a dam spewing out its waters; the crowd now completely drawn in and mezmorised with what they were witness to. I felt Sandra had to pray for that moment. Then she sent down the most loving glance over me and cupped her hands around my face.

"Conner James," she smiled with a kiss, "I will marry you for a lifetime of mornings and midnights," she cried, "and then some."

"She said yes!" I bellied out with a shout and a spinning hug of her, "She said yes!"

We danced to our own music there, though none could be heard by any other than the two lone serenaders, that we were directly in the middle of all this. I could hear the soft melodies of an orchestra playing in surround of us. Our eyes kept to one another; our kisses without shame or polite pause.

Many people were relit in their faith that day; that true love, when observed, could be seen and admired on.

It warms the heart; lights a flame to the soul. Makes real men weep; makes true women cheer. I heard all these things in the backdrop; a chorus riot of applause delivered us through the rest of that scene. It made out for what I wanted and wished for most; a magical moment we could forever instill ourselves with, and always remember.

"Thank you," she whispered in one final clinch.

"For?" I grabbed on her hand, and we made our waltz through the admiring looks about. I wanted her to tell me.

"For being the man of my dreams," she said, "From the very beginning, I saw you Conner. You were always there."

Plans for a wedding commenced immediately to occur the following June. Invitations were made up; wedding dress plucked from the lot of many; flower arrangements decided on; maid of honor and her matron's dresses detailed in every manner; my tuxedo along with the grooms and ushers were wrangled over until a final decision was made; catering; wedding cake, layered and style; ceremony procession; music arrangements; location of church and reception determined; the list went on and on into what appeared to be forever. Her family rejoiced in the entire mangled journey throughout, yet Sandra and I had lesser time for one another due to this. Still, we decided, for the sake of both our families this would be the path of least resistance; and so appease all involved.

Her parents eventually warmed up to me, though Dirk had always been their first choice. He was 'better stock' to come from higher breeding than from my humble beginnings. The fact that Sandra's grandfather had been a decorated fireman was perhaps my saving grace through it all. My parents were always very accepting of Sandra, and a genuine bond quickly formed as a result, especially between Sandra and my mother.

Whenever the two came into the same room they formed a party of two, chatting for hours until either the sun set into late evening, or their jaws fell off. I believe the former was almost always the case. I would admire them afar; sitting as they were out over the coffee table and in the kindest conversation, drinking their teas or cappuccinos in the family room and spouting off about every versatile subject they could think of; or minding the rockers on the back porch like two post guard watchers overseeing the sunset while they rocked away. Their bond became full in strength, and one of humility and respect.

We decided to hold the wedding at Trinity Church and we made no apologizes for it. Some may very well frown on the prospect of having your wedding at the identical church your grandfather had been laid to rest years before. But I suppose, according to American tradition it was indeed politically permissible to do so. So in mid-June, on a hazy and mild-tempered Saturday, Sandra and I were married as to the conditions of our mutual Christian tradition.

All of Boston seemingly was invited. The church was filled to the rafters, as I observed while coming from the side doors and into the main area of the sanctuary itself. My eyes kept constant watch over the far back double doors in anticipation for Sandra's grand entrance. A short measure of calm, silence, and then the bride's song began as the congregation rose and turned to face Sandra in her introduction; the doors swinging free and there she standing with her father in arm to her. My knees shook at their knockers; my eyes bulging wide as though I were standing in the middle of a highway and a deer was driving a car directly for me; headlights in high beam.

She floated more aptly than walked through the outlayed rose pedals before her. A bouquet enriched with the full colors of the rainbow sitting at attention within her grasp; the sun's light fixture dipped through the stained glass windows, adding even more color to the scene, and so lighting the way for her to walk by. The streaming rays beamed from all the angles possible; the music in play but I couldn't hear it. All my consciousness, waking moments; all thoughts and feelings were directed to her as she proceeded towards me.

Her golden hair pulled above her head, and her locks curled into a cascade of dripping ringlets and curls. A few stray strands twirled down each side to give it that elegant look. Her walk was slow and deliberate, and the whole world appeared to be watching.

The time seemed more surreal and illuminating with fantasy and reality. My princess had at last been born to me. I could not move in that instance; my eyelids stuck wide open and near to water from emotions and from not blinking. This was the final prize for me winning her heart; and she winning mine.

We dazed through the entire ceremony; followed the precise formation of that duty; said our vows and recited what was asked of us; made the exchanging of rings, was pronounced man and wife preceding our last kiss, and then, as we turned.

"Now I pronounce you Mr. and Mrs. Conner James."

At this moment, when the world felt to be in a blur, her squeeze in my hand brought me back to her. We waltzed down through the center isle as though we had been king and queen for the day, but I knew our kingdom would be the longevity of our coming marriage.

I remember catching her father in the hallway afterwards, though, to my amazement he had not spotted me. I kept my watch over his activities as he felt he himself was to be alone. I ducked behind one of the columns and out of his view. There was a string of silence; a shuffling of his feet to an unattended chair; another pause, and I could hear the soft, tenderly-affectionate weeping of a man who feared he had lost his only daughter forever. I debated, crumpled my chin into a frown as I bent around the corner to watch him, and I wondered if it would be my best venture to interrupt him.

I stood without movement; eyeing him with a sort of reverence, and so thinking someday I might be in those shoes. Would I, in such that fraction of a moment, have it lost to me?—Or to let the tears flow as a sort of release; a final farewell to an age gone by, and a 'hello' to the one to come.

He bent his head down into his chin and shook from his weeping. There, he covered his face with his hands. It was a frantic dam-breaking escape for him, and I chose to let him fill the moment with his special tears. Mr. Miller recovered nearly as quickly as he was consumed by his emotions; hastily looking about in every direction and discharging of those tears which had only moments before flowed without inhibition.

The reception was held in the same bay hotel where our final class prom was in. The day had drawn into early evening hours, where the sun shimmered off the bay's water's and sparkled out the waters as the waves pressed through the bay itself. The fading lights began to show twinkles of stars rimming with bright orange, reds, and soft blues stacking beautifully along the horizon.

Several hundred people were in attendance when we entered into the large open balcony. Throngs of cheers rose about in spontaneous applause. The masses surrounded as Mr. Miller took to a toast while raising his glass with a smile towards Sandra and me.

"I'll make this quick and fanciful," he grinned, "Martha and I have had our fill for emotions today, as any happy parents would be on the marriage of their daughter. You can see the love these two share, as Martha and I have had all these years we have been together. It's a love that means nothing to anyone else, but is the greatest gift between those two who share it. I believe my daughter has found that with Conner, and I am so proud and happy for her, that she can enjoy the very same love her mother and I have always had.

I remember when Sandra was such a little girl, trying to ride her first bike. No matter how many times she would fall off, she would get right back up again, and try, and try, and try, and when it seemed she wouldn't and couldn't try anymore, she finally learned to ride that bike. I was proud of her then; as I am so very proud of her now. I knew she would be a very special woman," he paused and raised his glass higher, "To Mr. and Mrs. Conner James; may life always give you safe passage to your dreams."

"Here!" we heard others sound of, "Here! Here!"

Jason stepped forward with a wink out of his left eye, and a smirk coming out of the right side of his mouth.

"Aptly put Mr. Miller," he lifted his glass to Mr. Miller, "Well said, and that which wisdom can only teach," a muddled laughter rumbled through the group while Jason took to pause, "I just wanted to say, knowing Conner as I have since we were blood buddies, or as early as I can remember. I may have been best man today, but I can assure you he is best man in life," his glass rose with all others in synchronized candor, "To my best friend, and to the queen of his heart. I knew you two would be together; I just knew it!" everyone laughed into a roar, "No serious now; let's start this again…To my best friend, and his most lovely bride. You both define what true love is. And I hope, as we all do; those that are still not married, that we can someday find this special place of love, that you both found with each other."

Another 'Here! Here!' rose all around us.

Mother came up to us just before the first song was to play. Her eyes were beading red from some tears she had shed all through the day, but now had given away to a reflective sort of happiness. Her expression told us all and it nearly brought me into tears when she came up to Sandra and I, held both of our outward hands, and so placed a warm hug around as we stood in a triangle.

"Dance with your mother," Sandra said.

"Oh no!" mother giggled, "This is your time."

"When father cuts in," she looked eagerly at both of us, "The first dance. Oh please Mrs. James! Dance with Conner. It would mean so much to me, and for Conner."

"Alright," mother bowed after thinking about it.

The song *'If I Never Knew You'* began to play; the dance floor cleared. Sandra and I took center stage there and we danced about in a swirl and sweet melody of sight and song. The moment was filled by magic and the most wondrous joy when, halfway through the song, as it had been planned, her father came forward and took Sandra through the rest of the song. I reached over and took mother to pair us both off. I knew it had been an uncommon occurrence for my mother to dance, let alone dance with the spectacle of all eyes on her. Though she did; being the wonderful woman she is. Little did I know this would be the final dance my mother and I would ever share together.

Chapter 18

Into the Dawn of Lights and Shadows.

Nine years had passed since my marriage to Sandra had begun. Our children, Cory and Tyler, had been promptly born two years apart from one another, and two years inside the beginnings of Sandra's and my life together. We remained in Boston to be close to all of our family members, but partly because this was our home.

We loved the décor, the history, the charismatic nature of the town itself; and so having our children being born and raised here was a dream we both shared. Sandra had left for college and as it was told to me, as soon as her departure began, she had such a hunger to return. This, being not a nature for lack of independence or maturity, but what was simply a case of being away from where she knew she belonged.

I had dabbled in politics for some time, landing a spot on the city counsel in the previous elections. I found some interest to further my career in this venue for the future, though my main core of business and trade was to be a commodities trader in the heart of Boston itself. I had brokered in my time a few influential deals on an international level; traveling to Hong Kong and Singapore, Ireland, Switzerland, and even Tokyo a few summers before.

Sandra had become a court-appointed attorney for the Boston court system. It had always been one of her loves. Neither the money nor the associated fame was of any appeal to her. But defending the defenseless, as she emphasized, was her greatest contribution. She quickly developed a reputation as being a tuff-minded, D.A.-circumcising, hard-core, don't-mess-with-me attorney. Sandra took the greatest pride in giving her all to her clients, helping and assisting justice to prevail, and receiving nothing more than a hug from the family and a 'Thank you' from those she defended.

I often went to the courtroom to see her during a high-profile, critical case. When the odds were stacked against her, was when she turned out her best performances. The D.A.'s office made tireless attempts to hire her on as well as some of the top attorneys and law firms in Boston. She remained as she had always been; a dedicated servant to those who needed her the most.

As the children began to wean from bottle to crawling to walking, and eventually (as unfortunate as it may be sometimes) to talking endlessly, I had made a practice to take the kids back to fire station 112. I remember my father's reaction the first time I had done so. He nearly wept at the first sighting of them there, recovering and showing about the place as though it was the most famous relic of Boston.

Cory had taken a especial liking to Gerry, who by his own aging charm, had turned fully gray now; though he never lacked the energy, smile, and gleam that made him such a dear friend to me. And yes, he still carried the autograph of Nat King Cole wherever he went. I, to this day, still marvel at his kindness and his charitable ways to all which engaged him.

"Still have that Yaz baseball card?" he asked.

"Haven't been to any fires of late," I returned with a smile.

"You still got it Little Pa?" Then he looked at me with a curious and confused look about him, staring out over my children who were playing in the front lawn, "Little Pa…Little Pa," he whispered, "Don't suppose I can call you that anymore. How about…Big, Little Pa now?"

"That gets a bit complicated," I laughed.

"We sure did miss you Conner," he became all serious in a sudden, "Strangers come more often than that son."

"I'll make better time, next time," I replied.

"Good," he slapped me on the shoulder with that powerful hand of his, "Cause if you do? I'll have to chase you down in my wheelchair; you hear?" He shook his finger on me loud and clear.

I turned with a serious look of my own sitting over my face. My motions were silent and I walked from room to room near the kitchen, wondering so as I looked down where Skip's bowl had gone to.

"Here Skip," I whistled about, "Skip. Skip."

"Don't you know," Gerry came over to me and placed his heavy arm over my shoulder, "You'se crazy you know? Dogs don't live to be twenty years Little Pa. Skip's been gone for eight years."

"So why didn't somebody tell me when he got sick?"

"He died in his sleep soon after your last time here. It was sudden like. Only nature I suppose, that he would pass peaceful like. They found him the next morning with his nose propped up on his bowl," Gerry gave me the saddest look when he spoke.

Meanwhile father had become much more dusty gray now in his hair. His reading glasses had become all-wear glasses. His walk was a little light in step and less sure; his stance more stooped than before. I could tell when he spoke that his voice sounded most tired and dry, and it took to quiver at times. He didn't go out on calls much anymore, but stood guard at the firehouse, and made all the dispatches.

"When you going to retire Captain?" one of the younger fireman jokingly spoke out.

"When I get good and ready," father grinned back.

"When will that be?" another called out.

"When I get good and ready," he grunted, "to be good and ready," and he shuffled off to sit up in one of those fire truck cockpits. I could sense he really missed making those runs.

"Someday soon," I looked over to Gerry, "You'll be Captain."

"Oh no Little Pa," he shook me off, "Your father's Captain. He was born for it; takes a special kind of spirit to do that deed."

I could see it in my father's eyes. He was caught in between something; a rock; no, two rocks of time. For some reason he felt out of breath running on the tracks of his own life; being caught now silently in his own memories, or wondering about the scarcity of his future and what it would hold for him. It was beyond the point of mid-life crisis, and it reflected in his expression like a shadow which was constantly pursuing him. Even in the brightest light, you could see the thorns of that shadow always mindful over him.

Something had passed him by, yet he didn't appear to know what it was, or how to remedy the situation. So he was continually reminded, caught in his own silent sorrows; wondering; always wandering. Perhaps this was the prelude to his own fears.

Now Lorie had married several years back to her long time love Marshall. She graduated from Boston College with her degree in Education, with an emphasis on Business and Economics. Within two years after this, she had acquired her master's from Boston College and held her dissertation on the mathematical influences of increasing foreign trade on the U.S. economy. She had devised a mathematical equation in taking 'What If' scenarios and applying them to current economic conditions. This astutely landed her a professorship at Northeastern University. Marshall on the other hand graduated with his degree in Business and he became a marketing director for a local firm in Boston.

Amanda had become quite serious about her acting career. Stage, film, dance, short plays, long plays, tap; Amanda had become so skilled; she could perform it all under the slight auspices of perfection, and so being employed within the theater district. A struggling actress of no doubt, but it gave her opportunity to spend valuable time with my children; and she adored every moment with them. Amanda had the natural instincts of a mother, and she held the uncanny ability to discipline and communicate with children all in the same stroke.

Adam had become well recognized in the art community of Boston. His paintings and portraits were hanging from galleries all over the New England area. I forever marveled at his increasing skill in this particular venue, but I could sense the very isolation which still had taken a more powerful possession on him, sitting there born in the strokes of his paint brush. He still held to his obscure social level and he seemed to shy away from any assemblage of admirers. It was the most difficult matter for him whenever they did an unveiling of several of his new works. He would show up only for the shortest of spells; stand over the podium, see the canvases brought into full view, hear the admiration, the applause, the handshakes from those around, then slowly dissipate into seeming thin air.

He had taken residence in a flat in southern Boston where he kept to his isolation and to himself most of the time. Of course there were rather rare visits from his most immediate family. Adam simply preferred the company of himself and his empty canvas; nothing more.

Grandmother had passed away in her sleep four years before. She never recovered from the unfortunate fire of her home and tender belongings. There were times when she would as suddenly appear, then disappear as quickly back into that private and illusive world of hers. I had not realized just how long grandmother and I had spoken. But at the outset of her funeral I came to the notion our final conversation was indeed on the night of my prom. Perhaps it was all she needed to give to me; to say her one final phrase, 'Find her.' This would always have a lasting affect over me.

Now my mother had aged as much as anyone through these preceding eight years. Her hair held threads of large sweeping white gray; her cheeks less of rose and flush; more textured to pale and puffy from her increasing weight. You could see her vintage smile whenever a happy thought crossed over her mind it and forced out the beauty in her expression when it passed by. Her voice had become more soft and soothing, and required less from her hard discipline of earlier years. Time had rather given to her a more vast resource of wisdom to utilize, rather what one might suspect as mere complacency. Her love had nurtured an endless well of kindness and charity that I had grown to admire beyond any measure I could have ever conceived.

Her talents grew to every corner and group whose first priority was to help others of less fortune. Whenever there was a rainstorm, she would be one of the first to help a family in need. If a fire had left a family without food, shelter, and clothing; mother would organize a drive in what she called her 'three-step process'. Food first; Shelter second; and clothing coming up in the rear.

But I believe her greatest love and fondest admiration was with her grandchildren. The duty to her family caused her the greater joy. It was her spectacular horizon that she awoke to every morning, and beamed the finest sunset just before she went to sleep. I would often see her reading to Cory and Tyler when we stayed at their house, or attempt to be in play in the backyard whenever the children wished to throw Frisbee, or play catch; dance across the lawn at dusk and try to snare a firefly or two in a jar. Her body was unwilling, but her heart held more to compensate for this.

It was her charm to life; to cast the lots of her love like ripples in the pond and watch them go wherever they may. She knew the influence of charity had the long, lasting affect she desired; to cast out the strongest ripples possible was her intent.

My siblings and I had been planning our parent's fortieth anniversary for sometime now. Though Adam was not a direct participant in this matter, he gave his lukewarm approval to it all. When all was set and placed into formality, he sprung it on me that he would not be attending any of the functions.

"Something has come up brother," he called me by phone.

"Adam," I huffed, "We have been planning this for four months now. Nothing is more important than this. You know mother would want you there, even if you were on your death bed."

"I know," he paused, "I can't go into any detail now, but something has simply come up that I can't avoid."

"Adam," I pressed.

"Trust me on this Conner," he fussed, "My work has precedence on this occasion."

"And your family," I stressed.

"They'll be there after it's all done."

"You just don't understand," I said in a cross fashion, "You are mindless to it all. It's totally inconceivable the resolve your actions have. Do you know brother?"

"I don't need a sermon Conner," he reacted.

"Good," I shot out at him over the phone. "Nor do I need a single, deaf-minded congregation to try to convert. I hope someday your paintings will talk back to you and give you all the joy you are currently passing up with the family, which cares for you most."

"It's never so easy," he responded, "You get involved…"

"Well you make the sacrifices then," and I hung the phone up on him, stewing about the house in quiet fumes for nearly an hour afterwards. Sandra knew to let me be; to simmer into a talkable conversation when all was clear.

I informed my sisters the next day on Adam's plans not to attend. Amanda figured as much from him; while Lorie made mention to give it a try on her behalf.

"Let him be," I said, "He's the greater loss for it."

The next day was indeed their fortieth anniversary. And as it so happened, Jason was to pitch at home for the Red Sox that very day. We had arranged it through their P.R. office to have my parents attend the evening game in prime seats; just behind the Red Sox dugout. To have their names flashed on the high screen in the middle of the fifth inning and to have someone sing their favorite song over the intercom during the seventh inning stretch.

A limo would come at their home around five to pick them up; a candlelight dinner awaited them on an exclusive porch overseeing the Boston harbor. I was to make sure they had not developed plans of any kind, though my father was in fits wanting to take mother out to a local lobster restaurant. It took all my foreseeable powers to keep them in bay until the limousine arrived.

Without a hitch, and to their gleeful surprise, my parents were whisked away to a fanciful night of celebration and fun. The July evening was crisp and warm from the humidity; the winds died down to nearly a crypt level, and without even a stir. The deep harbor shores echoed the sights of those flickering lights adorning the surrounds of that waterway. The skyline seemed to float in that calm night blackness and vast well of sparkled stars.

We were to meet them at the ballpark. And nearly six forty-five that evening, they would appear, coming down the high-arched steps. Father was wearing a Red Sox hat and a signed jersey Jason had supplied for them at the ticket counter; mother having a fine bouquet of flowers settling on her lap.

"Jason said he was going to win this one for you," I told them, as I leaned over in a whisper.

My father could hardly pull the grin from his expression. Though to my surprise, as I looked out over my mother, I could sense a weary spell dipping into her eyes. She kept to the pleasures of my father and she did not want to disturb the enjoyable time he was having; yet I could sense the tired nature in her look. Her smile was quick to fade; her cheeks drawn and not as responsive. She was most quiet and to herself, though she would force out a smile when the occasion called for it.

"Mother," I bent to speak with her, "Are you alright?"
"I am fine son," she gave a pat to my wrist, "Just tired."
"Perhaps a soda will do," I began to get up from my seat.
"No," she forced another smile, "Really. I am fine."

During the sixth inning, after making it as far as able, she had requested Sandra to accompany her up those long stairs to the bathroom. The evening activities had worn her weary thin.

"Watch the kids," Sandra instructed me.

"Maybe I should go," Lorie interjected, "We can both go."

They all three moved up toward the outer rim of the ballpark and dispatched out into the hoards of people going for concessions and breaks. The sixth inning came and went; the bottom half did the same with little fanfare. I stretched back my eyesight to view if they were on their back to return; still nothing. The seventh did as much, yet my father was quite involved with the game, and paid no mention to them being gone so long. I stood into the nearest isle, nervously pacing from one step to the next; still nothing. I gazed back over Cory and Tyler; Amanda and Marshall, as well as father. The visitor half of that inning was one out away from being complete.

'Surely they would not miss the seventh inning stretch, and the announcement of their wedding anniversary, along with a song dedicated to them,' my pacing grew more rapid; dread worry became more evident in my expression.

"You go and check on them," Amanda cautiously said, "We will watch the children."

This was my excuse to take leave on. I rushed up through those long stairs, nearly darting past several steps at one move. I dodged all the various vendors huddled about those steps like obstacles in my road. I kept my viewpoint constant in the upward position as I watched for any sign of them; still nothing. I reached to the top almost without my breath. Left, right, then left again; trying to gather my navigations and directions accordingly. I felt the hot sweat of that summer dripping from my forehead; the faces meshing into one blur. The calls; the screams; the muddled voices drove through my ears as I wandered about with apparent anxiety; purging with my dogged-look about.

The heaving of my breath; the palpable perspiration dripped from my cheeks as my clothes grew hotter still; nothing still. I asked a few people if they had seen three women pass this way; one more elder than the other two. No one seemed to know, nor had an inkling to them; everyone looked the same. I pushed beyond more vendors wanting to sell me a cotton candy, drinks, and a program; even pushing one to the ground when he became more insistent that I purchase something from him.

"Hey!" he cried, "Watch it buddy." I moved onward, looking with the piercing eye of a hawk; still hearing his voice echo in my ears, "Did you see that?"

I stalled, spun about in a three-sixty turn, watching for any movement faintly associated with Sandra's high-postured step, Mother's white-flame hair, or Lorie's astute-walking style. I wiped my brow free and my forearm nearly stuck to my forehead. My breath became more disturbed from the commotion about.

They had been gone for nearly twenty minutes to this point; still nothing. I stepped further, each pulling me farther away from our seats; the crowds assembling into a mob about me. My gaze pushed out further still; wanting, wishing to find them approaching me. I went to the first ladies, long-lined bathroom area.

"Sandra," I called out, "Sandra," I made further attempts, "Lorie," my cries were more desperate now, "Lorie," I could feel my breath escaping me again, "Mrs. James," I yelled like an intercom call, "Your son is looking for you." Still, nothing. The mass of faces all looked foreign to me; strangers of unknown quantity passing to me a sort of odd spectacle look as I went around.

Seventh inning now split into its stretch. I heard the announcement over the full stadium speakers.

"We want to welcome all of you to a very special event. Today is the fortieth anniversary of two long beloved Red Sox fans…Mr. and Mrs. Allen James!" a huge roar went throughout the stadium, along with the cascades of applause. Certainly now this would bring my mother forward to receive that acknowledgement; still nothing.

I sought the refuge of my hope; to find her as soon as I could and to discover her to be well. I glanced back into my mind when I saw her face last; the tempest shadow lurking in her eyes. Light; then shadows pulling through the horizon of her looks. Those eyes; so esteemed in every moment I had known her, was now fluttering in uncertainty. I knew something was amiss and it had frightened me whole.

"Now to sing 'Blue Dream Mountain', is Andrea Bright," Another roar, and so I thought this would bring mother out to the brink of those stairs; back near to the playing field where she could hear her most favorite song of all. She would always stop to listen when this song played about the radio, no matter what she had going at the time. It was her moment to smell the roses.

My pace took me to section C where another line of people were in wait to use the facilities there. I called out for all three; still nothing. Yet the song played from verse to chorus, then back to verse again. Jason had long left the game with a sizeable lead. If the Red Sox would hold to the lead, he was up for his eight victory of the year. But the game fell off the chart of importance to me; an instinct, something that held a tenuous implicit string from child to mother and from mother to child was pulling on me; tugging war with me as if indeed there was a fracture between us.

I pushed through more in haste now. People gazed in curious wonder as I vaulted from one section to another; nearly tripping, sometimes falling, running into the columns, bolting in every direction in hopes to at last recover them. It seemed a futile attempt to continue any further, so I moved back to our seating, and so found Lorie sitting near the children.

"Where is Sandra?" I asked her, "Where is mother?"

"They are up close to the exit ramp," she said.

"Why?" I was most aggressive with the word.

"Mother doesn't feel well," she replied, "She couldn't even make it back down the stairs. She was way too weak."

"Then we should go to her," I pursued.

"We are," Amanda stated, "We were waiting for you to return. We didn't want you to be looking for us, and we had already left."

"I think mother is the greater concern," I grabbed Cory up near to me, and began shuffling his things in my pockets.

"Where is grandmother?" he questioned with cherry icy dripping all over the rim of his lips.

"We will go to her Cory," I tried to reassure him with a smile, "Now get your things; help your sister please. Father, can you grab Tyler?" I rotated and pulled Cory up over my shoulders so he could sit around the back of my neck.

"Lead the way," I said to Lorie.

Our group moved as quickly as the slowest member would allow. Tyler seemed to want to view everything as we passed by, halting our progress further until we had finally reached the exit ramp. I saw mother sitting, huffing a bit, with tired eyes barely able to lift up to see us coming towards her. Sandra's expression spoke to me the magnitude of what was occurring.

"I guess today was a little much," she made a shaky and crumbled attempt to grin, "Little much indeed."

"What's wrong mother?" I pulled Cory off of me and I bent to her with my eyes exploding from their sockets, "Are you hurting?"

"No son," she dropped her hand on mine, "Just very tired. A good night's rest is the best cure and remedy for me."

"I'll take her home," father stepped in.

"Don't you think she might need to see a doctor?"

"She will be fine," he continued, "She has had spells like this lately. Your mother just needs her rest."

"Spells like this," Lorie questioned, "For how long?"

"A few months," father looked hard on us.

"No really," mother hastily took to her feet, "I am fine. Really. My sinuses have been acting up of late. Just worn down from this I suppose." She grabbed father's hand and they moved out into the parking deck area. I could see her walk was on the verge of dragging.

"Maybe she should go to the doctor," I spoke out, when father turned around and gave me a look to whip me with.

"Listen," he insisted, "We can handle this; between us. I know how to help your mother."

"She might need medical attention," Amanda spoke more freely on it, "There could be a problem."

"I am telling you children," he growled, "We can handle this. Your mother and I have been married for forty years. Don't you think I could tell if something was wrong with her?"

"I'm not questioning this," I replied.

"Yes you are," he spat, "I'll take her home. She will get her rest and she will call you tomorrow."

We all watched helplessly as they slowly made their way to the car. The misty grays of that night hovered low, as if the famed ghosts of Boston history had returned for one final venture into the living. The hoarish mist of fog and rolling, tumbling fumes filtered throughout the entire Boston area, appearing to be like tentacles of some larger beast probing within the low-lying streets; from the Waterfront, into Charlestown, the Back Bay, South End, and even into parts of Cambridge.

I could see the famous churches had lost their high liberty bells and chamber-top steeples as we drove homeward. Gases seemed to pour out of the cemeteries and spill out over the road curbs; streets lights dimmed from that particular excess, within those constantly roving and thickening clouds.

There was a war between the Lights and Shadows that evening; a convergence of conflicting souls re-enacting the wages of past battles which had been born by the peoples of the past. On this night they appeared to be as alive as we were. My soul was restless with worry; my voice silent, unmoved, as if I had found the therapy of muteness to guard me. My mind roamed no further than the duty of my mother's welfare. Something was wrong, as that instinct tugged on me like a constant vice with no cure.

Sandra drove us home; the kids as strangely silent as I was. Her hand touched my leg. I couldn't feel it. My thoughts were numbing my every sense into oblivion. I knew the night to come was to be an act of terror in my attempts to sleep. I saw the streets pass by the passenger window in the dripping fog and motion of our car. The haze cut across the hood of our car and drifted down into a silent wave of obstruction. The stoplights seemed faint in their yellows, greens, and reds now. The side lamplights were glowing as though they were a bulb too weak for this ever-increasing fog.

We saw roving souls quietly parading down the sidewalks in two's and three's; always looking back on us as our lone car traveled from street to street. The harbor seemed oddly baron now when we traveled over that long Charles River Bridge. The mist rolled out in a cussing sort, with a strange and uninviting cantation by its mere sight.

A few ships docked about. There still was no beacon accustomed to the harbor bay to call for more ships home. Even the waves beneath us looked cautious in the rolling in and out from shore. The pattering of their streams dribbled in a sort of dance with that ghastly hue.

I could see the reflection of my eyes in the window, so staring back at me with a measure of longing in their face. My hand propped my chin up for that view. I had traveled a long distance away from the car in my own mind. A world I was confused by; reflecting in a serenade of thoughts and visions from my own past.

There was a tint of stain in the air, and so clouded the skyward view with its glum appearance. Every so often, the moon would peek through for only a moment or two, and then dissipate underneath these converging waves of dew and clouds.

"She'll be fine," Sandra spoke out to break off the silence in the car, "I'm sure it is just the activity of the day."

"My mother's never been tired," I responded, "Not like this. Never like this."

"Conner," Sandra whispered, "Its best not to scare the children," she watched me stare back on their drooping selves.

"They don't know," I softly spoke, "You are right; it's best they do not know."

"I think we should hold off on that speculation."

"I agree," I stalled, "But I know there is something out there."

"How?" she shot back.

"Because my dear," I paused and drove a stare directly on her, "I can feel it."

We stepped back into our silence once more.

Our home was unlit when we approached; undisturbed and seemingly cold from the casting shadows of that night.

I gathered up Cory, as did Sandra take about Tyler. Still, they slept through it all. Even as they were laid to bed, placed about a goodnight kiss, and were tucked in for the night.

Sandra and I retired to our room, lapsing still in that same coma of silence. We stirred only for a short bit, readying for bed, and soon finding ourselves all tucked in for the evening. I rolled to the window side, felt the coffin air from the outside seeping through the cracks of that window. The curtains coursed a simple dance of their own as the low muddle of whistling wind faintly echoed in an aimless haunting about our room. I felt in my heart Heaven was sleeping, if only for a little bit. The blackened soot of night skyline and its replete spell for darkness cursed my hope for as long as the night would stay.

Dreams would not bring me refuge. I had to battle the fears which were cutting me from my sleep; to wrestle with an angel; to find light where only the night lay still. I stared into nothing, hearing only the fading sounds of reality around me, wondering what the morrow would bring. I again felt the touch of Sandra to my shoulder; still, I could feel nothing, nor did I move to recognize her care. She was like the rest of the world; a distance travels away.

I got from my place after an hour of simply wandering around the day dreams of my thoughts. I took nurture in that same chair my grandmother used to fall off from the world some years before, it now sitting closest to that window.

I stared most constant out into the world; it posing as nothing more than an empty black canvas. So I dreamed of a world. Painted lines, and coursing curves; bright colors and vacant shadows; texture moods in a stroke, the drawings of a dream.

I sensed I was becoming the artist of my brother; feelings now on display in that fictious artistic play. There was forever a sunrise and a sunset in that rendered picture. The dawn of lights and shadows; the dusk of lights and shadows, all poised to draw the eye into a constant viewing without even a blink.

The world had lapsed from me and I was in a strange place. Unknowing, insecure, the harbor of no dock for my ship; still I was wandered; hoping, still hoping, always hoping.

"Sometimes," I heard my mother's echo strike me like lightening to an apple's core, "The sorrows come before the Joys can follow."

I shook at this; these ghostly words from her remembered voice. It seemed at that moment she was reaching across the bay and attempting to touch me with the fingers from her heart.

I felt the breeze cuddle my soul; the breath stalled and unconvinced I still lived in that same world. I stared back out into this black abyss, searching for that painting I had drawn in my mind only moments before. It was gone and faded from all internal view; lost like all else into pictured memory. What remained were only the shadows on that infinite, dark, and listless night dripping against my window's view.

"Are you coming to bed?" I heard Sandra's whisper reach for me, "Come to bed Conner," she bent down to my side.

I lifted myself from that precipice; the vantage point surreal and lacking of Heaven's warmth. I went with her back to our bed, and so settled into that same position as I had before; this time I remained, waiting, pondering, and waiting for sleep to come.

I had wrestled with an angel that night and it was myself. And when the match had finally subsided I found my dreams waiting for me.

Chapter 19

The Colors of Reality Show Like a Rainbow.

A morning fog had replaced the heavy dew from the night before. All appeared normal, not obscene like the previous evening. I was early to rise with Sandra and I quickly hastened the children to be ready for school. Sandra was off to her law practice and I to go downtown for a day of office work. Morning coffee, a pastry, the morning paper, and light sugar awaited me at my office when I arrived. I flipped to the front sports page. I saw in full color my friend Jason plastered from one edge to the other.

'Jason Winchester wins Eighth for Sox,' he looked from a profile shot, stretching gallantly across the pitching rubber. I read through the article and the writer had made mention of my parent's fortieth anniversary in small print, down at the bottom of the page.

The day crept hour into hour, stepping into its constant pace of one second building on top of another second. I had several meetings to attend to; conference calls at eleven; client luncheon at the 'Bishop's Harbor Restaurant'; board meeting at two, and finally a proposal I had to draft up for the following day.

"Mr. James," my secretary stepped through the doorway of my office, "I believe it is your sister on line three." I hesitated to check my watch and see that it was nearly four.

"Hello," I picked up line three; nothing more than a crackle, honking of a horn, and the blaring sirens cascading off in the distance somewhere, "Hello?"

"Conner," it was my sister Lorie.

I heard a sniffle follow as though a cry had been sitting in her voice for sometime.

"Lorie?" I bent over my desk with a cutting expression.

"Conner," she paused to gather herself, "You need to come quickly. Something is wrong with mother."

"What's wrong?" I pressed, "Lorie, talk to me."

"Dad called a short bit ago," she continued, "They have been up all night. I'm not sure…" she babbled and cried again.

"Lorie," I pressed further, "What did he say?"

"They've been up all night," she came to a full cry, "Mother's legs have swelled twice their size. She's been in so much pain. He couldn't even touch her. Tried everything; cold cloths, warm water." She dropped in her speech.

"Lorie," I said, "You're not making any sense."

"I am trying Conner!" she yelled back, "Dad was crying."

"Where are they now?"

"He's getting her ready," she returned.

"Ready for what?" I stood and exclaimed.

"To take her to the hospital," she replied, "You have to go; he's not able. Not in any condition to…"

"Are they home?" I questioned.

"I think," She started, "I don't know. I think."

"Are they home??" I inquired further.

"I don't know," she wept in full tears then, "Conner…"

"Let me get off of here," I pushed, "Where was he taking her to?" I held the phone more tightly then.

"New England Medical Center," she said, "I believe. I am just not all that sure Conner."

"Let me get off of here," I nearly hung up on her.

"Conner," she cried, "Look…after…her; he's…not…able."

"Meet me there," were my last words to her.

I shuffled the phone about as my secretary began to drift in, dressed in a shocked and serious look on her face.

"Get me the McDonald's account," I asked, "Now Mrs. Simpson."

I dropped the phone and pushed it about the desktop in a near frantic endeavor to gather it up again.

"Is there anything I can do?" she spoke softly.

"Just get me the account please," I began to dial.

The phone; one, two, three rings. I slammed the phone down fist first; redialed; more rings. One, two, three rings; still no answer. One final try; pause, then a single ring-an answer.

"I can't stay," my father's voice weakly came on the line.

"Dad!" I cried, "Dad! Mother!" Another terrifying, painful pause, "Where is she? Dad! Please!"

"She's not well son," he wept, "She had a bad night."
"Where are you taking her?" I asked.
"Doctor," he leaned about in a single word.
"Which one?" I quickly blurted.
"Medical Center," he softly posed, "I believe."
"Do you need me to help you get her there?"
"I don't know," he seemed most confused.
"Can you get her to the car?" I was even most hasty in this.
"Yes," he said, "I can manage."
"Are you sure?" I called one last time.
"Conner," he wept, "She is in a lot of pain."
"Dad," I said, "Get her to the car. I'll meet you there."

There was silence, a click; the phone died. I felt my heart beat through and beyond the walls of my chest as I dropped the phone onto my desk. My secretary rushed forward with three files in hand, so pressing them inside my briefcase. I pushed the phone violently from my desk as it went crashing across the room; Mrs. Simpson jumped backward in near shock.

"Have to go," I sneered at the open door, grabbed about all my things, and I began for that opening. She moved aside.

"But sir," she called back, "Mr. Johnson."

"He'll have to wait," I looked quickly at her, then in my pause, "I have a more pressing issue. Be polite in my favor."

"I'll inform him of your emergency," she replied.

Such a long walk; such a very long walk; the steps to my empty car were like lands and oceans away from me. Travels were more of a voyage than a normal step to go home. But my destination would not take me there; rather, my destination was untold; a voyage with no compass; no map to guide me by. A captain without its ship of sails, as it so seemed I was wandering into a foreign land.

The long hallways were as caverns and caves with more twists than I could remember how to get through. As I passed, people stared in such strange wonder; some with grimace, others in a frozen and stunned expression. I paid no heed yet made my way from a quick pace into a trot, and then finally emerging like a thoroughbred in a race; the finish line somewhere in the distance.

I galloped down the stairs; their rotating turns nearly put me in a spell. I tried for the elevators; slow as cold and winter molasses dripping from an icy spoon. So I continued down each floor of stairs, as I skipped the stairs in a near freefall. The railing hugged me by my left hand; my right arm tucking away all of my papers. My suit was brushing against that self-made wind; the tie flipping from left to right shoulder, and then back again.

"Conner," a young lady I knew called for me. I passed her in-between floors. Still, I continued. I could feel the punishing moment drive me into further worry. The world I knew had halted to a stop; pushed its hand into my face and made me feel the pain from its forceful palm. After fourteen flights of stairs I had now entered the main lobby. Some were leaving from work at that hour; still, I rushed through their waves without reserve or caution.

"What the…" one man felt me clip his shoulder with mine; his face told all of his anger, "Hey butt nick!"

I ran for the turnstile carrousel just ahead of me. People unsuspecting were passing beyond its glass frame and out into the main street. The flesh from my face seemed to push past my cheeks as I vaulted down this long opening and into the carrousel itself. I thrust the long handle with the heave of ten men, while others on the other side felt the sudden rush of my force, and began to tumble through into the building.

Two blocks left; turn on Oaks street and down Barter's. My feet pressed forward; the open air now casting the hot sway of sunlight against my face. My brow beating sweat; my hands perspiring into a drip; my eyes blurring from the motions around me; the sounds merely illuminating into nothing more than people in glass cages of their own device.

My speed never slowed when I galloped reckless into the street. I was nearly being clipped by an oncoming truck. The lights green; the pedestrian walk sign red; still I ran from street corner to the next; down onto a side street, through the guarded parking lots; past construction, and onto a parking deck where my car sat vacant in lot B, second level.

I heard the echo of honking horns; tires grabbing the biting pavement as the cars turned down into the exit.

"How are you Mr. James?" one of the guards asked, losing his smile into a brisk gaze of concern, "Mr. James?"

Still I continued, tireless, undaunted, unwilling to yield, and finding my car where I had last parked it.

"You're in no condition," I saw a friend come to my window once I started the car, "Let me drive you."

"What?" I rolled my window down briefly.

"James," he exclaimed, "Let me drive you," he reached inside the cabin and grabbed for the ignition.

"No!" I pushed his hand off.

"Get out!" he demanded as he stepped back.

"Sorry Quinton," I forced the car in reverse, "I don't have time for this," I saw him step in front of my car as I placed it in drive.

"Come to your senses man," he pleaded, "You nearly knocked everyone over to get out here. You're going to kill yourself."

"Move Quinton," I responded in a stark and headstrong look back over him; his hands pressed to the hood of my car.

"Conner," he suggested, "Look at your self."

"Move Quinton," I became more aggressive.

"Listen," he posed, "I'll take you."

"Quinton," I bantered one last call towards him, "Move!"

"No," he shook his head nervously at me.

I rose from my car, slammed the door nearly to the passenger side; my eyes stern to his. I folded my hands around his lapel, forced him into reverse, and shot him across the parking deck against a concrete pillar, "I said…MOVE!"

"You are going to get yourself killed."

He watched as I headed out of the deck in a screeching heap of screaming tires and sharp, hair-pinning curves.

I reached the hospital within minutes, parking where I could and not caring if I was towed away or not. Attendants, nurses, and shift-changing physicians stared on as I pushed my way through the front doors, and flatly before the head secretary.

"May I help you?" she said with reserve.

"I need to know where Lauren 'Anne' James was taken."

"Was she admitted today?" she flipped through her charts; checked her screen, and spun back to me.

"Within the last few minutes," I said, "She had to be."

"It wouldn't show sir," she replied, "System updates only every thirty minutes; we only batch register here."

"Can you look further please?"

"Sir…If she were in the hospital, we would have been informed. If she were admitted through E.R., it will take thirty minutes."

"What about the clinic?" I pressed further; the intensity in my voice was rising near into a riled state, "The clinic; check the clinic."

"You'll have to check with the clinic secretary," she slipped her eyes back onto the papers she had been flipping through before I entered, "The clinic is adjacent to the West wing. You will have to go down this corridor, hang a left, up the escalator the third corridor on your right will lead directly into the clinic."

I made my best attempt to remember this; she looking up over me, and seeing the difficulty I was having with it all.

"Just," she lifted her pen up to keep me silent, "follow the signs. They will lead you to the clinic; color-coded orange."

I was off without another word. I clipped my hard shoes over that high-shine checkerboard floor with an eerie echo, as if I were some patron ghost now walking the hallways. Doctors came from every direction, with clipboards in hand and long white coats nearly tailing on the floor.

From every outlet and door people commenced; cleaning crews pushing mops to the side or carrying small white bags of trash to the dumpsters; LPN's darting with their stethoscopes dangling around their shoulders and pens clicking as they quickly walked; nurses shouting out directions to one another. People were sitting in waiting rooms for as long as eternity; their faces in a stoned, glassy stare, and looking into a blur. Some were transfixed to couches and sleeping in any manner comfortable to them. Others playing games; children dancing around a waiting room table while others were leaning up against the phone cubicles and talking in low muddles.

I saw an old man sipping to his late afternoon coffee, watching me impolitely over the top rim of his Styrofoam cup; the steam of its warming brew sitting in a mist at the front of his constant and wary stare. His face had been dried hot ash brown from too much sun; the hand wrinkled and worn; the lips parched and discolored. He displayed a beard unkept and only half-grown; white and made double coarse like hard string. His posture was in a lean, weakly pose yet indifferent as I approached onto where he stood.

"Room 212," he showed few teeth and he spoke through his gums, "Room 212."

"Excuse me?" I looked hesitantly out to him.

"They say she is asleep," he replied, "for awhile. She will be unsick soon…Just heard."

He sipped a longer drink into his cup; his reserve of coffee nearly gone.

"Who are you speaking of?" I wondered aloud to him.

"The misses," he grinned, "they covered her up; but only for a little while. They still have to fix her though." He paused with an unconvincing smile, "She'll be home soon. They promised."

"I'm sorry," I spoke in a turn.

"They say they all go home," I heard him yell towards me. I spun for one final glance over him. His cup slightly elevated as though he were in the midst of a toasting, "She'll go home. They will promise you the same." I sensed the dreadful haunting of his last words to me. That simple phrase landed over my spirits and my hope as a horrible premonition of what lay to come.

I discovered the door leading to the clinic; the doors sweeping back and forth until I pushed my way through, and found the nearest desk possible, "Mrs. Lauren 'Anne' James; Is she here?"

"Are you immediate family?" a nurse imposed.

"I am."

"Relations?" she questioned further, checking her charts.

"Son," I said, "Oldest son. Where is she?"

"Follow me," she directed me down a tight corridor and into an observation room. The heavy door lifted free and I could see my father standing in the corner; his eyes welting; face drawn into recluse. The shock of something seemed most evident in his look.

"Doctor Ogden will be available soon," the nurse left us to ourselves.

I turned to view my mother for the first time. She held out this enormously-tired look to me; nearly engrossing her every blink. Her reading glasses were now propped limp over the farthest edge of her nose; her hair in a fray, as if every strand were unwilling to cooperate with her attempts to brush it down. She still wore her nightgown with a cherry blossom tint to it; her body stretched over the table; back bending into a bowing sit.

"How do you feel?" I softly asked.

"Not too good," it nearly took all of her strength to say this. I observed her puffed hands, seemingly so swollen; the veins could not be viewed. Her legs were extended out on the table's length. And as if my horror had not been addressed, it would so rectify itself with me now. I witnessed her legs had shot up double the size; as they were limbs of no use, laying without motion, distorted, faintly recognizable to what I had remembered before.

My shock streaked across my face for only a brief moment, as though it were a lightening streak across a sunny sky. Then I shoved it back into my inner self again. I had hoped she did not see the strain in my expression, nor give to her more cause to worry with.

"Mother," I cautiously questioned, "how long have your legs been like this?"

"About a week," father answered, still standing in the corner; head down, jaw muscle contorting uncontrollable. His sights were square to the floor and not us.

She coughed; I could sense the congestion riling in her lungs. There was not an air of joy or contentment in her eyes; but grasping the idle whims of fear. I knew by how she took to look on me; wanting me to grab for her and pull her off the side of that cliff she now felt herself slipping from.

The door opened behind me. I turned to meet the apparent Doctor Ogden who was coming into stage there.

"And you must be the son," he extended his hand to shake mine, "Conner, I believe."

"Yes," I held to my own worry as he began.

"Well," he said, "As I have briefly discussed with your parents, there is some cause for concern. We won't have any answers until we run tests."

"What is causing the swelling?" I immediately went into it.

"A number of things may be contributing; possible slight congestive heart failure, perhaps a case of pneumonia. Your mother's symptoms are fatigue, chronic congestion, persistent cold symptoms, pain and swelling of the limbs, especially the lower extremities," he paused, "Mrs. James? Have you had any bleeding?"

"A little…of late." Mother responded.

"In your bowel movements," he pressed further.

"Yes," she continued, "a little."

"How long has this been occurring?"

"Perhaps a few weeks; off and on."

"Increased blood flow? Generally?" he asked.

"Some," she coughed out the word, "My legs felt like they were being attacked by pins last night."

"It could be as I stated. There might be some kidney abnormalities; but without the tests, we will not know for sure."

"Have they been scheduled?" I wondered.

"Not at this juncture. We will have to admit your mother for a few days in order to conduct the tests. It would be the wise choice."

"I didn't think there would be need for a choice," I struggled with my confusion on what he was trying to say.

"We didn't know, your mother and I, if it would be for the best." My father moved a little forward.

"What are you saying?" I strangely looked over him.

"Son," mother weakly stated, to the point it sounded more like a whisper than anything, "I would like to go home."

"The decision always rests with the patient," the doctor replied, in staring back on my gaze around that room.

"Doctor," I objected, "I am not a professional physician, nor would I claim to be one. But I know my mother; have known her for my entire life. I can see she is not well and it is apparent to me she needs to be admitted."

There was an odd silence as they all three watched my every move.

"You tell me doctor; if it were your mother, would you let her walk out without medical attention?"

Doctor Ogden switched his concentration to my father.

"I won't object if it is for the best," father gave his approval.

The doctor, in turn, measured his glance towards mother. She looked about with a most desolate gaze; her face nearly parched without sleep; she too, looked as though she had been wrestling with an angel, as I had done the same night before. She said nothing rather. She looked about the room at all of us, wanting someone to make the decision for her.

"Doctor Ogden, if there is reason to admit her, then we need to admit her today; without delay."

The doctor appeared to wrangle with this in his mind, deliberating as a jury to his own thoughts, and then gazing out over the three of us; his hand cupped underneath his chin.

"I'll have the nurse contact the admissions office. We will schedule tests to begin; perhaps this evening." The decision was made, "Otherwise, we will hold her for observation tonight."

He left the room, attending to his immediate call to the hospital. It was shortly thereafter when we made our way from clinic to the admission area. I knew my mother had a great deal of discomfort at this juncture. However she made no note of it, nor did she remark on the extent of her pain. She simply smiled with those tired eyes of hers; look about in a mist and fog, and squirm about in her wheelchair they provided for her when the pain became too great.

"Name; last name first, then first name and middle initial," the admissions officer asked as she began pulling forward a whole array of paperwork to be filled out.

"James, Lauren Annie," my mother commented.

"Date of birth," she continued.

"October twelfth, nineteen thirty-six."

"Location of birth..." the woman never moved to stare on my mother, keeping her pen to the point of paper at all times.

"Boston Mass," mother replied in more discomfort.

"Social Security Number?"

"Listen," I interrupted in a brew, "Is this really necessary?"

"And you are?" the strict, expressive officer said.

"I am her son," I stated, "She needs assistance, not a test quiz on her entire life. I'll be happy to supply the necessary information; all that you need when she is in her room."

"Mr. James," she started, "this is all required for insurance purposes," she flipped her pen upside, and began padding the form with the back end of it.

"Then I will take personal responsibility for it, until the forms are completed," I stood and pushed my chair from underneath me.

"Mr. James, we cannot..."

"Don't tell me what you cannot!" I angrily growled, "Admit her! Do it! Here! You want an insurance card?" I flung my wallet open and threw several cards on her desk, "Credit cards as well; max at fifty thousand each. That should do."

"Mr. James," she pressed further, "the procedures must be followed. I have very little latitude in the matter."

"So she sits," I exclaimed, "in obvious pain, while you sit there and take bland notes over her personal information."

"Don't paint me as unsympathetic," she warned.

"No," I pointed, "Just matter-of-fact about everything. I'm sure you see this all the time. For me? For her, this is our first time. So do us the general kindness and have her taken up to a room and attended to by the doctors and nurses she desperately needs now."

The woman paused, blinked a few times, stammered in her thoughts as she took a look at her papers in one final glance.

"If we are quick about this Mr. James."

"Dad," I looked over to my father, "When the nurse comes, can you escort mother up to her room? I will be there as quickly as I can. Leave all your insurance; Medicare, Medicaid information with me."

Within minutes a nurse's aid had appeared to take mother up onto the third floor of the hospital. The Cardiac Ward as they so called it. The concern here, being that whatever was causing her condition it was more likely to be inherent from her heart itself. This would be their first venture toward discovery, and little did we know to what extent and the powerful measures we would have to go through in order to finally determine the nature and cause of her illness.

I had learned later Amanda and Lorie entered the hospital at virtually the same time, and had made their way to mother's room within fifteen minutes of her arriving there herself. I, on the other hand, was spending the good length of an hour down with this plainly sadistic woman who held less personality than the very pen she was working with. I had forgotten precisely the time. I had no sense to whether the evening had arrived or if the afternoon was still in any delay of motion.

Sandra would be calling my work if I were much later than I had already been; she being totally unaware of what had transpired. I made quick change and I made my way to the outer phone area near the canteen.

"Conner," she sounded highly anxious, yet relieved, "Where have you been? I called the office. They said you left in regards to an emergency, but they could not explain what it was."

"It was mother," I spoke in a muddle.

"Where are you?"

"At the hospital," I returned, "We just had her admitted."

"Which one?" her stress level began to rise once more.

"New England Medical," I said, though there was deaf silence, a simple sigh, then a somber, moodish reply.

"I need to come down there…"

"No Sandra," I said, "Stay with the children."

"I can get our neighbor to watch them," she quickly responded, "Jill has always been great with the kids."

"I know," I suggested further, "There is nothing you can do; nothing I can do. I'll stay as long as I can, then I will be home."

"What time will that be?"

"What time is it now?" I asked.

"A quarter till nine," she shot back.

"Gees!" I fluttered, "I didn't know it was this late. I should have called. I left my watch on the office desk at work."

"Do what you need Conner," Sandra tenderly spoke, "If it were my mother, I don't know that I could track time either. How is she?"

I relayed all the evidence of this unknowing crime to her in feverish detail; the symptoms and the elements of what may indicate exactly the cause to mother's illness. It struck a chord with Sandra when I spoke of my mother's apparent duration of pain.

Sometimes they say silence is golden, but as I listened for Sandra's response, I knew there were tears behind her voice; shivering, clamoring to her intended words; keeping them from my ears, and sounding off the silent fears which were now consuming her.

Mother and Sandra had become immensely close over the years. She had been there, holding Sandra through both of our children's childbirths. During her pregnancies, mother came to our home and kept the house as well manicured as she had done with her own residence. There was nothing mother did not assist in with us during the last formidable years. Sandra had become so sequestered with my mother that she had virtually turned into her surrogate mother. My pain was Sandra's pain; of no doubt, but in the larger sight of things, she felt the more so pain my mother was now trying to fend off of herself.

We knew in our darkest intellect that a woman of such virtue and grace, of giving and charity beyond even what the immortal ones could share, was now fighting a lonely battle. A battle we all wished to take the yolk of, collectively force it into submission, and give back the world she had for so many years. But we were indelibly sidelined, unable to contribute to her relief; to share in her pain; to in-act our own sense of corrected fate.

I believe Fate has a feather on one end, and a sword on the other. It can fan us from the heat; yet cut us cold in the winter. This would be a journey whose destination and road held many turns, with no apparent cause or reason for even existing. Still, as fate had turned about its finger as a sword and shown the steely and cold blade it now possessed, it was now inevitably pointed squarely in mother's direction.

"I love you Conner," Sandra said through her tears.

"I love you too," my chin wrinkled in the onset of my own cry, though I held myself until I could find privacy about, "I'll be home as soon as I can."

These words ended our conversation. The warm handset dropped out over the lip and settled back into place. I had felt now the emotions of this time converging over me. Like an ocean tide roaring in from the seabed; when the night comes and you dance over the shorelines; feel the wind pressing your face, and hear those beacons of sound like mighty thunder unearthed from beneath, casting its powerful resonations just beyond your reach. You sense the waves, rising, pushing towards you; so hearing the rumbles coming from the belly of earth itself; rising still; the sound growing in intensity and strength. Then you feel the crash upon the shores and it is here when you feel most alive, and most conscious of your own mortality.

I went into the men's room; found the last stall unoccupied, and I slammed the door behind me. That emotional sea spawned the force of a hurricane within me at this moment. I was falling to the floor, writhing in my own torment as if I were a prince who had just lost his maiden, and now finding himself crying his own ocean of tears. Heaven must have wept with me then.

CHAPTER 20

The Portal Eye into Night.

Several days had come and gone, and I had spent most of this time wondering when time would move at its normal speed. The hours were endless, seemingly tripping over one another to see how slow they might proceed. I would daydream during my work hours; festering my sights on the doings at the hospital. In the evening hours I would attend to home for an hour; no more, then make my way back towards the hospital.

Sandra came each evening with me after the children had been whisked off into bed and the babysitter had come to oversee their activities for as long as it would take us. Cory and Tyler found it most odd that they would go off to bed at such an early time. And the questions began as to why, and for what purpose.

"Daddy?" Tyler would inquire, "Are you and mommy going off again tonight?" She always held that same disturbed look.

"Yes dear," I would respond.

"What for?" was always her answer back.

"There are some things we need to handle dear."

"Why won't you tell me?" The questions never paused with her, "You would always tell us before when you left."

"I know sweetheart," I somberly implied, "Maybe soon."

"When will you be back?" I heard Cory's cautious voice coming from across the darkened bedroom.

"As soon as we can...I can't say when it will be yet," I paused, going over to his bed, "How's the tooth partner?"

He smiled broad with oddball teeth and he wiggled the one in question, "Not ready."

"Now you know," I warned, "At some point in time, it should come out. You don't want to wait too long."

"But it's not ready," he pleaded.

"Well maybe tomorrow then," I whispered and placed a kiss on his forehead, "What is it?"

"You said grandpa was gone a lot when you were little…"

"Yes," I replied, "I did say this."

"You and mother aren't going to be like this," I could see the fit of worry shadowing over his face.

"Oh no dear," I grinned and gave him a fatherly hug, "My place is here, with you, with mother, with Tyler. When tomorrow comes and you awake, your mother and I will be right her—Alright?"

He was well with this and he rolled to his side to begin his rest.

I crept from the bedroom. I stilled their door into a crack; just enough for the babysitter to have ample sight through without creaking the door back and forth during the night.

Sandra and I made our way to New England Medical within moments of placing the children to bed. As we entered, Lorie and Marshall were standing to one side in the spare corner of the hospital room. Father had his seat by mother's bedside, where he had a cot open the two previous nights in staying with her; Amanda stood closest to the door, and so kept a quiet lookout for the nurse.

"I hope we are not late," I said.

"No," father spoke first, holding his arm over mother's bedside. I came closer for a more hawkish look.

"Mother?" I called for her; her eyes dropping over her pupils and appeared more swollen than before, nearly keeping her from seeing me directly, "Mother? Can you hear me? See me?"

"Conner," she weakly spoke, "I dreamed of you…"

"How long has she been like this?" I snapped a look back at Lorie, and found her eyes never lifting off of mother's estate.

"Most of the day," she stated, "But it has helped with the pain; the medication they gave her."

"They still don't know anything," I suggested, "Do they?"

"The doctor will be in shortly," father softly said to avoid mother from hearing him speak. I inspected her legs and feet, which were open from the blankets and still holding to their swelling.

"They stopped the Laysik," I asked.

"No," Amanda said from my rear, "they continued it today."

"Still nothing," I returned.

"Not for several days now," father sat up in his uncomfortable chair, "No movements of any kind. No bowel or urine."

"It should have helped with the swelling…" Sandra came forward, "By now anyways."

"Her legs have reduced," I looked out over to Lorie, "She still has pain in her ankles, feet, legs?"

"It is less," Lorie said, "But there is numbness in her arms."

"They have her on fluid restrictions, but still do not know what is causing her Neuropathy; not yet." Amanda said.

"Hello everyone," a voice from behind us came into the room; it was Doctor Ogden, along with an attending nurse.

"Mr. James," he came to me and shook out my hand, "Conner I do believe. I have some results for you, if you could step into the hallway for a bit."

We all went into the open, gloom-lit hallway. We surrounded him as he became the center of our attention.

"We performed a chest x-ray and there doesn't appear to be any extensive congestive heart failure, but we will keep monitoring her heart for the next thirty-six hours to see if anything will show itself. There is still slight bleeding coming from the uterus but it could be due to her low red blood cell count. An ultrasound showed there is a thickening of her uterus, and we may find cancer there; we'll just have to do a biopsy and see." He paused and his expression became increasingly more serious, "We did a stress test in her feet and ankles; they are very, very weak."

"What is causing that? And the swelling?" I asked.

"Her kidneys are simply not performing well at all. Dialysis is not an option at this point, but it could come to this. The laysik will continue due to her inability to release waste and fluids. There is a fine balance here with the restrictions; we don't want to dehydrate her, but we need to keep the fluids very regulated at this juncture."

"The urologist tests," Amanda blurted.

"They are showing inflammation of the arteries and nerves which very well could be contributing to her fluid retention."

"What could be causing this?" father asked.

"Best estimation at this point? Some form of autoimmune disease along the kinship of Lupus. We aren't sure yet and need more blood work. It's just too early to tell. We are also giving her a stool softener in hopes it will assist."

"And the blood work you have tested?" Lorie speculated.

"Her O2 level is good, as well as her salt level in her blood. She still is having a severe problem with her sinuses; almost to the level it is caked and hard-packed deep in her sinuses. We plan to do a nasal biopsy in the morning to determine exactly what is causing this." He stalled for a moment to allow us all to absorb what he just informed us of, "The CAT scan revealed a large concentration of blockage in her nasal cavities. It seems she has had this for sometime…" he looked about to my father for an answer there.

"Perhaps several weeks, "father stated, shaking off our looks with his head and shifting eyes, "The first I noticed it; and the first she ever complained of having this problem."

"Is there permanent damage to her kidneys?" I inquired.

"Some," he worried me with his own worried look, "To what extent, we can't well say at this time."

We stood, waiting for his next word; and so, by his polite demeanor and politically-correct ways, he summed it up in the best light possible.

"I want to caution each of you. Your mother, and wife, is a very ill woman. There are apparently many complex elements striking her all at once, and we are working to understand the source and reason for this. Until then? We will have to be diligent in treating whatever symptoms she has; as they arrive."

"Like putting out a forest fire in many locations at one time," my father commented, while staring into nothing.

"I am afraid so Mr. James." He said, "We just need to identify the culprit here, and treat it accordingly."

We all stood motionless in that hallway for several minutes or more. Alone in our own thoughts, we were now divulging what was said to us like a bad meal of indigestion. The words were cutting, and nearly heartless to the soul; still, they were necessary words to be spoken. Sandra came to my side and slipped her arm beneath mine in a supportive hug. I draped my arm around her and placed a gentle kiss to the side of her forehead.

"Who is staying with her tonight?" I wondered.

"I will," father quickly shot back.

"No dad," Lorie confessed, "You have been here two nights in a row. Please go home; get some rest. I will stay with her tonight."

"No," he countered, "I insist. I should stay."

"Dad," I interrupted, "Let me take you home."

"No," my father slightly pushed me off in a restrained form of anger, "Sleepless here; sleepless there. It makes no matter. I can't sleep in either place. She needs me."

"Yes she does," Amanda came to father and cuddled him in an embrace, "But she would want you to go home. I'll stay with you tonight; get you breakfast in the morning, and bring you back as early as we can get here to see her."

"But I promised your mother," he nearly wept on this, yet sustained himself as quickly, "All those years, I was away, when you were all so very young. I promised your mother then I would remain by her side, and never leave her again."

"And you have," I pushed my arm over his shoulder, "Don't labor on it like a long, lost, unforgivable sin. She wouldn't want you to sleep night after night in a bad-sitting cot. We will take turns, and make sure she is never alone."

Father looked out over my expression, and then finally conceded to give in. He was speechless all the drive back to his home, though Sandra attempted to comfort him. He instead, most politely, remained at a distance with all of us. I could see the diving remnants of his thoughts collapsing under the hard weight of this reality. He cupped his hand around his chin, stared out with a blank and unveiling stare over the streets as we passed by each of them. I saw him looking, yet his gaze was not where his eyes were. Rather, it was the look of a man in rapture; caught in a corner with his unforeseen foe lurking in the shadows. It appeared his eyes riveted to find this being as it hid and lurked around that unknowing darkness.

I watched my father through the rear view mirror. At every light, I would glance constantly at his continual pose and Sandra held her look to mine, as I were watching him in that similar fashion; a son mirroring his father, and so seeing him begin his own voyage into a dark and seemingly unholy place. His world was changing and he knew it; and the unknowing had become his greater fear. It was apparent to me my father was sitting in the shadows of a very dark place. He now had his own empty sea to cross.

"Good night Dad," were my parting words to him, as I left Amanda and him out near the curb, "See you tomorrow." He said nothing, only to turn and head toward the front door.

Sandra and I made our way back to our home. The lamplights burning low in the downstairs windows as was to the custom for our babysitter to indicate to us the children were still in their beds asleep. We would be most quiet in our entrance.

Little was said while we made our way into our own bed. I could see the register in Sandra's look speak volumes to me without a word spoken. Her eyes were saddened but unwilling to shed those inner tears just sitting on the other side of her expression. A crawl into the bed; lights out, and a simple embrace was all we could muster.

I turned to the outboard window, glanced into the empty and vacant skyline, and spotted the moon peeking back at me. I would not allow myself to wrestle with another angel this evening, so I forced my eyes into a shut and dreamed of the passages of time through my life. The days at the ballpark; trips to the zoo; roller coaster rides on the fourth of July; parades and dances for the seasons; church weddings and bible schools; music halls and arcades; recitals and baptisms; movie theaters and first kisses; all these things flipped through my memory screen in a jumbled, garbled, and incoherent timeline. Yet, in this expanse of my life, these things quickly brought me to my sleep.

I awoke most early the next morning to the racket sounds of the telephone ringing. I picked up the receiver.

"Hello?" I muddled, half asleep.

No answer, just an empty fizzle of a poor connection.

"Hello?" I was most quick this time.

"I think you need to come to the hospital Conner," it was Lorie on the other end; her voice somber and disapproving.

"What has happened Lorie?" I came to a sit in my bed. I checked the clock as it read nearly seven in the morning.

"Don't get dad," she insisted.

"Lorie, talk to me."

"Just come Conner," were her last words to me. I quickly roused from my sleep, made as much haste as I could in getting ready, instructing Sandra to call the office and inform them of my absence until further notice; a quick bite to eat and something to carry out with me, and I was out the door and driving through the streets as if I were a temperamental cab driver.

The hospital was in its early morning bustle with the shift change. I hurried about and made my way back to the third floor. I found my mother's room quarantined off; no one was allowed to enter. I insisted to see her, yet the nurse led me quickly to the chapel where Lorie was alone. I was informed she would tell me everything that had transpired the previous night.

The door swung free, allowed me to enter, and bent back to a shut as I passed through. Lorie was alone; the chapel walls silent and dancing with their stained glass windows. The vestibule holding center stage before me with the podium just off to the left; a Bible propped open and in a stand. The lone figure of my sister; distant and in a far away place I knew nothing of; bent over in the second pew. Her head cast up against the first pew's hard wooden back; her arms in a cross and pressing a sit on her knees as she rocked back and forth; the slight whimpers of tears that would not come to be.

She was lofting prayers to Heaven in hopes someone would answer. Her expression bent in a bow and her eyes tumbled to the carpet floor below. I came to her side, rested my arm gently over her, and tried to pull her into a sit next to me.

"We almost lost our mother last night," she said.

"How can that be?" I asked.

I could see by her look she had not slept any the preceding night. Her gaze was cast into its own weary shadow in the hopes she could find sleep, even for just a moment. The worry she held I had never seen before; the look of someone who had aged ten years in one night. Her voice was gruff and congested, with a cold that seemed to brew by that weak contagion; the hair drooping and unsettled, laying flat over her crown.

"Conner, there was so much blood," she began to massage her eyes, "So much blood. I thought it would never stop."

"Where was it coming from?" I questioned.

"It was like her bowels began to explode. It started shortly after eleven. She would have a movement; I would clean her up, and she would have another, and I would clean her up again."

"How often did it happen?"

"About seven or eight times; every forty-five minutes or so."

"Where were the nurses through all this?"

"Her nurse was on a smoke break when it first began. I went to the other nurses and pleaded for help. They simply told me that she was not their patient; her attending nurse would be back shortly."

"But you spoke of the blood…" I said.

"They said they couldn't chart it since they never saw what was happening, and since I cleaned her up."

"And the doctors?" I went further.

"No one called Doctor Ogden; I requested it however. I just had to wait until mother began all over again. I could tell she was very frightened," Lorie held to a pause for a moment in order to reorganize herself, "There was so much blood."

"They wouldn't let me in as I passed her room."

"And they are not going to. When the first shift nurses came in, they were horrified with what they saw, and called for STAT. Doctor Ogden soon arrived; said this was a simple backslide and she would recover within the next few days from this. Conner, she nearly lost half her blood; they are now stabilizing her with transfusions and IV'S."

"So what caused it; do they know?" I came from my seat, went over to the propped Bible and began mindlessly flipping through the books; from Psalms to Micah; from Micah to Malachi; from Malachi to Corinthians; from

Corinthians to Titus; from Titus to James; from James to John; making my way through the journey's of the Bible with the flip of my wrist.

"They believe it is originating from her intestines; called it G.I. bleeding of some sort. They just don't know precisely where it is. They have scheduled her for a Colonoscopy as soon as she is able. Could be a tear or lesions in her Colon wall; they just don't know."

"Dad will be here shortly," I pondered.

"I know," she fretted, "He'll never leave her side now; he's going to blame himself for this."

"Well little sister," I went back to her, "So why are you here?"

"Waiting," she sniffled, "Doctor Ogden sent me in here to wait for him. He would return to give me a prognosis and plan of action."

"Were you able to talk to mother?"

"Only for a bit," Lorie replied, "They had her stabilized. She seemed to be more comfortable thirty minutes ago."

"Then we will just sit here," I looked over my shoulder; the sight of no one penetrating through the front of this small chapel only made me more uneasy, "and wait for Doctor Ogden to return."

"And pray," she sounded, resorting back to the position she held when I first saw her, "Pray very hard. Conner, I have to feel something out there is telling me to still believe in miracles."

"You did the right thing Lorie," I comforted her, "Don't ever second guess yourself. The outcome is yet to be determined."

"I do believe," she stated, "I still do."

The door swung open from the rear, announcing the arrival of Doctor Ogden. His white jacket curling by his pace towards us; pens all aligned in his upper and lower pockets.

"Mr. James, Lorie," he began, "We had a slight setback last night, as you well know."

"Slight?" I sounded a bit irritated on this.

"A manner of speaking, yes," he said, "this is a rather unpredictable venture here. This certainly makes the biopsy more critical as well as a Colonoscopy. She has also suffered a partial lung collapse, and there appears to have been an allergic reaction to an antibiotic we prescribed her yesterday."

"And the bloody diarrhea?" I asked.

"We don't know if it is caused by a possible tear; lesions, hemorrhaging, or if it is the disease itself; or a combination of all three. We have detected a rather large mass in her rectum, and if cancerous, then we are looking at a very difficult scenario."

"How much so?" Lorie said.

"Enough to warrant," he stopped, "making arrangements."

I was stunned on the breaking of these words to me, nearly pushing me back into the pew. I caught myself, looked away for a moment to pause, casting out a startled air about my expression. And then I brought myself back to him.

"How long would she have?"

"Let me preface this however. It could be nothing more than a hemorrhoid, or a non-cancerous mass. In either case it would not be life threatening; the internal hemorrhoid can be attended to later. If, on the other hand, we are looking at a form of cancer…"

"How long doctor," I persisted.

"Maybe a few weeks…" he said, "Maybe less."

I struggled to stand, yet fell onto the pew in shock from the utter meaning of this. My eyes were unfocused; my voice gasped to speak as I felt Lorie's hand land over my shoulder. The silence prevailed for a second while the doctor allowed us to absorb it. My look ran up to Lorie's; her hand trembling and her lips were pressed hard on one another. This moment, like all others in your life, are known to come; eventually, someday, but never now. They just sit alone, somewhere in that future, yet never quite ready to materialize until you least expect it. We had been blindsided by all this.

I felt the earth was shaking; time stopping into a stutter, then stillness and nothing. You had been shaken from your world and wretchedly dumped into a new one; one which had far less appeal than anything you could have imagined.

"Father should not learn of this," Lorie announced, "Not unless necessary; not unless certain."

"And if it is certain?" I weakly asked, remaining unfocused as I was, "He has to know at some point…"

"Or perhaps not," she said, "Until we are certain; it's best to let it be, and not give him undue worry…"

"I'll tell him," I said, "If the moment comes."

"You will have to make that determination for yourselves," Doctor Ogden spoke, "Listen, we just aren't sure yet what we are dealing with here. It's unlike anything we have seen. I won't deny the terrible impact you are feeling, but this is the time for rational behavior, albeit the more difficult of the two to adhere to."

"Our life is not at stake here," I said, "The decision affects us least of all. How can we tell what decisions to make? Which are right; which are wrong, and have hope for the correct outcome?"

"You'll have to pray." He replied, "And trust on your instincts. This could be a long journey; or the decisions, the most vital, will already be made for you."

"The lesser of two evils," Lorie answered.

"Or," Doctor Ogden came, "The greater of two goods."

"You should have been a philosopher Doctor," I said, still staring out in a daze, watching the empty pulpit remain as such.

"I do better at medicine," he grinned, "My business is to save lives; to save your mother's life."

"We are indebted to you doctor," I could sense the care in his eyes; those stark gray pupils radiating some kind of spectacle thought which showed he was true to his word. His expression was fertile, which always indicated the thoughts and feelings he held deep within.

There were no heirs or 'a-front' to his impression; nor a mask he put on display when his patient's lives came too close to his own. Like a chiseled out piece of clay, showing the varying emotions inside, he worked his eyes; the flux movements and sounds of his voice; the twitching of his cheekbone; the crumbling formations in his chin; the careful blinks and moving stares he rounded about the room with; his high-ledge eyebrows crossing across his forehead in a continual line. All to this was something more than show. It was a man who truly endeared himself to those he deeply desired to save.

My eye caught the corner of his stare. And for a brief instant, when the blink brings it into your look, then blinks it away, I thought I saw the younger self of my father staring back to me. The fireman's hat tilted atop his head; the strong and demanding manner of his countenance beamed a man for sacrifice and duty. His gear sitting all about him just before he was to go; that strong smell of hovering musk odor all reminded me of my father there.

"You wear midnight shade," I asked.

"Yes I do," he replied, with a shy smile.

"My father always wore this," I said, "Its' one rare cologne. Why?" My pause seemed to place him on the spot.

"It's to my liking," he finally said.

"That's what he would say," I paused, "Do what you can Doctor Ogden. I believe you are a man to be trusted."

"I'll take that as a vote of confidence," he bowed.

"Take good care of her doctor," I returned, "She's the only mother I have. There isn't a more graceful person."

"Will do," he said, taking to his leave in a quick pace.

"Doctor?" I called for him just before he left, "When will you know?" I could see him hesitate to give me a bon-a-fide answer.

"Tomorrow, we will have more answers; perhaps THE answer we are searching for."

The nurse came in shortly afterwards and said it would be a few hours before we could see our mother. We knew the next twenty-four hours would be very crucial to her diagnosis. The events of the preceding night awoke us to the tenuous state our mother was in. We thought of what she must be thinking, surrounded by strangers she never met or knew before; all about her, hooking her to every wire and machine possible, drawing blood, giving blood, taking her vital signs; temperature, heart rate, blood pressure, and other elements she could never fathom. But to decipher the horrid reality she had found herself collapsing in could have only partnered her with a self-trapping fear. Fear so disseminating, it wrenches the soul from any hope and replaces it with the emptiness that such fear can only bring. That vacuum just a few days before had no existence in her life. Now, to this very moment, it was the only reality she knew.

I reached with my thoughts to touch her as I stepped back to the pulpit one last time. I searched the avenues of that Bible for comfort, reading verse after verse, and hoping that one would speak directly to me. Then, as the spell to time goes, I could think of it, recite it deep into my thoughts, and so bring it forward in hopes she could hear my inner voice calming the storm about her.

Somehow our own measure of time in life together could bridge our worlds once more, and I to be a harbor to her wrecked boat, giving her sanctuary from rough seas to calm waters. There were flashes of my memory playing before me. Like a reel from a lost vault of time just now discovered. The precious moments once escaping into my forgetfulness were now finding life in the emotional and tragic state I was in. I watched in sympathy; I watched in awe; looking, staring, seeing at last a glimpse of her former self. When happiness was young; when life had the beauty of flowers dancing in the wind; when hope was brighter than the Summer sun.

The season of Fall had displaced the Summer and I worried what Winter would bring. Its echoes shadowed the cooling winds; the breeze touching with a fit of its own, cussing me for not being more prepared. And as I closed out the Bible I could sense the seasons collapsing under the weight of its own breath.

Chapter 21

Into the Season of the Unknown.

The hours pressed by with the sludge of a rainy day. I found myself on constant watch over those two hands; one rolling by once every hour; the other rolling by once in a day. I never knew time had such a turtle's pace before until we waited for a few hours to finally see all had calmed down.

I had called Amanda and asked her to delay father's arrival from late morning to noon.

"Take him shopping," I said, "Get flowers and a card; be particular about both and make sure that nothing he picks out is quite right. He's got to find the perfect one."

She wondered why we wanted such a delay; noting father was already in the shower and would be ready within the hour.

"Keep a good face," I told her, "We'll take care of mother on this end."

She agreed, yet felt estranged by the whole situation; trusting in, rather, the better case of my judgment.

"Tell me about it later, won't you?" she asked.

"In private," I said, "And call Adam, will you?"

"He won't come," she sighed.

"Give him that chance," I replied, "Either way, he deserves to know. Whether or not he decides to come will be the judge of his own conscious. I couldn't face myself in the mirror each morning if I were him," and with this last volley, we disconnected from one another.

I made my way just outside mother's room where Lorie was still waiting to enter.

"Let me go first," I requested, "Alone."

"If you prefer," she returned, nearly dead-looking without her sleep, "Find a cot and get yourself an hour's sleep."

I looked to the nurse standing just within the doorway.

"Mr. James," she softly said, "You can come in now."

I walked partly through when she held me up.

"You'll have to be patient with her," the nurse whispered, "her answers will seem a little slow. She has been through an ordeal this morning and she may be too tired to stay alert for very long," she paused, "Watch her, and ease up if you sense her stress."

I moved forward and setting my eyes over the bed which had mother occupying it. I could see her heart monitor ticking away; the numbers flashing pulse rate, blood pressure with digits in full bright green colors. An IV was strapped to her arm, still hanging by a hanger; her forearms bruised and limp; the thumb fingers rolling about the other fingers in an uncontrollable manner, as though she were rolling up a fine twin of yarn into a huge ball.

Her hair was spanked into an ungodly look of medusa; her eyes glassy and misty from the lack of sleep, with the dim lights of their grays now momentarily faded into a darker shade. I could see her face had become puffy and discolored; her feet and legs slightly less swollen but still several sizes too large. They had her tilted upwards just enough to see those first entering the room. She seemed exhausted, and held a difficult breathing pattern.

I went to her bedside with a reassuring smile, leaned on the edge a bit, and crossed my hands over my front.

"You know," I grinned, "You didn't have to go to all this trouble to get our attention," I paused to see her attempting to smile, "You could have asked."

"Well," she muttered, "I got your attention."

"That you did, and many others," I said, "I could help you break out of here." I suggested in a tease.

"I might slow you down a little…"

"Mother," I said, with a straight look crossing my expression, "How do you feel?"

"Not too good Conner," she sounded, with a heavy breath and a wheeze in her voice, "Not sure what to make of all this."

"I think it took us all by a little surprise."

"How is Sandra?" she asked, "Tyler, Cory?"

"All doing fine," I said with a corner stare, "They all give you their love."

"And give it back to them in return," she appeared to be in an exhausted spell, thrusting a cough or two through her voice, "Little Cory," she started, "Has he dropped that tooth yet?"

"Not yet," I smiled, "He considers it too much as a trophy to let the tooth fairy have it."

"Maybe you can steal it from him while he sleeps," she cast only a shadow of a smile my way, when the clouds of her situation came rushing back through her eyes, "Is anyone else here?"

"Lorie is just outside, getting her rest a bit," I stopped for a moment, "Father and Amanda will be on their way in a few hours."

"And Adam?" she asked with an air of hope.

"Can't say mother," I sighed, "Adam is an odd one."

"Don't talk about your brother in such fashion," she tried to scold me but was unable to do so with any effectiveness; not like her hard line rule of discipline during the days of my youth, "He has his ways, just like his older brother."

"What is that supposed to mean?"

"Mean as said," she had a flash of quickness about her words, "You have the skittle of something unique like he does."

"It's true he is very gifted," I replied, "But that is of little excuse for any conduct related to this."

"Don't be hard on him," mother defended him as she always did; "He will come around."

"I suppose I should grant him some latitude."

"Do I detect," she rose a finger weakly in the air, "jealousy?"

"Why should I be jealous?" I pondered aloud.

"Conner," she laid her hand onto mine, "You are my first born. This makes you unique from all the others. When I first saw you," she smiled as if some happiness cuddled with her in that moment, "the wondrous joy I felt; to see you, baby-eyed, staring back up at me. I'll never forget that moment…This is one great memory you have always given me. The very first moment I became a mother. It transformed me; gave me rights I never had before."

"It could have easily been another."

"But it was you son," she squeezed to my hand, "You alone."

"Well in fact mother," I said, "I am honored."

"Sandra can tell you all about it," she lowered her tone, "You have a good wife there son. The pride of your heart it seems."

"Sandra has always been a blessing," I said, "Even in times I don't tell her so."

"Then tell her more," she paused, turning her head in a twist to look from side to side, "God gave me a river of love, strength, and appreciation when I met your father. The union of two hearts; it is so magical. Like a dream to believe in, until it becomes real. Those years together are only known by God. I believe."

She came even lower in her voice as she made a try to lift her head closer to me.

"God feeds this seed with true beauty; the beauty is comparable to the sweetness and fond nature sitting in the fragrance of a rose. Like the rich color texture found in a waning sunset, and to the power and kindness discovered in a friendly gesture."

"Mother," I whispered, "what is it you're saying?"

"Son," she came back, "You have a good one there in Sandra. The sky always has two colors, just like the union of a marriage; it has two people. That gradual union takes shape, with the food God gives it. That very seed planted so many years ago inside of you and Sandra is where a strong, wholesome, pure, and rich trunk is formed, and is the basis upon which you and Sandra will walk through life and create a home together."

"Mother," I smiled, "Always the low-key philosopher."

"And you work too much," she gruffed, while leaning painfully back into her bed, "Wonder if you know where your bed is."

"Now, now," I smirked back on her, "You and Sandra bare the burden of gabbing well enough…How about a sip of water…"

She shook me off, waving her hand weakly towards me.

"Doctor has you still on water restrictions?"

"They lifted it this morning."

"Do you need to sleep?" I tried further with her.

"Yes please," she rolled her head to one side; I standing to place a kiss on her forehead and rub the wild strands of white hair back from her eyes before I was to part from her.

"You need your sleep," I calmly spoke, "and an entire night full of dreams."

I could hear the shuffling in and around mother's hospital room. Near to the point I figured even a ghost could not get his eternal sleep through all that commotion and racket abounding about. Yet somehow she quickly found her sleep and those private dreams to keep her mind preoccupied with.

I moved to the outer regions of this hallway and I quickly made my search for a nice, private place of my own. I knew Lorie needed her sleep the same, and need not be kept from her rest. The night had been doubly long for the both of them. Though I was quite relieved Lorie had been with mother the whole night through. She always seemed to have this charismatic and calming influence on mother whenever mother became distressed, though being as rare as it had been in the past.

There was a man in the room two doors down who belched out a continual stubborn, cattle squawking, roof bursting, distastefully lingering, ear drowning wail that never seemed to cease. He was always in a nonstop fuss; never pleased with what the doctor's ordered, not content with whatever the nurses tried to do. He flung his food about like a caustic child and swore like a sailor with an ingrown cyst in his mouth; babbled the rhymes of an idiot all the day through. The nurses had to close his door and tie him to the bed, which only perfumed the air even further. If I had a parent who conducted himself or herself in such a manner, they would have quickly found their mouth taped shut from all the laced profanity.

"Keep it in pops!" I desired to say, as I moved up and down this hallway, and so stirred my attention directly through his door when I came close by.

"What is wrong with this guy?" I asked one attending nurse.

"Mr. McCall?" she questioned, "He doesn't want to be here."

"Giving you heaps of trouble I take it."

"You can say that," she grinned, "He's a fussy brute."

"How long has he been here?" I wondered.

"Six day." She replied, "And six days too long."

She prepared a shot for him, paused at the door, appeared to say a low-flying prayer, and then sighed a spell, "He isn't going to like this."

And in she went. The nurse cast out a phony smile directly at him in hopes, for once, he would buy that this would do him some good.

"Alright Mr. McCall," I heard her cheery voice perk up through the door, "I have a present for you!"

"I don't want any presents!" he belly ached, "Take it back to Santa! And tell him to get his reindeer out of my parking space!"

"Now Mr. McCall," she puttered, "We can't gripe forever."

"You can't!" he squalled, "But I can! Get that thing away from me! No! No! Get that away from me!"

I could tell he wasn't getting his way. I peered through the small, wired view box leading to his room, in an attempt to see him leaning out on one side of the bed, silly-strapped at every limb, while the nurse reached from the other end, poking him where she could get close enough for, "Not a hippo nurse!" he yelled.

"Well then quit squirming," she suggested.

"Your name must be Mary," he cried.

"No, it's Samantha," she cocked her arms on her hips.

"Well it should be Bloody Mary!"

"I am not drawing blood Mr. McCall," the nurse insisted.

"He did this all night long," I heard Lorie's voice behind me sound off, and I turned to see her near asleep, standing in the middle of the hall, "All night long…"

"You don't say," I grinned back at her, "Comical character isn't he?"

"The man never sleeps; the man never eats," she said, "He's a suffering fool; that makes everyone else pay for his contagious mouth. I swear. I have never seen anyone so possessed before; like a spirit which had forgotten to die."

"He kept mother up all night," I implied.

"No," she poorly and shyly puckered a grin, "Just me. Mother had her moments. I thought he would, but she rested as best as she could between her bouts. I asked the nurses first thing this morning if they would move her to another floor."

"What did they say?" I leaned up against the far wall, still hearing the violent soundboard within the next room.

"They plan to move her to ICU this afternoon," Lorie stated, "She'll get more regulated attention; ratio between nurse and patient is two to one. More restricted in seeing her, but it will be for the best I think."

As we moved toward her room, a nurse came towards us and seemed to want out full attention.

"Your father is here," she said.

I could see my father standing overly-clothed for the occasion; even wearing an oversized though slightly worn-through jacket. His pants were jumbled at the ankles as if they were too long. The look on his face was of a man who struggled now with the basic needs to his life; a man who seemed to have been thrown from the curb into a muddy pool of street water. Even brushing his teeth appeared to be an obscenity, which constantly sat in his expression.

My sister Amanda was just behind him and to his right. I could see he was rather perturbed about something, as though this undisclosed matter had found its way mistakenly into his knowledge, and he was angry for us not telling him what had gone on the night before. I could make no apologizes in this instance.

"You are early," I came over to him.

"No thanks to you," he clamped down on his teeth and rocked his jaw back and forth, "Son, she could have died last night."

"I know dad," I tried to temper the situation.

"But I didn't!" he strongly whispered back, "Next time," he stuck his finger out at each of his; his stare blaring the gleam white pupils in his eyes; his cheeks straining to keep from quivering; his hair shooting out like sparkling strings from his head, "everything is revealed without question. I am called with any change in her condition. Whether good, bad, or indifferent; I am to know about it regardless. Suffering! My children would keep me from knowing."

"I am sorry dad," I pleaded the guilt.

"Sorry almost wasn't enough," he said, "and nearly caused a tragedy that I would have to suffer through for a very long time."

"We thought it might be best," I explained.

"Don't challenge me son," his finger came directly towards me, "I have a right to know, and you know it!"

He spun about to take his attention into mother's room.

"Next time," Amanda leaned into me with her own version and whispered, "You'll need to come up with something better than 'take him shopping'. You know we couldn't keep him in a store for five minutes, let alone for several hours."

"I did my best," I replied.

"Suggest a fireman's charity fund raiser instead. You will keep him there all day then."

She began to shadow our father once more, but stalled to ask further.

"By the way, what are the doctors saying?"

"Newscast tomorrow," Lorie stuttered through the words, "We will know more results then."

"Can't they sooner?" Amanda asked.

"Biopsy's like this could take three to four days; they have done a rush on it, considering the circumstances."

"How many complications?"

"Too many to count," Lorie said, "The doctor did a quick inventory. There was so much, I could not tell you all of it."

"And they don't have a clue…" she continued with a cast-eye, suspicious glare in her look, "You would think they would have some idea at this point."

"Only the symptoms; not the cause," I said, gazing around as I did, "Adam decided to follow tradition and not participate."

"I called him," she re-iterated on her failed attempt.

"And?" Lorie folded her arms over.

"You know Adam," she spoke, "Our brother is such the mystery." She sent out a look of 'what did you expect?'

"Does anything ever move him?" Lorie questioned.

"A quick, swift kick in the…" I stalled as Lorie interrupted.

"Do you need to be strapped down as well?"

We three moved to enter through that narrow doorway leading into mother's dim-lit room. Father was standing above her quietly, watching her sleep, as he himself seemed to be in a gradual trance of his own. I looked about her window and saw nothing more than the gravel pit roof of the second floor. The glare from those white rocks shined through from the early sun's heated reflection.

"This won't do," I went to shut the curtain gingerly, in hopes not to awake her from her needed rest.

"Like a babe in arms," father whispered, "Don't wake her. We will wait until she decides to arouse."

And so we sat, each in one corner of the room, with father nearest to her side. I kept tower-watch about the bathroom and open sink; Lorie to mother's other bedside; Amanda most near to the door. No one spoke, yet we kept some level of inner conversation with our thoughts. The chairs were too small for a man of my bear size; father had as much difficulty, if not more.

Mother would snore in discontent for some time, then quietly waiver off into a distant dream; contorting, flinching, raising her forearms and appearing to direct some silent symphony while she slept. One set of fingers still continued to roll on with that increasing ball of fictious twine.

Then, when we were least prepared, mother came to awaken around like a snow spring child rising from her winter sleep.

"Allen?" she looked over to him with confusion, "Shadows and the mirror."

"What are you saying dear?" Dad took her hand gently.

"I see shadows in the mirror," she had this strange, cross-eyed look about her expression, "they are there. I see them."

"What are they?" I leaned in to ask.

"I don't know," she replied, "I haven't seen them before."

"What do they look like?" Amanda said in a concerned fashion, "Do you see them now?"

"Hold the mirror to me…" she requested, barely strong enough to pull her hand free from the covers, "Hand mirror will do."

Lorie pulled a mirror from the bathroom, brought it to mother, and held it about chest length away as mother took to raise her head, and struggle with her sight to see through to her reflection.

"Well?" Lorie asked.

"They are gone," she gazed into the mirror world with a most confused and confounded daze, "They were there before. I remember seeing them, like they were trying to haunt me."

"What do you think they were?" I softly inquired.

"A shadow that knew it just had been discovered, and slipped away into the light, where I couldn't see it," she paused, "There wasn't a face, a figure; nothing distinguishable, only like a shadow is; an image; a hollowed-out darkness that moves with a mind of its own," she looked over to me, "You see them in dreams always. But this time, I could have thought they were more real than this."

"It was only a dream Annie," father got from his chair and kissed mother to her forehead.

"You are not leaving, are you?" she looked at father with a sense of fleeting hope in her eyes; an expression all too described in the most evident scare to man; fear itself.

"No dear," he smiled, "I will be here as you need." Another kiss fell on her forehead, and this appeared to comfort her, at least for the moment.

"They planned to move you to ICU this afternoon," I tried to reassure her further, "You'll get better treatment there."

"That will be good," she laid her head back to the pillow and gradually drifted off into this world of shadows and mirrors once more.

The day drew into evening, until the night converged and forced us to make arrangements. Father insisted to remain this evening and none of us were in any position to object. Mother had slept until nightfall and then some. Plans of moving her before the evening were delayed until early morning, and all three of us siblings had decided to return before seven since the doctor had scheduled a meeting with us at that time.

When the morning arrived I made my early start just as the sun began its peek into sunrise. Sandra had the children for the day since it was a Saturday, and they would be off from school. We had made mention of bringing the children to see their grandmother in hopes of raising her spirits, but thought perhaps it might be best to wait, and so keep the children from such possible trauma unless the circumstances required it. Cory and Tyler were still in their beds when I politely entered their room; planting kisses on both their cheeks before I left. I said my tender 'farewells' to Sandra, and told her I would call before the afternoon set in; to give her an approximate update.

I made my way to the hospital and through the morning traffic. The streets were laden empty as though Boston had turned into a temporary ghost town. I felt an eerie remnant from the night before still in overhang about me.

Those shadows in her mirror; what were they? A premonition? A leery-eyed illusion from someone who had a near-death experience just the night before? A dream; a stop from reality; or something in-between settling and festering within her own mind, and something she was unable to let go of. A spectre; a haunting fettered spirit; something real yet not tangible and seen by the human eye?

This was a markedly different world we were now entering into, and mother, being the head of our group, was now holding the light along the way as we went.

There was a heart behind all this; a purpose; a reason for her now dwelling in the shadows of that darkness, and I spent the entire drive up mingling around with that thought, trying to figure out the pulse of it all.

As I entered the hospital, I summoned my sisters back to the hallway. We formed a circle in that midst. A trail of doctors and nurses all came to penetrate the room; converging if you will, as a swarm of new activity. Doctor Ogden was with them.

"May I see you?" he said to us all; his face stern to some painful knowledge, "We have further results."

I re-entered the room to gather father up, yet he declined and wished to further be by mother's side. He had been asleep by her bed the entire night without episode. I told him I would inform him of the news later on in the morning, and so he nodded to assure me this would be fine. I released back to those three awaiting me in a private room, further down the hallway.

"We have good information," he paused, "and not so good information; but, new nonetheless."

"So where do we begin?" I cautiously asked.

"As you wish…" he lowered his head at my admission.

"The mass," I said, "in her rectum."

"Hemorrhoid," he replied, which drew a sigh from the three of us, "Not a cancerous mass. It's something we can deal with down the road. We have other things to attend to that require our more immediate attention," he paused as we stopped breathing at this.

"Such as…" Amanda requested.

"We do know the cause of your mother's illness. The nasal biopsy results came back this morning. She has a rare disease caused Wegener's; a systemic, auto-immune disorder; chronic tissue and blood vessel inflammation."

"Is it fatal?" Lorie pondered in worry.

"Up until a few years ago, it was," he started, "The success rate is quite low now; somewhere around ninety percent survivability. I must caution you however, this is a very highly, most unpredictable disease, and can be catastrophic."

"Doctor Ogden," I recalled, "I don't desire to know the possibilities, as much as I desire to know what affects it has on her, and can it be treated successfully."

"It can," he said, "The disease can manifest itself in many ways. As your mother's symptoms indicate; crusting of the nasal passages which would leave the impression of an ongoing sinus infection; attacking of the kidneys which can be quite severe."

"And in her case?" Amanda interrupted.

"This is the sixty-four thousand dollar question. The most measured advance of the disease generally would be the affect it has on the kidneys. In her case however, the disease, although not infected for very long, has indeed damaged her kidneys to nearly fifty percent at this point."

"So when does dialysis come into play?" I asked.

"Twenty to forty percent, depending on the patient," the doctor responded, "There is more…Your mother still has bleeding and we still are unable to pin the source down. In the rarest cases, this disease can manifest itself to uncontrollable G.I. bleeding or gastro-intestinal bleeding."

"Then how can it be stopped?" Amanda stated.

"Stop the disease."

"And to treat the disease…" I spoke more freely, "With what?"

"Prednisone," he said, "Initially so. It will help suppress the disease. However it will also suppress her immune system."

"Unable to combat other ailments," I said.

"It's a precarious line," Doctor Ogden announced, "…we will have to walk over. She will be receiving her first dosage this morning and we should see some reduction of the disease, or at least the stabilization of it. Treatment generally takes between six months to a year. I must remind you there is no cure; only the ability to place the disease in remission."

"How advanced is it?" Lorie gulped when she said this.

"This is where the greatest caution lies," he began, "I don't want to dispel any hope, nor impede the prospects she may have to survive this disease. We have consulted with doctors from areas of the country which have greater exposure to this disease than we have, including John Hopkins Hospital."

"I don't think this will be good…" Amanda folded her head in her arms, "not in the least."

"Whether you wish to believe it or not, the probable chances are still good that she may and can survive Wegener's. As long as she is alive, there is hope. Your mother has perhaps the highest ANCA level ever recorded and measured for the disease."

"ANCA level," I struggled with the term.

"The level registered in her body; this is the indication of Wegener's she has. I will tell you, it has gotten a mighty hold of her and she is definitely fighting for her life at this stage. She even has it manifesting itself within her uterus, which, in the annals of this very young disease, it has never been recorded before. We are in consort with doctors across the country; the best doctors who have had the most exposure to Wegener's."

"Obviously," I said, "her chances are not at ninety percent."

"The fortunate thing here is we caught it early; not late, when the disease can become terminal. Your mother, even though it is at a very, very high level, has Wegener's in its infant stage. The damage to the kidneys still is minimal, and she could have near complete recovery in this regard; over time."

"Is there anything else we should know doctor?" Lorie came from her chair, turned, and headed towards the open window to peer out over the parking lot below.

"She has a bout of pneumonia in her left lung; her nasals are quite packed, crusty, whitish, and cobbled; bacteria gestation in her stomach; all this outside of the issues we discussed yesterday."

"She will be going to ICU this morning then," I asked.

"Immediately; treatment to begin as quickly. In forty-eight hours we should see signs of the disease going into remission. I think however she will need a measure of chemo therapy; perhaps as long as six months of treatment."

"How can she possibly survive all this?" I wondered, "If you're doing everything to suppress her immune system? I mean, she could die from the common cold if she contracts this."

"If she doesn't receive the treatment Mr. James," the doctor cut me with his look, "she will most definitely die from much worse. We can give her medication for more common ailments if it should arise. We take the lesser of two evils in this case."

"And hope for the greater of two goods," I concluded.

"That is the plan," he responded, "and it is an aggressive, necessary one at that."

"When can we see her?" I asked one final question.

He paused, checked about his watch, gave out a look which seemed to travel about his thoughts in a very deep-rutted road. His answer was one without any latitude in it.

"I would say sometime mid-afternoon. We would like to perform a Colonoscopy on her as soon as we have her settled in ICU. It is important we discover the source of her continual G.I. bleeding."

He stood as if to indicate he was taking leave from us.

"Do you think that would be wise?" Lorie wondered, "I mean—you are just moving her and all."

"We need to be able to treat the bleeding as soon as we can. I don't believe it is from hemorrhaging, but there is always a risk there. Not to worry, she will be sedated through the procedure."

"We have your number doctor if we should think of anything," I looked out from that window, stoned and thoughtless to my emotions; for I let them scatter in the winds which were currently blowing across the rooftops.

"Please, don't hesitate to call me."

I did not turn to give my expression on him. Rather, he left without a moment to ponder on. The room drew eerie silent. A word never passed between my sisters and me. I thought of the time when Jason and I were sitting alone in that administrative room; waiting, fidgeting, pausing for time to pass by as we sat in silence, and thought of why we were brought there. Only to find out that our dear friend Spike had passed away just the night before.

This time was similar in mood, character, and persuasion; the ending however still unknown. Yet in that oddest place, the place where the spirit wanders about without reason and has no place really to go, you think of the past as though it were a grand gift from time itself. You reminisce with yourself; standing there before the film of your life and looking in review. I had picked that moment when Jason and I sat there alone because of the recurring feelings I had begun to feel; a sort of reminder to the stir of that similar wind that was swirling about me then.

If I had been born at this moment in time; suddenly finding myself there, I would never have brought with me the fear I was currently possessed by. I struggled with it; those notions of preeminent danger cast out like poor lots by the hands of fate itself. As if I were the ghost of someone who had lived long ago, but still thinking they had somehow survived death and were still alive, now living in the reruns of their life. Perhaps, if I were the same haunting ghost, I would try to make amends.

"We should go now," I said, making my way past them and into the open hallways.

Chapter 22

I Have a Dream.

Sandra met up with me later that afternoon. I had called to inform her of the general changes going on at the hospital, and she was to see me at the front entrance into ICU. The doors opened from this long, bright hallway leading in, and she came through. Her golden hair was flying about the wind she made as she walked; dressed in her business suit, which did indicate to me she barely made it home long enough to settle the children and situate the babysitter for as long as we needed her for. I would miss Tyler and Cory before they retired to bed this evening; no tucking into bed; no pre-sleep bed time story; no quaint chat before the time they were sent to their dreams; no kisses to the cheek or hugs and embraces.

"Are you alright?" she asked, as she came up to me with a gentle kiss and embrace of her own, "How is she?"

"The Colonoscopy showed nothing," I stated, "the doctors just indicated she has loss of vision in her right eye, and a severe reduction in her left."

"What is that from?" she said with a stunned look.

"From Wegener's most likely," I said with a solemn expression, "Or perhaps the product of an old stroke; they just don't know."

"May I see her?" it was more of a desire than a question.

"In a bit," I replied, "They have her sedated so there will be little to no response for a time. The nurse will come for us."

We stepped into the ICU waiting room where my two sisters and father where sitting in wait. I saw the horror in Sandra's eyes when she first laid eyes to my family. Their looks were merely the remnants of what they had seen so far. Nothing masked over, yet all told with the snap of an eye; a turn of the cheek; a blink; a nod; a fractured stare which shadowed the hovering clouds of worry. Sandra stalled, turned, moved back out into the hallway, clasped her hands to her face, and began to shelter the tears welting in her eyes.

I went to hold her; her breath stuttered and heavy, as if her lungs were beginning to collapse under the weight of her emotions.

"This can't be happening," she wept into my jacket lapel, "Oh God! It was only a few days ago. Conner, how could this be happening? I don't understand…"

"Are you ready for this?" I whispered to her.

"I need to see her," Sandra said, "She needs to know I am there for her," she pulled free, held her hands long ways over her mouth and nostrils, "I can't be caught like this," she paused, made brave attempts to gather in her emotions, and then felt a sudden, though brief explosion come over her, "How can this be?"

"Maybe you should wait here Sandra…"

"No," she defied me, "No. It's a promise made, but never spoken. She just deserves so much better Conner."

I said nothing, bit to my lower lip, looked away to watch those coming through the hallways, and closed my embrace over her shoulders, "When you are ready…"

The nurse came forward, and counseled us briefly before we entered ICU. Her words were soft and direct, quick to the point, and lacking no less than what was minimally required.

"Only two at a time," she advised.

I would accompany Sandra in first.

The rooms lay in a broad circle around the heart of ICU; the main desk poised at the very center, with each nurse in constant watch over their two units of responsibility. Mother's drawn curtain sat only half-closed and yet half-open, nearly shielding the sight of all of her except for her limp hand hugging the railing beside her. A dim light played with the deep shadows which had entered her room; the curtain only see-through to the point of seeing vague silhouettes and nothing more. Even from this distance we could sense the loneliness and strange atmosphere she must have been feeling there. A few doctors were making their rounds nearby. I eyed the compartments in and about, and so finding the pulsing silence that was eroding from each area. I felt this was not a kind place, just a desolate one.

We stepped forward, most cautiously. Our surroundings were as foreign as a distant land would be. Our hands clasped tight, nearly in a desperate squeeze together; wrought with some tense level of dread and anxiety. I observed the scene from all about, keeping steady pace with Sandra. The curtain within hand's reach; the lone silhouette more pronounced, lying to the bed without motion. My hand crossed over our bodies and it settled over the edge of that curtain; a pause, lift, and we were within.

The room felt a wayward draft. Near deaf with a chill; the visitation of some reckless loneliness was now dancing in the deep and dark shadows lurking about. This single light anchored above and to mother's left cast out the torch of a hard and coarse illumination.

I looked to my mother; her body as limp as a lifeless body could be. Though she still lived, emptied out and tired from the intrusions she had been through over the last few days. I turned only for a brief moment, cupped my hand to keep any and all tears from dropping from the eye, then I yielded to a more powerful sense and composed myself with it before I turned around to her.

We moved slowly to each side of her bed. Both of her hands and forearms showed a clear indication of bruising from all the blood taking, IV'S, and lines now running into them. In the light of this new mother; a mother I had never seen before, I could see still the vacant shadows of her old self still residing in her expression. Her eyes were locked into a shut; her mouth gaping as if she were grasping for any air about; hands now in a light tremor; fingers still rolling that imaginative ball of twine. The registers above her were now showing constant blood pressure signs and heart rate.

"Mother," I whispered, as though I would be the voice in her dream, "Mother."

Her eyes rolled open, staring to the ceiling above. The caustic stare, blank and unobserved, seemed to be waiting for reality to kick in. There was no answer.

"Mrs. James," Sandra touched to her arm. Mother turned slightly her head towards Sandra's awaiting smile, "How are you?"

"Not," she weakly said, "too," she paused, "good…" Her stare went out with a cross, straining look, "Sandra?"

"It's me," Sandra's smile chuckled and grew into a most broad grin, "I am here."

"Did you see the shadow too?" mother cleared to say, nearly in a faint whisper that was barely audible.

Sandra sent a confused look towards me, then a smile back on my mother, "What shadow dear?"

"Mother," I touched to her other shoulder, and so she lifted her head from the pillow, turning my way.

"Conner," she posed, "It came back."

"The shadow," I replied, "This is what you mean…"

"I think it will come again," she softly said.

"Not in the mirror," I asked.

"The mirror," she remarked, "larger one, this time."

"Did you see it more clearly?" I pressed further.

"Still a shadow," she became weaker on her reply. Her hands took to grasp the railings without any measure of strength, though yet enough to hold firm on them, "Larger, than before."

"What does it want?" Sandra questioned as mother spun her head over to Sandra.

"Sandra," mother queried, "such a good child. Give…love…to…children."

It was apparent her body nearly had been depleted. The harsh weight of that stress now preoccupying her into delusion, or yet a world she could see, but unseeing to us. Sometimes milked with trauma, the mind has a power and a stage of its own to play in.

"Mother," I called to her, "was it a good shadow?"

She spun her head in a slow and tempered manner that I thought her eyes were too close from the apparent weakness she was currently exhibiting. The rational world had somehow dislodged itself from her mind, casting some strange and provoking shadow into the reflective place she was residing in. Our connection, as my eyes passed onto hers; thoughts once so gleaming and filled with roadways, now seemed a misty haze of confusion, and so lost in the shadows of darkness itself.

"I will ask him next time," she whispered, then dropping her head, and allowing her eyes to roll backwards into some forced stage of sleep. Her hands were still gripping to the railing sides; perhaps in hopes of slipping no further into that vault.

I lifted my head from where she lay and I came with a glance back to Sandra to suggest our time to leave. Sandra's hand reached for mine while her other palm bent wretched over her face to hide her dripping tears. She became more pronounced as we entered back into the mainstream of ICU. I came to hold her as we walked past the hallways, quickly down the elevator, and into the streets and night sky.

We spent much of our travels in a diverted conversation. Sandra speaking about the kids, their activities and schooling; I, of work and the accounts I would have to muster over the next few weeks. Times were hard; the agonies silent and haunting within the back of our minds, like a ghost who trailed our every thought and made it known to us it would not go away anytime soon.

When our car came to a stop in the driveway, I could see all the lights were dim and low, nearly in a sleep of their own. The babysitter was awake, watching television, and ready for her trip home. I checked in on the children as they slept, folded the blankets around their chest, brushed their fropped hair from their expression, and gave to each a kiss for good night's rest.

Sandra took to preparing for bed once more. I moved to enter the room in our house seldomly used; the misty spray of dull and unmoved air touched to my senses as I roamed about in search of the light switch. It was cold and damp, as if it were a place much like the world my mother was now finding herself in; unoccupied, unclaimed, unwanted, always vacant the charm of human contact. Yet in my wayward ways, as my mood and spirit began to drift into a journey of its own, I sought refuge where I could think in private for myself. Perhaps this same shadow would come to me, and I could find out the source and reason for its existence.

The light flew open; the shadows drawing into the crevice and corners about; nothing appeared; no silhouette or empty model of image to interact with. There was no mirror here for it to play in. I saw the canister of films all displayed in chronological order, sitting in a dust-filled shelf in one corner. The projector was lying open beside the wall; the empty reel sitting high in its perch. I pulled it free, moved the white backdrop down, took about the first reel made, and began to play it forward. The stage was set.

There, as the lights cast low; the square bright hue from the projector set the images all into motion. The memories I had so longed to remember; the whiffs of time, like a smell long forgotten yet sensed when the right wind blew, all came rushing back over me. I could hear the loud rumble of the projector's motor grind in my ear; the sounds mute, but as those visions came forward and tumbled into my view, I could remember the words spoken then, as if it were an old song playing in the tune box of my head.

There were my sisters; seemingly just born, holding steady to that rooster, carrying it around and looking for the eggs it was supposedly laying behind them. I watched with a smile, then the cascading echoes of my tears from some unmentionable emotion dripping from my eyes. Still, they carted this rooster around in hopes it would lay to that egg. The camera followed their motions; the tender smiling expressions all illuminated and locked into film; ageless; timeless; shadows of our past; the mirror reflection born; they danced, played to the camera as it spotted them.

There, as most unexpectantly as if I had never remembered, my mother came into view carrying about an Easter basket, stooping low, holding it close to my sister's side and just behind the rooster, and so trying to catch any egg it may by chance lay.

I could not see the basket, nor to the activities of my sisters any further, nor to the cackles of that old rooster in hand, nor to the clipping sounds of the projector itself as it wound around time and time again. But I kept a constant and wanted stare to my mother. Her eyes, of younger self and most clear, so filled with youth and dreams; her hair the raven color I had lost from my memory; the body driven to be active and free to roam from one side of the filmstrip to the other.

She laughed and giggled throughout, without a care or concern. Her heart was filled with wonder, of attraction and beauty, of hope and freedom to see the burgeoning world about her. This was a new land to her; a world fresh as a newly-cut daisy from the fields. A time then, as powerful as any known; yet now, a time lost and fading from some clear sunrise into a fog-laden sunset. It was the colors of the rainbow to life, as she would put it.

There were so many sayings and verses she had rendered to me. Like poignant tales and lessons for me to learn by. They all were whispering back to me while I watched her former self so alive on that one-dimensional stage. This tiny vault of time spread out through the long yards of my past, showing meadows and streams galore; of endless days when I was young. The memories so striking and stirring to my soul, I felt the world rushing back to them all in one eclipse. I would blink and see the world as it was; when the darker shades of life had no bearing to enter that world; the world now fashioned and playing before me against this bare wall.

But my mother's words and sayings played havoc in my thoughts, echoes and streams of sounds all from the same voice, dripping into where my mind would think next on, then following my trail of thoughts wherever they would lead.

I felt the tremor in my soul as she must have felt that evening. I was now watching those memories playing out before me like a pre-written script; yet to her, playing from the shadows of her memories as she lay in that hospital bed.

I shut the projector off in the middle of its play; I could take no more. My motions instinctively led me to my bed, and Sandra who, though lay silent as if to sleep, kept quiet throughout. I knew she was most soundly awake as I felt her stillness to be more common than to her normal tradition. I felt her touch in the night and how she bent over me as I settled beside her; her hand wet from the tears just touching over her fingers. A handkerchief followed with her other hand as she gave an embrace that felt firm, then softened after a few moments. Nothing was said; the words of conversation all built into the language of our bodies while we slowly drifted back into sleep. Her palms loosened; her hands now retracted.

It was then I felt the beginnings of my dream. The slow waves of transition flooded into my internal view. I was being transported; to what? I could not tell off-hand, but it was a place I had never seen before; and thought, if the dream was a kind dream, it would be a place where I could see my family not as it was, nor as it is, but as it could be without tragedy.

I landed along the long shores where the lines from sea and sand stretched in either direction, far beyond my own sighting of it; uninhabited, ancient, but new. Time had made it a place where Heaven could take notes from and make a copy of it in its own realm.

The drifting waves rolled from sea harbor to shore in calm rolls and distant claps of thunder-sounding calls. The white sprinkles of foam, especially from a distance, seemed to top off the waves in a cream coating of its own. The sun rippled through the outstretched waters, and rolled out into an endless horizon. The waves would come forward; drip onto the shores like flat fingers touching where both would meet, and then dive back into their sea body as before.

I could see no one, and though my search reached from the north shores to the south, there was nothing of evidence anyone had ever been here before. I looked for the echoes of footprints; pressed indentions into the sands; places where the waves would collect and cement that evidence just long enough for me to see; nothing. There was not a dock; no seaman ships passing along the faint horizons; no tow-ins or small bell towers bobbing about the water when the sea had a good mind to rush about it with a wave and so cast out a bell sound or two.

The seagulls passed overhead in a flock; small birds of prey prancing along the shorelines in rapid motion and dipping their beaks into the wet sands. I saw dolphins creating a half-circle as they rose from the waters' dome and crevice. One, then another, and another, then several in unison; all performing some inert serenade of dance and play as they came crossing into my view. There was a spray of spout water and air like a volcano shot from the sea rim; as it spewed high into the air, spread, and then faltering back into the oncoming waves; a whale was in passing.

I went from the top of the sand domes, down into the pits themselves and down further onto the wet shorelines. The wet sand clumped onto my feet and in between my toes, nearly making my feet into webs. I traveled the lot of these shores for what seemed an hour; in one direction, looking, sending a sight through the bow of my hand as it crossed over my forehead when I cut the sun's bright reflection from my view; still, nothing.

I walked further, knowing that when I reached my destination something good, and with correct purpose would find me; give me strength and courage. I felt the contradiction of hot and cold absorb me. At times I took a dip into the ocean; felt the waves touch me with their cool droplets and heavy sprays, then; as I pressed onto the shoreline once more, the sun baked me with its heat.

Down into the distance; into the simmering heat loops and waves rippling from the deep sands themselves, I could see a lone figure walking along the shoreline into my direction. The figure was faint, tiny, of no marking or gender offhand; almost without care, watching as it did off into the seas themselves. I pressed forward, and I still kept my constant sight over this lone figure.

It stopped and crossed halfway into the waters; the waves washed in and nearly half of it was now submerged. The person stepped free, dripping from the wash it received, and there continued on its march towards my direction. I felt the urgency; made my rush, scampering, finding the kicking of that wet sand flopping behind me. I came to a trot, stalled, then ran, full speed, almost feeling as if I were running in place. I pushed forward; the details more evident than before. The figure was of a woman; no, a girl; a young girl; perhaps ten, no twelve. Her hair in a heavy and harsh curl, bouncing against her shoulders as she walked; still, she had not seen me coming to her. My sight strained from the sun's glare; looking, pressing with my vision to know the identity of this young girl.

She looked to me; I stopped, shook to my bones; stuttered, stammered to a halt; my mouth gapping in awe. It was the child of my mother now coming to me, though she never paid heed to my presence, and yet kept her attention along the long divisions of this ocean.

It was a massive field; one where people drift off into their imagination with, like a raft made of rations and of dreams for the mind to travel with. She seemed to have already lifted herself onto this mindful raft, and it now was drifting her to the awaiting shores which lay before into that endless individual horizon. The distance unknown; nor to the days of travels, but she had gone on that boat, and was now watching herself and looking into that never-ending spectrum of light and beauty.

"Mother?" I called, though she did not respond.

Her head dropped onto the sands before her; she bending low, finding something of interest which cut her expression into a curious spell. It was a pebble; one of clarity and of glitter; seemingly to have the sun's brightness of its own within. It glowed and reflected as she shifted it from hand to hand. I saw the shimmer cut across her face; her eyes inspecting most deeply to its root. She held it deep into her palms, almost near into a prayer and a wish.

She whispered something, alone; only for her to hear. I watched, taken aback by all this. Still, she had not taken notice of me. Her eyes lifted back into sight; the gray glows of her pupils radiating out into my direction, yet looking through me. She turned, waltzed back to the foot of those seas, lifting one hand up and about, and then casting out this pebble where it dipped back into the sea's belly. I saw a wave, reaching high from somewhere underneath, now accumulate and grow until it reached some height.

It sounded that low rumble I had heard often, but stirring in what seemed to be its own stewpot; then lifting, reaching until it began its thrust inland. I ran to the spot where it would come through; mother now standing just off from me. She giggled, laughed, with apparent anticipation and knowing of what to expect next. I saw the wave crest and come forward as its cream-top foam towered into a heavy mist. The roar nearly deafened me, and so caught us both full force and hard on. It was as if it had a hurricane deep within its waters. And as it came to a settle I caught my mother back into my view.

She danced about the wading waters in glee; her face steady and viewing the waters and what they were reflecting. I looked low for myself and I saw the very same image she was in sight of. The waves shifted and eased, spread foams and debris throughout, but still the image was more than clear; it was precise.

It was her, most distinct, when she was an adult. The expression was as exact as if it were playing in my own memory of her. Though of her image when she had just turned away from childhood; vibrant, still of youth, ambitious, longing, wanting of the future to come as if it were her very own dream. The ripples formed and moved to change her expression, as though they were alive and in continual motion.

This was a special pebble she had found. One that could send a wave more than a ripple's size when cast out into sea. Mother had made a wish; a wish I knew only when that effectual ripple had returned, once the pebble was dropped back into the ocean. She had wished to see herself as an adult and what world she would later find herself in.

"Conner!" I felt myself rise from my dream.

I looked about; nothing astir; the night still deep into its darkness. Sandra had remained in the bellies of her own dreams. She had not called for me. Who did? That voice, as memories would drop a hint or two, left no evidence of whom it was. My mother was calling me through this unfinished dream? Sandra beside me? Who was it? Or was it another in between dream and awake.

I saw the shades of darkness, where the night had peeled back the hours into the very middle of that evening, and so crowned the atmosphere into its own sleep. The sounds were quiet, alone, giving off no residence but for an occasional honk, squealing brakes from some old worn car coming to the stop sign just down the street. That old tree just outside bobbed, bent, and moved with the insistence of a contrary wind gust that happened to blow by.

My eyes stayed awake, and so pierced out onto that tree limb; watching, waiting, figuring a bird would eventually come along and settle aboard it; none came.

I laid my head back to my pillow; the covers now drawing close and upwards to my chin. The dream had left me on that word; that calling to my name; abandoning, and escaping as quickly as it had announced itself before. I made my attempts to run back into my dreams with my mind, and to find that shoreline again where my mother, in her younger self. I am sure was must have still been dancing over those shores.

Sleep, so easily found before, was now in escape of me like the dream had become. And when I finally drifted off once more I could not find her. The dream now lost.

Chapter 23

Out of the Eternal Springs of Hope.

A week had passed and little word had surfaced on the cause and source of mother's G.I. bleeding. There had been several Endoscopies and Colonoscopies to determine the precise nature of this bleeding, but it was left to the conclusion that Wegener's was the prime culprit in it all. The bleeding had remained so continuous throughout, that a measure order of five to seven units of blood were transfused into her system to support the loss of her own blood. She had been left unstable enough to not be able to walk; her feet and legs were still coming to some swelling, and felt as though ice picks were yet stabbing her constantly.

The doctors reminded us of how delicate her balance would become; the immune system taking a radical jolt from the medication; her kidneys under attack to the point she had only forty percent usage left; her creaton level now falling to a mere three.

They dressed her with special boots, though of some discomfort by their very bulkiness. It was necessary however to keep the threat of clots from rising in her legs, traveling through her body, and entering into blood stream and lungs. They installed her with a floating mattress which gave her further support and reduced the chance of her lungs stiffening from all the lying in bed.

Her spirits remained as diverse as her moods. They would rise and fall; shift and ebb constantly throughout the day and evening hours. She was most apprehensive at night; the darkness and lack of human contact was a general fear of hers. Only an occasional 'checking up' by the night nurse was what she experienced through the night. As it stood, being under the government and supervision of ICU, no family was permitted to stay beyond nine at any evening. Her nights; alone, cold, restless, and most empty, found her wide awake; stilled on her back, staring upwards onto those square tiles hour after hour. During the days she would drift from sleep to awake in nearly a manic state of confusion.

There were few times of optimisms; moments when she would rise just high enough to take a spell for eating, and fuss profusely about the drab nature of the hospital food. I would see the small shadows of her true self-light up like a small and delicate Christmas tree light, then only to fade when she grew tired again.

The doctor had arranged for yet another meeting that late afternoon, and we were all to attend. There were several issues he had desired to talk with us on; issues of importance as we were now diving into the very 'delicate state of her disease', as he put it.

Still, Adam had not come to see his mother. His duties to his canvas work; introductions; travels; showings were all encompassing the vast portion of his time. All of us had left messages on his answering machine, and all unfortunately remained unanswered.

She had yet to ask for Adam a second time, though I knew it had been playing on her; noting by the very absence of him in any of our conversations, she too, had made no mention of him.

I would ask of her to look back over the open window, see the world beyond, and eye-cast her gaze over the lawns in her view box; she refused. I suppose the notion of seeing the world in beauty, and knowing the prison box she was currently in was too great for her to bear. My birthday came round with a large array of birthday cards; we taking our turns reading each and everyone to her, and so hoping we could have some small influence in raising her spirits over the cage she felt herself now currently locked within.

Sandra and I, along with Amanda, decided to take the children to the common gardens this Saturday morning and remain throughout the day until our meeting time with the doctors that same afternoon.

The day was a pitch-perfect day for outside affairs; unusually warm and fresh, akin to an early spring day we would often see during the months of April and May. We had not been back to this location since the day Sandra's grandfather 'Buck' had been buried here. My reasons were more obscure than hers; she not wishing the constant reminders on the tragedy she had suffered so long ago. But to this day, for whatever reason possessed her, she requested we do so. I was never one to question, nor to deliberate the issue in all, yet to give her due and make arrangements with the children.

We sat about the same large, overhanging tree my mother had so often enjoyed before during my early years. I thought I saw her shadow there, sitting along the width of that blanket, waiting for us with her constant and considerable smiles; the memories in an over sweep of me. As if the birth of their wind pushed me back into those prevailing thoughts. The mind's eye playing tricks with me once more; the shadows of my emotions like the reel player to these films; and so I sat, lying about with my head over Sandra's legs as she whiffed about my hair with her caressing hands; silently, quietly, as we watched our children out in play with Amanda in the fields just beyond us.

Our silence remained for sometime. But I could feel Sandra's love brightly over me like the brilliant sun the day had produced overhead. My thoughts of that distant misery had now crept away from my mind for a spell, and I thought of Sandra and her own plights coming into focus.

"Whatever happened?" Sandra's soft voice approached me.

"What do you mean love?"

"That day," she began, "The day of the fire…in detail, now."

"You haven't spoken of it since the prom. You sure you want to here this?"

"Yes," I could sense her stare reach out to the children, "A final time; maybe back then something was unsaid that should have been said. Maybe your memory on that day will give me more than it did back on the night of our prom…"

"Five firemen went in; the fire grew very rapidly. Buck stood about directing everyone, and then the explosion came. It rocked us all from our feet; threw me back to the curb and I stumbled for a few seconds. Within minutes, I saw Buck angrily pulling Joey into the house with him to go after those men still trapped inside. Said he was going to make a hero out of him that day. Little did he know he was going to make them both heroes," I stalled and waited for Sandra to respond.

With a moment to her silence to absorb what I was saying to her, I could see the shadow of her figure now stretching just before me. Her head bending low, as if to capture the start of her tears; the soft hand to my hair; the touch of love and gentleness so caught me in my stare on her silhouette.

"Please Conner," she choked slightly, "Continue…"

"They went in; disappeared from me. My father along with Gerry went to the rear of the home to take the back exit. I followed, against his wishes; saw the deck as they climbed it. Our dog Skip followed and I went up onto the deck, but the fire was so hot; so very hot. It pushed me back. I could see the flames crawling up the walls; the smoke billowing out in every opening. I could hear the crashing of the stairs within; more explosions; heat growing stronger as the house seemed to melt before me. Father and Gerry came forward with two men, but they went back in, hoping to find the others. Your grandfather was still in there; he would never leave; not as long as any one fireman remained inside."

"I knew he would be this way," Sandra sniffled a little through her emotions, and allowed me so to continue.

"They did their best; what they could do. They just ran out of time. We went to the front and that is when I saw your grandfather laying there. Paramedics were working feverishly to try to revive him; I started to walk forward…"

"What did you see?" she said, "Tell me…I want to know."

"I spoke of it before Sandra," I pleaded with her, "Why put yourself through the suffering all over again?"

"Because," she replied, "Just…because."

I reluctantly proceeded further into it.

"His eyes were open, staring at me. I thought for a moment he was actually seeing me, looking right through me. Then I felt it."

"What was it?" she bent down to kiss my forehead.

"The wind; a spirit in the wind. It was as if his spirit left just then, brushed past me, gave me a gentle hug or recognition. Maybe it was his way to say 'goodbye'; something to let me know it was him; that he would be alright; that where he was going would be a better place than where he was coming from. Still, he would miss me; miss all."

"Do you believe that Conner?" I could see her figure pose a look out to where our children were at play.

"I do Sandra," were my soft words back to her.

"Do you think this is where your mother will go?"

The question struck me to the very core of my feelings; my heart sinking into that wallow of emotions which had been sitting in the back of my mind; festering, stewing like the unrelenting force that would consume me at some point. I felt the brush of a wind ripple the tree leaves into a rustle and shimming sound; cast down a swirl, pick about those leaves which had fallen some days before, and pull them skyward into a rotating circle. Like the ghost of some small tornado with its outline formed by the dance of those leaves.

"I hope," I whispered, "I hope not."

Sandra came from her sitting and made her way to the outskirts of that cemetery; I in follow to her. She walked by her memory of those events so long ago; she moved as the thoughts of her grandfather stirred her to go. I knew where this would lead, and so my steps traced the very shadows of her walk, like the tracing shadow I was.

The wind seemed to follow us through the darkened alleyways of that cemetery path. The trees were most dense and shadowed the grounds about with bright clips of sunshine and silhouette images of their branches sprawling about. Still, the wind followed us.

Sandra had left me to my own demise; wandering about with my thoughts of what she was feeling; the turmoil in her mind, those elusive memories which remain always in the background. Sometimes they would show themselves in moments like this. What were her feelings? What was she thinking? I followed till we both reached the back edge of this cemetery; the newer plots where these three firemen were buried.

The crypts and head stones looked worn and aging, though still quite new compared to the others. The writings plain, sentimental, written on words of love and admiration, where the hearts of mourning are newly bled, and the words as ripe as a just-picked apple.

She went to their feet, facing away from me, still, motionless; the wind catching to her long blonde hair. Her stance was quiet and unmoving, as if her body was caught in a spell of total meditation. Her hands moved up to her arms, crisscrossing as though in a cradling; the wind blew forward, then crisscrossing her, the same. I could feel her shuttering, standing as I did a few yards behind her. She bent down, watching still the words on the headstone as she read them through, and they standing alone in her thoughts.

"Grandpa," she wept and pulled the cross she wore from beneath her shirt; touching it to her lips, "It's so strange Conner," she started, "I never cried for him before; not when I heard he had passed; not during the ceremony or the burial; not afterwards; not ever."

Her head bent low; the tears falling into her palms; the roaring of those emotions thundering through into their own storm of sympathy.

"I miss him no less. I was a good granddaughter to him, and he was a good grandfather to me."

I went to her side as she knelt to one knee, and then sat at the foot of his grave, Indian style. She picked at the grass in an arbitrary way, with no rhyme or reason for what she was picking on.

"You have nothing to be ashamed of..." I stated.

"Shame?" she reacted, "Shame is not the word; lack of connection is. I did not feel the loss as much as I thought I would. The feelings were strong during his life; his smile always reminding me of them. But when I discovered he was gone, my emotions froze; frozen into some icy, cold place; a place where I could no longer could find them."

She stalled on these words.

"You never grieved Sandra," I suggested.

"Now I cry," she said, "And I don't know why. Why so long? This should have come long before," she turned to me and wept into the bed of my shoulder. I clung to her with the wrapping of my arms while we sat there, "Does this make me a bad granddaughter?"

"No Sandra," I spoke, "Your only crime comes from forfeiting your grief for the sake of silence. You were young, as I, not knowing; being a child. The world is safe then, like a garden that never ends. Nothing is to touch you. And when it does, you can either choose to confront it, or push it further away from you, and still believe that this very garden, the only one you long to play in, never ends."

"Why did you stop believing?" she questioned through the soft echoes of her tears, which had found her eyes now in focus, dropping like starlight rain from the night skies.

"Spike," I whispered, "I couldn't deny his absence." I paused to hold her closer still, "The question is, do you still remember? Do you still hold true to the touching of your life by him?"

"I remember the shipboard trips along the bay," she began, "The summer days when he would take me out for fishing, and other times for sailing. I remember the way he would catch the wind in his sails and cut the water as if he were flying over the sea. Grandfather and I had many talks then," she peeled back from me as I wiped the tears from her cheeks, and there out-produced a simple smile when she caught her gaze with my tender stare.

"He was the one grandparent who adored the outdoors; his love for birds and seagulls; the sunsets that would cross the bow and touch the waterline with a red hot sun. He loved to watch the sun dip below the horizon, and think of the days when he was young."

"Then you have that treasure there," I said, "Something he gave you; something to hold true, deep, internal that can always find its way back to you again when you want to remember him."

"But I tried to cry when the ceremony came…"

"What is it you most remember Sandra?" I said, "Think of it."

"How, in his own way," she pulled my cross free to match with hers, "he brought us together; you and me."

I looked deep into Sandra's eyes as I had done so many times before. But to the stripping of our hearts, the souls met glance to glance; where I could sense in this moment the language of the most intimate could speak. I thought back onto that ceremony and so gazing up at my father in the pulpit; my mother's stare engaging his; the internal talk they shared. How their eyes blinked the words spoken; the voices of the heart turning sentences into tunes.

It was here when Sandra and I first began to speak in the same manner; when those unspoken words were translated into some deeper meaning. Her hair curled round her face when the wind blew about; those locks dipping in a dance of their own. She met my look with hers; the soft flowing embers of our love touching the other's soul in a most profound way. Where hands were tense and folding with their caress; the eyes left nothing to bare or keep into a secret; our thoughts united, weeping a cry she had never discovered before until now.

"I know why you never cried love…" I spoke.

"Why Conner?" she shadowed my look.

"Because you couldn't do it alone," I whispered as we embraced.

And so the silence met with us. The delicate tears were to flood through her emotions and find there home, a place, on my shoulder.

I think we made her grandfather most happy there. He must have been smiling from Heaven's view. That shadow of the day; soft pillars of clouds passing by overhead, so docked the sunlight into its own shores for the time it took to pass by. We felt the shades cool us; the returning sun warm us once more, and yet we felt so the shelter of his presence guarding us underneath his new birthplace.

We stood after a spell, walked hand in hand back to where the children were still in play with Amanda. The day had grown older since we left and the afternoon sun was beginning to peak and wane through those later hours. Amanda would take the children back home for the evening and Sandra and I were to apprise her of the situation, after the meeting with the doctors was to conclude.

The return to the hospital was less than climatic. That is until we reached the floor where my mother had been staying in ICU. The world had suddenly appeared to be in a violent and chaotic buzz. Nurses were stammering about; doctors in a hustle to and fro. A sort of delirious dance we had just found ourselves in.

"Nurse," I pulled one to me, "Can you help me please?" Just behind the awaiting door was the ICU unit itself.

"We are in a state of some influx at this moment sir."

"What is going on?" I stressed.

"I am not at liberty…" she was attempting to pull away from our conversation, "There isn't time sir."

"Time for what?" I pressed further.

"We are not at liberty to discuss anything at this point," the nurse spoke out as she left Sandra and me. I turned, and at this very moment father came from behind the ICU doors.

His stare glared a look of stone; disfigured in its expression; distant in its thoughts. His mind seemed to be lost from his body and now his body was walking about with the absence most apparent in the bed of his face. He took to not recognize me. His aging face seemed more aged than before; like the ghost of himself was peeling through the hollow gaze he was sending our way.

"Dad?"

I went to his side and pressed on his shoulder.

"Dad? What is going on? Is it mother again?"

"Your mother," he struggled to say, "is dying."

"Dying?"

I cut a most painful look over my face, so feeling the near dropping of Sandra to the floor next to me.

"This can't be."

"She may not make it much longer…" he spoke with a stunned, nearly fragile tone in his voice. His eyes shuttered and closed; the voice quivering while he made attempts to regroup and recover his composure, though his disposition never faltered.

"Dad," I pursued, "Talk to me. Look at me. Talk to me."

"There is little they can do," he stalled, "They will try, is all."

"What is wrong?" I asked further.

"Her platelet level has dropped below twelve thousand," he responded, "Blood clotting; heart attack at any moment. She may not make it through the night son…"

"I have to go see her," I began forward, though he held me to refrain.

"Dad! I have to go see her!"

"I think it would be best son," he paused, "to wait on the doctor to call. Doctor Ogden is with her now."

"Good," I started, "then he will allow me to see her."

Just as I spoke these words, Doctor Ogden came from the swinging doors; catching my eyes with his hard and worried look.

"Mr. James," he spoke with his hand out into another direction, "Please attend to me for a bit."

"I wish to see her," I made my case.

"This will have to wait…" he was more persistent this time.

"For when?" I was more the angrier now.

"Please," he came, "Do attend; in private."

"On one condition," I suggested.

"Be quick then," he responded.

"We see her afterwards," I said, yet there was no reply to it, "Listen doctor, I HAVE to see her. It's not a matter of 'if' I can. If there was any possibility, however remote, that this would be the last time you would speak to your mother, would you be denied?"

"Alright," he conceded, "For a few minutes," he shifted his eyes backwards, towards ICU, "But nothing more; nothing further. You say your peace, and then leave on my command. Her vitals signs are tenuous at best, at this time."

My wife came to my side, slipping her arm around my waist, and by doing so, she urged me to proceed quickly with the doctor.

We made our way into an isolated room. Simple, private, without any duty to comfort but for the lone purpose it would hold; to be exclusively quiet. We sat across from him, with hands draping over that small round table. I could feel the perspiration between my palms dripping with the weight of their own intensity.

"I will not deny you any measure of truth here. It's best to know, than for me to skirt around the issues. Your mother has had a significant setback. We have begun a plasma exchange due to the near fatal drop in her platelet levels."

"How far?" I struggled to ask.

"Far enough," he answered, "Too far; way too far for security sake. If not for the immediate plasma exchange, she would have died most certainly within the hour."

"Within the hour?" Sandra took tighter hold of me.

"What caused this doctor?"

He took to a sigh, a bending of his head below his chin, a harsh and grim look to the floor, "Sometimes when people have an auto-immune system disease, they can regularly contract another. It self-manifests itself into something new, more powerful. At any moment things can alter and change…for the better, or for the worst."

"And in this case," I spoke, "Hope failed us."

"This has gotten out of control," Sandra nearly wept.

"Your mother has many battles to contend with, and I could never make light of the fact it is an uphill battle at best."

"What are her chances?" I asked.

"I can never determine that," he replied, "Many factors play a role. Among the greatest is her will to survive. She is struggling against the more rare of all immune diseases," he paused, "and she has a very aggressive form of it; very, very aggressive."

"So, we wait," I concluded.

"She has other looming problems which are pressing," he continued with caution to expose them fully.

His eyes showed such reservation that I felt her chances slipping even further than what I thought they were already.

"The more prevailing now is clotting, which can result in hemorrhaging or even a massive heart attack. Outside of this, she has a staff infection and a viral infection; we drew cultures yesterday and they came back positive; antibiotics will resolve that. Beyond this, the most pressing thing to follow is she is beginning to show signs of ARDS or Acute Respiratory Distress Syndrome."

"I don't understand doctor," I questioned, "How can this be more severe than the Wegener's she already has?"

"Because it is a severe and permanent injury to the lungs; her current breathing patterns are quite irregular, and may require ventilation. We will have to perform a nerve conductor test to determine the nature and condition of her lungs."

"What could possibly be causing this?" Sandra asked.

"Wegener's," he closed his eyes on this, "It generally causes the vessels in the body to bloat and enlarge, and so breaking down the nerves. We believe this could be causing the related distress in her lungs and throat. It also is possibly suppressing her bone marrow and this could also be affecting her very low platelet levels. Without the nerve conductor test, we cannot say for sure. The disease is appearing to become more globalized in the body, finding more avenues to be destructive with."

"It's not giving her a chance," I whispered.

"Steroids are doing some good," he said, "We would desire for better results. But small victories are still victories."

"Anything else?" I inquired as I stood to circle about the room. My eyes were cast off into the corner wall, and I dreaming of a distant place to run to.

"Besides her demiliated nerves and her poor oxygenation," he began, "she has contracted a mild case of aspiration pneumonia, a yeast infection in her kidney; the continual fluid buildup; the vision problems are still apparent..." he stalled.

"Enough doctor..." I looked over to him, "Now its time for me to see her."

I felt his allowance come through clearly with his expression; the soft nature of his permission yielded us all to leave the room as quickly as we had entered.

Father had remained just outside the door where Lorie had come through, as well to give him comfort. She came to me with an embrace, without the penance for words to speak on; Sandra and I so proceeding forward through the ICU doors.

The shadows were as prominent as they had been before, perhaps even more so. The nurses who were hovering about the main station sent a look to where we stood; the concern in their eyes appeared more evident than I had remembered. Even the silence seemed to dim the lights into a low, muddling haze as we past through.

There were doctors and nurses congesting into my mother's room. A large machine heavily at work, spun next to her bed, grinding out in a deep humming sound of its own. The plasma exchange was commencing as quickly as the machine could flush her from old to new.

Every moment could be the last; the final pages were turning on our book in life; the chapters worn to the end, and Heaven perchance calling the end to what we knew. The bitter leafs of time had spun into a small accounting of what felt to be left between us; the words now becoming more precious than ever. I would drink out the final drop as long as the moisture was still remaining in this nearly empty glass of opportunity.

I felt the world had lost itself, and created an odd dream for me; a dream where things were not exactly as they should be; a place where life had trailed off into a downward spiral. I prayed I would awake soon and so find myself in the correct place I should be in. To call my mother in the morning and find all is well.

It is strange how the diversity of dreams and shadows can be. Their interlocking roles; the reversing traits would often confuse and confound a soul into defining which is real and which is actually the product of imagination. At this moment however I could never tell the truth between the two. That reality had been lost long before and was sitting in a fog far away from me; waiting, hiding until the sun would appear once more. To me, dreams and shadows had become nothing more than hollow corpses.

Sandra and I moved slowly to the very step of her room. Mother's hand was tight to a fist; clinching, neither unmoved nor shaken, still clinging to what life remained for her. I pressed past the curtain wall, lighting my expression to hers. Her eyes to a grinding shut; her face all puffed into a strange, white-moon glow, with eyes lost behind their eyelids. She blew out the air from her lungs; the breathing precarious but holding her at life's doorstep.

She must have been counting the rotation to the Plasmapheresis machine, for her breathing seemed to be aligned with its turning. I saw the sweat from her brow collect over her forehead; I went to wipe it free and press my palm along her eyelids.

"Mother?" I tried to wake her from her concentration.

"Conner," she called to me.

"How do you feel?" I wondered aloud.

"Not…too…good," she explained past her breathing.

"It might be a long night," I whispered in her left ear.

"I'm still here," she pressed to say.

"Looks that way," I smiled, though she never opened her eyes to look upon me, "This isn't the end mother…"

"I'm not done," she spoke, "Not yet anyways." I could sense the strength in her spirit when she spoke this, though the fear resounded as heavy from the tone of her voice. I sat there in silence, watching her and feeling the ebbs and flow of her breathing pace through that time without waiver. She had defeated death once before; now, she would do it again.

"Have you seen anymore shadows in the mirror?"

"He is there," she replied.

"He?" I asked, "How do you know it is a he?"

"Because," she answered, "he came with his voice this time."

"What did he say?" I wanted to know.

"It is a secret," she whispered, still heaving her breath as every moment passed into the next, "for now."

"You can't take it with you mother."

"In time son," she said, "the moment will arrive." There was a pause in that silence, "Now son, let me rest for a piece."

I kissed her to the forehead, pressing my lips to sooth her as my hand brushed back over her hair. My body went into retreat while I kept watch over her. Doctor Ogden took me by the hand and led me free from the room.

We sat by the waiting room for the hours to expel themselves out into the past. The waiting we shared together had crossed over into one bridge after another; the time pressing us into a further stall. It would be some hours before the doctor would reappear and so inform us, by some element of a gracious miracle, that mother had made it through the worst of it. Her platelet levels were beginning to rise and the chance for clotting subsiding; though she would need her rest and we were not allowed to see her until the morning hours.

Chapter 24

My Friend Calls for Me.

The harrowing tides from the night before had pressed us all into submission. The darker hands of time seemed more like shadows that hid in the late afternoon air, and would not speak of their presence until they became most prominent. I knew we had grown weary from the previous day's events, so it was to my delight when, after the early Sunday morning run through the park and a trip with the family to the restaurant for lunch, I had received a call from my good friend Jason over my answering machine.

"Conner; it's Jason. Meet me at Fenway around eight. No need to explain for now. Just be there; and no excuses. You know how I hate it when you wimp out on things; so be attentive." There came back his message as we replayed it.

"I wonder what he may want…" Sandra questioned.

"Knowing Jason…" I smirked, "No telling with him."

"What about your mother?" She asked.

"Lorie wants the day with her," I said, "She will apprise me if there are any changes. I have the whole day off tomorrow to be with mother."

I shuffled through my pockets in search of my car keys.

"Do you want me to go?" She continued to question.

"What about the children?"

I could see the frustrated look crawling over her face; her eyes darting and in a switch from one room-side to the other, "This was our night out this evening…"

"Don't start Sandra," I locked a corner stare over her. She pulled back, fumbled about with a distorted expression casting down over the sofa, as if she were a heavy weight with thought.

"Children," she grew a fake smile, "Why don't you go to your room and play for a bit."

They looked over her with curiosity, though not saying a thing in return; I knew I was in for it, "Go on now."

"Don't shut me out Conner," she began, "I am in this as deep as you are. She is your mother. But she is also my close friend."

"I am aware of this," I had no care to speak on this now, and my gaze told her as much, "Besides, I am sure Jason means nothing by all this; perhaps an hour or more, nothing further than this."

I watched over her, noting full well this was not in the least satisfactory to Sandra. She stalled about the room without meeting her look on mine. I could see the touch of one tear meeting on her disposition. A curling of her lips revealed the continual stress she was feeling. I came to her with a kiss and a hug, pressing my explanation with a whisper there.

"Its not a matter of shutting you out dear," I said, "It's a matter that some journey's are left alone; of letting in. There are times for family; there are times for friends as well. Jason has called for me; his schedule is very difficult to contend with, especially this late in the season," I looked onto her dripping stare, and so pulled it up to mine, "An hour; perhaps slightly more, then I will come home to be with the three most important people in my life."

"Is that a promise?" She smiled.

"Promises lent, is promises earned," I returned in a smile, "My lady; you've earned a lifetime of promises from me."

I brushed through her long strands of hair; the soft curls in their body dipped around the round features in her face. Her eyes were no longer discontent, but full in their warmth and humanity towards me. I could smell the sweet fragrance of her perfume sifting past my nose, "Pride is not the word to speak of when speaking of what I hold for you…"

"Then what is?" she dreamed with her look.

"A gift," I replied, "A treasure beholding the respect I have for it. Love as ours endures, and makes the meadows that much more green. Weathers the storms; and gives shelter when the need arises."

I felt her pulling me close.

"Just don't forget about that gift…"

"To lose this gift," I explained, "Is to lose myself."

Several hours would pass before I made my way to Fenway. The afternoon ballgame had long been played through. The Red Sox were in a tight race for a playoff berth, and had pulled out yet another victory; coming from two runs down in the eighth by way of a three-run homer and defeating the Chicago

White Sox 5-4. Jason, to date, had a very successful season, going 12-7 with the second lowest ERA on the team.

I could see the dusting of the sky beginning to melt deep into the sunset just off the bay's shoreline. The waters curled with that fading gleam, creating a sparkle in their waves as they rolled in and out of the bay. I stopped my car for a few minutes in an abandoned parking lot, coming to the forefront of my hood, and taking a few moments to be a spectator over these ocean seas.

There was a crawling of distant ships coming past the harbors and into the lime life of the endless rows of waters. The cascades of light and dying reflections warmed me to the soul; I hearing the long sounds of bells tottering along the tossing landscape in front of me. The hard working shore men cast out ships into the sea like the lots of pebbles my mother had held in that dream I had just a few evenings before. The docks were more vacant than normal; the anchors and hard wooden vessels not aboard and tipping along their lines when the sea yawned forward into the bay.

But the seagulls took their place; their shadows in flight along the vast escape of this horizon as I looked abroad. The world appeared to be an infinite land of horizons and ember-burning reds. The summer heat had now fallen into a humid, low-settling mist that seemed to roll dockside. There was a silence about; sifting past all the slow moving waves which lipped the shores every few seconds.

I closed my eyes, thinking of a ship that was currently in travel to where the dying day's sun was meeting the end of those seas; somewhere out into that infinity. Perhaps there was a world there of no sickness; a journey land to where my mother could be taken, and this terrible disease called Wegener's was unable to follow to. I would mast my own sails; calculate the direction with my compass aboard, and pray for the more favorable winds to brush us out onto this sea's cliff and edge.

Columbus' journey had less importance than my own, for the journey to the Americas was of lesser concern than the saving of her life to me. I would stand about the bow like the captain of my own dreams; eyes set in stern and forward, so watching my ship cut through those waves like a knife in the belly of that dividing butter. And just beyond this awaiting horizon, where the sea land met with the sun, she could find refuge and rescue.

I opened my eyes and found myself back in the reality of the world I found myself so in conflict with; it was a hope and a thought all rolled up into one. The remaining journey was not long in the least; however, as I drifted off into a daze, eternity seemed to be longer still.

I could see the bright harboring lights of Fenway gushing over the tops of her park; like a calling and a beacon to my passing car ship. Her brilliant lighthouse spectacles burned brighter still as I came closer. Though they did not turn into a rotating, their power was the more evident as I pulled into the parking space across the street.

I heard no activity within her fields. The echoes of cheers long passed from the afternoon before; now so subsiding into an eerie silence which prevailed throughout. Still, her lights were in full use. Normally, by the time a few hours had passed from the end of the game, all had been shut down unless the team had an after-game practice. Practices were usually reserved a few hours before game time. Perhaps Jason had been mistaken and wanted me to attend the game itself, or even come to practice to speak with him.

I came to the front gates, saw the front area abandoned but for the pedestrian traffic walking by along the sidewalks. A few cars met at the stoplight just down the street, waiting for the lights to go from red to green, and proceed forward.

"Mr. James," I heard a voice from within call for me.

"Yes?" I shot my head around to respond.

"May I see identification?" the man asked.

"Certainly," I pulled my license free from my wallet and handed it to him through the gate.

"Needs renewal," he smiled and returned it, while opening the gate and allowing me to enter, "follow me sir."

"Is it alright?" I asked.

"Yes sir," the man walked along side of me; his obvious limp hampered by his bowing legs. He wore a ground's keeper head uniform, a graying crew cut, a scar running along the downturn of his chin, and glassiest blue eyes I had ever seen. He was not much one for conversation, with a belly as big as his chest protruding forward. He surely showed himself to be a rather stout man. His tiny, truncated arms seemed to flop along his sides as he walked, appearing more as a penguin waddle than a walk itself.

"What is this all about?" I asked.

"Have to wait and see sir," he cocked his head in a grin.

"I don't remember you," I made an attempt to recall recognition of him when I had come during my boyhood days.

"Nor I you, sir," he shook his shoulders.

"How long have you worked here?"

"As long as sin," he replied, as we made our way down the runway, "Believe I have more years than all the Red Sox players in the majors."

"Do you remember Spike?" I pulled him to stop; we looking square eye to eye there, "Spike Johnson."

"Sure do," he gapped a smile, "My brother; got me started here." And he continued to walk near to the illuminated field.

"You don't say," I pondered.

His form waddled into the ambience of these sparkles and lights all embedding their force into the very centering of Fenway. Those green, lush foresting pastures groomed a pure plain of perfected lawns, with sprinklers all in full water from right to left fields. I could hear the constant buzz of those enormous lights reining down over the arena. The smell of freshly-cut grass; the looming, hollow, and ghost-feeling appearance of those empty bleachers; the overhanging green monster in left field standing thirty feet in height; the barren dugout crawls; the tall, high-reaching screen directly behind home plate; all standing to create a scene I would never have imagined from Fenway Park before this moment.

You could feel the games of the past, like specters and ghosts all in replay; the shouting echoes of their victories; the whimpering cries of their defeats, now cascading down like heavy droplets from a water faucet. The dew had formed into a symphony with that silence of this soundless field, rising in a low-settling fog and mist that only grew most dense when those sprinklers rotated to every corner of the outfields.

I saw Fenway as more of a remote, isolated treasure landscape; something of privilege and honor. I had dreamed from my very early youth for the chance and opportunity to one day step onto Fenway field and see the diamond as exact as my imagination had imagined it to be. There, as I took it all into my scope, was a lone figure standing squarely on the pitchers' mound, in uniform, like the grown-up actor of a child's dream he was; my friend Jason.

He stood high in his saddle, with an heir of confidence and acclaim shooting straight back at me. His brim hat settled just above his eye view; hand in glove and scuffing a ball. His jersey held as much intimidation as his look had, with the word 'Boston' streaming across his chest like a shield.

I could see the rise of a smirk rustling out of one corner of his mouth; the ball pumping in and out of his glove. His cleats were digging deep into the rubber; the belt gripping hard to his waist.

"So what brought me here?" I asked with a laugh.

"To settle a score," he grinned.

"What?" I threw my hands out as my voice radiated across the field from that outpost of the far foul line, "What score?"

"A long-time one," he replied, "Still, to see if you have it…"

"Have what?" I moved within the right field line.

"See if you still own my pitch," he called back, "Times have changed. Think I have proven a thing or two. Now, I just have to prove it to you my friend," he dipped his hat with respect. He stalled as I took a few steps further, then leaned his face towards home plate, "There..." he said in a single word.

I went to where his look had gone, and so found a bat leaning up against the far backstop.

"Black, lean," he returned to smile, "Just how you like it."

"Pearl black?" I wondered.

"As black as night," he responded.

"Slim handle?" I wondered again, "Trademark sliced in two?"

"Just how you like it," he winked, "Exactly; I remember."

"You know something?" I suggested.

"What is that?" he returned in a question.

"Never thought I would hear an echo at Fenway..."

"About as deafening as when you are pitching in the ninth of a 1-0 game," he pumped the ball hard-fisted into his glove.

I went to the backstop, took hold of the bat, with its heavy edge and hardwood nub at the handle's end, took a few gentle swings, and stood a moment to stare out at the seemingly infinite view of that entire field.

"Never thought I would get here," I said.

"Well you did," he took hold of some dirt near the pitcher's mound, "And it's no dream...Ready Casey?"

"Now hold on now," I urged, "Let me smell this for a moment."

I closed my eyes and began to smell the surroundings as if it were my sights that were all consumed there.

"You'll need to get ready," he spit to the side and began digging his cleats further off the rubber.

"Don't know if my shoulder will hold up," I worried, "It's been awhile," I took a few more swings.

"Dirt dauber," he muddled, "'Old man' it is."

"What's that Gum?" I shouted back.

Before I knew it, he spun about, thrust himself into a full pitching motion, and propelled the ball right along the inner, high side of home plate; nearly forcing me to the ground. I felt the sizzle of that ball steam past me in flames.

"There's more where that came from," he turned and ducked his eyesight just beneath his cap bill.

"Gees," I whispered, "You've gotten better; a lot better."

"What was that?" he turned to scowl me down once more.

"Ball one!" I yelled back, with a few more swings before he could re-arm again.

"I'm not responsible for what happens here on out!" He set up once more, sending a glaze-of-a-stare right down home plate.

"Nor am I," I called out, "Oh! Brother!" I whispered to myself.

"Not the same pitcher Sherlock…"

"We will test that arm of yours," I waited in still motion.

Our eyes forged to lock there in what appeared to be an endless, gut-wrenching stare; the pause, the quiet silence of all those empty seats; the buzz from the man-made lights; the glare from his looks, and the long-shadows of the fields behind him.

He steadied, took to his stance, held firm, then began that heaving twist of his frame, turning nearly one-quarter back, keeping hard-eye over me and the plate; his hands rising, ball-to-glove, glove-to-ball, as though it were all a ferocious dance to him.

I watched as his arm came forward with the ball displayed to me like a big volleyball to take swing-shots at. He leaned in with a horrid grimace writhing all over his face; his barreling shoulders with the force of a ship's cannon, then the baseball hard to blow like the wind, being sent right to my direction.

The sizzle from its velocity came thundering towards me and nearly took me off-guard; this throw being much harder than the first. I steadied, held to my stance, and when the ball neared, I moved back-foot forward with my weight while holding my shoulders in balance. My eyes grew bigger than gumballs at the sight of it. That white and red-stitch blur hurled directly down the middle of the plate. It seemed like a comet topsy-turning with a trail in its rear; the sound more heated and on fire as it came most close.

I swung, holding my eyes down, and so seeing the ball swiftly move past me, my bat felt as though it were still over my shoulders when that ball ripped through the gunnery of that batter's box.

"You've gotten slower in your old age; old man," he grinned and smiled, "Strike…one."

"Just for starters," he gulped. "Hope your head doesn't get too big with that fake out." He knew I was challenging him further, "Seen your soft stuff; now give me the big leagues. Or, is that the best you can do?"

I could see the flames rising from his ears.

He roared a pitch down onto me for the third throw; like a lion's growl in anger. It railed just underneath my chin and pushed me back-first onto the dirt floor below.

"Had one to waste," he turned from me and climbed the pitcher's mound like it was his lair.

I stood and dusted my clothes off, casting out an evil eye his way, which he caught the back end of it as I finished my cleanups.

"I do have a family you know," I suggested.

"Pitter pat," he smiled, "Pitter pat."

He commenced with the next pitch; it tumbling down off his arm in a curve that nearly hung seven feet tall, yet broke down as if gravity grabbed it whole and forced it down over my waistline.

"Strike…two."

"Whoa," my jaw dropped, "You've gotten a lot better," I whispered to myself, but still more determined than ever to put a pitch of his in play.

"Uncle?" I heard him echo to me, "Say please?"

"No pleasure here," I answered, "But to see your best pitch in a missile shot over the green monster."

"Dream on Shakespeare," he warned at the outset of his fifth pitch; I swinging nearly blind yet dribbling it down the first base line. I felt the numb hammer-shake of that vibration ring through my hands, which nearly caused my forearms to fall off.

"Hopefully I won't have to take you home to Sandra," he paused, "in separate parts."

I gazed over the third base line, and saw that old man leaning over the dugout railing at us; his hands tossing another ball back and forth between his hands.

"Go get him tiger," he yelled as encouragement to Jason.

"I see you have your own cheering squad," I replied, "Too bad he wouldn't look good in a skirt…"

"Maybe so," he grinned, looking about in a curious way, "but not half as good as seeing a pile of dirt on you're…" and with this he shot his sixth pitch right along my chest line. It quite literally put me back on the ground; tush first. I stood to clean myself clear once more.

"Hey!" the old man laughed, "I think he does tiger!"

"Full count," I sneered down at both of them as I climbed back into the batter's box.

"Ready, choir boy?" Jason pulled the glove just beneath his chin; still keeping sightline just above the tiptop of his gloves' lacings; never giving into a single blink.

"Been ready all my life," I took three mighty swings, "Bring it on pulpit pusher…"

"Here we go," he started his windup, high rising stance, lean forward, and there, in that moment of poetic motions, I saw more clearly than I had ever seen, felt the rush of some unshakable powers grab hold of me as his arm came forward and so shot-put his final pitch in my direction.

My swing met with perfect timing, balance, and lift; finding the mark as his pitch rolled in on me. Bat-to-ball, striking with the violent crush and wicked crashing that all but shouted out its own lamenting when they met in force.

The sound bellowed all throughout Fenway Park this night. Its howl even shuttered the furthermost walls of her reign, and crawled through the alleyways most near to her standing.

I saw the ball bend for that moment, nearly crack through its stitching, and send its way high into the night-soaked air. The arch was like the start of a rainbow, reaching high and higher still; going, elevating to the brisk of those lights; still climbing the mountain of the night without even a notion to fall from. This was not a comet, but the beginning of a new day when the sun keeps rising as long as the morning goes.

I stood there with my eyes falling out of their sockets; my jaw dropping to seemingly dust off home plate with my chin. The ball became a spec in the dark and light shadows about. I could feel Jason turn in amazement to see just how far this ball would travel. So too did this old man bend his sights around that railing, look upward, and appear as stunned as we were.

It was said that that ball traveled as far as any in memory; the type where legends were born; where feats of heroics stand through time and go from mouth-to-ear, and back again through generation to generation. I lost sight of it as it climbed long over that green, castle-wall monster, and so disappear into the depth of this low-misty night. The moment emptied out into a still wind there.

"Make your trip," Jason turned to wave me on, "Make your way around the bases to home; you deserve it."

I said nothing, yet made my slow pace around the bases as they both watched me ring around that diamond. The old man met me rounding third with his hand out-stretched and greeting me with a smile; I feeling the pat of his hand over my back.

"You're as good as he said you would be," he softly expressed, "You would have been a great one son…"

I stomped on home plate, raised my hands into the air, and felt Jason coming towards me. It was then I felt Spike's spirit seemingly pass by me in a whisper and a breeze. I rotated my sights all about the empty ballpark, felt the soft echoes of my memory storm through my imagination like a freight train, and then see the shadows of those who were there that day when I was the ball boy and Yaz making that hero's double to bring the Red Sox to victory. Even then I could hear the slow rumble of 'Spike! Spike! Spike! Spike!' captured within my ear.

"You want a bottle of water?" Jason punched me over the shoulder and pressed me back to the mound where we took to sit near the pitcher's rubber.

"You know you shouldn't have said that about me," I said, taking the water from him, and gulping it down as though I had just come beyond a long travel through the desert, "I appreciate your accolades, but I would have never been that good."

"What are you talking about?"

"The ground's keeper," I said, looking around to spot him, "You know...the one you had let me in."

"What are you talking about Conner?" he insisted.

"He was just over there," I pointed to third base, "he met me rounding the base. You know...the one you set out to let me in. He walked me down here to the field."

"There was no one here," Jason giggled, "You're seeing things in your old age brother," he laughed further.

"I'm serious Jason," I stressed, "He was just here. You didn't see him??" I was nearly beside myself.

"Listen friend," he leaned over to grab his glove, "there are only two people here...you, and me. I left the front open, against the best wishes of management. But hey," he smiled and pushed his fist on my shoulder, "What management doesn't know won't hurt them."

And just as he leaned down I saw that old man standing in my far sights; a smile crossing his expression, a whisper that even though sounded off in the distance, it touched my ears more clearly this time.

"Like he said; you would have been a great one." I felt his words pass into sound only for me to hear.

"Give my regards to Spike."

I was nearly in shock. My pulse almost riveting through my veins; my hand in a shake as I kept my eyes glued to this festering spectre of a man who as suddenly appeared, was now fading down the runway.

"Would you?" I softly said in a plea, "Good sir..."

"You bet..."

He saluted me one final time, now hobbling gently down into the deep and dark crevices of this runway. Spike's brother disappeared in the shadows that emptied out into another world.

"How are you holding up?" Jason's voice was becoming most tender with concern. I turned towards him and I sat across from him in a straddle on that slab of rubber. We took another swig of bottled water in unison there, "Your mother..."

"Days are long," I said, as I lowered my head into some thoughts of the mental pain I was suffering through, "Nights are longer still," I breached my sights throughout the lonely park again.

"You know," he said, "I am pretty handy with friendship."

"I know," I freely smiled, "I heard."

"How's Sandra?" he said, "the kids?"

"They manage," I replied, "I don't make it easy; I don't make it convenient for any of them."

"How can you?" he defended me, "The kids; they know?"

"No," I dusted down some dirt off my shoes, "If they did, too young to understand the magnitude of it all."

"You'll have to tell them," Jason rolled the ball on the ground, "If it gets so far; it's not like you can hide it."

"I'll manage when the time comes," I started, "You know Jason," my chin began to wrinkle a bit, "I am sort of new to this; have to play it through as I go; challenges everyday; heartaches and fears. You live life in such a smooth way. Then it hits hard to a stall and you just try to figure out a way to make it start up again."

"I could never win enough ballgames to match your battle friend," he looked over me with honor and pride, "they say wisdom is known by the one who understands their abilities…"

"I know," I drank further, "and their weaknesses."

"So which one are you?"

"Who has the greater glory?" I responded in question.

"The abilities?" he said, "Or the weaknesses."

"Ask me any time," I pondered, "and the answer always changes; from moment to moment; from time to time."

"Your mother's a special lady," he stared out into the deep haven of the outfields, watching the sprinklers shower those lawns.

"How so…" I wondered aloud.

"Just look at her children," he responded, "Its that clear…"

"She has shown me much," I replied, "more than I knew she ever had; the promise to have the will to survive."

"Not what I meant tush…" he pushed me backwards.

"So?" I leaned back to set the stars into my sights.

"To have a son like you," he said, "must make her proud."

"Ohh," I wondered, "I'm not the one making all the sacrifices."

"But you have the choices," he responded, "She doesn't. You can walk away; pretend none of this is ever happening. Say you want to remember her the way she was. But still you remain. Why?"

"Forgiveness," was the single word I spoke, "Forgiveness."

"Clue me in Conner…"

"I wouldn't have the right to this word; its meaning; the purpose for it being there if I walked away. To abandon her in her time of most need, regardless of the situation and circumstance, its not something you do, or ever do…if you love someone."

He kept to his silence, dropped his eyes to the outstretching grasslands, as if he were melting into his own thoughts for a second. I could see his mind was at play in front of me.

"Testament," he whispered, "who has the greater will; the one who gives, or the one who takes? You're a giver my friend, and that's what giver's do; beyond all measure."

"I believe," I propped my elbows over my rising knees, "That no matter how difficult life can be, no matter the harsh realities proposed to you; just look around you and observe. What do you see? You don't have to look very far to discover someone else who has it more difficult than you," I took to a pause to reflect, "In this particular case I don't have to look very far at all…not far at all."

"What are her chances?"

"I don't know Jason," I nearly crumbled at the idea of losing her, "The days before us are just as dark as night itself."

"But still you hope…" he said.

"But still you hope," I echoed him, "No other choice."

"Conner, she will fight it," he sounded, "If I know your mother, and I think I do, she will fight it, and win."

"But what if she doesn't?" I pressed, "Fight and fight, and fight some more, and yet still she losses; all that suffering to go through, and for what reason? Nothing; simply nothing…"

"You can't think that way brother," he shook his head, "If she gives up now, she will certainly lose…And you will never know if she could have won. That uncertainty will always live with you, haunt you, and you can never make peace with yourself over it…you, your sisters, and for sure, your brother Adam. Think of it…This is your chance to finish that unfinished business with her, if it were to turn out this way. Time is more precious than gold now. You know and understand the value of it here; right now, and still have the chance to do something about it."

"I know," I sighed, "Quitting is not an option."

"You're right," he grumbled, "it's more than that; it's a sin."

"I am trying to manage my feelings."

"Good," he said, "Do it. But don't let your mother see this in you. She has enough to worry about other than to worry how this will affect you, your siblings, and your father. She needs everything she has now to fight this."

"You know something?" I leaned back to eye him and smile, "Your smarter than a jock."

We sat there and laughed for a time; saying nothing, but drinking in the full view of Fenway Park. It felt as if we had an eternity to drink all this in; the key to that park and evening night, now thrown away and discarded for a time. No clock to register time with, but to allow the evening air to navigate its own way through into the morning. I was vaulted back when we were children together, wishing the bounty of our dreams to come true.

There we were, sitting upon this unmentionable field as young heartfelt boys, and drawing that fresh air into our lungs; watching the daylight dim into early evening sunsets. Jason and I shared so much back then; the solo games of pitch and hit, batting practices; all the scenarios we drew up with our minds, like painting to an empty canvas there; being the Picasso's of baseball. We were to at last play for the Red Sox; this being our final destination. And in this moment, when part was brought to reality and the other part to unrealized dreams, we shared the time of our life most influential to us in this community of strung-along moments; these being the most meaningful to us.

Somehow in the strange twists of fate we had accomplished more than we knew. True, we had the dream of playing for the Red Sox together one day. But here, now, when time held more treasure than any other, we were as we had always been; those two boys, lifting our sights to the stars, wondering how the future would be; and hope, truly hope, we would be together like we were now, sitting on the floors of Fenway Park, and so reveling in our successes.

If only that crystal ball had been turned on long ago. Perhaps we could have seen the smiles now currently sitting in our expressions. Sometimes prayers are answered in a different way than what we intended them to be, but they are answered.

"Do you remember long ago?" I asked of Jason, "What you told me long before; that evening, when I swore to never tell. I want you to know, I kept to my word."

"I know," he shut his eyes and nodded out his head, "I knew you would; that's why I told you to begin with."

"When did it stop?"

I could see the strain in his look cut across the outskirts of second base, as he blew out all his air like a balloon totally deflated. That little boy now was showing glimpses of his old self; those pang and bitter pills of old memories still lodged in the back of his mind. I could see them through his blinks; there, then falling back and undisclosed; another blink, and they returned. His expression bore the children of their wombs out, and I so knew he still lived some of his life still there. It appeared he had died a little during the years we grew up together.

"Probably when I was fifteen, I suppose," he softly spoke, "I guess I have less memory of it now than I ever had. Sometimes when a person allows themselves to forget, the healing begins and goes through more quickly. It dwindled over time, until it simply never happened again."

"You never told, did you?" I asked.

"To what purpose?" he replied, "I mean…he was my father. No need to say anything further. You do to survive; figure the best way to cope and handle. It becomes your poverty; you just have to figure out how to break from it, in the end."

"Well," I shifted my stare out and about, "I am loyal."

"That you are my friend," he took about another drink, "That you are. From time to time dad and I do speak; nothing more. I suppose it was better this way, to kind of implicitly agree to fall away from each other, and let the past go."

I could feel him stumbling through his voice, check his throat, and start again.

"I am guilty of envy though."

"What is that?" I looked to him.

"Because tush," he stared me down, "You always had what I truly, deeply wanted; and could never, ever have."

I knew what he meant.

"Make these moments count Conner," he warned, "and don't allow regret to play a part on what things are to come."

"I promise…" was my final word on the subject.

We gathered ourselves from the pitcher's mound, dusted ourselves off from the scattered dirt particles still clinging to our backsides, and we began a slow walk away from the fields.

The lights were hanging lower still; the buzz beginning to resound out once more and take precedence through Fenway. I checked back with one more glance at the green monster; her towering wall seemed like a galactic vessel from the medieval bygone era. And where its king would sit perched atop its highest peek and look out over his lands called Fenway.

Jason dropped his arm over my shoulder for a moment. We looked back, eyed the world of that empty baseball field one final time, and returned to our steps.

"Would you miss it?" I asked, "If it ended tomorrow?"

"Of course," he responded, "Would you?"

"Can't miss what I never had," I said, "But thank you Jason. Just to have a moment here in the moonlight will have to do."

Another smile and shoulder hug draped over me.

We passed through the runway and we finally met up with the outer gates. The walk to the parking lot felt as though we were journeying through a lonely trek across an empty wasteland. A trickle of rain began to fall and dropped before us to make it look like the night held a tear or two for us. The lowly misty rolls of dew had dissipated into a faint wisp of fog; the night air more damp than before when I had entered Fenway.

We spoke our farewells for a time; Jason had a west coast trip leaving early the next morning, which would last all of two weeks. He would call me when the opportunity would arise to check on the status of my mother. We stood to my car; his vehicle only being a few yards from mine. His hand went to my shoulder as we faced one another; his eyes dipping to a close, then he began to pray; and I too, bowed to my head to listen to his words.

The words of a gentleman; the words of a friend. Hope was held into each sentence; the prayer rising up towards Heaven as he went from pause to pause. I knew God was listening there. It was for my mother; it was for my father; it was for my sisters; it was for my brother; it was for me and my family; but nothing for him. The speech made the night air seem like a cuddling blanket on a winter's day. Or, if only a moment, as such the season can go; a brief eclipse in time, it becomes nothing more than Winter's Moment.

We parted as the rain began.

Chapter 25

The Serpent Strikes Again.

Several weeks had passed, and the change and alteration in my mother's condition had slowly deteriorated. Not in the manner of gross negligence or the condition of dire need, but in the scope and realm of a gradual sliding and slipping lower into the grasp of this disease itself. My fear had grown worse; my anxiety stemmed harder to isolate me from myself, and from those around me.

It was a terrible weapon, this strike of venom. The affects lingered like a haunting ghost to an old house; searching, probing, looking for places inside of her to strike next on.

Mother's irregular breathing patterns became most disjointed; her oxygen support required with a mask at all times now. They had supplied her with a steady stream of morphine to calm the pain, and her conscious state faded in and out like a bad reception. There were times when she was in fact alert enough to speak and communicate, but her state of affairs drew into a more sleep-like way than anything at all.

The swelling in her limbs would rise and fall without warning; her kidneys teetering on a place between total failure and barely surviving. The bruising on her limbs grew worse as each day passed. A simple bump to the railing could persist into a dark spot for a week or more, if it were to ever heal at all.

There began a seeping of fluid from her arms. Small, insignificant at first, then it seemed to turn her forearms into damp, wet cushions with yellowish seepage which required towel wrapping from the nurses on the hour every hour.

I would come to visit her after work everyday; Sandra to join me at the hospital until ICU would be shut down for the evening around nine each night.

Sometimes, if her attending nurse were kind, they would allow us to remain thirty minutes longer. It was always a torment to me to leave mother alone; desolate and empty, in that tenuous box of night and hospital room.

The monitors remained on constantly, and so her blood pressure, white cell count would play adverse roles in dipping from time to time; though her lung issues were the biggest obstacles at this point. The doctors feared for this ARDS they spoke of earlier; the beginning phases of it already set in. There were signs of immobility on her right side; a possible affect from clotting in her lungs for which they performed several ultrasounds on her legs and chest—to see if they could locate precisely where it was, if a clot were to be found.

Father had become more reserved in nature; the seeds of his disease growing in the long days before us. I would catch him staring out into a far place, sitting alone in the corner of the room; his fingers bent around his face, and his teeth chomping incessantly at his nails until they were nubbed. I saw a man fixed in an illusion of his own design; a land only of his knowing; a place where he could sit and ponder through his own mind's eye. He wandered there often; always when he was in the hospital room. At dinners and times at his home; alone, in the newly darkened spaces of his place, we could feel the young emptiness of mother's absence there, like a ghost not yet born, but the seeds of its birth beginning as though the house were its womb.

The low dimming lights would display their sights through the dining room when we would make supper for father. He would sit at the front of the table, stare to the edge and occasionally look over to mother's empty space, and seem to spot the shadows of her ghost beginning to settle in that seat. The silence grew longer at each eating; Lorie, Amanda, and I clearing the table even before everyone were to be finished with supper. The melancholy nature of his particular disease, however imprecise it may be, was as strong to blowing as mother's disease was to her. Still, I wondered if hers was so far gone as well.

There was some joyous news to encounter then.

"Conner," Lorie and Marshall pulled me to the side one evening, "I am pregnant." I could see the happiness in her smile as Marshall stood behind her for support.

"Oh Lorie," I gave her a hug, and a handshake to Marshall, "I am so happy for you both. You will both make wonderful parents."

"Thank you Conner," Marshall smiled, and cast a gruff hug to me as well, "You'll make a great uncle."

"Two months along," she grinned ever more loudly.

"Already?" I gave to her another, more bearish hug, "Have you told anyone else?"

"No. Just you," Marshall said, "Amanda and your father will be next." He sniffled as he brushed off the chill from his shoulders.

"Don't tell mother," I explained, "Not yet anyways."

"Why not?" Lorie appeared lost by this.

"Wait," I replied, "Until she is more alert. You will know the time for it. I think it would make her very happy."

"I am sure of it," Lorie whispered, trying not to think of the dilemma mother was currently in.

"What of Adam?" I asked.

"Don't even know if he would want to know."

"Lorie," I sighed, "Don't give up on Adam. There will come a time soon when he will know he needs us. It is then we have to be ready to accept him; this, will be the time he changes."

"We can hope," Marshall was more to the positive.

"We have no other choice," I said, "This is OUR family."

And as to my children, their regular routines were to school, back home again, a night with the babysitter, and then to bed, making ways to try to sleep but always failing at it. They would peer from their bedroom windows just at the striking hour of ten, and watch about the streets in anticipation.

During this time Cory and Tyler sat up on the window ceil in one room, crouched about in their bed clothes, and settled in to wait for us as we returned from the hospital each and every night. I could see their tiny heads along with the backdrop of waning lights, through their bedroom window as we approached. Their expression always appeared as if they had awakened from Christmas Eve night and had found the greatest present waiting for them underneath the Christmas tree. Those bushy hairs and wayward lots seemed to crawl about their heads in every direction; eyes disjointed and somewhat confused; their expressions longing and full of anticipation. And when so spotting us, they would rush to the front door to greet us.

One evening, as Sandra and I always with our custom to put them back to bed thirty minutes after we made it home, we held the most intimate conversation.

"When will we see Grandma and Pa again?" Tyler spoke from her bed; her hands propping her head right by that pillow.

I made no further move to explain immediately, but to bend my head down in a long and deep gaze towards the floor, move to her bedside, and watch the light by her bedside mantle flicker.

"In truth," I said, "I can not say for sure."

"But why not?" Cory interjected.

"Is there something wrong?" Tyler seemed to not detect anything other than the change in our daily patterns.

"You have no idea do you?" I asked softly, propping my head at an angle as I looked over her.

"You have been gone much," she replied.

"And why do you suppose?" I kept to my stare on her.

"I don't know," she remained steady.

"Mother cries sometimes..." Cory shook me to the core with this; "I can hear her just after we are put to bed. She closes the door, but we can still hear her."

My eyes grew strong with a constant look. It radiated through my expression, and so nearly exploded through my eyes by the very thoughts that brought them to harshly bear upon me. I reflected there, looking inward, thinking of my own lost past. Those days, off in the distance of time, where the past played hard to the memories and made me think of them in retrospect. My father's allegiance was on many things; and to his travels abroad, so too did my mother cry to her sleep at nights. Have I born the same measures my father had so instilled in me? The reckless shadow had I become also?

The silence in the room dripped in that short season of moments. I thought more loudly than my voice could air, and surely the children heard my inner voice speaking. I turned back to look down that vacant hallway in hopes of spotting Sandra. She was alone in our room; the door cracked with that single light creeping past into the hallway. I stared out into this crevice and I could see on occasion the silhouettes and shadows of her being, lurking and pacing within.

I blinked; the time returned; I staring down my childhood hallway and watched the same parched light proceeding forward. The television was on and in a soft whisper; I moving to inspect, step to step, and sensing the emotions high within this bedroom. The curdling and tender tears falling in that weep, and I felt insecure by the very turmoil my mother was feeling then.

"Dad?" Tyler swept me back to them.

"Do you know why your mother cries?" I asked, still phased and glaring nearly a stoned look about.

"She never tells," Cory said, "She just gets really quiet."

"Do you ever wonder why?" I continued.

"You're not here Dad..." Tyler responded.

"Do you think this is it?" I was heavy to my own sorrow. The pains to that stabbing more severe than if a true weapon and spear struck me time and time again.

"What else could it be?" Cory replied.

"Son…" I started, "There are many things a child can wonder on; many things that you do not know of. I have been the cause to some of her tears; true. But there are other things you don't know about…"

I tried to make defense for myself.

"Like what?" Cory asked.

"Your grandmother has a little problem right now," I was careful in choosing my words, "We are trying to fix it."

"What is it?" Tyler, being the curious child she was, had more meddling in her than her brother.

"I can't say," I honestly said, "I don't know the remedy yet."

"Will she be alright?" it was Cory's turn this time.

I thought for the moment, delaying my answer to ponder exactly what I should say then. If she were to return to her old self and I to say she would be fine, then all is good. In any other scenario the water could be as deep as the deepest ocean with my next step, or as shallow as a faucet wave in a flat sink. I could no more bare the truth than a lie; each, being a weapon for sin with no retribution for good. However I knew Truth would live beyond the legends of a lie, and so I must speak as quietly with its verse as I could.

"I hope so Cory," I answered, "I pray hard; very hard. Pray for her before you sleep each night children. God hears the prayer of a child beyond all others…And he will hear yours."

They both grew deafly silent there. The hearts, which beat so rapidly before, were sinking into a stalling by their pulse. I could see they were frightened and concerned, yet not knowing the full ramifications of what was impending in their grandmother's life.

"I hope to see her real soon," Tyler whispered near to my ear. I bent low to kiss her on the forehead.

"I hope so too," I returned with a whisper. I stood and went by to Cory's side to tuck him in.

"See?" He opened wide to let me view his front tooth dangling most precarious. His tongue poked through and wiggled it back and forth as though it were a door to his mouth.

"Son?" I looked to inspect, "It nearly is ready to fall out."

"I'm ok…" he pulled the covers up over him.

"Don't you think its time?" I pulled them back to retrieve him once again, "The tooth fairy is probably wondering."

"She can wait," he said in a convincing fashion.

"I think we should pull it son…"

"No…" he was sturdy in his response.

"Cory," I pressed, "It could come out any time now."

"No…" he was more steadfast than before.

"Tooth fairies prefer not to have lost teeth running about."

"I don't care," he swore on it, defending his position.

"Alright," I agreed, "If not in three days, we agree to pull it then," my eyebrows shot up and I was waiting for his reply.

He said nothing, but kept to himself and folded his arms out over his shoulders in a huff.

"Or," I offered up another suggestion, "We pull it now. Which will it be? Your choice…"

He remained as obstinate as before; cross-eyed and in a hard frown. Cory never took to blink through it all.

"I'll make the decision then," I started in on his tooth.

"Three days," he fussed, "Three days."

"Agreed," I placed out my hand to have him shake it; he did so reluctantly and with grave reservation, "Get some sleep."

I moved to cut out the evening lights into darkness. They both watched me as I retreated from the room, gently cut the door into a crack, and quickly move down the hallway to my room.

"I heard you have been in tears," I whispered out to Sandra as she turned to meet my look with hers.

"Who told you this?" she asked, looking down at her brush.

"Little spies," I moved deeper into the room; softly, patiently stepping to her side, and coming to a crouch beside her and her chair. I now looked up at her with wanting eyes, "I hope I have not been the product of those tears…"

She leaned in on me, cupping her hand to my face, and casting out a rainbow of a smile towards my way.

"I fear for your mother, and my friend."

"I see things I could never imagine Sandra," I said. She leaned further in to place with me a soft hug, "And this scares me more than I would have ever thought. I ask myself what will become of her. And will this end in a tragedy, or end in a miracle."

"We can pray for one," she spoke, "and hope against the other."

I felt the pressing of her lips to my empty cheek. We kept to this embrace for sometime, and not allowing the escape of it until we would both feel more secure.

Sandra and I moved to our bed to retire for the evening. The lights drew into a deeper darkness, to the point I could nearly smell the nightfall over us; cast us out, and spin us into our own bed of sleep and dreams. I feared the dreams now, wanting to go no further than I had before; but still, the edge of curiosity bore me to that God-forsaken precipice once more. The harbors of that illusion began in the same manner and fashion as it had in the first installment.

I heard the oceans' roar before I saw them. Like a blind man who sees with the sounds. I too, saw those sounds coming in the tranquil realm of my dream. The thunders inland; the crushing, fevered crashes came in with each tide. The waves rumbled into a heave and bellowing, as if the sea had a heartache of its own. Then always it had finished in the same crumbling shoreline, giving way to the powers of those waters.

My eyes drew into a focus; dim at first, secondly coming into a haze; light casting down within my tunnel of vision until it grew into a full spectrum of sight and sound. I could feel the curling of that wet sand mesh between my toes; my feet sinking slightly from my weight. The land was barren; unsightly to the human eye. No one remained; as if the world had abandoned all but for nature itself.

The sea was more into a mighty thrust than before. The torrid ocean currents were humbling the sands and shorelines just in front of me. I spun into a drunken twirl; the edges of my gaze pushing ever farther out to spot what was to be likely that end. Mother was there; I knew it to be so. Somewhere in this vastness and empty shell of natural wonder, she was stepping her own footprints in the sand.

To me, it was the lost treasure a pirate always dreams of; but to this, I was only in search of the mother I knew, with no compass, sexton, or map to guide me with. So I walked, as before, feeling the waves curl more violently up to my knees as I stepped. The wind blew in as if it were in an elongated yawn; the clouds above circled and rotated into a haze, then cast away into the unseen horizon.

I looked for any hope of human connection; nothing was immediate. The seagulls parleyed above as before; the sea serpents roved in a swim all about the distant waters; still, no manner but for this to engage me by. I walked the shores as though the lines of water and sand were my director; my navigator to where I was to go. The shadows of that day never seemed to change; stuck in a time of their own, never bending from high day into afternoon.

The caustic rumbles of the seas ahead of me grew in intensity; the shoreline growing more by a mist than waves. Then, as I traveled without recognition for a time, I remembered the spots, as they were many nights before. Everything seemed so familiar to me. Even the crystal waters and blue haven of their colors appeared identical. There; as my eyes stretched into a blur, I could see a lone figure strolling nearly in a transit walk. The figure was older now; full-grown, charmed by the sea, and was now looking out onto this endless horizon with a daze and a hypnotic stare.

How strange this was to feel the memory of something not yet known, but to know that it was from a time long ago in my past. My logic felt stirred by a curious flood of thoughts while I bent low to see the pebbles in the sand. Which one was it? They all looked so seamlessly similar to all the others.

I came to a stand; stalled on this very step of shoreline as I waited for this figure to come closer; to so conquer the distance between us and make its way towards me. The wind had now pressed my shirt against my chest; my heart stopping in mid-pulse. The anticipation drawing nigh as each stepping drew this figure closer to me. I wondered would it be her.

The person stopped, lifted its hand across the bow of its eyebrows, and so viewed the ocean like she or he were to have smelled the fragrance of a rose. By the stance and look, I discovered it to be indeed a female; a woman of tribute and graceful verse.

She was the muse of a poet long lost from life. Death had taken him, but left his words behind to reflect on the memory of her. Her garment was long and black; sleek and sheltering her frame. She began her walk towards me once more. I could not move, though stand in the shadows of that tall sun. Her blackened hair once looked as though it were a scarf dangling in the wind from that distance; now, the shortened curls of a child had grown with her into that woman. How they danced in tribute to her shoulders, and so pranced about in mighty wonder.

She turned and met her face in my direction; squarely seen. It was indeed the young passage of my mother. These were the earlier lands to her life. And though she possessed vacant stares of someone most young than I could remember; still I could see the sweet shadows of her before she was born to me. How youth glowed most warm than the soft tempered wisdom which eventually took over. Unbridled and un-cast; no restraint dawned to her, nor kept her from the woman she was. Life; as she was seeing it then was as vast as the deep horizon now consuming her and her dreams of adventure.

Her heart there showed me of wanting travel; to see the world and all of its' glow; to smell the rose and every pedal which adorned it; to taste the waters of many lands; and to brace the highest cliffs for the chance to view the longest sunset possible.

She came closer as my eyes grew wider and more intense. I could not swallow; not blink in that moment. But stare with a mind-full eye onto my mother there. My steps moved me closer; nothing more than ten yards away.

She turned and grinned; the pastel gray eyes shinning more brightly than the sun itself.

"Mother?" I chanced a whisper.

She did not answer.

I saw her bend down and capture the sands below with her look and soft, embroidered gaze. She pushed about the grains as if she knew where to look, pressing deeper into the sands until she found that golden pebble; now sitting from its long journey from when she had thrown it out before.

Many years had passed since then. The sands called it back from the seas; and she so finding its refuge only an inch below the sand lines. Without a word, but for her motions to speak the verse in her heart and mind, she clutched to that pebble. Her eyes closed into her deep-set thought; perhaps a wish, a dream yearned for but not yet delivered. A moment stirred into another; the winds kicking about in glee; the waves stretching just now to the tips of our standings there. I said nothing more, but observed.

Her pearl eyes opened with a new-born hope; the hands spinning and locking back into a throw; the pebble cast out once more with a purpose, and dipping within the belly of that sea. I could see the foam stew in a waterspout and swirl, cascading down towards us under a wall of water and tide. The roar and rush was greater than the first dream and so sent a force that once again nearly knocked me onto my seat. Though, as the waves leveled off, I could see her still standing, looking down within the face of these waters. I moved most near, staring down the same; searching, pushing the foam aside, and to now view the reflection just coming of age.

I fell down in shock until the edge of that sea nearly submerged on me completely. My heart raced and almost came through my throat there; my mouth gaped more for what I had just seen than for air itself.

"What does it mean??" I yelled over to her, "Why is this happening?"

I wanted back from that dream; to awake and find myself next to my sleeping Sandra once more.

I could even see within these shallows the very face of my father staring back; though his expression was of the same youth unborn to me. I had seen his look in old snapshots and photo clips; of a day and time before me; yet, in this avalanche of thoughts, had it never appeared more real to me than now.

Mother had made her second wish off the duty of that magic pebble; to see the man she would eventually marry, the very man my father would become. I saw the casting of myself in those waters, and as much of me than of him. Still it was he who stared most glaringly back. My eyes bent higher to watch her in her dance of joy.

How she danced to the tune of her own silent song. Her hands were clasping and wailing to reach for the skies; her expression glowing from the bright emerging lights of her own thoughts. I saw the footsteps in that sand press from the weight of her dips and twirls in every direction.

The wind and sea came to converge one final time; she moving back from the brink of both and not allowing herself to be captured so. Though, to what the dream did say to me, I saw the newfound harbor of happiness engulf her expression.

"BRING! BRING!" a sound came uncommon to the scene, "BRING! BRING!" there, it came again.

I felt the dream disappear in a wave of something stirring outside. The darkness came and sped the dream away. I rose from my sleep to a sit and so discover the phone next to my ear sounding off again. A small flicker of light perched next to our bed had come on, and so I answered the call as it blared out one last occasion.

"Hello?" I spoke, though not knowing the time.

"Conner," it was Lorie.

"Lorie," I looked about, "What time is it?"

"The hospital just called," she paused, "We need to meet there as quickly as we can."

"What time is it?" I could feel the lump in my throat in astir.

"Don't mind this," she weakly said, "It doesn't matter."

"What's wrong?"

"There are more complications…" she halfway proposed.

"Well?" I pressed further.

"I don't know Conner," she was stressing at the tone of her voice, "Must you persist? Just meet me there in thirty minutes."

"Lorie…" I called.

"Just meet me there," she said, "the doctors are waiting."

"Doctor Ogden is there?" I inquired, though no answer returned; only the deaf pause of silence, then a dial tone fell into the line, "Lorie?" I spoke, "Lorie?"

"You have to go," Sandra muffled and turned my way.

"I have to go," I struggled from the bed.

"I'll take the children to school," she groaned, "Meet you there afterwards; have a court case at two."

"Then you should wait afterwards," I suggested.

"No," she replied, "I'll be there."

"You have to prepare," I insisted.

"It will be alright Conner," she began to shuttle out of the bed.

"Sandra," I countered, "Not fair to your client."

"Nor fair to your mother," she waltzed to the bathroom; half-asleep, and the rest of her now waking, "I'll be there."

I was out and about within less than fifteen minutes, with no time for my particular duties to prepare for the day. My hair only partly combed; teeth brushed but no flossing; hasty bathroom duties yet no shower; a dirty shave and facial wash but nothing further; car keys in hand; wallet to the back pocket, and I was off.

The memory of that advanced dream overplayed in my mind all during the drive to the hospital. My thoughts were preoccupied by its constant rehearsal and variables. I felt to be stolen from myself and from my normal concentration. It was quite unlike me to have the second party to any dream, let alone a replay of a dream from a prior evening before. But it sat there like a live memory from a distant age I had gone through and could reflect on; a reflection born from some history in my past, but nothing ever I had observed before the time of that initial dream.

I felt there was great purpose in it. A destination lay somewhere in future installments; a message; a mark and key of something I should know, but have yet to realize. Perhaps some remarkable end lay in the vestige ahead; I could only ponder now.

As I entered the main corridors Doctor Ogden spotted me first, and so quickly pulled me aside.

"I was alerted a few hours ago," he rushed past his words. He was nearly in complete disarray, which almost put me in hysteria. Something most dreadful and harsh had occurred.

"What are we dealing with here?" I asked.

"As I had feared," he said, "ARDS has taken a full strike."

"But I thought this was manageable…"

"Not to the degree we are seeing it," he replied.

"What does this all mean?" I felt myself repeating the very same sentence I had asked in my dream; the striking sounds of it echoed me back there again, as if the whispers of its prediction struck me with the deadly potion of a vile and inhuman serpent.

"I will not deny," he worriedly responded, "This is distressing; very distressing indeed."

"Can she die from this?" I was nearly beside myself.

"She can," he said, "And most likely will, if we can not moderate her…And soon."

"Then we should do what is necessary then."

"Everything is being expedited," he cautioned, "as soon as feasible," he stalled, "but there is required prodigal here."

"I am confused doctor…" I shook my head clear.

"The respiratory specialist is currently trying to setup an Endoscopies as soon as we can; to establish the level of damage to her lungs, and place her on a ventilator as quickly as possible."

"So why not now?" I pushed further.

"Mr. James," he pulled me closer to the edge of the corridor, "Your mother could die before, or even during the procedure. It is that tenuous. I will need you to sign a waiver form in order for us to proceed with the procedure."

"Anything," I said in a stunned whisper, "Whatever must be done." I stared about the blank floor line before I continued, "May I see her? I think it is important."

He paused, lowered his head to agree, and so pressed me to the desk where the paper was readied for my signature. I was quickly rushed into ICU, past the main central desk, and into the covered segment housing my mother.

I moved without reservation beside her. Her look of worry and alarm quickly met with my expression, which in turn was attempting to calm her as best as possible there. Her oxygen mask covered about her look mostly; the inerts of it steaming from her constant strain to gather oxygen. She grabbed to my hand, held tightly in a struggle not to slip any further down. I could see her violent convulsions vibrating through her chest; her air passages apparent to be in constant stress and turmoil.

The palms of her hand dripped with sweat; her upper brow rolling down from the perspiration. Those pearl gray eyes I had just seen so happy in a dream; now aged, revolted into a near-hysteria gaze back at me. I saw her mouth gapping for air, but consenting to gather only a morsel and nothing more.

"Calm," I said quietly, "Calm; don't speak; shh," I looked as pleasant as I could on mother, "Easy; relax; don't press; concentrate."

Her eyes began to close as her head rolled to face the ceiling above; the grip now more powerful than before.

"Conner," she gasped, "I can't breathe."

"Then do nothing else but this."

"There is more," she recalled, "the shadow; mirror."

"No time," I required, "Doesn't matter."

"It does," she claimed, "You don't know…must tell."

"Not now," I resisted her advances.

"If you knew," she nearly could not speak any further, "It would. Please…if…I…go…"

I felt the rush of nurses and doctors pulling about me, and calling me back to the edge of the room. Mother found herself now being wheeled to the second floor. The corridors were long and bumpy; the light above whisking by as they pushed her through. I could view the five or so attendants guarding every edge of her bed as it rolled down the long, far-reaching corridors.

My hands dove into my pockets; perhaps looking for a good luck charm or a bible passage I might install into a prayer; a prayer that I would be hastily sending to Heaven only a few moments away from now. The chapel was only a few yards from me. I pressed to engage it.

I was angry; furious; the disease of my heart growing from the horrible fate now consuming the most graceful person I had ever known. The serpent's lair had no remorse, nor aid to our sympathy, but was unholy-bent to punish her; ravage her; and steal the very life she was due.

My walk bent within the chapel walls; I closing the doors shut behind me as I entered. The pulpit was sitting alone; a bible now open and in frontal display.

"No!" I roared to the front, "I won't let you do this to her!"

I yelled at the open bible.

"Don't you know she doesn't deserve this!"

I leaned back, spun into a desperate circle, and folded my hands to press back my flopping hair.

"Do something! Anything!" I enraged.

"Don't sit there like words in a book! Be what you say you are!"

I felt the wrestle of that angel entangled with my own spirit. The hands of its spectre now wringing my heart and soul out like they were two old sponges filled with unspent tears. My world was collapsing and I felt the shadows of some dark place now engulfing the very surroundings about me. There was no whisper in my prayers; only contempt, frustration, and craving anger spinning out of me like a twirling shell. The lambs of those unkind angels seemed to glare over me with the weapons of their looks.

The haunting and shallow souls about seemed to encircle me in a dance of predator to its prey. Those words so born to me in my youth felt to be the hollow corpse of a world lost in its own scope and measure. I had no fear; only desolate hope now withering on that vine of a single belief and religion I had so long held close to.

I was torn; raptured between solemn prayer and disgust. At moments, I would bend into a solemn kneel and pray harder than anyone could. At other times, I would be enraged like the traditions of a mad man, scoffing the very faith I held so endearingly to.

At last, I bent low and repeated, "Please, don't turn your back on her, please, please, please, please," the echo of that word growing softer as they passed from one plea to the next.

The back door opened. A lone figure entered and so spotted me in my dismay; it was Lorie. She came to my sitting, said nothing but with a stare, and laid her head alongside my shoulder.

"You did all you could do," she whispered to me.

"But that's still not enough," I replied, "It's not enough."

The silent air moved to a stale and unprovoked halt about the room, as though we were in a locked chamber for thousands of years; inescapable, enclosed, with no exit or entrance. The solemn promises of hope and life had disappeared in an instant, and were so replaced by the frank reality we now found ourselves submissive to.

There was discord and tragedy all around us. We huddled close like a child sister and her brother would when most frightened by the world about; where fear shakes the very marrow of your bones and you find yourself withdrawn from all else but yourself.

The haunting melody of this silence played in our ears like the peddling ghost it sounded out to be. Those former prayers sent Heaven-bound by loved ones from so long ago, as they too sat on these pews and prayed, rocked, and recited their heart's words for God to hear. Those tearful echoes of the past still lingered and mingled about this room, trapped as we were, and they singing the chorals for this deaf symphony of silence currently in our play.

Lorie and I felt the hardened pain of not knowing, yet realizing all too well what end could be awaiting us when we got there. It held ground here and I could feel it, smell it, and nearly touch the very trail to its path. We feared for our mother and her life; what dread may sit in her future, and yet most of all, we feared the world would change forever.

Chapter 26

We Call Upon the Children.

Our waiting time was akin to the time spent from cradle to grave. All members of the very immediate family, with the exception of Adam, were present through the next twelve hours. A variable number of doctors came in to give us constant updates, request our permission to go forward, and detailing the elements of concern as they proceeded.

Mother had suffered a severe bout with ARDS. It had struck quickly through that previous night, and had basically forced the doctor's hand in pressing for her to be placed on the ventilator. Her condition was already destabilized by the continuous infections, pneumonia, by-products of Wegener's, and Wegener's itself. As it was placed to us, the feared worst scenario had come to play.

Her chances of surviving the procedure and placement on the ventilator were hovering around 50%. However, not to have anything done would have placed her in inevitable danger. So, the course had already been set for us. There was no decision to be made but to proceed on the path given to us.

I could see the hardened sorts of expressions pressing into everyone's face. Nothing was said, nor explained, though to see how their disposition settled in their eyes, it was more than written within the measure of their looks; this was a language unto itself.

After knowing someone all your life, you begin to taste the food as they eat, smell the flowers as they drift their noses into bouquets, feel the warm sunshine on their faces as they raise their attention into the sun, saw the wonderful sights they had just been to on their vacations. You knew them all too well.

My father's disease had taken hold and it seemed to have bitten his soul in half, leaving the shell of his spirit there before us. His heart had bellied to the floor, kicking across the corridor as he paced back and forth incessantly, and without rhyme of reason; just to pace, stare down into the blocks and think of nothing else. He had turned into a man shadowed by the very things that were consuming him excessively. Alas, he had been stolen from us, and from himself.

Sandra held to my hand all through the day, connected as we were in the hopes the power of that bond would somehow save my mother. Lorie and Marshall studied each and every resident which walked by; the nurses who carted back and forth on this floor; the janitor, supply personnel; specialists and doctors all esteemed and high ranking. Even other patients and their families fell under that constant watch and observation.

Amanda however sat alone; fidgeted, crossed her legs and rocked her ankle back and forth, turned her expression from side to side, and so buried her self in her brief episodes of tears when she could no longer contain her emotions. I felt compelled to go to Amanda's side but she resisted me. She held me off with her hands and pleaded for me to let her be.

Later that afternoon, Doctor Ogden returned to us. The procedure had been completed and mother was now resting more comfortably than she had been in some time. The ventilator was currently breathing for her, and they would be checking to see how much damage had been done by the ARDS. We were warned her sedation would keep her near a dream-like state for an indefinite period of time, and this time would be strictly determined by her ability to recover. A window of one year had been thrown out at us to suggest her recovery from the ARDS would take this long.

"I must warn you," the doctor explained, "She has a tube inserted down her throat. It is required without a trach."

"What is a trach?" Lorie asked.

"An insertion through the windpipe here," he displayed where the hole would be present and exposed, "with the ventilator feeding her supportive oxygen by the tube."

"Why not do that initially?" I questioned.

"We would prefer not to," he said, "If the patient is on the ventilator for just a few days, it becomes an additional, unnecessary procedure. Outside of two weeks on the vent, we would prefer not to perform it unless it is really needed."

"You will allow us to see her..." Amanda said.

"Two at a time," he advised, "and for five minutes each."

Father and I went in first; he peeking about the door chamber without speaking a word. His eyes in a droop and seemed terribly shadowed by exhaustion. I could see the strain in his expression becoming most tired; the burden he was cast with becoming too great to bear. He watched her from the doorway; stopping, terrified at the sight, observing the manner of expression drawn on mother's face. I could see nothing, but attempt to control my own shock I was feeling at the sight of her.

Her eyes were shut hard; mouth gaping open with a solitary tube seemingly driven and thrust harshly down her throat. Tape surrounded it at every angle, and so gave her the appearance of someone who was continually gagging. Her arms were tied to the bed; her hair rolled back from her forehead and pulled up in a bow atop her head.

"This is medicine?" father angrily asked, "Do you see this? They are killing her!" I came to his side and stayed close.

"She can't live without the ventilator dad…"

"This isn't the way; there has to be another. This will not do," he moved closer to inspect her further.

There was a drawing up of his chin as he fell silent once more; he pulling his handkerchief from his back pocket and trying to dry his tears with it.

"She is in good care," I said, coming to his side and standing over mother, "I trust Doctor Ogden."

"Everyone says that," he muttles through, "They say she is getting better; will improve. But son, I look over her and I see different; she is not improving…not improving."

And with this, he turned to head out the door without my companionship. I held to my mother's bedside, felt the soft whispers of my abandoned prayers I had left still lingering in that chapel and I bent low to mother, kissing her over the forehead.

The others were to follow with similar reactions. And as each one came to exit back into that corridor I could see the residue of tears still close to their shadows.

Nothing more could be done this evening and all else would have to wait for the next few days to tell the tale of her condition. Sandra and I made our way home along that misty and cloud-covered night, though we stopped along the bay to catch a glimpse of passing ships. A new chill was entering the harbor.

"Perhaps we should tell the children," she said, leaning out over that railing into the bay. The soft winds curled her blonde hair into a frazzle as she leaned forward. She spotted the wayward glows of that night and she seemed to think of the world we once knew.

"I have thought of that Sandra…" I said, standing beside her.

"Tyler and Cory are so young," she said, "to ask them to be able to handle this, perhaps is asking a bit much."

"It's a nightmare, either way."

"Whichever ends first, is the way we should go," the idea forged war within her thoughts, "Would I have wanted to be there when my grandfather passed away? You were there Conner. Which one of us is more haunted by that?"

"I can still smell the air," I gazed out over the sparkle lights reflecting through the water's plain, "See the fire; feel the heat from its flame. And to see the expression on Buck's face has always been with me. I can close my eyes, and I still can find it there, waiting for me," I paused, "always."

"We have to be fair to the children," Sandra began to cry as I held close to her, "And not think what would be best for us."

"Well then Sandra," I came to a whisper, "You have to ask yourself that all important, honest question."

"What is that?" her cold, wet nose fronted her expression to meet with mine; eyes to eyes.

I could see the youthful, vibrant woman yet posing through her look of innocence; unwavering; lightly tamed, but still free in heart to be most honest with her self and me. My heart nearly stopped before I spoke again.

"Would you have wanted to be there," I replied, "That day; that moment, and would you be strong enough to battle through the very trauma you found yourself exposed to. If you can answer 'yes'; honestly, reflecting truly back to what you feel, then you have partly answered your own question."

She gazed out over the bay and the far-exceeding shore to think about this. The lights round us rose with the height of those buildings, as they ascended through the fog and mist for that evening. I could tender her silence; feel her thoughts rolling through her mind as if it had a fog of its own.

"What would be the other part?"

"Can Cory and Tyler reflect the same opinion?"

"I don't know," she turned to me, "on either point. I didn't have the choice. I was never given that chance. Now, Cory and Tyler do have this opportunity by which way we decide. We either give them this very same chance, or take it away from them; without them ever knowing about it."

"Then which is the greater sin?" I pulled her near for comfort.

"The one that causes the greatest pain to them," she quickly responded. My brow bent to meet hers. We looked to one another without even a faint blink to interrupt us.

"We have to know before we decide…" I suggested.

"How can we?" she asked in a calm and polite voice.

"Trade our own experiences with each other. Swap that day and see that event as the other did," I pulled her close; held her in my loving embrace;

peeked over her shoulder to continue, "Oh Sandra, we have to know already what their favored course is."

"And what do you feel it is?" I heard her speak.

"To have the chance to say 'Goodbye'…"

The long, tempered night sprayed the surroundings about us with its deep and blackened air. The shorelines were aghast with the twinkles of Boston's city lights and the smoky waters below us. We were treading in the quicksand of our own emotions, and so feeling the weight of every precarious decision we were forced to make.

I knew what answers lay before us, but how to proceed? Our two children were the greatest persuasions in our lives, beyond the love we held for one another and the love of God. We would only have one chance at this; and if all goes right except for one element, we could discover the event as a total tragedy through their young, impressionable lives.

We held in a clutch, so cast in the bed of that cooling night. Sandra held warm to me; with love and dependence all rolled up into her embrace. When she thought more precious of our special relationship, she held to me tighter, not wishing ever to let go. A boat passed by very close; the ship mates waving out to us in friendship. We both returned them a wave, a smile, and a continued stare as they steamed out of harbor and into the open seas.

That night as we made our travels homeward bound, we at last turned down onto our street. Cory and Tyler, as was to their frequent tradition, were still holding vigilance in that very same window. The lights were peaking out from the backdrops, with our children's teetering expression brushing back the sheers in the window. Those innocent stares landed on our view as we looked up to; we stepping from the car and onto the walkway.

They sent down to us two simple, though frantic waves; and I, in turn, returned a correspondence of waves back to them. I could hear the measured stroll and runs they made from second floor to first; running, sometimes tripping, but always loudly down the stairs and onto the front steps, even before we could reach them.

They forever greeted us with a warm, heart-glowing, timber burning, raging-hearth smile and embrace. It felt almost wicked to turn their happiest joys into concern with the news we were about readied to beset on them. Our goal was always to protect them; provide them a world of security, even if it were to be entirely make-believe. This, above all else, seemed to fly in the very face of all this. Tomorrow perhaps would be too late, and my mother's passing becoming all too real; tonight was the inevitable evening to displace all else with the truth.

I could feel the weight of that decision falling through my expression, and Cory was the first to pick up on it.

"What's wrong daddy?" he asked, still propped in my arms.

"Nothing son," I lied, and he knew it, "time for bed."

The time was nigh; the moment closing in for something to be said. I had been calculating my words and how I would approach this ever since Sandra and I had decided to tell them what was occurring.

Sometimes I had hoped the truth would not be so grave. That the illusion could remain in place until some remedy would be found to improve my mother's well being; alas, none was found, and we were faced with the harsh, embedded realities a hard world can present. I had hoped for better results in the end.

Sandra held to Tyler; I encompassing young Cory. All four of us made our way up the stairs and into their rooms. The dim-light glows softened the room with the playful shadows of a child's world. The toys were sprawling about from one side of the floor to the other, as if they had been in play all the day long and had found a still place to rest in when we made our entrance.

"I have something to tell you," the babysitter followed us.

"What is it Stacey?" I asked.

"Don't tell," Cory commanded.

"Cory!" Sandra infused, "Behave your self!"

"I fed Cory his dinner; during which he accidentally swallowed his loose tooth," she was propped at the doorway, with her hands clutching her jeans and hips.

I turned over to Cory, pushed his mouth open, and so discovered the gap now exposing the empty spot where his tooth used to be. I paused to collect myself.

"And what did I say?" I sternly reported, "Cory, you should have let me pull it when I wanted to. Now you are out a tooth, and it being replaced by an upset belly."

"What do you think the tooth fairy will do?" he looked over at me with a terrified, worried look on his face.

"I don't know," I shook my head.

"I earned my dollar," he quietly pleaded.

"You'll need to explain that to her," I advised, "But I would imagine she will be none-to-happy over the affair."

"What should I do?" he was nearly beside himself, "I know," A light seemed to go off in his head, then glow through his eyes and spark out some grand invention he had.

"I'll write her a letter."

"Ok Cory," Sandra pulled up to the small table in one corner of the room, sat with an empty chair beside her and she grabbed a pencil and a blank sheet of paper, "We need to start."

Cory shyly moved next to his mother, picked up the pencil, and began to scribble slowly the letter he was proposing…

'Dear…Mr. (no) Mrs. (no) Miss tooth Fairy.
I…am…sorry…I…ate…my…tooth…while…eating..supper…tonight…Please…would…you…except(no)…acept(no)…accept…my…word…as…g old…and…true…and…put…one…dollar…under…my…pillow…tonight?…I…promise…to…let…dad…pull…all…my…other…teeth…when…they…needs…to…be…pulled.'

"Now Cory," Sandra instructed, "you need to end it correctly."

"How so?" he looked up at her glaringly, with a startled look in his eyes and a mouth gaping, with his tongue hanging through.

'Best…wishes…and…good…tooth…hunting…Sincere(no)…sincerely(no)…sincerle(no)…thanks…oh…p.s…have…another…tooth…loos(no)…lose(no)…loose…now…please…come…again…soon…Cory…James.'

"Take the envelope."

Sandra gave further instruction.

"Seal it."

She continued.

"And place it underneath your pillow."

Cory did as he was instructed to do, with the pillow now propped up more than normal. We could see the fringes of that letter sticking out from the corner side of that pillowcase.

"Think she will see it?" he asked, climbing back into bed, looking down, and checking to make sure the letter was partly exposed for when she would come. Sandra came to his bedside and placed over him a smothering hug, a gentle push of his hair from his eyesight, and a rub over his check with her thumb, "How will she come? How did she come before?"

"So many questions young man," Sandra whispered, "Is it not enough, when you wake in the morning, a dollar is there?"

"I guess so," he figured.

"What do you think son?" I asked.

"Well," he began to contemplate, with his expression growing into a disconcerted frown and thinking manner, "Probably through the window; the easiest way. The window's not locked is it?"

"No," I said with a smile. I moved to sit beside Tyler's bedside, much the same way Sandra was to Cory. Sandra looked to me with a sort of uneasy stare, loaded heavy with the thoughts of what was to happen next. Her eyes parted through the air, blinked, and there came a nod from her to go ahead.

"Children," I softly gained their attention, "There are some things I need to tell you, and some things you need to know."

"What is it papa?" Tyler looked up to me.

"I can't always guard you from bad things little girl," I looked into Tyler's innocence and engaging eyes reflecting back over me. Those early toddler expressions seemed so fraught with purities that not anything punitive would ever arise from them, "Though how hard I wish to try; I simply can't, not always."

I kept to my seat, though looked out through this window into the darkened night; empty as it was, and hollow from the lack of any shadows or light about. The world had appeared to fall into a void then, where nothing escaped, and nothing entered; like the corpse of 'nothing' had taken over and spilled into the air.

"Do you know why we have been gone so much?" Sandra bent low to ask on Cory; their eyes transfixed to one another, "Why your father has been absent so much of late?"

"I believe it has to do with work," Cory replied, playing about with his favorite lion stuffed animal.

"No," Tyler interjected, "Because of Uncle Adam."

I looked directly onto Tyler, pulled the braids of her hair by her ears, played about my expression with a comforting smile, and then returned back to the serious matter at hand.

"Have you not noticed your trips to grand ma's and grand pa's house have not been happening of late?" I spoke, yet they said nothing, though they breathed the slow sighs of dread, "You haven't seen them at all; not once."

"Dad," Cory began.

"Cory," Tyler interrupted, "We never said we would talk about this; you promised." She leaned to look on her brother.

"Promised?" I questioned, "Promised what Tyler?"

"Promised," she started to bury her attention into the doll she was clutching, "Promised to never talk about this, so mother will not cry," her voice began to grow softer still into a muddle.

"And what would make your mother cry?"

"To see daddy's mother so sick," she replied.

"How did you know Tyler?" I whispered deep into her ear.

"Grand ma said she would be sick," she played on with her doll, "Said for us not to worry, and to make sure we look out for you daddy."

I heard her words as if I were seeing the slow melting of an icicle after a heavy ice storm. The air had more frost and chill in it than the dead winter could impose. I was fractured by her announcement; to have thoughts my mother knew of her impending illness before it ever occurred, and to so advise her grandchildren before anything grew from this. It seemed more than ordinary to me.

The wisdom of such a woman who held more concern for those around her than for her own welfare, even as she began to stare down the impending storm just before her, and to see the flashes of its lights as it was approaching; to hear the thunder in the fore ground, and so know this was all meant for her and her alone.

I thought as she must have thought then, sensing the premonition on the edge of her life and still yet had the fortitude to conceal it from all those around her; having enough care for the youngest to help prepare them for that same journey, but only they would see it from the roadside.

"When did she speak to you about this?" Sandra was in as much shock as I was.

"Awhile ago," Cory whispered over to me.

"When son?" I pressed on.

"I think it was," he paused, "I think a few months ago, when school was out, and we were on her back porch in the swing."

"Where was I?" I questioned, "And your mother?"

"You were out in the back yard, playing with the neighborhood children," Tyler took her turn, "Mom was inside getting drinks for everyone."

I flipped to that moment like it were a page from my most immediate past; the flashbacks reverting back into time, deeper and deeper until I reached that moment with my memory. I heard the voices and echoes charging forward like whispers in the field, when the wind blows the meadow into a bend, and whistles the leaves into a chime; the flowers into a flutter and a uniform choral spark or two commencing. I could see the clashing shadows play as ghosts in that mind-field of mine. I slowed it down, in a pause, and so I collected that remembrance, in this split moment when I stalled in my play with the neighborhood kids; looking up, and seeing my mother staring so freely back at me.

There was a speech in her expression there; one that in this moment I forgot to read. She was speaking to me, and as so often before, I could hear her words that were unspoken; a collectable language like two related hearts from the same blood lines. This most important time was in escape of me. I was not listening to her by what she was saying to me through that expression. But in reflection, when the important moment is so realized, you look back, eyeing that replay to see what you missed.

I saw her face; that galactic and towering tale written in her eyes. When you see the face of a thousand words glaring back at you so evident; I seemed to hear her voice there while I sat amongst our children, attempting to tell them a tale they already knew. And in a strange sense, they were giving me something of greater value.

It was at this moment I could sense my mother had indeed told me of the impending world which was about ready to overcome her; and me, and all of us. The sentences dripping from her sight and look to me, though I never paid heed to listen then. Perhaps this was the reason she told Cory and Tyler instead, in hopes I could find some comfort in their own preparation.

"Then you already know…" I proclaimed.

"Grand mama is sick," Cory spoke.

"She is son," Sandra caught Cory with her stare.

"What will happen to her?" I heard Tyler's angelic voice rise from those sheets, and so bring us to the heart and course of our time there; the silence kept hold for a moment or two.

"It's not over Tyler," I calmly said, "Hope is never lost, even when hope doesn't seem to be there; hiding, like a friend who doesn't wish to be found when playing hide-and-go-seek. It's still there."

"I miss grand mama," Cory somberly said, which was met by Sandra's hug even before he could finish with that statement.

"I miss her too darling," Sandra kissed Cory.

"What will happen to her?" Tyler asked once more.

"She could get better," I said, "and be able to play again; have you over to her porch swing, and you and she and Cory can swing away until you all fall asleep."

"I would like that," Tyler laughed and smiled at the possibility.

"Or," I could feel my expression grow dim, "she could get most sick; very sick, and end up in Heaven."

"You mean," she nearly cried, "Die?"

"She may never come back home love," I wiped away her faltering tears, which were running down the far side of her cheeks, "But find a new home in Heaven."

"Then we wouldn't see her again," Tyler responded.

"Someday, we will," I tried to console her. Cory suddenly jumped from his bed and he went to the largest window where his telescope was sitting out; lens pointing more skyward and out through the open, cracked window. A breeze cut the curtains out deeper into the room and began to crisscross over the telescope itself. Cory paid no heed to any of it, though seemed a child in a hurry, directing his telescope high into the northern and seemingly empty, night sky.

"Cory, we don't have time for this," Sandra said, "Come to bed son." He gave Sandra little attention; instead, he just kept scoping through his telescope and spotting out elements in the endless beacon of stars about.

"Cory, you heard your mother," I reinforced her command, "Cory, Cory, what are you doing son?"

"Which one is Heaven?" he said, though continuing with his search, "Which planet is Heaven? So I can see where grand mama will be living. Then I can wave to her, and see her waving back."

I went over to his side, pulled his look squarely to mine, and bent low to match my eyesight with his. I could see the soft embers of a young man growing through his face, like the speckles of some fire flint that would soon become greater than the spark they had started from. There was curiosity and fear all deeply woven within his look, as if the new world he was realizing was not as friendly a world as the one he was currently in.

"Son," I briefly smiled, and pulled him by his waist, trying to turn him where he stood in a twist, "There isn't a telescope that can reach Heaven; no earthly realm that can spot it in a view."

"Why not?" he seemed most confused "Is it not real?"

I must confess, in this time of my most relinquished faith, I too struggled with the very heart of this question. The phantom I was currently wrestling with had provoked such ire in me that I wandered the phantom's true origin; Heaven-bent or Hades-bound. The haunting trial of it played in my mind, ran unaffectionately through my heart, and coursed the very veins in my soul to the point I had lost some measure of myself from my faith. I had to front an expression which would assure him of more than what I currently had belief in.

"Should you question whether Heaven exists?"

"If it's not there," he replied, "then where is it?"

"There are some things," I said, "that we can not see, touch, hear, or have any other way of knowing, but only to believe that they truly do exist…Why else would we ever have faith at all, if we first do not believe?"

"I don't understand," he looked hard at me.

"Do you believe," I began, "when you awake tomorrow, I will be there waiting for you, as well as your mother?"

"Of course…" he insisted.

"But the morning hasn't come." He replied, "How do you know Cory?"

"You always have before…" he answered.

"Then what makes you feel your grandmother will not always be there for you, even if she goes to Heaven?"

"Because," he confessed, "I don't know where Heaven is."

"Does it matter?" I asked.

"I want to see her," he held a cross look at me.

"I want to see her also son," I said, "But perhaps a little bit of Heaven is here," I pointed to his heart, "And here," I rose my finger to the side of his temple.

"If you believe," I whispered, "Then she will be there at both places waiting for you, just like I will be waiting for you to awake in the morning."

I looked over to Sandra and I noticed she was looking in return over me with the sweetest embrace of affections in her eyes. The smile and soft dimples rolled past the dim lights like fireflies in the deep part of that night.

"We will not die in this Cory," I said, "Nor will she; but we will always have her if we remember her, the way she holds her heart close to us, her love and caring ways." I paused to see his expressionless, drifting gaze appear to shoot past me without listening to a word that I had just spoken.

"Son," Sandra asked Cory to come over, waving him through with her hand, as both he and his sister sat up to each side of her, "Think of your grandmother as I thought of my grandfather."

"What about your grandfather?" Tyler questioned. Sandra stared over to me; her eyes showing the shadows of that long-ago pain now seeping through her expression. Then she smiled as if it were the cure to her ills.

"I think about my grandfather," she said, "Sometimes when I am sad, and it makes me happy to remember. The way he used to toss me in the air. I thought I could fly. And all the while I felt he was getting my own wings prepared to fly with; kind of like testing me out a bit."

"Was your grandpa like grand mama?" Cory wondered.

"Oh yes," she clung to both of them tenderly, "like brother and sister. You could never tell them apart."

"Do you see him in Heaven?" Cory continued. I rose to the window and gazed skyward in hopes I too, could cast an eye shadow to see Heaven with. If only for a glimpse; a blink; a moment where both Heaven and Earth could bridge that eternal gap, and show to me once and for all—Buck standing on the mountain he had built since he had passed away so many years before.

"I see him in my thoughts and in my dreams honey," I heard Sandra's voice behind me, "I close my eyes and my heart takes over. He is there waiting to say 'Hello' again. Just for me; only for me. A special message reserved for his grand daughter."

"Then what is Heaven?" Tyler said, "Where people go?"

"They go there darling," I could hear Sandra kiss Tyler on her forehead "to help make a home for those they love more than anything. The most gifted go first because God wants them to make a very special place for us all."

"Do you think your grandfather is doing this now?"

"Oh Cory," Sandra came lower still, more to a muddle than a whisper, "He already has. He just waits with a smile."

"I want to see grandmother again…" Tyler was near to her own tears, wiping her face both in sleepiness and sadness.

"You father and I will discuss it…"

"I want to see grandmother too," Cory employed. I could sense Sandra's eyes wander my way, though I had taken a fixation upon the night about our window. The vast quantity of space and time boggled my mind into a frenzy. Perhaps, if I looked hard enough, I could see Buck's face staring back at me with that same 'Hello' smile Sandra spoke of. His blink would be like two comets crossing over the faint horizon there and his smile would be like the moon turning belly up on its back.

"Children," I said, "We will take you to see her."

"Conner," Sandra interjected, "not here."

"It's alright," I turned to face all three, "When the time comes, we will take you to see your grandmother."

This seemed to ease the children into their beds and they quickly found sleep before too much longer. Sandra however was distressed in my decision to permit this, as we both made our way to our bedroom.

"Conner," she angrily spoke, "Think of the children…"

"I am," I threw my shirt over the post.

"Doesn't seem that way," she frustratingly said, "I worry about the stress this will cause our children."

"And not give them the right to say goodbye?"

"I didn't say that…"

"Then what are you saying Sandra?" I looked directly at her, "Don't you wish, for once, you had that same chance as they do?"

I had crossed a harsh line with her. And in this instant Sandra crumbled to the floor, gushing with her own tears for her grandfather.

"Oh Gosh…" I ran to embrace her, "I'm so sorry Sandra; I didn't mean it that way."

She clung to me and wept.

I felt the emptiness in this room crumble with us in that embrace. The ghostly haunts of our past rolled in as if the fog had sent them to our stage. I prayed for them to pass and not recognize us, yet it seemed they found us most vulnerable. They were playing around our huddle.

"I wish they had neither to choose from…" Sandra sobbed through their tears, "Because, if then, I had the choice to choose with, I would have been so afraid I would have made the wrong choice for myself, and could never live with myself afterwards."

"It's a chance for them to say goodbye," I whispered, "If the need should arise."

"I believe Conner," she looked to me with a most frightful gaze, "that moment is quickly approaching."

The night had crawled in from the streets below, settled high into the trees, than descended within the crevices of those upstairs windows. I feared what the morning might bring; another call; an urgent message; one which comes with two rings of the phone; a clamoring voice on the other end, and word of some tragedy which was lurking in the shadows of that tomorrow soon to come.

I wanted to sleep an endless dream; one where no death prevailed; and the plight of long separation would be nothing more than a thought which never existed. Alas, dreams are only those that we are to awake from. They play only for a time for us to frolic in. For even my dreams seem to betray me, casting out the good parts it was supposed to have, and leaving me with nothing else but the product of an unfinished world; a world where Truth lies somewhere in the sea.

Chapter 27

The Lost Birthday.

It was a bitter month which lay before us, or nearly so. My mother had been on the ventilator for the better part of that time; the tube always a matter of great discomfort to her. You could see through her heavy sedation she was in some manner of pain; the grimaces as common as a blink; the eyes rolled back with some thought of hysteria. At one juncture, she was in such a diverse level of pain, she nearly bit her upper lip off in an overt attempt to slice open the tube which had been sitting down her throat for as long as the inclusion of this month.

She would wake, on many days, for no longer the length of time than five to ten minutes. The radical and heavy sedation was causing no greater spell of alertness than this. Ativan and morphine both were used for this purpose. There was no word on how the ARDS actually found its onslaught; only that the damage was severe and inevitably irreversible. The use of her lungs had left her with minimal ability, and caused her to be so dependent on the ventilator for support.

Plasmapheresis was discontinued, for a time, due to the fluid buildup which could be possible in her lungs. If perchance her platelet level were to tumble once more, her fate of doom would be sealed. The doctors had discussed with us, with the prospects of her being on the vent for longer than two weeks, there was a graver chance she would have to remain on the vent for the remainder of her life.

We took turns attending to her, watching over her condition day in and day out, flexing her legs, changing her boots, working her arms and hands, and placing lotion to her hard calluses; changing her arm wraps after the seepage nearly soaked through the fabric; the stench was as though it were raw fish. Her hands had grown so stiff that her fingers could no longer be moved or mobile; as though they had already died. We placed washcloths within her palms to keep her hands from curling up any further.

Patients with ARDS, if they are to display improvement, this improvement begins to show signs within the first two weeks of the initial attack. The x-rays were showing 'crusty' patches in both lungs where the damage had occurred, like scabs to the soft tissue there.

During this time, a few birthdays, as well as my mother's, had come and gone. I celebrated with the others by a loving call from Sandra, Cory and Tyler, and the vast part of the day within the confines of ICU. I sat in the corner, at times watching my mother for movement, checking the vitals above and about her, then proceeding to read the endless volumes of novels I had brought with me. Every hour on the half hour I would check her bandages, replace her foot boots, work her arms and legs, and then commence back to the stories which were keeping me company during the times she was asleep and in her own world of dreams.

Within a few weeks mother's birthday, her sixty-sixth, came about, with as little fanfare as mine did. I pulled out her birthday card reserved especially for her, read it aloud with a voice and a tear, and placed it about her chest when I was done.

'The mother for All Seasons
She gives the flower breath,
Of sunlight to grow in the spring,
She warms the rose from bud to grow,
In the early birth of summer,
She blows the winds of autumn,
To touch the trees in giving
Their leaves the path to journey by,
And when so winter comes,
And top the mountain tips white,
She sings to us a soft lullaby,
For us to sleep softly in,
For all these wondrous things,
She so gives to the world and its seasons,
But more she gives to me,
A golden heart of ember glow,
A higher joy of the purest Hope,
Yet most of all she gives to me,

> As it shows in her graceful smile,
> And in her caring, tender ways,
> The eternal Love that only a Mother knows.
>
> To my beloved mother; no man could ever have a finer mother than I do.
> I love you mother, as long as eternity is.
> Your loving son, Conner James.

I heard the soft voices of a group of people in transport. There, along the lines of this room's curtain, I could see an assembly forming just on the outskirts; the curtain drawn free, and there was Gerry with the finest smile in glee; one hand holding a set of balloons, and the other hand holding a miniature card.

"Hello little Pa," he laughed and whispered all in the same motion, "Nurses says I can't bring flowers and cakes, but says the balloons and cards will do just fine!"

He pulled free a card, brought it over to the vacant side of the bed, and shuffled the card from its envelope. I watched as he read aloud, though my mother was far in her own distant lands. Still he read with the soft temperament of a parent reading for their own child to sleep by; underneath those whispering words. I kept my eyes to her, clinging to any hope she may suddenly and without cause, react to his kindness. She never moved.

Yet I felt the words and phrases were a calm symphony to her soul; the dungeon which caged her still allowing the echoes to pierce through their walls for her to hear him by. Perhaps even in the darkest places of life there is still warmth there to be found.

Gerry was steady in his prose, though he looked up from time to time, past his small-framed reading glasses to spot her. He read with the elegance and the ability of one who had done this all his life. He propped open the card, flat to the bed, and out popped a red rose rising from the middle.

"Sees Mrs. James," he whispered, "You can see the rose; just dream to smell it and it will become as fresh as any rose garden."

"You know," I cautioned him, "You didn't have to do this."

"Yes I do," he softly said in my direction, "Because it is what I want to do. That's what makes the 'haves' in doing."

I looked down to see my mother's hand with a washcloth rolled underneath her crippled fingers. It ever so slowly shifted from one side to the other, and lifted up the card Gerry had brought to her. Her eyes rolled free; her expression drawn into a look as she tried to speak through the tube stuck in her throat. I stalled, wondering if I should gather in a nurse, and so thinking she might be in some measure of pain. That glassy-eyed stare, which sparkled out the reflection of a thousand glistening thoughts, so pushed me back in my chair.

"Look Little Pa," Gerry leaned forward, cupped his massive hand tenderly over her forehead and caught his sight with hers, smiling those white pearly teeth through, "She's come to talk a spell."

Mother leaned up her head to see Gerry more clearly.

"Did she say anything?" I asked.

Gerry paid me no heed, though bent low to kiss mother on her forehead, and speak two words, "Your Welcome."

She took to relax once more, faltering back into her sleeping beauty spell; a place where she had grown accustomed to; a place I knew nothing of, but seemed to spectre itself in my own dreams.

"Mrs. James," he whispered, "A rose like this is special; this one always lives through the four seasons; like you."

All the other firemen began to gather round, smile down on mother, and touch a segment of her body with their free hand.

"What did I ever do to deserve such a friend," I said, looking over to Gerry as he kept his gaze over mother.

"Be human," he replied, "is all."

"Where is father?" I questioned in a stern manner, "Gerry?"

"You's don't want to know," he shied away.

"Yes I do," I pressed, "Where is father?"

"At the station," he spoke after a slow, meandering pause.

"And why is that?" I gripped my teeth with my jaw, "It's her birthday; he should be here."

"Don't suppose he wanted to come," Gerry responded.

"And leave her without even a gift," I stated, as I rose to pull him just outside of earshot from mother, "What is he thinking?"

"I can only imagine Little Pa…"

"What must she be thinking?" I wondered.

"Dreadful," he said, "to even think of this."

"Was he coming?" I inquired further.

"Didn't say," Gerry quickly shot back.

"Didn't say," I stalled, "I see…How one's character goes with the virtue of a man. A fireman at this even. When you come to the back end of your life; when you're needed most, and you decide it's too much for you. Gerry…you put your life on the line everyday, without even a 'thank you'; sometimes in order to save others you don't even know. Now here sits the idol'd woman of your dreams; the woman you have spent most of your life with. And when she is in her greatest need, you aren't there."

"I knows Little Pa," he sank his stare to the floor and shook out his head, as if he were trying to shake out the disappointment he was feeling, "Fear does strange things to a man."

"Fear?" I said, "What does he have to be afraid of."

"Being alone," he softly replied.

There was a moment of poignant silence that sat between us there; a stutter in time when the world seemed to take a few seconds to listen by. I withdrew, not realizing before the horrible ramifications it must have been playing over and over again on my father. I made an attempt to sit in his shoes, then to sit in the entrapment of my mother in her bed and try to make sense of this all. I felt the weight of a pondering jury in measuring the guilt of his crime, and the judge's pressing wonder on the level of his punishment. There were no simple answers to the questions, for the questions themselves were as complex as any I had ever come across in all my days. The greatest statute to wisdom then would have been a galactic leap for me. Still, mother had been struck by the worst of those two villains.

"It's still not right," I gazed back to see her through the shadows of those men watching over her, "It's still not right Gerry."

"What will you do?" he put his hand to my shoulder.

"Do what I can," I said, "to make things as right as they can be. There's a woman in that room," I looked back in her direction, "who could have everyone else show up to see her, and if that one person, her husband, is not with her, she still will feel as if she were in the loneliest world. The weight of a thousand people couldn't bring her enough company."

"So you will speak to him..." he suggested.

"I plan to," I said, "Yes..."

"Just to keep one thought Little Pa," he held me firm with his arm to mine, "You may not be able to save your mother, but you stills can save your father; as cruel as this may sound, it may play out to be true in the end," he paused and lowered his voice further, "Your father's a great man. He saved me; I woulds not be here otherwise. I owe him this; and to you. He saved a lot of folks, and they have a rescued life because of him..."

I started forward but he held to me.

"Don't lose sight of this Little Pa," he warned, "Man's a victim just like yous and me. If you paint him out to be somethin else, you could lose him through and through."

"I'll keep that in mind," I nearly swore on this.

I made my way down to the main floor of the hospital with the fullest intention to see my father before the night was over. The main lobby was more packed than usual with people of all shapes and sizes mulling about; some with flowers and candy; cards and decorating items. A few were wheeling out newborns with their mothers in tow. The smiles they shed along their route showed of the most unbelievable joy; their eyes lit up with glowing candles of joy and pride. I stopped to remember when my two little ones were first brought into the world, taking Sandra and each one out on their initial journey into that new home. I could feel the echoes of her laughter tickle to my ears as I waited in this lobby, feeling the shuffle and mix of people passing me by. I was stuck in a realm where only my own time had stopped and all others remained in full motion. You sense the rule of spectator there, casting out your look on the sights of that moment, and hearing the resonating sounds of so many people muttering about in their own span of conversation.

I saw the toddler of a little girl dressed in a pink shirt and pants, with orange shoes that glowed on her every step; her bright golden hair pulled back in a ponytail with a yellow ribbon wrapped nicely into a lavish bow. Her tiny hand was in grasp of her mother's larger one, though she kept her stare in my place; and I, watching on her the more intently as she approached, passed, and descended to the steps leading towards the upper floors. I could see my Tyler in her; I could see myself the same. But as I rose deeper to spot her more closely, I could see the youth of my mother looking back at me; alas the vintage notions of that first dream cast into the seas of my night just weeks before.

"Conner," I heard a voice call for me. My thoughts dispersed. I looked hawkishly about to see perhaps who it was, "Conner."

From behind, I turned and found my sister Lorie waiting for my response. She had been in tears; her eyes drawn low and frazzled from the emotions she had spent out like a river that would not run dry, "Can we talk?"

I pulled her to the small gardens the hospital had kept up; a tiny sprawl sitting between the two main buildings. We sat over one bench and I kept my attention fully towards her.

"What is it Lorie?" I asked, "Have the doctors told you something more. It's mother; the news. It isn't good."

"No," she shook her head, squinting to hold her tears in check, "It's not our mother."

"Then what is it?" I pursued.

"You would have thought," she started, "The news of me being pregnant would be such a happy thing."

"Lorie," I reminded her, "It's the best news."

"Conner please," she employed of me, "I talked with the doctors this afternoon. Mother has a viral infection which is very contagious and deadly to an unborn fetus. I can no longer see her; not now, not at anytime. They pulled one nurse from her duty; she too, is pregnant."

I pulled back; my eyes bulging from their base as I felt the harsh meaning behind what she had just said to me.

"Have you told mother you are going to have a baby?"

She shook her head as though to say 'no.'

"Does father know?" I made an attempt to comfort her, yet she held me off with a corner glance, "Anyone?"

"No," she explained, "Marshall and you. I have over seven months Conner; seven months of quarantine in front of me. Mother's condition may not allow her more time; not enough anyway. She could die tomorrow."

"Don't say that," I warned her.

"Oh Conner," she fussed, "You know this to be true. I haven't talked to anyone about it, not even with myself. Marshall asks, but I never speak of it; I can't. There is too much burden in those words."

"True," I leaned forward to cuff my hands together in a grasp; my elbows to my knees, "I can only live for now. The future will have to hold to its own predictions," I paused, "I won't allow myself to lose sight of reality Lorie. But at the same time, I will not allow my own fears to control my emotions. This is for her; not for me."

"To put up a good front…"

"We have to," I stressed, "What else can we do? She looks to us as the hands that hold her from slipping further off that rock. If we should lose hope or give into those fears, she will detect it. Mother is a brave woman. We know this. But if she is to survive this, she will not be able to do it by herself; not alone. We have to be those hands of hope which hold her from those rocks below."

"We can't make miracles happen," she buried her head deep within her own hands, as if to release the stress she was feeling.

"No we can't," I looked to her, "But we can pray for them."

"What if the end is the same," she said, "but by our asking her to hold on, she only suffers more?"

"We don't know this…"

"But even still," she cut me off.

"Lorie," I commented, "We can't ask her to live or die. She has to know herself when, and if that time ever comes. I can only hold her hand through this journey; a journey we have never taken a walk through before; not together," I paused as the silence bore in on us, "I am not going to her and asking her if she wants to give up."

"That's not what I am saying Conner," her voice rose higher.

"Then what are you saying sister?" I stood angrily.

"I just want what is best for her," she turned and began to cry, "I want her not to suffer anymore than she has to."

"Nor do I," I turned to Lorie, eyeing her very sensitive mannerisms at this moment, "I'm not a professional at this…Don't claim to be. I only do what I feel is best for her, if she can't make those decisions for herself. If I were to make the wrong decision? Well, I will bear the guilt for that; it's my lot for being the firstborn."

"I think that is something dad needs to decide…"

"Well," I forced my hands outward, "he isn't here."

She cried further and came to me with a hug and an embrace, "I am not blaming you Conner. I am just so afraid, so very afraid."

"I think we all are," I whispered in her right ear. I felt the moisture from her tears dropping down onto my comforting shoulder, "But not as afraid as mother is."

I held my sister Lorie for as long as time would allow. The torture and storm of her emotions were flowing like the ancient river gone mad. We looked onto even the most immediate future as a pervasive window of darkness and shadows. The world had been swallowed whole, and nothing remained around us but for the continual and peril status of our mother, sitting three stories above us, and fighting dearly for her life.

We could have been anywhere, living in the household of any city within the United States. Still such an outcome would remain constant and be as universal as if we were merely a spectator in this unfortunate scale of events.

But we were not; we are intimately involved; our emotions; our hopes; our dreams; the materials of our lives all interwoven into that same melody of harsh reality. Somehow life had momentarily faltered and fallen from what it promised us; stolen our season of dreams and replaced them with brutal fate, and made those dreams nothing more than a fading hope and fantasy.

I was at war with my soul and I found the devil sitting on the right shoulder of it; toying with me, mocking my every thought and feeling as if they did not matter.

The events of tomorrow were cast in a fog so dense I could no longer see any further than just a few moments before me. Elementary things were even being forgotten and I was losing sight of my life-long journey to that very point. I looked high above me and I made an attempt to pick out the window to my mother's room. I counted over on the third floor, thought surely I had found the soft brilliance of light cascading down from that particular cell, and wondered what she was feeling then.

"I suppose I will tell her," I remarked, looking high.

"I'll never know the joy of seeing her face when you do," I heard Lorie speak through her tears.

"And she'll never know the joy of seeing your face as you tell her Lorie," I looked back and saw Lorie reaching her eyes into the stars about.

"You know, I even see the stars differently now; as if I were thrown onto a new earth. Like they were sparkles from a different planet."

"I know what you mean sis…"

"I wish I could see how this will end," she said, "But either way, I don't know if I could emotionally prepare myself on what will come, if I ever knew. I don't know if it would help."

"It may," I replied, "If we knew, perhaps we could help better prepare mother for what she is about to go through. Isn't that the reason? The reason why we are here?"

"For her?" she responded and nodded her head.

"Then nothing else matters more," I looked back to find mother's window, "Time is more precious now than ever."

"I wouldn't know," she came back, "I have spent all mine with her," I could hear the soft muddles of her tears still calling out.

"Lorie," I looked over to her, "I'll do what I can. To see her make it through so that the day comes you and your newborn can walk in that room, see mother smile at you at first-sight, and all these tears now were nothing more than wasted ones."

I saw her send a gentle grin towards me, as though a sprinkle of hope had been cast down from Heaven on her.

"I pray you can Conner," she whispered.

We sat down over that long park bench, and so we began to talk of our childhood days; of moments that still yet whispered sweet memories into our thoughts; those deeply forgotten days when we were younger and held more of life ahead of us; the thoughts of our travels to the outskirts of Boston; the trips to our grandmother's and the seasons which fell in rows of anticipation, and how we longed for our next time to visit her. The birthday parties; the outings to the oceans and mountains; the school days of spring and the hope summer brought every year.

How Lorie and I walked along that path to melancholy, and felt those moments around us as if they had just been born. In every case mother was there; always there, so entrenched in our lives that life itself would have been far less grand without her in it.

She was the feeder by which we fed life from. Mother never allowed us to go without a day's dose of wisdom to be instilled within us. And by these long yards of history, it was apparent we had become the man and woman we were by her very hand and nurturing. Like the breath to wind itself; the strings to a harp; the tempered waves to a shore. She had molded us and so in turn, given the love only a mother can bestow to her children.

Lorie and I ventured a slow walk out into that night, arm in arm, where laughter replaced the tears. We had found a small cubbyhole inside our conversation to feel secure within, though however brief it would become. It seemed like the sun just after the clouds had parted from the rainstorms. We walked and spoke for more than an hour, and so found the shelter of many scenes as we went.

The night had turned into a clear one. Where shadows only meet deep into the distance and the bay waters below us glistened with the moon's own prevailing light. I saw the ripples dip and roll as if the moon had dropped its own dusty pebbles from its lands onto the ocean plains before us. And one by one, as they descended from that long journey, how the waters received them with a welcome and those ripples reached the shoreline where we stood in a continual embrace.

I wondered if perhaps one of those pebbles were indeed magical, and I could reach down at that moment and capture one; close my eyes, holding that pebble deep within my palms, make a wish, and cast it out as far as the seas would receive it. Then, as I watched in a hope only as strong as a dream, I could see that ripple reach far and wide, touching every base of the Atlantic; and a dream as precious as a pebble would at last come true…

Chapter 28

Father, Please Come Home.

I called Sandra later that evening to inform her that I would not be home until late; perhaps quite late. I explained the purposes for my delay, and her reply was to hold an ominous silence over the phone. It was apparent there were words to be spoken behind the silence but she rather played the cautionary tale, and said nothing at all. Biting her lip instead and holding her objections to herself seemed to be her play in the matter.

I knew this, I must admit, but cared nothing for creating a stir between us, least of all by phone, where cross words would begin and no resolution found; hanging up the phone, and we dwelling on that argument for the remainder of that evening without any hope of reconciliation. It felt we had come to our own sport of 'white flagging' the situation when the matter could be brought to a head the moment I entered the house. It was then I would get the full belly of her concerns.

I left the hospital. I stayed as long as I could with mother when, at 9.30 that evening, the nurse came in quietly, gently, to inform me visiting hours had concluded. I said my 'goodbye's' to mother in my normal fashions; not being certain that when I return the next day that she would in fact, be alive. There was always a sort of semi-bonding farewell I would cast her way. And I am sure if she had not be so sedated as she was, she would have realized this for herself, and had been stunned by the very look on my face as I left.

Lorie accompanied me out and was quizzing me on how mother faired, looked, her reactions; all sorts of details which may give her imagination some sense of what was transpiring in that 'forbidden' room. I advised Lorie that perhaps it would be best for her not to come to the hospital; that the pain of being so close, yet not being able to see mother would be too much for her to bare. She said she would take that into counsel, but nothing more.

I decided to return back to my parent's home on the chance my father had left the firehouse and was present there. As I pulled down the street; this lonely enclave of narrow roads, side-sitting cars, street lights that flickered and dimmed, sidewalks buckling from the age they were under, and the occasional lamplight which set aboard a house every so often like beacons in a storm. I could see the lonely rapture of the world had seemingly taken place. No one was about; not the Ferguson's nor their neighbors the Jones's; Mr. Fedigrin, who often sat by his porch late at night, was neither present nor accounted for; Mrs. Sparrow, alone for as many years as I could remember was not available either, and her Terrier dog that forever barked at the least little bit of sound had fallen strangely silent as I passed by.

Even as I slowly made my way down that final turn and onto the street where my parent's home lay, no one was around. The world had gone and left itself alone, and not a soul was present. I pulled into the driveway; the home empty, cold, echoes of ago even lost and silent. The screen door had come loose, and as a gust or two blew to bellow into that narrow way the door would pop free, stall at full open, then slam shut as if it were in a ghost town of sorts.

The shudders seemed parched and worn, so needing new paint. I had not been here for a few weeks since our last family get-together, and yet the home appeared as though it had aged a thousand years in time since then. Perhaps the gloom of night and the often wisp of that silver hue left such a foreboding look that I could not imagine it being the place of my birth and childhood.

I knocked first; no answer; came again; still nothing; the insides as empty and cold as the streets below. I wrestled with my keys, discovered the correct one, and so entered without further introductions. The door squeaked hollow, aged, tired and restless as the house seemed. Nothing was on. Not a single light, not even the stove timer was on. I flipped on the tall lamp next to the front door; the shade of light sprayed the room about with a cosmic ray of weak brilliance. The table about was filled with mail, unopened, not touched; just picked up from the mail slots and left there to sit and rot in the corpse of this house.

The mood and scenery stunned me. Like the warmth of this home had abandoned it and I was looking at nothing more than the hollow shell which remained. I walked the halls and rooms without emotions or feelings, but trying to measure the history this house and I shared. The vaults of those times, so spent in my own memory, left no trail in the home as though it had never existed here. As if it appeared a simple, happy dream in my own mind, and it never lived anywhere else. I stepped into my old room now turned into a study place; that old window and the curtain which flopped and danced about in my youth, was so vacant and abandoned; still, limp as death must have taken it over the same way.

I saw where the grooved old rings, where my bed posts once lay on the floor; that same creak in the floor just left of where it stood; the shadows of banners which hung to the walls; the closest store; my jars of pennies once lay here; nothing was as it once was. I could feel the slowing of my heart into a weak pace; I finding no refuge wherever I looked to, yet going from room to room, perhaps hoping to see, finding that home I remembered from so long ago.

The lack of upkeep had been apparent. My father was not living here anymore, or so it seemed. The heart of those memories had fled with his escape; our adolescent demise into adults had weakened it, and like a good faithful home that it was, it had spent its usefulness and died a silent death.

I felt as though I were a ghost in return; a spectre that had lost his way and suddenly found his home again, but not as it was. This hollow grave held no shadows of the past; even too, it was emptied out with not a marker to spare.

I could stay only for the short time I was there. The discovery was all too real and hard for me. Father had left here only to stay and visit a few moments every few days; to gather the mail, check the messages, and abandon it once more. I knew then his life was lost, sitting beside my mother's hospital bed in his mind, or drifting off in a cast boat in the Boston harbor, sending him self out to sea and waiting for land and fate to rescue him.

My plans were to find out where he was in his mind, his heart, and try to make some remedy of the situation. I collected my words and recited them back to me as I drove down to the fire station, which lay only a few miles away. I felt the anxiety in a loom, pervading and constant to hover over me like a dark cloud ready to rain.

The firehouse 112 was indeed active; I coming from my own distant past to revisit it. And as I entered, all drew oddly silent. The stares of a dozen men were looking my way; some knew of me, others did not. But they were all the same in a halt of their activities; gazing, eyeing over me like an alien who had lost his way home.

"May I help you?" a younger fireman walked up to me.

"Captain Jones, please," I responded.

"Whose calling?" the man did not back down.

"Is that you Conner?" I heard a voice from the rear sound off, and out came Crew Cut from their mist.

"Crew Cut?" I smiled and took his hand in a shake, "But you aren't a crew cut now."

"No," he grinned and then flopped his hands into his back pocket, "They just call me Spiker now," he laughed.

I could hear the hoarseness of his voice from all those years of smoking.

"Where is my father?" I asked of him. I noticed how his laughter and smiles turned into a serious frown.

"Second floor," he whispered, "He...hasn't been the same for some time. We got concerns. He comes in, tries to keep order, but not able to carry on much for conversation these days."

"Does he go out on runs now?" I questioned.

"Hardly ever," he said, "avoids it as best he can. But, he's the captain and we abide by that."

"Do you mind?" I asked again.

"Conner," he went to shake my hand once more, "You are always welcome here. Will do him some good I believe; maybe."

I looked above us and noticed the vacant stairway. The firehouse had not changed since my last visit. The way was set and I knew my father was in that loft above me. My intensity began to ring about my face; my hands in a clinch, driving the sweat through my palms as I went. My jaw locked up, hardened, as I started to grind down on my teeth; the moment at hand was about ready to occur.

"You were absent today," I called down the corridor as soon as I saw his frame sitting amongst the beds, still aligned as they were from so many years before.

"I have little to excuse myself with," he remarked; not turning towards me, but keeping to his thoughts and duty.

"Why?" I pondered aloud, "Her birthday? Of all days?"

"I don't ask for forgiveness..."

"None given," I stepped closer; my sharp shoes clopping to the wooden floor, and so producing an echo fade of my steps as I went slowly.

"Then what is the matter between us?"

"My mother," I said, "Your wife; as it always has been."

"I love your mother no less," he offered, trying to catch me with a corner look as he partially turned.

"Then show as much," I responded, "She is aware."

"She is asleep Conner," he said, "Always; nearly every moment of every day. She can not know."

"You have no excuse; yet you would excuse yourself so easily?" I wondered, "How do you know?"

"I know your mother greater than you," he refuted.

"Oh you do…" I spaded him, "and how is this? By time? You have known her longer, yet she and I are of the same blood. You are not…"

I could hear the echo of my voice ricocheting down through those rafters. I moved ever so closer to where he sat.

"I am your father," he replied, "You should honor me."

"At the expense of dishonoring my mother?" I came with that rebuttal, "It's been three weeks dad; three weeks since you have seen her last."

My statement did not draw an immediate response.

"I have been busy son," was his explanation.

"Busy…" I recalled, "Work? Errands? Day-to-day activities? What is it? What keeps a man from his wife's bed side in her time of most need?" I stopped in my steps and I held about ten yards away, at the foot of the first bed.

"I have my reasons."

"What could possibly be a more formidable reason for being away from her? This makes no sense…"

"Nor to me!" he shot angrily back.

"I am trying to understand…" I became more volatile.

"Understand what son?!" He stood into a stance to face me.

"You!!" I paused, "You. It's that easy. All my life, you taught me honor, dignity, never fail your fellow man; always be the rescue of them in their greatest need."

"I did," he sighed, "I tried to teach you well."

"And you did," I swallowed hard, "And I thank you for this. But where is he?—The man who was that teacher. Where did he go?"

"He is still here…" he countered.

"Where?" I replied, "I don't see him?"

"Right here!" he stomped his foot in futile anger, "He never left; never abandoned anyone, least of all your mother."

"Is my mother the same as your wife?"

"One and the same," he returned, shuffling about with his uniform, and he so trying to dress himself better.

"Then why leave and never return; after three weeks or more? The others came; Gerry, the other firemen all were present. They were there to keep her company, but you were not."

"Just say what you need to say son."

"I'll say plenty."

I rushed closer to him, nearly defiled with anger and frustration on his continual hardship ways. He never budged, even as I approached, but held his strong look squarely onto mine.

"She needs you dad. She asks for you…"

"How so?" he exclaimed, "She can't speak."

"With her look," I cried, "Five minutes of everyday she wakes, and when she does, she says nothing. But do you know what she does dad? She looks throughout the room, probing, hoping to see you; to find you there waiting for that moment."

"You don't know this."

"She speaks with her eyes dad," I slumped to the bed, "Her expression tells all. Every day when she comes to, just for this brief time, she looks all around, into every corner, hoping to see you," I paused, wiped away my short-lived tears, and stammered about, "and you aren't there…"

"I am sorry son," was his only words to me.

"Tell her," I recalled, "She is the one you need to apologize to."

There was a brief moment of silence.

"I need to get ready for another run," he began to shift around, looking for all his uniform, as if he were going to leave.

"Run away?" I replied, "You mean."

I felt the thrust of his hard hand grab hold of my shirt and force me to the wall.

"Don't you EVER question me son," his eyes were in a bloodshot and in a bulge. They shot dual weapons of fear towards me; my frantic looks being that of peril, "I have always been a good husband, and a good father!"

"Has," I softly spoke, "Is past tense father."

"You disgust me," he shoved me loose. I fell in a free-fall to the floor, "Why don't you get your things and go."

I said nothing, feeling the terrible rejection as I stood and gathered myself with what dignity remained for me to polish up; set my clothes back in order, and so stalled before I made my steps in retreat. Our eyes collected one another; more of a sneer and anger reclamation than with any other manner of expression.

"Just tell me one thing," I turned to face him.

"Do you love her? Do you really love her? That's a question you will have to answer for yourself, and for her…Because I am sure, sitting alone in that hospital bed as she is right now, she probably is wondering that as well."

I could sense the shock rippling through him where he stood; his eyes cascading down from the stern impressions of before. As if I had struck him with my own version of lightening. Father seemed to return back to that disillusioned, lost soul he had been transformed into over the last six weeks or more. I could feel him leave me in that moment, walking away in his mind, and leaving the shell of that man now standing before me.

He had been emptied out; his air gone; wasted, spilling from his chest as he slumped back to the bed. His eyes wavered off onto some distant and incoherent shores; shores where men of strange behavior go to; shores where the quirks and oddities of one's soul can be realized; shores where the freedom and abandoned dream of hope is lost; shores where loneliness prevails.

"You will excuse me," he said in that long-looking gaze, "Grief does strange things to a man's soul," he looked up at me, "This tragedy is not so great for you. If all is finished, you have your wife, your children to go back to...I have nothing."

"Is this what it is all about dad? Being alone?"

"It's a terrible spectre son," he glanced up to me, "It never ceases; always follows you wherever you go. No manner of repenting can stop it from haunting you."

"Then it is about you dad, not her..." I suggested.

"It wasn't supposed to be this way!" he yelled.

"Then how was it supposed to be?" I went closer still, "Huh? The world according to how you see it?"

"I was supposed to go first," he nearly returned in tears; his face caught in a wretched stare with which no tears dripped from, "It was me; not your mother. I am older still...Your mother was supposed to live past this."

"Well dad," I replied, "See reality for what it is. You will probably survive her no less. And from this day forward you might have to live with that. However unnatural it may appear in your eyes; that's how fate sees it. And if you falter, now, when it means the most, I fear a haunting of a hundred times greater for you than what you feel now...about being alone."

I saw him dispatch his face into the belly of his palms; more of horror than in shame. Slowly he rose to meet his look on mine; that crippled gaze aged his look ten more years in only a few moments.

"She will not live Conner," he proclaimed, "I know this."

"You don't know dad," I shot back.

"Oh yes..." he whispered and shook his head, "Oh yes...Son...I do. So many years I have lived, saving lives; saving people. I swore the duty to it like an oath a man never forgets, and always holds his memory steadfast on it. Each day, I rose and went with this one decree; to honor my duty and save lives. One hundred eighty-seven men, women, and children I have saved over the years; one hundred eighty-seven. I have spent all my life saving others Conner. It's what I was made for. I knew this even when I was a young boy, sitting on my parent's porch, riding that horse, and wearing a fireman's hat. I was so proud then; so very proud."

"Dad," I sat near to him, "And you should be proud of this."

"All of it means nothing," he shook me off, dropping his head again, "I never had affections for any of these people; just do it, and make sure they survive to live beyond that single tragedy. Now? The very woman I love and adore; have lived my life through all these years for…I simply can't save."

I felt the hard whip of that silence strike me; the heart of his essence spewing and gushing out in front of me as if it were a hundred year old volcano; silent for as many years, now rupturing and spouting out before my very eyes.

"I don't know what to say pop…" I softly said.

"Nor do I son," he hung himself low, "I lived my life in her shadow for all these years, and now that shadow is gone, and I am exposed. For the one who means the most to me, I cannot be the man I need to be. The fireman, taught and trained, is not able to do as he should…This, above all else, has broken me."

"She isn't gone dad," I tried to ring up hope.

"I'll have all the more suffering son," he stood, turned his back towards me, and his face directed into the darkest shades of that room, "How a man's life goes, is never how he thought it would be."

"So you are giving up?" I replied, "Written her off; gone, already emotionally buried and 'may she rest in peace'."

"I can't stop the inevitable…"

"Nor can I," I stood to come closer, "But I will move Heaven and earth to alter it. I owe her this dad; as you do."

"Do you know she hasn't given up?" he put it to me.

"No dad," I responded, "She hasn't…nor have I."

"I don't want to fight son," he claimed.

"Then if you can't fight for yourself," I said, "Help her fight for herself. Listen, she can't do it alone. What she is facing is worse than anyone of us has ever faced, or can even imagine. It will take all of us to help, aid, and assist her. If this still takes her, then, well, we did all we could do; and she did the same."

"You love your mother, son?" he turned again to face me.

"I can't do anything else but that for her."

"Then what are you afraid of," he asked, "Hmm?"

"Losing her," I recalled from my weighted feelings I had recycled over and over again, "But this is not as great as…If she was to die, and I quit now, then she will die alone. I won't allow her to go through this by herself."

He said nothing, yet held a frown to his expression, pacing solid with one step to the next, clipping about the floor in sharp reversals, and keeping his thoughts closed in that silence.

"It would bare my heart to split in two," he began to break into a full, all-gushing cry, "to see her struggle, waste away, and die, and I can do nothing!"

He stood with the violence of a man in rage. He took to thrust his helmet hard against the corner as he bent to his knees, and then crumbled to the floor.

I looked about him in shock. My eyes were galvanized by this sudden burst to emotion. The man I had known; the man I had always revered through life had suddenly become too human for me. He was the idol to my youth; the bearing mantle of my admiration, and in one wink of an eye, one swift motion on that stage, all had crumbled at the alter of this inhumanity, and the utter humanity he was now displaying was all too real to me.

This unpredictable realm we had all found ourselves in had changed us, shifted the weight of all our souls to be out of balance, nearly tipping over at the roar of this hideous disease. How one single, hollow pin thrown into our lives was now making us change, evolving us into beings once foreign to what we knew.

It was like a world that had become so different in the matter of one night's span. I go to sleep, seeing the world as it was. And once I awake, the world had altered the very source of its scenery. I felt the milk of this evolution to be as bitter as churn-made butter itself. Everything was compromised, and as I took a view of this new world, this new place I would be forced to call home, I felt myself in a land of no beginnings, no birthplaces, or forms and moods of history. The beauty of that lost yesterday had vaporized into the wasteland of today, sitting now before me.

I saw no shadows but the shadows to my own fears. That wicked fable called life had thrust me forward, or backward, sideways, or to no place at all; perhaps I standing still at the sight of something different and not realizing it until now. Tomorrow was nothing more than a new beginning; they all were new beginnings from this day forward. The strings of time had seemingly been dislodged and broken from that normal and patterned sequence.

I had fallen deep into myself. I could no longer hear the measured cries of my father. He was alone, and so was I. The rip in our relationship fell with him to that floor. I had nothing more to spare, and so I rose from my seat like the sight of a mummy just rising from its own catacombs. My expression was unaltered and looming into an endless peak of that inner horizon; something you see which no one else can see.

My thoughts were sitting in their own harbor; thinking amongst themselves, and so wondering what the next stage of life would bring and turn out to be. I could not even remember how I left that fire station that night. Yet soon, as my thoughts numbed every other notion around me, I found myself within my own car, driving home in a slow, pondering manner.

I could not find the essence for tears; I was too cold for this. Much like when the temperature drops too low for snow to fall; the atmosphere appears stuck in its own empty comb until something dislodges it. My drive home seemed an eternity in time; a book whose pages turned so slowly, the lamplight would go out before I could finish the story, and never truly know the final ending to its truths.

This story had no ending; just a perilous journey into an infinite place of time and space. The chapters of its root would linger about with a pondering, sluggish read; its idea born from some strange and unknowing imagination, and it seeming to embellish the path it was taking until the ending was changed or altered many times over.

One can always see the scale to a books' measure; the chapters born and bred for that read; finite, enclosed within the belly of its covers. The pages set; nothing greater or less than what was before you. Life is a terrible misfit in comparison. It has no bounds, no limits to its passage, but the scattering debris to your former life all strewn behind you, and sitting in the path you had crossed over from. And once you look back with a bit of reflection, you finally see the world you once knew as no more.

A catastrophe was born; a mother's life in jeopardy; a father torn from his well being; a sister anguished by that forbidden wall; another so young and fresh in life, one pedal to her rose may be forever lost; yet another brother abandoning his roots and his self all with the simple, unthinking stroke of his paintbrush; and my dearest Sandra, Cory, and Tyler banished, if only briefly, from the sweetest treasures of my heart.

Chapter 29

The Long Journey of a Dream.

I entered the dark, clammy home where my family all lay in sleep. The children were long past their bedtime, and sweetly embroiled in the fancy of their own adolescent dreams; my wife Sandra now tossing about the sheets of our bed, occasionally spotting the bright red numbers on our clock to see what time it was, then tossing about in the other direction; still waiting, wondering where her husband had gone to.

There were parts to my journey which must be taken alone; there was no other rightly course than this. The road was too hazardous and treacherous for those most close to you. Either they would have to meet with you up ahead, or sit back and wait for you to return. I had neither the pleasures of these; this journey being so affixed with my preoccupation that no one dared to follow in the long shadows of my footsteps.

I moved as quietly as able down the long corridors of the upstairs rooms. I carefully skirted the normal squeaks and aches coming from the wooden hallways and tired sub floors beneath my feet. I learned from past experience which blanks to walk on and which to avoid. My last encounter with Sandra had not been on a friendly sort and she would be most definitely waiting up for me, even if she desired to place with me the impression she had been retired and asleep the long while.

"How did it go?" I heard her voice ask me in the dark night, as I settled to sit on my side of the bed.

"I fear I have lost my family," I whispered back.

I felt her hand engage my back as it reached upwards to connect with my shoulder.

"What makes you think so?" she wondered.

"More than what a premonition would tell me."

"Your father called," she paused, and then spoke.

"What did he say?" I asked.

"Nothing," I heard the voice below me speak out in that calm.

"Then why did he call?"

"Because," she paused once more, but to say nothing further.

"There isn't much for a reason there," I replied, "Sandra."

"Because means many things Conner."

"And in this particular case…"

"Only he knows," she turned about to face me in the bed; the deep endless breach of light gave me little to see her by, "You can speculate on your own terms. You know your father well enough."

"What would you say?" I asked.

"To say the words that can't be said; just felt. When one can't bring themselves to say such things, and they want a pause, a look, an act to speak for them…It's all the same."

"I am not sure what he wants," I responded, "I am sure he doesn't know either."

"Oh Conner," she leaned up to pull my face next to hers, though we were unseen to one another.

We could sense the soul of comfort settling to do what our eyes could not view. That transfixed voice; the smell of your mate; the cream touch of their hands; that breath which breathes the identity to their wind, has all the essence of their presence to sooth you.

"You feel him better than this," she softly whispered.

"I think I have lost touch Sandra."

"With what? Yourself?" she questioned in that broken phrase.

"With life," I said, "And all that goes with it."

"Do you think it is more convenient for your father?"

"No, worse," I met my face across hers, "I don't discount his pain, nor his grief."

"I think you do," she pondered.

"How so?" I was not angry by her persistence.

"Because," she paused again, "now you fill in the rest."

"I can't" I exclaimed.

"Why love?" her voice grew more tender and soft with each breath of her sounds, and the touch of her body to mine, "Think Conner, more deeply than you have ever thought before."

"Because," I spoke in that thought, "I am not him."

"Then you know the way you have never seen before…" she said, "Some things can only be left to the experience; not to the observation. Sitting so close to the wind doesn't tell you how fast the wind blows. You can't know his full share of grief, without first experiencing it yourself."

"God forbid," I clung to her with a hug, tightly spun that only hardened as the embrace continued, "it would happen to me."

"You haven't lost your way Conner," she stroked the back of my hair, "the road just bent in a turn, at this point in your life."

"I can't make sense of all this."

"Shh," she faded back into a calm whisper, "Don't try. You can't go back to find the life you once had Conner. It isn't there. You will have to learn to build a new garden."

"This wasn't supposed to be this way."

"How was it supposed to be?" she asked, "Winters are never known; only that they will come; but you will never know when the snow's will fall."

"I think a better metaphor will do," I tried to laugh through my tears, but failed to do so, "Something more spirited."

"Conner," she pulled back from me, so placing her palms full flesh to both sides of my face, "Oh Conner, if it were so easy, we could all live without trial. I love your mother, as much as I ever thought I could love someone outside of my immediate family. But there she is. So close to my heart that I could feel her heartbeat with mine. I don't know your troubles, but I am here for you; Tyler and Cory are the same. We are your family; your new garden."

"I haven't lost sight of this…"

She said nothing more, but only to hold my hand as we both fell back into the bed, and slowly finding ourselves drifting onto the canopy and canvas of our own dreams.

I had no thoughts that I would ever re-enter this same dream again. No fettering notions; no weary hesitation that I might be drawn unwillingly to this same beach once more. I had persisted for as long as that day did last; to quantify the allowance of my father to miss mother's birthday. It seemed to be a greater cloud to overcome than what lay ahead of me this very night.

The painter's brush, worn and discolored from all the former paintings done before this, seemed now clogged with the variable spectrum of a rainbow. The ocean pearl blue as before, with waves so clear to the eye, one would have seen the other side of earth through them. The daylight streams of clarity rose along the panoramic horizon; that very place where Heaven and sea did meet in a thin line which went from east to west. I saw a heavy rainbow dip from that distant ocean towards the northern coastline ahead of me.

No seamen were abroad this ship of scenery; no material wands of humanity to cut the land and sea from its natural setting. No docks or harbor bounds; no cast-off boats or fluttering buoys by the sea; the sands and shoreline free and undisturbed. The long yards which stretched beyond my sight or limb showed not a sign man or his kind had ever been there.

The scene seemed most warm, and touched only by wind and previous storms. Its habitat was more overflowing than before with a stream of flying birds wandering about the open skies. Some would fly just above the curve of the waves; others were like tiny dots coasting about the highest winds.

I could see the community of the sea congregating in patches around those plains where sky and water converged with one another; dolphins and whales; fish and jelly fish, all making traffic just beyond my view of them.

That shoreline bent much the same; unprovoked by the steps of man, as if I were the discoverer of its hidden world. I watched as the waves kicked up along those natural bays, bringing with them sifted debris and shells from the long journeys of that sea.

I went to the very edge and I spotted just how blue those waters were; ghostly blue, with cantations which would make a man's look turn into a stare. Like a spell with no cure. Even the foam resting above held a tint hue of blue in their bubbles. Those warm cascades sent down from the fountains of some ever-flowing waterfall, with roars in their engines and thunders in their thrusts; one could see the purity in those watery quarters.

If one could turn that portion of earth upside down, and those waters dripped like a forever faucet into Heaven's skies, what earth would be revealed, and how so this perfect, pearl-blue sea would produce the most perfect rainbows. Those undiscovered mountains, sitting now at the deepest parts of that ocean's belly would rise up and touch the new sky and have such glorious rainbows dancing across their low-lying meadows.

I saw the world sitting beneath this sea where some would call it an endless and infinite watery grave. I saw the channel of paradise instead, below me just a swim away. The dusting of those waves brushed my feet into a cool sensation, and thus called me back to my surroundings. The sun was cast more deeply into that day. This old sky looked most worn from when I had remembered it. Yet it still brushed out with the flints of red and orange, and seemed to be trimmed in variable streaks along the deepest portion of that horizon.

Time had not touched this landscape, nor given it the virtue and wisdom of age; but holding it still, by lock and key, within its own sanctuary. I would be witness to that stage once more; alone, separate from the parched life I had left behind. Those gallows of fate could not grasp for me here, though I found this prison of a dream more like freedom than a dungeon.

I sat along that shore for the spell of some infinite time. I had been sent here before; unwillingly, and by the hand of some force that only played in my dreams. Still, like a man who had more time to dally with than to be pressed by; I sat, alone with my thoughts, akin to someone stranded on a deserted island and waiting for that one ship of rescue to somehow discover me.

When you have so much time with your thoughts you become best friends with them. There becomes a sort of equal partnership which develops; a bond and truce where your discourse and thoughts communicate equally so.

I thought I had aged a thousand years; my beard grown long; my hair frazzled and in tightly spun braids; the skin parched and deep with that olive tone and shade; the shirt and pants ripped along the limbs as though I had worn that fabric and nothing else for as long as I could remember. I felt I had indeed turned into Robinson Crusoe. And then, as I reopened my eyes, I was back to my former self once more.

I stood upon the edge of that ocean and shoreline. I made a full turn to see the world about me, but only to discover my voyage into this dream was a lonely journey. As before, I began my walk on that unmarked trail. It seemed the destiny of my steps to take and I decided to go as if something directed me to do so. I had lost the purpose to resist with, and so I walked along that shoreline under the power of some unknown will that either inadvertently possessed me, or took me by design.

Somehow this dream had more color in its stage; the sounds most riveting; the smells and distinct measures in this world more alive than the two dreams I had weeks ago. The vivid crust of that world had given sparkles more of its gleam; the waves more to its crest and lush cool feeling. I felt the wind hurl at me with the thrust of some mighty blow; an exhale by nature itself with a faint fragrance sitting in its breath.

I sensed the outcome nearing; my world ready to collide with my mother's again. She was there, though I could not see her or view the presence of her step there. Yet she was indeed the duty and point of that dream. I knew each step brought me closer still; the footsteps were like shadows trailing from the path I had just crossed over. I looked back, saw the waves rush behind me, and wipe out those indentions in the sand. As if I had never been there.

Alone in the bounty of a long-reaching stare I saw a frame; a figure aimlessly marching towards me. The figure seemed first like a dot in the sand; a moving crawfish or crab; perhaps a tiny bird darting along that wet sand. But as I moved further into this inlet, I could see more securely the frame was human, a feminine shape and posture; the waltz of an angel dressed in a pure white robe.

She danced and spun almost gently in the breeze, though finding her way in my direction. I had no reason to doubt it would not be her. Should I wait? Should I proceed? No matter, the terminal outcome was the same. I moved further towards where our meeting place would be.

The distance shortened; the seas rumbled into a stir; the pebble spit out along the shores and was waiting for her hand and wish. I saw this golden speckle lay reflecting in the sand before us, poking the bright sun's glare in every direction.

I found her older now; the product of some passage in time. The clothes loose; not secure; those graceful hands dipping into the sand and ocean. There, in that wisp of moment she bent low, collected a palm full of wet clumps and appearing clay, turned her palm skyward but still in a grasp. She looked at it in this moment, eyeing it with firm concentration, yet letting her fingers part and permit the sand to drop in what would seem packs of wet particles. Rather, as her hand did open, the sand was bone dry, running past the sides of her fingers like the ankle of an hourglass just turned over; slowly, grain by grain, now casting a swirl in the brushing winds about.

I froze at the sight of all this, as though she had some unforeseen, strange power I had ever to observe. The dream was like a melancholy approach to a nightingale. Her ways were a song unversed ever before this time; the melody of a beautiful note which played in the day of its own harmony. You could sense her presence like it was a part of the scenery. It appeared she was more like the ocean and sea than human itself.

Her greater voyage had begun. She had traveled like myself from one dream to the next, and then again. This was not the same shoreline I had come to realize, but the third in her journey to some final destination. She had a raft of time which took her from place to place; abandoned her here, as before, to discover that same pebble having crossed the seas by its own long passage.

I thought she looked at me; stalled, blinked, and kept her look steady in my stream. I said nothing, but stopped in life to keep my watch with hers. Mother gazed directly through me with those pearl gray eyes of hers; nothing whispered; nothing said.

She bent low to study the waves as they crossed before her; her ankles sinking slowly in that wet sand around. The pebble was only a few feet away yet she paid it no mind initially. I feared it would be dislodged and taken back into the sea, and as the waves rolled in, the glowing pebble always remained, seemingly untouched and unmoved.

There was a calm persistence about her. Unlike the ages before, she appeared to have grown wiser by her ways, and only moved when the moment called for it. The time had come; the pebble most near in grasp, and just before a wild rush of water came crashing forward, she pulled the pebble within her grip and she stood.

It went from palm-to-palm like a plaything, and while as I viewed her most intently she pressed that pebble in a cherishing way to her belly. Her figure was showing. I felt the rush and pulse of my life beating into a halt; mother was with child. Me, the man I am, so cast in her womb; my life yet to begin, but begun. I felt like the ghost spotting a scene of my own review. The start of my world; genesis, the harbor by which my creation had been sparked; the birth yet to be, and now like some flaw in nature, I was seeing my life before it was even spun before birth itself.

I began to shake, unknowing the cause or reason for it. My thoughts collapsed; my vision blurred and then brought acute once more. The world as it was before I knew it. Those long years of memory recalled me back to their beginnings. I recounted every step to all the paths I took in life; from that day forward until I met with myself where I currently stood. Like a script of the past, those voices all accumulated and now streamed from their collective vaults; speaking, talking to me in a uniform whisper, like they were chimes singing by a cuddle wind passing by.

"This is your life Conner," I felt and heard their words pronounce, "The wish is yours…"

"Oh Gaa…" I nearly came to a faint, backing up and feeling the world in a spin, "This isn't for me…"

I stood straight, looked into my mother's younger self, and felt her gaze staring straight for me.

"But it is," mother whispered to me, "this is all for you…as a gift should be."

She moved forward; I taking a step back by my fears.

"I can't," I heard myself say, sensing my soul beginning to pull from the boundaries of my own body, "I didn't ask for this."

"Life never asks for our permission," she sweetly proposed in a smile that nearly cut her gray eyes from my view.

"How do you know it's me?"

She smiled once more and cocked her head to the side.

"A mother always knows her son. My wish was granted before I cast the pebble…Now, the wish is yours."

She lifted her arm forward which held the pebble abroad; I took another step in retreat.

"Where are we?" I asked as the fear struck deeper still.

"Where Hope lays son," she spoke.

"No," I looked at her hand, pressing my fingers hesitantly around hers, and so forcing the pebble back, "The wish is yours."

"Do you see?" she pointed down upon the wave cresting at our feet. I saw the steady vision in those waters. The reflection was most clear by the clarity of that ocean, as I could see the essence of what the mirror shows, and it staring back at me with the same expression I bore myself.

My hands touched to the waters, though the seas did not ripple, but accepted my hand-to-hand as though I were greeting myself. I looked backed to mother; her hand still outstretched.

"I have found my wish," she spoke, "And it is you. This pebble is free to be wished again…"

"What will I wish for?" I speculated before entertaining the idea of accepting her offer.

"A dream your heart has longed for…"

"And will it come true?" I asked.

"The sea will know," she touched her palm in my hand and she released that glistening pebble to me, "It always knows."

"I have nothing I want for myself…"

"Then it will have to stay a dream," I felt her smile glowing in the dimming fabric of that day.

"How will this all end mother?" I asked, nearly engaged by my tears. My face began to crumble from the weight of my fear.

"It ends all the same Conner," she gracefully said. A smile sparked in her expression anew, "with a tear and a 'goodbye'."

"Then what good is a wish?" I replied, "nothing more than a dream that would be never realized."

"It's all the varying colors of the rainbow son."

I felt her hand touch gently to the side of my cheek, as if she were the good mother comforting a disturbed child of hers.

"It doesn't have to be," I pleaded.

"But it is," I saw her view cast out in the shadows of this dying sun. The looming horizon was like the harbor to it, "It's life Conner," she drew in a heavy sigh, "Its life."

"I will live beyond you," I swore, "and I am so afraid of that."

"It's the ownership of Love," her tightly squeezed hand embraced mine, "and without Love, you will never know the rainbow. You will never see the beauty of the seasons. Love gives all our hearts life; to live the life we should live."

"Life and death?" I looked over to her.

"It's just another color Conner," she smiled, "another color to the rainbow." I felt the supreme warmth of her saying guide me away from my caution.

We stood alone at the mouth of this inlet, where the seas and surrounding shorelines seemed to curl and converge upon us. I heard the harsh banter of a wave strike out on some rocks an eye look away, behind where my mother had come from. The shores were different from where I had come; rocky, indisposed, jagged and torn by years of a fierce and mighty ocean's hand. Those waves lipped up with the fume and foam from its increasingly sturdy rushes inland, cutting top-over those rocks and shading them from view only too briefly. When the seas subsided and the waves went in retreat, we could see the white foam dripping down the rock's sides.

"Is there more to come in a dream?" I questioned her, hoping she would know the answer, "More wishes to ponder?"

"Life is a wish," she whispered, "and what reality is made of."

"Stay with me," I asked of her, "for awhile."

We traveled along these gateless shores for the length of a day which would not end. I wanted my time with her, to know the life she held before me; and perchance, someday in the time vault of my future, I could come back again and tell her of my life I had been living past her. Those mitigated gaps we know little of; of days lost, fleeting where death takes us all.

Mother never spoke of her past; not ever. The days before we, her children, were born into this family never existed to us. They were as droplets of water sucked into a dry lake; never seen; never observed. It seemed she was born with us upon the moment of our escape into life; so too did her life begin there. The tales of reflection; the embers to her memory were as locked treasures without a key. I wanted to know of her family, her home, and the life she led and held. The persistent dreams she played upon before the duties of her motherhood took over.

She told me of her desire to travel to Africa and become a missionary, and how she longed to be in a world and land she could make a true difference in. One by one, those within her life shattered that dream, telling her of what dreams she should adorn herself with. Those fretting moments of her life when a simple turn in direction could mean a lifetime of alteration, simply never came. No one held to her passion, yet so instructed her on the course she was to claim; that of being the wife to my father; a mother to her children. I wondered then if she had regrets for our being present in her life, and so becoming more of a barrier than a longing.

"If all the days of my life had been changed," she softly said, "and I would not be the mother that I will become, then I would have lost all the rich treasures of my life I will own."

"Do you wish to know what the future will hold?" I asked of her, "I can tell you what you would wish to know mother."

"And I forfeit faith for knowledge," she drove her sights deep into the ever-motioned seas, "No Conner; no one should know the bounty of their life before it happens."

"But imagine what I could share with you…"

"I would lose more," she replied.

"There is much to tell," I insisted.

She turned her look at me, sitting as we were close to those waves and shoreline, "It's a truce Heaven has with Earth. Live your life as the free soul you are, and allow it the direction it was meant to take," her eyes never lifted from me.

"Like Africa?" I spoke aloud.

"There was a greater gift," she smiled broadly and returned to run her hand round about her belly, "A son; you, Conner."

"I suppose," I replied, "If I were to know my life from this day forward, I don't know if I could find the joy in living it afterwards."

"Would you want to know the sight, before you saw it?"

"No," I responded.

"The smell of a rose, before the scent touched your nose?"

I again shook my head in that plea of agreement.

"See the mountain rise before you reached the top?"

My head dropped to spot the sand as she continued.

"Then tell me son," she began, "How much I strip from myself if I were to know the future of my life with my children, before I first had the joy of experiencing those moments with you; the 'first' to everything; the 'first' gaze; the 'first' diaper change; the 'first' crawls; the 'first' steps and walks; the 'first' words you speak to me; in the comical, uncommunicating speech and language you will say then at that moment, hoping I would know at least one word you spoke," I felt her calm laugh hit the air.

"Everything is original," I stated.

"Reflection should only come by your memory of things," she said, giving to me a hug, "Life is like a candle that burns only once."

There was a long pause. I could sense the time drawing nigh, and I was to return back to the world which I was sleeping in. It sounded as though a most natural calling; as if an inner voice imposed on me that regulation of time was nearly ready to conclude. The fire of our moment was growing dim and I could see in her eyes a sort of empty, tired way entering into her expression.

She had smiled in her final gaze to me; a gleeful simmer and transposing grin that held a sort of sweet kindling in her eyes. Mother took my hand and lifted me from our sit, parting ways as we did with one final embrace. I watched her move slowly off from whence she came. Her step was more of a dance than a walk.

There, in times, she would dally at the edge of that sea, allow the waves to roll by and clip her feet and ankles. Time had no insistence for her as it did for me; though still I was much the captivated one now as I pawned my gaze off as far as I could see her ascend away from my sight. I dare not turn in retreat; the tears would be as mighty as the mighty ocean about me.

It was a longing which only grew; a hope sitting in the fancy of a dream; a place where summer never falls into winter, and the seasons forever stalled. I had hoped for more time with her; the drink of that potion all too sobering for me.

The presence of my mother slowly drifted into a spec along those distant sands; nearly untraceable until at last, she was gone. I waited for some time and hoped she would return. The shores brought about those waves but there was no sighting from her. I paused to think, wondering what had happened to that magic pebble when, as my recollection recounted its misplacement, I could feel it tickle in my hand. My palm opened as I looked down and there in its glowing wonder I still had possession of it.

"What to wish for?" I asked myself, "Her life back; her sickness defeated; one day to freely roam about and smell that rose one final time; drive along the ocean front from sunrise to sunset; see the grand canyon and yell out over its massive frame; taste the freshly-brewed water of a mountain stream; see the highest peek and mountain range; or have one concluding embrace with all the children she so loved."

I paced about, calculating, thinking, and weighing my options. I pressed my eyes forward into that endless land of water; spun about, tipping my balance into a spin, then releasing the pebble as far as my throw would send it

"Noooooooooooo!"

I rose from my bed; the dark air surrounding me and converging on me as I awoke. The dream was lost, sent out by the flight of that pebble, "No! That's not fair! I deserved that wish!"

"Conner?"

Sandra quickly rose from her sleep.

"Conner?"

I felt her hand press over my shoulder. I began to fumble search for this pebble in the sheets.

"It must be here somewhere Sandra," I stressed, "It's here; help me find it."

"What are you looking for?"

"It's here!" I insinuated, "Please help me find it!"

"Conner," she pulled me into a hug, "It's only a dream."

"It glows," I said, "You can't miss it."

"Shh," she tightened her grip over my shoulders, "Conner; its over. You're awake now; the dream is over."

"It can't be," I whispered back, "It was promised to me."

I struggled in that realm of where reality and sleep meet. Everyone knows there is a distinct line between the two, yet somehow in this very time I was in, the line had become frayed. I held close to Sandra as if she were the mother that had just escaped me. I closed my eyes to see if I could hear those heavy waves beating through from that dream; the rush of waters; the calypso cries and pulse beats by this unrelenting sea only gave way to the local streets and their common sounds resonating from below.

I drew back, saying nothing more of my experiences. It was better left as a silent thought; a crisp illumination of light and hope which had dominion for a short time over my dream. I wondered where it had gone; which part of the world it had fled to. Perhaps it was playing in the mind of another who was still caught in the heart of their own dream. I was the least fortunate and I was left with the mere hope it would someday return.

I could see however the lantern sitting on the bow of its ship like a guard post to its port, haunting the ocean line with its passing brilliance as it went. A ghost ship of a dream that crest the waves as it traveled. I believe my mother was on the lookout; watching, observing, and waiting for me to fall back into my dreams once more.

CHAPTER 30

A Season With My Brother.

The next morning I found myself waiting for the time I could attend to my mother in ICU. Amanda and Sandra both had accompanied me to the hospital and we quickly found ourselves stalled in the hallway, and patiently holding there until the nurse shift-change had been completed.

"We have a little surprise for you Mr. James," one of the nurses commented to me, with a very sly look and smirkish grin.

"What was that all about?" Sandra fussed on me as we entered ICU, "At least she doesn't know you on a first-name basis."

The entire unit was alive and busy with early day activities. It is the time when the doctors make their initial rounds, review the patient's charts, check on their condition, and commence to the next patient. Interns, resident student physicians, and nurses are all about preparing medications according to the doctor's orders.

We sifted our way through and caught the eye of those nearby, once we found ourselves in front of mother's location. I could see several nurses within her room, as well as Doctor Ogden, standing post around the monitors, checking about the figures, and commencing to spot me, Sandra, and Amanda as we entered.

I looked to mother first. To my surprise she had been totally freed of the ventilator, and seemingly now able to breathe on her own. I was gratified by what I saw; the look about their faces, and the apparent pleasant news I was soon to be informed of.

"Mr. and Mrs. James; Amanda," the doctor took note, "A slight word please. This will only take a minute."

He pulled us just outside of her room.

"As you see, she has been able to sustain her own breathing through much of the night. We had lowered her support, gently weaned her off the morphine as well as the sedation. She has made general improvements over the last few days. By sometime this mid-day, she should be more alert as the morphine and sedation wears off."

"Was this to be expected?" I asked.

"More of hope than expectation," he smiled slightly, "Her lung dead space is slightly below fifty percent, so she is border-line without use of the ventilator. We will see how well she tolerates it. And if she has generally improvement, then perhaps her recovery from the ARDS can begin."

""And if not?" Sandra said, "She is only stable, or even regresses back…"

"Then we will have to look at alternatives."

"Such as?" Amanda spoke up in her turn.

"Miss. James," he directed himself towards her, "If there is a return to the ventilator, a tracheotomy will be the most appropriate option. There is simply too much risk placing the tube down her throat again. The trach procedure is not without risk. Her condition being in the state it is in, it could result in a heart attack, stroke, bleeding. And without the trach, she may become further weakened by the tube, and not able to pull out of it; the sedation creating more problems, as well as the her vocal chords becoming damaged and closing around the tube in her throat; perhaps even pneumonia may ensue. We just don't know at this juncture."

"How is her breathing?" I questioned.

"Better," he came, "We have seen a general decrease in the stacking of her breaths; also, she would hold her breaths from the agitation. They are non-existent at this point."

"Do we know how severe the ARDS has become?" I moved past them and began to watch over my mother, as she was quite and tempered in her sleep."

"I won't lie to you Mr. James."

"Please," I asked, "I would rather be told, than to be considered the lesser fool in this."

"Fair enough," he moved to my side, "The situation with her lungs is of the greater concern. The attack of ARDS was severe and life-altering. She will never return to her former life. Not as she, nor you, nor any member of your family knew it. Recovery, if there is any, will be long; months instead of weeks; perhaps a year or more. Frankly, we are rather surprised she came off the ventilator. And the likelihood is that she will return to it."

"Greater mysteries have occurred doctor," I turned to direct my sights on him, "Miracles born from no explanations."

"We are on the front line of miracles Mr. James," Doctor Ogden smiled and peered back at mother, "I hope infection does not strike before she has a chance to exhibit some level of recovery."

"Is there anything else?" I pondered aloud.

"We repaired her lip," he replied, "It should heal nicely without further complications. There is still continual swelling in her feet. The Laysik is filtering the fluids from her body. However she is retaining her bicarbonates due to the dysfunctionality of her kidneys, and dialysis maybe be required in the near future. Again; that is a wait and see approach."

"Any sign of depression?" Sandra commented.

"None," the doctor quickly stated, "Nothing we can pinpoint, and there is no evidence of this."

"Just do what you can doctor," Amanda came.

"Your mother is doing more," he reacted, "I think all of us are surprised by her fortitude. The fact that she has survived this long with the continual maladies and trumping symptoms she has encountered is highly unusual; this 'stacking' of events should have taken her after only two weeks inside of her disease. Her form of Wegener's was so very aggressive and rapid. I just marvel at her will and strength to survive."

"I think we all do doctor," I moved inside the room.

By this time the nurses had been cleared to allow mother to settle more deeply into her sleep. I, on the other hand, measured my motions most cautiously, observing her sound and restful nature. Amanda quietly pulled three pictures from her pocket; one of Cory; one of Tyler; and the final one an empty pose of a frame. I asked Sandra and Amanda to assist as we slowly maneuvered a chair just to the side of her bed, as if we were three mice in theft of a slice of cheese just under the watch guard of the house cat lying above us.

One by one the pictures were posted on the ceiling, there, directly in her sights whenever she awoke.

I nudged her once; nothing, then a second time; still she slept.

"Maybe we should wait," Sandra whispered across the bed.

"We may not get another chance," I replied, there commencing to nudge her further, "Mother." I called briefly, though she did not answer, "Mother."

Her eyes drifted open. She appeared caught in the shock and surprise in seeing all three of us standing before her. Her look went cross, heavy, appearing coarse, over-absorbed and distant, and then settled back into a resting pose.

"We see you are getting better," Amanda smiled and shook at mother's left knee, "It's wonderful you are breathing on your own."

She nodded her head in approval at this. Her eyes probed our faces one by one; calculating, inwardly thinking along with her mind, as though the shadows of something more deeply loamed there.

"Mother," I brought her back to me, "Do you know what day it is?" I asked with a smile.

She paused and nodded her head side-to-side to indicate she did not know, but still retaining that confused look of hers.

"Do you remember anything of what happened?" Sandra bent lower to whisper out at mother; again, a nod of 'no'.

"Your birthday has come and gone; Gerry and many of the other firemen stopped by with balloons and cards."

I felt her tug on my arm, attempt to lift her head up closer to me, and desire something which was not self-evident.

"Where is your father?" I felt her mouth the words, though little, if any voice came in that tumbling whisper. I felt it to be more of a general plea than a curious question.

"He will be here," I lowered my sights away from her eyes, not able to speak more than this, and she knowing the heart of my thoughts to the point where she could read right through me.

"Mother," Sandra diverted her, "Look above."

My mother stalled for a second. She shifted her strong gaze to the ceiling. I could see the fancy of her eyes begin to glow that gray pearl vision of hers; the vision of my dream, as though they were the very waters of that sea coming from the night before.

"Your grandchildren," Amanda winked, "Every time you wish to see them, they will be there."

"There is one missing though," I leaned forward in my chair, propped my hands along the width of my arms, and rested my chin squarely so I could see her more closely, "You see mother? You have another grandbaby coming. Lorie is now pregnant."

We all stopped in this moment to peer with the most intense observation. She calmly waited, like she had been spent into some level of suspension; where time stopped and made her think through that moment. The light of her look transferred from look-to-look on us. There, a tender smile crept into the lower portion of her mouth.

"Lorie," she whispered, "Pregnant? Here?"

"Lorie isn't here mother," Amanda returned.

"I want to see," she announced, "her."

"You have to get better mother," I said, by the stroke of a serious gaze in my own expression, "then she can come."

"No?" she mouthed the word; that cross, stern look returning.
"Not yet," Sandra said.
"When?" she continued.
"Soon," Amanda calmed her.
"Is there anything you wish for us to tell her?" I asked.
"Love," mother whispered more clearly this time, "her."
"You need your sleep now."

I pulled the covers up closer to her as our eyes did meet again. I was nearly swept into some moving emotion there, watching the casting eye of her expression sitting on my face. The look seemed most indelible from the night before when she and I had spoken most intimately along that shoreline. We were two people in different paths of time then, yet still could share; mother to son and son to mother.

I had seen the verse of my life in the shadows of that dream; stretching long and deep, as if a tall tree had reached across the world in one late afternoon, and so extended itself by that shadow onto the very path I was walking under. Like a bridge over an ocean; a walkway from sea to sea, casting a point and place where, being exclusive of time, mother and I could meet, speak, talk of our lives, and grow our bonds together ever closer still.

It was a precious gift and I knew it to be so. Those eyes would never change; unaltered, even when unspoken. Still, the thoughts of love sat behind her voice and words like a tender box and treasure she held for me. I could hear her voice through the whisper of that dream; long ago, but only from the night I had just awoken from. They were there, those words of love and kinship; just a heartbeat away, trapped in that lonely verse of time in her life.

I knew those volumes dripped through her expression; and I let her know as much.

"I know mother," I spoke as a tear tumbled to my cheek along with a smile; joy and sorrow all mingled in that rainbow she so often spoke of, "It's alright."
"Adam," she whispered out to me, "Bring to me."
"I will try mother," I promised, "I'll do what I can to get him here; we all three will, if need be."
"Important," she weakly proposed, "Something...left...undone."
"Do you want to tell me?" I tried to persuade her.
"No," she leaned back on her pillow, keeping her look and gaze over me, "Adam...must...see."

I watched as her eyes dip back behind her eyelids. Like a brief moment when the wind blows your way and you feel it. I felt her spirit touch me and then fade back into the precocious nature of that sleep. I thought of my grandmother and so remembered how she was. The illusions and brief episodes where she would rise from that sea of her own illness, peak her head through the waters, and speak some volume of wisdom to us.

We knew time was escaping away in those moments. We simply could never tell which moment would be the last time, until the last time came. I feared this could be the last we would talk to one another, speak the words 'I love you' in a final phrase, as all the times before this one had held us constant in our fears.

I pulled back, not saying anything further, yet feeling the sound and tender arm of Sandra cast over my shoulder and neck. I leaned back, felt her bosom close as her other hand dipped around my body and the embrace consumed us. Her falling hair crowded around my face as I felt her lips touch and kiss the top of my head.

"I have to go get Adam," I spoke, rising from my seat, "I need to make that call."

I left the room, made motion down the hallway; past three long and enveloping corridors to the elevator. The doors opened and all activity surrounded me; to the phones I went.

"Pick up," I echoed into the receiver, as Adam's phone rang once, twice, a third time; no answer, "Come on Adam. For once in your life, be dependable."

I slammed the phone down, made another attempt, and paused as my heart raced with the anxiety of not completing my mission. Another ring; yet another, still, Adam was not to pick up. I knew his patterns; his mannerisms of isolation. Nothing could ever stir him from his paintings when he was living in one. The long hours; from early morning to late evening would draw out from eternity to infinity with him. Nothing more existed but for his canvas, his easel, his paintbrushes, the paints themselves, and that vision co-existing in his mind.

I would try every hour on the hour that day. The morning cast shadows longer as the day wore on. Mother kept to her sleep for long spells; the nurses made their constant rounds of medication, checking for signs, and proceeding to chart their observations accordingly. The three of us remained all through the day; our babysitter knew her time with the children might last well into the night. I saw the weary notions pass from Sandra and Amanda, then back again. When three o'clock came I asked both of them to take time for lunch, or supper; whichever they preferred, and that I would keep mother's company in the event she would awake. Before five minutes was up, mother and I were alone.

"I am sorry mother," I came to her bedside, "This is hard for you; month's in the condition you are in." I began to play about her covers, and fiddle endlessly with the threads, "It seems to never end, where you are; like a season that can't find its' finish. I don't know what that's like; I can only imagine it. And where you are, I haven't traveled to; but still even yet, it is like a season—a season with a birth, but no death; cold, dark, and lonely, kind of like winter; a harsh one. But mother," I looked deep at her as she sat in her well.

"I promise you."

I began to tear at the thought.

"It will end; this season you are in. Winter is a season; a moment, and no matter how cold it gets, it is only Winter's Moment. And behind every winter there is a spring; a point of re-birth. And you will have your spring; a very special one."

Time had melted from one second to the next. I stared out into the ocean blue sky from the window set just over her bed. Those pearl blue waves and endless vibrant textures of blue were indeed another color in the rainbow; a beautiful one. I watched for it as the day marched from mid-day to afternoon; those dimming lights of the sun cascaded a whole array of bursting, seamless rays from yellow to orange and red. My posture held throughout my blinks; that tapestry from nature's own beauty hole held my attention for as long as I could remember.

I walked back into my memory; those stores of thoughts with every imaginable thing to look at. No price tags were on those shelves; nothing to buy but the treasures of a lifetime full with experiences and joys, and were as priceless to me as the most valuable item.

My mother sat before me then; perhaps at the edge of her life. I would count the moments we shared together as though they were numerous pedals on a flower. I dare not pluck them, but watch them as they bristled in the wind. I saw their glow in the evening ray of that dawn; a dawn to a new world we would both share in.

Perchance this would be our long goodbye. Where the road to life ends and puts both of us on separate paths. I remembered her counsel of me in the previous night's dream. I watched her sleep in that indigo shade of her own dreams, now alone in this hospital bed. Maybe I was walking along her shores as she waited for me to encounter her; a pebble, nice to the glow and golden hue, sat at the floor of that sunrise and the foot of this beach, and how I would take it upon myself, cast a wish out with that pebble in hopes she would awake to her own recovery.

"You have nothing to prove to me," I smiled, "You have proved all, and I am proud of you for this."

Her eyes peeled back from their lids; her hand held touch to mine, and she forced a smile across her dry and weary face.

"I will bring Adam to you mother," I said through a smile of my own, "This, I can promise."

"I know," she mouthed; her hand crumbled and ripped from its natural use, laying then over my crossed hands.

I waited for Sandra and Amanda to return which they did in due time. My intentions were more headstrong than before; Adam must be brought here, whether kicking or screaming, or by his own choice; Adam will be returning with me.

I had visited Adam a variable amount of times at his studio. He had become rather well known throughout the eastern seaboard for his prolific painting; his dubious works for art, and but for the introductions and shows he would be performing from time to time; 'Art Fests' as he would call them. Adam could almost always be found in his long and expansive studio. Little did he know I was to interfere with the security of his home and work; make announcements and commands he had not heard since leaving our family's home many years ago. I was willing to sacrifice our relations if he again, attended to this pattern of self-righteous rebuke towards his parents, and mine.

There was only shame in his approach and I was prepared to let him know this. Time was calling him to action. If he were to stand by his introvert convictions any further, he would stand-alone and our brotherhood would cease; to no longer be. Adam was to become the man he should be; or remain, as he was, alone, unavailed by his immediate family; no longer to see myself, Sandra, or his niece and nephew.

I feared the seemingly inevitable conclusion that lay in front of me. If I were to lose a mother, I was as much to the hesitant to lose a brother on top of this. Knowing Adam as I do, this was a very real and distinct possibility.

My car pulled down onto south Boston; the rain going from a drizzle into an outright pour. The skies had as suddenly been clear that afternoon, were now dripping with so much moisture, the heavens had altered its plan for a bright evening sky and given us rain instead. I marched from my car, and stopped for nothing. His studio lay on the third floor. I could see from the outlaying streets below, a lone light from his window had been lit.

There would be confrontation; angry words to pass between us; harsh, adolescent skirmishes now all grown up like we were. This was not something I had a great desire for, yet something I must do.

I rang his door; no answer. I tapped and banged; rang again, still nothing. I moved back, leaned forward with one foot in the lead, and so jammed it up against that door to produce a horrendous thug. Surely this would get his attention.

"What on earth!" I heard his aggravated voice scream from behind that door of his.

"Who the devil has gotten up to disturb me at such an indecent hour!"

"Your brother," I responded as he flipped the door wide free.

"It's you," he turned down the volume in his voice; bringing his back to me and allowing me to enter without saying so.

"Yes; me; your brother," I entered behind him; watched him with a leery, detective eye. He moved back over to his half-empty canvas, still spawning itself from his mind into a provocative painting.

"Another work in progress brother?"

"Always," he leaned back over to his painting, measuring the remaining unfinished parts with a look, grave and hollow in its composition, yet hard onto his exposed, blocked canvas, "What brings you to this neck of the woods?"

"A matter of purpose," I said, moving deeper into his vast and open studio, and now settling my sights on the various oil paintings he had displayed all throughout, "But you know what it is."

"Will need to make it quick," he settled back into his work.

"I think not," I objected.

"My assistant is due any minute," he replied, "Connoisseurs of the art world; prospective buyers from Japan and London have interest in my work; seven pieces to be exact."

"I am sure it will be a prime cash cow for you."

"Undoubtedly," he brushed a stroke or two, "Conner, is there something you need?"

I could feel him pressing.

"Much, brother," I said in a disturbed manner, "I am certain the art business can wait for a little while."

"You have a reason for being here," he spatted, "I am sure of this older brother, noting how mindful you are of preoccupation."

"I have come to transact a ledger of business with you Adam," I came closer still, "Call it a 'second calling' if you will."

"And what might that be Conner?"

"You know," I scowled, "Or you swear at me with your own ignorance in not recognizing this."

"Prattle," he stalled me, "Intellectual or no; it is still prattle."

"Is that what you call this?" I stammered.

"Does it matter?" he elevated his voice.

"Yes!" I pointed my strong finger at him with my eye squinting like a pin shot.

"How can you be so unreal; a sterile man without emotions?"

"I don't know what you are referring to brother…"

"No you don't!" I fussed, "You won't discount me like that! I won't let you…" my eyes bulged out at him.

I heard the slamming of his paintbrush, hard down to the table sitting below his hovering, "You have some nerve Conner!"

"And you," I shorted, "A mother sits on her death bed, asking for you, and you have not a single nerve to feel for her."

"What can I say?" he threw out his arms.

"Anything!"

I stood closer still.

"Anything at all! Anything; something, a single word beyond the 'nothing' you have given her."

"You know I am not good at relationships."

"That's no excuse," I grumbled, "and you know it!"

"I haven't been a good son," he cried, "Is that it?"

"No," I agreed, "You have been a terrible, awful son; and that is it!"

Our looks were now at war with one another. Though by our bloodlines we were prevented from an all our brawl; still, we rather much despised the other.

"Alright," he said, "You have come to insult me, at my place."

"Where else am I going to find you Adam?"

"Anywhere but here would be better," he explained.

"And this would make it all better," I mocked on him, "You know? You have one advantage over all the rest of us; you truly do."

"What is that?" he carelessly asked.

"You don't feel," I walked up to him, "Pain doesn't touch you, but nor does Love, and that is the price you pay for what you are; for who you are. You go about without a care; as if nothing has happened; unaffected, a dreamer that you are. Yet the rest of us pay dearly for it all. Mother most especially. She calls for you, though you can blink a tear away rather than shed one."

"I am not as cold as you make me out to be Conner."

"No," I replied, "Your worse. How can these canvases; your paintings replace all that you could own with your family? I can't imagine the lifeless life that you have. It's beyond my knowing about it, and yet you can be the more complacent by it. Like you were perfectly content that this is all you need."

"Perhaps it is," he exclaimed.

"Then I feel the more sorry for you brother!"

"I don't need your pity," he spoke in a cross fashion.

"Then I have nothing else to give you," I replied, "because there is nothing more you deserve from me than this…"

"I think you should leave," he started towards the door.

"I am not finished with you yet!" I yelled.

"You most certainly are," he nearly popped out of his skin.

"You have one chance Adam," I said, "Just one chance; one final hope, to finally make a difference; in your life and hers. Don't blow this opportunity…You can't go back if you do."

I could see the expression in his eyes withdraw him deep into himself.

"The road ends here brother. If you do? All I can say is don't look back. There will be nothing left for you to see; to visit again."

"I'll think about it," he weakly proposed.

"And you will think," I said, "And think further; let time pass, then it will be too late. If I walk out this door alone, it will already be too late," I walked over to Adam with a gentle gaze in my eyes, near to the point of a single tear dropping about my cheek, "If I were you; really you? And I had this chance and let it slip by me, I could never walk through the rest of my life and hope to ever look in the mirror again without a mountain of regret looking back at me."

He wanted to speak; to find the words in a phrase that would calm the situation into a simmer. Though when he made the fair attempt to produce any utterance, nothing came; only the silent partner of his thoughts could remind him of the loss.

"Don't hide behind your talent any further; to keep yourself from being human," I said, "That's what you are; that's what we all are. To deny this, is to deny ourselves."

I felt the shuttering of his walls cutting past his expression; his heart in a tremor; the earthquake in his soul beginning to rumble, and his eyes said as much.

"Do you want to be a man of good intentions?" I questioned him, "Or be the true man to act on them?"

"You don't know all Conner," he tried to defend himself.

"What?" I pressed further with a hard and steady look, "Another excuse; victim? Adam, all you own for the rest of your life is the time you have now until you die; nothing more; no canvases or paintings; no arts festivals can give you more, or something more valuable to replace it with. There is no pardon for excuses."

"I don't feel like I belong," he began to shake; his jaw in a quiver, "An outsider; no relating to me."

"Your half of the equation," I said, "Half of the fault you own."

"But still," he came, "When I paint, write; its' just me. I belong there, but with people, there is an empty place I can't fix. I don't know what it is; like I wasn't born here or something, or a part of me is missing. A part of me was left behind, and lost."

"Adam," I placed a hand to his shoulder, "You're my brother, and I love you." I took to a pause, "But just imagine how lost mother feels right about now. It is like she were out of place; not belonging; here, there. You and I have a choice. We can deny her and be totally selfish in favor of our feelings. Or, we can sacrifice to make her life what it is, and what it could be. Hold her hand, and if her journey takes her past what we know; well, we can at least say we never abandoned her, and we could live our lives beyond this; without any guilt," I paused, "Unfortunately, mother doesn't have the luxury of such a choice."

"What if I say the wrong things?" he pleaded softly.

"How can you?" I questioned, "If it comes from the heart?"

"Conner," he stumbled, "I am terrible with words."

"Look," I said, "And listen. The rest will follow. Mother has called for you; has for some time now. I will be there; just look to me and I will intercede."

I walked over to the wealth of his paintings, viewed the cosmic and exceptional view once buried deep within Adam. It was now sitting in eye view on that wet canvas strip before me. I looked to my brother as he seemed to be most worn down by our conversation. I had broken him; like a wild mustang that had lost its girth and strength for freedom. It was a lesson well learned; something as foreign to him as a distant language. But I could see in his eyes that this newborn knowledge was sinking in. He was quickly discovering that his world was not the only one which existed; and I had profoundly touched him so.

I pardoned him with my look. The testament coming from his gaze was showing to me he was evolving before my very eyes. The distant, aloof brother I had always known was no more, and a new brother was taking its place.

I felt his isolation; the torment of his loneliness. This sanctuary he held for nearly all his life, appeared to be more of a prison in his eyes now that he had left the boundaries of its guard. He was retracting, reviewing this ecliptic moment in his life. What did it mean? The purpose and reason for it now? Those questions were better left for another day, another time, with a bit of reflection behind him to sort it all out with.

Now, at last, I could be the brother to him I always and forever wanted to be. Finally Adam would let me be his brother and his true friend.

"What is this?" I observed his newfound work, standing before it as I did.

"A simple piece really," he explained, "the complexity lies in its simple nature. The lines provoke inner thoughts that, at first, seem shallow and elementary. But as one studies it further, you can see the illusion and symmetry of this complicated world just below the surface," I could see in that review what he was saying to me.

"What is the piece called?" I kept my look steady to it.

"Shadows in the mirror," Adam responded.

"You what?" I spun around to see his stare.

"Shadows in the mirror," he repeated.

It hit me as if a clap of thunder rode right past my ear. I felt for the first moment in my life, that of all the times I sensed that inner connection with my mother; that stare which meets with the eye, forms a sentence in its blink, and calls back to me for me to listen to her, meant now that I was not the only one she made such a connection with. This very same power of connection had not only been reserved for me, but to all my siblings, including young Adam. He was the more estranged of us all, yet, in this fortune of a mother's calling whisper, she had stretched through the boundaries of time and space, and had somehow pressed upon him her own continual dream.

"I think we should go," I sparked.

"What is it Conner?" he replied; I looking to my watch, and so in notice that visiting hours at the hospital had concluded for the evening, "I don't understand."

"I have to make a call," I went to his phone, "May I?"

Quickly I made a call out to Sandra on her cell phone. She answered promptly, and was on her way home.

"I will be staying here for the evening," I implored.

"Where is here?" she asked.

"My brother's," I shot back, "We will be at the hospital first thing tomorrow morning."

"You don't have to do that Conner," Adam put up a small measure of resistance, "I will promise to meet you there."

"I think it would be best Adam," I clearly said, "if I remain."

"My assistant will be here," he responded.

"Whatever you need to transact," I came, "If in private, I can go into the other room…not an issue."

"I have only one bed."

"I will make do on the couch," I returned, "Really, I can make do anywhere. In the hallway if need be."

"Suit your self," he turned from me and picked up his brush once more, taking sights back on his painting.

"Conner," Sandra's voice came over the line, "Talk to me."

"Can you meet me in the morning?" I questioned.

"I have a court appointment at ten and it could last all day," she stressed, "I will come as soon as I am able to do so."

"I plan for Adam and myself to visit mother."

There was a stunned pause of silence which filtered through her side of the line, nearly as though she could not even measure a single word for response.

"How did you possibly manage that?"

"Tapping," I whispered back, "Tap the heart; move the soul."

"I am so proud of you Conner," she began to weep, "It will do wonders for your mother."

"That is the hope," I reacted, "Give my love to the children."

"I will," she quickly spoke.

"And to my wife," I said, "She deserves the greatest portion of this. Until tomorrow love…"

"Until then dear," and I heard her leave with a click.

"You have yet to answer my question," Adam pursued me again; his eyes bending the width of his canvas.

"Which question was this?" I held tight to the receiver.

"A shadow in the mirror…"

"Let's just say Adam," I looked back over to him, "You are far less removed from the nucleus than you hope to realize."

"But why the sudden shift?" He asked, "Was there something I said?"

His eyes bent harder around that corner.

"You will know better of it tomorrow," I answered. "Sometimes we think the wind blows in one direction, because it is blowing our way. Little do we realize, it can blow in every way possible."

"I am not sure I follow you."

"The ripple brother," I said, "touches every corner and on every shore." I paused, "Sometimes, it just takes a little time to get there."

I took a seat to the couch, staring out in a space and place of my imagination; not really looking ahead or seeing the objects in front of me. It seemed there I was, painting my own portrait to that picture. I heard the dribble rain pounding the roof above us.

Adam's assistant came for a short while, and both bantered back and forth on his business proposition and venture that would occur over the next coming days. I made myself scarce and entered about one of the other rooms in his sprawling studio.

Later that evening, Adam and I took in an old western movie; one we had seen countless times before. But by that comical verse and heart-known wording to every scene and line to the movie, we took up the varying parts from one character to the next, reciting the lines as if the movie had become a part of his studio box, and we were the prime players on that stage.

We did this for hours on end; laughing, joking, and producing waves and waves of comical errors with the words and influxes. I felt my partnership with

Adam beginning to nurture itself once more. I saw him laugh for the first time in years; reflect back in a greater sway than the constant melancholy he seemed to always own; nearly to the point they had made up that word just for Adam.

I watched the sparkle in his eyes rise, yet never fade; glow and warm as the evening waned further into the deepest part of that night. The rain never faltered, but crisply patted his roof with a comforting sound all throughout this evening. He stared now in the bounty of my affections for him.

Sometimes you lose, but in the same occasion you find the slightest gains to grow upon. I had found my brother; those prodigal lands he once traveled over only built the distance between us. Now he had come home again and he found the purse of his true treasures sitting across him; acting out the goofiest scenes ever to be shown on big screen. He laughed and it made my heart soar to see him so encouraged. The light of his world had suddenly reappeared.

Prayers are forever answered in never-ending cycles; we just don't know which one will be answered first. The others will come in their own good time. I had waited for this one for as long as I could remember; and now, gazing back on that very special season I spent with my brother, it was worth the wait for me.

I went to my place of rest down on the first floor. He settled in his loft bed above from where I was sleeping. I could see him relentlessly tossing about his bed, as if a great disturbance was now wrestling with his soul; like the dark angel it seemed to be. I knew then this was no 'goodbye' but a 'welcome home' to my brother. In this light I found the comfort of my sleep to guide me to my dreams.

Chapter 31

The Shadow in the Mirror.

The sunlight warmed to my face in that early morning dawn. Those rays of bright cascades filtered through his blinds and cut across my cheeks to tickle me into an awake. I heard the steam of a fresh brewing pan of eggs, sausage, and the sizzle of bacon. The aroma was like an unseen fog rolling past my smell, and it arising me quick from that couch. Adam was making us breakfast.

Our conversation was warm and delightful. We had years to make up for; and we did so, courting our friendship with each other as we went along. I had discovered that we were more similar and alike than different. Adam was affectionate with his words, like he had them bottled up all these years and they were now exploding out from him in streams. A river held back by that imprisoning dam was bursting at its seams, and the water flowed out at every breach.

We hurried our way to the hospital, making quick time through the entourage of people and check points along the way. I passed by the closest waiting room and there, having two chairs pulled together to produce a makeshift bed, was my sister Lorie sleeping quietly on her side. The tussle of people about her; the cackling and loud noise, never seemed to bother her. She just remained in her sleep all the while. I moved to her side, bent low in a crouch, so staring at her face-to-face, and watching her angelic expression sit in some dream she only knew of.

"Lorie," I whispered out to her; her eyes popping free.

"Conner," she startled, holding her position.

"What are you doing here sister?" I asked.

"I can't see her," she said, "So I thought I would do the next best thing; be here in case something were to happen."

"But this isn't the way," I answered, "Not like this. If you are going to stay close, you will stay with Sandra and me."

"I can't impose," she countered.

"I insist," I converged, "Gladly. There is no sense in your staying the full night like this; you being pregnant and all."

"Pregnant?" we heard Adam shutter behind us.

"Adam?" Lorie rose to view her brother, "Adam," she smiled, keeping her eyes steadfast to his, going to him and gently crossing her hands to his face.

"Adam!"

She nearly wept, yet held her tears within, "It's so good to see you. Mother will be so pleased; so very pleased."

There was a pause, though Adam held such a curious stare in his expression that we thought it might be stuck in that pose.

"You're pregnant?" he stated, "Really?"

"Yes," she giggled into a silly, goopy mess.

"I am so happy for you," he smiled, and hugged her, "Mother will be so happy to know as well."

The smile once registered over Lorie's face transformed itself into a disconcerted, off-base stare; nearly predisposed to tears.

"Mother won't know," she claimed.

"Mother does know Lorie," I responded, "I told her."

"What did she say?" Lorie sniffled and bit her lower lip.

"The true words a mother has for her daughter," I said, "Pride and Love. I made a promise Lorie…I aim to keep it."

"I'll hold you to that," she cried and laughed all in the same spell. We embraced; all three of us in this crowded, busy waiting room. Adam and I parted and made our way to ICU.

Adam had a stroke of fear pulling his face into worry. That sensation of not knowing what to expect was something more to battle with than he first thought. I could see it in his eyes, and sense it coming through his hesitant body posture.

"You'll have to excuse me Conner," he said in a low tone, "But it would be best for you to take the lead."

"Remember what is said yesterday," I returned, as we entered this expansive area, "Look and listen. The rest will follow suit."

"Understood," he replied.

I pointed in the direction of her room; that open glass window stretched nearly from one length of the room to the other. Mother lay close to the corner with her head turned towards the open window. We could see the brilliant sunlight filtering through and so casting ray beams right across the full spread of her bed. She appeared despondent in her reclining; still, unemotional, limp and harboring nothing but the inept overabundance of time. I am sure the nights are always long for her; torture in their long patterns and overused moments.

I had come through at the beginning of many mornings; seen her face as soon as I walked through this door. And on every occasion her look was the same; enclosed, lonely, and expressing a sense of being abandoned by fate and good fortune. There was nothing I could do, nor anything anyone could do for that matter. I had hoped this day, above all others, would be different; it was not. That shadow of crawling desolation had again walked with her through the previous night and it left the stain of that expression still biting at her face.

We walked forward, holding our stance close to the door. I stalled, poked a look at Adam to make certain he was prepared. He nodded for us to go forward. Our walk pulled us to the close side of her bed, though her head lay bent toward the window.

My hand touched hers; cold and bent into a hard grasp like before. She rocked her hand back and forth, trying to raise it but unable to do so. I wrapped my hand between her fingers, taking my other hand and touching the top of her shoulder with it.

"Mother," I whispered to her exposed ear, "I have something for you. I know it's a little late for your birthday, but I am sure you will think it was worth that few days' delay."

She began to pull her head over; her eyes blinking from the pain.

"Conner," she whispered on her turn.

"Mother," Adam stepped forward and stood beside me as she rotated her sights further our way. It was a look of disbelief, as though her dream had come true, yet she was unsure it was real and before her now. I saw the different shades of emotions cutting across her expression, as though she were to be running through shadows and light.

"Adam?" she whispered, releasing my hand and making a desperate attempt to grab onto his. I moved away and allowed Adam beside of her. She lifted her head; strained her sight, grasping her other hand, and so tugging him closer still.

"Hello mother," Adam sent a smile her way.

"Adam!" She wept with a grin; grabbing him tighter still, and seeming to wrestle him forward, "You came. God…forbid."

"I am sorry for being away," he apologized.

"Don't," she stressed, "No."

"I found my way mother…" he looked deep at her.

"And," she grinned, "So…you…have."

"Is there anything I can do for you?" he asked.

"Yes," she replied, "Listen…Listen."

"I am here," he pulled a chair forward; sat about it, leaned into her, and was eyeing her continual movements.

"Dream," she said, "Do you know?"

"Dream?" Adam wondered.

"Dream," she paused to catch her strength, "Shadow…mirror. You know Adam…you know."

I saw Adam bend back a little, delve into his thoughts in that moment, and was attempting to put the two together.

"That dream," he answered, "I have had."

"Yes," she patted her crippled hand over his, "Shadow in mirror." I had yet to see her more animated during her illness.

"What of it?" Adam softly said, "Its meaning."

"Something…you…must…know," she tired a bit on this, "I wondered…myself…the shadow. Dream…many nights. Come…go…then…return. Always progressed…came more clear."

"What does it all mean?" Adam questioned.

"Something missing Adam," she began to say, "Hole all your life. I know…you feel it."

"What is it mother?" he responded, "If you know the answer."

I watched from the rear as she shook her head in agreement. In my own mind I wasn't fully aware of what was about ready to transpire; yet I held to my breath just the same. They were not in notice of me. I had seemingly disappeared in their eyes, and Adam and my mother were as though they were alone. Mother reached deep within herself, gushed out as much energy as she could possibly muster, and spoke as close to her normal self as she was able to; her eyes were all in a grayish glow.

"Time; long time, at birth…You, Adam were not alone. I nearly lost you, and feared I would. Prayed to God that if you were to go, and God's will…I accept. This…is…when he gave…you…Adam…back to me. I knew…you had gift; wondrous gifts."

"You don't need to…" he wanted her to rest.

"No," she patted his hand hard, "Listen boy…You were given gifts; gifts for two. Shadow and Mirror."

"What does that mean?" Adam moved closer in.

"It came," she replied, "Many times. Came more clear. He wanted me to see…"

"Who wanted you to see?" Adam returned, "What is the Shadow? Mirror?"

"Mirror," she sounded weakly, "Is life. The shadow is your brother Adam." I watched Adam turn about to look at me.

"You mean Conner," he spun back around.

"No son," she reacted, "No…your brother; your twin."

I felt the world coming to a collapse with the sound of those words. The shock on my face nearly dropped me to the floor. My feet were propping up against that far wall and nearly faltered me into a tail-first sit. Adam froze like an ice cube in his position; holding calm and still, not making a sound, nor moving either way. I thought he had died or had turned into the tin man at that very moment.

I heard a soft, wavering whistle in my ear; a melody from a lost brother. There were no words; just the sound of his faint and contrary whistle stirring about my hearing then. One I never knew or ever heard of; his was as foreign and as strange to me as anything or anyone I had ever known.

Such a secret born at Adam's birth had been held as closely guarded as one could be. Once exposed, the world we once knew was no longer to be, and was now replaced by a world we had no identity with.

I tried to collect myself but could not; my chest pounded into a roar. My heart fled like the wings of Pegasus from my chest. I felt that disease of ignorance, undetected all these years, and was now showing to me I was most terminal with it. Frankly I did not know what to think or feel, only to sit in that moment, and stumble from one second to the next.

That silence; that eerie silence struck out like it were the hard striking of midnight by the largest clock tower known. I looked to my mother; saw the back of my brother so undisturbed. They were both frozen together, sealed complete by this odd occasion and incredible revelation. The shadow in that mirror was my brother; a brother I never knew. Mother had talked of it often, but never revealed any more to me, other than the shadow was unidentified.

He had come from his own lost world; perhaps to comfort her, or perhaps to expose the truth which had been buried all these years. We would never know, only that such tragedy remained illusive to us all; except for the walled knowledge my father and mother had kept from us.

I gazed back into my own time, reflected to remember that day when they first brought Adam home. I had always wondered why there was such a celebration on his arrival, and the moments before when father whisked us away to our aunt's house for several weeks. The gap in time we were separated from our parents was surely the time when the one brother was lost and Adam was saved.

"What was his name?" I could hear Adam weeping into mother's bed. She placed her loving, though crippled hand over his head. She looked out to me with a crafted smile.

I felt her communicating with me once more; to say thank you for bringing Adam. We shared more than a glance there, where the moment sits in a frame of time; a moment most concentrating and poignant; a moment where our hearts would meet and mend.

"Joshua," she whispered out, "Joshua."

She kept her look on me, and I spoke to her with my eyes that I had felt I had abandoned Joshua, and left him behind.

"No," she whispered to me, "You didn't."

I went to Adam and I placed a hand over his bent shoulder. He stirred into a full, engrossing cry now. His emotions flooded those banks of his heart into an overflow. There was nothing left to crest from those shores of his; the message my mother wanted to deliver was now sitting in his emotions.

Adam bent upward and placed his elbows to the bed, so leaning his face forward into his hands to cover up those tears; though they still seeped through the cracks of his fingers.

"I never knew the answers," he claimed, "Why my distance; why am I so estranged," he came to a pause, "Now I know."

"Shadow in the mirror," I called from behind him, "now you can finish the portrait you started Adam…A portrait of yourself…"

"Adam," mother spoke, "There…is…meaning…in…your'…survival…God made…the…rainbow…and…the…colors…in…it," she paused again to gather what little strength she held onto, "You…have…greatness…in…you…Now, go…and let…the world…see it; rejoice…in…it…"

I could see in her eyes she was beginning to falter once more; the fear rising, and she slipping on that wet rock, down further onto that slope, "Why didn't you tell me mother?"

"What…would…it…have…changed?" she responded. She turned her stare back onto Adam, "Promise me…"

Adam looked back to her; the redness of his eyes so bent his face into a sorrow that mother made attempts to rescue him from, with her embittered hand; it seemed to comfort him nonetheless.

I felt for Adam; all this escaping right before his very eyes. He had neglected his life; his home; his family for so many years, and now it was like a haunting from a newborn ghost he would have to encounter for what remained for him in the leftover portions of his life. I felt the same loss as he did; for the brother we never had the opportunity to mourn. The day seemed more like a lifetime;

a brother is born, he lives, and then passes all in that same moment. Something was left out; something important, for Joshua, for myself, and for Adam.

The world had been fractured and we felt the pain for it.

"Promise me," she started over, "College…finish it."

"I have no desire to mother," Adam rejected.

"Finish it," she countered, more strenuously.

"I don't need…" he began.

"Finish it!" she forced, "Promise me…this."

Adam stalled to think on it, looking through the windowpane about, and seeing the sun rising from the east borders.

"I promise," he shook his head to agree.

"Make him stick to it," she looked over his head at me, "Make him…work…that…promise."

"I will mom," I smiled at her in return.

"I will…be…watching," she leaned back into her bed; the strength moving away now, "you…"

Adam and I watched her leave into a place and setting all her own. She faded deeply back into her mind; the eyes tilting to a close; the head wandered away to the other side of the bed. It was time for her rest; a long, enduring rest. I held onto Adam's shoulder; squeezed it out a bit, and felt him quiver in that residue. I felt the pause in that room govern us to remain for a time while she slept. Sandra would come, and more likely Amanda to follow her.

I decided to return back to Lorie who had stayed patiently in the waiting room. Adam was close behind me.

"What shall we tell her?" he whispered to me before we entered; she sitting by the corner in a small and inconvenient chair.

"I think you need to tell her the truth."

"You mean we should…" Adam shot back.

"This is something," I said, "that would be best coming from you…A chance to have your sister in your life again."

"I don't think I can," he replied, "the words."

"Adam," I looked to him, "Wherever there is love, there are also words which can make a bridge between you. Now, go."

I inspected his walk as he followed my command, and entered the waiting room. Lorie spotted him after he had made it halfway; coming to a stand and meeting him in an open area. He began, and by his speech her face grew into many expressions; the final, of which, was in shock and disbelief. She nearly collapsed at this spot and Adam helped her back into a chair. Her mouth gaped in amazement; her hand clasping about her flushed and reddening face; the cheeks turning a rose shade in an increasing measure.

I turned back into the hallway as my eyes rolled up into the ceiling, and I took about me the biggest swallow. I could see from the corner of my eye a figure standing in the open passageway; it was my father. His hat was in hand and his eyes trailed now my every move.

We detected one another on this moment; holding, and then moving to greet one another. There was a look of distance which still remained in his expression; locked hard in his look.

"Why didn't you tell me?" I asked, "the children?"

He didn't speak directly at first; rather, he fumbled with the brim of his hat, locating it downward with his dropping sight.

"I imagine she told you," he sounded.

"Yes," I replied, "she did."

"Well," he returned, "I thought the day would come when it might be out. Don't suppose you can keep a secret like that forever."

He appeared distressed by its exposure.

"Why would you want to keep it from us for any length of time?" I remarked, "Because you could? Because it seemed more convenient at the time?"

"Among other things," he said, "Yes."

"This was your idea," I fretted, "All your idea."

"Son," he grumbled, "I thought it was best for the family."

"Better for you," I snarled, "instead…"

"It wasn't like that Conner," he defended, "It was never my intent to do you, or anyone else harm; let alone your mother."

"Well I will say this father," I explained, "You need to show that woman in there a great deal of appreciation. She honored you; whether good or bad; she honored you. Did by your wishes and never went against them, no matter what her own judgment determined."

"I didn't come here to make war with you Conner."

"Then make peace with her," I shot back, "And give her the peace she needs." I stalled in my approach of him.

"Listen," he shortly pleaded, "I need my family."

"Then start with her," I expressed, "She needs you."

"I just wanted to apologize…" he continued, "My actions were more from grief than from me. For this, I have nothing to bear but an apology for. Things were said that should not have been said."

"Then be the man I always thought you were," I confessed, "The man who cared enough to light the world for me, and show me the wonderful things that was in it. Go sit with her dad; as long as it takes. Go sit with her. She's been waiting longer than you have."

"I'm not a villain Conner," he said.

"Nor do I think you are," I replied, "Those matters can be settled once we know which way this will turn. Put your feelings; your emotions behind you, and let hers take over."

He kept his look in a humbled posture as he moved forward, and made his way down the corridor towards mother's room in ICU. I made a short prayer then; a hope, a desire that he would go to her, and she still sleeping in that tiny window for her to see him in. For if this were the moment for 'goodbyes', in the least, she could hear his voice and see his smile; and know that he resided close to her when she needed him the most.

I felt there were many shadows in the mirror. I, above all else, had more than I could bear. The tempest stares of that reflection could never tell me for certain who, in fact, was staring back at me. Perhaps my shadow was a dream; the dream where my mother gloriously played upon. Would I ever see it again? Or to only realize that she had picked up, held, and cast out to wish for, her last pebble, and I was never to revisit it again. It troubled me that the finality of things always sat just around the corner; waiting, observing the moment when it would strike upon us as some unlucky fate. It was as if the showers came upon the seas and never relinquished to stop the rains. I felt I should be along those shores with buckets to capture those Heaven's tears as they fell.

There were scores of victories to cherish; one above all, was to see Adam home again. His place was here with his family, and as I peered back into that waiting room and saw Adam; Lorie in a full, loving embrace, that renewed hope found me in my own joy. We all made vows with our blood and beginnings to forever be present for one another; in good times and bad; in times of joy and in times of sorrow. The moments would pass like sunrises and sunsets to be experienced over and over again, but when I would look most close to me, I would see my family along with me, and I with them.

Chapter 32

I am Home Again.

Sandra was unable to make the trip to the hospital that day. Her court case kept her tied up for the better part of its duration. I made a point to call her to tell her I was on my way home to be with the children. She, in turn, would meet me there as soon as she was able.

The late afternoon drifted into the evening hours as the sunset began to crawl about the sunlit sky. As soon as Sandra's car pulled into the driveway, we made our way to the harbor so the children could play about the dock while we watched over them. Cory and Tyler found this to be such an amazing treat, that they held no bounds but to enjoy the frolic underneath that evening sun.

I sat with Sandra along the waterways there. The day was basking in its own bright fireworks, flickering along the dune of that rustling ocean and her partner waves. The sparkles spent about the horizon and stretched so into infinity. They made like tiny fireflies dancing and parading across that watery, flat land.

I looked over at Sandra; her profile stretching her romantic sight all along the long Boston harbor. There was something of thought there. For as she blinked, I thought I could see those calm, mindful tidbits lighting up past her gaze. Her breath was like a sigh; content; at peace, not worried for the days ahead, just in a stance of her own and finding joy in the simplicity of that moment.

"There is something you need to say," she spoke first.

"What makes you think this?" I wondered.

"Why else would you have us here?"

"To enjoy a good sunset with my wife and children," I answered, casting a smile into her expression, and a comforting arm over her shoulder for an embrace.

"Conner," she grinned, "how long have we been married?"

"Forever," I goofed a boyish smile, "and loving every minute of it."

I took to squeeze her close.

"Then you should know," she explained, "I know when something has you in a bother."

"You think so," I kept my grin square to my face, "huh?"

"Yes," she dreamed into my eyes, "the wrinkles on your forehead wrinkle further; your eyes, they dart full of something that preoccupies your mind; your hands always are in a rub, as they are now; and your lips, they always perk about."

"You know me well Mrs. James." I laughed.

"I should," she smiled, "That's why I said…'I do'"

I looked back over this drowning sun, falling as it were in the wet horizon before us. I pressed my lips hard together as I made my attempt to form the words most suitable for her discovery. The matter was a delicate one, and I had hoped I held the ingenuity to ease the shock of it in her mind when I told her of it.

"It's your mother isn't it?" she pressed.

"The shadow in the mirror," I said, "do you remember?"

"She spoke of it," Sandra replied, "Adam was there today; it must have something to do with him."

"The day is as long as it is short Sandra," I softly spoke, low enough to where the children could not hear, "Adam has always been a lost soul. From near the moment he was born, something off-center was sitting in him. There was a reason for this; a secret."

"A secret…" she drew back.

"It has been well-preserved all these years," I returned, "Adam was one of two sons born that day; a twin to Adam, and a younger brother to me."

I could feel her shock radiate and tremor through her eyes and sight of me.

"Oh Conner," she gasped, pulling her hands to her face, "How could you keep this from your family?"

"Its design was to protect," I said, "not to injure. But the irony of it is that the injury is all it ever did."

She bent closer to me and laid her head over the bow of my chest; her hand reaching for my shoulder as we watched the sun lower in its final farewell for that day.

"Adam must have been devastated," she whispered.

"More relieved," I responded, "Now he knows; now he knows."

"I am so sorry Conner," she muttered, "A brother you never knew; an uncle, our children will never know."

"His name was Joshua," I announced.

"It must have been something weighing heavy on your mother all these years," she peeked up to watch me.

"Enough to desperately want to stay alive..." I replied, "To tell his story. If she were to die, Joshua would have gone with her."

We stayed in this pose for as long as the moment would allow. It was a brief eclipse of joy in a long day of sorrow. I remember my mother always saying that sometimes the sorrows have to come before the joys can follow. That's what makes the rainbow so colorful; I was still eagerly waiting for that rainbow.

"And the children?" Sandra spoke.

"Soon," I replied, applying a kiss to her forehead, "Have they asked for her?"

"Everyday Conner," she responded, "and I tell them the next day might be the day."

"We will have to watch and see," I finished, "when that day will come. We will know; we just have to prepare them for it."

We retired to our home. I had said nothing to Sandra of the dreams I had been a part of thus far. She only knew that some reoccurring bad visions in my night had come to visit me. She never asked, not did I tell. It was left in a place undisclosed; a matter she felt was insignificant and held no meaning whatsoever; the reasons for their existent, arbitrary and incoherent. They were merely a product of my internal stress and nothing more. It was strange however; I held a want and a fear all in the same emotion for those dreams.

The night was in starlight for fresh new beginnings and perhaps sad endings. It wasn't until I found myself captivated within the bounty of those dreams that I would witness something more special than I could have ever imagined on my own. Something else was driving it and not of my imagination, or I might have held to them as some evolving premonition all these years.

Instead, they appeared in the longest journey of my life; created a refuge by the sea, and brought to me the person more endearing to me than life itself. The roars of that ocean bellowed out their long and constant calls as soon as my eyes dropped behind their eyelids, and my head hit the pillow.

I wanted nothing more than to enter that dream once more; to see her rising along the shores by her steps, and show to me the world of her wisdom once more. There was a strain of comfort built into it, yet it was a place I feared quite regularly.

This night was akin to the others before it. Within moments of my delivery into sleep, I fell out along that fuzzy and vague image on this shoreline. The waters crashed wave after wave, like a precluding hurricane ready to strike. Those skies were the play fields of every bird imaginable, and how they spread their wings high-arching above me. Most were indigenous to the region but for one lone bird, cast out of its own season and so flying freely into this one. It whirled and danced in that vast pearl background like a dancer of some lost harmony song just found again. I could feel the spirit in its wings while the other birds seemed to chirp out the song in the backdrop of it.

My eyes kept interest to it for a good minute or more, and it so spiraled about to keep watch over its movements wherever it went. It soared and reveled in the sky as if it were the owner of that inescapable world. I wondered what the bird felt as it frolicked in the skyline, dipped about the horizon, and then raced back overhead, over and over again. A dove, of pure white gleam, with feathers so porcelain that they seemed to glow by the sunlight when it hit them; still loft high in what appeared a late afternoon sun.

I peered out over the sunset; the birth of it in its earliest stage, where the vibrant colors of red and orange were just beginning their streams beyond the hemline of earth. There flowed into that intermittent stage these drifting clouds to make out its burgeoning shoreline. There, in that mist and hue, the dove rose onto that stage with so the majesty of a birdly king. And how I could see in that part silhouette, something held within the grip of its beak; a flower, more to a rose than any other tradition.

The dove rolled about with some internal navigation only a free bird could have; and in that wisp and tranquil art, the rose remained with it all the while, dipping at points just below the dove's wings, and so causing that rosebud to spread into a full flower.

The tide was rolling in and so it touched the edge of my feet when the initial waves cut across my steps. It crept up on me like little fingers of a hand from that sea, reminding me where I had returned to. I was there again.

My breath drew long and deep; my memory serving me on the manners of that procession. I was to travel for as long as the shore would lead me to where my mother was. Who would she be? How old would she become? And what would the pebble speak on her wish? Every visitation brought more and further questions. Only the dream would hold faithful to those answers.

I strolled along those shores as if I were a schoolboy kicking home in my long walk after classes. Instead of a can, I found rocks and seashells to peddle along, punt, and toss about the edge of water and land. I dallied for a while, collected my thoughts, and so noted the importance of our next meeting here. The disease which held her in her cage made light of her emotions, and kept her from all of us; it was unavailed in this place. She would be free in this beautiful setting to speak; to have a voice of her own, and speak it so to me. I knew I would sit on her every word, make a recording of it in my memory, and find the treasures embedded within every sentence.

I felt a sense of longing for that loss that had yet become so to me; something that was not fully realized; something that was escaping and in arrears of me. I had no control of what was to be. But still I felt it slipping past the seas beyond my reach or view of it.

It was a time where a man only sees himself; a moment where he reflects not on his life, but who he really is. These hands of clay makers who shaped and molded me; still, even unto this day, held their loving grasp over the person I am and would become. Perhaps the shadow in my own mirror was truly my self; a man who still was only partly made, pressed into some form, but still not the man I would be; not yet anyways. The power of love would create this vintage person; this one I would see myself as some long years pressed out over the pages of time. Not one who was more of fiction, nor one of impression; but real, personable, holding to the brand of what my destination was to be fulfilled as.

I wondered what that moment would look like. This very second where, as I looked onto the past yardstick of my life; how I had progressed through all these years, and to possess such a smile for that joy I will have then. To know I had finally become rather than to always be. Maybe I will see my rainbow then; the most glorious kind one only sees once, just once, in a lifetime.

I wanted to lock myself in this dream; to have the moments never escape, like a vapor to the wind; I reaching for it, and making an attempt to hold them in my palms, but to only find out they had faded back into my memory like all the rest.

I bent low to meet the forwarding waves with my hands, bring the waters towards my face, and hide the tears which were melting from my eyes. It seemed the sea had enough moisture to hide them away, but as with tears from two different origins, one could always tell them apart.

"Conner," I heard a voice behind me call; it was my mother.

My gaze spun around with the instinct I had.

"Mother," I stood as the sea droplets dripped from my fingers.

"I knew you would come again," she smiled.

She looked and felt in the age I had most recently seen her as. It was just a few years from that moment when her life, and all the lives around her, were to change. Her smile still enveloped the earth in joy and there was no peak of sorrow evident yet; no shadows present or any clouds of discontent sitting off the shores of her life. Clear sunshine sat in her gleaming eyes, without a fog or cloud mingling in that window of hers.

She had golden hair which seemed to be bleached by the sands behind her; reading glasses worn but not too distinct to take away from her glowing cheeks, or to those haven gray eyes that blossomed when her smile roamed her expression freely. There was nothing about her appearance that was unpleasant; her beaming personality always radiated from within, and it cast out streams of goodwill even without her having to say a word. It was just her nature; the deep belly of her essence.

"There is another wish," I replied, "But I don't see the pebble."

"The wish is already made," she said.

"Made?" I asked, "But I was not here. What was it?"

"Look," she remarked, so pointing out to the sea below my stance; I looking below me and brushing back the foam to see.

My eyes widened out into a strain, in order to form the image as it rippled in that water. I saw Cory and Tyler before me, like a picture frame but more perfect than this. As though they were there and I could touch them through this reflection. Their smiles were forever curled around their cheeks, and one could see they had the happiest thoughts behind their expression.

"Your grandchildren," I stalled, "but where is Lorie's child?"

I feared the remedy this may well impose. Like the brother Joshua I never knew. There would be a tragedy fall over my sister in the same manner.

"Please tell me she will not bear a terrible loss like this," I nearly wept, bending to a stoop, and brushing back the water's vision to and fro; hoping, wishing to find another face hidden somewhere beneath those soft-cupping waves. My mother stared over me as the tears rumbled and crashed my look, sending waves of rain along that shore. Still I pushed the waters away; pleading for another sight.

"This can't be," I suffered to say, "Please, not this."

This was supposed to be a dream; not a nightmare.

"Conner," my mother's comforting word sent my fears into retreat, "that vision was not for me, it was for you."

"What do you mean?" I was shocked by her words, "Oh no mother," I rushed onto the shore, "You can't see them, can you?"

"Conner," she smiled, cupping her hand up to my face, "my son. Do not fear what you can not change; learn to live through it."

"We need to make another wish," I asked, "and find us a pebble that will tell us something different."

"There is only one magic pebble," she smiled, "just like there is one future with many roads to that place. It's not the destination Conner; it's the journey by which you travel. This will be the heart and treasure to your memory."

"But what of Lorie's child?" I pressed, "I told you she was going to have a child. I placed an empty frame above your hospital bed."

Upon saying such a thing, I suddenly realized I had broken the world into two halves. Her eyes indicated as much; the shock she bore, and the way her eyes fell below mine told me she did not know, as of yet, her own fate. I had broken the cycle I had so revered, and longed to see once more.

"Mother," I nearly gasped, out of breath, "I am so sorry. You didn't know," I tried to comfort her.

"What is to happen to me?" she asked, "No," she broke, "Conner, you know the world ahead of me; please, make no mention of it. I already know too much."

"I should tell you," I stressed.

"No," she argued, "We can not."

"Perhaps you can better prepare for it," I followed her along those shores to the sea, "do all the things you wanted to do, but didn't have the chance to do."

"Why?" she turned and shot back." Because? You were going to say…" her eyes became hard and stern over me.

"I," I stuttered, "I, want nothing more but to be there."

"And you are," she said, "and here. There are places Conner, you can't follow me to."

"Where are they?" I pleaded softly, "Please tell me. Where do you go?" I paused, "I want to know."

She smiled, relaxing her expression into full pleasantries before me; the waves cutting through our feet and stance; the winds dotting our hair in the breeze, though her smile remained as constant as the sun, and so glowed as bright.

"You wish to know what is behind me?" she gazed to where, in all those dreams, she had traveled.

"Yes," I replied, "That way, I can better understand all this."

"You find no purpose in being here?"

"I wonder," I remarked, "as much as you wonder what the future now holds."

"It is not for me to wonder on Conner." Mother softly said, "The future will bear its own fruit; in time, and I will be but the player in its hand. We all have one sunrise and one sunset; some of us have longer days than others, but still, nature will call the day to end."

"But what is behind you?" I looked over her shoulder.

"The same as what is behind you," she replied.

I looked down to the sands, saw the wave cut across in speckles and so flood the land only in that instant, until it returned back into its brethren sea, "Your speaking of my past."

"As with yours," she stated, "we all have one."

"But I know nothing of yours," I explained, "So very little. You kept it from us all these years and never spoke of it; like you were born to you when we were born mother."

"I was," she grinned, "You, Conner, you." She grabbed a hold of me.

"As with all your siblings; you were and are, the joy to my life. I see my legacy going forward in you. My life could have been spent achieving other things in my day; to be recognized for; to be seen with greater influence," she smiled so broadly then when she took to pause, "But you, to me, are the sunrise and sunset all at once. The very day I created, molded into the beauty of nature you all are to me. Represent me," she stressed, "Represent me in every moment after this one; in the part of that day you live beyond the conclusion of mine. Mine will end Conner; the sunset falls as though it had just begun. The moment lost, but the memories remain."

"I don't want your day to end," I stuttered.

"But it will," she came, "I was born to live Conner; and I was born to die in the palm of God's hand."

"All the things I wanted to do for you."

"Then wrap them up," she announced, "like a gift you will give to your own children…and that legacy is passed on."

"Nothing I can give you then," I concluded.

"No," she shook her head in the bed of another smile, "nothing more to give; all has been given to me," she paused to see the day as the sun started that descent lower onto our sights, "You have given me more treasures than you will ever foresee."

"I have done nothing mother."

"Only to be the son I have always dreamed of," she sounded, "nothing greater a mother can be given by a son."

Her words were like the melody of a song I had never heard. But once it went to tickle my ears, I could feel Heaven breathing over me.

They say if the heart becomes the speaker to the soul, the soul will be transformed from its potential into the humanity it was supposed to become. It is the sad gesture of one's life to not evolve into such a person; to only see half the beauty in your day; to not feel the wind cutting across you face, force your eyes into a shut; to observe the whispers and roars of earth clipping on your ears; to smell the wind and fresh flowers all in the same aroma. Almost as if the sunrise and sunset of your life just wasn't as bright.

Some will concede not to glow as much, but to reside in and be content with a dimmer day; not ever realizing just how much they could own, and share all in that world they live in. This much understanding I knew my mother had given to me.

"Mother?" I wondered, "Why did you never tell me, or any of us about Joshua; his death?"

"I told you this?" her face nearly gasped.

"A time ago," I replied, "Yes."

She contemplated this for a spell, walked within her thoughts until she was ready to answer.

"I knew it would happen someday, when you were all older; when the shock of it all would not be so severe. I never prescribed the moment for you to know about Joshua, but I will say that everyday I mourned for your brother as if it had been you. With Joshua, there is a portion of me which will never be realized; the moments we would have shared with him, would never be a part of our lives together as a family."

"I would have liked to have known," I said, "so his life would have been always remembered; to go to his grave on his birthday; to visit him when the need arose."

"And you can still have those things…"

"How did he die?" I asked.

"I never spoke of this," she wondered again.

"You never said," I responded.

"He was stillborn, the second twin; Adam was the first," she replied, "The doctors feared Joshua had been lost. They were not sure. But at the time of birth it was confirmed."

"That is why we were sent away for so long."

"Adam was very sick as well Conner and he nearly didn't make it. Your father and I decided through that ordeal to leave things as they are, if Adam were to survive; to allow you children to carry on with that sense of security and home; to leave things as natural as possible for you."

She stalled to reflect, and then proceeded.

"Was there anyone else that I told?" she came again.

"Adam," I said, "You told him directly. And I was there."

I could see her heart dip from her chest; the fear she feared the most seemed to crisscross in her eyes; like lightening strikes in a stormy sky.

"How did he react?"

"With shock," I returned to say, "and with tears and amazement."

"I had only wished to save Adam from this."

"It was best he knew," I defended the actions she would take in her own future, "It helped define who he is. Now, his healing will begin,"

I looked over to her with a caring and loving stare.

"You will need to be there for him," she said, "Promise me this Conner; that you will always be there for him."

"It goes without saying mother," I assured her.

I stared back over the waters of her wish, still seeing the sights of my two children still rippling in that sea, and how I wondered and feared once more for my sister Lorie and her unborn child.

"What will happen to Lorie…and her child?" I whispered.

"As it should be," she said, "to live in the joys and sorrows of their own day, after I am gone."

I was certain what she meant by this. The pebble would only reveal those things of a wish important to her; and her alone. She would never see the child born to my sister. Her day in the sunset would have fallen by then. It felt as though the piercing of fate's knife had stolen from me the last measure of hope I held out for.

Mother knew her end was near and I knew now when it would precisely be. In her life there, she only had a moment of her day left to live; and in my time that I had taken a walk from, the day had nearly spent all of its waning light as it was bending most near to that long and escaping horizon. The shadows were dark and dissipating as the night filled in along the sky's length. A breath or two away, is all.

I turned away from her at that moment; the emotions all too shattering in my heart as it bled. My life had never known life without her in it. We were to soon part ways, as fate would ask of us to do so. I wished to go no further; to halt time and space and cause it to remain for as long as I wished. That day was not to slip into night, but hold in a stillness I would wish for with my own pebble from the sea.

"Conner," she calmly proposed, "don't fight it son. It's the call of nature; of God's will in our lives."

"And when it is done?" I spoke with those tears facing the palm of her hands, as she pressed them from my cheek.

"You have a wife, a son, a daughter to go home to," she stared over me, "A home to grow that legacy with."

"May we walk for awhile?" I asked. She smiled one last glee in my direction; taking her arm underneath mine as we walked along those shores.

I will always remember the treasures of that dream we shared there. The moments basking upon us; the tumble waves beyond our reach sprayed the sea lands with white foams and tipping waters. The dove above followed us as we stepped; the lone cloud in a sunny, late afternoon. That rose was still embedded within its beak, and was so bouncing while that dove dipped and rolled as though the wind made it do so.

Mother talked of her former life; the days I wanted to know most of; her childhood, early years, the moments of her college days, and those times before she met my father. I listened with such intent, not even willing to breathe for a single breath as sand in that hourglass might drop below without me seeing it.

She governed me in our steps and I felt I was being escorted onto that dance floor of my wedding a second time. I thought of our first dance after my wedding vows to Sandra; such the memory shot back into my mind, and a grin curled up on the corner of my mouth because of it. It would be our last dance together, and though in that moment I never knew the significance of it; still, my memories were the saving grace, and I could savor that long lost vintage tale all over again.

I reasoned why I had faced death at such a young age. First there was Spike and his sudden departure; then Buck followed in the tragedy of that long-ago fire; and so too my grandmother, as she passed most silently than all others. These moments were to prepare me for what was to come; a training course in life. That graduation would soon be tested, and so I began to feel the presence of her departure beginning to show in that offshore wind there.

I could no longer battle fate, but only to make preparations for it; a storm in brew; an adverse wind and hurricane just sitting a day's measure away. Mother was still there and I could not fully sense the loss yet, for fear of depriving what little time we had left.

"Will I see you again?" I mustered to say, "Another dream?"

"There is one final wish," she proclaimed.

"Then I will see you in that dream," I spoke one last phrase through our embrace. I watched most silently as she turned to step from me. The walk was aging, but still care free and never pressed for time; it went on its own good terms. I stood to watch her in her leave; every moment without a blink, but a stare that held to her like a forever eclipse. Those basking emotions went to nearly every extreme; inwardly so, though I held to an outwardly, peaceful stare all the while.

I could see her turn in that distance, pause, and raise her hand to her lips, blow me a kiss, wave, and then proceed to fade along that shoreline. I felt the travesty of being alone there, as before, but more so now. The world wouldn't be the same without her.

Even when I was no longer able to see her, I remained with my stare. I cast out my look as if to have some idle hope she would return and find her way home again. As with the previous dreams, once the parting waves made their returns, there was nothing more for me there. I began my walk back from the dream, back into the bed I was still sleeping in.

I felt the loving hand of Sandra bring me home. The gentle rub; that soft caress only soothed by love, caused me to wake. I gazed to the dark ceiling and felt a single tear drop past my left eye and down to stain the pillow, though I never moved; just laying there and sensing the wetness of that emotion draw me back into my thoughts.

My legacy lay in the other room; my true love beside me.

"Ocean of tears," she whispered.

"Sandra?" I called for her.

"Ocean of tears," she repeated, "I cry them too."

We embraced and held to one another for the longest while. The love was sustaining; the hope somehow alive but sleeping within some meadow in paradise. I knew the rapture was sitting near the sea; perhaps a happy life was playing in the soft meadows in the mountains of those shores.

I have always believed that words and writings carry thoughts through time and place for those beyond me to read, to reflect upon, and to ultimately understand the joys and sorrows I enjoyed through the meadows and seas of my life. It would be the witness and true testament of the man I was to become.

Chapter 33

The Light Grows Dimmer Still.

Over the next few days, as I had observed along with my father, Amanda, Sandra, and my brother Adam; mother's condition took a general trend downward. I had feared her window would be soon to close. And as unfortunate as it was, this very fear was realized. That next morning she had taken to be placed back on the ventilator with the use of a trach. This would disallow her any further contact through voice or speech. We would have to make do with other forms of communication in other manners, at least on her behalf.

Doctor Ogden pulled both my father and I aside to discuss the particulars. Her lungs were not improving and in fact, had destabilized and were also taking a bad jolt from bacterial pneumonia she acquired over the previous week. This was also the first of two bouts of Sepsis, a deadly blood disease that she would encounter. I could tell this very element possessed greater fear for the doctor than anything else, at least at this point.

The tremors in her shoulders and hands continued without fail; the seepage from both forearms became slightly more exaggerated; nausea bouts only increased and were quite common; the rattling or 'gurgle' sounds became much more frequent from her throat, and so caused her suction to be rather continuous through the day; and with full observation throughout the nighttime hours.

"Doctor," I asked, "how can someone acquire so many elements; to become so sick after a full life of apparent health?"

"We can't say," he looked at me and shrugged his shoulders, "Honestly. She could have acquired some elements of bacteria many years previous—such contracted 'embryos' could sit in a body dormant for years and years; perhaps decades. The trigger mechanism goes off, along with her weakened and suppressed immune system from the disease and the steroids, and these related events could be the very source of her catastrophic, domino affect."

"Is there any relief?" I stated.

"Mr. James," he replied, "I pride myself on being forthright; especially in such matters as these. Your mother quite literally, should have passed within two to three weeks at the onset of these multiple and very deadly disorders, illnesses. Now, here we are over four months later, and she is still battling them along with new elements. Her state is quite weak, compromised, and something of the minor ailment could push her through; we just can't say."

"You sound so optimistic," I nervously looked over him, "Are you saying she could die at any time?"

"No," he returned, "However, the probability does exist. And if she does remained within the estate she is currently under, the risk is highly probable. We will do our best to aid her in that fight, and at the same time relieve her irritations and discomforts as well as we are able."

I had heard such fears in the nightmares of my dreams; now, in that illusive play of fate, they became all too real to me.

My father turned about and walked away, clutching his hand to his face and made an attempt to push back the commencing tears. Amanda came from mother's room; Adam was in her shadow, and so noted the affect this news had on our father. She went to him for comfort as Adam came to me with all questions.

"What did he say?" he leaned into my left, back shoulder.

"Nothing," I called, not turning to meet Adam.

"Just like that," he came, "Nothing."

"He said," I voiced, "Time is precious."

I spun about to enter the room once more, so finding Sandra had stepped to the side, watching the happenings with my mother. My feet stalled in the doorway; my eyes hovering about the attendant who was in charge of my mother's care in that moment.

The woman had so the loving grace of a seamstress with care; her black curly hair rolled down the sides of her face and sat limp to her shoulders. The eyes were stark black, though as enduring with a smile as the expression which was sitting around her face.

She would dip the rag into this bowl of cooled water and so wipe my mother's brow, cheeks, chin, and face as she went. I heard the sweetest old Negro tunes resonate in a hum from her; cast down from generation to generation without a halt or stop in its play. Every so often I could hear a word whisper through the song from that attending nurse, near like a whisper to comfort and sooth my mother.

I could see the view in my mother's expression; her eyes locked to the ceiling and in constant watch over the pictures of her grandchildren staring back upon her. Her breathing stalled but totally in rest; her eyes looking with a sensation of hope that was filtering through for me to see. Those loving hands, so true to the word, brought my mother a moment of refuge.

"Thank you," I softly spoke to the nurse after she finished and passed by me with a smile, "She truly adored your singing."

Sandra caught me all the while in her look and gaze; her hand reached for me as she pulled us both closer to the bed.

"You wish you could talk," I frowned on mother as she spotted me with a turn of her head, and nothing more.

"Yes," she mouthed my way.

"Well," I grinned, "We shall see if we can remedy this."

She made a rash attempt to smile but was unable to; only meeting me with a long blink and a slow nod to her head.

"How do you feel?" I questioned. She only shook her head in neglect, and to affirm all was not going well.

"Mother," Sandra caught to her attention, "you know there would be setbacks; this is only a small one."

Mother shook her head, in faith, with more of an attempt to wish it to be true than to believe it for herself.

"You know," I gathered her attention, "I won't let you give up. You have this to live for," I looked above to bring her attention to the grandchildren sitting, in picture, above her bed.

Her stare became stuck there. Nary a blink she sent to the ceiling, but with the appeal of her grandchildren's permanent smiling faces glaring back at her. I am sure she wondered when the day would come for her to see them again.

"How would you like it for us to have Cory and Tyler visit you?"

I tugged at her sheets and I caught her look once more.

She grinned most briefly, stuttered in her thoughts, and then shook her head as if she thought it would be a good idea.

"I take it, Sandra said, "that is a 'yes'."

Again, another nod to confirm it to be so.

Adam entered the room; this garnering mother's full attention when he did so. I looked over to Adam and sensed still the notions of his awkwardness seeping through his stance and expressive, though he forced a smile. He poked his look at all three of us, we gazing directly towards him, and the awkward ways became more evident as he sheepishly smirked, stopped, and through a slight wave with his hand.

"What did I do?" he asked.

"I think your mother wants you beside her," I said, as I lifted myself from mother's side and allowed Adam to take over my place.

She grabbed for Adam's strong, sculpting hands with her weakest one; patting him by that crippled hand with a persistent and vibrant stare centered in his direction. Mother was speaking to him with her look; those eyes now in full communication and giving him exclusive air, as if to say 'keep well; keep well'.

"I think it's time," I whispered over to Sandra.

"Yes," she agreed, "it is."

We would take our leave while Adam, Amanda, and Father remained with our mother for much of the remainder of that day. We debated that principle issue all the way home, re-dress ourselves, and proceed to pick up the children from school. We were to head directly back to the hospital once, both Cory and Tyler, had been picked up. As usual, along the winds of that late autumn and early winter day, the children burst from the school as the bell sounded off onto the outlaying fields and parking areas.

Some bustled through so quickly, they nearly dropped their book bags and satchels as they went. I stood on one edge while Sandra stood to the other side; the children now flocking out all around us like little geese and wayward lambs. Yet I could still view Sandra in all her loveliness, spotting her as she was to me.

Cory came first, with bag in hand and eyes darting about until he saw me. A most stunned and studious look hit his face when he stalled right near me; noting how unusual it was for me to be there.

"Cory," I waved him over, "Let's go; where is you sister?"

He said nothing, only to slowly make his way towards me, limp to my side, and pause for my further direction.

"How was your day at school?" I asked.

"Fine," he simply said, not ever taking a glance up at me.

"Is your sister close?" I curiously wondered.

"Her class was a little late," he explained. Then seeing his mother watching from across the way, he ran to her side; felt her kneel before him, and give him the most gracious hug possible.

I eyed this as though a moment from my past interceded on me there. Twenty-five years removed from, though still as fresh as the spring meadow that breathed out those sparkling flowers only a few months before. It was a blink only; a moment when my eyes closed and I could see myself as the toddler I was, rushing towards the awaiting arms of my mother. Her embrace was exact to Sandra's; engaging, the bright sunshine of love and endearment, opened to my every whim, and the embrace of a cherished and bygone age.

I thought I was seeing the reel of one of my old movies, sitting aloft in a canister in the downstairs room at home; those voices cut from the past and the sound of that projector replacing it with a 'tic, tic, tic, tic, tic' sound. That time was a blissful gaze; a blink of emotion shortly looking back on that time in my youth, and a time when my mother held life in the palm of her hand.

The blink returned; I was seeing my son Cory and Sandra still captured in that embrace. They were involved with one another, and I watched them most intently until a little tug came to my pant legs, seemingly out of nowhere. Tyler stood below me and gazed upwards to meet her glance with mine.

"Howdy do, little cup," I picked her up and I held her in a sit underneath my forearm.

"You don't ever come to pick us up dad," she stated.

"Well," I said, "Today is kind of a special day."

"Really?" she smiled, "To the park? Zoo?"

"No," I said to both, "No."

"What then?" she asked as we both moved closer to Sandra and Tyler; her look kept steady over me.

"Your mother and I made a promise to you," I replied, "If you and your brother are up to it, we plan to visit grandmother."

Her face did not change on this, but rather stayed in the compact, unemotional look without turning into another season.

"Why?" I wondered, "What is wrong? I thought that is what you and your brother wanted."

"I know," she fiddled with a button on my shirt.

"Well," I spoke, "Why the glum face?"

"Just afraid," she weakly proposed.

"Ahh," I deducted, "Your mother and I will be there. What is there to be afraid of?"

She said nothing in response. By the tell tale sign of her outward look, Tyler wanted to make no mention of it further. I looked over at Sandra with a sort of stress gaze in my stare, and I made every attempt to communicate to her that the children may not be up for that visitation.

"Tell you what," I determined, "out to eat? Or see grandma."

I looked to them both as they stood short and close by me.

"Grandma," Cory gleefully replied.

"Tyler," Sandra wondered, "What would you like?"

"Go home," she shyly said.

"I don't think that is an option," I announced.

"But dad," she pleaded with a hurting look.

"Then we go see your grandmother," Sandra confirmed.

Out on the roadways we could see a light mist beginning to fall. The clouds above were in a heavy overhang, creeping along the harbor with a sort of ominous faction. I felt Sandra's hand crawl to my leg as I drove, and my free hand grasped to hers as we drew closer.

We were caught between two seasons; the time of year when nature isn't really quite sure which way to turn. The days were either too cold or too warm for the tradition. The wind was always kicking; the harbor waters bristling into ripples in and out to sea. Leaves of the deciduous kept to their trek for turning from green to yellow and burgundy, and then a dry crusty brown that enveloped the dormant, green grasses below; about the meadows around Boston. On occasion the temperature was so cold you could begin to see the exhale on people's breaths as they walked through the streets.

I thought of winter's moment; the time of year so apt for mother's dilemma; the meaning to its sound, the purpose in its phrase, and how the world could be relegated into three simple words such as this. I would look into my mind's eyes as we drove along; silently, almost as if in a pause for prayer, and to see my mother staring above in her hospital bed without a blink; so she watching the smiles of her grandchildren frozen in that clip of time; they always smiling and so staring back into the face of her eyes.

I began a solemn tear there, without warning. No reason to account for, but it settled over the bridge of my eye most close to me, and as the waters warmed from that tear, falling more heavy in their stream, it rolled through my cheek and onto my chin. I felt Sandra's hand wipe it free, and I turned to her to see her smile engrossing me.

"We'll make it through," she promised through her grin.

"Love always does," I smiled in return.

We were at the hospital without much delay. The traffic was unusually sparse along the way. Before we knew where we were the four of us found ourselves in front of ICU, and penetrating through. I could sense the whole area was more dark than normal; activity placid and calm as many nurses were checking their charts, administering medications, and overseeing their patients. Few doctors were about, with their cloaks of white coats offering up their standing within the hospital.

I felt the clutch of Tyler growing tighter as we went; she cowering more behind me with the look of some foreboding escape through her expression. She was tense, uncertain, and wary of everything and everyone around her. Cory made no evidence of his leering nature, if he possessed any. Rather, he bounced about with his mother as though he wasn't prepared for what he would see.

"Dad," Tyler whimpered, "I don't want to go."

I stopped, bent down to her size so I could see her close, eye to eye, "Sweetheart," I whispered, "I can't make you do what you don't want to do. This is your chance to be with your grandmother, and it may very well be your only opportunity."

"What does that mean?" she cried slightly.

"I don't think you will want to walk away from this dear," I patted her on her stomach, "Darling, do what your own mother wished she could have done. Speak with your grandmother."

She nodded her head, took about my hand once more with that same squeeze, and we moved forward to the foot of that hospital room doorway.

We caught a glimpse of mother; alone, still saddled in her bed. Her face and aged look bent to stare out the window with the soft pelts of rain touching against the glass. She made no movements towards us, so we entered. Sandra and Cory moved to one side; Tyler and my self moved around to the other side.

"Hello mother," I called out to her. To the inner window and at the doorway, several nurses had stopped what they were doing and were in heavy watch of us.

Mother looked weakly to me; her eyes glassy and worn, nor as pearl gray as before; her face torn by the misery of her disease.

"Conner," she mouthed without voice.

"I brought you a present," I pulled Tyler up into my arms.

Mother steadied her hand, elevated it with a tremor, and so touched Tyler's foot at its tip.

"Hello Tyler," she versed to mouth further.

"And we have a second present," Sandra interjected; she too, raising tiny Cory up for mother to see.

"Hello Cory," she managed to smile, if only briefly.

"Will you go to Heaven?" Cory bluntly asked.

"Maybe," mother smiled and closed her eyes for a moment.

"Can I go?" he asked, clutching close to his own mother.

"No," she worded, "In time."

I let Tyler down to see her grandmother more closely; she touching the railing which stirred mother to turn her way. Their eyes met; I feeling the slight tremble in Tyler's body rivet through. Tyler remained in her stare, holding to that railing as mother pressed her hand upwards and lay in gently over the back of Tyler's hand, stroking it all the while.

"Love you," mother moved her lips to say.

"Love you too grandmother," Tyler whispered. Mother took her view upwards to where the pictures were set in the ceiling. I pointed to show both of my children to where their exhibit was.

"See?" I whispered, "Whenever grandmother wakes up, she sees you. You both are always there with her," I gazed over to Cory who was keeping his bright-eyed stare directly at the photos.

"Now you know how important you are to her," Sandra spoke in Cory's ear, placing a hard kiss to his cheek.

Mother began to shake her head in agreement. Then, without any sudden measure for movement, she motioned for us to let both children close to her. Reluctantly, Tyler edged in further with a sense of fear dripping from her face while Cory stepped up to the bed and pulled himself up by the railing; now, both were eye on eye with mother's stare.

"Be good to Daddy," she mouthed, "Be good to Mommy."

Neither child seemed to know what to say; only to stare with that blank inference and fractured look.

"Promise," mother said, though she wished to say more.

"I promise," Cory announced.

"Promise," mother looked squarely onto Tyler, and I felt her trembles growing stronger.

"Promise," Tyler finally whispered, then backed away and up against me; I clutched my hands around her shoulders.

"Thank you," mother mouthed one last couple of words to me.

"I will be back tomorrow," I leaned in on mother, "that's my promise."

I knew beforehand this visitation would need to be most brief; the children, in their early manners and needs, were of the greater concern. The stress they would sense was something we desired not to extend any further than necessary. They were above all else the large measure of joy in our lives.

I felt the pangs of some discomfort in what was occurring before me; noting how the children were. Tyler was more so because she was older and a little wiser to the world. Fear had become more realized than the bouncy, carefree nature Cory exhibited. I suppose I pondered which had the lesser evil in it; to shelter the children as long as possible and not allow them a moment, even if it were only a moment, to see their grandmother one final time; or to give them this hope in chance to see her, and have what may pass between them be as it is, before the end comes.

Sandra was crying, and so too, the nurses about as they viewed from their outward posts. Many nurses had told me that they worked feverishly to distance themselves from their patients in an emotional sense. The care would not be denied nor would it be lessened by this sense, but this was a self-preservation mechanism they had instilled within; a way to set them selves apart from the inevitable agony they would feel otherwise.

This, above all others, was the immortal heartbreak to their jobs. Nothing can prepare one for the lost innocence of a child; to be so forced to encounter the world in such an erratic behavior as it can display. Cory and Tyler were now playing cautiously with that demon, and their eyeful stares showed as much.

I had seen my own ghosts with Spike, Buck, and my own grandmother. I knew they had played in the backgrounds of my life. Still, I would have wanted the wish to say goodbye.

"Goodbye Grandmother," Cory waved to her; she waving back with a return, though gravely weakened smile.

"What do you say Tyler?" I bent down to pick her up.

"Goodbye Grandmother," she spoke; mother again teetering Tyler's foot with her right hand; the stares past amongst us all in that time of pause; mother being quite constant in her looks toward the children. She knew this more than anything that this would be the last time.

Cory seemed unaffected by this as we left the room; Tyler taking the adverse side, and appeared quiet and reserved; nearly cowering as we went.

Father, Amanda, Lorie and Marshall were all in the waiting room as we passed by; Father coming up to us.

"Conner," father called for me as he shuffled the rim of his hat in circles, spinning it with his hands, "May I have a word with you?"

"Sure," I lowered Tyler to her feet, and went with him. We began a walk up the opposite way through that long corridor.

"Again, my apologizes for what has happened son."

"Well," I pondered, "I think the important thing is, whatever happens from here on out, you can live with yourself afterwards."

"I believe I can son," he stopped me, caught my look with his.

"After forty years of marriage," I sounded, "I wouldn't want her to think of you in any different light; to always believe you are the man she married, trusted, and has known. It's a long time for one to believe in someone, something, and to find out they were truly mistaken."

He looked at me slightly cold when I spoke this.

"I haven't given her a reason to doubt me."

"Then I hope and pray it stays that way," I said, "No matter what happens. The chances are she will die dad."

"I know this," he closed his eyes, rolled his lip for a moment, and inhaled to continue, "Your mother has the most honorable traits of grace, and for this plight to be hers…it isn't fair."

"A great injustice also would be if her family fails her."

"A ship without an oar," he whispered in a smile.

"Or a heart without a way," I returned.

"I'll be here son," he was stern in this, "I was not myself at the fire station. Every man has his weak moments in life."

"Yes we do," I came, "and I saw yours."

I paused to look up and down the hallway.

"Promise me you will not lose contact with her again; her time is so small now. Three weeks is an eternity for her. I just don't want her to have that sense of abandonment a second time around. I think it would simply be too much for mother."

I stood before him with a sheltered look and I allowed him to speak.

"Son," he began, "There are things which have passed between your mother and I which you will never know, nor have any clue to; moments that only can pass between two people as close as she and I are; moments which can only pass between a man and his wife."

"I accept that," I shook my head in agreement.

"I need you to come back to the house with me," he said, "after I take good care with the business, with your mother."

"What for?" I questioned.

"Something of importance," he replied, "It is important."

"Let me inform Sandra," I stated, "See mother and I will meet you in the waiting room."

I went back down the corridor and I caught all three waiting for me. With a quick embrace, Sandra and the children were in leave of me; I standing alone in that dense corridor, yet feeling the sense of being alone. Father and Amanda had gone to see mother; Lorie and Marshall had left for the evening. So I stood, alone, in the embryo of my thoughts. The world was passing about me like fireflies in the night. Only by their illumination would I know they were even there.

My body bent back up against the wall. The murmurs and muddled voices of unknown people echoed in the backdrop of my thoughts. I had known this inner world for as long as my life, yet, in that moment, I felt myself to be a foreigner out of place in my own lands; as if I was just born there and so discovering it for the first time.

My mother was becoming the spiritual butterfly that Heaven so requires for entrance; the cocoon of earth only a momentary place, where the spirit yields to that time for growth. And when nature calls like a desolate whistle in the hills and mountains of life, it is time for you to go. It's an internal hum; one that when it blows as the wind, you discover this evolution into a new world.

You see Heaven marking the path to your voyage; the road; the path bristled with signs and directions all about.

I could not imagine the elements to her fears; only that they existed. I could view it in her eyes; see it in the trembling of her hands. She was caught sitting on the shores of that sea, waiting for her raft to be readied. Her voyage was to begin and I, as she, feeling the loneliness prevail. I did not know precisely when it would all begin for her; only that it was very soon to commence.

Father returned with Amanda by his side. We all took our exit and made our way to father's car. It was alone except for Amanda's parked by his. I cast out a hug to Amanda, crept in the car with my father, and we were off for a quick ride to our family home.

The house looked as it did before; dark, cold, embedded with emptiness and an air for vacancy. Even though winter had yet to show itself, the home was as wintered as one would have been after a full year unoccupied. The door ached free as he pushed it ahead. The house was damp, uninviting, and so purged from the joys of its long and storied past. I followed my father like the shadow he owned, for as dark as the home was, his shadow was nowhere to be seen. There was a purpose and message for me being here, though I waited patiently for him to settle into his reasons.

We went from first story to second, clicking the lights about as we went; the house now showing some endurance to life. The rooms we passed were with an uneventful stare until we reached my old room. It now had been converted into a simple study for dad.

The shelves along the long bookcase held volumes of moderate interest, none that would stage my interest any further than a few chapters in reading. He initially said nothing; just prodded around the room as if he were a ghost in search of a good haunt, yet finding nothing for him to spectre about on. I looked out over my old window; the tree grabbling the pane, and yet it still had some fight in it. The lamplights below illuminated those streets even when the nighttime sky was filtering in the rain.

"Take a seat Conner," he offered me one of the two chairs in the room. I watched him clamor about for a spell; so buried in his thoughts as he was. The fear in his eyes; the cascading droplets from his expression were seemingly no longer sheltered.

I knew father had been having his fits before, especially at the fire station. I did not have the heart to tell him the image I once held of his reverence had been so disturbed; his impeccable unstained image; that plight of ill manner that I once thought could ever touch him; all altered into some measurable review of who he truly was to me; all of this impenetrable image had evaporated from before this moment. He proposed a weak smile as he sat; those reading glasses now fixated firmly over the bridge of his nose.

"You and I have had a long journey without one another," he started, "A long journey indeed. But, here we are, finding ourselves in the exact and identical destination; the roads different, but the end being the same."

"I suppose you are right on that," I bowed my head to look at my hands, cross my legs, and stare back on him.

"You know I haven't been one for sentimentality for a long time," he said, "Perhaps this was born when my mother died. I don't know Conner."

"Dad," I interrupted, "Is this a confession?"

"No son," he smiled with a shake of his head.

"Then an excuse."

"Not this either," he quickly shot back.

"An explanation," I found a quick answer.

"Just a talk Conner," he said, "with its own end purpose."

"Well," I fretted, "we are here; talk."

"I am sorry," he said, "I am sorry," he paused, "I am sorry."

"For what dad?" I asked.

"For not being there," he sounded off, "All the years you came to the fire station, bent on my every word, followed me around like a loyal son, and I was so proud to have you there. As you grew older, I allowed my connection with you to go; to somehow grow in distance. I wasn't showing the interest I once had and I left you to fend for yourself; without warning. You grew up and I didn't know it. Nor did I recognize all the changes going on around me. I was too involved; too wrapped up in the duties as a fireman. For this, I am truly sorry, and for all that escaped us."

I paused for a minute, waited for a spell.

"You know dad," I continued, "I remember so many years before you spoke of your father; the times you played catch with him. One day, without warning, he let it go, and no longer made those moments with you. I felt in telling me so you were making a vow to me that this would never happen. These similar mistakes would not be repeated on your behalf. You were to be smarter; more acute, and most aware."

"And lightening struck twice in the same place, at two separate spaces and times in history," he stopped to grin with a saddened look, "and I should be so lucky."

"We have the power to change," I suggested.

"But to my fear," he said, "not the powers to go back with; to alter the past into something different and new."

"I am afraid not," I closed my eyes and shook out my expression with a nod, "I can make all the promises to Cory and they would not mean a thing if I can't, or won't keep them."

"All of my life son," he whispered, "I wanted to be a good father; to you, to Lorie, Amanda, and young Adam."

"And you think you have not been?"

"I hope I have had some influence in your life Conner," he bitterly spoke, "That it was good, and that it aided in making you the man you are," he paused to keep his tears back into the crevices of his heart; those wounds and scars of a long life which beacon the memories to stall and forget at last, "Because I am most proud of you son; for who you are, and the person you have become. If this is a testament to being a good father then I must have done better than I originally thought."

"I think mother had equal part in it," I responded, "and where some of the credit needs to lie."

"Inevitably so," he wrinkled his mouth into a small wad, waited for a moment, and then shook his head to agree with me. "You are the benefactor of the most wonderful mother; and I the most fortunate benefactor of the most gracious wife. For whatever discounts I have, your mother certainly made up for them; and more."

"I am glad you see it this way."

"I never stopped," he said, "no, no," he stood and circled about. "Quite the contrary, I have been most intimate to this."

I watched him prepare his next words as though they were the beginning of a very important speech; a speech one would give at a lodge or a politician's words formally announcing his candidacy.

"What do you think will happen Conner?" he asked, "Where does the end lie for all of us?"

"If I only knew dad," I smiled, tired-like, and massaged my face as I were to lean forward and prop my chin on my hands, "I wish I knew how this all will play out."

"Your mother knows…" he suggested.

"How does she?" I sounded.

"Things she tells me; in preparation for. The look in her eyes; that expression," he said, "After so many years, you know what the words are without the voice to speak them in; a language all its own; the verse incalculable to all but me. It's almost as if you know she will breathe before she does it; clears her throat before the cough comes; a sneeze, the blink before it sets it off."

"I have seen this in both of you," I answered.

"Then you understand," he softly spoke, "how the heart goes."

"And what is her feeling?" I wondered.

"Her time is near," he responded, "she knows. It is not her wish, nor mine, nor anyone's; but that is what fate has delivered. We accept it, and she has accepted it on her behalf."

"But still she fears…"

"Of course she does," he peered out the window and looked along the thick branch of that tree, "I am sure I will as well, when the time comes; as you will son, when your time calls to you."

I felt the shift of a cold frost breeze jaunt through the room; timber its way beyond the cracked door from the first floor below, guide its navigation in a swirl around the room, and settle in a brisk sentiment about me; to the point of making me shiver. Father looked at me with an upward stare; high-bridged nose with his eyes staring down on me as though he was high to the ceiling. He stalled in that formation; frozen for a second in time, calculating, brimming with as strange of a look as I had ever seen. I didn't know him there in that phrase of an expression.

"I pray for her every night," I swallowed hard.

"Do you feel no deliverance in that prayer son?"

"I feel it is being neglected," I replied, "so to answer your question, honestly; yes."

"Don't feel that way son," he stepped closer, "God always has an answer. It might not be what you want to hear; not the choice you desire for; but an answer is there. There is purpose for whatever outcome comes to us; a better choice than what we perhaps can see."

I felt his hand glide about my shoulder, softly pressed, and gripping me into a caring hold.

"Your mother and I have had some discussions, of late."

"I am sure it has little to do with me," I sparked.

"Oh to the difference," he circled to face me, went to the edge of his bookcase and he began to pull a series of envelopes from some hiding place he had in the back edges of one shelf.

"It has been all about you, your sisters, and your younger brother."

"I don't understand," I grimaced.

"You wish to know the purpose of you being here," he looked at me from over the small-framed glasses of his. The eyes rattled off a course of rapid blinks. His face was now studious, learned, and thoughtful to what he was feeling there, "and I will tell you as such."

He gathered up those envelopes; gently, as if he were the procurer of them; handling them in such reverence that there was so much greater meaning in them than the simple, white envelopes which contained and held their message.

"What is it?" I kept my eye squarely to them.

"A message," he replied, "a message in a bottle, but without the bottle," he grinned. "Your mother has always been profound in her constant lessons to you children; antidotes, and prescriptions to the soul as she would call them. The learning process never stops learning; it pushes you farther than you thought you could ever go."

"There is something you wish to give me."

"With conditions," he stuttered, "yes."

"And what are they?" I asked.

He said nothing initially; rather, moving in a circle till he reached the chair opposing mine; sitting about it with a calm elevation for wisdom. He attended to his place as if he were meant for it, and all the wiser for being there. I watched as he withdrew for a spell; to collect the better words for him to speak with.

"Your mother was quite fervent in this, let me tell you," he flopped up one to display it for me.

"A promise is a promise to keep. The other night we discussed, as best as she could, letters she had started to write for you children years ago. And ones she had finished about a year since. She kept them handy, thinking of things she wished to individually say to each one of you; in her own hand, and from her own heart. It was only to be given out to each of you at the time of her death, or near to it."

"And the conditions?" I pondered.

"For you Conner..." He spoke. "Not to be read until she has passed; not ever before..."

"What about the others?" I questioned further.

"The others?" he claimed, "Lorie and Amanda, the same."

"And for Adam..." I continued.

"He is to finish school; to graduate from college," father looked down, eyeing each one of the thick envelopes, "If he never goes to school and gets his degree, he is to never, ever know of this letter. The letter is to go back to a vault at the bank, with clear instructions for it never to be opened."

"Doesn't seem fair for Adam," I objected.

"Her wishes son," he was stern in this, "no compromise."

I looked to the floor and I saw the blackened wood stains from the years of my youth; the knots with a deep rosy outlay, so ran across the boards in varying styles. To honor my mother's wish was to keep her honor, and I would not press any further on the issue.

"She felt it was time Conner," he said, "For you to have yours."

He slowly lifted the white, brown-edged envelope towards me; his hand extended forward to me. "You are the oldest, and your mother felt you should have yours first."

I took the envelope into my palms and I held it with the approach it was the most fragile of things; a harbor of some lost words she wanted me to have. The sea had brought it back from its long journey; cast off from that separate land of her thoughts. A time when she was to be alone, thinking of me, and so wishing to dispel some words of comfort.

I would read it along the shores; at home in front of the fireplace on a long winter's night when all the rest had gone to bed; on the airplane during my flights of business overseas; during vacations, and waiting for my children to gather outside the school; soccer practice and baseball practice; summer leagues and freshman orientation; during service and along the bays of Boston; the sweet summer evenings sitting by the harbor and waiting for the sunset to give its last 'goodbye'. All these times, so precious before, would be all the more precious with her newfound words reading along my mind as I read them.

Their meanings never to lose their luster, yet, as the years rolled along and made me the elderly man I am to become the words would always find new ways to reinvent themselves to me. The phrases still so fresh; moving, and inviting as if her very voice was in whisper to my ear.

There is a special providence a mother gives to her son. The heartwarming venture she shares through her love, and displays it in all the ways a mother can. My mother chose her own message in a bottle; the letter from the sea; in keeping the greatest verse and jewels of her life on record for me to read, and re-read again and again. I discovered the reason for me being here once more.

"Take this in confidence Conner," father said, "and let me do with the others as your mother wishes. Say nothing, but hold to that promise we both now share for her."

"I will," I said, clutching the envelope inside of my jacket.

"I want you to come again son," he smiled, "whenever you like. It will always do my heart good to see you here, in our family home."

I smiled to meet with his and we left for the outdoors. A handshake and a simple wave sent me along my way.

The drive home was to be a brief spell. But as my mind wondered around in the dismal setting and landscape of that down-pouring rain, I felt I had long past an hour or more in drive time.

It was not to be. The moments were truly shorter than I thought, and my wife was waiting up for me as I pulled into the driveway. Sandra met me at the door; the children already tucked to their beds. Lamplights were low and dimmed to allow them their sleep; we tipping about the house in our own version of 'Santa Claus is coming to visit', though I never saw the cookies and milk sitting anywhere on the kitchen table.

"How was it?" she softly whispered with a kiss.

"Something from mother," I produced the envelope.

"Why? You didn't open it Conner," she fiddled with it.

"Not yet," I said in a low tone, taking it from her, "Not yet."

We worked our way upstairs; the letter sitting about the top of my dresser. The long evening would shorten a bit while in our sleep, and so we found ourselves nestled in for as long as the night would draw out to be. I wondered if I would go back to my dream once more, and as those thoughts rung deeply within me, I reminded myself all the more, "Not yet. Not yet."

Chapter 34

I am Visited by the Past.

Several weeks had passed; the winter growing stronger to the day. Seasons of change had bent nature into its strike for fury; an unusual snowstorm had quickly commenced and whitened all of Boston from nearly every peak, every street corner and parlor, and to all the surroundings about and around the city.

This was a fantasy to winter it seemed. Everywhere you turned, all white was showing, and it appeared a sort of melancholy breeze cutting through our lives. No one had prepared for this one; it being too early in the season for such a discharge as we found cropping all over Boston that day.

Three weeks had passed and mother's condition further worsened. From day to day one could not see evident her general digression, but to see week to week there seemed a world of difference in her. The infections in her lungs had nearly made her teeter on terminal; fibrosis struck along with another bout of bacterial pneumonia; a second case, more severe than previous was Sepsis; the lung capacity reducing even more which only increased her anxiety and anxious spells.

She held the continual dependency for the trach and ventilator. And no matter the times off of this machine, or the durations she spent in the cardiac chair, respiratory therapist, and breathing treatments, her condition never made any significant improvement. I had often heard the doctor speak through his glaring words.

"We need to see improvement," he would say. "Otherwise there is even a stronger risk of further infections and disease from her lowering immune system. Her status is tenuous at best, and with these increasing complications it would only lend to her demise."

"So you are saying there is no hope doctor?" I asked.

"If hope does exist," he replied, "it better show up very soon."

"Her lung cavity," I said, "how much does she truly have to utilize in her breathing?"

He held up both fist in a strong curl, and tightly wound.

"This much; with her lung capacity so depleted by the ARDS, she struggles, even with the ventilator, to keep oxygen in her lungs. There never seems to be enough. No matter how hard she tries to breath, she always feels desperately out of breath. We encourage her to cough rather than be suctioned, due to the fact this will only strengthen her lungs. But she has to pool all her energies just for this one simple function; something we entirely take for granted. To have come off the ventilator twice, as she has, is a feat for someone like your self to perform. Even in your healthy condition it would take some measure of performance to do so."

"Do you think she will live doctor?" I spoke, as he looked squarely over me, "Honestly."

"Everyday she remains in this condition leaves her in a status of a ticking time bomb. Her low and compromised immune system coupled by the varying illness, diseases, and deadly infections she is battling, drives her in a very high mortality ratio."

"She only wants to talk," I whispered to him, viewing her through the lines of that window leading into her room.

"I know this has been enormously difficult for you and your family," I felt his hand wrap around my shoulder for comfort.

"True," I speculated, "But I have always been told; no matter how difficult it is, no matter the tragedy you are faced with, the least amount of fortune a person can have. With all these things accumulating against you, you still do not have to try and work through anything that comes your way."

I paused as we both looked into where mother was being attended to by two nurses, "In this case doctor, I don't think I have to look very far at all to find a person who has it worse; do you?"

"No," he shook his head with an attempted smile.

"More than five months," I counted out the long days into months within my mind, "Five very long months for her."

"To have lived this long Conner," he stated, "in the condition she has endured, you are looking at a one in seven million chance."

"Then I wonder," I replied, "who has the greater misfortune."

That evening, our virtual entire family came to the hospital. The children were of course left at bedside under the care and supervision of their sitter.

We discussed many things this late afternoon; difficult, immeasurable things. If she goes into cardiac arrest, what do we do? If she were to lose all consciousness, do we shut the ventilator down? What drugs are to be administered, if any? Should we have her moved? Delivered home and therefore conceding her eventual death from all this. Experimental drugs? Any new programs where her results would be published in a medical journal; apart of a testing group for highly unusual cases? How much morphine to administer? What manner of drugs, therapy would we still have her under course in?

We struggled with all the factions to these problems and we never could reach a determined, unified, and clear solution for which we agreed upon. It was our communal habitat to do and perform what was best in her interest above all else, without consideration to any other. This much we knew then. Her standard of living through what remained in her life had been so severely compromised, we simply knew, though it was never freely spoken, her time was inevitably near to passing. That struck me more than any other. And as we disassembled from the meeting, the mood was quiet, somber, self-evaluating, and very little was said.

Sandra and I walked out into the atrium, found a seat near to the falls and glassed birds singing away. We talked for a time, fought with our own consensus, and tried to make peace with it all. She drew silent through my tears, waited for them to pass like a good rain, and then continued on with our conversation.

Lorie came running forward in a frantic spell.

"Conner!" she yelled, "Conner!"

"What is it Lorie?"

"You need to come quickly," she huffed, "something is wrong with mother. I don't know if it is another breathing spell. The nurse alerted me to get you, dad, and the others."

"Is she alert?" I asked.

"I think so," she wept, "please go, now!"

I ran through the mass of people, down several corridors, to the elevator, and to the floor above us. The sound of those bells; the awkward slumber of that elevator's pace and its inability to go any faster, so nearly forced me out through the top hatch to pull it up by its cable lines. It finally reached the upper chamber floors and I burst from the gates of it to explode down the hallway. I made such a commotion as I went. A few doctors stopped to watch me in my full sprint. I saw one of mother's nurses waiting for me directly in front of ICU; her eyes full to the terror of that moment.

"Mr. James," she said, "please; quickly."

She led me through, and so I found mother wrestling as able as she could, with her straps that were binding her to the bed. She had an explosive look in her eye, as if the end was near; as though she had seen an angel sitting in the corner, quietly waiting for her to pass. The strong glow in her look gave me the sense of her in seizure, or provoked by some hideous devil of a spirit pounding on her. She jerked, yanking at those straps as if they were the only thing between her and her freedom. I made my way forward, and so entered the room to gather by the side of her bed. She took to look at me; straining with that expression like the fight she was currently under.

"Conner," I saw her mouth, catching me eye to eye.

"Mother," I stressed, "mother, calm down. What is it?"

"Don't want to sleep tonight," she desperately mouthed without a sound, though I leaned in closer to try with my hearing.

"Why?" I whispered, "Why mother?"

"Afraid," she jerked. I could see the secretion from her forearms oozing once more through those towel wraps of hers, "So afraid," the trach around her neck nearly popped free.

"There is nothing to be afraid of," I made my attempt.

"Sleep," she replied, "Yes."

"We can help with whatever needs to be done."

She pointed to her call button, clapping her crippled hand on its red push button, and no matter the effort made there was no sound coming through to alert the nurses of her needs.

"Breath," she mouthed, "Can't…in…sleep. Afraid; very…"

"I don't understand…" I grimaced towards her in my own attempt to grasp what she was saying.

"Who…will…know," she weakly said.

"The call button will not work," I looked around, "Nurse, the call button will not work."

"Let me try," the nurse came over, pressed the button, and soon thereafter another nurse came in attendance.

"Not for her," I fussed, "She doesn't have the strength to push it. Not anymore. Don't you see? She is afraid to be alone, and not able to call out; this won't do…This won't do…"

Mother was looking intently at my explanation; all the time shaking her head as if to tell me all was correct in what I was saying.

"If you don't mind; I think a family member should stay the night," I suggested to the nurse.

"Rules are rules Mr. James," she explained. "The hospital strictly forbids overnight visitations in ICU. You may stay in the lobby, waiting room, or downstairs; but not in ICU."

Mother tugged to my arm; I spinning about to see for her concerns once more; her face now more in ease.

"Bell," she whispered without a sound, "Bell."

"Bell?" I was confused.

"Yes," she shook her hand back and forth, "Bell."

I paused and stared out to her with the glimmer of her idea sitting now within my expression. She rattled her hand back and forth, in keeping with that bell image; never relenting until I made some motion to her in further explaining that idea.

"You need a bell," I lowered myself to her, "to ring; in case you need a nurse to come in."

She shook her head to affirm.

"Any bell will do?" I asked. Again, she agreed.

Amanda, followed by father and Adam, came rushing into the room; Sandra was in pursuit shortly thereafter.

"I'll be back mother," I assured her, taking my leave and making quick exit. I stalled to speak with Sandra.

"She needs a bell," I announced.

"A bell?" she questioned.

"Hand bell," I said, "to ring the nurse."

"It's late Conner," she looked at her watch, "half-past eight. The weather is not going to allow for it; nor the road conditions."

"I have to try Sandra," I confessed.

"I'm sure most stores are closed due to the weather."

"I don't know that," I stressed, "I have to try."

"It's too late," she said, "We can talk her into not requiring one. Conner, she doesn't need one."

"Yes," I forced, "she does. Sandra, I have to try."

"It won't matter," I felt Sandra's distress rising.

"To her, it will," I called, "and that makes it all important."

"The nurses will not be able to hear it Conner."

"Tell her that," I was becoming angry by her delay of me, "and then watch her go into a fit; cardiac arrest from that stress. I'll get her the liberty bell if I have to."

"I'll go with you," I felt Sandra's concern coming in her voice.

"Stay with her," I replied, "She needs you."

"But the others are there…"

"She needs you Sandra," I ended, "Keep her calm."

I felt the rush of that situation consume me; unbridle the shackles which bound me no further to that hospital. I was on a search; a rapid, fevered hunt for a single hand-held bell. The symbol of its wake was something of dire comfort to mother, noting how the look of her anxiety pushed past her expression there.

The gift shops, the malls, the downstairs hospital store had nothing from that venue. I ran from the hospital towards my car, which was sitting nearly two blocks away.

The early snows of that day discontinued as they were and reverted into a soggy, drenching, shiver-bone, skin-achy, nose-numbing, blistery-eye rain that consumed every article of my clothing. The whites of the streets had turned into a dirty, muddy, gritty slush with pockets of ice dabbled all about. The forecast was not more to my advantage, but rather for it to continue throughout the night. The cloak of those clouds hung so low, that barely a few feet in front of me was all I could see.

The roads around were desolate, isolating, brittle to human contact, though the homes from street to street all bustled with the warm fires, the cooking chimneys, and night lamps sitting lit in front of windows ceils throughout. I waited for streetlights to change; beating my steering wheel and begging them to go from red to green, though they appeared to stall at every turn.

Many of the stores had disbanded for the evening; the lights hidden in the dusk of those inner shadows; the sign to the front doors flipped to 'closed'. I did find however, a strip area open and still in order of business; a local gift shop still stirring about.

The manager met me at the door and must have thought I was a beggar or vagabond wishing to get out of that torrid rain. My look was appalling; drenched; hair wet and matted, like soggy sticks to my head with rain dripping from my nose, chin, and eyes. I squeaked when I walked like a wet rubber duck; and so looked pitiful as a lost puppy wishing to discover a dry spot.

"If you're looking for money," he stammered, "we have none."

"No," I paused and smiled, "Just need a bell."

"A what?" he strained one eye at me, while the other shut hard, causing his face to grimace in that spell of exaggeration.

"A bell," I repeated, "simple hand, dinner bell."

"Have none," he fussed, flailing his hand upward, "We are closed," he turned his back from me.

"But you haven't looked," I pleaded.

"Sorry," he walked away, "We are closed."

"This is important," I stated.

"Me getting home to a nice and warm evening meal, and a good sturdy pipe smoke is important," he went back to the front door and flipped his sign to 'close' in so the disgruntled manner.

"Fair enough," I pushed through the door, "Give my regards."

I steadily made my way back through that pressing, pinching, pinpointing rain; finding my car as I fumbled with my keys. I looked back, opened my car, and saw that old man re-flip his sign back to 'open'. My gaze shot through to where he stood, bullish in its look and grunting attitude. Yet I continued down the road and discovered the local 'we have everything' shop still open.

"Sorry sir," the man at the counter told me there, "We don't carry anything like that here."

I traveled further west, some four miles to the mall. It also had disbanded for the evening, earlier than expected due to the inclement weather; three stops and nothing; simply nothing for a dying woman to have her wish fulfilled; a simple one of little cost, but holding the key to hope in her eyes. I was to find that bell; relentless to my pursuits, and so I drove further west to where there was a card and knick-knack shop that still happened to be opened.

"Back in the corner; to the left of the journal and diary sections," the woman working the counter instructed.

Indeed they did have hand bells; a dozen to choose from. I did garner the stares of a few hovering folks as I moved through the store. Some attendants kept watch of me, making certain I would not steal or be a thief finding their store as an easy target—I just wanted a bell is all.

And there, to the bottom shelf, sitting alone and dusty from being untouched for months on end, was a 40th anniversary bell. White with pink trim at the base and along the top of the rim, and in golden lettering was to read '40th anniversary' with flowers streaming in two rows. The handle was plain, imperfect, and nearly tilting to one side. But I knew; picking it up, make it rattle in that high-pitch tone it had; this was the bell for her.

I rushed to the counter, in a hurry, did a quick check of my watch to see the hour had just dipped past nine, and now made my way through that all-consuming rain; driving east and pulling back to the parking lot about a quarter past. Through the puddles, slipping past the dark ice, along the catwalks and potholes, through the open ramps and dripping overhangs, I made my way back into that hospital. I shook myself free of all the wetness I could like a drenched dog, and so rushed from front door to elevator.

My family was waiting, breaching the door to her room as if they were a bubble which had surfaced from that edge. They stared on me, mostly in shock at my appearance, though saying little and parting to let me through. Mother had her eyes steady to mine, gifting me a little smile upon my entering. I shuffled forward, seeming as to be the boy she used to send off to school and one who would walk home in the wet rain, snow, or ice; still smiling, brimming ear-to-ear, and shining my white teeth into a sparkle as I went. For that instant, I noticed a little bit of her coming through.

"Thank you," she mouthed, as I placed the bell in her hand.

"Now try," I grinned, and watching her weakly lift her hand, shake the bell from side to side, and the 'ching ching' ring throughout the room and into the ICU main hallway; 'ching ching' 'ching ching', as the melody went. Orderlies, nurses, and night doctors heard the ruckus, and peered in from the open window, listening for the next chiming to commence.

"Thank you," she replied, seemingly reassured.

"We have a date tomorrow," I bent to kiss her forehead, "Agreed?" I winked on her.

She smiled and nodded out her head as I backed away.

I was flushed with emotions; stirring within the stewpot of my soul. I had expensed all out, pulled out the pennies I thought Heaven had sent down for my namesake; they sitting in the loaves of my pocket; wet as I, cold and clamming, and I placed them on the table for my own display out in the waiting area; three shining pennies and a fourth, dull and copper-looking one. I rocked in my sitting, clasping my hands around my belly; the emotions tearing through me; my face in a wrinkle as I bent lower. I could sense the tears emerging from my own eyes, as if my soul was beginning to rain as hard as the weather outside.

"Conner," my sister Lorie came to my side; her shadow dark and converging, "Are you alright?"

"No," I pulled my hand to my brow, weeping noticeably then, "Don't; give me room, give me room."

I stood to see Sandra coming from mother's room. She stopped; mouth gaping free, and her eyes bulging at the contact of mine. I knew she could see the rapture I was under.

"Conner?" she asked, though I looked, backed away, and said nothing, "Conner?"

Our look disconnecting there; I wandering away into the bed of that elevator and motioning my self down.

It was as if I had entered the loneliest period to my life; a passage to self-discovery; a night where the world rocks on its axis and I no longer know where reality lies. It is a time of pivotal beginnings, of somber endings; of emotions that delve into the very essence of ones' heart to see the mirror to your soul. Suddenly, the deepest light in your being comes to a brighten shade; you, sitting amidst this realm and so seeing the very elements of your life, and you can sense the very heartbeat to your spirit.

It is a time when you speak to yourself; a moment, however fractured from time and space, as endless as the wondering seas to the Atlantic. I was not sitting on the Boston harbor and shores, and looking out into those infinite waters. I was inside, looking deep into myself, and so seeing there was no horizon there as well. Only the forever ghosts to my life; the hauntings of my past; of those long lost friends and family before, now escaping from their box to tell me of my mother's soon travels.

I ran to no place intended; there was no prescription to my navigation—only that I must run. The rains were beating forever harder, pressing on me, and nearly weighing me down. The streets bellowed with their ancient history and calls; I feeling the walks of those before me from long ago. I held no sense to where I was or to where I was to go; my destination as un-approaching as if I were to be just born and I had no clue to the life I was to have.

Those shadows of the night cloaked the city in grays and black. So dismal were they in that mist and fog, the harshest demon of showers fell and converged from all around. At first I had no gumption to where I had ended up at; whirling about as I sat in my confusion until the landmarks close by told me my approximate vicinity. I was very close to the Common Gardens.

I thought Buck must have been calling me and perhaps the overture of Spike's voice as well. I went through those long yards and short grasses, beyond the hedges and trees, and so reaching the Central Burying Ground. I was being governed by nothing but instinct now; my thoughts and my ongoing actions were only colliding in the dark hue of that night.

I spun in a three hundred and sixty degree rotation, capturing the aurora of my surroundings; the shivers of my spine were cascading up and down my body and I fell into a huge puddle at the outset of their affliction.

At last my world had collapsed; the hope of all, seemingly gone; evaporated, escaping into the night air and midnight rains.

"Oh father," I prayed in tears; mine and Heaven's both, "not like this. Show her mercy; a woman as graced as any, should not suffer so much. She deserves better, and you know this," I wept deeper still "You have to know this."

I bent lower to touch my face with the puddle. Those pelts of rain pinning me down in the darkest shade of that rainbow my mother always spoke of; that rainbow to life. I could see no colors, and I had discovered there was no beauty in that shade.

"Conner James," I heard a voice whisper through that wind and rain, "Conner James, attend to me."

It was like a whistle in the midst of a hurricane; with winds so in howl, and rains so driven like horses to a race, yet even in its softest verse, I could hear it as plain as if the whole world had grown silent in its wake.

"Who is calling me?" I lifted my head up.

"Have you forgotten?" it spoke.

"Do I know you?" I squinted about, rubbing the rain from my face. I dried out my eyes, "Where are you?"

"I am here," I heard it again.

"Where?" I pleaded, looking around me.

"Do not deny what you can not see off-hand, and say that it is not real…" the voice advised me.

"Then how will I know who you are?"

"Think," It whispered, "And remember."

The silence fell through that rain and downpour; a moment; an etching in time where some string of life from Heaven became as rope to my rescue.

"I don't have any money," I cried, thinking perhaps a robber had followed me to this gravesite.

"I require none," the voice came back, "Only you to attend me, nothing more."

"You must want something," I advised.

"For you to reflect is all," it was a man's voice.

"And what am I to see?" I wondered, squinting further into that drowning-out lash of rain, and still seeing no one on the bay edge of it, "I am in no mood for riddles."

"A boy; a man," he described, "Only time and space tells of those differences. You are still the boy I once knew, for the shadow to your soul follows you like a silhouette; never leaves you, like an imprint to your life, and the man you are, and have so become."

"You knew me once then," I applied.

There was a shortness in that pause, when, at the length of four grave rows, I saw a figure standing still in the outpouring of this rain. He was as drenched as I, though no identity of him directly prevailed. Still, I could see the outline of the man he was, and I watched his every move with the intent to picture him from some period in my past.

"You were a boy, standing along at this grave; your sister and you were sitting below, thinking the words to a flower," he said.

"Daffodil," I whispered with a sense of awe; my expression straining further out to see him, "Mr. Haberstaff?"

"And there," he pointed out, "We rode your kite to the skies; the river and the bridge; I spoke to you then," he slowly began to step closer to me.

That image of him coming toward me there was as locked in my mind as the impression I held for him from so many years ago. There wasn't a single difference; no separation, and he so appeared as if he had come from my yesterday like it was truly yesterday.

It is like a time when you blink, keep your eyes closed for a spell, and then re-open them; time, space, history have all changed, yet he just walked out from the long yards from my past and into the present time of my life.

My heart nearly roared like a lion at such a sight and I thought the moment was hanging in its own camouflage, trying to trick me into believing something that wasn't truly real.

I had imagined what ghosts would look like before this moment; a prescribed idea and notion of the garments; their wears, looks and mannerisms, and this defied all of my former ideals.

"Mr. Haberstaff?" I said with a stunned gaze, "How can this be?" My mouth gaped wide as he came into the dimmest light.

"It redefines all that we know, doesn't it Laddy?" he spoke.

"Do you normally skip along time like this?" I curiously asked, "Like skipping a rock along the waters instead of being pulled out by the tides," I suggested, "You haven't changed."

"We all change Conner," he said, "in our own time."

"You are an angel," I inquired, seeing him as each step he took made him most clear to my eyes. And the deeper he came, the more amazed I became at the stuttering sight of his presence.

"I am a messenger," he politely bowed, "from God's wing."

"I held out such hope," I prayed, "that the end would be better than it has been; that somehow God would intervene."

"And God has," he stated.

Mr. Haberstaff was now in full view; his eyes glowing with the ancient wears he held. Those harsh lines sitting in his expression brought his look back into my memory, though his smile seemed warmer than before.

"I don't see it," I somberly replied, "If it is there, I can't see it."

He placed his hand onto my shoulder, though I was not reluctant to allow him to do so.

"And so is the wind," he returned, "and you can't see this either, but for the things it blows upon."

"I don't know how to make sense of this."

"Do you remember Laddy, what I once spoke to you?" he said, "Upon the bridge; the years before. Do you remember?"

"No," I shook my head, "I don't."

"Those words," he seemed to plead, "Please remember."

"I can't," I fussed.
"Laddy…" he tried a second time.
"I can't," I was more aggressive, "Alright?"
"Then we must take a walk."

He guided me around the varying grave plots, and past the hedges. And as we approached the Lagoon Bridge the rain faltered in its pace, seeming to withdraw from the downpours of before. I could see the shadows of those clouds above rip apart in that fairing weather moment. The gilded stage of dark sky and speckled stars above began to illuminate when nature withdrew its waters, and so allowed the beauty of that night to glow through. The evening suddenly turned into an enchanting one; the insects and frogs made their calls from every pond shore; the waters were in a gentle ripple and cascade of their own devise, like a deep river motor which was churning those tiny waves to bubble about and lip the shores.

I saw the canvas of this picture appear like a refuge to me. The trauma I just felt before seemed to dissipate. And how I felt like a child again, rediscovering for the first time a friend once lost to me who now had returned. I stopped at the edge of this quiet bay and lagoon; the freshness of that air, and how it interacted with the wind to blow against me and speak out those soft whispers of nature into my ears.

It was the glory of that moment. It was the glory of that time. It was a moment in time when your hope is reborn; alive and well, and smiling through your eyes and expression.

There were silhouettes of geese drifting along the waters there. Some were sifting through the outer rim of that lake while others made motion for the bridge and gently paddled out in circles for a time. One could see the last remnants of these clouds drift away. How the white torrent moon poked through to shimmer along those dipping waves. I could see the moon in every fabric of the lake, as if it were stitched on its blanket.

The whole scene was as though a dream lost from the memories, now reconstructed before your very eyes. I marveled at how that glow from the moon burned so white and how it held such an illumination all throughout this venue. It appeared like an eye from some Heavenly ghost watching and inspecting us as we strolled along that little harbor.

How moments become so diverse, even in short installments as before. How alone I felt just a short time ago, and now, standing on the edge of the bridge and looking out over that rippling glow of the moon's reflection, I felt the warmth and comfort of my friend beside me.

"Look upon the waters Conner," he whispered; I bending low to send my sights within that strange well, "Look deep."

"What am I to see?" I asked.

"The truth of your life," he responded.

I kept to my stares; never to blink, but to remain as I was; looking, straining with the power of my lenses to see what he apparently could see, and I was just beginning to realize.

"Your life is like the history of a river," he announced.

I looked further and out the murky depths just below me, I could see something rippling through. The days of my past coming in review; places and times, events and occasions, parties and celebrations, moments of happiness and cheer; all days when life was a fruit bowl filled with fruit for me to taste.

The memories sent shock waves through me as if I were there, reliving my life all over again. Those joyous times were the sweet taste from so long ago when I was younger still; hoping, wishing for the days I would come to know as part of my life. My father, mother, sisters, brother, friends, and grandmother were all in the belly of that little sea; showing to me what had become a part of my past. At last I saw myself at the very moment when I was staring into those waters. It was now a reflection to me from my past; the time when Mr. Haberstaff spent that Saturday with my family and me.

"Do you remember now?" he whispered; a hand to my shoulder, though I kept to my stare.

"Yes," I returned in a whisper, "I do."

"Through time," he stated, "This lake; this river; this pond, becomes as old as you. Shows to you how the future will become in your life, then slowly descends like the moments of life you go through; once a river of the future, it now becomes the river to your past Conner." He paused, "You asked me once what it shows to me. Conner, I have lived my life; a good life; a life that when I reflect on I can always smile at and remember on; always remember on."

"But there is still more to come," I said, "for me."

"Yes," he replied, "this river for you is still in transition."

"Not yet the river to my past then..." I suggested, "But if my mother were to come, would it be like your river? A river from years gone by; no waters to show her what will come?"

"Remember Conner," he seemed to plead, "Those moments; that time we shared together..."

"I can't" I said, "I was so young."

"When the time comes, be there for your mother. There will be a time she will need you most. This time, this very moment, is now."

I felt his hand leave my shoulder, as I lifted my eyes to see the moon glow warm on those ripples out along the long stretches of this river.

"Do for her as she has done for you. Be brave and be ready."

His voice trailed off as he spoke this last phrase.

"If only I knew," I spoke, "I could have better prepared myself for this moment. It was coming; you warned me, and I didn't see it still. I should have been better prepared."

"How can you?" He pondered, "You never observed it before. How can one prepare them selves for a time like this? There isn't a way. It's a time where fate delivers you through those doors to the very man you are to become."

"Then why tell me?" I looked up to him.

"Because Conner," he bent down to me, "God wanted you to know there was comfort even at the darkest days of your life; her life, and he wanted you to know this."

"Is that your purpose?" I asked, "Your reason for being here?"

"I am here for you Conner," he smiled.

"And what about her?" I wondered.

"That is for you," he responded, "for you to do. You are like me Conner in that sense. It's time for you to hold her hand through this last age of her life."

It struck me harsh by his words that I knew then it was her design to leave her life, her home, the ones she loved, and to be separated from us for the many years to come.

I wept hard on this; so very hard on this, clutching my hands to my face and going into an Indian-sit. I felt the well to my soul was expensing out all my tears from my life; drying the very resource of my emotions into a desert. I felt the fear and horror of it all engulf me; those shadows I was sitting in were from the darkest place in my life. I wanted to run from it; hide somewhere where I could find light. But there was no place to go; only to descend into that tunnel. Be brave and wait for that travel to bring me back into light once more.

"There isn't enough prayer in this world to stop this…" I asked, clutching my hands hard to my face, "nothing I can say to God to convince him to intervene on her behalf."

"Conner," he pulled my hands free from me, "What is to be, is as though they are shadows in those waters already in place. They will come; those moments; those times; just like the winds to your life will blow in every direction. There is greater purpose than just in this particular moment you are sitting in. You just can't see it. Someday you will know and you will understand all the virtues of these events which are unfolding…"

He looked at me heartfelt, and with a speckled smile.

"But when?" I gazed out over those waters again, "tell me…"

"You will know," he said, "and your faith will tell you so."

I gathered myself to my feet and I leaned out over the railing before me. I stared out onto the moon now sitting higher in its perch. The cold breath of that coming winter chilled me to the bone; though only a moment in time, it still held the force of a most perilous breeze, and I shuttered when it hit me.

Mr. Haberstaff was the prayer I had asked for, though it was not my initial intent. It was indeed the answer to that prayer I had so often lofted toward Heaven's ear. I looked at him and saw his smile engage me, be the warming influence to my soul, and now so give me the strength to continue.

I feared what was to come. Yet in knowing some element of conclusion to it, I could now learn to rest at peace with it. The fear of not knowing was greater than the fear of what might inevitably be the outcome to this all. I would miss my mother and I knew the time was even more precious now. Every breath she was taking was bringing her ever closer to her last, and I felt the need to go to her side and be there for as long as it would take.

I would not speak of this to my siblings or to my father; Sandra and my children would never know of this. It was to be my secret and my secret alone. There are times in one's life when only you know the very heart to your world; places where you go, and you alone. This was one of those places. A room where Heaven and God wants to talk with you, speak with you, and send some feather from Heaven to make sure you know they are there. Mr. Haberstaff was to be the very wing for which I was to fly on; the kite to soar with. All I needed was to take a running start and watch myself fly.

Our time was to come to an end; and on the shores of a hug and a long farewell, this time came to pass in my life. We walked from the bridge, and I found myself constantly looking out over those waters. The moon and her brilliant glows sat along the bed of this pond and they seemed to shadow our every move.

We reached the outskirts from where we started; our ending was to be here, along the graveyard where I learned the meaning of that daffodil.

"Will I ever see you again Mr. Haberstaff?" I looked to him.

"There is always a tomorrow Conner."

He smiled, bent his head in a slight bow, turned, and made his way through the grave plots. I watched him go deeper into the night; the moon's ire reflecting along his path as he went until the distance and landscape caused him to disappear from me.

I wondered where that place would be, where he and I would meet again; what it was like; how Heaven would be when I first see it. I felt at this moment I was standing on the edge of this new world; that precipice reaching far with its viewpoints, and I, standing alone, looking out over her infinite shores, and seeing the world my mother would be seeing soon.

Chapter 35

Friendships and a Story.

Time has its own memory and they call it history. Those patches of our lives we reflect on; absorb like a sponge when they occur in our lives, and how we move on into a solitary path to be called our own destiny. We can look back and remember, see the world as it was, and reminisce in those times as if we were spending a most special, sunny day in the meadows of a beautiful park.

I was in one of those times in my life; always reminiscing, looking back with a sense of fondness and duty to where my life had come from. We tend to remember the goodness of what was, hold onto those virtuous clips from our growing years; like tethering stitches to keep us together through the tough times we experience. Alas, we revert back to what we know, and knew, and so recall from our own memory.

It was like a fog in my mind; occasionally becoming clear and so showing me the world of my life in replay. I could smile then in the feast of my reflection and I could drink from its free-flowing wine.

Several days had passed since my eclipsing, unexpectant interlude with Mr. Haberstaff. I took to heart what he said; locked away the advice he rendered to me, and went to my mother with the idea and hope to stir within her all the good times we shared.

I spent the betterment of two days by her side, and as long as she could stand it, I spoke freely of my days from memory and from hers. It was then I saw more smiles from her than in the previous five months collectively. I believe it did her heart good to see just how much influence those times, and her self, held in my life. She made a difference and I made her aware of this.

Adam and Amanda always came in tandem; father was escorted by Lorie to a certain point through the hospital. With a gentle kiss and a hug she let dad go to check in on mother while she took to wait; sometimes alone in that crowded, stuffy waiting room. I knew she was left to the affects of her own tears during that time, though Marshall would come once he got off from work.

Mother's condition had changed toward more deterioration. It seemed a foregone conclusion to me now and as Hamlet would say, 'the readiness is all' seemed rather profound to me.

Doctor Ogden had a brief moment with the family. His grim face spoke volumes more than what his words could possibly say.

"If you please," he began, pulling us like cattle into a private room, "We have had to move her central line for the antibiotics; for the simple reason her old line could blow. She has acquired a blood bacteria infection which we are rigorously treating with new antibiotics; as well as a urinary infection."

"How was this caused?" Amanda worriedly asked.

"Possibly from her old central line," he said, "Quite frankly, this is a very resistant strain of bacteria; more potent. It is a setback," he trailed off with this.

"How much more can she take?" father whispered.

"Not much," Doctor Ogden spoke, "She is very tenuous now. We are giving her Laysik to help relieve her lung congestion. She is also showing signs of infection in her kidneys; however unrelated to the Wegener's itself—we believe."

"That's not it Doctor," I looked at him with a stone stare, "There is more; I can see it in you."

"There is," he paused, "of greatest concern is a disease called Anthrosepsis; bacteria infection. It's new, relegated only in the last few years. A counteract of bacteria to the measure of antibiotics we have instituted over the years."

"The infections are becoming smarter," Amanda stated.

"In a manner of speaking," he said, "You have to treat them like living organisms. They are simply looking for ways to survive. In my experience I have never had a patient survive this particular bacterial infection before. Not to say it would ever occur. It just has not been my experience to date."

"Is there really any good things we can hope for?" Lorie questioned, as I could see her flushing of tears begin again.

"Life," he replied, "Is always Hope…"

"That's a generic reply," Lorie wept and rushed out of the room; Amanda took to following her for comfort.

"I know what you are saying Doctor Ogden," father stammered through his speech, coughing back his own tears, "but there must be something, anything we can do."

"I pride myself on being honest," he said, leaning toward dad, "Even when there seems to be no remedy for it. Your wife is simply being overwhelmed by all her infections, her continual bouts to fight off disease. Each time she has to endure another setback it further weakens her. We are giving her Linezolid and Synercid to assist in her fight, but ultimately the fight is hers. She has to win it and she has the greatest influence in the outcome."

"Then do what you can Doctor," dad said.

"Anything else?" Adam seemed to be fit for anger.

"Don't be alarmed by the crackling sound in her chest, especially when she breathes. It's a mere element to her lung infection. She is running a fever; has continual nausea as you well know; gagging and vomit episodes throughout each day."

"Then maybe we should pray for her death," Adam angrily stood to face the outer window leading into the hospital gardens.

"Mr. James, I am not the convict here."

"I didn't say you were," Adam shot back.

"Adam," I stressed, "this is not the time."

"Then when is it?" He fussed while coming to me, "Huh?"

"Get a grip," I grunted.

"Don't you see?" He grabbled with me, "Maybe we should have her moved. She obviously isn't getting the needed care here."

"I wouldn't advise that," Doctor Ogden spoke out.

"Why?" Adam forced.

"Your mother is teetering on going back to the vent. Mobility will only traumatize her to the point she will require it again. She has no reserve in her lungs; none. The significant impairment of her lungs from the ARDS has not reversed itself like we had hoped."

"What are you saying Doctor?" I looked at him more seriously.

"The damage to her lungs," he paused, "in essence is permanent; non-reversible. In the best-case scenario now, she will need a 24-hour skilled nursing facility. And if she were to go onto the ventilator once more; for the third time, it is likely a life-long, though very brief occurrence. Moving her would undoubtedly seal her fate in this."

"I just don't think you want her moved is all," Adam grumbled.

"At this juncture, yes," Doctor Ogden stressed, "She needs more time to recoup; gain her strength so we have the chance to place her on portable oxygen."

"I think otherwise…"

"Think what you like Mr. James," the doctor stipulated, "We are having the most difficult time balancing her fluids. One rush of such fluid to her lungs, with their limited capacity as they are, would drown her. And in the very least condemn her to the hospital under ICU for the remainder of her life."

"I think she might give up what she had left," Adam suggested, "just for one last day at home."

"In normal circumstances," Doctor Ogden proposed, "I would agree; whole-heartedly. However, if we were willing to make such an attempt, she would not survive the trip, and would so perish en-route."

"She would not even make it home," dad replied.

"I am afraid not," the doctor shook him off. "Her 'O2' level simply isn't strong enough to support such a venture. She would die within minutes of leaving this hospital."

I lowered my head between my arms in hearing all this, "then our choice doctor is really that we have none."

"I think this is safe to say," he reacted, "yes."

"Adam," I looked to my brother, watching him pace more nervously than ever, "go sit with mother."

He said nothing, though cast down a formidable stare at me and took to exit the room where only father, the doctor, and my self remained.

"I suppose we need to make arrangements," I weakly said over to my dad. I looked into his eyes and I could see the horrible burden dripping from his expression; like cascading waters from a waterfall. He said nothing, though pondered the meaning to my words, and so shook his head to agree with me.

"I don't believe we are at that point," the doctor suggested.

"But close," I responded.

"Close," he said, "yes."

"Thank you Doctor Ogden," I sighed, "for your honesty."

"Might I say," he sounded, "I know your family has been through much. This has been very hard on all of you; in different aspects and in different manners. We see this much too often, though not nearly to this grave extent. I admire you all; dealing with the length and duration of what you all have been through. It has been honestly a source of inspiration to many of us here at the hospital. To see a family so dedicated to a loved one."

"Well you know doctor," I leveled to keep my tears at bay, though they seemed to drip through as I spoke, "That woman in there; you will never fully know just how much, is one of the most special creatures on this earth. It's a shame you don't know this; not like you could; not like we do. But I suppose many families before us have said the same, and the families after us will as well. But still; even still, her qualities are more than you can imagine."

The room settled into its own spell of silence; where expressions spoke the words which were left behind in that deafness. I stared back into my own world of remembering; of days in youth when we were all younger still; thinking, remembering as if I were still there.

The doctor became more thoughtful; grinning, shaking his head as if he somehow understood the extent of what I said. Father delved back into his isolated world of depression; where shadows grow long and deep into one's eyes to become stoic and cold. He was frozen there; his heart showing the initial signs of rupturing like a dam once more.

I stood, pardoned myself; going to mother's room and finding Adam alone, sitting religiously by her bed. She was fast, sound asleep; now in a better world of her dreams while Adam held his head down into her covers. He was weeping at her side with a muddled grown that seemed to muffle in her sheets. The winter was beginning to takes it affects on us all now.

I left the hospital for a spell there as I moved to the gardens, which were sitting between an array of buildings. The wind was brisk and confining me to my heavy clothes. Much to the point I bristled when even the least of dustings stirred about those general gardens. I looked above at the pearl sky of blue; those mountains of soft pillow clouds rising from some unseen bay, moving in slow motion from left to right. Those gusts and blows had their own language it seems; dying in the midst of the previous rush, then picking up speed again and blowing around me in a whirl. The leaves danced to their own muted songs.

The grounds were vacant; no benches were in full, nor was anyone there for the sitting. The brown patches, once flowing with every breed of flower, now only held to the late perennials, which somehow festered to stay alive just before the winter would hit.

I heard the traffic to my rear. The buses pulled out and to a halt at the light, and yet screeched from some old and tired brake pads still in service. There were the streetwalkers off in the distance, though they looked like tiny men and women seemingly taking forever to travel along that long bay and harbor.

The world never stopped; never appeared to take a care for the sudden rupture of my mother's flower. But little did they know time had stopped; rather, held something in reverse, and as I sat along that cold and black bench, I went back in time in my own mind.

My history was like my brother's paintings; reflections; still; colorful, yet unique, and when one looks upon them, they see something of themselves between those wooden frames. A pastureland where I used to play upon; a landscape where the summer sun danced in the meadows and hid behind those brushing clouds above; it is a cross between what was once real and what was imagined; something of mutual influence.

And as it hangs on the wall to his studio as it would hang from the vaults in my own mind, those who would cross it would reflect, perhaps even smell the rose of its stem and ponder the illusion to what it was showing them.

I could have stayed there for hours and so see the world around me never change; never show cause for concern. The day was only as long as their memory would be, and I could sense they were doomed to repeat themselves just like the next day and the next day after this. The cycle of ever life would continue without pause. I felt a heavy, stiff hand collapse over my shoulder.

"Little pa," I heard a voice call; unmistakably Gerry. I turned to see his smiling and broad face glaring down over me like a dark cloud obstructing the sun from my view.

"Gerry," I squinted and smiled, "good friend; you have come."

"I just sees what it is," he grinned and sat beside me as we both looked out over the harbor.

His tight curl hair was noticeably gray now; the punctuating smile and long gaping grin were older, more wrinkled than I remembered. Still you could see the heart of his soul still beaming through, "Come by to fancy a call on my friend; you see?"

"It's good of you to come," I stated.

"Born out of nature than anything else," he smiled, "I just hads to come; like an old habit that dies hard…You can't get rid of ole' Grumble."

"Nor would I want to…" I remarked, leaning forward and looking at him with a smile of my own.

"How have you been Little Pa?" he looked serious.

"As good as expected; as well as one anticipates."

"No time for speeches," he gazed out into the harbor as he spoke, "don't claim to be very good on that…"

"You do better than most…"

"And what of your ma?" he asked.

"Gerry," I softly spoke, "She is going to die."

"Don't suppose nature has a choice in the matter," he responded; more serious in his expression than ever.

"If it did," I replied, "it never asked me for my opinion."

"There is always hope," he stated.

"Sometimes I wonder," I returned.

"The cross?" he questioned, "You have it?"

I said nothing but to pull it from beneath my shirt.

"Then you wears it for a reason. Otherwise you would have it sitting at home, locked away. Good and shut in; not like how Buck would have wanted it worn."

"It never leaves me," I said.

"Then Hope doesn't either," he placed his large hand over my shoulder's edge, "Buck would have been mighty fine proud the way you kept your duty to it Little Pa."

"You think?" I laughed.

"I knows," he stressed, "That's why he wanted you to have it. That's why the misses has one just like it. He brought you two together; like a good influence long after he is gone. It's like a wind that starts here. You don't see it, hear it, feel it, until it moves all the way to where you are. It was always there; it just hadn't reached you yet. Like a good prayer's answering."

"Well I have sure prayed enough…"

"And like a good wind," he said, "it will blow your way; the answering. Just has to reach you is all."

"Hope," I sounded off, leaning back.

"Hope lasts as long as your faith does," he announced, "as long as you have faith; God-given; Heaven-inspired kind, then your Hope will never die and it will live long after your mother goes."

"Where did you get such wisdom Gerry?"

"Doesn't go to the smarts or to the rich…Just goes to the simple ones," his face grew a smile that nearly burst out his white teeth in every direction.

"You came all this way to talk to me about a cross and a prayer?"

I smiled at seeing his broad river of teeth glaring on me.

"Well, well," I heard a voice from the rear intercede on us, "If it isn't little Conner all grown up."

I could tell, though somewhat aged and farther along in years, it was the voice of Kelly. I turned, lifted myself from the bench, and so saw the smiling, attractive woman she had become staring back at me.

She pressed forward and came to me with a hug and a further whisper, "I knew you would turn out to be a handsome beau."

"I thought you had left Boston years ago," I stated.

"I did," she smiled, "But at some point in time I knew I had to return home; and so I am here. Just moved back from Washington a few months back. Retired politician's wife, and looking for a little leisure before I get too old to enjoy it."

Behind Kelly came three young women and girls. Two were appearing to be in their very early twenties; the other just crossing out of her late teens. They all, in their own separate and unique manners, carried the shadow of Kelly in them; the eyes were all the spitting image of her pupil's own.

"And I knew you would always be a good mother," I whispered through my hug to her after I reviewed all three of them standing politely behind her.

"I suppose we held that dream for one another," she pulled free and held me there with her loving expression.

"I think we did well."

"Well," she gifted me with another grin; "I suppose we met with each of our expectations for the other."

She turned to her eldest daughter and began to introduce them one by one.

"This is Karla; the sudo-graduate student whose major is everything Georgetown has to offer," she took to pause, "Reba; all batting eyes and beauty starlit queen, and I might add Junior Miss. Illinois two years ago—Now grand master hostess as newspaper editor for a regional news group at Temple University."

"Then this leaves you much to live up to," I looked to the youngest daughter, "much to aspire for…"

"Melanie," Kelly was formal to say, "Hasn't found much by way of her niche yet."

"Oh mother," she shyly interjected, "orthodontics."

"A formidable aspiration then," I reacted.

"May we take a walk?" Kelly asked of me and I so obliged.

We took out to our stroll without much a word said. She clutched tight underneath my arm as we went along the harbor's side. There was something of great and enormous weight building in her thoughts there. And the more we stepped into that silence, the more I could feel the difficulty she was apparently having with it.

"How is your mother?" she asked.

"As well as her dilemma would allow."

"If I had known," she replied, "I would have come much sooner. Your mother has always been there for me; more than you know Conner. She actually taught me in Sunday school; was a mother figure when I had none."

"Is that why you are here?" I questioned, "I do appreciate your condolences and your' reflecting…"

"Its not that Conner," she stopped me, "I just wanted you to know; to let your family know that by your mother's hand, I have been so blessed; beyond belief. My husband and I are starting a scholarship fund in your mother's name at Georgetown…with your permission of course."

"That's not for me to decide," I said, "but I am sure she would feel it to be a gracious honor."

I watched Kelly as her look fell back into herself; thinking of the days many years ago; the time just after Buck passed away.

"Do you think still unkindly towards Heaven?"

"No," I shook my head, "It's a place where dreams go to stay; waiting for me to get there."

"And is it where your mother goes also?"

I leaned out over the hedging on that bay; the waters more crystal and crisp in their waves as they washed by me with the glimmer of that sunny, bright day.

"I am no longer a child," I began, "You think of the world differently. You have gotten bigger while the world seems to grow smaller. The vastness of it; once so infinite, seems now so finite. That somehow your childhood was merely an illusion. I look back now and think of the world I came from; all that it was, and the one person who made it all so special to me. Now I see that her life too, is finite; fading just like the days of my childhood are."

I paused to glimpse back over at Kelly.

"Heaven you ask? It hasn't changed. But I wonder if I ever had the right perception of it to begin with," my voice faded into a whisper, "Just like my childhood…Just like my childhood…"

"You'll find your own peace with this Conner."

"I suppose," I weakly smiled, "Time will tell."

"You will," she responded, "Because I did with my father. It always does; it's the nature of things, and how they progress."

"Maybe it's her time to go," I wondered, "Seems fitting the matriarch of the family goes first. I'm sure it takes some time to set up a good home in Heaven for your family."

"You'll miss her no less," she grinned; the heavy lights of that day basking in her lighted expression, "You told me once your mother spoke that Time has a present each day for you; some good; some bad. It's all in the rainbow of Life." She moved closer to me.

"Conner, what present do you think these days hold for you?"

I nearly wept on how she spoke this to me, looking at her thoughts as they fell past that glare of hers; coming so sweetly and sincerely through her eyes as she stared over me.

"To have a chance to say 'goodbye'…To know nothing is left unsaid; undone…"

"Then you should go out and embrace this dear," she held my face in her hands, pointing her eyes in look of me. In our embrace there along that waterway, I felt the moment stop longer than the moment should. Kelly had embodied the truth of her motherhood at last.

"It's a hard thing to endure," I pulled free.

"No one said it would be easy," she returned, "But everyone will tell you, those who have gone through it, it's a gift to cherish…At least this much for me that I can say for myself."

""How did you feel when you lost your father?"

"Terrified," she said, "Alone; empty. That the world had become more cruel that at any time in my life."

"So why go through with it?"

"If you don't? You will agonize over it for the rest of your life," she stalled in her words, "And if you do? Then as time goes by; gives you a chance for you to reflect on it. You will always see it as a treasure box in your life. A moment when you gave completely, without purpose for yourself, but with the greatest purpose for someone you love."

"There should be an easier way," I kept my head low.

"Oh Conner," she smiled, pulling my chin to face her once more, "Your not a child, but some things never change."

"You've been praying for me…" I stated, "It's you."

"I have," she said, "and your mother."

"You said once if you pray real hard, you will see the ones closest to you in your dreams that same night."

I looked at her with a sense of awe.

"Yes I did," she replied, "How thoughtful of you to remember."

I pulled further away from her, but kept to my smile.

"Thank you Kelly," I said, "You are grace to kindness. I must go and attend to my mother."

We held to one final embrace; a stillness when the seconds collapse and halt their procession forward. It was a moment when two kind souls collide and find a connection with one another, as Kelly and I did then.

I made my way back towards the inner halls of that hospital. The floors were uncommonly active for that time of day. The bustle crowds and roving personnel seemed to stop-up those hallways in a heavy bottleneck; still, I made my way through.

Her room was teaming with nurses, two doctors, my father, and my sister Amanda. All were settled by mother's bedside as she appeared to be sound in some sickly sleep; not normal to rest, but such a retirement one feels when they have continually battled against all odds, and seemed now to be slowly losing that battle.

"May we be excused?" I asked all to permit a moment alone.

The doctors reluctantly agreed; father and Amanda included, and as quickly I found myself alone with my mother.

She never made direct movement towards me; rather holding to her idle, precarious sleeping posture as I moved about her and settled to a seat across from her window. I looked out partly to that dimming day and partly to her still and motionless frame. Her eyes were gently tucked behind her eyelids, though they seemed to bob about, as though they were fractured in that rest.

"I read a book once," I began, "called 'A Diary's House'. In it, the grandmother told her grandson of a story many years before, of a woman who lived in this village. She was so well liked. All the townspeople knew her by her first name. And when she came below into the town where the vendors and local shop owners were, she would brighten up their day with her laughter and her cheer. They so enjoyed her company and her friendship. She was like bright sunshine. She had a son who followed her everywhere, and he was like the spitting shadow of her. Wherever she went, he went with her. One day a drought began throughout the land; was so severe and appeared to last for weeks-on-end; into months. So much so, the crops and livestock began to die. People were afraid of starvation, sickness, and were certain they would have to leave or face dying."

I stopped to watch her steadily, though she never parted from her motionless lay on that hospital bed; I continued.

"This woman's son became sick; deathly ill and he died. The mother cried for days-on-end; her echoes and tears could be heard long into the nights. The day became a very sad place. The mother wept and wept for her lost son, and as she cried, her tears created a river which flowed into the entire town. This river saved the village from the drought; a river of tears. The woman reappeared one day; as she was; as she always was; still full to the happiness she always endeared herself to.

She had conquered her sorrow and everyone revered her for it. All the townspeople went to this river of her tears; taking these small vials and filling them up with her tears. They sent them far and away; these vials, along with her story; a story of hope, of endurance, and of love; for a woman who loved her son, and she never forgot this love…"

I kept to a moment of silence; moving closer still and sensing the presence of her soul near me.

"Mother, I believe you are this very woman I read about so long ago; a children's tale come to life, right before my very eyes…In you…"

I saw the tears of my mother rolling down the sides of her upper face, though she lay there without recognition. Beyond all that this illness prevented her from doing; during the ravages it set to her body, casting out hope and replacing it with fear, the one thing which always remained was her feelings for us all; her love to surpass through each second in Winter's Moment.

Her hand came slightly to a sit. Her head rolled into an angle and motion that settled to the point she could view me with her look.

"Loving son," she mouthed, barely audible above a whisper, "I will never forget you."

I felt a hand slide over my shoulder from behind. It was Sandra who had entered without me knowing. I bent upwards; clasping my mother's hand as I rose, and catching her square look towards my gaze. And with a strong and firm disposition I sweetly smiled.

"A son never forgets the mother he loves," I returned as I kissed her to her forehead, "Mother, I don't now how this all will go, what will become of us in the end, nor how this all will turn out. I just can't say, but we will all be OK through this. I will be OK, Amanda, dad, Lorie, Adam, Sandra, and you. We will all be OK."

"I know," she muffled to say without her speech.

I could see the light of her gray eyes beginning in a fade. The once stilled soul packed up its things from the body and was readying itself for the long journey home. The collective embers of her life were smoking into a simmer; sparking a fuse every now and then. But as each moment passed, the fireplace to her heart was starting to cool. We were not months away from that time, but only days, perhaps even hours from it now.

There was a wrestling in my soul; an unpardonable grabbling which ensued and so caused my heart to race back into its own emotions once again. It was that emptiness; that terrifying, wrenching sensation Kelly had only spoken of minutes before.

My mother's eyes locked hard onto me without a blink and I suffered the royal pains of her dilemma in every moment of her stare. I never flinched, yet made my attempts to warm my expression well enough so she would not feel so cold. This was the beginnings of our 'goodbyes' and I knew it to be so; she in her own hollowed-out way, knew as much.

There was fear in those eyes of hers; deathly fear, and I could hear the whispers resonating from her soul, ascending from the lost breath she fought to take, "God is good; God is good."

To this day those words ring continuously in my ears. Like the long rattles of that bell I bought her, chiming its tune through the echoes of our collective past. Those words were as the lyrics to that melody, but not cast from the dye of some haunting nightmare. Yet they were the sounds of an active shore even the blind know of. You here the rumble of the ensuing seas; their start, beginning rolls into waves; the thunder of those waves, and how they move forward to lip out the shores before you. One can even close their eyes and see the onslaught of it before it comes.

I heard the rumble of those seas long before this moment, but now I could feel the spray of those waves casting me into my own silent chill. They say such moments are brief, though I could sense the longevity of their infinite ways, and how they may preclude themselves to be the long-living ghost that sits waiting for me in my own future ahead.

Mother-to-son; son-to-mother. It was the final glimpse of a lifetime as we sat in that moment together. We gazed back and forth, and we knew in our hearts time was spinning its last threads for us. I wanted to cry; to break down and sit in the shadows of the boy I once was; but not to be, for the moment was filled with more than sadness. The moment of parting times, of the most tender whispers coming from our own expressions. And a time, just a glimpse, where words speak less in value than the loving looks which transpired between us.

If you could capture it, you would. But as the treasures from a life of living so goes; they come into your world, place with you their profound message, then leave and so escape as most capable winds may do. They show you just how fleeting those times can become.

It's as if you try to capture that very vapor in your hands, yet the very moment you attempt to re-look upon it, it goes to flight once more, and so finds a new wind to travel by.

I saw my mother with her expression on me for the final time; one last embrace with her smile; a slow blink and a slight nod to her face. It was time for me to go now; to see this new world for the first time, alone; without her. I was slowly being born, revisiting the time of my birth, but born not of the child, a scream, and first awakening. It was an awakening where there was a past to my life though the future was as open and as unknowing as before. This was a new awakening; a time which held some memory, some point of reference, and the vast and incredible thoughts of what this woman meant to me, and would always be so to me.

"I will be back tomorrow," I whispered to her. Her hand slipped from mine and I could see one last nod settle from her there.

"Yes," she sent out the word to me, "Stay with me."

"I'll be back tomorrow," I returned, "I promise."

I left the hospital without pomp or ceremony, absent any victories or celebrations, yet allowing Sandra to drive us both home in that silent car. In my mind I would sit in the catacombs of my spent life like a boy who possessed a new toy to play with; alone, in the room of my thoughts; a single light penetrating the place to my sitting where I was in review of all those segments of joy I could remember. The reels to my previous world were in play; the pictures, the memories; like echoes to my ears; gifts from the reminiscing whose patterns and replays were as the long lost play of an old record.

I did my piece with the children once we arrived home, and after a reuniting we scurried them off to bed. Sandra made one play to intercede on me but she quickly backed away when knowing I wished to be separate from everyone. She retired to bed with a kiss and a leaning hug; I sitting in the loft of that couch, and staring through the clear shadowy window.

It was here the echoes turned into voices; shadows turned into sunshine; and the moments from so long ago came back to be in reunion with me. I would sit and stare, and note just how the world was being ripped apart; the tremor as the world shifted before the freefall. The colliding of two worlds, which were at war with each other merely by the differences they possessed, and nothing more. Somehow I knew a new beginning would come from all this, as I drifted off to my sleep unaware.

Chapter 36

One Final Dream.

There was one final canvas shore to look upon; one final pebble that held such promise to find; one last wish; one final goodbye. I was sent back into that dream and I knew it would eventually come. The timing was just unknown to me.

The expanse of that shore rode through my sights while it held a horizon as vast as the seas themselves. The pattern of sands sitting by those waters rolled longer than my gaze could collect them in a view, and further beyond. I noticed the deep roll in of those waves as if the tide had to tumble about, fester, and then settle inland before it went into its own natural retreat. I marveled at how the waves, further down, came forward in succession; one by one, like they were in this delay until the next series of tides began.

I could see the deep-set horizon; the day had been worn down and was bending further into the early evening times; night was soon to come. The brilliant array of colors, which were dancing about those skies, were of a spirit my brother could never paint more to perfection. God had a better canvas to work with than he did. The bursts of red, flaming orange, sifting blues, trite yellows, and scorching burgundies bent around the fireball sun in a cascade of backdrops that made the sun brighter still. Its eye peered back over me, and so reflected that gorging of colors through the ripples of those seas.

My walk took me east once more. A walk I had seen numerous times before. The steps into the wet sands implanted my presence until the sea rolled in and washed away all the evidence; the waters cold, uninviting, bitter to the chill, yet clear to the crystal-eye. I wondered if this would be the revolving world I was left with after the wars from what seemed only moments ago. Or would it be nothing more than a solemn refuge for us to speak one last time in.

I kept my gaze ahead and waited for the inevitable hue of a distant figure to penetrate my long vision. With each step I felt the hurry to increase; to continue on, without fail, and to abandon all else but this; this moment in a time that had no time at all.

I went from a walk into a trot; a trot into a sprint; sprint into a full galloping run. My breath was in a sweat of its own; the perspiration was glittering in that fading sun; yet nothing. I bent low trying to catch my breath; my hands buried into my knees; mouth gapping as my wind escaped out. My look ventured out to spot the sun once again and then I reached my gaze eastward to see if something was moving through the distant sands before me. There were shadows I could see; short drifting ones which rippled past that late afternoon heat. Some seemed to cast out an image; a figure in step. But I went to see more clearly in a squint. It was nothing but the heat rising from the outstretching backdrops which sat just beyond the shoreline.

"Mother," I whispered, "Where are you?"

I continued my way for what seemed the length of an hour, though the day appeared to sit still in that time; the sun keeping its hedge about the horizon to my right. I again went into a sprint; my heels clipping the wet sands into clumps as I ran. The jolts and force of it all weakened me to the point of nearly dropping me into a one-knee kneel. Though I stopped, collected myself, and continued further in a slow, pondering, wayward walk. My hands were to my hips; my lips widening for me to breathe deeper with. There, in the vast measure of this endless shoreline, a lone figure appeared to be in wait of me.

Once locked into view, I took my pace steady until I reached her; mother in a stance, never moving, but keeping her eyes towards me as though she had waited for me all along, and all this time.

Age had graced her complete. Her white flowing hair revealed the fairer complexion dawning her face, though her glaring gray eyes shown brighter than I had ever remembered. The gradual lines would sit around her eyes in rows of wrinkles. And when she smiled, her expression brightened into a glow.

"Its' good of you to come," she remarked.

"How could I not?" I explained.

"If we could only make the moment stand still…"

"I do wish," I expressed.

Without a word she lifted her hand out, rolling her fingers free and exposing within the bed of her palm that invaluable magic pebble. I gasped as my thought reached hers.

"If it is your wish," she suggested.

"Is it possible?" I moved closer to her.

"All things are possible," she stated, "You and I here, sitting in a dream for eternity; you to never awake, and me lying in the hospital bed always, your children and Sandra going on to a new life of their own; all the years before you escaping without you. Those moments to cherish, watching your own children grow into the man and woman you will eventually see them as. This is more of a gift than I could ever give you son," she grinned, "but all things are possible."

"I would not want you to suffer any further," I said.

"Through your love," she spoke, "you would sacrifice for me."

"I never wanted for myself," I replied, "Only for you."

"The greatest gift I ever gave you Conner," she said, "is my unconditional love. Beyond this is the life you possess. Now go live it son. This is your greater duty."

"I never wanted our time to end," I swallowed hard.

"The spirit never dies," she smiled, "nor the measures of our lives to ever disconnect completely. Heaven knows the verdict, as you and I know as well."

"I should accept fate then…" I looked hard on her.

"Fate is the greater reasoning of what Heaven decides." She remarked, "If I can accept it freely, then so should you."

"The final wish is not mine," I said, "but yours."

"Then we will value what is left and treasure what short time we have to share," she continued, "and say our goodbyes."

We sat upon those sands for as long as the sun would sit in the sky in front of us. Mother would often twist and turn the pebble in her hand, and at times I would look down over it with the full concentration of my gaze; the reflection in its firing seemed to light her hand up with such illumination.

We talked of my days to come; the hopes and dreams I held for my children, and how their lives would unfold over time. I mentioned Heaven and she grew with anticipation; a sigh, a gaze out over the seas, and a thought which held her in her silence for a moment or two.

If our choices were to be realized, she and I would have more years together. Yet knowing the moment of separation would eventually come, but not now. She was only sixty-six and it felt like such a travesty that it will end so soon, and as it seemed to be playing out the way it was to us.

"Each day is a color in life, painted by the hand of God; now you are seeing the full colors of life; all at once. It's the whole rainbow Conner, and look at just how beautiful it really becomes," her smile stuck in her expression while she looked out over the seas and fading horizon.

"How does it feel?" I softly asked.

"Like being born Conner," she replied, "All over again."

I placed my arm around her shoulder; felt the warmth of her presence soothe me into nearly a tranquil emotion.

"Tell Joshua 'hello' for me, when you see him," I requested.

"He knows," she grinned with a look my way.

"Would you do anything different?" I questioned, "With your life I mean?"

I could see her thinking past those vaulted seas, and though they held more of the world than land itself, I knew she had reached far past this in her mind.

"Just to embrace it more," she replied, "and to share more of my time with my children. The world had to be so busy, and I had to be busy with it. To think beyond the moment I was in; to really think about it and to see truly the time and how my own decisions affected my life. I suppose to have a little bit of the wisdom before the wisdom was learned," she smiled on this.

"To smell the flower before it blooms," I grinned.

"The smell would have been most sweet…"

"I would never have another," I looked at her with a gaze that if it were a smell or fragrance, it would be sweeter than the flower she just spoke of, "there could never be another mother like you…"

"Nor a first-born like you son," she settled a hug to me.

"I suppose I am not afraid of dying anymore," I whispered in looking out over the half-sinking sun.

"Oh Conner," she reveled, "The only fear one should ever have is to be afraid of not living your life; never giving yourself that chance to explore your world, your dreams, your hopes. Death is nothing more than a mystery which is eventually revealed in the end. It comes like birth; once in your life."

For every passing moment there, I held more to my wish in having time stop from its normal pace. Seconds slipped away like sand grains were filtering back into the ocean. Each tide pushed further in, taking with it more of those sands from that hourglass itself. We sat for a spell without saying a word; the venture of our lives trailing away and the road splitting now before us. I sensed the beginnings of her falling away from me and as she went, her tailing shadows felt as vapors in my dream.

She bent to hold my hand one final time; I knowing the measures of what it meant and so I stood, holding her hand in return as she came to a stand alongside of me. Our walk together was a time-honored step; her arm slipped beneath my inner elbow and now two sets of prints were crossing those shores, side by side; together, and how I knew what the morrow would bring for the both of us. I felt as if I were leading her up to the door of some new beginnings I had never seen, though I had only heard of.

We could see the hallway leading to it; the corridor of our departing. I would go as far as I could with her, say my 'farewells', and permit her to enter alone. This was my promise to her; this experience we all must travel through once in our lives, as we do with birth itself. It should never be one she would encounter by herself. I was with her for as long as God would allow it to be so.

I gazed ahead along those deep shores before us, and to my astonishment I could see a solitary figure off in the long distance. I studied it; observed it as it moved, somberly, simple, unimposing, and seeming to have no certain awareness we were there with it.

"Who is it?" I stated, moving just ahead of my mother while I kept constant watch over that figure.

"It is time…" she remarked.

"It is time?" I spun back to catch her with my look, "No, it isn't."

I moved closer to her side.

"Does he have anything to do with this?" I asked.

"Conner," she looked in a wanting manner at me, "It is time."

"No; not yet," I fussed, "Tell him we need a little more time. Go to him, then come back and stay a little longer."

"Conner," she cupped my face within her hands, tearing out a cry as she closed her eyes, "We must part…It is time."

"Just a little longer," I was breathing heavy.

"Conner," she looked square to my expression, "It's your brother Joshua. He is waiting for me."

"Joshua?" I whispered, sending out a deep stare onto that distant, blank, and empty figure standing alone along those further eastern shores, "I will go with you."

"It is time," she repeated, "But it's not yours."

"I can't go with you?" I questioned, "But why can't I see him? He is my brother."

"You're not ready Conner," she explained.

"But what of the pebble?" I felt her hand clutching it, "A wish still remains."

"I have had all my wishes fulfilled," she smiled through one of her tears, though it was gently pelting the flush measures of her cheeks, "There is no other wish I can ask for."

"There must be something," I persisted.

"It will be here waiting for you," she replied, "when you come."

I felt her hand release it freely into the wet shores between us. The tide pushed through, rolling over the pebble and drifting it back into the sea. I bent low and made a rash attempt to rediscover it. My hands plunged past those freezing waters in hopes I might find it once more; but to no avail, the pebble was forever lost.

"There must be something more," I felt the sudden trauma of that moment consume me, "another chapter to all this; another dream."

My hands went to my face as I felt the stampede of emotions I thought I could contain; yet, as the moment pressed deeper into our lives, I sensed the weight of it all crushing me.

"You will live in your happiness Conner."

"Tell me mother," I pressed, "When I awake, will you be gone?" The very presence of those words choked in my throat.

"Soon," she answered, "you will wake from this dream and see my end. I just want you to go from this with a full heart. Nothing left; nothing more you could have done, or performed differently to change or alter the outcome. It was meant to be this way."

"I know," I lowered my head, "I know."

"But I ask this of you," she stepped closer to me, "Take care of your father, and be there for your sisters and brother."

"I will," I looked away, not wanting her to capture my look with hers for fear my emotions may collapse before her.

She pulled me close with a farewell embrace; a moment where all earth, Heaven, stars, and moon were to stop in their very midst, unbeholding to time and all its measures. The force of nature seemed to unravel and lose all its dimensions, and the regulations it normally sustains were thrown out, disposed of if only for that single eclipse; a speck of time where time could not exist or enter into.

"How does one say goodbye to a mother you admire as much as you love?" I wondered by a whisper in her ear.

She pulled free; slowly with a look and smile, "You don't son…it's only 'until'."

I shook my head to agree with her, though in my heart I felt the forbidden notion that this was all wrong; that this could never be. That in a moment as quickly as the wind comes, blows, and fades away, that she would be gone. A memory, which to the inescapable powers of the human heart and mind should dim somewhat over time, and many of the precious elements of those days you shared together would be forgotten and lost in the former time box of your life.

This was the inevitable course of life; a breach of transition where death plays a significant role, greater than the distant fear it used to be; now transforming your world into something new, something radical and unforeseen; those experiences, those feelings all newly born to you. In a sense you are born separate, but along with her. The once ruptured womb becomes yours. Now, as we stood folding in the expressions and arms of one another, we knew that particular time of separation was quickly in approach of us.

"I don't have the words to say anymore," I bowed my eyes to the sands, and hoped I would awake now.

"There is no need," she brought my look back to her.

"Then this is 'until'...."

She shook her head as she took to send one last gaze over the dying horizon. The glimmer of light began to descend quickly now, and the fuse and cascade of colors started to assemble into a unique pigmentation.

"Now," she replied, "It is time for me to embrace my new birth; my new life; my new beginning. As you Conner must embrace yours..."

She kissed me to the forehead; one fainting look, and she turned away. The hue of night faltered my sight as she trimmed those shorelines just above me. And though I took a few steps forward I felt her leave escaping more severely than I could ever hope to keep pace with. So I watched; tempered without a breath or a heartbeat, gazing towards that mist of a world she was walking into. The fragments cast those long shadows just when sunset is at its highest point. Those figures seemed more of an illusion than real to me. My eyes wandered through that landscape, hoping that no tricks abound in my sightline, though I looked deep into that window and I found her so in flight. Within moments mother had filtered away without a trace.

The ravages of this dream had appeared to dwindle down into nothing more than a nightmare. The lamplight of the world had gone out suddenly; the darkness in surround of me; the shores, the waters to the seas seemed all to dry up in an instant. But the wind so silent and unknown before now blew about me with the force of a hurricane. There was no refuge but to stand in the midst of a place unknown and wait for myself to awake from the shadows of this very dark place.

A ring; a deafening call of a phone; I arose.

"Hello?" I instinctively spoke, "Is anyone there?"

Chapter 37

Into the World of Another Land.

"Conner," the voice returned, "It's me, your sister, Amanda."

"Is something wrong?" I asked, though still unaware of my fullest faculties at the moment. I could see by the light shadows casting past the window, a very early morning sunrise had commenced, "I am here; give me a second."

"The hospital tried to call you."

"What do you mean?" I pondered with a muffle.

"They rang you three times Conner," she replied, "no one answered."

I could sense the increasing stress in her voice.

"We have been here all along Amanda," I insisted.

"I was second on the call line."

"So they called you," I affirmed, "Mother's condition is worse." I spoke, though I knew by the preclusions of my dream what to expect now. The end was drifting into our collective world.

"Her kidneys are failing," she cried from the other end.

"Have you seen her?" I wondered, "Where are you?"

"At the hospital," she answered.

"Why didn't you call me sooner?" I pushed, "Have you seen her?" I was more insistent this time.

"No, not yet," she sniffled, "Just get here."

"What are they saying Amanda?" I heard nothing at first, "Amanda?" the phone dropped, "Amanda!"

"You know the situation," she weakly replied, "Under normal conditions, to call in the family. Mother has nearly died five times so they are not sure if this is it. Conner," she took to pause, "it is time…"

I vaulted from the bed when she phrased those last three words from her side of the receiver.

"I will be there shortly," I proposed, "You need to call dad."

"What should I say?" she was in full tears now.

"Tell him the truth," I suggested, "Nothing more can be said…" then I thought, "Call Adam first. Tell him to go pick up dad. I will call Lorie and Marshall, and let them know."

"How long will you be?" she wept.

"No more than thirty minutes," I pressed to release her from the call, "we need to get going."

A few moments further Sandra awoke to place her hands over my shoulders. I rushed frantically to fumble Lorie's number through the dial. She said nothing, yet looked at me with fear and trepidation. Our thoughts were not communicated through words, but with expressions alone.

"Lorie?" I hastily spoke when the phone was picked up.

"Conner," was her single word back.

"We have some quick decisions to make," I started, "And you above all else have the most difficult circumstances, but I am calling to let you know your mother will die today."

There was a pause; a lift of the phone, then a tear could be heard faltering in her voice; shaky as it was.

"You promised Conner…"

"We can't stop what is happening," I muddled; my chin in a wrinkle from her response, "I don't want you to blame yourself. Whatever you do, please, don't blame yourself. If you should go or if you don't; either way, I think mother would understand."

"I have every reason to believe this…"

"I know I promised Lorie," I began to weep and so cup my hand over my brow, "I wish I could say sorry is enough."

"It is," I could hear her breathe a smile over the line, "We can't think of what we wished for, but just be prepared for what is to come."

There was a point of silence for both of us.

"You will be there?" I questioned.

"I don't know," she explained, "Marshall fears the stress for me and the baby."

"Then you shouldn't," I implored, "It isn't fair for you to feel any guilt for not coming. It would have been what mother would want. I feel this more than anything."

"Conner," I heard her say, "Give her my love."

"I will," I sounded, then disconnecting from the call.

"I am going with you," Sandra announced.

"The children," I resisted slightly.

"I'll make some calls…"

And with this I was off to the bathroom in a rush. Sandra quickly found a morning sitter from the local neighbors. She ran down to the children's rooms, made a hurried but 'pleasant as needed' arousal of them from their sleep, and so readied them into their dress. The children were grumpy; I could hear the objections echoing down from the hallway, though by Sandra's motherly hand she had them quickly in line. A shuffle or two, and as I exited from the bathroom, Sandra was nearly dressed with a package in her hand.

"What is that?" I inquired.

"Something I was hoping to give as a present," she responded, "But it holds a different meaning now."

"What is it?" I asked.

"No time to explain," she persisted.

It was nearly eight when the young teenage sitter rang the doorbell, with her mother closely knit behind her. Sandra and I made our way to the hospital by the shortest route possible; defending against rush-hour traffic and placing our hazard lights on in the hopes people would be kind enough to let us pass through.

The hospital, as usual, was full in a bus; hectic and looking like ants in a swirl of morning activity on every floor and in every room. We had seen rain the last few days and this day was no different; the skies a cream gray color and heavy with the dew, and now pelting the sidewalks with a constant and dismal spray of drizzle. Raincoats were not in order, and as we entered the front of the hospital, Sandra and I were nearly wet from the shoulders up.

We rushed through with a reckless manner, nearly knocking over the unobservant in every corner as we went. The hounds of people; the orderlies, doctors and nurses, and the feverish attendants and residents seemed to be all amassed in our way. I held hard to Sandra's hand as I pulled her along; she grasping tightly to the wrapped package in her left hand.

I peered back to check over her every few moments; the stare in her eyes; that gasp, almost a fugitive from any breathing, like her face had grown cold from the lack of oxygen. She was terminal with fear and so was I. The hopeless fortress we had to overcome seemed like mountains that reached farther than the sky itself. I pressed forward, sensing the pillar of time measured by the sand droplets in an hourglass were growing ever thin. Each breath, each exhale mother was now succumbing to, was bringing her closer to that doorway; and I was to be there to hold her hand through it all.

The time was now; the world of another land was being put into place of which I knew nothing of. I could feel it in the changing air; the heavy clash of cold and heat seemed to be that Heaven and Hades were wrestling at that very moment for her soul. But such the grace of this woman; her lifelong gift of love and to God had already decided this raging, current battle. I could hear the whispers of it going on and the mantles of some ghostly weapons crashing around us. Yet there was indeed a sense of calm as well; where whispers so soft are heard plainly through the vaults of the most violent clashes.

I feared what I would see; the images surreal and haunting, waiting for my view; the convictions of what is not known; the horrid shade of dim lights and shadows prevailing in disturbing silhouettes. We were most close to this door now.

Sandra and I turned the final corner still hand to hand. The distressed nurses pulled us closer as we shuffled forward. The window to mother's room was half drawn and the lights inside darker than I could ever remember. Amanda came first into view, standing quietly beside mother's bedside. I saw the look of dread in her eyes; of half tears; of half sorrow, with no harbor for her pain. She rushed to me, slowed, and then collapsed into my arms. I moved forward, standing tall to see my mother straining from breath to breath. Her eyes were fixated upwards; unmoving, constant, unblinking, and cold as ice, streaming a constant light of gaze towards Heaven like a beacon into the fog-laden night for ships. She was almost there, holding briefly on for us and wanting her last goodbye's before the time was to come.

I lost my breath there; I bending over slightly near to mother. Her mouth was wide open, gasping for the air the vent was now pumping into what was left of her lungs. It was apparent she had a devastating stroke that early morning just before we arrived. The signs were there; the blank, cosmic stare; the lack of motion or movement in her body.

"I wanted to speak with your family collectively," Doctor Ogden entered the room and said, "as soon as all the members are here."

I looked about him and saw the look of a defeated warrior who had lost his queen. The eyes dropped suddenly, discouraged, and worn from the long night he appeared to have undertaken.

"The others should be here within the hour," I whispered.

"I have a meeting room set aside," he replied, "when they get here." He paused and came forward, "Your family has been through so much Mr. James."

"Please," I replied, "Its Conner."

"She has fought very hard Conner," he said, "We simply don't see this everyday; in fact, rarely do we ever experience this."

"I think a strong soul never fades doctor," I responded, "It simply disappears."

"It's Frank," he smiled slightly, "and I believe you. It certainly is the case here."

"She suffered a stroke…" I asked, though not in a question.

"Her brain activity is far diminished," he announced. "We can presume this, yes."

"How long can we estimate?" the fear rode in through my voice and mostly trembled my words into their shaking sounds.

"Hour," he spoke. "Perhaps two; maybe less…Nothing more than a day, if God's speed wills it. Such are the things I need to address with the entire family unit, as a whole."

I turned to mother lying as she was; a shell no longer the whole woman who birthed me, raised me, and now saw me reach this stage of my life. She was only a fragment there, holding her grip on the slipping precipice she had found herself sitting on for all these months. I pondered that illusive moment as it also slipped away from us all. The tragedy was born with so the introduced labor pains of a very difficult delivery. I was just looking for the most humane road now for her, regardless of the consequences for me.

"So this is it…" I whispered to myself.

I bent lower; my head most near to hers; eyes engaging upward, though the blank stare fused no expression but for the stilled soul which lay within. The shell was growing cold; the soul shedding from within and appearing to pull away from this failing body of hers.

"I am here mother," I chanted in her right ear, "I don't know if you can hear me, but I am here…and will be for as long as this takes."

I could sense the exhaustion in her dimming pulse; the breaths' becoming more labored than the last. The pumps to the vent pushing forward, releasing, and then allowing the air to escape her; it would all begin again.

Her lower jaw was withdrawn; the mouth still yet gapping, reaching for air, though all would pass in and out of the trach itself. She never blinked. Not once. No faltering in her look or a faint change in her gaze to show even the shadows of what she was.

"Dad will be here soon," I bent over her, and placed a kiss to her forehead; so turning to meet with Sandra once more.

Father entered within a few minutes, alongside Adam. He stirred to the door, said nothing but for the shudder in his own stance; thinking long and hard in disbelief at what was before him. He remained silent as though none of us were there; whimpered, stepped to the edge of the bed, took his hand gloves and thrust them hard against the wall. His chin wrinkled as he took his handkerchief and blew into it.

Adam moved forward with a combined look of terror and awe. I grabbed him by the wrist, pulled him closer, and wrapped my arm over his far shoulder. Yet his hypnotic stare only grew more intense as he proceeded forward.

"Will this be all?" Doctor Ogden looked about and asked.

"I believe so," Amanda replied.

"Shall we proceed?" he led us out, single file, down one corridor and into a solitary room.

"I think we all know the situation at hand." he began, "I stayed through the night; observed Mrs. James' charts and her condition as it progressed. Simply, the signs are not very good at all. Her condition has worsened and I do believe beyond repair now. Her lung capacity is now the size of half one fist; nothing more. She is more comfortable relying on the ventilator as it stands. Otherwise, without it, she would not be able to breathe on her own, and would quickly go into cardiac arrest. But I assure you she is comfortable. At this point we are keeping her alive with the stabilizer drugs. And with them we could possibly keep her alive beyond a twelve hour period; perhaps a day, but no more."

"What has caused the downturn?" Amanda questioned.

"The blood disease Sepsis has returned." He replied, "Her unwarranted condition and fragile state; Wegener's; her ARDS. A whole multitude of factors are involved here. It is simply too much for one person to sustain, let alone a completely healthy person."

"So what is the offering here?" I questioned.

He remained in his stance; stalled, seemed to think at depth on it, and then, "Your wishes primarily. The decision is yours; however you wish me to proceed, we will abide by it."

"There is no other alternative doctor..." Sandra spoke.

"I am afraid not," he shook his head, "Her health is severely damaged; the conditional state of the body is far exceeding recovery. There isn't even a hope for a stable vegetative state," he paused on this, "We can do nothing more for her but to keep her comfortable, and allow the rest to take its course."

"Without the stabilizer drugs?" father proposed, "How long would she have?"

"Minutes," Doctor Ogden quickly returned, "Not even an hour."

The room fell into deaf silence on this; the pressure of that moment in time held us all victims to it. We wallowed about in this stewpot of emotion; holding to our innermost thoughts while gazing to one another and waiting for someone to take an approach. I swallowed hard; sensing the weight of all eyes patrolling the room, passing over me like spotlights in the night. I held stone motionless, unwilling to move in all, and so hoping another would take directive there. I surfaced back into my dream; thought of what passed between mother and me there. The words I could build my precious memories with all stilled in my mind, locked as they were in the deepest corner of my heart.

I was caustic numb; idled by the moment. No stirring, not even for a fraction of a second. I could feel the weight of my beating heart press against my chest, push forward, and heave out a cry of its own.

"Then we should do what is best for her," dad wept through these words. My sister Amanda tilted low by the weight of her own tears. Sandra rushed to her side for comfort.

"I think it is best…" Adam agreed; his eyes drifting away into the far away lands of his own thoughts.

Amanda bent upward and shook her head to agree.

"Conner…" I heard the doctor's voice gently call for me.

I said nothing, yet held to my possum pose.

"Conner…" father interceded, "son…"

"I agree," I shuddered with fists' clinching, and so squeezing out that time as though it were a poisoned sponge.

"When you are ready then," the doctor paused, stood, and stepped from the room. I heard the soft cries of my family members breach into a more steady flow.

"Its' not time," I spoke, "for this. She isn't gone yet. I, for one, will not waste any more time sitting in a room and letting her lay in that bed alone. There is enough time for sorrow later."

I jumped from my far seat, rushed through the door, galloping down that long and darkened corridor; sprinting as it were for freedom and life. I heard the roar of the battle enraging within me; the heavens and the Hades of that galactic struggle all molded into those wayward spirits diluting my own soul. I felt to be nothing more than the tiniest pebble in the vast throngs of a large sea.

As I entered ICU, all manner of doctors, nurses, attendants, and resident students from the university were clamoring round, catching me face-first when I drew inward. The strong weight of their stares pushed onto me with one uniform expression; that of solemn and mortal gloom.

I seemed to look into the fashion of all their faces, and they seemed to be born from the same mother and father to me. There was a great hush as I moved through and entered mother's room, so finding her as she was; ceiling-gaze struck, and vaulting every ounce of energy she possessed to breathe with. Several nurses were to her side. I approached.

"Mother," I stumbled, "It's Conner; the rest are coming. Winter is almost over," I leaned in to rub over her dry forehead, "It's time mother. It's time to go to Heaven."

The other's entered as I moved to the opposite side, facing the doorway. Sandra glared onto me until I reached my look into hers; she bending low to her package and releasing what was within. There were two pictures; one of Tyler and the other of Cory. She moved forward with both in hand, as if she were Moses carrying down the two hard-carved stones of the Ten Commandments.

The room drew into reverent, eerie silence. A hush and roar all in the same moment stilled the air as she pressed forward. All gave her passage to mother's bedside, and so permitted her to go first.

"Mother?" Sandra whispered with an attempted smile, which only failed when she was near. "I have a present for you…Pictures of your grandchildren…"

She laid both on each side, and then held one upwards for mother to see by. Sandra shifted her hand to a button on the frame and out played a message from Cory.

"Happy birthday Grandma," Cory's voice rang through the muffled speaker, "Please get well soon."

Sandra pulled the second one up; the one from Tyler.

"Please get better grand mommy," Tyler's voice resonated in the same manner, "We want you home soon so you can read us many more bedtime stories…We love you…"

I felt the air collapse in the room and mother drawing what remained of life, within her frail lungs. Several nurses from the edge pulled down the windowed curtains to each side. Doctor Ogden hung behind us all like a lighted ghost in one corner; waiting, watching the drama as it unfolded.

I took mother's hand within mine; the flesh cold, dry, feeble and worn, and near the land of death. She made no furthering motion other than the stilled and oppressive image of her staring upward; without a blink, and gasping for every breath. I gazed behind me and I saw her vital signs beginning to press lower still.

"Father," I looked then behind me, "Do you want to be near?" I asked, though he shook me off and withdrew into his silent tears.

Amanda came forward with a bible in hand. Her face was blushing red from the emotions already exposed and the inner trauma consuming her. She paused and waited; held herself most near to mother's ears, and though I watched most silently on this episode, I could see the tears beginning to fall from mother's gaze. A trickle; a ball of water, then the tears rolled downward along her sides. The streams were coming from the onset of hearing her grand children's voices. I went to press my hand along the side of her cheek and catch those tears as they fell.

Amanda looked very grieving to me; nothing said, not even a whisper or a muted and sorted response. We all felt the surreal moment touching us, as if it were an illusion more real than a dream, but less real than reality itself. The entire world had dove back into this room; nothing else remained. The fire flies of all that was, was no more; this room being all that was left.

This was a land of tragedy; of inescapable drama which had pulled us each into its reign; most of all, our dearest mother who lay near to her death. The shadows of life appeared to hide in places most concealed, and allowed something more mysterious to take over for a brief time; as if the sun had suddenly, and without anticipation, gone out.

My sister split the bible at a marked spot.

"Psalm 23," she began, clearing her throat, "The Lord is my shepherd; I shall not want. He maketh me to lie down in green pastures; he leadeth me beside the still waters. He restoreth my soul; he leadeth me in the paths of righteousness for his name's sake. Yea, though I walk through the valley of the shadow of death, I will fear no evil; for thou art with me; thy rod and thy staff they comfort me..." Amanda drew into silence and looked to fumble through the remaining passage. Her hands came into a shiver; head drawn, deep-holding into a stare settling onto mother's sheets, "I love you mother; please go in peace."

She lifted herself away while sobbing within her hands, leaving the bible sitting by mother's side; open, a rose settled amongst the leaf pages. Cory and Tyler's pictures lay over her breast, softly bobbing up and down as her aged lungs continued to struggle for air. The morning hour read thirty minutes till twelve.

I sanctioned Adam to approach, and so he sifted through those standing over the opposite side of the bed. His gaze never wavered from her and it kept his good counsel by her side. There was a tremor in his walk; perhaps the shadow of the old man he would later become long after this day. Those banished ways he once held so steadfast to, had all but crumbled in the mirror of his own self-reflection. He was a different man now; educated, sympathetic to the arts of his emotions and his soul.

He stalled into a still for that moment. He grasped about her hand and pressed with his own grip. I, holding mother's other hand akin to his posture. We stretched our look to one another and then slowly he dipped his back to hers. His breath was heavy and tired from this tragic abuse we all suffered under; his mouth opened to a pause, a tear jolting down his left cheek.

"I lost more time than I could have ever imagined with you." He softly spoke. "Please forgive me. I will learn somehow, someday to forgive myself for it. I made a promise mom, and I plan to keep it; for you, for all of this, for all that you are, and what you have shown to me. The time that I have lost with you is worth more than I ever realized; now, it is too late."

He crumbled only for a second into a cry, but held his composure to speak further.

"I would have changed the world over for just a chance to alter how all this is ending for you. It should never have turned out like this…You are my hero."

Adam began his retreat to the bottom of the bed. He stood, gazed over mother; there, placing his hand over her feet.

I set my hand over mother's brow, slowly brushing back the small strands of hair that still remained over her balding head. Doctor Ogden approached and pursued to settle close behind the front of the bed where all the wires, machines, and medicines were dripping into her.

I felt his stare hit me, stall for a moment, and proceed to cut the stabilizer drugs off. I could see the confession of 'I'm sorry' falling from his expression towards me. It was then I squeezed mother's hand tighter still, and how I could feel the final sand droplets moving through the hourglass.

She never whenced at any time. She stayed as she always was; looking Heaven-bound, absent a single blink. Those seconds dropped into a slumber as they sped through time. I heard the beeps of her pulse from the machine beginning to falter even more. So much so like a clock ticking to a slow stop. Her heart rate fell deeper, colder, and lower from the seventies and into the fifties. I turned to watch the monitor; the thump of that machine growing dimmer and most weak in its reading.

I glared around the room in that silence for only a brief spell. More tears drew from her stare as they rolled all the way to the bed sheets; and as they dampened around her, my family members drew out their own sorrows in watching this.

"Now," I whispered close, "It's time to go home…It is time."

I felt the birth of her soul coming to bear; Heaven's singular call going out. The heart monitor was collapsing still more, into the thirties; the pulse dipping deeper into its own permanent mark.

I drew one last breath; a shudder in my eyes, then my blink found the world had changed forever. She reached high for that final breath, holding it for only a fraction; still, and then at its release she was gone. My hand was in hers; her hand now frozen.

I turned in a shattered phrase, holding my hand across my mouth.

"She's Gone! She's Gone!"

I went to the dark corner of the room, bent myself into a stoop with my hands converging fully over my face.

"Oh God! No! She's Gone!"

I felt the fragile shakes in my palms pulsating uncontrollably and pushing against my face; the tears in a torrid rain from my eyes as they gushed in that rampant river of sorrow that was consuming me.

The gravity of it all had struck me harder than a bolt of lightening. The shattered dreams; that series of eclipses I had falling in my nights were now ruptured from the shores of that illusive sea. For in this ravaging time of raptured emotions and startling thoughts, I felt all of Heaven and earth crashing through my chest and into my heart. The wearing of it seemed too much to bear then. I wanted to run, hide, find refuge in any place where relief would be; but nothing, no solace from that eternal tragic moment. Her passing door was like a force of nature I had never experienced before, nor could ever fully prepare for.

I felt the grasping of hands over my shoulders. The full explosion of Amanda and Sandra's own emotions caused me to stand and we embraced in our trio to comfort one another. Through the clouds of my own tears I saw more doctors coming within the room and settle around the bed. The ventilator went off; everything was being shut down.

"Time of death," one doctor stated, "Eleven fifty-two a.m."

Amanda went to mother's bedside one last time; Sandra collecting the personal items within the room. Both gazed forward to catch her glimpse, stunned as they were, as I moved from side to side. I looked onto her motionless frame. Those pearl gray eyes were holding steady in their look still Heaven bound.

Father and Adam drifted from the room, staring with those glassy, disbelieving gazes of theirs. I passed close to mother, rubbed her hand with a gentle collection of thoughts and memories streaming through my mind.

"I will make you proud mother," I softly spoke, "I promise."

My look kept a watch through that glass window leading back into her room. The halls of ICU had many inspecting the scene and I could sense the massive strokes of their looks pestering my want and desire for privacy. But still, even still, I could no more force myself into a leave, than for me to stand and ponder through my own, most sentimental stare on how someone that I loved was now forever separated from me.

I felt the trinity of spirits to be complete. First was Spike, then Buck, and at last my mother would go beyond my ability to reach her. I had wrestled with the scope and measure of all that had transpired for the last six months, and now it was over. By the dim light of that former evening sun, a new day of sorts had dawned.

Sandra held close to me for the remainder of my stay in the hospital. The hours would peel back until two or so in the afternoon. We took our exit hand in hand; she going to gather the car for our ride out. For the last three days the weather about was blistering, cold, damp, drizzling, wet, and brushing along the edge of winter itself. The gray clouds hovered about without pause, and so took out the bright blue sky and sun we had been so accustomed to.

Now, as we walked from that hospital, the blue etchings of a mid-day, vibrant dome had cast out the unmistakable beauty of that color; as if the rainbow of this particular color filled the whole sky through. The dotting sun was arched high, and birds-to-the-feather took to flight along the rim in every direction.

I stood alone at the curb waiting for her when Wanda, mother's respiratory therapist, came stepping from the hospital front door.

"Mr. James," she called, "Conner."

I turned to greet her.

"I heard," she with a yearning stare most accompanying the subject of death, of love, and the ones close to us that its touches.

"Just a few hours ago," I said in a brief way.

"Sorry isn't an able word is it?" she asked.

"No," I gazed into the sun, "Doesn't seem apt at all."

"I felt an intrusion to have come this morning," she returned, "But I decided to stay away; not to interfere."

"I think she would have wanted you there Wanda," I replied, "She was entrusting to you, especially the last few months."

"And I take kindly to this…"

"There were many who came to see her go," I spoke.

She paused, looking anxious; wanting to find the word or phrase that would invoke the thoughts she felt or wished to say.

"You're the reason…" she announced.

"I am sorry," I responded, "what do you mean?"

"You're the reason," she repeated, "Why we all are here, doing what we do. Mr. James, you don't realize just how special your family is. We all noticed; the doctors, nurses, and staff recognized just how loving and special your family really is. The care she received from you, your siblings, and your father was a tender thing to see. It makes what we do have purpose, and every so often we see this type of love; real, very real, imagined, but from time to time we can actually see that royal monarchy of love."

She nearly cried on this, as was uncommon to see.

Being her trade and position in life, there is a sort of distance one needs to address; to hold at bay your emotions and allow things to occur as they were meant to be…And when fate falls with its decisions; except it, without emotion, and go on. The scope being to try to save all that you can, and to know that those which are lost, were the ones you do your best to aid, help, and give comfort to.

I saw the seeping of her humanity shadow through. Not of apathy or of sympathy, but to experience the similar pain and sorrow I was feeling. She was, in essence, becoming one of us.

"She is in a better place now Wanda," I softly declared, and so feeling her place a gentle and pervasive hug over me.

"I believe so."

"Someone once told me," I said, "When someone you love passes away, think of them just before you go to sleep at night, and they will be there waiting for you in your dreams."

Wanda pulled free, collected herself and her tears.

"I do feel this to be true," she cried, "Your mother will be missed."

I held her once more for that tiny moment.

"Sometimes the sorrows have to come," I replied, "before the joys can follow."

I felt the nod of her head in approval as it shifted politely over my shoulder; the release, one final gaze, and we parted never to see one another again.

If I could fracture time and have it hold for just a spell; to give me chance and hope to reflect without measure, even if it were a morsel of my life which would expend, then I would take the opportunity to see my mother one last time. I thought of her in every form of nature. I saw her sitting there that day, representing all that was good in the world.

My daze was just as reflective when Sandra drove us through the hazy traffic; I watching the curbs and people walking from street corner to street corner. I had no idea she was taking us to the harbor. That is, until we had actually pulled close to the bay.

"Why are we here?" I looked to her.

"You have some unfinished business Conner," she whispered. I could see she had been crying all through the ride. Her eyes parched red, drowning in the soft wetness of her cheeks, shuffled to pass a kiss to me, "Let's take a walk."

"But the children…"

"Let's take a walk," she stressed, "There is time."

Sandra led me through that stroll with little to say, yet forming her body close knit to mine. Our strides were in unison; collective and synchronized, as though we were taking the longest hike of our lives.

The water rippled gently to the shores; seagulls darted along those endless blues and streams of white sunrays, which were beating through our expressions while we stepped to face the seas.

We walked as far as the dock way would permit us. The ropes and railings were holding us in our bends over them.

"Have you forgotten?" she asked.

"I suppose if I were to ask what," I said, barely able to look at her, "then I would be convicting myself of my own sin."

"It's no sin Conner," she replied, "All that has happened today. It seems the world never took notice after all."

"I don't want to discuss it…" I said, "If you are asking."

"I'm not asking," she returned, "Just don't bury it…"

"In time," I said, bending to look out over the harbor and the long seas beyond this, "But there is not a clock to it. I don't think it will ever know what time it is."

"You say that now," she bent beside me; a hand reaching around my waist, "But 'Now', will not always be that way."

"You haven't experienced this…"

"You're right," she said, "I haven't. But it doesn't make me immune from being sympathetic to it. I loved your mother as well. Just don't bury it; you'll bury yourself instead, and shut me and the children out along with it."

I gazed to her lovingly; patted her on the wrist, pulled her close, and felt the sun warming to my face, "You are asking for a promise then…"

"No Conner," she kissed me to the forehead, "Just the Gift you owe me and the children. We have a right to it."

"This," I frowned, yet keeping my emotions within, "I can do."

"But there is one gift you haven't realized," she stated, "Something very important you have forgotten."

"What is it Sandra?" I whispered.

She drew from within the lapel of her jacket the envelope my father had placed in my confidence some time ago.

"A letter from your mother…"

I took it from her clutch as I eyed it with the most observant stare; bug-eyed and casting all of my attention to her very hands; the possession of that letter, and how I had misplaced it in my mind during all that time.

"I'm not sure I am ready for this…" I held it limp in my one hand, "I don't know that I can Sandra."

"You have to Conner," she whispered, tilting her head at an angle and rolling her hand over my wrist.

"Why?" I pressed.

"She wanted this from you," she persuaded, "It's like opening up your present the first Christmas you had together with her. Do you remember how happy you were, and how happy you made her?"

I said nothing, though I kept my inspection of the letter.

"The joy you gave her," she softly spoke, "Was more than what was within that present box."

"She's watching..." I replied, looking more intimate to Sandra. She remained in her silence and smiled a half-joy, half-sorrow grin. The kind which doesn't know if it were raining or basking in the midst of sunshine; but between the two, the emotions are well-meaning.

This was to me a message that reached far beyond my mother's leaving of this world, and it was to be her design to speak to me through the greatest trial of my life. Even then she was more in thinking of me than of herself; the truest gift of charity.

"I'll be over here," Sandra began to back away, "When you are ready," and I watched her slowly move back down the dock; yards by the shore, and drift out into the parking lot.

I gazed over that aged envelope; the ends worn and tattered; the sealant to the back of it was coming loose. But upon quick inspection one could see it had been sealed for sometime; perhaps even years. The envelope was of odd shape, as if it were no longer the size they had been making; the edges brown, musty, smelled of some faint or long ago whiff of perfume, or a mist of fragrance my mother must have worn years before. I took to smell over it; my nose running along those ends and sensing that scent that was born from so many years in the past. How it cast into my mind the memories of her from the age of my own youth. For a moment I felt I was there, and so I moved to break the seal and read out her words to me. The message was not from a bottle, but a message written from the pen of her own spirit.

'To my dearest eldest son, Conner:

I suppose the time has come for us to part ways. The reading of this letter signifies I am gone from this world, and it is not to my liking that we are separate from one another for a span that I no more can predict or estimate, than I could have ever desired for us. I have the burden Conner that you are in trial now. And the world will seem as no sense to you, as it was for me when I was in loss of my own parent's years ago. I often wondered what words would be appropriate at this juncture; what measure or saying that would fit the tragedy you and I now feel so strained with.

It is for me, the first moment where I knew the loss of someone I loved, and also to have become that very same loss to my own child. Beauty is always born, even in the worst of tragedies; you must be assured of this, know this, and understand it, even at the time of your life where emotions are as enraged as a stallion in the midst of a heavy rainstorm. Speaking from what I remember in my own loss, I know all things will pass and so will the hardships that are associated with it. I have always told you that the simple colors of the rainbow to life have the beauty only when they are all together, in a mix, and shining across the sky in their brilliance.

Even in the very moment of my death, especially then, I knew that what I spoke to you as a gift all these years was indeed true. This is the beauty of life; the rainbow we all admire. Every season has its duty to succeed one another, and I grant you as much Conner; you have the duty to succeed me. Go out into the world and mark your trail with the full admiration of others; represent me, and all that I have taught you these long years of our lives together. Nothing would make me happier; nothing would prove me more that I now live within you, even after my passing.

You have always been a great son to me; the finest a mother could ever wish for. When I look to you, even now, I look with the pride I always wanted to own; not for myself, but for you. I hope I have taught you well, given you the resources to live your life with the utmost success, and endeared you with the spirit I felt only my son would be worthy of. God graced me with the chance and hope to pray for this very thing, and I believe it has all come true.

Someday, somewhere in the vaults of time and future, you and I will be together again, and Heaven will be a more joyful place for it. In the meantime, be the gentle giant I know you will be with your children. Grant your wife the most blessed husband a wife could ever have. And when the light shines greatest over you, just know that it is the eyes of my smile from where the light comes from.

Remember these things, and that which I have always spoken with you on; and life, and God will bless you always.

Your loving Mother—Annie'

I folded the letter back into its proper place; the words now dispelled to me and locked into my memory for as long as I would live. The final touching of the most brilliant torch, even in its dimming airs, that I had yet to know. And as I gazed out over those waterways and shot a glance at the ships tumbling into and out of the harbor, I knew I had been graced with the most wondrous of mothers' a son had ever the fortune to have.

I bowed for a short and inviting prayer; one that I had hope for that God and my mother would overhear on. There seemed such a divinity there; a calm for peace; the magistrate for compassion, and as I felt the gentle wave sounds of those ever-flowing waters touching into my ears, I could see for one final moment my mother standing along the shores of my dreams. I took one last look through the harbor and I felt a stillness, which nearly gathered, in the most panoramic view and gracious tranquility. The scene seemed to be companioned with the both of us there. She was there, with me.

"Thank you mother," I whispered out into the air. Grief, in fact, would be short-lived; by the power of those words written in her letter to me. The purpose of it had sent shockwaves through my emotions; stilled them, calmed them to believe that beyond death, she still lived as vibrant as before.

I stepped back towards Sandra.

"Are you alright?" she questioned, looking up to me with the embrace of her eyes; a smile parting with those words.

"You were right," I returned with a smile, "It was like the first Christmas gift she ever gave me; truly a gift."

The following days were spent with reflection and preparation. Many would come with their condolences and flowers. The community of friendships is more aligned then, like the stars above are when the earth tilts a certain way. Hundreds would gather during the receiving of friends, and even more would attend the following day's funeral.

As nature would have it, not a speck of cloud entered the sky that day. The pearl blue Heavens were like the clearest oceans, and the horizons appeared never-ending. Like they were in the very dreams I had come so accustomed to before my mother's death.

I remember how Lorie re-acted going to the funeral home and observing our mother in her casket for the first time. The emotions were overwhelming; contentious, and warred with her soul to the point she nearly collapsed right there at the foot of mother's view. Marshall reached for her; lovingly so, and pulled her into retreat. Lorie never wanted to leave as she overflowed with her tears, even without a moment's reservation. I went to her and held her in a warm embrace; the tears now a steady flood over my shoulder as Marshall and I both helped her to the rear.

Tyler and Cory were in hand with Sandra, side to side, and so watching the on-goings of their aunt Lorie. I could see the hesitation and fear in their eyes as they peeked through; spotting me, and wandering what the full term of meaning this all had. I went to them, pulled them both up to my shoulders and carried them just underneath the various chandeliers that were ascending down the hallway. Cory held such a fascination with each one, and how he gazed bright-eye upward in an attempt to touch and grasp each and every crystal; the glow and reflection held to his attention as though he were star gazing in the clearest of nights.

"Jason," I saw my friend standing in the doorway. He walked to me in a serious pose, rolling through the brim of his hat many times over. His expression remained steady and with conviction, "Don't," I suggested, "There is no need to, really."

"She was a great mother," he proposed, "and she raised a fine son. I suppose that is as good of a testament as any."

"No greater than the friend you are to me," we sent a hug to one another, "It is good of you to come."

We attended the service together like a family. The sanctuary was full and in overflow; so much so, chairs were brought in from the fellowship hall. The cast of congregation adorned the pulpit with the sights and gazes of so many who loved and adored her.

The ceremony was polite, traditional, and had the venue of reflection and admiration. Gerry came up to me just after the funeral concluded and gripped my hand with a more sturdy vice.

"Little Pa," he smiled with those white teeth of his, "Holds onto that cross, cause you have more angels looking out for you."

"I intend to," I faintly smiled his way, "It has more meaning than ever." We shook hands, held for a moment in that grasp, then parted with a shy and distant, final glance to one another. Perhaps he knew this was not a time to re-invent old friendships.

There was a bit of a delay in the parking areas. The long processions of cars pulled up to the front limousine's rear, and were held in check with their headlights beaming until all was readied. What family members could, began to cram into that small compartment. The remaining members were escorted to the second and third limos just behind ours.

I cast my attention out over the church's front lawn; the birds in flight, resting as they would on the Bedouin branches of any tree that would support them. Their chirps and vicarious calls echoed through to us in a muffled sound, as they quickly filled up the trees with what looked to be flickering and darting leaves. The branches all seemed to be alive in that moment, and so singing the carols of their own tunes. The trees swayed and bounced, nearly appearing to walk along the front lawns; all within their own powers to do so. Then, as one car door took to slam, the birds scattered in a haven of one singular, roving, active cloud of seamless colors. Branches were bare once more with the shadows of this fleeing mass crossing the beds of that entire landscape.

My children held close to us; vice in their grips; a hold, longing in its scope; loving and warm but filled with some element of fear. These were not the hugs of bedtime or comfort, but hugs where the world had changed and altered from what they knew. I looked over to Sandra, and with my expression, in telling her I had always desired to keep our children from the unknown; to protect them for as long as protection could hold them in some security. I knew then the reasons why my parents kept Joshua's death from me and my own siblings. Perhaps, in the end, they knew wisdom before it could be known.

I saw little Cory gazing through the window. His glance torn, afraid, grasping with his child-like sense of hope, and wanting the remedy of the past to make this all nothing more than an episode we would be absent in. His grandmother would be sitting in her back porch rocking chair on a quaint Sunday afternoon; rocking and waiting with anticipation for her grandchildren to pay her a visit.

What words could counteract this and fold out the world of innocence once more for them to play in? I felt myself to be human for the first time in their eyes; no less loved or longed for, but the duty of invincible strength had forever escaped me; lost in the vapor winds of time itself.

The trail to the cemetery held such an eerie realm about it. The browns of the earth; the lack of green and vegetation made the roads appear more fragile with the soon onslaught of winter. The speckled and flowing meadows glimmered with tumbleweed leaves and grass uncut for sometime. Our walk held the journey of our family in four, hand to hand; the children between us. On occasion Cory and Tyler would look skyward at us; crouching their eyesight to catch us more clearly with their gaze.

I saw where mother was to be laid to rest; the green canopy had been pulled about and in overhangs with the casket sitting on its individual pedestal, and with chairs all aligned in rows before it. I stalled, took a short spell to breathe with, then I continued. I sat somber through the brief service; heard nothing of what was said, though staring onto the ambiance of this casket; still, motionless, feeling the echoes of my mother's words ringing to me. The children each lay a rose over the top of the casket, in single file, until a dozen roses sat in lay over her.

The crowd dispersed and we all took our leave, yet I remained behind, looking, watching the grave preparations continue shortly after everyone left. Sandra came to me, clasping to my hand; the children, the same, and we made our passing away to go home.

"Could I say anything of convenience?" she stated.

"There are no words Sandra…"

"When joy is not around," she replied, "love still remains."

"There isn't time in the shadows of a day," I said "to know when joy ends, and fear begins, and the moment when joy returns."

"Then why question what has happened?" she asked.

"Because its' there," I sounded, "When there isn't a better reason, you always question. And because, perhaps, you know there will never be an answer to it."

"The unsolvable world," she said, "A world without clues."

"It's a different place now Sandra," I turned to her. "It's not a place I remember, or know of."

"So what do you do?" she whispered, holding my face in her hands; her eyes locking onto mine.

"Go on," I whispered back, "and live."

"An answer with no clues," she softly smiled, "A wish of a parent. Her desire for you was to remember; never to forget, but to live this day forward in your own happiness."

I looked about this new world; an eye displaced and seeming to search it out for my new home; a home for my family and myself.

"You have two children to raise," Sandra further whispered, "to teach, to love and embrace, and to show just how this new world will be for them," she paused, silently, holding her breath into her lungs until the remaining part of her sentence spilled over me, "and to be the husband I know you will be to me. I want to see the world in your eyes forty years from now Conner. As we are, even if we are ancient…I still want to see this."

"Then I think we have a new journey to take," I held her close, whispering alike to hers', feeling her embrace envelop mine.

We walked along those meadows as if we were taking a stroll through the park. The flourish of winds seemed brisk, and so challenged the warmth of our jackets to us. Still we managed and the children began to play about, much like Lorie and I did so long ago.

Chapter 38

A Promise Kept.

"Mr. Adam Benjamin James," my brother's name sounded out for all to hear. He was next in line, beaming with the pride of one who had accomplished all of his life's goals in one day. Now he would have his diploma; a college diploma, and so fulfill that long remembered promise from four years before.

All of the family was in attendance. This was a special day and we rejoiced in every moment as though it held the sunshine of Heaven in it. We stood when Adam moved across our view. We cheered and clapped as he went; flashbulbs in a flint that seemed to sparkle in the sunlight. He stalled, shook the chancellor's hand, grabbed his diploma with the other, turned to us, and smiled through with the happiest expression I had ever seen him with. He raised both hands while he stepped further across this stage, and I felt the pride like his mother would have felt for him then.

That May morning was the birth of spring to us all. It was as if the trees had come alive with their blooms; the grasslands all about were ripe with the most beautiful green stitchings; the flowers engorged with every color; violets and purples in cascade; speckled whites and blues dripping from every stem; the yellows and burgundies rushing through with their vibrant textures.

Cory and Tyler were older now, sitting alongside Sandra and myself. My wife was as lovely as ever; sitting proper there in her flower dress and touching me with her warm smiles. Father sat most near, dressed in his dark, pin-stripe suit; pressed from end to end; the one he had had for decades and the same one he used to preach with on those Sunday mornings. I looked over to spot Lorie and Marshall sitting hand in hand. Their little Gloria, now nearly four years old, so gaily propped between her parents. Her little golden locks seemed as long as Sandra's, and how this child gazed through the world in such awe. I watched as Lorie bent low, cuddle her little girl, and kiss her to the forehead while looking out towards me with a smile of 'thank you'.

Amanda and Jason were also present sitting to my left. Every once in a while Amanda would glance over to me, smirk with a portion of her face; wink, and engage a full smile as if she were that wonderful actress just receiving the most rousing applause for her performance.

The years had rolled by as time has a tendency to do so. This was indeed a new world; a world we had learned to embrace, live in, and become successful to a flourish; each, in our own method and manner. This was another verse in our lives; a pinion of fate and circumstance, which also cast to us a newfound hope that we had never realized before it came to us.

Generations will be born; generations will be lost, but the memories run as thick as the oldest of wines. The river has many waters, but it still is the river that remains; holds true, and outlasts even eternity. We were this river; our family. We were born to survive and the bloods to our line and vintage would endure.

"I have something to tell you friend," Jason said in all seriousness to me, after the commencement.

"Don't tell me," I looked at him with a sense of dread, "You've been traded from the Red Sox; west coast team. Probably the worst team in the league, I'll bet."

"Not quite," he grinned with that goofy, tushy grin of his, "But it does alter the family status...a little."

I noticed Amanda walking up beside him, gleaming in her newborn smile; her shoulders shrugged, then her arm dipped underneath his. My pause grew terminal; my eyes bulging, my expression came to a stiff pause.

"Wake up you ghost," Jason giggled, "Or you look like you have seen one. Get with us here."

"Now wait," I held my hands about, "Am I?" I paused again, "Are you?" another pause, "Is this?"

All the time Amanda shook her head to agree with my thoughts, becoming all the more expressive with each shake.

"Conner," she burst softly, "we are engaged."

"But you are not even dating..." I suggested.

"This is true," Jason shuffled, "But...What the hey?"

"How?" I stumbled, "Where?" I tripped, "When?" I fell flat in my speech, "Did I miss something?"

"I've known Amanda just about as long as you have friend," Jason smiled and gushed, "Not too often you can say that about a dear friend, can you?"

"But when did this all happen?" I pushed to know.

"Last week," Amanda replied, "We wanted to tell you then but we decided to wait. I didn't want to steal from Adam's thunder; being that this is his graduation and all."

"So what do you think partner?" Jason looked at me, yearning for my approval, "Life-long friend turns into a brother-in-law. How does that suit you? How about a blessing…"

"If only I had holy water now!" I laughed and took to embrace both of them, "enough to fill a river with," I stood back and smiled, gazing with admiration.

"Blessing?" Jason smirked, "or condolences?"

"Goof," I hugged him once more; more bear-like this time, "Do you have to ask such a Tush question?"

"Have to speak your language Conner," he shouted.

"I will be honored to call you brother," I swallowed proud in catching them with my radiant, over-bending expression.

I quickly looked about and I saw father standing to himself, glass in hand, fidgeting, and looking as a manner of being out-of-place and not holding favorable to his own company. I went to him.

"Dad," I began, "How are you holding up?"

"We will see," he appeared heavy with his serious look.

"What do you mean?" I questioned.

"The letter," he replied, "Do you remember the letter?"

"Which one…" I offered.

"You received yours four years ago son," he stated, "and now, your brother Adam has received his."

"You gave it to him," I was as serious as he was.

"Yes I did," father looked about, not wanting to stare over in my direction. "He fulfilled his promise to your mother."

"Do you think," I suggested, "In all this time, after all these years, that was a wise thing to do?"

"It was your mother's wish Conner…"

"I know," I paused, "But he never knew about the other letters dad. Would it have hurt to at least wait a few more days? This is his day to celebrate; nothing so prominent to bring his spirits down."

"Your mother would do best by him," he explained, "She desired for him to have it the day he graduates. As good as gold is to her word; your mother would find the perfect things to say."

"I agree," I sighed, "and you're the executor. Perhaps it was to his favor then."

I glanced about and noticed the mass of people converging near to our conversation.

"At the base of the fountain son," father said, "this is where your brother is. Go to him."

"I will," I stalled, shook my head in honor, bowed slightly, and left to find Adam.

I knew where the fountain was; it being the very aesthetic centerpiece to the entire college. I held hopes that Adam would not yet take to mother's letter; though rather wait until the moment when he could be more private with himself, her words, and his own thoughts and feelings. I pushed myself into a rush, bantering about and around all the hoards of people; searching, in a quest for my brother. The walkways were long and hard to breech. But as my step grew to a quick hurry, I came around the last bend and I discovered Adam sitting alone on the shelters of that enormous fountain.

His stance was in a profile, deeply woven into thought; bending, still, glancing downward as his hands propped out the open letter. The words were crossing his mind like the very thoughts my mother possessed then to write them with. A haunting verse of unknown quantity; the quality to speak of wealth and grand volume, yet, in this new embryo and idea Adam would have to deal with, I had prayed his heart was strong enough to handle it.

I saw in his eyes the sediment of a forgotten world; not lost mind you, just in a brief spell of suspended imagination. The feelings he held were cursed to live with him, and he, with them; wounds never to be discharged, but to heal with time and conviction, and the earnest desire to move on. He was sitting in his own shadow then and I could see its silhouette propped there beside his still body. The papers were open and in full display; his hands to embrace, though in some intense dramatic shake. Adam was locked into this world; a tiny speech and collective phrases our mother had endeared to him. I could sense he was being moved by them.

Even now her strong hand for wisdom was reaching back for him; unknown to me the exact mechanism to her words; it being only the converse and conversation meant exclusively between her and Adam. I slowly made my way towards Adam.

"I can't cry." He softly spoke out, looking ahead, and away from me. "I could never cry; not again. I can try, but the tears would never come. The river is dry Conner."

"There is no need Adam."

"If I had my wish," he paused, "I would write a letter, send it to some future of hers, and make sure it was special-delivered…To Heaven." I went to Adam. He remained unmoving; my hand placed over the back rim of his neck.

"And what would you say?" I questioned.

That's for me," he replied, "and her to know."

"I think we all have that intimacy with her." I said, "That's what made her so special. Our relations with her were so individual, and so unique. We were blessed brother."

He froze for a moment, shook his head out to agree with me, without a word spoken on that behalf.

"Those words were meant for you; alone," I sat beside him, catching his glare, eye to eye, "As she had for me years ago."

"You have something as well," he suggested.

"A treasure like yours Adam," I said, "I memorized every word. The letter sits in a frame in our bedroom."

"I'll do the same." Adam swallowed hard. "How all this turned out, it was not from my imagination."

"Nor mine," I stated, "But it is what we have, and share. And we go on with our lives. Adam, we are family…This is what we are."

"I hope I made her proud," his look nearly faltered into a brief and eclipsing stage of sorrow, though he refrained.

"No Adam," I clasped my hand behind his head; our foreheads touching into an embrace of their own, "You are; and always will be. This, you take with you through what is left of this life of yours; to cherish, endear yourself to…As much as this letter is, and will become a sign that she still lives in you."

"I miss her…"

"That will never change," I suggested, "It's a sign you remember and care. 'Missing' can sometimes be a good thing."

Father appeared just behind me, catching the duty attention of Adam who looked above me, and caught dad in his stare.

"A thousand paintings," father said, "nor a thousand novels, screenplays could ever bring me more pride or honor than this moment now…when my youngest boy Adam filled out his dying mother's wish card. She wanted this for you son. And in return, you discovered something so much more."

"Myself…" Adam softly spoke. Father smiled and shook on his head in approval when he came and gathered us both in for a hug.

I felt the fusing of my entire family soon to envelope us. The collective embraces were all spontaneous; without thought or reason, yet they were upheld by the enduring feelings we felt for one another. My sisters and Marshall, along with Jason, filtered in front of the fountain. Sandra came to me last, with both Cory and Tyler in tow; she clasping one hand to the side of my cheek, and so smiling past the grimace of her face. I tossed both of my children into my arms, swinging them about; tempting them there in a frightful tease that I was ready to throw them aboard into the fountain and its placid river. I felt the tug of a tiny hand below me; the hand of Gloria.

"What is it Gloria?" I asked.

"Come here," she requested, and I followed her so.

She led me to a view between two bushes outlaying the grounds all around. There between those sights we caught the collective view of those dipping meadows all strewn together in a sea of greens. The leaves had popped from their buds and were now gushing out a full spray in every tree, in every turn. How the birds danced from perch to perch; flying from one limb to the next, hopping along those limbs as they went, taking to flight, and crisscrossing the low-level sky lines until the atmosphere was drenched with them.

I saw a family of bunnies propped in the shadows of one tree, and I so pointed this out to her. Gloria gazed in astonishment at such the sight; her eyes gulping the scene with the thurst of that view. The enormous canopy above was glowing about the bluest haze, as if it were the starting arch to a rainbow. The wails of those leaves as the wind blew through; the uniform carols to that nature's song all appeared as a quiet symphony to me.

A pond settled just below at the belly of the first meadow before us, nearly a hundred yards away. I thought on that river of time and reflection; you know the one, where Mr. Haberstaff and I played upon with our thoughts. How it held its own refuge of sorts. And perhaps this one would be like it, and show to Gloria her life-long images she can look forward to. Her young life was like this: still a little river and tiny pond. It was indeed a quaint, twisting body of water. Ripples were cascading across its top whenever the wind blew by it. I could see the reflections of that blue-sky shutter in its lines.

We could view the association of ducks trimming the waterline, spreading an 'arrow' ripple of their own as they went. I looked over the ridges to see if the image of my mother sat on her blanket; still, looking out over the other side of the world at me; smiling, engaging me with her expression there. I knew there was birth in the eyes of this child; a sense of wonderment that would play along the long string of history in our family tree.

You could smell the freshness in the air; those whiffs from the breeze; the adolescence of a new season, a rebirth of old into youth again. I thought of how the seasons so radically change throughout the year; but yet, having that mixture of calendar and time on its side, nature seemed to be forever, and it would be alive long after my own passing.

Gloria pulled me through with a tug on my hands; releasing me as such, and rumbling down the slow decline towards the base of that pond. I watched her precariously stumble, nearly fall, but somehow keep her balance with her hands propped skyward; her legs jaunting out as she went, still attempting some measure of running in her step.

I followed her till we both met at the foot of that tiny sea. She was in want of a closer look; I picking her up and raising her to match my more-elevated look. There, in that kaleidoscope of beauty, where nature seemed to have been born anew for a new cycle of seasons, we studied the surroundings about us, and observed what was before us.

She stared about, eyes kept in a squint. I could see the value of what she saw sitting there in her view box. The wonder; that stare of curiosity played in her expression for as long as I looked over her.

"Does this mean spring has come?" she asked.

I stalled with her announcement; pondering the deeper meaning of it as well as the remedy life itself seemed to have for us all. Winter had indeed passed as it always does, and the birth of a new spring had taken its place.

"Yes dear," I smiled, and looked over her innocent expression, "I believe it does," I hugged her into a tender squeeze, "I believe it does."

The measure of life sits in its own eternity. The joys and the sorrows are but the different colors we all see through the lives we individually experience. Those transposed and transfixed wonderments are but the tales we live through, and so cherish for all the days we live in. I, for one, had learned the more valuable of lessons through the death of my dearest mother.

The pain of loss really never goes away. It just mingles with the other feelings and emotions you end up discovering throughout your life. Through the burdens of tragedy and the ultimate despair which follows, you find some level of cure in joy, and the relationship with those that still remain with you in your life. There is a harbor called love; a vantage point where the world seems at its highest beauty when you reach for it. I had learned to travel to that land; those mountain peaks where I could see the greatest views in life. It's a stillness; a contentment for peace and tranquility. You remember the quiet sounds that it makes; you listen for it and when it comes again, you relish in that joy.

My mother always spoke that sometimes the sorrows have to come before the joys can follow. I had found the most endearing meaning of this and I knew it to be true. Through all that had ensued, I had discovered such a joy as she spoke of; the meaning, the purpose; the relevant answers to all my questions I was so possessed by during her illness.

It is true when life throws you a mystery, a riddle of its own for you to solve, there are always answers. You just have to go out and find them.

I have seen the full colors of the rainbow; the darks; the lights of its realm and stature. This flavor called life, where the meaning of it is born in your own experiences. I suppose I went through all that I did to tell you of a story; a story about a beautiful life lost, yet always remembered. Through these pages, these volumes; through the measures of what beginnings' and ends' contain, and all which lies in between; the life of one person is simply muted to some level and never really, truly exposed with the justice it deserves.

A promise given; a promise earned. Hope reinvents itself in the tender waves of youth. The majesty of innocence is always reborn; kind of like the seasons as they roll and evolve in that continuum rotation. Winter has its place, but only for the moment. Time holds the holy grail of spring and summer to follow; and hope, faith will forever take us there.

The deliverers of our history are always held in what we remember and pass on to those who will live beyond our years. As I turn to the second chapter of my life, the pages before are as extensive as the pages to follow. The past leaflets worn, bent from that use; yet those pages to come are as fresh as the newborn daffodil sitting in the isles of spring. I will go there with faith and hope to accompany me, and to see what the next adventure to my life shall hold.

The lessons taught from one so prominent in my younger world will be the roadmap to what remains of my life. Thus the influence, the cherishable influence from what love bestows in all its glory. A glory that shadows the love of one mother to her sons, her daughters, her family, and to those lives she touched throughout her own life. Indeed the joys have passed through the rains of the greatest sorrows; and there, before Gloria and myself, sat the high arches of a most beautiful rainbow cutting through the skies.

THE END

Coming Soon...

Coming in February 2006 is the new novel *A Diary's House*.

Landon Hampshire never knew that the boyhood adventure he takes with his friends would ever yield the incredible journey he ultimately experiences—going down the mysterious and mighty Randola River. It is a ravaging, mighty, heaving frenzy of water which has taken the lives of so many; those who dared to travels within its waters. At the base of the Randola is an island even more mysterious than the Randola itself.

Born in the vast and looming mountains of North Carolina during the 1870's, Landon always remembered the folklore and legendary tales about the people of the Kituhwa (Cherokee). Incorporating the aid of an eccentric old French trapper (old man Montague), their initial belief was to discover treasure and become men in the eyes of those within their immediate township. But what Landon will eventually come to discover is more than he ever bargains for.

The island releases many of its mysterious, yet even many more are created when Landon discovers on the island a diary of a young woman who lived forty years during the 1830's (Trail of Tears). The diary entries are hopeful, though haunting, and show in intimate detail the life and dreams of this very special young girl who is turning into a woman of beauty and adventure. Her story unfolds through the reading of her diary, and Landon suddenly finds himself caught up in a sweeping, empowering world of re-invention and ultimate redemption.

A Diary's House is about love, lost love, and the hope that dreams, even those in the latest time of life, can come true. It is of a young boy's attempt to become a man, the once-lost secrets of a diary, a sweeping romance which transcends time and place. It is more than a boy's journey into manhood, but the mysteries of so many lives unknowingly intertwined, now brought together in a climatic ending; all from the engrossing world embedded in a forgotten diary; a diary of a woman.

Contact Information

We welcome any and all comments you might have about our books. In fact, we encourage your response. The reader's voice is even more important than that of the writer. Drop us a line; we want to hear from you!
Our email addresses are as follows:

epicnovelist@carolina.rr.com
murphyturf@carolina.rr.com

For more information about this book, upcoming books, ordering information, please visit our websites:

Epicbooksonline.com
Inwintersmoment.com

All orders can be placed through our website, email, or iuniverse.com/amazon.com

Also please note autograph copies can only be purchased through our website/email address.

Happy Reading!

For mail orders/contact:
David Murphy
P.O. Box 23836
Charlotte N.C. 28227-2014

978-0-595-36754-2
0-595-36754-2

Printed in the United States
42157LVS00003B/58-255